August /54.

To "Jeremy"

The path of a Jew is not strewn with Roses, but covered thickly "thorns". Therefore please accept this book so that the prick of the thorns will be less severe by a knowledge and understanding of our Jewish Heritage.

Sincerely,
Adele Garfinkel.

A Treasury of

JEWISH FOLKLORE

A Treasury of

JEWISH

FOLKLORE

STORIES, TRADITIONS, LEGENDS, HUMOR,
WISDOM AND FOLK SONGS OF
THE JEWISH PEOPLE

EDITED BY NATHAN AUSUBEL

CROWN PUBLISHERS · NEW YORK

PRINTED IN THE UNITED STATES OF AMERICA
BY AMERICAN BOOK—STRATFORD PRESS, INC., NEW YORK

TO MARYNN

*who shared with me the labor as well as the
delight of rediscovering the beauty,
laughter and wisdom of our
people's lore.*

Contents

NOTE: All items not otherwise credited are the work of the editor. These are stories from Oral Tradition and adaptations from foreign-language sources.

v

2. HOLY MEN

3. MIRACLES

4. FIGHTERS AND STRONG MEN

Part Three: THE HUMAN COMEDY

1. DROLL CHARACTERS

x CONTENTS

2. ROGUES AND SINNERS

CONTENTS

3. TRADITIONAL TYPES

4. HUMOROUS ANECDOTES AND JESTS

Part Four: TALES AND LEGENDS

1. BIBLICAL SIDELIGHTS

CONTENTS

2. THE WORLD TO COME

3. THE TEN LOST TRIBES

4. FOLK TALES

5. DEMON TALES

6. ANIMAL TALES

Part Five: PROVERBS AND RIDDLES

Part Six: SONGS AND DANCES

1. FOLK SONGS

xvi

CONTENTS

Introduction

Like other children brought up in an orthodox Jewish environment I was immersed in Jewish song and story as soon as I became aware of the world around me. Years later, I discovered that the lore of my people had entered into my blood stream, as it were, and had become a part of the cultural reality of my life. Who has not had this experience? Melodies sung in childhood have a tendency to linger persistently in the subconscious and the stories and sayings we heard time and again from the lips of our parents are never really erased from our memory.

While my main purpose in compiling this anthology was to present the spontaneous folk-creation of the Jewish people, I was also motivated by the desire to recapture the fading memory of the wonder and the beauty that had inspirited my childhood in the Old World. And so I began to gather all the myths and parables, stories and legends, the songs and the wise sayings upon which I, and millions of other Jewish children throughout the many centuries, had been nurtured.

But what was my delight to discover in the course of the work that a unified portrait was shaping itself in an almost sculptural sense out of all these materials. This portrait was of one I knew intimately, of some one endowed with a well-defined character, familiar psychological traits, ethical values and emotional responses. And before long I knew with certainty whose portrait it was—it was the composite portrait of the Jewish people.

How could there have emerged such a remarkable unity from all this variegated mass of folk-materials? For one thing, Jewish historic experience has been disturbingly similar in so many ways, in every age and in almost every land of the Diaspora. Jews have never been allowed to sink their roots for long anywhere; they have been forced to be everlasting wanderers on the highways of the world. They have been perpetually faced with the same kind of slanders and persecutions in almost every country and in every generation. And their folklore naturally is but a faithful chronicle of these historic experiences. Then again, we cannot avoid the fact that for three thousand years the remnants of Israel have maintained their ethnic-cultural identity, which too is an unparalleled historical phenomenon.

Like children who had no father to give them protection, no home they could call their own, they developed a feeling of deep emotional insecurity in the world. They found comfort in devotion to their faith and their religious literature, of which much of Jewish folklore is a significant part.

xvii

For sacred writings, such as the Talmud and *Midrash*, are almost inexhaustible repositories of the legends, myths, and parables of the Jewish people. In almost perpetual study of this literature as a devotional obligation, the Jew of every age and every country absorbed these elements of folklore and entered them into the cultural experiences of his life.

By the humanizing art of the legend such foremost heroes as Moses, Jeremiah and Hillel, have been transformed into well-loved ancestors—we might say members of the same family. Even God has lost his awesomeness in the folkloristic transformation. "And nowhere indeed has God been rendered so utterly human, been taken so closely to man's bosom and, in the embrace, so thoroughly changed into an elder brother, a slightly older father, as here in the *Midrash* . . . God has not merely become a man, he has become a Jew, an elderly bearded Jew." *

There is no folklore that can claim such a long and continuous history as the Jewish, that has had such a vast range of productivity in both time and geography. It is richly varied and colorful with the imprint of the many diverse cultures that Jews have assimilated everywhere through the many centuries. Nonetheless, despite the absorption and adaptation of non-Jewish elements from without and despite the consequences of more than twenty-five centuries of wide dispersion in almost every part of the world, Jewish folklore probably possesses an over-all unity greater than that of any other. It is noteworthy, for instance, that, while American folklore has had a continuous three-hundred-year history of creativity in a unified geographic area, it nevertheless can claim a lesser integration than the folklore of the Jewish people with its several thousand years of turbulent history in so many parts of the globe.

Folklore is a vivid record of a people, palpitating with life itself, and its greatest art is its artlessness. It is a true and unguarded portrait, for where art may be selective, may conceal, gloss over defects and even prettify, folk art is always revealing, always truthful in the sense that it is a spontaneous expression. It is therefore three-dimensional with the sense of "life" and "people." It proceeds in a straight line to the significant and ignores the trivial. By juxtaposing good with evil, light with shadow, grief with laughter, and honesty with sham, it achieves the harmonious unity of opposites that resides in objective truth.

The Jewish people has fathered many talented and profound sons and daughters but no less talented and profound—in a somewhat different way perhaps—has been the people itself. Because it hides unpretentiously behind its anonymous creation like the unnamed master-sculptors of ancient Egypt, few have learned to recognize it as the creator of significant culture. Certainly, men of eminence could never have arisen in any of the arts of civilization had it not been for the molding force of the people's mass-genius which serves to them as the fertile soil to the seedling. The fundamental role of folklore in the creation of culture is yet insufficiently recognized except by those who have succeeded in freeing themselves of

---

* Professor H. Slonimsky, *On Reading the Midrash.* In *The Jewish Institute Quarterly,* January, 1928, p. 3.

the "Great Man" theory of history and culture so eulogized by Carlyle in *Hero and Hero-Worship* and in *The Aristocracy of Talent*.*

Some writers have expressed astonishment at the marked intellectual and sophisticated character of so much of Jewish folklore. But seen within the context of its social and cultural history there is nothing at all baffling in this. Jews became an intellectual people not because of any innate mental superiority over other peoples, but because of the peculiar nature of their history. They have cherished and preserved their tradition of learning ever since the Age of Ezra the Scribe and the public teachings of the Men of the Great Assembly during the Sixth Century B.C. In large measure this tradition was derived from the religious obligation of every Jew to study Scripture ceaselessly, for it must always be kept in mind that Judaism was cradled in a theocracy, a priest state. In later centuries, this study also embraced the *Mishna*, the Talmud and the *Midrash*, of which folklore was an integral part.

This activity was not only unprecedented in its mass scope in the intellectual history of mankind, but, within its limited religious framework, it represented the most democratic philosophy of education in Antiquity. This universal duty to study *as a religious act* broadened the base of Jewish culture and, in consequence, elevated it.

It was this general and sustained intellectual activity among Jews that, in the process of refinement and sensitizing through many centuries, led to a razor-edged sharpening of wits, to a verbal ease of articulation, and to an unusual preoccupation with abstract ideas and philosophical speculation. In the plain Jew this differed from that of the scholar only in extent and intensity. Sometimes this virtuosity led to an intellectual sterility, defeated its own avowed ends. The scholar so often became entangled in his own complicated web of hair-splitting. This fruitless type of mental gymnastics, even in the Talmud, drew forth the ironic retort from an exasperated rabbi in debate with a casuistical opponent: "Aren't you from Pumbeditha where they draw an elephant through the eye of a needle?"

But by and large, the Rabbis of old who compiled the Talmud and the *Midrash* were neither pedants nor closet scholars. They were down-to-earth teachers of the people, robust with the life-urge and endowed with good practical sense. In their desire to make their teaching intelligible to the people, they drew with canny pedagogy upon the familiar tales, legends, witticisms and sayings current among the Jews. Being men of talent and of considerable profundity they in turn took fire from the uninhibited folk-imagination and themselves adapted innumerable folk-stories and sayings which they wove ingeniously into the fabric of their learned homilies and discussions. In their turn again the common folk, who revered as sacred these tales and their source in Talmud and *Midrash*, adopted them and, in the process of telling and retelling them, embroidered them with their inexhaustible fancy, invention and wisdom.

---

* "With the modern trend of seeing the individual as a part of the whole social organism, folklore is becoming an auxiliary science for a social and religious history as well as an integral part of the history of literature."—Abraham Berger, *The Literature of Jewish Folklore*. In *Journal of Jewish Bibliography*, V. 1. Nos. 1-2, 1938-39.

The practice of employing the old legends, parables and the ethical exempla of the sages for didactic ends was continued by the rabbis and preachers of later days down to our own time. Thus, like the complementary interaction between the shuttle and the loom, the Jewish people and their teachers together wove a tapestry of folklore of the most exquisite designs and colors.

What are the salient features of Jewish folklore which distinguish it from other bodies of folklore?

To begin with, it is most frequently of a poetical and introspective nature. It is philosophical and subtle, pious and moralistic, witty and ironic. But it is almost always ethical, pointing a lesson of right conduct, ceaselessly instructing, often even when it is being entertaining or humorous. To be sure, other peoples' folklore also possesses some of these characteristics, but the nature of their culture and history led them to make other emphases.

Wit and irony can be regarded as the likely attributes of a civilized mentality. In Jewish life, as reflected in its folklore, these traits have been nourished by a macerated national sensibility, by a disenchantment with a world not of its making or choosing. Jews have received their tempering from an unflinching realism learned for a high fee in the school of life; they have always felt the need of fortifying their spirits with the armor of laughter against the barbs of the world.

Despite the tragedy of their historic experiences, Jews have always been life-affirming or they could not possibly have survived the ordeals they had to go through as a people. In fact, if anything, their troubles made indestructible optimists of them. The therapy of gaiety and laughter was as necessary to them as the very air they breathed. The life-force within them was far too vital to be dissolved in tears and perpetual mourning. Neither persecution, nor grief, nor the poverty of their dank ghetto-prisons could keep Jews from laughing. But their laughter had to be something more than gay frivolity, something more than mere diversion. It had to be an affirmative and defiant answer to the world's cruelties. And so within Jewish humor there is a unique type of wit that serves, not only as a trenchant commentary on life, but also as a corrective, as a mellowing agent which helps draw the string of grief from tragedy. This mellowing humor may very well be called "Jewish Salt," an indefinable quality comparable to "Attic Salt" except for a distinctive flavor of its own which helps establish the character of Jewish folklore. For this reason the book begins with a touch of this seasoning.

Many Jewish legends and folk tales are suffused with a deep sadness. Like so many of the Jewish folk songs they too are keyed in a haunting minor. But somehow this sadness rarely degenerates into despair or even self-pity. Almost always it bears within it the saving-grace of catharsis, of the ennoblement of grief in the steadfast spirit, of the moral triumph of the righteous even in defeat.

As we have already noted, Jewish folklore is knit together by a remarkable unity of both subject matter and world-view despite its vast time-place sweep. This cohesion also has been due to the fact that the most significant tales were found in the *Agada* in the Talmud and in the *Midrash*. Later Jewish folklore, to a very considerable extent, was merely poured into the traditional matrix of form and content established by the ancient Rabbinical folklorists.

Jewish folklore treats of Heaven and Earth, of Paradise and Hell, of Good and Evil, of the natural and the supernatural, of the spiritual and the material, of the sacred and the profane. A large number of legends and myths, derived from their neighbors in Persia and Babylonia among whom the Jews lived for so many centuries after the Captivity, tell of angels and demons—all mediators between God and man's destiny of which he is the architect according to the good or evil of his conduct. In hundreds of other tales, with the humanizing intimacy of the true folklore spirit, there passes through a procession of the Patriarchs and the Prophets, of the Jewish kings and heroes, sages and scholars, saints and sinners, martyrs and renegades, rationalists and mystagogues, men of faith and also men of little faith. One of the objectives of all these tales is didactic—to hold up to the view of the Jew the inspiring example of his eminent forefathers in righteousness. They have still other objectives—to offer consolation and hope to the afflicted, to reconcile for the simple Jew the unhappy destiny of his people with his own trust in God, and also to explain to him those Scriptural passages and incidents that baffle his questioning mind. About these legends Tolstoy wrote in the 1880's: "They contain something unendingly gentle and movingly great, like the rosy morning star on a quiet morning. The most precious quality in them is their agitation over the eternal mysteries of the human soul."

Folklore is a continuous and unending process and flows along with the stream of life. There has not been yet sufficient time for the recent historic experiences of the Jewish people to crystallize into folklore. It is perhaps too early for the emergence of legend out of the staggering tragedy of the six million Jews murdered in the charnel houses of Hitler. And time must elapse before the Maccabean grandeur that infuses the struggle of the Jews of Israel against the combined might of their enemies will kindle the folk imagination to give it utterance. Yet that time will surely come, for life, with the deft fingers of a weaver, tirelessly draws the crimson thread of human anguish and struggle into its magical patterns.

In conclusion, I would like to add a personal note. The years of labor which have gone into the preparation of this work will be more than rewarded if it will reveal to the Jewish reader the existence of the little known cultural treasures of his people and, in consequence, will fill him with the sense of human dignity and worth that is his birthright. To the Gentile reader Jewish folklore addresses itself with its myriad implications because it is but a colorful part of the kaleidoscope of universal culture. May it make plain the common humanity of all races and nations and thus draw them closer in the bonds of brotherhood and understanding.

MAJOR SOURCES OF JEWISH FOLKLORE

Most of the old legends contained in this book are naturally from the *Agada* of the Talmud and the *Midrash*. But of the character and contents of these vast repositories of folklore many people, Jews included, have but the haziest idea. For instance, the French historian Bossuet, who was a bishop as well as a famous savant, once appealed to the philosopher Leibnitz to procure for him a translation of the Talmud by "Monsieur Mishna." Therefore, to those readers who may find themselves in the predicament of Bossuet, it might be useful to explain in the barest outline what the *Mishna*, the Talmud and the *Midrash* actually are.

As is well known, the Pentateuch, (the Five Books of Moses) contains the Jewish written Law, or Torah. In time, beginning with the era of the Scribes *(Soferim)* who succeeded Ezra, it was found necessary to add to the written Law a second body of Law consisting of traditional doctrine that had been orally transmitted through the centuries. The *Mishna* (repetition or doctrine) constituted this Second Law. It was compiled in Palestine and composed in Hebrew by one hundred and forty-eight teacher-scribes called *Tannaim (Mishna* teachers). It was a Code that developed but slowly, taking almost five and a half centuries, from the era of the Scribes to its final redaction by Judah ha-Nasi in the Third Century A.D.

However, the oral traditions contained in the *Mishna* were found urgently in need of interpretation. In answer to this need emerged the *Gemara* (doctrine) or, as it is more often called, the Talmud (explanation), as a commentary on the text of the *Mishna*.

The Talmud, which constitutes the *Corpus Juris* of the Jews, was created by several hundred rabbis who went under the collective name of *Amoraim* (expounders); they regarded themselves as the continuators of the *Tannaim*, the architects of the *Mishna*. The Talmud is not just one book but a great collection of many books; it is not the product of one age but of several centuries. With the meticulous care of practiced legal scholars the *Amoraim* examined the *Mishna* sentence by sentence, carefully traced every source and tried in cool objective discussion with one another to reconcile the contradictions they encountered in the *Mishna* text. It was a rare instance indeed when they attempted to lay down the law dogmatically—they merely gave their reasoned opinions, presented their views in the course of discussion, the dissenting one side by side with those of the majority. The laws that they discussed and interpreted touched on a vast number of subjects concerning every minute circumstance or problem arising in contemporary experience. Not just religion, but philosophy, hygiene, ethics and other matters of a civil and secular nature came under their purview.

There are actually two Talmuds—one which was developed by the *Amoraim* in the Rabinnical academies of Babylonia where a great settlement of Jews had been established during the Captivity, the other which was created by the *Amoraim* of Palestine. The Babylonian Talmud received its final redaction in the Fifth Century A.D. by the Rabbinic editors, the *Saboraim* (ponderers), who were the successors to the *Amoraim*. The Jerusalem Talmud was closed by the Palestinian *Saboraim* a hundred years before, in A.D. 370. Of the two the Babylonian Talmud, which is about three times the size of the Jerusalem Talmud, is by far the more important, although both are commentaries of the same *Mishna* text. However, the Jerusalem Talmud is incomplete. Out of the sixty-three treatises contained in the *Mishna,* it deals with only thirty-nine; it is assumed that the rest were lost.

Both Talmuds consist of two elements. One is called *Halacha,* which is the juridical exposition and interpretation of the Law; the other is called *Agada,* the ethical and poetical interpretation of Scripture by means of the story-telling art. The sages of old described the complementary relationship between these two methods: "Bread—that is *Halacha;* wine— that is *Agada.* By bread alone we cannot live." It is from the *Agada* that so many stories with profound ethical meanings have been culled for inclusion in this collection.

Finally, we come to the *Midrash.* This is a body of interpretative literature which was begun by the *Tannaim* simultaneously with their work on the *Mishna,* and was continued for many centuries by their Rabbinic continuators until the closing of the great Jewish schools in Babylonia in A.D. 1040. A perceptive scholar has given an accurate description of its contents and the spirit that animates it: "The *Midrash* is art in the interest of religion; but above all it is art. It is the flowering of the art creative instinct, snubbed and repressed elsewhere, which here finds full freedom and scope. The amazingly fecund and vital principle which shoots forth and blossoms in this endless garden is a repressed instinct. The Jews were forbidden the plastic arts, because the Deity was not to be modelled or drawn; and the mytho-plastic urge generally was frowned upon. But the myth-creating phantasy, the mytho-poetic urge, banished and forbidden in the official halls of the religion, finds its outlet here. And so we find this starved power driven underground, emerging here in the endless plenitude, from mere story-telling and parable and play of fancy to images of tragic beauty and to supreme flights of the creative imagination."*

During the Middle Ages it was the Jews who served in Christian Europe as the most important intermediaries for the diffusion of the tales and fables of the East, such as the Bidpai and Barlaam cycles. (For more on this subject see the introduction to ANIMAL TALES.) Nonetheless, Jews remained skilful originators of tales in their own right. There was, for instance, the notable collection by Rabbi Nissim of Kairwan (11th Century). While many of his stories were adaptations from *Agada* and *Midrash,* quite a number were from other Jewish sources. Another celebrated compilation, *Sefer Hasidim* (Book of the Pious), adapted for the most part by Rabbi Judah Hasid of Regensburg (c. 1200), consisted of legends into which were patterned the cabalistic beliefs and fancies of medieval German Jewry.

The invention of the printing press by Gutenberg marked a great advance in the democratization of learning in Europe; it stimulated a broader diffusion of culture even in the ghetto. Yiddish compilations of

---

* Professor H. Slonimsky, *On Reading the Midrash.* In *The Jewish Institute Quarterly,* January, 1928, p. 2.

folk tales, and also moralistic works in which folk tales played an illustrative function, came off the printing presses in considerable numbers during the second half of the Sixteenth Century. The most widely read of these were the *Teitsch-Chumesh, Brantspiegel* and *Leb-Tov*. However, the most popular of all Yiddish folk tale collections was the *Ma'aseh Buch*. More than half of its two hundred and fifty-four tales were adaptations of *Agada* and *Midrash* originals; many were of medieval Jewish vintage; and some were even variants of Christian stories.

With the upsurge of the *Cabala* during the Fifteenth and Sixteenth Centuries it was but natural that there should have originated a great number of cabalistic legends in which the drama of the miraculous and the demonological was fully exploited. Finally, with the advent of the mystical *Hasidic* movement during the Eighteenth Century, a unique body of legendary literature appeared in Yiddish concerning the continuators of the cabalists—the wonder-working Rabbi Israel Baal-Shem, the founder of *Hasidim*, and his principal rabbinic disciples. (For more on this subject see the introduction to CABALISTS, MYSTICS AND WONDER-WORKERS.)

I wish to acknowledge my indebtedness to Edmund Fuller for his sensitive understanding and the discriminating taste he brought to the shaping of this volume, and to Bertha Krantz for the skilful and devoted hand with which she piloted the book through its technical stages.

I also wish to thank Dr. Joshua Bloch of the New York Public Library and his assistants: Marie Coralnik, Dora Steinglass and Fanny Spivack; Abraham Berger for generously allowing me to draw from his wide erudition in Jewish lore; Mendel Elkin and the Yiddish Scientific Institute; the library staff of the Jewish Theological Seminary; the Jacob Michael Jewish Music Collection and Joseph Levisohn, its librarian. I also am indebted to my friend and father-in-law, the late Morris Older; Ethel Older; M. Vaxer; Hillel Ausubel; Bertha and Philip Shan; Ruth Rubin; Samuel Feldman, who copied the music; Jacob Richman, author of *Laughs from Jewish Lore;* and a great many other individuals too numerous to mention.

Finally, I wish to acknowledge my deep indebtedness to my wife, Marynn Older Ausubel, who worked side by side with me in gathering and preparing the vast amount of materials from which this volume has been culled; it was her enthusiasm and perceptive understanding that helped bring this arduous work to fruition.

N. A.

PART ONE

Jewish Salt

Jewish Salt

Such Odds!

Two Jews sat in a coffee house, discussing the fate of their people.

"How miserable is our lot," said one. "Pogroms, plagues, quotas, discrimination, Hitler, and the Ku Klux Klan . . . Sometimes I think we'd be better off if we'd never been born!"

"Of course!" said the other. "But who has that much luck? Not one in 50,000 . . ."

The Realist

AFTER the smoke and thunder of the battle had died down at Austerlitz, Napoleon wished to reward a number of men of various nationalities who had fought like heroes that day.

"Name your wish and I will grant it to you, my gallant heroes!" cried the Emperor.

"Restore Poland!" cried a Pole.

"It shall be done!" answered the Emperor.

"I'm a farmer—give me land!" cried a poor Slovak.

"Land it will be, my lad."

"I want a brewery," said a German.

"Give him a brewery!" ordered Napoleon.

Next it was the turn of a Jewish soldier.

"Well, my lad, what shall it be?" asked the Emperor, encouraging him with a smile.

"If you please, Sire, I would like to have a nice *schmaltz* herring," murmured the Jew, bashfully.

"*Ma foi!*" exclaimed the Emperor, shrugging his shoulders. "Give this man a herring!"

When the Emperor had left, the other heroes gathered around the Jew.

"What a fool you are!" they chided him. "Imagine, a man can choose whatever he wants and all he asks for is a herring! Is that the way to treat an Emperor?"

"We'll see who's the fool!" retorted the Jew. "You've asked for the independence of Poland, for a farm, for a brewery—things you'll never get from the Emperor. But you see, I'm a realist. If I ask for a herring— *maybe* I'll get it."

Higher Mathematics

Two wise men of Chelm lay sweating in the steam bath one day. To drive away the boredom of doing nothing they began to discuss deep mathematical problems.

The first one said, "If, for instance, it takes four hours to drive to Dvinsk with one horse—wouldn't it be right to say that if I drove with two horses it would only take me two hours?"

"Correct as gold," answered the other sage, filled with admiration.

"Now, why couldn't I drive to Dvinsk with four horses so I'd get there in no time?" continued the mathematician.

"Why trouble to go to Dvinsk at all?" exclaimed the other. "Just harness your four horses and stay right here."

Richer than Rothschild

"IF I were Rothschild," said the *melamed* of Chelm, "I'd be richer than Rothschild."

"How is it possible?" asked a fellow-citizen.

"Naturally," answered the *melamed*, "I'd do a little teaching on the side."

A Lesson in Talmud

ONE day a country-fellow came to his rabbi. "Rabbi," he said, in the tongue-tied fashion of the unlettered in the presence of the learned, "for a long time I have been hearing of Talmud. It puzzles me not to know what Talmud is. Please teach me what is Talmud."

"Talmud?" The rabbi smiled tolerantly, as one does to a child. "You'll never understand Talmud; you're a peasant."

"Oh, Rabbi, you must teach me," the fellow insisted. "I've never asked you for a favor. This time I ask. Please teach me, what is Talmud."

"Very well," said the rabbi, "listen carefully. If two burglars enter a house by way of the chimney, and find themselves in the living room, one with a dirty face and one with a clean face, which one will wash?"

The peasant thought awhile and said, "Naturally, the one with the dirty face."

"You see," said the rabbi, "I told you a farmer couldn't master Talmud. The one with the clean face looked at the one with the dirty face and, assuming his own face was also dirty, of course he washed it, while the one with the dirty face, observing the clean face of his colleague, naturally assumed his own was clean, and did not wash it."

Again the peasant reflected. Then, his face brightening, said, "Thank you, Rabbi, thank you. Now I understand Talmud."

"See," said the rabbi wearily. "It is just as I said. You are a peasant! And who but a peasant would think for a moment that when two burglars enter a house by way of the chimney, only one will have a dirty face?"

Hitting the Bull's Eye

ONCE Rabbi Elijah, the Gaon of Vilna, said to his friend, the Preacher of Dubno, "Tell me, Jacob, how in the world do you happen to find the right parable to every subject?"

The Preacher of Dubno answered, "I will explain to you my parabolic method by means of a parable. Once there was a nobleman who entered his son in a military academy to learn the art of musketry. After five years the son learned all there was to be learned about shooting and, in proof of his excellence, was awarded a diploma and a gold medal.

"Upon his way home after graduation he halted at a village to rest his horses. In the courtyard he noticed on the wall of a stable a number of chalk circles and right in the center of each was a bullet hole.

"The young nobleman regarded the circles with astonishment. Who in the world could have been the wonderful marksman whose aim was so unerringly true? In what military academy could he have studied and what kind of medals had he received for his marksmanship!

"After considerable inquiry he found the sharpshooter. To his amazement it was a small Jewish boy, barefoot and in tatters.

" 'Who taught you to shoot so well?' the young nobleman asked him.

"The boy explained, 'First I shoot at the wall. Then I take a piece of chalk and draw circles around the holes.'

"I do the same thing," concluded the Preacher of Dubno with a smile. "I don't look for an appropriate parable to fit any particular subject but, on the contrary, whenever I hear a good parable or a witty story I store it in my mind. Sooner or later, I find for it the right subject for pointing a moral."

Lost and Found

THE old rabbi had left the room for a moment, then returned to his studies, only to find his eye-glasses missing. Perhaps they were between the leaves of his book? No. . . . Maybe they were somewhere on the desk? No. . . . Surely they were in the room. No. . . .

So, in the ancient sing-song, with many a gesture appropriate to Talmudic disputation, he began:

"Where are my glasses? . . .

"Let us assume they were taken by someone. They were taken either by someone who needs glasses, or by someone who doesn't need glasses.

If it was someone who needs glasses, he has glasses; and if it was someone who doesn't need glasses, then why should he take them?

"Very well. Suppose we assume they were taken by someone who planned to sell them for gain. Either he sells them to one who needs glasses, or to one who doesn't need glasses. But one who needs glasses has glasses, and one who doesn't need them, surely doesn't want to buy them. . . . So much for that.

"Therefore . . . this is a problem involving one who needs glasses *and* has glasses, one who either took someone else's because he lost his own, or who absentmindedly pushed his own up from his nose to his forehead, and promptly forgot all about them!

"For instance . . . *me!*" And, with a triumphant sweep of thumb to forehead, signalizing the end of his analysis, the rabbi recovered his property.

"Praised be the Lord, I am trained in our ancient manner of reasoning," he murmured. "Otherwise I would never have found them!"

One Big Worry

SEVERAL days before Passover a poor man came to the rabbi for advice.

"Rabbi!" he complained bitterly, "I'm in desperate circumstances! Passover is almost here but I haven't the means with which to observe it properly. I must get money for *matzos*, meat and sacramental wine. My family and I dare not show ourselves in the synagogue for the holiday services—we are all in tatters!"

The rabbi tried to soothe him. "Don't worry—God will help you!"

But the unhappy man would not be comforted.

"I've too many worries, Rabbi," he wailed, "I'm afraid they're too much for me!"

"In that case," said the rabbi, "let's see what your needs are." And he began to figure.

"How much do you need for *matzos*, meat and wine?"

"Sixteen rubles."

"Clothes for your children?"

"Eighteen rubles."

"A new dress for your wife?"

"Eight rubles."

"A new suit for yourself?"

"Ten rubles."

The rabbi then added up the various items and said, "You need altogether fifty-two rubles. Now at least you won't have to worry about *matzos*, meat, wine and clothing—you'll have only one worry—where to get the fifty-two rubles!"

So What?

A YOUNG boy approached his father, saying, "Please, father, may I have an increase in my allowance?"

The old man stroked his beard reflectively. "And if you have an increase in your allowance, so what?"

"Then I'd be able to go to night school."

"And suppose you go to night school. So what?"

"Then I could get a better job."

"Suppose you get a better job. So what?"

"Then I could dress better and go places."

"And suppose you dress better and go places. So what?"

"Why, I might meet a beautiful girl."

"All right. You might meet a beautiful girl. So what?"

"I'd get married."

"So, you'd get married. So what?"

"Why, papa, then I'd be *happy*!"

"So, you're happy. So what? . . ."

Why Only One Adam?

WHY did God create only one Adam and not many at a time?

He did this to demonstrate that one man in himself is an entire universe. Also He wished to teach mankind that he who kills one human being is as guilty as if he had destroyed the entire world. Similarly, he who saves the life of one single human being is as worthy as if he had saved all of humanity.

God created only one man so that people should not try to feel superior to one another and boast of their lineage in this wise: "I am descended from a more distinguished Adam than you."

He also did this so that the heathen should not be able to say that, since many men had been created at the same time, it was conclusive proof that there was more than one God.

Lastly, He did this in order to establish His own power and glory. When a maker of coins does his work he uses only one mould and all the coins emerge alike. But the King of Kings, blessed be His name, has created all mankind in the mould of Adam, and even so no man is identical to another. For this reason each person must respect himself and say with dignity:

"God created the world on my account. Therefore let me not lose eternal life because of some vain passion!"

WHY ONLY ONE ADAM?: Adapted from the *Agada* in the Talmud.

His Fault

I ONCE saw a man with a long beard who was riding upon an ass which he was beating. He said to him, "Oh cursed beast! If you did not wish to be ridden why did you become an ass?"

Bad Business

THE Evil Spirit once came dejected before God and wailed, "Almighty God—I want you to know that I am bored—bored to tears! I go around doing nothing all day long. There isn't a stitch of work for me to do!"

"I can't understand you," replied God. "There's plenty of work to be done only you've got to have more initiative. Why don't you try to lead people into sin? That's your job!"

"Lead people into sin!" muttered the Evil Spirit contemptuously. "Why, Lord, even before I can get a chance to say a blessed word to anyone he has already gone and sinned!"

It Was Obvious

A TALMUDIC scholar from Marmaresch was on his way home from a visit to Budapest. Opposite him in the railway carriage sat another Jew, dressed in modern fashion and smoking a cigar. When the conductor came around to collect the tickets the scholar noticed that his neighbor opposite was also on his way to Marmaresch.

This seemed very odd to him.

"Who can it be, and why is he going to Marmaresch?" he wondered.

As it would not be polite to ask outright he tried to figure it out for himself.

"Now, let me see," he mused. "He is a modern Jew, well dressed, and he smokes a cigar. Whom could a man of this type be visiting in Marmaresch? Possibly he's on his way to our town doctor's wedding. But no, that can't be! That's two weeks off. Certainly this kind of man wouldn't twiddle his thumbs in our town for two weeks!

"Why then is he on his way to Marmaresch? Perhaps he's courting a woman there? But who could it be? Now let me see. Moses Goldman's daughter Esther? Yes, definitely, it's she and nobody else . . .! But now

---

HIS FAULT: Adapted from Bar-Hebraeus (13th Century, Syria).

IT WAS OBVIOUS: Adapted and translated from *Royte Pomerantsen*, a collection of Jewish folk humor, by Immanuel Olsvanger. By permission of Schocken Books. New York, 1947.

that I think of it—that couldn't be! She's too old—he wouldn't have her, under any circumstances! Maybe it's Haikeh Wasservogel? Phooey! She's so ugly! Who then? Could it be Leah, the money-lender's daughter? N—no! What a match for such a nice man! Who then? There aren't any more marriageable girls in Marmaresch. That's settled then, he's not going courting.

"What then brings him?

"Wait, I've got it! It's about Mottel Kohn's bankruptcy case! But what connection can he have with that? Could it be that he is one of his creditors? Hardly! Just look at him sitting there so calmly, reading his newspaper and smiling to himself. Anybody can see nothing worries him! No, he's not a creditor. But I'll bet he has something to do with the bankruptcy! Now what could it be?

"Wait a minute, I think I've got it. Mottel Kohn must have corresponded with a lawyer from Budapest about his bankruptcy. But that swindler Mottel certainly wouldn't confide his business secrets to a stranger! So it stands to reason that the lawyer must be a member of the family.

"Now who could it be? Could it be his sister Shprinzah's son? No, that's impossible. She got married twenty-six years ago—I remember it very well because the wedding took place in the green synagogue. And this man here looks at least thirty-five.

"A funny thing! Who could it be, after all . . . ? Wait a minute! It's as clear as day! This is his nephew, his brother Hayyim's son, because Hayyim Kohn got married thirty-seven years and two months ago in the stone synagogue near the market place. Yes, that's who he is!

"In a nutshell—he is Lawyer Kohn from Budapest. But a lawyer from Budapest surely must have the title 'Doctor'! So, he is Doctor Kohn from Budapest, no? But wait a minute! A lawyer from Budapest who calls himself 'Doctor' won't call himself 'Kohn'! Anybody knows that. It's certain that he has changed his name into Hungarian. Now, what kind of a name could he have made out of Kohn? Kovacs! Yes, that's it— Kovacs! In short, this is Doctor Kovacs from Budapest!"

Eager to start a conversation the scholar turned to his travelling companion and asked, "Doctor Kovacs, do you mind if I open the window?"

"Not at all," answered the other. "But tell me, how do you know that I am Doctor Kovacs?"

"It was obvious," replied the scholar.

He Had Him Coming and Going

A POOR shopkeeper listened raptly to the rabbi's sermon on that Sabbath day in the synagogue. The rabbi preached, "He who is poor in this life will be rich in the world to come; he who is rich here, by God's decree, will be poor in the next world, for all men are equally God's children and he is just to them all."

Several days later the poor shopkeeper went to see the rabbi.

"Rabbi," he asked anxiously, "do you really believe that those who are poor in this world will be rich in the next?"

"No doubt about it!" emphatically answered the rabbi.

"You know I'm a poor shopkeeper—do you mean to say I'll be rich in the world to come?"

"Of course!"

Overjoyed, the poor shopkeeper cried, "In that case, Rabbi, lend me a hundred rubles. When I collect my riches in the next world I'll give them back to you."

Without a word, the rabbi counted out one hundred shiny silver rubles. The poor merchant could not believe his own eyes. As he stretched out his hand to gather in the money, the rabbi stopped him and asked, "What do you plan to do with your money, my friend?"

"Buy a new stock of merchandise."

"Do you expect to make money on it?"

"It'll sell like *Channukah* pancakes!"

"In that case," said the rabbi, gathering up the money himself, "I can't give you the hundred rubles. If you get rich here you'll be poor over there. So how in the world do you expect to return the loan?"

The Fine Art of Fanning

FOR a full hour Mrs. Gutman from Suffolk Street handled every fan on the pushcart, feeling them, smelling them, weighing them, trying to decide which one to buy.

"I'll take this penny fan," she finally said, giving the disgusted peddler her coin.

She then went home with her purchase.

The following morning, bright and early, the peddler saw her standing big as life before him.

"What is it now?" he asked.

Mutely she held up the broken remnants of the fan she had purchased the day before.

"What's the matter?" he asked.

"I want my money back!" she demanded.

"How much did you pay?"

"A penny."

"And how did you use it?"

"What kind of a foolish question is that? Naturally I waved it in front of my face from side to side."

"Is that what you do with a penny fan, Mrs. Gutman, eh?" cried the peddler, outraged. "That's what you do with a five cents fan! With a penny fan you hold the fan still and wave your head!"

For Honor

A STRANGER came to town. He stopped the first Jew in the market-place and asked him, "Can you please tell me where *Reb* Yankel, the warden of the synagogue, lives?"

"Oh," said the man, "you probably mean *Reb* Yankel, the Stutterer, whose father is *Reb* Avremel 'Eczema.' He lives further down near the church."

When the stranger reached the church he asked a passerby, "Can you please tell me where *Reb* Yankel lives?"

"Oh, you mean *Reb* Yankel with the hernia, the wife beater?" answered the passerby. "He's buried three wives already. You'll find him over there."

The stranger went on to where he was directed, but, to make sure, he asked a shopkeeper.

"Can you please tell me where *Reb* Yankel lives?"

"Oh, *Reb* Yankel!" answered the shopkeeper. "You mean *Reb* Yankel-*Goniff*, who goes into bankruptcy every other year! There he stands—over there!"

The stranger approached *Reb* Yankel and, after introducing himself, asked him, "Tell me, *Reb* Yankel, what on earth do you get out of being warden in this town?"

"Nothing! Not even a groschen!"

"Then why do you do it?"

"What a question to ask! I do it for the honor!"

Iron Logic

AN OLD Jewish woman, just turned ninety, became ill and called the doctor. He examined her carefully and looked doubtful.

"Can you cure me, doctor?" the old woman asked, hopefully.

"Dear Granny," said the doctor, soothingly. "You know what happens when one gets older. All sorts of ailments begin to happen. After all, a doctor is not a miracle man. He cannot make an old woman younger."

"Who's asking you to make me younger, doctor?" protested the old woman, irritably. "What I want is to grow older!"

No Target

To A rabbinical school in Old Russia the military came in search of recruits. The entire student body was drafted.

In camp, the students amazed their new masters by their marksmanship on the rifle range. Accordingly, when war broke out, the *Yeshiva* youths were ordered en masse into the front lines.

Shortly after the contingent arrived an attack began. Far in the distance, in No Man's Land, an advancing horde of Germans appeared. The Czarist officers called out, "Ready . . . aim . . . fire!"

But no fire was forthcoming.

"Fire!" yelled the officers. "Didn't you hear? Fire, you idiots, *fire!*"

Still nothing happened.

Beside himself with rage, the commanding officer demanded, "Why don't you fire?"

One of the youths mildly answered, "Can't you see . . . there are people in the way. Somebody might get hurt!"

Pain and Pleasure

A JEWISH father took his little boy to the bath for the first time. When they jumped into the pool the little boy began to shiver with cold and cried, "*Oy*, papa, *oy!*"

His father then led him out of the pool, rubbed him down with a towel and dressed him.

"Ah-h, papa, ah-h!" purred the little fellow, tingling with pleasant warmth.

"Isaac," said the father thoughtfully, "do you want to know the difference between a cold bath and a sin? When you jump into a cold pool you first yell '*Oy!*' and then you say 'Ah-h.' But when you commit a sin you first say 'Ah-h,' and then you yell '*oy!*' "

The Rabbi's Nourishment

A VILLAGE Jew was asked, "How can your rabbi survive on the small salary you're paying him?"

"Our rabbi would have died of hunger a long time ago. It's just his luck that on account of piety he has decided to fast every Monday and Thursday. That sustains him."

Cheap

YOSSEL and Mendel were partners in a small village inn. One day, having scraped together a few rubles, they drove to town to buy a keg of whiskey.

On the way back the weather became cold and blustering and the two partners were teased by the desire to take a drink of whiskey. But to do so became a serious problem. Had they not solemnly promised each other when they had placed the keg on the wagon not to touch a drop of it? Their entire livelihood for the week depended upon it.

Now Yossel was a resourceful man. He looked into his pockets and found a five-kopek piece, so he said to Mendel, "Here is a five-kopek piece. Sell me a drink of whiskey from your half of the keg."

Mendel, being a businessman, answered, "Since you have cash I have to sell you a drink."

So he poured him a little glassful. . . .

No sooner had Yossel downed the drink than he became warm and cheerful. Mendel's nose, on the other hand, got bluer from the cold. How he envied that rascal Yossel for his luck in having the five-kopek piece!

But suddenly he felt the coin in his pocket. After all, the coin is mine now, he said to himself. Why can't I buy a drink from him now? So he said to his partner, "Yossel, here is a five-kopek piece. Pour me a drink from your share of the keg!"

Yossel, being a businessman, said, "Cash is cash!"

And he poured Mendel a drink and took back his five-kopek piece.

In this fashion Mendel and Yossel kept on buying a drink from each other with the same five-kopek piece. By the time they reached the inn they were thoroughly drunk.

"What a miracle!" cried Yossel. "Imagine, an entire keg of whiskey sold for one five-kopek piece!"

He Ran for His Health

IT WAS in the days of Czar Nicholas II. Two Jews were walking along a boulevard in Moscow. One had a residence permit, the other didn't. Suddenly a policeman appeared.

"Quick—run!" whispered the one without the permit. "When the policeman sees you run he will think you have no permit, so he will run after you. This will give me a chance to get away, and it won't hurt you any because you can show him your permit."

So the Jew with the permit started to run. As soon as the policeman saw him do so he went in hot pursuit. After a few moments he caught up with him.

"Ahah!" gloated the policeman. "So you have no permit!"

"No permit! What makes you think I have no permit?" asked the Jew, showing it to him.

The policeman looked bewildered.

"Why then did you run away when you saw me?"

"My doctor told me always to run after taking a physic."

"But didn't you see me running after you?"

"Sure, I did. But I thought your doctor had given you the same advice!"

World-Weary

FOR two and a half years the rival Talmudic schools of Shammai and of Hillel debated the question but they could not resolve it.

The adherents of Shammai argued that it would have been far better for man had he never been created. The followers of Hillel maintained that it was good that man had been created.

Finally, both schools concluded their controversy on a compromise: that it would have been far better for man had he never been created, but, since he is already here on earth, it is his obligation to make the best of it and live uprightly.

Truth in Gay Clothes

THE Preacher of Dubno, Jacob Krantz, was once asked why the parable has such persuasive power over people. The Preacher replied, "I will explain this by means of a parable.

"It happened once that Truth walked about the streets as naked as his mother bore him. Naturally, people were scandalized and wouldn't let him into their houses. Whoever saw him got frightened and ran away.

"And so as Truth wandered through the streets brooding over his troubles he met Parable. Parable was gaily decked out in fine clothes and was a sight to see. He asked, 'Tell me, what is the meaning of all this? Why do you walk about naked and looking so woebegone?'

"Truth shook his head sadly and replied, 'Everything is going downhill with me, brother. I've gotten so old and decrepit that everybody avoids me.'

" 'What you're saying makes no sense,' said Parable. 'People are not giving you a wide berth because you are old. Take me, for instance, I am no younger than you. Nonetheless, the older I get the more attractive people find me. Just let me confide a secret to you about people. They don't like things plain and bare but dressed up prettily and a little artificial. I'll tell you what. I will lend you some fine clothes like mine and you'll soon see how people will take to you.'

"Truth followed this advice and decked himself out in Parable's gay clothes. And lo and behold! People no longer shunned him but welcomed him heartily. Since that time Truth and Parable are to be seen as inseparable companions, esteemed and loved by all."

What Is Greatness?

ONCE there was a man of great learning, versed in every branch of knowledge. In addition, he had a beautiful voice and played on the violin like

---

WORLD-WEARY: Adapted from the *Agada* in the Talmud.

WHAT IS GREATNESS?: Adapted from the *Parables of the Preacher of Dubno*.

a master. One day he fell sick and the doctors advised him to move to a warm climate. This he did, and settled in a small town among ordinary people of little education.

As is customary, they asked him, "What is your calling?"

"I do cupping."

Afterwards, when they were alone, his wife said to him, "I can't understand how a great scholar like you, with so many accomplishments, should have mentioned cupping as the one thing you know how to do! What kind of honor or profit do you expect from it?"

"The people of this town," explained her husband, "are poor people with simple needs. Were I to recite to them my important accomplishments they simply wouldn't know how to value them, nor would they know what to do with them. They would only look upon me as a superfluous man who could be of no earthly use to them. But, ah, how different with a man who can do cupping! To them he is a very important and useful person. They will have great respect for me, I assure you."

The Modest Saint

A DISCIPLE once was boasting rapturously before strangers about his rabbi:

"My rabbi, long life to him! He fasts every single day except, of course, on the Sabbath day and on holidays."

"What a lie!" mocked a cynic. "I myself have seen your rabbi eating on weekdays!"

"What do you know about my rabbi?" the faithful disciple snorted disdainfully. "My rabbi is a saint and very modest in his piety. If he eats it is only to hide from others the fact that he is fasting!"

The Poor Are Willing

THE rabbi had prayed long and fervently.

"And what have you prayed for today?" asked his wife.

"My prayer is that the rich should give bigger alms to the poor," answered the rabbi.

"Do you think God has heard your prayer?" his wife asked.

"I'm sure He has heard at least half of it," replied the rabbi. "The poor have agreed to accept."

There Are Miracles and Miracles

A *Hasid* had heard so much of the sanctity of a certain rabbi that he journeyed all the way from his village to the town where the great rabbi lived.

"What miracles has your rabbi performed?" inquired the visiting *Hasid* of one of the rabbi's disciples.

"There are miracles and miracles," replied the disciple. "For instance, the people of your town would regard it as a miracle if God should do your rabbi's bidding. We, on the other hand, regard it as a miracle that our rabbi does God's bidding."

The Expert

WHEN you tell a joke to a Frenchman he laughs three times: once when you tell it to him, the second time when you explain it, and the third time when he understands it—for the Frenchman loves to laugh.

When you tell a joke to an Englishman he laughs twice: once when you tell it to him and again when you explain it—but understand it he never can, for he's too stuffy.

When you tell a joke to a German he laughs only once: when you tell it to him. First of all, he won't let you explain it to him because he's so arrogant. Secondly, even if he did ask you to explain it he wouldn't understand because he has no sense of humor.

When you tell a story to a Jew—before even you've had a chance to finish he interrupts you impatiently. First of all, he has heard it before! Secondly, what business have you telling a joke when you don't know how? In the end, he decides to tell you the story himself, but in a much better version than yours.

No Loan!

TWO chance acquaintances, both recent arrivals from Poland, met on Delancey Street in New York's East Side.

"Hello! How's business?"

"All right."

"In that case, will you lend me five dollars?"

"Why should I lend you five dollars? I hardly know you!"

"A funny thing! In my town in the old country people wouldn't lend me any money because they knew me, and in this country they won't lend any because they don't know me."

A Quick Prayer

ONCE, after prayer in the synagogue, the rabbi asked Hershel Ostropolier, "How is it you pray so fast? It's a disgrace! Why does it take me twice as long to say my prayers?"

"Who can compare with you, Rabbi?" answered Hershel. "You, Rabbi, have, may no evil eye fall on you, a lot of gold and silver, a fine house, four horses and a carriage, and money in the bank. It takes time to go over all these matters with God when you pray to him to preserve them for you. Now take me, on the other hand, what have I got? Only a shrewish wife, eight children and a flea-bitten goat. In my prayer to God, all I have to say is: 'Wife, children, goat!'—and I'm through!"

Schnapps Wisdom

THE old *shammes* began to lose his hearing. The doctor, whom he consulted, told him that too much alcohol was making him deaf.

"You musn't drink anymore!" he rebuked him.

For one interminable month the old *shammes* scrupulously avoided liquor and his hearing gradually returned. But suddenly he was tempted and took to the bitter drop again. This time he became deaf as a door-post and used an earhorn.

Once more he came to consult the doctor.

"Didn't I tell you not to drink any *schnapps*?" roared the doctor into his earhorn.

The old *shammes* shrugged his shoulders wearily.

"Sure you told me, and I did exactly as you told me," he answered. "But, believe me, doctor, nothing I heard was worth one good *schnapps*!"

He Should Have Taken More Time

THE rabbi ordered a pair of new pants for the Passover holidays from the village tailor. The tailor, who was very unreliable, took a long time finishing the job. The rabbi was afraid that he would not have the garment ready for the holidays.

On the day before Passover the tailor came running all out of breath to deliver the pants.

The rabbi examined his new garment with a critical eye.

"Thank you for bringing my pants on time," he said. "But tell me, my friend, if it took God only six days to create our vast and complicated world, why did it have to take you six weeks to make this simple pair of pants?"

"But, Rabbi!" murmured the tailor triumphantly, "Just look at the mess God made, and then look at this beautiful pair of pants!"

It Pays to Be Ignorant

A POOR *luftmensch* came to New York from Kovno. He had neither trade nor calling and, when he found that the streets of America were not lined with gold as he had been told in the old country, he became a peddler of needles, pins, and hooks and eyes. Life was hard, insults were many, and the profits were small. So he kept his eyes open for something better. When he heard that a *shammes* was wanted in a synagogue on Attorney Street he hurried to apply for the post.

"Can you read and write English?" asked the president.

"No," answered the peddler.

"Sorry, mister," replied the president. "In America a *shammes* has got to know how to read and write. New York is not Boiberik, you know."

So the poor man sighed and went sadly away.

But in the course of time he began to prosper. He turned to real estate and amassed a fortune.

One day, when he needed a quarter of a million dollars to finance a real estate venture, he went to his banker and asked for a loan. He got it instantly.

"Write your own check," said the president of the bank flatteringly, handing him his pen.

"I—I can't write at all," stammered the realtor in embarrassment. "I've only learned to sign my name."

"Tsk-tsk, how wonderful!" exclaimed the banker. "If you have accomplished so much without knowing how to read or write, imagine what you would have been today if you did know how!"

"Sure!" muttered the realtor. "I would have been the *shammes* of the Attorney Street Synagogue!"

Equally Logical

A GROUP of Nazis surrounded an elderly Berlin Jew and demanded of him, "Tell us, Jew, who caused the war?"

The little Jew was no fool. "The Jews," he said, then added, "and the bicycle riders."

The Nazis were puzzled. "Why the bicycle riders?"

"Why the Jews?" answered the little old man.

The Life of a Jew!

IVAN SERAFIMOVITCH, the driver, was taking his Jewish passenger, Shmul the *melamed*, from Boryslav to Drohobycz. From the other end, from Drohobycz, Mikhail Stepanovitch was driving Moishe the *shammes*, to Boryslav.

When Ivan and Mikhail met on the road, each going in the opposite direction, they drew up their carts and exchanged a pleasant good-morning.

"I see, Mikhail Stepanovitch," sneered Ivan, "that you have that horse-faced Jew Moshka for a passenger."

"What's the matter? Don't you like him?" Mikhail snapped back. "He's nicer than that scarecrow of yours, Shmul."

"I want to serve notice on you, Mikhail Stepanovitch," threatened Ivan, "that no pot-bellied sot like you can abuse my passenger and get away with it."

"Just look who's talking, you goggle-eyed pig!" snorted Mikhail. "One more word from you and I'll give it to your Shmul in the snout!"

"Just try and do it!" challenged Ivan, defiantly.

Without a word, Mikhail jumped off his cart and crossed to the other side of the road. Climbing into Ivan's cart he punched Shmul in the nose.

When Ivan saw that his passenger's face was covered with blood, he was incensed and began to tremble with rage.

"How dare you hit my Shmul! I won't let you get away with it!" he shouted. "Since you hit my Shmulka I'm going to hit your Moshka!"

He wasn't at all lazy and got out of the cart, crossed the road to Mikhail's cart and let fly with his fist into Moshka's face.

When Ivan saw Moshka's eye swell up, he was speechless with rage.

"With God and the Czar as my witnesses, I warn you, Mikhail Stepanovitch—this is the limit!"

And, so saying, he fell upon Shmul, the *melamed,* and pounded him within an inch of his life.

"Never fear," shrilled Mikhail. "I'll match you in everything anytime. I'll turn your Moshka into pulp for what you've done to my Shmulka!"

A man of his word, Mikhail fell upon Moshka and knocked him unconscious.

For a moment Ivan Serafimovitch and Mikhail Stepanovitch glared at each other with a deadly hatred. Then each spat out contemptuously, mounted his cart and rattled away.

Nebich!

IT HAPPENED in a Russian town in the days of the Czar. A party of convicts was being lead to prison. It included three Jews. As they shuffled through the streets loaded with chains some Jewish women began to commiserate loudly with them.

"Why are they taking you?" they mournfully asked one Jewish convict.

"It's on account of my residence permit," he answered with a sigh.

Hearing this, the women wailed, *"Oy, nebich!* What a wrong! and just for a mere residence permit!

"And why are they punishing you?" they asked the second Jew.

"It's because I didn't want to be a soldier in the army of that Haman, Czar Nicolai!"

"Oy, nebich!" wailed the women even more loudly. "What a shame— what cruelty! And just because he didn't wish to serve that dog of dogs, that anti-Semite!"

Then the third Jewish convict, a muscular fellow with squint eyes and a scar on his face, passed by.

"Tell us—why are they taking you?" the women inquired.

"Who, me?" he asked piteously. "I am *nebich* a *goniff*."

The Modest Rabbi

THE wonder-working *tzaddik* seemed fast asleep. Nearby sat his worshipful disciples, carrying on a whispered conversation with bated breath about the holy man's unparalleled virtues.

"What piety!" exclaimed one disciple with rapture. "There isn't another like him in all Poland!"

"Who can compare with him in charity?" murmured another ecstatically. "He gives alms with an open hand."

"And what a sweet temper! Has anyone ever seen him get excited?" whispered another with shining eyes.

"*Ai!* What learning he's got!" chanted another. "He's a second Rashi!"

At that the disciples fell silent. Whereupon the rabbi slowly opened one eye and regarded them with an injured expression.

"And about my modesty you say nothing?" he asked reproachfully.

The Secret of Power

THE waters were rising until they almost reached the Throne of Glory. Thereupon the Almighty cried out: "Be still, O waters!"

Then the waters became vainglorious and boasted: "We are the mightiest of all creation—let us flood the earth!"

At this God grew wrathful and rebuked the waters: "Do not boast of your strength, ye vain braggarts! I will send upon you the sands and they will raise up a barrier against you!"

When the waters saw the sand and of what tiny grains it consisted they began to mock: "How can such tiny grains as you stand up against us? Our smallest wave will sweep over you!"

When the grains of sand heard this they were frightened. But their leader comforted them: "Do not fear, brothers! True enough, we are tiny and every one of us by himself is insignificant. The wind can carry us to all the ends of the earth, but, if we all only remain united, then the waters will see what kind of power we have!"

When the little grains of sand heard these words of comfort they came flying from all the corners of the earth and lay down one on top of the

THE SECRET OF POWER: Adapted from the *Midrash.*

other and against each other upon the shores of the seas. They rose up
in mounds, in hills, and in mountains, and formed a huge barrier against
the waters. And when the waters saw how the great army of the grains of
sand stood united they became frightened and retreated.

Circumcisional Evidence

A YOUNG Talmudic scholar left Minsk and went to America.

After many years he returned to the old country. His aged mother
could hardly recognize him. He was dressed in the very latest fashion.

"Where is your beard?" his mother asked, aghast.

"Nobody wears a beard in America."

"But at least you keep the Sabbath?"

"In America almost everybody works on the Sabbath."

The old mother sighed.

"And how is it with the food?" she asked hopefully.

"Ah, mama," answered the son, apologetically, "it's too much trouble
to be *kosher* in America."

The old mother hesitated. Then, in a confidential voice, she whispered,
"Tell your old mother, son—are you still circumcised?"

The Sled Story

THE snow was beautiful, but Mendel felt that each snowflake was a dagger
thrust into his heart.

"Everything happens to me!" he moaned. "Just when I get my home
fixed up okay, the landlord tells me the building is coming down. I gotta
move! I slave and I slave and at last I find a place around the corner.
How shall I move? I struggle and I struggle and I get everything arranged
for moving tomorrow. And now it snows! And what a snow! Everything is
upset. Woe is me!"

It was truly a dark, dark night for Mendel. Shaking his head, he undressed wearily and climbed into bed, but he couldn't get settled. "Such
troubles, what'll I do?" He twisted and turned restlessly. "What is there
to do?" He twisted and turned again and this time a thought struck him.

"I know! I'll borrow Goldberg's sled. It's simple. I'll pile the stuff on
it and one trip—two trips—ten trips. It's done. Wonderful. Okay. Thank
God." He turned and settled back comfortably. He was just about dozing
off when another thought struck him.

What if Goldberg won't lend his sled?

"Nonsense! Why shouldn't he lend his sled? Of course he will. Forget
it!"

What if Goldberg won't lend his sled?

"Why not? What am I going to do to it? Can you imagine that—Goldberg not willing to lend me his sled? Oh! The scoundrel! A plague on him! What a nerve! Not to lend me his sled! No! No! It can't be. Of course he'll lend it to me."

He turned around and settled himself for sleep.

Goldberg won't lend his sled!

"Goldberg not lend his sled? It's unthinkable. After what I did for him! Who got him his first job? Who showed him the ropes? Where did he get his meals when his wife was sick that time? I even introduced him to his wife. And wasn't I his best man? Didn't I sign the paper for him for the Morris Plan? When he had the trouble that time didn't I give him the money out of my own pocket? And now he wouldn't lend me his lousy two-dollar sled! That's too much. I won't stand for it. Why! Why——"

He scrambled out of bed, pulled on his trousers, thrust his coat around his shoulders, dashed out into the street, ran to Goldberg's house, and started jabbing crazily at Goldberg's doorbell, muttering the while, "The stinker—the low-life—the no-good—" until finally the sleepy Goldberg came to the door.

"Goldberg," shouted Mendel, "Goldberg, you no-good, you ingrate, you loafer! You know what you can do with your rattle-trap sled? You and your sled can go to hell! Good—bye!"

A Rabbi for a Day

THE famous Preacher of Dubno was once journeying from one town to another delivering his learned sermons. Wherever he went he was received with enthusiasm and accorded the greatest honors. His driver, who accompanied him on this tour, was very much impressed by all this welcome.

One day, as they were on the road, the driver said, "Rabbi, I have a great favor to ask of you. Wherever we go people heap honors on you. Although I'm only an ignorant driver I'd like to know how it feels to receive so much attention. Would you mind if we were to exchange clothes for one day? Then they'll think I am the great preacher and you the driver, so they'll honor me instead!"

Now the Preacher of Dubno was a man of the people and a merry soul, but he saw the pitfalls awaiting his driver in such an arrangement.

"Suppose I agreed—what then? You know the rabbi's clothes don't make a rabbi! What would you do for learning? If they were to ask you to explain some difficult passage in the Law you'd only make a fool of yourself, wouldn't you?"

"Don't you worry, Rabbi—I am willing to take that chance."

"In that case," said the preacher, "here are my clothes."

And the two men undressed and exchanged clothes as well as their callings.

As they entered the town all the Jewish inhabitants turned out to greet the great preacher. They conducted him into the synagogue while the assumed driver followed discreetly at a distance.

Each man came up to the "rabbi" to shake hands and to say the customary: "*Sholom Aleichem,* learned Rabbi!"

The "rabbi" was thrilled with his reception. He sat down in the seat of honor surrounded by all the scholars and dignitaries of the town. In the meantime the preacher from his corner kept his merry eyes on the driver to see what would happen.

"Learned Rabbi," suddenly asked a local scholar, "would you be good enough to explain to us this passage in the Law we don't understand?"

The preacher in his corner chuckled, for the passage was indeed a difficult one.

"Now he's sunk!" he said to himself.

With knitted brows the "rabbi" peered into the sacred book placed before him, although he could not understand one word. Then, impatiently pushing it away from him, he addressed himself sarcastically to the learned men of the town, "A fine lot of scholars you are! Is this the most difficult question you could ask me? Why, this passage is so simple even my driver could explain it to you!"

Then he called to the Preacher of Dubno: "Driver, come here for a moment and explain the Law to these 'scholars'!"

All Right

THERE was once a rabbi who was so open-minded that he could see every side of a question. One day a man came to him with the request that he grant him a divorce.

"What do you hold against your wife?" asked the rabbi gravely.

The man went into a lengthy recital of his complaints.

"You are right," he agreed when the man finished.

Then the rabbi turned to the woman.

"Now let us hear your story," he urged.

And the woman in her turn began to tell of the cruel mistreatment she had suffered at her husband's hands.

The rabbi listened with obvious distress.

"You are right," he said with conviction when she finished.

At this the rabbi's wife, who was present, exclaimed, "How can this be? Surely, both of them couldn't be right!"

The rabbi knitted his brows and reflected.

"You're right, too!" he agreed.

Why the Hair on the Head Turns Gray Before the Beard

THE Czar once went on a journey. On the way he met a poor Jewish farmer who was cultivating his field. The Czar saw that the farmer's hair was gray while his beard was black. At this he was filled with wonder.

"Do explain this mystery to me," the Czar asked him. "Why is the hair on your head gray and your beard black?"

"My beard didn't start growing until after I was *Bar-Mitzvah*," replied the Jew. "Consequently, since the hair on my head is many years older than the hair in my beard, it turned gray long before."

"How clever of you!" cried the Czar with admiration. "Promise me, on your word of honor, never to repeat this explanation to anyone. I will allow you to reveal the secret only after you have seen me one hundred times."

The Czar then continued on his journey.

Upon his return home he assembled all his ministers, wise men and counsellors.

"I will put to you a very puzzling question," he told them. "See if you can answer it."

"Speak, O King!" cried the wise men

"Why is it," asked the Czar, "that the hair on the head becomes gray long before the hair in the beard does?"

The wise men remained mute with astonishment. They did not know what to answer.

"Take a month's time to think it over," said the Czar. "Then come back to me with your answer."

The wise men went away and devoted themselves single-mindedly to the solution of the problem the Czar had put to them.

As the month was nearing its end and still they had not found an answer they were filled with gloom. But they found a straw of hope to clutch at when one of the ministers recalled that on the day the Czar had put the puzzling question to them he had come back from a journey outside the capital. So he undertook to track the matter down to its source.

The minister followed the route the Czar had taken and he chanced upon the same poor Jewish farmer with whom the Czar had spoken. He recognized him by the fact that the hair on his head was gray and the hair in his beard was black.

"What is the explanation for this strange fact?" he asked the Jew.

The Jewish farmer answered, "Alas, I'm not allowed to give you the answer!"

"I'll pay you well if you'll reveal your secret to me," coaxed the king's counsellor.

WHY THE HAIR ON THE HEAD TURNS GRAY BEFORE THE BEARD: Adapted from *Yiddishe Folksmaisses*, compiled by Judah Loeb Cahan. Ferlag Yiddishe Folklore-Bibliothek. New York and Vilna, 1931.

The poor Jew hesitated. Then he said, "I'm a poor man. I'm desperately in need of some money. If you will pay me a hundred silver rubles I'll reveal to you my secret."

After he got the hundred silver rubles, he gave him the answer he had given to the Czar.

The minister then returned to St. Petersburg and gave the Czar the answer. But the Czar understood immediately how he had gotten the answer. So he sent for the Jew.

"Do you know what punishment you deserve for breaking your promise to me?" cried the Czar, angrily. "Didn't I ask you to keep your answer a secret?"

"Indeed, you did!" replied the Jew. "But you must also recall that you gave me permission to talk about it after I had seen you a hundred times."

"Insolent fellow!" cried the Czar. "How dare you lie so brazenly to me! You very well know I only saw you once!"

"I've told you the truth!" persisted the Jew. And he drew out of a bag a hundred silver rubles.

"See for yourself," said he. "On every one of these rubles is graven your image. And, having looked upon them all, I have seen you one hundred times. Was I wrong in giving your minister the answer?"

"What a clever man!" exclaimed the Czar with rapture. "What you deserve is a reward, not punishment! Remain with me here in my palace so that I may always have the benefit of your counsel."

And so the poor Jewish farmer lived with the Czar in his palace in St. Petersburg, and was the first among his counsellors. The Czar never made a decision without consulting him first, and, wherever he went, the Jew went along with him.

The Way Anti-Semites Reason

As THE Emperor Hadrian was being carried through the streets of Rome a Jew passed by.

"Long life to you, O Emperor!" the Jew greeted him.

"Who are you?" asked the Emperor.

"I'm a Jew."

"How dare you, a Jew, greet me!" Hadrian raged. "Chop his head off!" he ordered his soldiers.

Another Jew, who chanced to pass by just then and saw what had happened to the first Jew, decided not to greet the Emperor.

"Who are you?" Hadrian demanded.

"I'm a Jew."

"How dare you, a Jew, pass me by without greeting me?" raged Hadrian. "Chop his head off!" he ordered his soldiers.

THE WAY ANTI-SEMITES REASON: Adapted from the *Midrash*.

The Emperor's counsellors were filled with astonishment.

"O Emperor, we cannot grasp the meaning of your action," they said. "If you had the first Jew decapitated because he greeted you, why did you do the same thing to the second Jew because he did not greet you?"

"Are you trying to teach me how to handle my enemies?" retorted the Emperor.

The Relativity of Distance

THREE weary Jewish refugees stood before the Paris representative of the Jewish Joint Distribution Committee.

"Where are you all going?" he asked them.

"I'm on my way to Rome," said the first.

"London is my destination," said the second.

"My plan is to go to South Africa," said the third.

"South Africa? Why so far?" the agent asked wonderingly.

"Far? Far from where?" wistfully countered the refugee.

PART TWO
Heroes

INTRODUCTION

"Who is a hero?" rhetorically asks a sage in the Talmud.

"He who becomes master over his passions," is his own answer.

The pursuit of virtue as a heroic quest is a fundamental tradition in Jewish life and lore. It is the seal of the Jews' ethical individuality as a people. It is their moral justification in their own eyes. For countless generations they have been encouraged by their leaders and teachers to pattern their lives on this religious-social ideal in both thought and action. Their folklore reflects this with dazzling clarity. The righteous, the wise man, is the hero, not the warrior who sheds human blood.

This extraordinary attitude was induced by the peculiar historic experiences of the Jews and was conditioned by more than twenty-five hundred years of this mode of living, thinking and feeling. "Sons of the Compassionate"—is what Jews proverbially call themselves. In their traditional view the moral and physical powers are everlastingly opposed to each other. For precisely that reason the warrior-hero, so overwhelmingly adulated by other peoples, was largely neglected by them. The folklorists of the *Midrash* almost gloss over the exploits of Samson against the Philistines. They glow with more genuine excitement over David, the sweet singer of Zion, than over David, the slayer of the giant Goliath, or David the triumphant warrior-king. To be sure there are exceptions—such as the heroic deeds of the Maccabees and Bar Kochba. But their celebration in Jewish legend does not rest on their warlike exploits or their feats of bravery alone. It is primarily because these men were the inspired leaders of their people in its struggle for liberty.

The characteristic attitude toward the warrior is quaintly described in Jewish lore by the contrast made in the characters of the Patriarch Jacob and his brother Esau. The latter, surnamed "the Wicked" in Jewish folklore, is portrayed as a fierce warrior and hunter, preoccupied with fighting and the chase. Jacob, on the other hand, is depicted as a gentle scholar, always found in the House of Study in pursuit of divine instruction. The same attitude is expressed in the amusing medieval engraving found in many editions of the *Haggadah*, the liturgy for the *Seder* which is the home service of Passover Eve. The picture presents four types of questioners: the sage, the wicked man, the fool and the idiot. The sage is lovingly portrayed as a scholar in the eloquent attitude of expounding the Torah. The wicked man, on the other hand, is represented as a fierce knight in armor running with spear in hand.

This does not by any means suggest that Jews were like the Buddhists, unalterably opposed to war. Their struggles for their national freedom, beginning with the Egyptian bondage, refutes this idea. Jews were always opposed to war and violence on moral and humanitarian grounds, except when they fought in self-defense or for the preservation of their country and faith. Then they fought as did only few other peoples in history— with valor and an utter disregard for their lives. For instance, during the two-year siege of Jerusalem by Titus, more than a million Jews perished resisting the hated enemy, an event hardly paralleled in the wars of Antiquity. But fighting as an end in itself, or to acquire ill-gotten gains, was considered wicked and anti-social beginning with the era of the canonical Prophets.

In place of the strong men and the warrior heroes of other peoples the Jews substituted *tzaddikim,* saintly and righteous men. But these were far from being insipid in their gentleness, hangdog in their piety, or submissive because of their abhorrence of violence. They were in reality men who stood up with dignity for their beliefs, and often sacrificed their lives in defense of them. In medieval, and in later folklore as well, these *tzaddikim* took on the sublimated character of the hero-knights of chivalry. In battling against the brute violence of their enemies they let their virtue be their sword and their Torah-learning, their shield. When the rabbi-knight was obliged to defend his religion and his people in disputations with Christian theologians before great throngs who treated him with scorn and mockery, he had to endure an infinitely more hazardous ordeal than that required of the Christian knight who went jousting cap-a-pie against friendly rivals at the tourneys of chivalry. The Jew was rarely the victor in this unequal contest and the direst misfortune fell upon entire communities of his brethren because of it. And yet, strange to relate, he remained a hero in the eyes of the people, for he had fought without fear or compromise as their champion, and with the only weapons sanctioned by their morality—wisdom and truth.

Those legends and tales, dealing with cabalists and *Hasidic* rabbis, endow their *tzaddikim* with invincible wonder-working powers. Many of them, like the knights of chivalry, sallied forth into the world to pursue quests of high valor. They were not accompanied by armed esquires, but by worshipful disciples. Their aim was not to rescue beautiful maidens held captive by wicked knights or to win a king's ransom by feats of arms. They went forth to battle against the power of evil, to redress wrongs, and to protect their people against threatening dangers. By the supernatural power of their virtue, and sometimes with the magical aid of the *Shem-hamforesh,* the secret name of God, (as in the case of Joseph della Reyna) they fought and triumphed over the wicked, even over the Angel of Death and Satan and over all his hosts of darkness. It even happened that these *tzaddikim* rose up to question God himself. This they did, not out of blasphemous intent or an arrogant spirit, but with the flame of truth and compassion burning within them. We have only to turn to the *Kaddish* of Rabbi Levi-Yitzchok, the Eighteenth Century *Hasidic tzaddik,* in which he questions God's justice toward his people. Jews in all parts of the world still sing its stirring strains:

> Therefore I, Levi-Yitzchok ben Sara of Berditchev say:
> *Lo azus mimkomi!* I shall not stir from here!
> An end must come to all this!
> Israel's suffering must end!
> *Isgadal v'iskadash shmay rahbo!*
> Magnified and sanctified be the name of the Lord!

N. A.

Wise Men

WISE AND LEARNED MEN

INTRODUCTION

The *chacham*, the wise man, has always been the beau ideal of Jewish tradition, and therefore of folklore as well. To a considerable degree, the *chacham* resembles the Greek conception of the philosopher. Knowledge and reason lead him to wisdom. And what is the highest wisdom? Virtue, of course. For this reason the *chacham* is required to be not only learned but righteous! He must have a passion for truth and possess genuine piety which dwells in the pure spirit alone. Above all, he must love people and seek justice. This pattern was laid down by Moses and the Prophets and it is remarkable how many Jews have attempted to emulate them ever since.

Before one could become wise one first had to acquire knowledge. "He who lacks knowledge lacks everything," said the sages of the Talmud. By knowledge was meant, not just any kind of knowledge, but knowledge of the Torah. And yet all knowledge, regardless of the source, was revered. That is why so many rabbis studied Greek philosophy, the natural sciences, medicine, and other peoples' wisdom literature. One of the rabbis of the Second Century expressed this very directly: "The man who understands astronomy and does not pursue the study of it, of him it is written in Scripture: 'They regard not the work of the Lord, neither have they considered his handiwork.'" One over-enthusiastic writer in the Talmud even went as far as to say: "A scholar is greater than a prophet."

The Yiddish-speaking Jews of the East European ghettos, until very recently representing the great majority of the Jews of the world, took this rabbinical dictum quite seriously. They venerated the role and function of the *lamdan* (scholar) above all other callings. For generations fond mothers would put their children to sleep with the haunting lullaby:

> What is the best *schoirah* (merchandise)?
> My baby will learn *Toirah* (Torah),
> *S'forim* (holy books) he will write for me,
> And a pious Jew he'll always be.

30

Wise and learned became synonymous concepts in Jewish thinking and the man who possessed both learning and wisdom was known as a *talmid chochem* ("a disciple of the wise"). This was a title of honor that represented the ultimate in social appreciation and recognition. Quite generally, although not always so, learning for Jews did not serve as an end in itself but as a means leading to a higher goal; it had to be endowed with the rapture of consecration. Therefore, the ancient rabbis said: "As with God, wisdom is a gift of free grace, so should man make it a free gift."

This was a conclusion that patently arose out of a profound social conscience; it was an impulse of democratic urgency in which learning and wisdom found their validity in improving men's minds as well as their way of life. Jewish tradition could see little merit in the saint who chose to prove his virtue by living alone in the wilderness. Likewise with the scholar. It was not enough that he sought knowledge and understanding for his own illumination. Possession of them imposed upon him the higher obligation to share them to the utmost with others less knowing or less fortunate than he. This exalted conception of learning led to the rabbinic opinion that it was wrong of the teacher of the Torah to accept remuneration for his instruction, for one must not traffic for gain with sacred values. With this in mind most of the *Tannaim* and the *Amoraim,* the architects of the *Mishna, Midrash* and Talmud, did not teach for gain but earned their livelihood in other ways at various trades and callings. Thus the illustrious Rabbi Hillel toiled as a common wood-cutter; Rabbi Yohanan ha-Sandler was a maker of sandals; Rabbi Isaac Nappaha had a smithy; the great Rabbi Joshua ben Hananiah was a skilled maker of needles; Rabbi Resh Lakesh was a night watchman in a vineyard; Rabbi Abba Hilkiah, the famous "rain-maker," was an agricultural day-laborer and Rabbi Shammai, the rector of a famous Jerusalem academy, was a land-surveyor. Thus, the dignity of labor was given increased luster by this example of the rabbis.

The scholar, the wise man, had no obsessive need of worldly goods. The pampering of the senses and a life of ease and luxury were interdicted for him by tradition. It was considered that they would only lead him into error and corrupt his moral values, and thus, without virtue, he no longer would be wise. In the great academy that Yohanan ben Zakkai founded in Jabneh after the destruction of Jerusalem, the sages taught the social creed of the scholar: "I who study Holy Lore am a man; my brother, the unlettered one, is also a man. I do my work in the House of Study—he is occupied as a tiller of the soil. I rise in the morning to earn my bread; he too with his toil. Even as he is not vainglorious about his work so am I humble in my own. Perhaps you will say that I do important work and he not. That is not true. Our sages have taught us that he who does much and he who does little are equal if only their intention is good."

Of course the Jews were not the only people in Antiquity who revered wisdom. The Egyptians, the Babylonians and the Greeks were equally devoted to it. For instance, the Book of Proverbs owes much to the sayings of the Egyptian scribe Amenemope. Greek philosophical ideas, and even modes of expression, are found in Jewish wisdom literature. The *Book of Ecclesiastes* is full of Stoic and Epicurean doctrines. And as for *Job,* which contains a panegyric to wisdom (*chochma*) in Chapter Twenty-eight, it is soaked in the twilight skepticism of Hellenist thought. No less Greek are the sayings of Ben Sira and yet, like *Job*, they are so profoundly Hebraic. None but a Jew trained in the ethical rationalism of Judaism could have possibly written his biting social satires so graphically full of the turmoil of the age. And his wisdom is the wisdom of the lucid mind, of the critical and appraising faculty that receives its impulse from a worldliness that is not parochial, but recoils from the obscure and the mystical.

> What is too wonderful for thee, do not seek.
> What is hidden from thee, do not search.
> Understand that which is permitted thee;
> And have no concern with mysteries.

The Hellenist intellectuals among the Jews of the first two centuries B.C. did their best to reconcile Jewish wisdom with Greek philosophy. For instance, Aristobulus, the first Jewish philosopher in Alexandria (180–146 B.C.), claimed: "Plato followed the Laws (i.e. the laws of the Torah) given to us, and had manifestly studied all that is said in them." He also tried to show the similarity between the teachings of Moses and those of the major Greek philosophers, saying that wisdom or *chochma* was esteemed equally by the Peripatetics and King Solomon. This belief had wide currency and even became a fixed tradition among the Christian Church Fathers.

So many of the stories in this compilation, whether serious or humorous, reveal with folkloristic directness the Jewish attitude towards learning and wisdom, scholars and wise men. Of great interest is the *Midrash* parable, *The Most Valuable Merchandise*. In a world in which the homeless and driven Jew was forced by his enemies to become a despised huckster of material goods he discovered by experience that learning was the only "merchandise" that had enduring value. It could neither be lost nor stolen nor snatched from him by violence as in the case of his material chattels. Therefore, the moral of the story, bitter-exalted in its flash of insight: "Learning is the best merchandise." Ever since the Talmudic era this saying has been on the lips of Jewish folk, uttered with a certainty and an intensity that has had few parallels in general lore.

Jewish learning never holds a recommendation for the wise man or scholar to become divorced from life. The rabbinic anecdote, *Learning That Leads to Action*, carries its own answer and justification for knowledge. Also the mind, by which one is able to comprehend learning and wisdom, must not be exalted above all other human faculties. Feeling and sentiment are never to be divorced from wisdom. We find this truth dwelled upon in the *Agada* piece, *The Best and the Worst Things*. What is the best thing? *A good heart*. The worst? *A bad heart*.

N. A.

The Romance of Akiba

IN JERUSALEM there once lived a very rich man whose name was Kalba Sabua. He had an only daughter, Rachel, who was beautiful and clever. The sons of the best families in the land proposed to her in marriage but she rejected them all.

"Neither riches nor good family concern me," she said. "The man I will marry must, above all, have a noble character and a good heart."

Among the shepherds who watched over her father's flocks and herds was a youth whose name was Akiba. Rachel fell in love with him and one day said to her father, "I want Akiba for my husband."

"Have you gone out of your mind?" cried her father. "How can you expect me to become the father-in-law of my servant? Never mention this to me again!"

"Father, give me Akiba for my husband!" pleaded Rachel. "I will not marry another."

"If you insist on marrying him you must leave my house!" threatened her father.

Rachel said no more but her mind was made up. She left her father's house and a life of luxury and fled with Akiba.

When Kalba Sabua heard of this he took a solemn oath: "My daughter shall not inherit even the least of my possessions."

Outside the city Akiba and his wife put up a tent. Having but little money they suffered privation and lived on dry bread alone. None the less, Rachel was happy and sustained the spirit of Akiba.

"I would rather live with you in poverty than without you in riches," she told him.

Their bed consisted only of a straw pallet. If a strong wind began to blow at night it would scatter the straw about. Rachel noticed that Akiba no longer slept but was wrapped in gloom.

"Why are you so sad, my husband?" she asked.

"It's on your account, Rachel," he replied. "You must suffer so, and all on account of me!"

At that very moment someone called from outside their tent.

"What is it you wish?" asked Rachel.

"Have pity on me!" answered the voice. "My wife has fallen sick and I have no straw to make a bed for her. Give me some, if you can."

And Rachel gave him some straw. Then she said to Akiba, "Just see— you consider us unfortunate but there are people who are even poorer than we."

"Bless you for your words! They have consoled me!" cried Akiba.

Often Akiba had expressed the wish to attend the Houses of Study in Jerusalem in order to acquire learning.

THE ROMANCE OF AKIBA: Adapted from the *Agada* in the Talmud.

One day Rachel said to him, "You must carry out your plan to become an educated man. I know it will be very difficult for you but I will gladly remain behind and not stand in your way. I will patiently wait for your return."

Thereupon Akiba arose and made ready for his journey to Jerusalem. His wife accompanied him on the way for a distance. Then she bade him fond farewell and turned sadly back.

As he walked along the road Akiba said to himself, "I'm almost forty years old and now it may be too late for me to study the Word of God. Who knows if I will ever be able to achieve my goal!"

Suddenly he came upon several shepherds sitting near a spring. At the mouth of the spring lay a stone which had many grooves.

"What caused these grooves?" he asked the shepherds.

"They were made by drops of water that steadily trickled upon the stone."

Hearing this Akiba rejoiced. He said to himself, "If a stone may be softened how much easier will it be to soften my mind!"

And he continued on his journey until he came to a school for children. There he learned how to read and write and was not ashamed to study with children. After that he entered the Houses of Study. He became a pupil of Rabbi Nahum Ish Gamzu. Afterwards he studied with Rabbi Eliezer ben Hyrkanos and Rabbi Joshua ben Hananiah.

Each day, before he went to the House of Study, Akiba would go into the forest to chop some wood. A part of it he sold in order to nourish himself, a part he kept for his own use, and the rest he used to pillow his head at night.

When Rachel heard of his hard manner of living she wished to help him. She cut off her hair which she sold, and sent him the money.

Despite his poverty, Akiba studied night and day. Before long he outdistanced all the other students in knowledge and in wisdom. When they met with a difficult problem they asked him to solve it.

Once Akiba stood outside the House of Study. At that time his comrades were discussing a very difficult question in a matter of Law. Akiba suddenly heard one say, "The solution is outside."

By that he clearly meant Akiba, who was capable of answering the question.

Akiba heard him but he did not stir from his place.

The students then continued to discuss another passage of the Torah but soon discovered that they did not understand it.

"The Torah is outside!" called another student.

Akiba heard him but pretended he did not understand the words. And still he did not enter the House of Study.

Once again the students met with a knotty problem.

"Is Akiba outside?" one of them cried. "Do come in, Akiba!"

This time Akiba, since he had been addressed, entered and sat himself at the feet of Rabbi Eliezer and his face was filled with the radiance of illumination.

For twelve long years Akiba stayed away from his wife. One day he said to himself, "It is high time that I return to her and give her some happiness."

As he reached her door he heard a woman's voice saying, "What has happened to you, Rachel, happens to all disobedient children. Your husband has been away twelve years. All this time you have been living in solitude and poverty. Who knows whether he'll ever come back again! Had you but listened to your father you would have been rich and happy today!"

"Were my husband here to take my advice," replied Rachel, "he'd remain away another twelve years and continue his studies, undisturbed."

When Akiba heard her speak thus he suppressed his bitter yearning for her and turned away.

For twelve more years he continued his studies, this time away from Jerusalem. His fame became so great that the number of his students grew to twenty-four thousand.

When the second twelve years were completed Akiba decided to return to Jerusalem. The multitude of his students accompanied him there.

Soon the report of his return spread throughout Jerusalem. All the inhabitants streamed into the streets to welcome him back. Among them, unknown to each other, were also Kalba Sabua and Rachel; they had not met for twenty-four years.

Rachel was so poorly dressed that her neighbors had said to her, "Let us lend you some good clothes. You cannot go forth dressed like a beggar to meet such a great man as Akiba."

"A man such as Akiba is unconcerned with the way people are dressed!" replied Rachel.

When Akiba appeared among his students Rachel elbowed her way through the throng. She fell at his feet and with streaming eyes kissed the hem of his robe. Akiba's students wished to drive the intruder away.

"Let her be, she is my wife!" cried Akiba. "Know that had it not been for her I would never have been your teacher. It was she who urged me on to devote myself to learning. She has waited for me for twenty-four long years!"

And speaking thus he raised her from the ground, kissed her and went with her into her poor hut.

In the meantime, Kalba Sabua, who did not know that Rabbi Akiba, the foremost sage in Israel, was his former shepherd and his son-in-law, was determined to see him. He wished to ask Rabbi Akiba to release him from the solemn oath he had once taken to disinherit his daughter. So he went to Rabbi Akiba and laid the matter before him.

"And why did you reject the shepherd?" asked the sage, without making his identity known.

"He was an ignorant man!"

"And where is your daughter now, and where is her husband?"

"I do not know, Master. I haven't seen them for twenty-four years. If you will release me from my oath I will go and seek them to the ends of the earth."

All this Rachel heard from an adjoining room. Unable to restrain her feelings any longer she burst into the room, crying to her father, "I am your daughter, Rachel, and Rabbi Akiba is your son-in-law!"

Amazed and overawed, Kalba Sabua regarded his children. Then he embraced them and cried, "My good daughter, you were right when you married Akiba against my wishes. Blessed be both of you!"

The Rabbi and the Inquisitor

THE CITY of Seville was seething with excitement. A Christian boy had been found dead, and the Jews were falsely accused by their enemies of having murdered him in order to use his blood ritually in the baking of *matzos* for Passover. So the rabbi was brought before the Grand Inquisitor to stand trial as head of the Jewish community.

The Grand Inquisitor hated the rabbi, but, despite all his efforts to prove that the crime had been committed by the Jews, the rabbi succeeded in disproving the charge. Seeing that he had been bested in argument, the Inquisitor turned his eyes piously to Heaven and said:

"We will leave the judgment of this matter to God. Let there be a drawing of lots. I shall deposit two pieces of paper in a box. On one I shall write the word 'guilty'—the other will have no writing on it. If the Jew draws the first, it will be a sign from Heaven that the Jews are guilty, and we'll have him burned at the stake. If he draws the second, on which there is no writing, it will be divine proof of the Jews' innocence, so we'll let him go."

Now the Grand Inquisitor was a cunning fellow. He was anxious to burn the Jew, and since he knew that no one would ever find out about it, he decided to write the word "guilty" on both pieces of paper. The rabbi suspected he was going to do just this. Therefore, when he put his hand into the box and drew forth a piece of paper he quickly put it into his mouth and swallowed it.

"What is the meaning of this, Jew?" raged the Inquisitor. "How do you expect us to know which paper you drew now that you've swallowed it?"

"Very simple," replied the rabbi. "You have only to look at the paper in the box."

So they took out the piece of paper still in the box.

"There!" cried the rabbi triumphantly. "This paper says 'guilty' therefore the one I swallowed must have been blank. Now, you must release me!"

And they had to let him go.

Shallow Judgment

A PRINCESS once said to Rabbi Joshua ben Hananiah, "It is true that you are a sage, but why are you so ugly? Imagine God pouring wisdom into such an ugly vessel as yours!"

Rabbi Joshua answered, "Tell me, O Princess, in what sort of vessels does your father keep his wine?"

"In earthen jars, of course," answered the Princess.

Rabbi Joshua pretended to be amazed.

"How can that be?" he exclaimed. "Everybody keeps wine in earthen jars, but your father, after all, is the King! Surely he can afford finer vessels!"

"In what sort of vessels do you think my father ought to keep his wine?"

"For a King, gold and silver vessels would be more fitting."

The Princess then went to her father and said, "It is not fitting that a King like you should keep his wine in earthen jars like the commonest man."

The King agreed and ordered that all his wine should be poured into gold and silver vessels. This was done, but before long the wine turned sour.

Angered, the King asked his daughter, "From whom did you get the advice you gave me?"

"From Rabbi Joshua ben Hananiah."

So the King sent for Rabbi Joshua.

"What made you give my daughter such wicked advice?" he asked angrily.

Rabbi Joshua then told him how the Princess had referred to him as "wisdom in an ugly vessel," and that he had wanted to prove to her that beauty is sometimes a handicap.

The King remonstrated: "Aren't there people who combine in themselves both beauty and great talents?"

Rabbi Joshua answered, "Rest assured—had they been ugly their talents would have been better developed."

The Vanity of Rabbi Mar Zutra

RABBI MAR ZUTRA was on his way from Sikhra to Marhuza at the same time that Rabbi Raba and Rabbi Safra were on their way from Marhuza to Sikhra. When Rabbi Mar Zutra saw them approaching he was under the impression that they had come to welcome him to Marhuza. So he

SHALLOW JUDGMENT: Adapted from the *Agada* in the Talmud.

THE VANITY OF RABBI MAR ZUTRA: *Ibid.*

said to them, "You really didn't have to go to all that trouble and come out so far to welcome me!"

"You are mistaken, Rabbi," Rabbi Safra replied. "Had we known that you were coming, rest assured we would have gone to even greater pains to greet you!"

Then they parted.

When Rabbi Mar Zutra had passed Rabbi Raba reproached Rabbi Safra.

"Did you have to tell him the truth, that we had not come to welcome him? You offended him."

"Had I not told him the truth it would have meant that we were deceiving him," Rabbi Safra insisted.

"Not at all!" answered Rabbi Raba. "We would not have deceived him; he would have deceived himself."

Grief in Moderation

WHEN the Temple was destroyed by Titus the Wicked, there were among Jews many, particularly Pharisees, who took a vow never again to eat meat or drink wine.

"Why don't you eat meat and drink wine?" Rabbi Joshua asked them.

They lamented: "How can we eat flesh that formerly was brought as a sacrifice upon the Temple altar when now we may no longer sacrifice? How can we drink wine which the priests used to pour upon the Temple altar when now we no longer have any altar?"

"In that case," argued Rabbi Joshua, "we shouldn't eat any bread either, because, since the destruction of the Temple, sacrifices of flour also have been abolished."

"You're right," they answered, "we can substitute fruit for bread."

"How can we eat fruit?" Rabbi Joshua asked. "The first fruits were also brought to Jerusalem for the Temple's use and now that such offerings have been abolished, we shouldn't eat them."

"Possibly we could eat fruits from which such offerings did not have to be made," ventured the Pharisees.

"Let's stop drinking water," Rabbi Joshua continued, "because the water-libation for the altar has also been abolished."

At this the Pharisees fell silent; they did not know what to answer. Seeing that he had brought them back to reason, Rabbi Joshua said to them:

"My children, pay heed to what I'm going to tell you. It would be impossible to expect us not to grieve, for indeed a bitter fate has befallen us. However, one must not indulge too much in grief. It is wrong to impose upon the Jewish people burdens that they cannot bear."

GRIEF IN MODERATION: *Ibid.*

The Virtue of the Commonplace

A RABBI once had a dispute with a Jew-baiting theologian. Said the latter, "You Jews brag about your world-mission and are proud of the fact that you are God's Chosen People—yet everybody tramples you underfoot! Aren't you deceiving yourselves?"

The rabbi replied, "When our Father Jacob fled before the wrath of Esau, God appeared to him in a dream and said: 'And thy seed shall be as the dust of the earth.' What, may I ask, brings greater use to man than the earth? Just the same—men trample it underfoot. . . ."

Why God Gave No Wisdom to Fools

A WOMAN of high rank once asked Rabbi Yose bar Halaftah, "Why is it written in the Book of Daniel that God bestows wisdom on the wise? Rightly, shouldn't God instead have bestowed wisdom on the fools who really need it?"

"Let me explain this matter to you with a parable," answered Rabbi Yose. "Imagine that two people wish to borrow money from you. If one is rich and the other poor, to which of the two will you lend the money?"

"To the rich, of course," the woman answered.

"Why so?" asked Rabbi Yose.

The woman answered, "If the rich man loses the money I lend him he'll find some way to return it to me. But where will the poor man get the money to repay me?"

"May your ears hear what your lips are saying!" exclaimed Rabbi Yose. "Were the Almighty to bestow wisdom on the fools, what do you think they would do with it? They would only sprawl themselves licentiously in the theatres and at the baths and play at being clever the livelong day. That's why He gave His wisdom to the wise who seek after wisdom in the Houses of Study."

The Consecration of Eliezer

ELIEZER BEN HYRKANOS wished to become a scholar, but his father, who was a wealthy landowner, would not let him. He forced him to work in the fields side by side with his farm laborers.

Once Eliezer was sent to plow a field in which there were many rocks. After working for a while he sat down exhausted on one of the rocks and wept.

WHY GOD GAVE NO WISDOM TO FOOLS: Adapted from the *Midrash*.

THE CONSECRATION OF ELIEZER: Adapted from the *Agada* in the Talmud.

"Why do you cry?" asked his father. "If this work is too hard you can begin working tomorrow morning in another field which has already been plowed."

On the following morning Eliezer was put to work in the field that had already been plowed. He had barely begun to work when he started to weep.

"Why do you weep now?" his father asked.

"I want to study the Torah," replied Eliezer.

"What nonsense is this?" cried his father impatiently. "You're already twenty-eight years old, and it's too late for you to become a scholar. Better get married, then your wife will bear you sons whom you will send to school and they will become scholars."

For three weeks Eliezer grieved over his father's refusal to let him become a scholar. Then one night the Prophet Elijah appeared to him in a dream, saying, "Go to Jerusalem and find Rabbi Yohanan ben Zakkai! He will teach you."

Eliezer left home without telling anyone. He arrived in Jerusalem, tired and a stranger, not knowing a soul there. He asked where Rabbi Yohanan ben Zakkai lived and went to his home. Then he sat down at the door and waited.

As Rabbi Yohanan looked out of the window he saw a young man sitting at his door and shedding tears.

"Why do you weep?" he asked.

"I weep because my heart breaks with longing to study the Torah."

"Whose son are you?"

Eliezer did not answer.

"What learning do you already have?"

"None."

Rabbi Yohanan then began to teach Eliezer the *Shema*, to say grace at meals, and to pray. In addition he taught him two sections of the *Mishna* daily.

Eight days he studied in this fashion, and all this time Eliezer did not eat. He was penniless and too proud to ask for alms. Because he had not eaten for so long his breath became unpleasant and Rabbi Yohanan found this very offensive. So he dismissed Eliezer as a student.

But Eliezer would not leave, and he sat outside the door. When Rabbi Yohanan passed by Eliezer reproached him, "Why did you drive me away as though I were a leper?"

"Whose son are you?" Rabbi Yohanan demanded.

"I am the son of Hyrkanos," Eliezer at last confessed.

"What?" cried Rabbi Yohanan, in amazement. "Why didn't you tell me that you belong to the great family of Hyrkanos! You must come in with me and partake of my hospitality."

"I have already eaten," Eliezer answered.

Secretly, Rabbi Yohanan made inquiry at his lodging and was told that

Eliezer had not eaten for eight days. When he heard this Rabbi Yohanan rent his garments and cried, "Woe to you, poor Eliezer, who blundered into our midst and we were not even concerned with your desperate need! But because you have suffered so much your glory will reign from one end of the world to the other!"

In the meantime, during Eliezer's absence in Jerusalem, his brothers persuaded their father to disinherit him. In order to legalize this Hyrkanos journeyed to Jerusalem.

As soon as he arrived he went to the house of Rabbi Yohanan ben Zakkai and found there a great festival in progress. The most eminent men of the land were present. When Hyrkanos entered he was invited to sit in their midst.

Then Rabbi Joshua ben Hananiah and Rabbi Simeon ben Nethaneel went to Rabbi Yohanan and whispered, "The wealthy Hyrkanos, Eliezer's father, is here."

"In that case," Rabbi Yohanan replied, "find a place for Eliezer at the same table."

And so Eliezer was seated among the men of eminence. Then Rabbi Yohanan addressed him, saying, "Honor us with a discourse on the Torah."

"How can I, Rabbi? Not I—not I!" answered Eliezer. "I may be likened to a well that cannot give forth more water than it possesses. How can I expound the Torah when I know no more than what I have learned from you?"

"A good student like you may be compared to an inexhaustible spring that gushes forth fresh water from its own source," said Rabbi Yohanan.

Three times Rabbi Yohanan asked Eliezer to expound the Torah. Still Eliezer held back. Suspecting that his presence was over-awing him, Rabbi Yohanan left the room. Eliezer then began to discourse, and as he did so his face shone like the sun.

After a while, Rabbi Joshua ben Hananiah and Rabbi Simeon ben Nethaneel went without to look for Rabbi Yohanan. "Come and hear how Eliezer discourses before the multitude and observe how his face shines like the sun," they said to him.

Then Rabbi Yohanan returned with them, and kissing Eliezer on the forehead he exclaimed, "Blessed are you, O Abraham, Isaac and Jacob, because from your loins has sprung such an illustrious son as Eliezer!"

Now Eliezer's father, Hyrkanos, failed to recognize his son.

"Who is that young man whom Rabbi Yohanan praises so highly?" he asked.

"Why, he is your own son, Eliezer," they told him.

"Blessed am I to have such a son!" he exclaimed with joy.

And he rose to his feet out of respect for his son who continued to discourse.

Seeing his father standing before him, Eliezer halted in his words and said, "O my father! How can I sit and hold discourse while you stand?"

And Eliezer seated his father next to himself.

When the discourse was over Hyrkanos said to Eliezer, "My son, I must confess that I came here with the object of disinheriting you. But now I am ready to make you my only heir and disinherit your greedy brothers instead."

And Eliezer answered, "No, father! I want nothing that belongs to my brothers. I did not ask the Almighty for gold or estates. I have only implored Him to give me the opportunity to devote myself to the study of the Torah. And this blessing, praised be He, I have already been granted. I am happy now and want nothing else!"

Learning Knows No Class

THERE were two families that lived in Sepphoris. One consisted of aristocrats, educated people who were wise in counsel. The other one consisted of common, undistinguished people.

Each day, when the two families proceeded to the house of the *Nasi* to pay their respects to him, the aristocrats would enter first and the common people could go in only after the others had left.

Now it happened that these insignificant people began to apply themselves to study, and in time they became great scholars. Then they demanded that they get precedence over the aristocrats when they went to pay their respects to the *Nasi*.

This incident raised a great deal of discussion everywhere. When Rabbi Simeon ben Lakish was asked for an opinion he passed the question on to Rabbi Yohanan who concluded:

"A bastard who is a scholar is superior to a High Priest who is an ignoramus."

Learning That Leads to Action

RABBI TARFON sat conversing on serious matters with other learned men in a house in Ludd. The question was raised: "Which is more important—learning or action?"

Rabbi Tarfon replied, "Action is more important. Of what earthly use are fine words and preachments unless they are put into practice?"

Rabbi Akiba upheld the contrary viewpoint.

"Learning is more important," he said.

The sages finally concluded that both were right.

"Learning is more important when it leads to action," they declared.

LEARNING KNOWS NO CLASS: *Ibid.*

LEARNING THAT LEADS TO ACTION: *Ibid.*

The Parable of the Two Gems

ONCE, after he had listened to his counsellor, Nicholas of Valencia, speaking evil against the Jews, King Don Pedro was very much perplexed in his own mind.

"There is a wise man among the Jews whose name is Ephraim Sancho," the king recalled. "Bring him to me."

So they brought Ephraim Sancho before the king.

"Which faith is superior, yours or ours?" the king sternly demanded of Ephraim.

When Ephraim heard the king's question he was thrown into confusion and said to himself: "Be wary, for the enemies of Israel have laid a trap for you in order to do you harm."

But to the king he said: "Our faith, O King, suits us better for, when we were slaves to Pharaoh in Egypt, our God, by means of many wondrous signs and miracles, led us out of the land of bondage into freedom. For you Christians, however, your own faith is the better because, by its means, you have been able to establish your rule over most of the earth."

When King Pedro heard this he was vexed. "I did not ask you what benefits each religion brings to its believers," he said. "What I want to know is: which are superior—your or our own precepts?"

And again Ephraim Sancho was thrown into confusion. He said to himself: "If I tell the king that the precepts of his religion are superior to mine I shall have denied the God of my fathers and shall therefore deserve all the punishments of Gehenna. On the other hand, should I tell him that the precepts of my religion excel his he will be sure to have me burned at the stake."

But to the king Ephraim said: "If it please the King—let me ponder his question carefully for three days, for it requires much reflection. At the end of the third day I will come to him with my answer."

THE PARABLE OF THE TWO GEMS: From *Liber Shebet Yehuda* (The Book of the Rod of Judah) by Solomon ibn Verga (16th century). Adapted from the German translation in *Der Born Judas*, compiled by M. J. bin Gorion. Insel-Verlag. Leipzig, 1919.

Ephraim ben Sancho, Twelfth Century Talmudic scholar of Aragon, was ordered by Pedro the Great, King of Aragon, to engage in a public disputation with the Christian troubadour, Nicholas de Valencia, in which each was to prove the superiority of his faith. Although learned religious disputations between Christians and Jews were usually of a harmless nature in early Christian times, during the later Middle Ages they took on an ominous character, for the spirit of the Inquisition had begun to enter the Church. The public disputation, particularly under Dominican auspices, became a Christian weapon of conversion and invariably the Jewish debater was declared the loser in this joust of theological wits. It was used by Christian rulers and clerics as a great public spectacle, Jewish apostates being employed to bring against their former coreligionists false accusations of blasphemy against the name of Christ, of the desecration of the Host, and of ridiculing Christian doctrines. The direst consequences to the Jews resulted from some of these disputations, such as forced conversion, being expelled from a city or kingdom, the payment of an enormous collective fine, and the banning or the burning of the Talmud.—N. A.

And King Pedro said: "Let it be as you say."

And for the three days that followed the spirit of Ephraim was rent within him. He neither ate nor slept but put on sackcloth and ashes and prayed for divine guidance. But, when the time arrived for him to see the king, he put all fear aside and went to the palace with his answer.

When Ephraim Sancho came before the king he looked downcast.

"Why are you so sad?" the king asked him.

"I am sad with good reason for, without any cause whatsoever, I was humiliated today," answered Ephraim. "I will let you be my judge in this matter, O King."

"Speak!" said King Don Pedro.

Ephraim Sancho then began: "A month ago to this day a neighbor of mine, a jeweler, went on a distant journey. Before he departed, in order to preserve the peace between his two bickering sons while he was away, he gave each of them a gift of a costly gem. But only today the two brothers came to me and said: 'O Ephraim, give us the value of these gems and judge which is the superior of the two!'

"I replied: 'Your father himself is a great artist and an expert on precious stones. Why don't you ask him? Surely he will give you a better judgment than I.'

"When they heard this they became enraged. They abused and beat me. Judge, O King, whether my grievance is just!"

"Those rogues have mistreated you without cause!" cried the king. "They deserve to be punished for this outrage."

When Ephraim Sancho heard the king speak thus he rejoiced. "O King!" he exclaimed. "May your ears hear the words your own mouth has spoken, for they are true and just. Know that such two brothers as these were Esau and Jacob, and each of them received for his own happiness a priceless gem. You have asked me, O King, which of the two gems is superior. How can I give you a proper answer? Send a messenger to the only expert of these gems—Our Father in Heaven. Let Him tell you which is the better." *

When King Pedro heard Ephraim Sancho speak thus he marvelled greatly. "Behold, Nicholas," he said to his counsellor. "Consider the wisdom of this Jew. Since he has spoken justly then justice shall be done to him. He deserves, not rebuke and harm, but respect and honor. You, however, deserve to be punished, for you have spoken nothing but evil slanders against the Jews."

---

* Lessing effectively adapted this story for the parable of the three rings in *Nathan the Wise.*

The Best and the Worst Things

ONCE Rabbi Yohanan ben Zakkai said to his five disciples: "What is the most desirable thing to strive for in life?"

Rabbi Eliezer said: "A good eye."

Rabbi Joshua said: "A good friend."

Rabbi Yose said: "A good neighbor."

Rabbi Simeon said: "Wisdom to foretell the future."

Rabbi Eleazar said: "A good heart."

Rabbi Yohanan then said to his five disciples: "The words of Eleazar please me most, because his thought includes all the rest."

At another time Rabbi Yohanan asked his disciples: "What is the thing that man should avoid most in life?"

Rabbi Eliezer said: "An evil eye."

Rabbi Joshua said: "An evil friend."

Rabbi Yose said: "A bad neighbor."

Rabbi Simeon said: "One who borrows money and doesn't return it."

Rabbi Eleazar said: "A bad heart."

Rabbi Yohanan then said: "The words of Eleazar please me most because his thought includes all of yours."

The Optimist

RABBI AKIBA once went on a journey. He took along with him an ass, a cock and a torch. The ass was to ride upon, the cock to wake him at dawn, and the torch to light his way in the dark.

At last he came to a village and asked for a night's lodging, but every door was closed against him. Good-humoredly Rabbi Akiba said, "Whatever God wills is for the best."

He then went into the fields to spend the night.

As he slept a lion came and devoured the ass. Then came a wildcat and ate the cock. Finally, a strong wind blew up and put out the torch.

When dawn came Rabbi Akiba learned that during the night robbers had fallen upon the village and looted it. He then said to the hard-hearted villagers, "See, how everything works out for the best—even your inhospitality! Had I lodged with you the robbers would have caught me too. If my torch had burned, if my cock had crowed, and if my ass had brayed, then the robbers would have discovered me even in the fields."

THE BEST AND THE WORST THINGS: Adapted from the *Agada* in the Talmud.

THE OPTIMIST: *Ibid.*

God's Delicacy

THE Emperor once said to Rabbi Gamaliel, "Your God is a thief! Why did he make Adam fall asleep and then steal a rib from him?"

The Emperor's daughter interrupted and said to Rabbi Gamaliel, "Let me answer my father." Then turning to the Emperor, she said, "Call a judge!"

"What do you need a judge for?" the Emperor asked in surprise.

"Thieves entered my apartment at night," the Princess replied. "They stole a silver jug, but in its place they left one made of gold."

"May such robberies occur every night!" laughed the Emperor.

"Well then," cried the Princess. "Didn't such good fortune happen to Adam? God stole from him a rib, but in its place he left him a devoted wife."

"In my opinion," rejoined the Emperor, "it was wrong of God to make Adam fall asleep. If he wanted to take his rib he shouldn't have done it stealthily."

"Father!" cried the Princess. "Order that a chunk of meat be brought." Wonderingly, the Emperor did as she asked.

The Princess then took the raw meat and in the presence of her father, put it into the hot ashes to roast. When it was ready for serving she said to him, "There now, father, eat the meat!"

But the Emperor shuddered with disgust and refused to eat. He had first seen the meat when it was raw and after that, when it was still covered with ashes.

"It nauseates me!" he cried.

"There you see!" said the Princess triumphantly. "Had Adam been awake and seen how God cut out his rib and created a woman from it he would have forever been nauseated at the sight of her."

The Cave of Simeon bar Yohai

ONCE Rabbi Simeon bar Yohai and other scholars were disputing over the matter of Roman rule in Palestine. Rabbi Simeon said, "Whatever improvements the Romans have made, they have made for their own benefit only, to facilitate the carrying out of their wicked designs. They have made baths to cleanse their own bodies, they have built bridges in order to collect tolls; and they have established markets for the purchase of slaves."

GOD'S DELICACY: *Ibid.*

THE CAVE OF SIMEON BAR YOHAI: From the *Agada* in the Talmud. Reprinted from *Legends of Palestine,* by Zev Vilnay. With the permission of the copyright owners, The Jewish Publication Society of America. Philadelphia, 1932.

When this became known to the authorities, the Roman governor sentenced Simeon to death. Rabbi Simeon and Rabbi Eliezer, his son, fled to a cave.

Miraculously there appeared a carob tree and a spring of fresh water; so they cast off their clothing, embedded themselves in the sand up to their necks, and studied Torah all day long.*

In this manner they lived in the cave for twelve years. One day, seeing that a bird had repeatedly escaped the net set for it by a hunter, Simeon and his son were encouraged to leave the cavern, taking the escape of the bird as an omen that God would not forsake them. When they stood outside the cavern, Elijah the prophet came to them and said:

"Who can inform Simeon bar Yohai that Caesar is dead, that his decree is null and that they are free?"

In the great pilgrimage to the tomb of Rabbi Simeon they sing:

The story will never die
Of Rabbi Simeon bar Yohai.
From the day of his birth
Blessed was his name on earth,
The bright shining star of Galilee.

In a cave he lay hidden,
By Roman law forbidden
Our Rabbi bar Yohai.
In the Torah he found his guide,
With spring and carob-tree by his side,
Our Rabbi bar Yohai.

The Slander against Rabbi Moishe ben Maimon

THERE once was a rabbi whose name was Moishe Maimon (Maimonides). He was a great master in the Torah, as one can readily see by his books, including the one whose title is also *Maimon*, and many other works that he had written. At the same time he was also a great physician. He wrote one book that nobody in his days could understand for it was very difficult. And so he lived in Spain among many other rabbis who did not agree with him. They considered him a *Min*, which means a heretic: one who is neither Jew nor Gentile. He chose to interpret the Torah according to his own ideas, just like a *Min* and not as our sages intended.

The other rabbis in Spain wrote to Germany, expressing their opinion that he well deserved to be excommunicated because he was the sort of man who did not truly believe in God, praised be He.

As soon as the German rabbis received this letter they met and said, "It is inconceivable that such a man as he, who has always been a pious Jew, should become a heretic, despite what the Spanish rabbis write."

---

* Simeon bar Yohai, who lived in Palestine during the Second Century A.D. under Hadrian's tyranny, was reputedly the author of the cabalistic work, the *Zohar*. Tradition claims he wrote the *Zohar* during his sojourn in the cave.—N. A.

THE SLANDER AGAINST RABBI MOISHE BEN MAIMON: Translated from the *Maasse-Buch*. Amsterdam edition, 1723.

The German rabbis therefore decided to send a German Jew to Spain on a visit to Rabbi Moishe. This man was to examine his book and his conduct. Possibly he would be able to learn what sort of a man he was and thus get to the bottom of it all.

And so they went to one who was called Rabbi Meier and explained to him the entire matter regarding Rabbi Moishe Maimon. They also showed him the letter the rabbis of Spain had written.

"Therefore," they said to him, "we beg you to go to him. You'll quickly learn on the spot whether he is a heretic or not."

They said this because Rabbi Meier was also a greater master in the Torah, even half a prophet. So they discussed the whole matter thoroughly with him.

Rabbi Meier then started out on his journey to Spain. He took along with him a *Masorah*.*

He was only a half mile away from the city where Rabbi Moishe Maimon lived, when he came to a spring. So Rabbi Meier sat down at the cool spring to study the *Masorah* and to eat and drink. And after he had finished, he continued on his way. But he forgot his book and left it lying near the spring.

At last he arrived in the city and asked where Rabbi Moishe's house stood. People directed him to it.

Rabbi Meier knocked on the door. A servant stuck his head out of the window and said to Rabbi Meier, "No one is allowed to come in now, for the master is eating. You will have to wait until he is finished."

"I well know that your master is eating now," Rabbi Meier told the servant. "Do you want a sign? He is having eggs for his noonday meal."

When the servant heard this he went to his master and said, "A man just knocked at the door. I told him that you were eating, to which he answered: he knew that very well, and for a sign he said that you were eating eggs."

"Go and tell him that he was right," Rabbi Moishe bade his servant. "For a sign tell him that he has forgotten his book at the spring."

At this Rabbi Meier reminded himself of his *Masorah;* he searched for it but did not find it. Then he recalled having studied it at the spring.

"I well see that he knows more than I," thought Rabbi Meier.

So he returned quickly to the spring and there he found the *Masorah* lying in the hollow where he had studied it. He then took the book and returned to the city.

Again he stood before the door of Rabbi Moishe Maimon and he knocked upon it. It was already sundown. They let him in immediately, as it was near suppertime. The servant came and set food on the table, food that looked just like human hands. Seeing this, Rabbi Meier declined to eat of

---

* A system of critical notes on the external form of the Bible text. Originating in pre-Maccabean times, it was concluded in A.D. 1425.

it, excusing himself on the ground that he was not feeling well and would rather not eat this day.

"Perhaps you would like to drink?" asked Rabbi Moishe.

And calling to another servant he said, "Peter, go and draw for me a jug of wine from the same barrel we drank from before."

Rabbi Meier became troubled.

"What! Shall Peter bring wine for me?" he thought. "He is a Kutite and will only make the wine undrinkable for me." *

As soon as Peter brought the wine Rabbi Moishe said to Rabbi Meier, "Since you haven't eaten you ought to drink at least."

"I don't care to drink either," replied Rabbi Meier, for he was not in good spirits. He was also tired, had walked too much, and felt he would rather sleep.

At this Rabbi Moishe said to a third servant, "Rise early in the morning and fell an ox so that tomorrow we'll have fresh meat for our esteemed guest; he is not in the best of health."

When Rabbi Meier heard this he said to himself, "Everything is indeed true what the Spanish rabbis have charged against Rabbi Moishe. His ways are not good, and there are far too many of such!"

The following morning, as soon as Rabbi Meier arose, Rabbi Moishe led him into a private chamber and said to him, "My dear Rabbi Meier, I know very well why you have come from Germany to see me. I also know who has sent you to me. Furthermore, I know with what I am charged. However, I would like to tell you that one has no right to accuse another regarding anything without first making sure that it is true. I know very well why you declined to eat and drink with me. You didn't want to eat because the food looked exactly like human hands. Let me inform you: that was a vegetable that you saw."

Rabbi Moishe then let him examine the vegetable for he was a great doctor and knew what vegetables were good for the health.

"I will also tell you the reason why you didn't want to drink," continued Rabbi Moishe. "You thought, because I called my servant Peter he was a Gentile and thus would make the wine undrinkable. Indeed, his real name is Peter and he is as pious a Jew as it is possible to find. He is named after an eminent Talmudic scholar."

And he showed him in the *Gemara* (Talmud) that a certain scholar was named Rabbi Peter.

"Thirdly," said Rabbi Moishe, "you declined to eat of the fresh meat of the ox because I ordered that it be felled instead of slaughtered. Let me explain the reason for this. Know that when a cow is with child and she is slaughtered and after they take from her carcass a live calf, such a calf need not be slaughtered ritually, nor does it require the benediction when killed. It is made kosher with the selfsame benediction that is recited over the mother."

---

* Wine handled by a non-Jew is prohibited to a believing Jew by ritual law.

And Rabbi Moishe illumined him on many other matters. He complained to him about the hatred his colleagues bore for him and of the persecution he had to suffer at their hands because they did not understand his book. Then Rabbi Moishe studied the book with Rabbi Meier, the book that is called "Maimon." * There were many new ideas in it, so that at any time one can, on reading it, perceive what sort of man he was. For it is written in his introduction that from Moishe our Teacher to Rabbi Moishe Maimon there never arose a Moishe like unto this Moishe.

As soon as Rabbi Meier heard these words from Rabbi Moishe's lips he begged that he forgive him. And Rabbi Moishe forgave him everything.

Rabbi Meier then started out on his journey home. He saw to it that Rabbi Moishe was again held in the great esteem he deserved. And it also happened, that all those of his colleagues who had slandered Rabbi Moishe were stricken in their bodies, for it is written, "He who accuses another of a wrong he has not done, that one will be stricken in his body."

From this one must learn that he who wishes peace must avoid having unworthy suspicions of his fellowmen.

An Author's Life After Forty

A YOUNG Talmudic scholar who had just completed a learned work came to Rabbi Elijah, the Gaon of Vilna, and begged him for a testimonial.

Rabbi Elijah regarded his visitor with gentle compassion.

"My son," he said to him, "you must face the stern realities. If you wish to be a writer of learned books you must be resigned to peddle your work from house to house like a vendor of pots and pans and suffer hunger until you're forty."

"And what will happen after I'm forty?" asked the young writer, hopefully.

Rabbi Elijah smiled encouragingly, "By the time you're forty you'll be quite used to it!"

An Unpredictable Life

ONE day, centuries ago, as a rabbi was on his way to the House of Study he suddenly met the duke of the province followed by his retinue.

"Where are you going this bright morning, Rabbi?" the duke asked him sarcastically.

"I'm sure I don't know, Your Grace," replied the rabbi with a doubtful air.

"You don't know where you're going? How dare you speak so impudently to me, Jew? I'll teach you to have proper respect for a Christian

---

* Probably the book referred to is *The Guide to the Perplexed*, Maimonides' most celebrated work whose unorthodox views aroused so much opposition.

prince!" cried the duke, and he ordered the rabbi thrown into a dungeon.

"What did I tell you, Your Grace?" called out the rabbi. "Now you see for yourself that I was right when I said I did not know where I was going."

"How so?" asked the duke curiously.

"You see, Your Grace, I left my home this morning in order to go to the House of Study—and where do I wind up? In a dungeon!"

Stale Ancestors—Stale Learning

USUALLY the orthodox rabbis of Europe boasted distinguished rabbinical genealogies, but Rabbi Yechiel of Ostrowce was an exception. He was the son of a simple baker and he inherited some of the forthright qualities of a man of the people.

Once, when a number of rabbis had gathered at some festivity, each began to boast of his eminent rabbinical ancestors. When Rabbi Yechiel's turn came, he replied gravely, "In my family, I'm the first eminent ancestor."

His colleagues were shocked by this piece of impudence, but said nothing. Immediately after, the rabbis began to expound Torah. Each one was asked to hold forth on a text culled from the sayings of one of his distinguished rabbinical ancestors.

One after another the rabbis delivered their learned dissertations. At last it came time for Rabbi Yechiel to say something. He arose and said, "My masters, my father was a baker. He taught me that only fresh bread was appetizing and that I must avoid the stale. This can also apply to learning."

And with that Rabbi Yechiel sat down.

The Most Valuable Merchandise

A GREAT scholar went on an ocean voyage together with a number of merchants who were conveying goods to sell in distant lands.

"What kind of merchandise do you carry?" they asked him.

"My merchandise is more valuable than yours," he answered.

But what it was he would not say.

The merchants were astonished and looked high and low in every part of the ship. But there was no sign anywhere of his goods. So they laughed at the scholar.

"He is a simpleton!" they said.

After they had sailed several days pirates attacked them and robbed the passengers of all their possessions, including the very clothes on their backs.

THE MOST VALUABLE MERCHANDISE: Adapted from the *Midrash*

When the ship reached port at last, the merchants found themselves without any money or clothes. Being strangers in a foreign land they were in a sorry plight and endured great hardships.

The scholar, on the other hand, had no sooner disembarked than he made his way to the House of Study and sat down to expound the Law. When the people saw what a learned man he was they showed him great honor. They gave him clothing, food and lodging. When he went into the street the dignitaries of the town escorted him with great deference. Seeing all this, his fellow passengers, the merchants, were abashed.

"Forgive us for having mocked at you," they begged him. "Help us! Intercede for us with the Elders to give us a crust of bread, for we are hungry! Now we see that it was no idle boast when you told us that your merchandise was more valuable than ours. Learning is the best merchandise!"

The Foresighted Father

IT CHANCED that a wealthy merchant, accompanied by his steward, a slave, left the Holy Land on a long ocean journey. Being a widower he left behind him only a son, who was pious and a student of Holy Lore.

On the way the merchant fell sick. At the point of death he made a will, leaving all his possessions to his steward. To his son he wrote that he could choose one thing only among all his possessions.

After the merchant's death the steward-slave took all his money and the will and returned to the land of Israel. He told his master's son, "Your father is dead. He has left a will bequeathing his entire fortune to me. He allows you, however, to choose any one thing from all his possessions."

When he heard the words of his father's slave the orphaned son was sorely troubled. He went to the rabbi and told him all that had happened. The rabbi then said to him, "Your father was a sage and had great foresight. I believe he must have thought to himself: 'If I leave my fortune to my son, my slave, as the steward, will pilfer it. Far better that I make the slave my heir. In that case he will guard it as the apple of his eye. Therefore, it will be enough for my son if he chooses but one of my possessions.'

"My advice to you," concluded the rabbi, "is that when you go to the judges and the slave shows them the will, you must say to them, 'My father has stipulated that I can choose only one thing from his possessions. I therefore choose this slave.'

"Rest certain," continued the rabbi, "that if your slave belongs to you all the wealth he has inherited from your father is also yours."

The orphan son did as the rabbi told him. Consequently, he came into

---

THE FORESIGHTED FATHER: *Ibid.*

all of his father's possessions, for the law is that whatever a slave owns belongs to his master.

Learning and Knowing

ONCE there was a prodigy of learning at a Talmudic College in Poland. His fame was spread far and wide and great scholars came to talk to him, and marvel over his wonderful store of knowledge.

One day an eminent Talmudic authority arrived and asked the head of the institution, "Tell me, Rabbi! Is it true that the young man knows so much?"

"To be candid with you," answered the rabbi with a smile, "the young fellow studies so much I don't see where he can find the time to know!"

Two against One

A SICK man called a doctor. After the doctor had examined him, he said, "My friend—you, I, and your disease—are three. If you will take my side the two of us will easily be able to overcome your illness which is only one. However, should you forsake me and not cooperate with me but hold on to your disease, then I, being alone, won't be able to overcome both of you."

Spinoza

A FREETHINKER once said mockingly to Rabbi Pinchas of Koretz, "Would you like to know what the philosopher Spinoza wrote in one of his works? He wrote that man in no way stands higher than an animal and that he has the same nature."

"If that is so," remarked the rabbi, "how do you explain the fact that up until now the animals haven't produced a Spinoza?"

Double-Talk

ONCE there was a young sinner whose conscience bothered him, but because he was vain he found it hard to confess his sins to his rabbi. So he fell on a stratagem. He went to the rabbi and pretended that a friend had sent him to beg for the remission of his sins. He therefore recited all the

---

TWO AGAINST ONE: Adapted from Bar-Hebraeus (13th Century, Syria).

misdoings of his "friend" who he said was too ashamed to appear and plead for himself.

Now the rabbi penetrated his pretense, so he said to him, "What a fool your friend must be! Couldn't he come himself? After all, he could have said just what you have told me—that he had come in the interest of a friend. In that way he would have spared himself any embarrassment."

A Reason for Every Custom

IT HAPPENED once that a well-to-do merchant, who was a clever and worldly man, maintained his newly married son and his wife in his household. The son had a fine character and a good heart. He devoted himself to charitable works and helped every poor man who asked for his assistance.

In time the young wife gave birth to a son; and so, in honor of the occasion, the happy grandfather arranged a great feast on the day of circumcision.

Shortly before the festivities were to begin the merchant's son asked, "Tell me, father, what arrangements have you made for the seating of the guests? If you do the conventional thing and seat the rich at the head of the table and the poor near the door, it will distress me. You know very well how I love the poor. At my own celebration, at least, let me honor them who get no honor. Therefore, father, promise me to seat the poor at the head of the table and the rich at the door."

His father listened attentively and answered, "Reflect, my son: it is difficult to change the world and its ways. There is always a good reason behind every custom. Try to see it this way: Why do poor people come to a feast? Naturally, because they are hungry and would like to eat a good meal. Why do rich men come to a feast? To get honor. They don't come to eat, because they have enough at home. Now just imagine what would happen if you seated the poor at the head of the table. They would sit there, very self-consciously, feeling everybody's eyes on them, and, naturally, they would be ashamed to eat their fill. And what they'd eat they wouldn't enjoy. Now, don't you think it would be better for their sake that they sat unnoticed at the door where they could eat to their heart's content without being ashamed?

"Then again, suppose I were to do what you're asking and seat the rich at the foot of the table. Don't you think they'd feel insulted? They don't come for the sake of the food, but for the honor. And if you don't give them that what will they get?"

A REASON FOR EVERY CUSTOM: Adapted from the *Parables of the Preacher of Dubno.*

Why Jerusalem Was Destroyed

"WHY was Jerusalem destroyed?" asked the Sages of Israel.

Jerusalem was destroyed only because of the desecration of the Sabbath.

Jerusalem was destroyed only because the morning and the evening prayers were abolished.

Jerusalem was destroyed only because the children of the schools remained untaught.

Jerusalem was destroyed only because the people did not feel shame towards one another.

Jerusalem was destroyed only because no distinction was drawn between the young and the old.

Jerusalem was destroyed only because one did not warn or admonish the other.

Jerusalem was destroyed only because men of scholarship and learning were despised.

Jerusalem was destroyed only because there were no longer men of faith and hope in her midst.

Other sages of Israel said: "Jerusalem was destroyed only because her laws were founded upon the strict letter of the Torah and were not interpreted in the way of mercy and kindness."

From the day that the Temple was destroyed, men of sound judgment were cut off. Confusion of thought prevailed, and the heart did not seek after purity but decided according to appearances. The shedding of blood profanes the holy soil and is an offence against the Divine Presence; it was because of the shedding of blood that the Holy Temple was burnt.

Where Is Paradise?

A RABBI fell asleep and dreamt that he had entered Paradise. There, to his surprise, he found the sages discussing a knotty problem in the Talmud.

"Is this the reward of Paradise?" cried the rabbi. "Why, they did the very same thing on earth!"

At this he heard a voice chiding him, "You foolish man! You think the sages are in Paradise. It's just the opposite! Paradise is in the sages."

WHY JERUSALEM WAS DESTROYED: Reprinted from *Legends of Palestine*, by Zev Vilnay. With the permission of the copyright owners, The Jewish Publication Society of America. Philadelphia, 1932.

PARABLES

INTRODUCTION

Of all elements in Jewish folklore the parable is probably the most distinctly Jewish. The Hebrew name for it is *mashal,* but *mashal* has a wider meaning; it also includes fables and brief allegories. In all of the Pentateuch there are only five parables, but they abound with prodigal lavishness in the *Agada* of the Talmud, in the *Midrash,* and in the books of the *Apocrypha* which are the non-canonical, extra-Biblical writings. The generous use of the parable by Jesus and the Gospel writers was but a natural consequence of their Jewish intellectual training. Jewish medieval literature abounds in a wealth of parables.

The most indefatigable collector and adapter of the parable was Rabbi Jacob Krantz, the celebrated "Dubner Maggid" (Preacher of Dubno). During the last decades of the Eighteenth Century he traveled from town to town in Poland and Lithuania, a true wandering preacher, admired and beloved in all of Eastern Europe. He drew vast throngs with his eloquence and homely wisdom, making both moral ideas and rabbinical learning painless and pleasurable with his delightful story-telling art. Some of the parables he developed from germs of ideas he found in the Talmud and *Midrash,* but the bulk of them he picked up from the plain folk as he traveled from place to place. They were the folktales of the people, only he, with his creative ingenuity, adapted them to serve didactic ends, in the manner of the sages of the *Agada* and the *Midrash.* In turn, the refined parable would go back to the people and undergo ceaseless variation and adaptation at their hands.

The attitude of the rabbis of the Talmud to the parable was one approaching reverence. Not only did it make their teachings easier for the students in the academies to understand, but it kept their congregations from nodding. No doubt with the intellectual snobs in mind the teachers of the people wrote admonishingly in the *Agada:* "Do not despise the parable. With a penny candle one may often find a lost gold coin or a costly pearl. By means of a trifling simple parable one may sometimes penetrate into the most profound ideas."

According to the universally accepted tradition it was King Solomon who "invented" the parable. "The Torah until Solomon's time," commented Rabbi Nachman in the *Agada,* "was comparable to a labyrinth with a bewildering number of rooms. Once one entered there one lost his way and could not find the way out. Then along came Solomon and invented the parable which has served as a ball of thread. When tied at the entrance of this labyrinth it serves as a secure guide through all the winding, bewildering passages."

Taking up the thought, Rabbi Nachman's colleague, Rabbi Hanina, said: "Until the time of Solomon the Torah could have been compared to a well full of cool refreshing water, but because of its extraordinary depth no one could get to the bottom. What was necessary was to find a rope long enough to tie to the bucket in order to bring up the water. Solomon made up this rope with his parables and thus enabled everyone to reach to the profoundest depths of the well."

A characteristic of the parable is that it is not just an ingenious and entertaining story but it is wisdom instinct with spirit. It is subtle and imaginative, penetrating to the very heart of an idea or a truth. Wise in the ways of the world and of men, it is mellow in its common-sense understanding of both the heights and pitiful limitations of the human being. We find in the parable *Truth in Gay Clothes* [see JEWISH SALT, page 13] the gentle understanding of how hard it is for many people to accept the naked or obvious truth. To become agreeable to some, Truth must first be adorned in attractive clothes. And that, concludes the narrator slyly, is why Parable is always seen in the company of Truth.

Often the parable is a bitter commentary on the perverseness of man's reasoning and conduct. *The Poor Man's Miracle,* which the Preacher of Dubno used to tell, has the ironic bite concluding on the thought: "Most people would sooner help one who has fallen than help keep him from falling."

Very often the parable was told, not so much to instruct, as to offer solace to the Jewish people. And, like the method of the Yiddish literary master, Sholom Aleichem, it sparkled with the wit and laughter of courage in adversity. Such a parable is *The Last Trouble Is the Worst,* offering to the sorely beset the following ironic moral: "New dangers can make them (i.e. the Jews) forget the old ones."

N. A.

Man Understands But Little

ALL their lives the two young brothers had lived in the city behind great stone walls and never saw field nor meadow. But one day they decided to pay a visit to the country.

As they went walking along the road they saw a farmer at his plowing. They watched him and were puzzled.

"What on earth is he doing that for!" they wondered. "He turns up the earth and leaves deep furrows in it. Why should someone take a smooth piece of land covered with nice green grass and dig it up?"

Later they watched the farmer sowing grains of wheat along the furrows.

"That man must be crazy!" they exclaimed. "He takes good wheat and throws it into the dirt."

"I don't like the country!" said one in disgust. "Only queer people live here."

So he returned to the city.

His brother who remained in the country saw a change take place only several weeks later. The plowed field began to sprout tender green shoots, even more beautiful and fresher than before. This discovery excited him very much. So he wrote to his brother in the city to come at once and see for himself the wonderful change.

MAN UNDERSTANDS BUT LITTLE: Adapted from the *Parables of the Preacher of Dubno.*

His brother came and was delighted with what he saw. As time passed they watched the sproutings grow into golden heads of wheat. Now they both understood the purpose of the farmer's work.

When the wheat became ripe the farmer brought out his scythe and began to cut it down. At this the impatient one of the two brothers exclaimed:

"The farmer is crazy! How hard he worked all these months to produce this lovely wheat, and now with his own hands he is cutting it down! I'm disgusted with such an idiot and I'm going back to the city!"

His brother, the patient one, held his peace and remained in the country. He watched the farmer gather the wheat into his granary. He saw him skillfully separate the grain from the chaff. He was filled with wonder when he found that the farmer had harvested a hundred-fold of the seed that he had sowed. Then he understood that there was logic in everything that the farmer had done.

MORAL

Mortals see only the beginning of any of God's works. Therefore they cannot understand the nature and the end of creation.

Where Is the Head of the Table?

A MAN once made a feast. He invited many townsfolk. Among them was a man of great distinction. He was a scholar and a sage, but a very modest man who disliked being honored. The host wished to seat him at the head of the table, as was his due according to custom. Instead, the man chose a place among the poor at the foot of the table near the door. Now, when the host, who was an understanding man, saw him do this he seated his other distinguished guests near him, saying:

"My Masters, wherever this man sits is the head of the table."

MORAL

It is not the place that honors the man but the man that honors the place.

The Poor Man's Miracle

No ONE showed any compassion for the poor man as he went from house to house begging for a groschen or a crust of bread. Many a door was slammed in his face and he was turned away with insults. Therefore he grew despondent.

One wintry day, as he was trudging through the slippery streets, he fell and broke his leg. Thereupon they took him to a hospital.

WHERE IS THE HEAD OF THE TABLE?: *Ibid.*

THE POOR MAN'S MIRACLE: *Ibid.*

When the people of the town heard that a poor stranger had been taken to the hospital suffering from a broken leg, they began to feel very sorry for him. Some went to comfort him, others brought him good things to eat. When he left the hospital they furnished him with warm clothes and gave him a tidy sum of money.

Before the poor man left town he wrote to his wife, "Praise God, dear wife! A miracle happened: I broke a leg!"

MORAL

Most people would sooner help one who has fallen than help keep him from falling.

Everyone Loves a Compliment

A KING's son once fell critically ill, so his royal father called for the greatest doctors in the land. They tried all kinds of cures on him, but to no avail. In despair the king had a proclamation read to his subjects calling on all who thought they could cure the prince to come to the palace.

Now it happened that in a distant city of the kingdom there lived a doctor who was both poor and without reputation. When he heard the king's request he travelled to the capital.

"Lead me to the prince!" he said to the king.

He had no sooner examined the youth when he knew the nature of his illness which was a very ordinary one. It could be cured by boiling various herbs that grew everywhere in profusion. But because the greatest doctors in the land were present, he was afraid to mention the matter of the herbs lest they laugh him to scorn as a concocter of old wives' cures. So he thought the matter over very carefully, and, choosing his words with great deliberation, he addressed himself to them:

"Most distinguished doctors! According to my poor understanding the prince can be cured by boiling certain common herbs, but, inasmuch as my healing knowledge is small, I very much doubt if I'm competent to prepare this medicine. Therefore, I most humbly beg you to let me lean on your greater knowledge."

Delighted with the compliment the celebrated doctors accepted their poor colleague's counsel and prepared the herbs he specified. The prince recovered.

MORAL

Tact is an aid to knowledge.

EVERYONE LOVES A COMPLIMENT: *Ibid.*

The Veneer of Silver

A RICH but stingy man once came to his rabbi to ask for his blessing. The rabbi suddenly arose, took him by the hand, and led him to the window looking out on the street.

"Tell me—what do you see?" asked the rabbi.

"I see people," answered the puzzled rich man.

Then the rabbi drew him before a mirror.

"What do you see now?" he again asked him.

"I see myself," answered the man, bewildered.

"Now, my son, let me explain to you the meaning of my two questions. The window is made of glass—as is also the mirror—only the glass of the mirror has a veneer of silver on it. When you look through plain glass you see people. But no sooner do you cover it with silver when you stop seeing others and see only yourself."

The Giant and the Cripple

Two paupers wandered from town to town begging for alms. One was a giant who had never been sick in his life, the other was a cripple who had never known anything but illness.

The giant used to laugh at the cripple constantly. His unfortunate companion took his mockery very much to heart and in his resentment uttered the following prayer: "Lord of the World! Punish this man who humiliates me all the time and makes sport of my deformity, for, verily, he is a wicked man!"

At last, the two paupers reached the capital city. They arrived just at the time when a great misfortune had happened to the king. Two of his most trusted servants had died suddenly. One was his personal body-guard, the strongest man in the land; the other was the most skillful physician among all the royal healers. So the king sent couriers into all the towns and villages of his kingdom to gather into the capital all the strong men and doctors who wished to compete for the vacant court posts.

The king finally chose one strong man and one doctor from among all the applicants. He then asked them to furnish proof of their fitness for the posts they were to fill.

"My Lord the King!" said the strong man. "Let there be brought before me the strongest and biggest man in this city and I will kill him with one blow from my fist."

The doctor said, "Give me the most helpless cripple you can find and I will make him well in one week's time."

THE GIANT AND THE CRIPPLE: Adapted from the *Parables of the Preacher of Dubno.*

So the king sent messengers scurrying throughout the city looking for the strongest man and the most helpless cripple. Luck was with them, for on the street they chanced upon the two paupers. So they brought them before the king.

First came the strong man, and with one blow from his fist he killed the giant. Then the doctor examined the cripple, and after one week of treatment he made him well again.

MORAL

The strength of the strong proves sometimes their misfortune, just as the weakness of the weak ofttimes brings them good fortune.

The Last Trouble Is the Worst

ONCE, while on a long journey, a man met a wolf on the road. And when he escaped from this danger he went about telling people the story of his meeting with the wolf.

Further on the road he met with a lion, and again he escaped from certain death. After that, the man went about telling people of his escape from the lion's jaws.

Still later on he met a snake. When he escaped from its poisonous fangs he forgot altogether about the dangers he had met before. He talked only about his escape from the snake.

Similarly with the Jewish people. New dangers can make them forget the old ones.

The Parable of the Wise Fishes

THE authorities in Rome had issued a decree forbidding the Jews to study the Torah. Thereupon, Rabbi Akiba arose and, at the risk of his life, went about from town to town establishing academies. He himself held forth in learned discourse to great throngs.

One day Rabbi Akiba met Rabbi Pappus ben Yehuda, the sage and patriot.

"Aren't you afraid of the authorities?" asked Pappus.

"You speak like a fool, Pappus, even though many people think you're wise!" exclaimed Rabbi Akiba. "Let me tell you a parable that has a bearing on your question.

"A fox one day was walking along the shore of a lake. He noticed that the little fish were scurrying to and fro in the water. As he looked at them he had a great desire to eat them.

THE LAST TROUBLE IS THE WORST: Adapted from the *Agada* in the Talmud.

THE PARABLE OF THE WISE FISHES: *Ibid.*

" 'Foolish little fish—why do you scurry about like that?' he asked them.

" 'We are fleeing from the nets of the fishermen,' the fish replied.

" 'In that case,' cried the sly fox, 'why don't you come ashore and we will live like brothers just as your parents lived with mine.'

"The little fish laughed and replied, 'O you foxy one! You talk like a fool even though many think you're clever. What silly advice are you giving us, anyway? If we are in constant fear of our lives in the place where we live, how do you suppose it will be on dry land where we cannot live? Surely, death awaits us there!' "

Then Rabbi Akiba concluded: "It is with us Jews the same as it was with the little fish. We are afraid of the enemy even when we study the Torah, which is our support and life. Can you imagine what fear would fall upon us were we to abandon this study?"

Know Before You Criticize

A YOUNG, half-baked Talmudic student, while talking to his rabbi, expressed a heretical view about prophets and the nature of prophecy.

The rabbi bristled with indignation.

"Shame on you!" he cried. "How can you speak that way about the Holy Prophets?"

"But that's not my own opinion, Rabbi," the student apologized. "I'm only quoting the *Rambam*. It's written in the *Guide to the Perplexed*."

The rabbi smiled wryly.

"Let me tell you a parable," he began.

"A merchant once came to buy goods in a large wholesale establishment. Quite by accident he broke the glass in a showcase. This filled him with confusion.

" 'I'm terribly sorry about this,' he said.

" 'Oh, that's all right—it's only a trifle,' said the proprietor minimizing the loss. 'May no worse damage happen to me. Thank God none of the flying glass hurt you! Tell you what—let's have a drink of *schnapps* on it.'

"So the two drank in very friendly fashion, as if nothing unpleasant had occurred.

"Now there was a simpleton who saw all this happen with his own eyes. He was very much impressed and said to himself, 'If for breaking a single pane of glass the proprietor gives this customer a glass of *schnapps*— what will he give me for breaking his big front window? He'll feel so sorry when he sees how upset I am about it that, likely as not, he'll have me drink a whole bottle of *schnapps* with him!'

"So he picked up a rock and, with all his might, threw it at the front window, smashing it. Thereupon, the clerks in the store who had seen him do this ran out and gave him a good trouncing.

" 'Stop, stop, you fools! Why do you hit me?' yelled the simpleton.

'Your employer gave that customer a glass of *schnapps* to quiet his nerves, and me you hit?'

" '*Schlemihl!*' answered the proprietor. 'That man is my best customer. If he broke a pane—*nu*, so what? But you, idiot, who broke my front store-window—what profit do I get from you?' "

The rabbi then concluded: "It's the same with you and the *Rambam*, my son. About Rabbi Moses ben Maimon, it has been said: 'From Moses our teacher to Moses ben Maimon, there has been no Moses like unto this Moses.' He was a Prince in Israel. He wrote wonderful books with deep meanings. It was perfectly all right for him to express a heresy, so to speak—to break a window pane. But you, ignoramus, what have you done for the world to allow yourself the luxury of breaking the store-front window of our faith?"

The Man and the Angel of Death

A MAN was carrying a heavy load of wood on his shoulders. When he grew weary he let the bundle down and cried bitterly, "O, Death, come and take me!"

Immediately, the Angel of Death appeared and asked, "Why do you call me?"

Frightened, the man answered, "Please help me place the load back on my shoulders."

MORAL

Even though life has its griefs man prefers a life of wretchedness to death.

Barking Dogs

A PREACHER once came to town and entered the synagogue. When he went up to the rostrum to speak the audience began to make a terrific racket and rudely yelled, "We don't want any preachers here! We won't stand for sermons in this synagogue!"

So the preacher asked the sexton to tell the audience that he had no intention of preaching. He merely wanted to tell a short story about a Jewish merchant. The story was a good one and the audience would enjoy it.

The audience agreed and the preacher began to tell the following story:

"Once a Jew was walking along the street with bowed head, looking greatly worried. On the way he met an acquaintance, a kindhearted old man.

" 'What's wrong with you, Uncle? What has happened to make you look so distracted?'

" 'Why shouldn't I be worried? I suffer from a great misfortune and it's the more aggravating because it's on account of a trifle.

" 'As you know, I am a merchant. At present I'm negotiating with the local nobleman about an important business deal. I have the bright prospect of earning quite a bit of money on it. This would indeed be very welcome because it would enable me to marry off my daughter and still have a neat sum left for myself. Unfortunately, I cannot close the deal on account of an idiotic trifle. The nobleman invited me to his house and when I entered the courtyard a pack of angry dogs fell upon me like tigers and wanted to tear me to pieces. I ran away almost leaving my soul behind.'

" 'Rest easy,' the old man then told him. 'I have good advice for you. Go again to the nobleman and utter the following words of the psalmist when the savage dogs come out:

" ' "Cease from anger, and forsake wrath!" Then you'll see that they will stop their barking and will start licking your hands like lambs.'

"The merchant went again to the nobleman and entered his courtyard. But the dogs fell upon him as fiercely as before, and before even he had a chance to recite the words of the psalmist, they nearly tore him to bits. He barely escaped with his life.

"Thereupon he went back to the old man who asked him, 'Did the psalm help?'

"The merchant heaved a deep sigh and replied, 'Possibly it would have helped but to my misfortune they were such nasty dogs they wouldn't even give me a chance to begin.'

"This, my friends," concluded the preacher, "is the short story I wanted to tell you."

He then descended the rostrum and quickly left the synagogue.

By Loving Man You Honor God

IN A certain city lived a rich man who had three sons. Two had left home to seek their fortunes in a distant town. One prospered but the other became poverty-stricken. Many years passed since they had left home, but one day their father wrote them a letter inviting them to attend the wedding of their youngest brother.

The letter was addressed to the son who had prospered and it read, in part, "Therefore, return home, my son, and be sure to bring with you your poor brother so that we may all rejoice together. I promise to pay all the travelling expenses that you may incur in fulfilling the Commandment 'Honor thy father and thy mother.' "

Immediately after reading the letter the wealthy son paid a visit to all

---

BY LOVING MAN YOU HONOR GOD: Adapted from the *Parables of the Preacher of Dubno.*

the drygoods shops where he bought the most expensive materials for himself, his wife and children. Then began feverish preparations for the wedding.

When they were all ready to start and the horses were harnessed for the journey the wealthy son suddenly recalled that he had forgotten to extend his father's invitation to his poor brother. So he called out to his servants, "Make haste and call my brother! Bring him here as quickly as possible and tell him that it's important!"

His servants did as he bid them and brought back his poor brother who, all out of breath, said, "I'm greatly surprised, brother, that you've called me. I can't understand why you should suddenly develop an interest in me after neglecting me all these years."

"Ask no question!" his rich brother replied. "Get into the carriage and come with me!"

And so the poor brother climbed into the carriage and away they whirled.

Upon their arrival their father and all the relatives came out to welcome them with great joy. First to alight from the carriage was the wealthy son, dressed up like a lord. Then followed his wife and children, dazzling in their finery. Passersby inquired with curiosity, "Who is this prince?"

And the relatives answered, "Why don't you know? This is the son of the town's richest man, and he himself is very rich, too."

Then, with great embarrassment, the poor brother slunk out of the carriage. His clothes were threadbare and there were patches on his shoes.

"And who is this one?" asked the passersby in astonishment.

"Oh, he?" evasively replied the relatives, somewhat ashamed. "He is from the same town."

"Maybe he's his brother or some other relative?" asked the passersby, slyly.

The relatives did not answer.

As the new arrivals entered the house the musicians played a merry tune in their honor. The wedding-guests waxed gay and they sang and danced in honor of the bride and the bridegroom.

The rich son and his family stayed two weeks in the house of his father. Then he said, "Dear father, as you see I have obeyed you in everything you've asked of me. I came to rejoice with you, but you know that I'm a merchant and my time is valuable, so, as much as I regret it, I must prepare for the journey home."

"Do what is best for you, my son," his father answered.

When the son was ready to depart he was filled with chagrin, for his father, who had promised to pay him all his expenses and give him a fine gift besides, did not even mention a word about it. So he handed him an itemized bill: so much and so much for his clothes, his wife's, his children's —so much and so much for what it cost him in the inns at which he stopped on his way, as well as for several other items.

"How nice!" said the father. "I am happy, my son, to see that you can afford such fine expensive clothes! May you, your wife and children, wear them in good health."

"It isn't that, father," replied his son in embarrassment. "Let me remind you of your promise that you'd repay me for all my expenses for the wedding."

The father regarded his son in astonishment.

"I never made any such promise!" he insisted.

Without a word, the son handed his father the letter of invitation he had sent him, saying, "There it is, in your own handwriting!"

His father then took the letter from him and read what he had written aloud, pronouncing each word very carefully: "I promise to pay all the travelling expenses that you may incur in fulfilling the Commandment, 'Honor thy father and thy mother.'"

"There, you see!" cried his son triumphantly.

"Now just let us understand what it is that I wrote to you," said his father. "I promised to reimburse you for all the expenses that you would incur in the fulfillment of the Commandment, 'Honor thy father and thy mother.' Had you really wished to honor me you would have taken pity upon your poor brother and not brought him here dressed in tatters. You would have known that the way to honor me was to clothe him decently. So you see, therefore, that the expenses you incurred for the wedding were only for your own honor. And these, my son, I did not promise to pay for."

MORAL

When a Jew celebrates the Sabbath and invites the hungry to his table it means that he has done so to honor God, and for that the Almighty repays him a hundred-fold. But when he eats the delicious Sabbath fare alone it signifies that he celebrates the Sabbath for his own honor only.

The Blemish on the Diamond

A KING once owned a great diamond of the purest water. He was very proud of it for it had no peer in the world. But one day an accident happened and the diamond became deeply scratched. The king then consulted with several diamond cutters, artists in their line. They told him that even if they were to polish the stone they would never be able to remove the imperfection.

Some time later, at the king's command, the greatest lapidary in the country arrived in the capital and undertook to make the diamond look even more beautiful than it was before the accident.

With the greatest art he engraved a delicate rosebud around the imperfection, and out of the deep scratch he cut a stem. When the king and the

---

THE BLEMISH ON THE DIAMOND: *Ibid.*

diamond cutters saw what he had wrought with so much ingenuity they were filled with admiration.

MORAL

With perseverance a man can transform his worst fault into a virtue.

The Rosebush and the Apple Tree

A ROSEBUSH grew near an apple tree. Everybody admired the beauty and the sweet scent of its roses. Seeing how everyone was praising it the rosebush became vainglorious.

"Who can compare to me? And who is as important as I?" it asked. "My roses are a delight to the eye and the most fragrant among all flowers. True enough, the apple tree is much larger than I, but does it afford as much pleasure to people?"

The apple tree answered: "Even were you taller than I, with all your vaunted loveliness and all your sweet fragrance—you still could not compare to me in kindheartedness."

"Let me hear!" the rosebush asked challengingly. "What are the virtues you boast of?"

The apple tree answered: "You do not give your flowers to people unless you first prick them with your thorns. I, on the other hand, give my fruit even to those who throw stones at me!"

The Parable of the Old Cloak

A STRIP of new linen lying upon the table was very proud of its beauty and fine quality.

"What a handsome garment I will make!" it exclaimed vaingloriously.

Suddenly, the strip of linen noticed a soiled, well-worn cloak that had been thrown carelessly into a corner. Scornfully, the new linen said to the old cloak, "Woe to you, you hideous old rag! What a drab appearance you make!"

Several days passed and the owner of the new linen sewed himself a garment from it. Nonetheless, when he went out upon the street he put on his old cloak over it. When the new garment recognized the old cloak it was filled with resentment.

"How did you suddenly become so important as to be above me?" it inquired.

THE ROSEBUSH AND THE APPLE TREE: Adapted from Rabbi Hillel's Parables in the *Midrash.*

THE PARABLE OF THE OLD CLOAK: *Ibid.*

The old cloak answered: "First they brought me to be laundered. They dealt me heavy blows with paddles until they beat the dust, the sand and the mud out of me. When they had finished I said to myself: 'It certainly was worth all that pain to become clean again! Just look at me! Don't I look better and handsomer than before?' And, as I was thinking thus, they threw me into a kettle of hot water, and after that into a kettle of tepid water. They washed, rinsed, dried and pressed me. And, suddenly, I saw that I had been transformed into a handsome garment! I then realized that before one can be elevated one must first suffer."

THE ANCIENT ART OF REASONING

INTRODUCTION

The use of the Talmudic art of reasoning, tortuous and oblique in its technique as it may sometimes appear, is frequently applied in humorous tales and anecdotes for the discomfiture of the wicked, the pretentious and the designing.

Sometimes Talmudic logic by its realistic application finds common sense answers to the most perplexing of human problems. This adroit use of casuistry is found in the two classic Yiddish anecdotes: *It Could Always Be Worse* and *One Big Worry* [see JEWISH SALT, page 5]. By viewing trouble relatively and from the perspective of the totality of all troubles, it loses some of its alarming character. Such wryly humorous anecdotes have arisen in great profusion among Jews and represent a highly individual type of folklore which is social documentation in the most genuine sense.

N. A.

Always Two Possibilities

WAR was on the horizon. Two students in the *Yeshiva* were discussing the situation.

"I hope I'm not called," said one. "I'm not the type for war. I have the courage of the spirit, but nevertheless I shrink from it."

"But what is there to be frightened about?" asked the other. "Let's analyze it. After all, there are two possibilities: either war will break out, or it won't. If it doesn't, there's no cause for alarm. If it does, there are two possibilities: either they take you or they don't take you. If they don't, alarm is needless. And even if they do, there are two possibilities: either you're given combat duty, or non-combatant duty. If non-combatant, what is there to be worried about? And if combat duty, there are two possibilities: you'll be wounded, or you won't be wounded. Now, if you're not wounded, you can forget your fears. But even if you are wounded, there are two possibilities: either you're wounded gravely, or you're wounded slightly. If you're wounded slightly, your fear is nonsensical, and if you're wounded gravely, there are still two possibilities: either you succumb, and die, or you don't succumb, and you live. If you don't die, things are fine, and there's no cause for alarm; and even if you do die, there are two possibilities; either you will be buried in a Jewish cemetery, or you won't be. Now, if you are buried in a Jewish cemetery, what is there to worry about, and even if you are not . . . but why be afraid? There may not be any war at all!"

It Could Always Be Worse

THE poor Jew had come to the end of his rope. So he went to his rabbi for advice.

"Holy Rabbi!" he cried. "Things are in a bad way with me, and are getting worse all the time! We are poor, so poor, that my wife, my six children, my in-laws and I have to live in a one-room hut. We get in each other's way all the time. Our nerves are frayed and, because we have plenty of troubles, we quarrel. Believe me—my home is a hell and I'd sooner die than continue living this way!"

The rabbi pondered the matter gravely. "My son," he said, "promise to do as I tell you and your condition will improve."

"I promise, Rabbi," answered the troubled man. "I'll do anything you say."

"Tell me—what animals do you own?"

"I have a cow, a goat and some chickens."

"Very well! Go home now and take all these animals into your house to live with you."

The poor man was dumbfounded, but since he had promised the rabbi, he went home and brought all the animals into his house.

The following day the poor man returned to the rabbi and cried, "Rabbi, what misfortune have you brought upon me! I did as you told me and brought the animals into the house. And now what have I got? Things are worse than ever! My life is a perfect hell—the house is turned into a barn! Save me, Rabbi—help me!"

"My son," replied the rabbi serenely, "go home and take the chickens out of your house. God will help you!"

So the poor man went home and took the chickens out of his house. But it was not long before he again came running to the rabbi.

"Holy Rabbi!" he wailed. "Help me, save me! The goat is smashing everything in the house—she's turning my life into a nightmare."

"Go home," said the rabbi gently, "and take the goat out of the house. God will help you!"

The poor man returned to his house and removed the goat. But it wasn't long before he again came running to the rabbi, lamenting loudly, "What a misfortune you've brought upon my head, Rabbi! The cow has turned my house into a stable! How can you expect a human being to live side by side with an animal?"

"You're right—a hundred times right!" agreed the rabbi. "Go straight home and take the cow out of your house!"

And the poor unfortunate hastened home and took the cow out of his house.

Not a day had passed before he came running again to the rabbi. "Rabbi!" cried the poor man, his face beaming. "You've made life sweet again for me. With all the animals out, the house is so quiet, so roomy, and so clean! What a pleasure!"

The Wheel of Fortune

A MAN of great riches lived in a certain city. He had an uncounted treasure of gold and silver and dwelt in a fine mansion where he was waited upon by many servants. He, his wife and children dressed like members of the nobility. But no one knows beforehand how the wheel of fortune will turn. And so it happened that in an important business deal this man lost a great deal of money and was bankrupted.

His creditors had no pity on him and took away his fine mansion. All that remained to him of his great wealth was a modest cottage and a garden patch. He became a shopkeeper, and in time he adjusted himself tolerably well to his new position. Although he earned enough to support his family comfortably, nonetheless he yearned after the seven fat years of his life when he had lived in a mansion in luxury.

Thinking about his past glory he lamented, "Alas, that I no longer dwell in my beautiful mansion! Gone are the happy years when I lived in luxury, waited upon by many servants. No longer am I and my household dressed in silks and velvets but, like insignificant shopkeepers, in plain cottons and woolens."

Several years passed, and the mysterious wheel of fortune again turned. Fire broke out in his cottage and burned it and all his belongings to the ground. Thereupon, he sold his garden patch and with the money, bought a horse and wagon and became a carter.

His life now was full of trouble. To feed his horse he was obliged to eat less himself. Now he no longer wailed about his mansion and the many servants that waited upon him, but said, "How well I lived when I had a cottage and a garden patch! Now just see what I am—a poor carter!"

Shortly after, misfortune struck again: his horse sickened and died. Not having any money to buy a new one he gave up being a carter and became a porter. He went about doubled up under heavy loads that he carried on his shoulders. Now he did not earn enough for bread. So he

THE WHEEL OF FORTUNE: Adapted from the *Parables of the Preacher of Dubno*.

lamented, "How well off I was when I was a carter and owned a horse and wagon and carried passengers and merchandise to market! Now, just look at me—I have to carry everything on my poor shoulders!"

One day, as he staggered through the streets groaning under a heavy burden, he met a friend of the days of his glory who began to commiserate with him loudly, "What terrible luck! Just see what has become of you, my poor friend! Where is your magnificent mansion? What has become of your great wealth and your fine carriages?"

Angrily the porter replied, "Don't bother me with such nonsense! I've forgotten about the mansion and my life of luxury long ago. What I yearn after now are those wonderful days when I had a horse and was a carter!"

MORAL

New misfortunes make a man forget the old ones.

Wishes Must Never Be Vague

A Jew was once trudging along the highway. From much walking his feet began to ache. So he prayed, "O Lord! If I only had an ass to ride!"

No sooner had he uttered these words than a Roman trotted by. The ass on which he rode had given birth to a little ass.

"Here, fellow," cried the Roman. "Take this little ass on your shoulders and carry it for me!"

So the Jew did as he was ordered and he trudged behind the Roman with the little ass on his shoulders. As he staggered along, bent double under his burden, he said to himself, "Truly, my prayer has been fulfilled! To my misfortune, however, I did not express my wish clearly enough. I should have stipulated that I wished to have an ass for me to ride—not one to ride me!"

Damning with Praise

The Rabbi of Tarnow, hearing that the post of rabbi was open in Sambor, applied for it. One Sabbath afternoon he preached there in the synagogue, but the congregation didn't like him and turned him down.

Disheartened, he returned home the following day. On the way he met his old acquaintance, the Rabbi of Landshut, and he unburdened his heavy heart to him.

"Was that a nice thing to do to me, Rabbi?" he asked, boiling over.

"To be frank with you," replied the Rabbi of Landshut, "the people of Sambor are perfectly right. Furthermore, going a little deeper into the matter, I think I have more right to the Sambor post than you."

WISHES MUST NEVER BE VAGUE: Adapted from the *Midrash*.

"How so?"

"It's clear as daylight. In your case, all of Tarnow would like to see you Rabbi of Sambor. In my case it's the same. All of Landshut would like me to become Rabbi of Sambor. But because my town is bigger than yours, I believe I have a better right to the post."

Seeing that the Rabbi of Tarnow grew despondent, the Rabbi of Landshut hastened to say, "But don't take that to heart, brother. Let me assure, you that if the post of Rabbi of Cracow were vacant you'd have a better right to it than I. You see, in my case only the Jews of Landshut would like me to become Rabbi of Cracow, but in your case not only the Jews of Tarnow but also the Jews of Sambor would like to see you Rabbi of Cracow. And against such a combination I couldn't beat you!"

A Brief Sermon

THE Rabbi of Ropshitz was a great scholar but had eccentric habits. He would concentrate on some particular point in his studies to the utter neglect of his routine duties. One Sabbath day he mounted the rostrum to preach, but suddenly panic seized him. He faltered for only a moment. Then he plunged into his sermon.

"How should a rabbi preach?" he asked.

"He must always preach what is true," he answered himself. "His sermon must be brief and to the point and his subject must be based on the Scriptural 'portion' of the week. Since a rabbi must speak the truth, I would like to say that I have no idea what this week's 'portion' is. Now, that I have spoken briefly and to the point and have based my sermon on the subject of the Scriptural 'portion,' I wish to conclude and say, 'Amen.' "

Mikhail Ivanovitch Makes a Discovery

IN A certain town there lived a rabbi who had taken on his holy calling late in life. Once, when he was asked about it, he replied:

"Let me tell you the story about Mikhail Ivanovitch.

"Now this Mikhail was a great soak. He used to roll in every gutter of the town, drunk as Lot.

"One day, the landowner's small boys decided to play a prank on him. So, while he lay in a ditch, they dressed him in an Orthodox Russian priest's black robe and high stovepipe hat.

"When Mikhail finally sobered up and rubbed his eyes, he could not believe what he saw.

" 'What the devil am I doing in a priest's outfit?' he wondered. 'Can it be—Lord preserve me—that I've become a priest—or is it only a drunken dream?'

"Carefully, he felt his priestly garments from top to bottom.

" 'They're real as life!' he muttered to himself.

"There was only one conclusion: somehow, sometime, he had become a priest!

"Bewildered by his discovery he lay with closed eyes, thinking hard.

" 'Let's see now,' he speculated. 'If the priest's breviary is in my pocket, then I'm surely a priest.'

"So he stuck his hand in his pocket and, sure enough, he drew out a breviary.

" 'So, I'm actually a priest!' he laughed.

"Still he would not believe it. He suspected something was wrong somewhere. He needed more proof.

" 'Let's see now if I can read,' he speculated further.

"So he opened the breviary and dug his nose into it.

" 'No luck!' he muttered, dejected. 'I can't read. It's proof, then, I'm no priest at all. On the other hand, how do I know that a priest must know how to read? I'll go to the priest and find out if he can read.'

"He found the priest at home.

" 'I've come to find out whether you can read,' Mikhail Ivanovitch said, handing him the breviary.

"The priest put on his spectacles and dug his nose into the breviary.

" 'I'm afraid not,' he said. 'I can't read.'

" 'In that case,' cried Mikhail, overjoyed, 'I'm a priest!' "

The old rabbi then concluded, "It was the same with me as with Mikhail Ivanovitch. At first I thought I didn't know enough to be a rabbi. So I studied night and day, year in and year out, in order to become worthy of the rabbinate. Later, however, I discovered to my amazement that other rabbis didn't know much either, so I said: 'Now I see I can be a rabbi too!' "

A Remedy for Ugliness

A TALMUDIC student was engaged to a very ugly girl; his father had forced the match on him. He therefore took the matter very much to heart and went to talk it over with the rabbi.

"Really, Rabbi," he complained, "she's so ugly she'll make me miserable if I marry her!"

"My son, use your head!" rebuked the rabbi, with impatience. "Now let's examine the problem at issue. All right—she's ugly. *Nu*, so what? Just answer me: when you're in the House of Study all day—will you look at her? No! When you come home for meals—will you look at her while you eat? No! When you go to bed at night—will you look at her in the dark? No! Furthermore, when you are asleep—will you look at her? No! Finally, in your leisure time—will you want to look at her? No! You'll go out for a walk. So I ask—what's all your excitement about? *When will you look at her?*"

There's Virtue in Misfortune

AFTER the armistice was signed in the first World War a young Jewish soldier returned to his village in Poland. In the fighting he had lost his left arm.

"What can I do now?" he said sadly to his rabbi. "Without an arm I'm not like other people."

"Foolish boy!" chided the rabbi. "Why do you exaggerate? Do you think there's no God in Heaven. Whatever He does He does with reason and with justice. For instance, if a man has lost his hearing in one ear, he gets to hear twice as well with the other. If a man loses an eye he begins to see twice as well with the other. Furthermore, if one has a leg that's a little shorter—what has he to worry about? The other leg becomes a little longer!"

The Cheapest Way

THE wonder-working rabbi held forth learnedly before his disciples. He told them a story out of the *Midrash:*

"Once, an infant was abandoned in the forest by an unfortunate mother who was too poor to feed it. So it lay there alone among the trees and cried and cried. A woodcarrier heard it and came running to where it lay. He picked it up and hushed its cries. While he was kind and gentle he was also very poor. How could he buy milk for the infant, for he hadn't earned a kreutzer all day?

"So what do you think God did? He caused a miracle to happen, the kind of miracle that hasn't happened since the creation: He made a mother's breasts grow on the woodcarrier! This miracle the good man understood to be a command from God. So he went home and suckled the infant without it even costing him a kreutzer!"

When the rabbi had finished his story he looked around him. Amazement was written on every face. Only one of the disciples had a troubled look on his face.

"Don't you like this story?" the rabbi asked him.

"No, not very much," muttered the man. "I just don't understand it! It seems to me that God's mercy could have been shown in other ways without having to reverse the laws of nature. Why did God have to give the man a mother's breasts? For instance, He could just as easily have dropped down from heaven a bag with a thousand gulden. Then the poor man could have engaged a wet-nurse to suckle the infant."

The rabbi mused, "It's not so, not so, my friend! You're a sensible man —say yourself: If God has the power to make breasts grow on the wood-carrier why should He lay out a thousand gulden in cold cash?"

Two Schools of Thought

Two gendarmes came into the home of a poor teacher of Scripture, and for non-payment of taxes carried off a goose-down pillow and a pair of brass candlesticks. The following morning the teacher went into the House of Study and, seeing the rabbi, he told him everything that had happened, complaining bitterly:

"I cannot begin to understand the sense of what they're doing, Rabbi. If they were among those who believed that the night was made only for sleep then they had no right to take away my pillow without which I cannot sleep. On the other hand, if they were among those who believed that the night was made only for study—why did they take away my candlesticks, without which I cannot see to study."

"How many gendarmes were there?" asked the rabbi.

"Two."

"It's all very simple!" cried the rabbi, triumphantly. "One of them belonged to that school of thought which believes the night is made for sleep—so he took away the candlesticks; the other that the night was made for study—so he took away the pillow!"

Why Scholars Have Homely Wives

AN INQUISITIVE young Talmudist asked his rabbi, "Why is it that most pious men and scholars marry homely wives? Is that their just reward?"

"Let me tell you a story," answered the rabbi. "A rich man once invited some strangers to dinner. Unluckily, the cook burned the greater part of the roast so the hostess, out of courtesy, had the good portions served to the guests. The members of the family were given the burned parts to eat.

"Now, my son, this also holds true with regard to the women apportioned to pious scholars. The Almighty in His wisdom created good-looking, amiable girls as well as homely, shrewish girls. The pretty ones, out of courtesy, He allots to the strangers, the libertines—the homely ones He reserves for the pious scholars who are, after all, members of His own family."

The Arrogant Rabbi

ONCE there was a rabbi whose son was also a rabbi. Whereas the father was gentle and considerate, the son was aloof and arrogant. For that reason he had no success with his congregation.

One day, when he complained about this to his father, the old man said, "My son, the difference between your ways and mine as rabbi is this: when someone puts a difficult question of Torah to me, and I give him an answer, my questioner is satisfied and I'm satisfied—my questioner with his question, and I with my answer. But, when someone asks you a ques-

tion, both of you remain unsatisfied: your questioner because you tell him
his question is no question, and you, because you don't give him an answer."

Love of Perfection

RABBI SIMEON BEN GAMALIEL once stood on Mount Moriah and saw a
woman pass by. She was unusually beautiful.

As he looked at her Rabbi Simeon exclaimed, "Wondrous indeed is your
handiwork, Almighty God!"

Did Rabbi Simeon grow enthusiastic over the woman?

No, he only admired the perfection of the Creator's handiwork.

WISE JUDGES

INTRODUCTION

If it was important to have wise teachers and scholars as an indispensable
social necessity it was no less desirable to have wise and incorruptible
judges. "To do justice and judgment is more acceptable to the Lord than
sacrifice," the proverb states. While wise judges are extolled in Jewish
folktales they are invariably delineated as scrupulously honest men who
have both the will and the courage to cut through the underbrush of deceit
and legal technicalities in order to discover the truth and to dispense justice.
According to the Jewish view a corrupt judge cannot be a wise judge.
"Presents and gifts blind the eyes of the wise," dourly reflects the worldly
Ben Sira.

In the legendary lore of the Jews concerning wise judges, King Solomon
naturally takes the foremost place. Who is not familiar with his stratagem
to discover the child's true mother? However, much more profound and
ethically stirring was his judgment in the litigation between the otter and
the weasel in the fable: *Whose Was the Blame?* It concludes on the stern
moral: "He that soweth death shall reap it." More significant yet, this fable
gives devout utterance to the Jewish ideal of the sanctity of all life.

In the parable, *The Saving Voice,* we see the traditional bending backward by the rabbinic judge in order not to be the cause of possible injustice.
Better to let ten guilty ones go unpunished than to unjustly condemn an
innocent man! And the ethical conclusion of the story: "To do a man harm
requires a decision from a high authority—to save him from harm, only a
word from the most insignificant person." It vividly recalls God's promise
to spare the wicked city of Sodom if only ten good men be found in it.
This ethical attitude is made explicit even in the many jests and anecdotes
in wide currency among Jews. It is present in the merry story, *He Didn't
Deserve His Fee.* If the rabbi sitting in judgment here became a casuist
and juggled deftly with legal technicalities and verbal sleight of hand it
was not with the intention of confusing the issue before him or to pervert
justice. On the contrary, it was to defend a poor man in adversity against
a heartless and mercenary doctor.

LOVE OF PERFECTION: Adapted from the *Agada* in the Talmud.

The Old Man and the Snake and the Judgment of Solomon

IT CAME to pass in the time of King David, when his son Solomon was still a young lad, that an old man, walking along the road in winter time, found a half frozen snake in the road. The old man, bethinking himself of the command to take pity on all creatures, put the snake into his bosom to warm it. No sooner did the snake recover than it coiled itself round the man's body and squeezed him so hard that he nearly died. And the old man said to the snake, "Why do you harm me and try to kill me when I saved your life? If not for me you would have frozen to death." Continuing, the old man said: "Let us go before the court that they may decide whether you are treating me justly." The snake replied: "I am willing to do so, but to whom shall we go?" The old man replied: "To the very first thing we meet." So they walked together, and first they met an ox. The old man said to the ox: "Stand still and judge between us." And he related to him how he had saved the snake from death, and now the snake was doing all in its power to kill him. The snake replied: "I am acting properly, for it is written in Holy Scripture, 'I will put enmity between the man and the snake'" (cf. Gen. 3.15). The ox replied: "The snake is right in doing you harm, though you have treated it kindly, for such is the way of the world, that if one does good to another, he returns evil for good. My own master does the same. I work all day long in the field and benefit him a great deal, and yet in the evening he eats the best and to me he gives a little oats and straw. My master lies in a bed and I must lie in the open yard on straw, where the rain comes down upon me. This is the way of the world, and therefore the snake is right in wishing to kill you, although you have saved its life." The old man was very much hurt by these words. Farther on, they met an ass. Addressing the ass, they said the same to it as they had said to the ox. And the ass replied in the same manner as the ox had done.

Then the old man came before King David and complained of the snake. King David replied: "The snake is right. Why did you not carry out the word of the Scripture, which says: 'I will put enmity between you and the snake'? Therefore I cannot help you. You did wrong in warming the snake. You should have let it die, for the snake is our enemy."

The old man left the king with tears in his eyes, and as he walked on, he met young Solomon in the field near a well. He had dropped a stick into the well and was ordering the servants who were with him to dig deeper below the source of the well, so that the water should run into the well and fill it, and thus carry the stick up, so that he could reach it. When the old man saw this, he said to himself: "He must be a clever lad, I will put my

THE OLD MAN AND THE SNAKE AND THE JUDGMENT OF SOLOMON: Reprinted from the *Ma'aseh Book,* edited by Moses Gaster. With the permission of the copyright owners, The Jewish Publication Society of America. Philadelphia, 1934.

case before him, maybe he can protect me from the snake," and he told him the story of what had befallen him with the snake. Solomon replied: "Have you not been before my father?" And the old man said: "Yes, I have been there, but he said he could not help me." Young Solomon said: "Let us go to him again."

So they went together again before King David, and the old man had a stick in his hand upon which he leaned. When they appeared before King David, Solomon said: "Why do you not deliver judgment between this man and the snake?" and King David replied: "I have no judgment to declare. It serves him right. Why did he not keep what is written in the Torah?" Then Solomon said: "Dear father, give me leave to pronounce judgment between the two." King David replied: "Dear son, if you think you can do so, go ahead without hesitation." Then young Solomon, turning to the snake, said: "Why do you do evil to a man who has done you good?" And the snake replied: "The Lord, blessed be He, has commanded me to bite the heel of the man." Then Solomon said: "Do you desire to observe the Torah and what is written therein?" And the snake replied: "Yes, most willingly." Then Solomon said: "If you desire to do what is written in the Torah, then release the man and stand on the ground beside him, for it says in the Law that the two men who have a quarrel with one another must stand before the judge (cf. Deut. 19.17), therefore you must also stand alongside of him." The snake replied: "I am satisfied to do so"; and, uncoiling itself from the man, he stood next to him. Then Solomon said to the old man: "Now do to the snake as it is written in the Law, for it is written in the Torah that you should crush the snake's head (cf. Gen. 3.15). Therefore do as is written in the Torah, for the snake has promised to accept the judgment of the Law." The good old man had a stick in his hand which he used in walking, for he was a very old man. So he lifted the stick and smote the snake on the head and killed it. And so the clever Solomon saved the old man from the snake through his great wisdom.

Therefore, no one should do good to a wicked creature, as the old man did.

Whose Was the Blame?

AN OTTER came one day and complained before King Solomon, saying: "Alas! my Lord and my King! Was it not thou that didst spread good

WHOSE WAS THE BLAME: From *And It Came To Pass;* legends and stories about King David and King Solomon, told by Hayyim Nahman Byalik. Translated by Herbert Danby. Hebrew Publishing Co. New York, 1938.

The legendary aspect of Solomon's wisdom took on a supernatural and semi-divine character. According to the Rabbis, before Solomon's fall from grace, he held dominion over the angels, over all humans, demons and spirits, the beasts of the forest and of the field, the fowls in the barnyard and the reptiles that crawled. King Solomon could speak the language of animals and birds and they frequently came to tidings of peace and truth to all dwellers upon the earth in thy time? Didst thou not likewise ordain peace between one wild creature and another?"

"And who hath broken this peace?" asked Solomon.

"I went down into the water," answered the otter, "to hunt for food, and my whelps I had entrusted into the hand of the weasel. But it rose up against them and destroyed them. And now the blood of my innocent children crieth out to me, Death to the Slayer!"

And the King commanded that the weasel be brought before him, and he inquired of it:

"Was it thou that slew the otter's children?"

And the weasel said:

"It was I, my lord the King, but, as the King liveth, it was not with intent or evil purpose. I heard the woodpecker as he thundered with his beak, giving forth the sound of the drum, proclaiming the summons to war. And so it was that, as I sped to the battle, I trampled on the children, but it was not with evil purpose."

And the King called the woodpecker and asked:

"Didst thou sound an alarm to summon people to the fight with a thundering of the drum?"

And the woodpecker answered:

"I did so, my Lord the King. But I did so because I saw the scorpion whetting its dagger."

And the King called the scorpion and asked,

"Why wast thou whetting thy dagger?"

And the scorpion answered:

"Because I saw the tortoise furbishing its armor."

And when the tortoise was inquired of, it said in its defence:

"Because I saw the crab sharpening its sword."

And the crab answered:

"Because I saw the lobster swinging its javelin."

And the King commanded the lobster to be brought, and he reproved it, saying:

"Why didst thou swing thy javelin?"

And the lobster answered and said:

"Because I saw the otter going down into the water to devour my children."

Then the King looked towards the otter, and said:

"The weasel is not guilty. The blood of thy children is on thine own head. He that soweth death shall reap it."

---

his aid when he needed it in time of danger or to furnish him with sorely needed information when he judged his subjects. The eagle particularly served him best acting as his messenger and as his fastest means of conveyance. In fact, the animals so loved him that of themselves they entered his palace kitchens to be served up as food for him and his thousand wives.—N. A.

The Receiver Is Worse than the Thief

ONCE there was a ruler who had a quaint way of judging criminals. For instance, he would condemn to death all dealers in stolen goods, but the thieves he would leave unharmed. His judgments perplexed his subjects, and they often murmured against them.

"How ridiculous," they complained, "to let the thieves go when they are real criminals!"

When the ruler heard that his subjects were dissatisfied with his judgments he assembled them all in a great arena outside the capital. He ordered that a number of rabbits be brought. Then various greens were placed before them. Whereupon each rabbit picked up whatever he could and scampered away into his hole.

On the following day the ruler again assembled his people in the same place. Again the rabbits were brought and greens were thrown to them. But before feeding them the ruler made sure that all the holes were closed.

Taking up the greens the rabbits ran home with them as they had done the previous day. But when they came near the holes and saw that they had been closed up, they dropped their greens and scurried away.

Turning to the assembled throng the ruler said, "Now you can see for yourselves that the thieves are less guilty than those to whom they sell their loot. Were the thieves to find all their outlets blocked and no one to buy their merchandise, they would give up stealing immediately."

A Very Ancient Law

RABBI ELIJAH, the Gaon of Vilna, had a distaste for presiding over the routine affairs of the Jewish community. He was a great Talmudic scholar, and he found that his studies suffered when he became involved in trifling disputes. Accordingly, there was a tacit understanding that under no circumstances was he to be called to communal meetings unless a new law was to be legislated.

On one occasion he was summoned by the communal leaders for an emergency meeting. When he arrived he listened with shocked amazement to the proposal that poor Jews living outside the city of Vilna should not be allowed to come into the city to collect alms.

Rabbi Elijah arose and asked, "Is it for this proposal that you have taken me away from my studies? I was under the impression that this meeting was called to legislate a new law."

"But that's exactly so, Rabbi!" explained the head of the community. "We are trying to draw up a new law against the outside poor."

"Do you call that a new law?" asked Rabbi Elijah scornfully. "Why that law was introduced more than five thousand years ago in Sodom and Gomorrah!"

THE RECEIVER IS WORSE THAN THE THIEF: Adapted from the *Midrash*.

The Discerning Judge

A YOUTH, who had not even reached his twentieth year, sold his father's possessions which he had inherited. Immediately afterwards, he was sorry about the sale and went to Rabbi Raba to have it nullified. The youth's relations instructed him beforehand, "When you go to Rabbi Raba be sure to eat some dates and shoot the pits right into his face."

The youth followed this advice and threw the date pits at the great rabbi.

Rabbi Raba regarded him with amazement and compassion. "Poor boy," he thought. "He is mentally deficient." So he nullified the sale.

Before they sat down to draw up the document of nullification the purchaser secretly instructed the youth to say to the rabbi, "A scribe is paid one gold piece to transcribe the entire Book of Esther. Why then does the rabbi charge one gold piece for just a few words?"

These words the youth repeated to Rabbi Raba who, when he heard them, said to himself, "In truth, this boy speaks sensibly! In that case the sale was valid."

And when the youth's relations heard how Rabbi Raba had reversed himself they protested, "The boy didn't say these words out of his own head! He must have been instructed to say them by the purchaser."

"In that case," said Rabbi Raba, closing the hearing, "since the young man has enough sense to remember and to repeat what he is instructed it's a sign that he is fully aware of what he's doing."

"But Rabbi!" protested the relatives. "Didn't he throw date pits at you?"

"As for that," answered Rabbi Raba, "that was just plain impudence!"

What's in a Name?

WHEN the time came for naming their firstborn son, a husband and wife began to wrangle with each other. She wanted to name him after her father; he wanted to name him after his father. Unable to agree, they went to the rabbi to referee the dispute.

"What was your father's name?" asked the rabbi of the husband.

"Nahum."

"And what was your father's name?" the rabbi asked the wife.

"Also Nahum."

"Then what is this whole argument about?" asked the puzzled rabbi.

"You see, rabbi," said the wife, "my father was a scholar and a God-fearing man, but my husband's father was a horse-thief! How can I name my son after such a man?"

The rabbi pondered and pondered. It was indeed a ticklish matter; he

THE DISCERNING JUDGE: Adapted from the *Agada* in the Talmud.

didn't wish to hurt the feelings of the husband. So he said, "My decision is that you name your son Nahum and leave the rest to time. If he becomes a scholar, then you will know that he was named after his mother's father. If, on the other hand, he becomes a horse-thief, it will be clear that he was named after his father's father."

Equal Justice

RABBI WOLF of Zbaraz had a stern sense of justice. Far and wide he was famed as an incorruptible judge. One day, his own wife raised an outcry that her maid had stolen an object of great value. The servant, an orphan, tearfully denied the accusation.

"We will let the Rabbinical Court settle this!" said her mistress angrily.

When Rabbi Wolf saw his wife preparing to go to the Court he forthwith began putting on his Sabbath robe.

"Why do you do that?" she asked in surprise. "You know it is undignified for a man of your position to come to Court with me. I can very well plead my own case."

"I'm sure you can," answered the rabbi. "But who will plead the case of your maid, the poor orphan? I must see that full justice be done to her."

The Saving Voice

RABBI MOSES LEIB of Sassov was a very tolerant man. Whenever he acted as judge in a dispute he would look for any possible excuse to be lenient. Upon one occasion, the lax conduct of the community *shochet* was cause for much complaint. His dismissal was demanded by all. Only one man appeared in his defense when the case was brought up before the rabbi. The good sage listened, his brow knitted, to the testimony of the witnesses. Then he announced his decision: "I absolve the *shochet* of all blame and rule that he retain his post."

Thereupon a clamor arose.

"Rabbi!" cried one. "How can you take the word of one single man against the testimony of many!"

The rabbi replied gently, "When God commanded Abraham to bring his only son Isaac as a sacrifice upon His altar, didn't Abraham listen then to a mere angel who stayed his hand? Yet God found this just, although it opposed His will. And God's reason for this is plain. To do a man harm requires a decision from high authority—to save him from harm, only a word from the most insignificant source."

Shadow and Substance

MISTRESS and servant had never gotten along. The servant was proud and the mistress was abusive.

One day, while her mistress was away, the servant went to the butcher's and bought three pounds of meat. She salted it and soaked it according to dietary law. But suddenly she saw the cat pounce upon the meat, carry it off and devour it.

When the mistress returned she asked, "Where is the meat?"

"The cat ate it up!" wailed the servant.

"All of you servants are liars and thieves!" snapped her mistress.

"Do you accuse me of being a thief?" cried the maid indignantly. "Then come with me to the rabbi!"

So they went to the rabbi.

"Did the cat eat up the meat?" the rabbi asked the servant.

"Yes, Rabbi, I saw it with my own eyes!"

"Very well then, bring the cat and we shall soon see."

So they brought the cat. The rabbi placed it in the scales and it weighed exactly three pounds.

"There are your three pounds of meat!" cried the rabbi triumphantly to the mistress. Then, to the maid in perplexity, "But tell me, girl, where the devil is the cat?"

He Didn't Deserve His Fee

ONCE a small town doctor, who thought more of his fees than of his patients, was called in to treat the sick wife of a poor tailor. After examining the woman he turned to the husband and said, "This case will take a lot of my time and I can see that you won't be able to pay me for my services."

"Please, doctor, save her life!" begged the anxious husband. "I promise to pay you even though I'll have to pawn everything I own to get the money!"

"What if I don't cure her—will you pay my fee just the same?" insisted the doctor.

"Whatever happens, whether you cure her or kill her, I promise to pay!" cried the husband.

The treatment was started, but within a few days the woman died. Shortly after, the doctor demanded 1500 rubles as his fee. The bereft husband informed him that he was unable to pay and, as was the custom among the Jews, they brought the matter to the rabbi for settlement.

The sage understood right away what had happened.

"Tell me again," he asked the physician, "what was your contract with this man?"

"I was to get paid for treating his wife regardless whether I cured or killed her."

"Did you cure her?" asked the rabbi.

"No."

"Did you kill her?"

"I certainly did not!"

"Then, since you have neither cured her nor killed her what right have you to the money?"

The Blessing

A WOMAN once came to lay her complaint before the rabbi.

"Rabbi," she began bitterly, "my husband is a wastrel—he gives away all his money to the poor. Please make him see that what he's doing is a sin."

And even as she spoke a poor man came in and interrupted vehemently, "Rabbi, my wife is gravely sick and my children are hungry, but my brother, who is rich, refuses to help us."

The rabbi thereupon said to the woman, "Go and bring your husband." And to the poor man he said, "Go and bring your rich brother."

The two men came.

"Why are you so impractical?" the rabbi asked of the charitable man.

"Man's life on earth is as brief as a heart-beat," replied the man. "Therefore, I fear that death may cut short my opportunity to do good. So I give away my money."

"And why are you so tight-fisted and cruel?" the rabbi asked of the rich brother. "Why don't you aid your own flesh and blood?"

"Rabbi," answered the miser, "what man knows the day on which he'll die? What if I live to be a hundred and twenty? Would you wish me to remain unprovided for in my old age?"

The rabbi mused awhile and then, with a faraway smile on his face, he said, "May God preserve each one of you from what he mostly fears!"

For Whom the Cock Crowed

Two pious scholars lived in neighboring houses. One was poor but quarrel-some, the other was wealthy but a miser. Now the poor scholar bought himself a rooster so that its crowing at dawn might wake him for the study of the Torah. So the cock crowed and its owner arose betimes for his sacred labors. Also the miserly scholar heard the cock crow and he too got up to study at daybreak.

Once the owner of the rooster said to his neighbor, "Since you share in the benefits of the rooster's cock-a-doodle it would only be fair that you also share in its upkeep."

"Did I ask you to buy the rooster?"

"No! But I see that you profit from it."

"Does it cost you anything if its crowing wakes me too?"

"Since you won't pay, let's go to the rabbi."

"Agreed!"

So they went to the rabbi. The rabbi pondered the matter long and gravely.

"It's a difficult case—a very difficult case!" he mused, stroking his beard reflectively. "Because of this I'll have to charge each of you a gulden for the hearing."

The two scholars were taken aback but nevertheless each paid the rabbi a gulden.

"Hear my judgment then," said the rabbi. "You, the owner of the rooster, say it's your rooster and therefore it crows only for you. Your neighbor, on the other hand, says that since he isn't deaf he too can't help hearing the rooster crow. But I say: it neither crows for you nor for him but for me so that you two blockheads can pay me a gulden each!"

Too Clever Is Not Clever

ONCE upon a time there was a *schlimazl*. He never earned anything and he never found anything, so he cursed his luck. But one day, as he was walking with eyes downcast, he suddenly saw a little bag lying on the path before him. Out of curiosity he picked it up and, to his amazement, found a hundred gulden in it.

That very day the sexton announced from the pulpit in the synagogue that the richest man in town had lost a large sum of money and that he had promised a substantial reward to the finder.

When the poor man heard this, he began to struggle with his conscience. Should he or should he not return the money? After all, no one had seen him find it, and at home his children were crying for food. Besides, wasn't the loser of the money rich? He'd hardly miss it!

Abashed suddenly by the wicked temptation that had come to him, the poor man hurried to return the money.

The rich man accepted the money without even a "thank-you" and began to count the guldens leisurely, one by one, in the meantime saying to himself, "This man is a ninny. I won't have to give him anything."

"May I have my reward?" mumbled the poor man timidly.

"Reward!" cried the rich man. "Reward for what? Before your very eyes I've just counted one hundred gulden. Yet I had two hundred gulden in that bag. Since you have already stolen a hundred you have some nerve to ask a reward."

"Then let us go to the rabbi," demanded the poor man.

"Very well," said the rich man.

The rabbi listened attentively to both men. Then he turned to the rich man and asked, "How much money was in the bag you lost?"

"Two hundred gulden."

"And how much money was in the bag you found?" asked the rabbi of the poor man.

"One hundred gulden."

"In that case," said the rabbi to the rich man, "the bag of money he found is not yours. I order you to give back the hundred gulden to this man!"

It's All the Way You Look at It

A MAN had two daughters. The elder one was as ugly as a scarecrow, the younger might have been called pretty but was made hideous by her shrewish mouth. She was constantly abusing people. The poor father would sigh deeply every time he looked at his daughters, for he knew that such "goods" would find no "buyers" on the marriage market. He was reconciled to the thought that they would both remain old maids and would hang like mill-stones around his neck as long as he lived.

But God is good, and so one day a marriage-broker called on the father and told him that he had just the right husbands for his daughters.

"Tell me about them," asked the father eagerly.

"Your ugly daughter I will supply with a groom who is stone blind; for your quarrelsome daughter I have one who is entirely deaf. Let her shout at him—let her abuse him! He won't hear a thing."

The father crowed with delight. He gave his daughters good dowries and packed them off with a magnificent double wedding.

Several years passed. The two married couples prospered and led a happy life. But what should happen one day! A celebrated doctor was passing through the town and, when the townsfolk got wind of it, they descended upon him with their physical complaints. Among them were also the blind and deaf husbands of the two sisters. The doctor examined them also and told them that he would undertake to cure them. Later he operated on them. Then the blind man began to see, and the deaf one was able to hear.

But horrors! No sooner did the man who had been blind cast his eyes on his wife's face, and the other one, the deaf one, hear his wife's abuse, when wedded bliss forever vanished from their homes. Now each man began to plot how to rid himself of his disagreeable mate.

When the doctor came to collect his fee, the two husbands became indignant. They argued that, not only had he not done them any good with his operations, but in fact had done them great harm. As long as the one

IT'S ALL THE WAY YOU LOOK AT IT: Adapted from the *Parables of the Preacher of Dubno*.

could not hear and the other could not see, life had its charms, but now their peace had come to an end.

The doctor then summoned them before a rabbinical tribunal. The rabbi listened to all the arguments and was convinced in his own mind that the doctor was entitled to collect his fee. However, he rebuked him, "You have done these two men great harm, much greater than the good you have done them. Therefore, I order you to make them blind and deaf again."

"It will be easier to do that than it was to cure them," said the doctor angrily.

When the two men heard what the doctor said they raised an outcry.

"What! Make me blind again?" cried one.

"What! Make me deaf again?" cried the other.

"Aha! I thought so," cried the rabbi. "And now, like good fellows, pay the doctor what you owe him and consider yourselves very lucky."

RIDDLE SOLVERS

INTRODUCTION

Talmudic dialectics developed in the Jew a penetrating subtlety; and also stimulated in him a love for cerebration for the sheer pleasure of it. Complicated bits of argumentation, mathematical puzzles, conundrums, clever retorts, ingenious word-play—all were pleasant diversions to drive away tedium, especially during the long winter evenings in the ghetto-towns and villages. Hundreds of riddles and stratagems which taxed the ingenuity were thus cooked up in those idle hours by the plain folk and bequeathed from one generation to another like precious gifts. Some of these were obviously borrowed from other peoples and adapted to suit Jewish folk-taste.

As with other Eastern peoples, the riddle-story was always popular among Jews. We hear Arab overtones, for instance, in *The Plucked Pigeon*. For centuries Jews lived in large numbers in Arab countries. Arab and Jew naturally borrowed readily from each other's culture. And so Jewish folklore shows Arabic influence to a marked degree, just as it, in turn, grafted its legends, tales and wise sayings on Arabic folklore. The riddle, *Rabbinical Arithmetic*, has an Arabic analogue, but it is indeed difficult, if not impossible, in dealing with intercultural fusion to determine primary origin. Attribution is frequently arbitrary and suppositional. This also holds true for *The Story of Kunz and the Shepherd*, taken from the *Maaseh-Buch*, the Sixteenth Century Yiddish folk-tale collection produced in the Rhineland. It has points of similarity to the English story, *King John and the Abbott*, and probably was an adaptation of a German variant.

N. A.

The Plucked Pigeon

IN WINTER-TIME the water at the creek was icy cold and the Jew who stood there washing sheep's wool felt his fingers grow numb. As he stood thus at his work the Sultan passed by.

"Tell me," the Sultan asked the Jew, "what is more, five or seven?"

"What is more, twelve or thirty-two?" answered the Jew.

"Have you ever had a fire in your house?" continued the Sultan.

"I've already had five fires, but I expect two more," replied the Jew.

"If I send you one of my pigeons, will you be able to pluck him?"

"Just send him to me and you'll see," answered the Jew.

The members of the Sultan's retinue listened to this conversation in amazement but they said nothing.

Suddenly the Sultan asked his Vizier, "Did you understand anything of the conversation the Jew and I had?"

"How should I know?" answered the Vizier. "You spoke in riddles."

"Aren't you ashamed of yourself?" cried the Sultan angrily. "You are the Vizier, supposedly the wisest man in the land, and yet a simple Jew understood me and you didn't! I give you three days' time to give me the right answer. If you fail to do so I'll fire you from your office."

The Vizier was stunned. He hastened home and called together all his sages and counsellors, but not one of them could tell him the meaning of the Sultan's questions to the Jew. Thereupon, the Vizier summoned the Jew to the palace.

"Tell me, what was the meaning of the questions the Sultan put to you?" he asked him.

"I'll tell you if you'll give me a thousand dinars," the Jew replied.

"What insolence!" shouted the Vizier angrily. "Do you expect me to pay you a thousand dinars for explaining to me the meaning of a few wretched words?"

"If it's not worth the money don't pay," retorted the Jew and went home.

But when the morning of the third day arrived the Vizier sent hurriedly for the Jew.

"Quick—here are the thousand dinars . . . explain the questions!" he cried.

Having pocketed the money the Jew gave the Vizier the following explanation, "When the Sultan saw me washing wool in the icy stream he asked me whether seven was not more than five. He meant to ask me whether I did not earn enough during the seven warm months to make unnecessary my work during the five cold months. I answered that thirty-two was more than twelve. By that I meant that with my thirty-two teeth I could eat up more than I could earn in all twelve months.

"The Sultan further asked me whether I ever had a fire in my house.

THE PLUCKED PIGEON: Adapted from *Yiddishe Folksmaisses,* compiled by Judah Loeb Cahan. Ferlag Yiddishe Folklore-Bibliothek. New York and Vilna, 1931.

He merely wished to know whether I had married off any of my children,
for when you get through marrying one off you emerge from the whole
business as destitute as from a fire. So I answered that I already had
five fires and there were still two to come.

"Lastly, the Sultan asked me whether, if he'd send me one of his pigeons,
would I be able to pluck him? To this I answered, 'Just send him to me
and you'll see.' As you see he sent you to me. So you now go and inform
the Sultan whether I've done so or not."

Alexander's Instruction

AFTER HIS triumphal entry into Jerusalem, Alexander of Macedonia and
his legions drew southward. When they reached the first city the wise men
there came out to greet the conqueror.

"I have ten questions to put to you," he told them. "If you are able to
answer them for me I will know that you are indeed wise, and will let you
go in peace."

"Speak, O King!" they replied with one voice.

"What distance is greater," asked Alexander, "that between Heaven
and Earth or that between East and West?"

"That between East and West, O King! The sun rises in the East, therefore it can be observed easily, without the eye being dazzled. It is the same
when the sun sets in the West. However, when the sun sits high in the
center of Heaven it is impossible for the naked eye to look at it. Its
splendor blinds the eyes, for at that point the sun is nearer to man than
East or West."

"Which was first created—Heaven or Earth?"

"Heaven! For Scripture says: 'In the beginning God created *Heaven*
and Earth.' "

"What was first created—Light or Darkness?"

At this question the wise men hesitated before giving their answer.
They thought, "If we say that Darkness is mentioned first in Scripture, he
will want to know more and more and ask us ever harder questions, such
as—what there is above Heaven and under the Earth, and what existed
before Heaven and Earth were created, and what will exist after they pass.
Therefore, let us better say that the question is too difficult for us to answer." So they said, "O King, the man does not live who could answer you
this question."

"In that case," answered Alexander, "I will stop asking you such difficult
questions and put to you easier ones.

"Tell me," he continued, "who is wise?"

"He who can foresee the future."

"Who is a hero?"

"He who conquers himself."

ALEXANDER'S INSTRUCTION: Adapted from the *Agada* in the Talmud.

"Who is rich?"

"He who rests content with what he has."

"By what means does man preserve his life?"

"When he kills himself."

They meant: when a man destroys within himself all passion.

"By what means does a man bring about his own death?"

"When he clings to life."

They meant: when he holds on to his passions and belongs to them.

"What should a man do who wants to win friends?"

"He should flee from glory and should despise dominion and kingship."

"That is a very foolish answer!" cried Alexander. "It is precisely he who wants to win friends that must strive for glory. Then he will be in a position to do good to people."

"Is it better for man to live on dry land or on the water?" Alexander continued.

"Dry land is better for man. Ask anyone who has been to sea and he will agree with what we say. They who live on the water never find peace of mind and live in constant anxiety."

Having concluded his questioning Alexander asked the wise men, "Which one of you is wisest?"

"We are all equally wise, O King! You must have observed that all of us replied to you at the same time."

"Why then do you shun us and don't obey my laws? Have you no fear of me, the great Alexander?"

"O King, the Angel of Evil also seeks daily to command men and to force them to obey him. Glory to him who disobeys him!"

Alexander was filled with rage, hearing such words.

"How dare you speak to me in this manner!" he cried. "Don't you know that one word from me and you will all die?"

"That we know most certainly, O King," the wise men replied calmly. "But do you think it is becoming for a mighty king like you to lie? Recall that you promised to let us go in peace after we had answered all your questions."

At this Alexander quieted down and gave the wise men presents of costly garments and golden neck-chains.

"I will now leave you and sail for Africa," he told them.

"For Africa!" cried the wise men in astonishment. "Why, you'll find there mountains so high that they reach the sky! They'll surely obstruct and darken your way."

"Advise me then!" asked Alexander. "How can I find the right road there?"

"Get the asses from the far-off land of Luw to ride on," replied the wise men. "They can see in the dark. Bind on them threads of flax and hold firmly to them. Then you will be able to pass safely through the mountains."

And Alexander did as they said and reached his goal safely.

The Wisdom of the Jews

Two Jews were taken prisoner on Mount Carmel by a Persian, who then made them walk before him. Suddenly he overheard one prisoner say to the other, "I can see that a camel passed along this road before us who was blind in one eye, was loaded with two kegs: one with wine, the other with oil, and that of the two drivers who led the camel one was a Jew and the other a Persian."

"O you stiff-necked race!" mocked their Persian captor. "What peculiar people you are! How do you know all that you are saying?"

Thereupon, the Jew explained how he knew. "A camel usually grazes on both sides of the road, but you can very well see that only the grass on one side of the road is nibbled. This indicates that he could see with only one eye. For proof that the camel was loaded with two kegs, one of wine and one of oil, look on the ground. You will notice tell-tale drops. Also, it is easy to tell the nationality of the camel-drivers. When a Jew eats he throws the crumbs aside, but a Persian throws his crumbs right into the middle of the road."

Curious to find out whether what the Jew said was true, the Persian hastened ahead until he overtook a camel with two drivers. Questioning them, he found out that it was exactly as his captives had told him. He then returned and, kissing both Jews on the forehead, took them home with him. He made a great feast in their honor and sang and danced before them, exclaiming, "Praised be the God of the Jews who chose the children of Israel as His people and endowed them with a share of His wisdom!"

The Way to Serve

A MERCHANT from Jerusalem travelled on business to a distant city. While there he fell sick and before long found himself at the point of death. Thereupon he called the man in whose house he lodged and entrusted him with all his possessions, both merchandise and money. He then said to him, "A young man will soon be coming to you from Jerusalem. You will know him by three clever things he will do. He is my son, and you must give him all my possessions."

All this time the dying man's son waited impatiently for the return of his father. Worried by his prolonged absence, he decided that his father must have met with a misfortune. He therefore journeyed to that distant city in search of him. He knew the name of the man in whose house his father lodged, and so as soon as he arrived he went to look for him.

Now the townsfolk had agreed amongst themselves that should a

---

THE WISDOM OF THE JEWS: *Ibid.*

THE WAY TO SERVE: Adapted from the *Midrash.*

stranger arrive and ask for this man no one should divulge where he lived. They did as they had agreed, and the poor orphan was very much puzzled.

He finally fell upon a stratagem. He called out to a woodcutter carrying a load of wood, "I would like to buy your wood."

And after they had agreed upon a price and he had paid for it the orphan mentioned the name of the man for whom he was looking and asked the woodcutter to deliver it to him.

The woodcutter walked ahead carrying his load and behind him followed the orphan. When they reached their destination the woodcutter cried out within the gate, calling the man by his name: "Come and get your wood!"

"Wood? What wood? I never ordered any wood from you."

"Maybe you didn't," replied the woodcutter, "but this young man here did. He paid for it and he asked me to deliver it to you."

Surprised, but grateful, the man said to the youth, "Peace be to you," and he invited him into his house.

"Who are you?" asked the man.

"I am the son of the man who lodges in your house and who has failed to return home."

The man entertained him graciously, and in his honor ordered a feast prepared. When they sat down at the table the servants placed before them five roasted pigeons. The host, wishing to show his guest honor, said to him, "Be good enough to serve."

But the young man declined the honor, saying, "No thank you! You are the host and the honor belongs to you."

However, when his host insisted, the young man agreed and began to serve. One pigeon he gave to his host and his wife. Another he gave to the man's two sons, and another to his two daughters. For himself he kept two pigeons.

His host was astonished by his action but did not say a word.

For the evening meal they had a stuffed chicken. Again the host very politely asked his guest to serve. The young man agreed. He gave the head of the fowl to the host, the gizzard, heart and liver to the hostess, the legs to the sons and the wings to the daughters. For himself he kept the body.

Out of patience with his guest's conduct, the host said to him, "Is this the way you serve in Jerusalem?"

"Did I not decline the honor when you tried to force it on me?" answered the youth. "However, I will explain to you what I did and then you'll see that I acted correctly. At noon today I had to serve the five roasted pigeons. I gave you and your wife one, and so, together with the pigeon, you numbered three. Your two sons and a pigeon, also your two daughters and their pigeon each numbered three. And so to keep the number just and equal I had to take the two remaining pigeons for myself.

"With regard to the chicken—because you are the head of the household I gave you the head. I gave the insides to your wife because from within her came forth your children. Because your sons are the pillars of your household I gave them the legs. As for your daughters—I gave them the wings because in God's own time they will fly away from you with husbands. For myself I've kept the body, which, as you see, has the shape of a boat, for tomorrow I'm sailing home."

"The Lord be praised!" exclaimed his host, overjoyed. "You are truly the son of your father, for I know you by the three clever things you have done: the first with the wood, the second with the roasted pigeons, and the third with the hen."

Then he returned to the young man his father's fortune.

How to Replenish a Treasury

THE Emperor Antoninus once sent a messenger to Rabbi Yehuda Ha-Nasi with the following question: "The Imperial Treasury is rapidly being depleted. Can you advise me how to increase it?"

Rabbi Yehuda did not answer. Without a word he led the messenger into his garden. Then he went quietly about his work. He dug up large turnips and in their place planted little turnips. He did the same thing with beets and with radishes.

Seeing that Rabbi Yehuda was not inclined to answer him, the imperial messenger said to him, "Give me a letter."

"You need none."

The messenger then returned to Antoninus.

"Did Rabbi Yehuda give you a letter for me?"

"No."

"Did he say anything to you?"

"This neither."

"Did he do anything?"

"Yes, he led me into his garden, dug up large vegetables and in their stead planted small ones."

"Now I understand what his advice is!" exclaimed the Emperor.

Immediately he dismissed all his governors and tax collectors and replaced them with less illustrious but more honest officials who, before long, replenished the Imperial Treasury.

Rabbinical Arithmetic

THREE men pooled their money and for twenty-seven hundred rubles bought seventeen horses in partnership. One had paid half of the money, another a third, and the third man a ninth. But, when the time came to divide the horses, they did not know how to do it. So they went to the rabbi for advice.

HOW TO REPLENISH A TREASURY: Adapted from the *Agada* in the Talmud.

"Let me sleep on the matter overnight," he told them. "Come back tomorrow morning and bring your horses with you."

At the appointed hour the following morning the three partners brought their horses to the rabbi. The rabbi then went into his stable and led out his own horse. Mounting it, he drew up alongside the seventeen horses.

"My good friends," he said, "there are now eighteen horses here. You, who paid one half, take nine horses. You, who paid a third, take six horses. You, who paid one ninth, take two horses. Altogether you, therefore, have the seventeen horses disposed of."

Then the rabbi led his own horse back to the stable and returned to his Talmud.

The Real Son

A MAN once overheard his wife admonish their daughter: "Why aren't you more careful? If you want to sin make sure that no one suspects you. Follow my example! Here am I, a mother of ten children, yet your father doesn't know that only one of our sons is his!"

Her husband never betrayed the slightest sign that he had overheard her, but on his deathbed he had a will drawn up leaving all his possessions, "to my only son."

Everybody was confounded! No one knew who "the only son" was. So all the sons went to see Rabbi Banna'ah to have him decide who was to be the heir.

Rabbi Banna'ah pondered the matter and said, "Go, all of you, to your father's grave and clamor loud and long until he reveals which one of you he had in mind as his true son and heir."

All the sons hastened to the cemetery, except one. He was really the "only son." But, unlike his brothers, he was determined that he would rather lose the inheritance than insult the memory of his father.

Rabbi Banna'ah then gave his decision. "The inheritance belongs to the son who didn't clamor at his father's grave."

The Mother

A KING once determined to build a town and selected a site. The astrologers approved of the place on condition that a child be walled in alive, brought voluntarily by its mother. After three years a woman brought a child of about ten years.

THE REAL SON: Adapted from the *Agada* in the Talmud.

THE MOTHER: From *The Exempla of the Rabbis*, by Moses Gaster. The Asia Publishing Co. London and Leipzig, 1924.

When ready to be walled in, the boy said to the king, "Let me ask the astrologers three questions; if they answer correctly, then they have read the signs aright but if not they must have been mistaken."

The king granted the request and the boy asked, "What is the lightest, what is the sweetest, and what is the hardest thing in the world?"

After three days the astrologers replied, "The lightest is the feather, the sweetest is honey, and the hardest thing in the world is stone."

The young boy laughed and said, "Anyone could answer like *that*. The lightest thing in the world is an only child in its mother's arms. It is never heavy. The sweetest is the mother's milk to the baby, and the hardest is for the mother to bring her child willingly to be buried alive in the wall."

The astrologers were confounded and had to own that they had read the stars wrongly and the child was saved.

The Innkeeper's Clever Daughter

ONCE there was a nobleman and he had three Jewish tenants on his estate. One held the forest concession, another operated the mill, the third, the poorest of them, ran the inn.

One day the nobleman summoned the three and said to them, "I am going to put to you three questions: 'Which is the swiftest thing in the world? Which is the fattest? Which is the dearest?' The one who answers correctly all of these questions won't have to pay me any rent for ten years. And whoever fails to give me the correct answer, I'll send packing from my estate."

The Jew who had the forest concession and the one who operated the mill did not think very long and decided between them to give the following answers: "The swiftest thing in the world is the nobleman's horse, the fattest is the nobleman's pig, and the dearest is the nobleman's wife."

The poor innkeeper, however, went home feeling very much worried. He had only three days' time to answer the nobleman's questions. He racked his brains. What answers could he give?

Now the innkeeper had a daughter. She was pretty and clever.

"What is worrying you so, father?" she asked.

He told her about the nobleman's three questions.

"Why shouldn't I worry?" he cried. "I've thought and thought but I cannot find the answers!"

"There is nothing to worry about, father," she told him. "The questions are very easy: The swiftest thing in the world is thought, the fattest is the earth, the dearest is sleep."

When the three days were up the three Jewish tenants went to see the landowner. Pridefully the first two gave the answers they had agreed upon

THE INNKEEPER'S CLEVER DAUGHTER: Adapted from *Yiddishe Folksmaisses*, collected by Judah Loeb Cahan. Ferlag Yiddishe Folklore-Bibliothek. New York and Vilna, 1931.

beforehand, thinking that the landowner would feel flattered by them.

"You're wrong!" cried the nobleman. "Now pack up and leave my estate right away and don't you dare to come back!"

But, when he heard the innkeeper's answers he was filled with wonder.

"I like your answers very much," he told him, "but I know you didn't think them up by yourself. Confess—who gave you the answers?"

"It was my daughter," the innkeeper answered.

"Your daughter!" exclaimed the nobleman in surprise. "Since she is so clever I'd very much like to see her. Bring her to me in three days' time. But listen carefully: she must come here neither walking nor riding, neither dressed nor naked. She must also bring me a gift that is not a gift."

The innkeeper returned home even more worried than the first time.

"What now, father?" his daughter asked him. "What's worrying you?"

He then told her of the nobleman's request to see her and of his instructions.

"Well, what is there to worry about?" she said. "Go to the market-place and buy me a fishing net, also a goat, a couple of pigeons and several pounds of meat."

He did as she told him and brought to her his purchases.

At the appointed time she undressed and wound herself in the fishing net, so she was neither dressed nor naked. She then mounted the goat, her feet dragging on the ground, so that she was neither riding nor walking. Then she took the two pigeons in one hand and the meat in the other. In this way she arrived at the nobleman's house.

The nobleman stood at the window watching her arrival. As soon as he saw her he turned his dogs on her, and, as they tried to attack her, she threw them the meat. So they pounced on the meat and let her pass into the house.

"I've brought you a gift that is not a gift," she said to the nobleman, stretching out her hand holding the two pigeons. But suddenly she released the birds and they flew out of the window.

The nobleman was enchanted with her.

"What a very clever girl you are!" he cried. "I want to marry you, but only on one condition, never must you interfere in my affairs!"

She gave him her promise and he made her his wife.

One day, as she stood at the window, she saw a weeping peasant pass by.

"Why do you weep?" she asked him.

"My neighbor and I own a stable in partnership," he told her. "He keeps a wagon there and I a mare. Last night the mare gave birth to a pony under my neighbor's wagon. Whereupon, my neighbor insisted that the pony rightfully belonged to him. So I haled him before the nobleman who upheld him and said the pony was his. How unjust, I say!"

"Take my advice," the nobleman's wife said. "Get a fishing-rod and station yourself before my husband's window. Nearby you'll find a sand-heap. Pretend you're catching fish there. My husband will surely be amazed and will ask you: 'How can you catch fish in a sand-heap?' So you will answer him: 'If a wagon can give birth to a pony then I can catch fish in a sand-heap.'"

The peasant did as she told him and it happened exactly as she said it would.

When the nobleman heard the peasant's answer he said to him, "You didn't think this up out of your own head. Confess, who told you?"

"It was your wife."

Angrily the nobleman went to look for his wife.

"You have broken your promise not to interfere in my affairs!" he stormed at her. "Go and choose from all my possessions that which you deem the most precious and return to your father's house!"

"Very well," she answered, "I will go, but before I do I would like to dine with you for the last time."

He consented, and during dinner she plied him with much wine. When he had drunk a great deal he became drowsy and fell asleep. Thereupon she ordered that his carriage be made ready. She then drove him, as he slept, to her father's house.

When he sobered up and discovered where he was he asked in surprise, "How did I ever get here?"

"It was I who brought you here," his wife confessed. "Don't you remember telling me to choose the most precious possession you owned and then to return to my father's house? So I looked over all your possessions, and, not finding any of them as precious as you, I carried you away with me to my father's house."

The nobleman was overjoyed.

"Since you love me so, let's go home!" he said.

So they were reconciled and lived in prosperity and in honor for the rest of their lives.

The Farmer's Daughter

ONCE there was a king who was wise and mighty. He had a large harem of many wives and concubines.

One night he had a troubling dream. He saw an ape out of the land of Yemen sitting astride the necks of his wives and concubines and then leaping from one to another.

In the morning the king awoke feeling sad and depressed. He thought to himself gloomily, "The dream can mean nothing else but that the King of Yemen will conquer my country and will take my wives away from me."

When the chamberlain entered, as was his daily custom, he heard his master sighing.

"What makes you so sad, O King?" he asked. "Reveal your secret to your servant. Maybe I will be able to help you in your trouble."

The king told him, "I had a dream last night that made me have bitter

---

THE FARMER'S DAUGHTER: Adapted from *The Book of Delight*, by Joseph ibn Zabara, Spanish-Jewish satirist and poet of the 13th Century.

forebodings of death. Do you know of any man who can interpret dreams well?"

"I have heard that only three days' journey from here there lives a man of great wisdom who can interpret the most confusing dreams. Tell me what troubles you, O King, and I will go to ask the help of this interpreter of dreams."

The king told him his dream and then said to the chamberlain, "Go now in peace."

And so the chamberlain mounted his mule and started out in search of the wise man.

On the following morning he met a farmer riding on an ass.

"Peace be with you, you tiller of the soil," he said, "you who are of earth and who eat earth."

The farmer laughed, hearing him speak so.

"Where are you travelling?" asked the chamberlain.

"I'm on my way home."

"Will you carry me or shall I carry you?" asked the chamberlain.

The farmer laughed again, saying, "Why should I carry you when you are riding on a mule and I am mounted on an ass?"

Then they rode on together for a while.

Soon they came to a field covered with ripening wheat.

"See how beautiful the field looks and how full the wheat spears are!" said the farmer.

"Indeed, it's so," answered the chamberlain, "but the wheat has already been eaten."

They rode on and came upon a tower built upon a high cliff.

"See how strong this fortress is!" cried the farmer with admiration.

"It looks well fortified but it may be destroyed from within," replied the chamberlain. Further on he exclaimed, "Just look at the snow on the summit!"

Again the farmer laughed because it was in the middle of summer and there was no sign of snow anywhere.

Soon they approached a city and saw a dead man being borne on his bier to the cemetery.

"Is this one dead or alive?" asked the chamberlain.

At this the farmer thought to himself, "This man thinks he's clever, but he's the most stupid man I've ever met!"

When the sun began to set the chamberlain asked his companion, "Is there an inn in the neighborhood?"

The farmer replied, "Ahead of us is the village where I live. Bestow on me the honor of lodging with me. I have enough straw for your bed and fodder for your mule."

"I will gladly accept your hospitality," said the chamberlain.

Thus he accompanied the farmer to his house. The farmer served him food and drink, fed his mule and showed him the place where he could lie,

The farmer then went to sleep beside his wife; his two daughters also slept in the same room.

At night the farmer woke his wife and daughters and said to them, "What a simpleton is our guest!" And he repeated all the remarkable things the chamberlain had said during their journey.

Now the farmer's youngest daughter, who was fifteen years old, was very clever. She said to her father, "Why do you call this man a fool? In my opinion he's very clever and wise. What he said is full of deep meaning and of great significance. I don't think you understood what he meant."

And then she went on to explain: "When he said that he who cultivates the soil also eats earth he referred to the origin of all food which springs from the earth.

"When he told you that you were of the earth, too, he was referring to the Scriptural passage: 'From dust you spring and to dust you shall return.'

"When he asked the question which one of you shall carry the other he was merely asking which one of you should entertain the other, for he who lightens the spirit of a fellow-traveller also lightens his journey so that he feels as if he were being carried.

"When he spoke of the wheat growing in the field he could very well have been right, for if the owner of the field was poor and in debt he most likely had already sold the crop in advance.

"When he held that the tower was not strongly fortified he merely pointed to the possibilities of traitors being within its walls and of there being an insufficient stock of food and water inside.

"When he said that there was snow on the mountain he was merely referring to your grey hair and beard. You should have answered: 'Time has done that to me.'

"When he asked whether the dead man was dead or alive he merely wished to inquire whether he left children behind, and if he did he was alive, even though dead."

The farmer was under the impression that the chamberlain was fast asleep, but in fact he was very much awake and had eagerly followed the daughter in her explanation.

When the morning came the daughter said to her father, "I want you to give our guest before he leaves us whatever food I'll give you."

So she placed before her father thirty eggs, a bowl of milk and a whole loaf.

"Now go to our guest and ask him how many days are still required to complete the month, whether the moon is full and the sun is whole."

Of the food that his daughter had served him the farmer ate only two eggs and a slice of bread, and also drank a little milk. The rest he placed before the chamberlain. Then he put to him the questions his daughter had instructed him to ask.

The chamberlain listened and then replied, "Tell your daughter that two days are missing to complete the month and that neither the sun nor the moon are full."

The farmer went to his daughter and reported to her what the chamberlain had answered.

"Tell me truly, isn't the man a simpleton?" he asked. "We are right in the middle of the month and here he claims that it is only two days before its end!"

"Tell me, father," asked the daughter. "Did you taste any of the food I gave you?"

"I ate two eggs, a slice of bread and drank a little milk," answered her father.

"Now I know that the stranger is a wise man!" cried the daughter.

When the chamberlain heard of the cleverness of the girl he was filled with astonishment.

"Let me speak with your daughter," he asked the farmer.

The farmer consented and the girl was introduced to the chamberlain. He asked her some more questions and she knew the right answers. Having convinced himself of her wisdom he told her the reason for his journey and gave her all the details of the king's dream.

When he had finished the girl said, "I know well what the ape that the king saw in his dream signifies but I will not confide it to anyone but the king himself."

The chamberlain now revealed his true identity to the farmer and his wife and begged them to allow their daughter to journey with him to the palace of the king. Her parents gave their consent, so the chamberlain brought the farmer's daughter before the king and she found favor in the king's eyes.

He led her into a private chamber where he repeated to her his dream and after he had spoken, she said, "O King, banish all worry from your mind! The ape you saw had no evil significance. But I dare not tell you the meaning of the dream in order not to cause you suffering."

"I command you to speak!" cried the king, sternly.

"Very well then," the girl answered. "Make a thorough search of your harem, and among your wives and your concubines and their maid servants you will find hidden an evil man who is disguised in woman's attire. He is the ape you saw in your dream."

So the king commanded that the matter be investigated, and it was as the farmer's daughter had said: they found a youth among them masquerading in woman's clothes. To teach his wives and concubines a lesson the king ordered that the man be cut down before their eyes and his blood be sprinkled on their faces. He also ordered killed all the women who had sinned with him.

And when all this was done he made the farmer's daughter his wife, and placed the royal crown on her head. He swore to give up all of his wives and concubines and the clever girl remained his only mate.

The Story of Kunz and His Shepherd

THE proverb runs: "You will be left behind as Kunz was left behind to look after the sheep." And if you ask how Kunz came to be left behind to look after the sheep, I will tell you.

Once upon a time there was a mighty king, who had a counselor called Kunz. Whenever the king needed advice, and the counselors in conference came to a decision, the clever Kunz would go to the king and say: "This is our decision." This fine gentleman always took the credit to himself, pretending that he was responsible for the advice and that the other counselors had to agree with him, for they had neither sense nor understanding. And the good king believed what Kunz told him and considered him as much wiser than the other counselors.

Now the other counselors noticed that the king loved Kunz more than he loved them and they resented it very much, for he was the least important among them. One day they took counsel together how to get the better of Kunz and humiliate him. So they went to the king and said: "Lord king, we beg of you to forgive us, for we wish to ask you how it is that you think more of Kunz and hold him in higher esteem than the rest of us, although we know that he is the least important among us?" The king replied: "I will tell you how it happens. Whenever you come to a decision on any matter, he reports it to me and says that the idea is his and that you have to acknowledge every time that he is wiser than you and that you have no sense at all. But I do not hold you in disrespect, for you are all good to me." When the counselors heard this, they were very glad and thought: "We will soon bring about his downfall." Then they said to the king: "Be assured that all which Kunz said is a lie, for he has no sense at all. Try every one of us separately and you will see that he cannot give you any advice by himself." The king said: "I will find out very soon," and sent for his beloved counselor Kunz and said to him: "My dear servant, I know that you are loyal and exceedingly wise. Now I have something in my mind that I do not wish to reveal to anyone. Therefore I want to ask you whether you can find out the truth for me, and if you do, I will reward you liberally." The clever Kunz replied: "My beloved king, ask me and I hope I can give you an answer. Tell me your secret." The king said: "I will ask you three questions. The first is: Where does the sun rise? The second is: How far is the sky from the earth? The third, my dear Kunz, is: What am I thinking?" When Kunz heard these three questions, he said: "Lord king, these are difficult matters, which cannot be answered offhand. They require time. I beg of you, therefore, to give me three days' time, and then I hope to give you the proper answer." The king replied: "My dear Kunz, your request is granted, I will give you three days'

THE STORY OF KUNZ AND HIS SHEPHERD: Reprinted from the *Ma'aseh Book*, edited by Moses Gaster. With the permission of the copyright owners, The Jewish Publication Society of America. Philadelphia, 1934.

time." Kunz went away and thought to himself: "I cannot concentrate my mind very well in the city, I will go for a walk into the country. There I am alone and can reflect better than in the city."

He went out into the country and came upon the shepherd who was tending his flock. Walking along, he talked as it were to himself, saying: "Who can tell me how far the heavens are from the earth? Who can tell me where the sun rises? Who can tell me what the king is thinking?" The shepherd, seeing his master walking about wrapt in thought, said to him: "Sir, pardon me. I see that you are greatly troubled in your mind. If you ask me, I might be able to help you. As the proverb says: 'One can often advise another, though one cannot advise oneself.' " When Kunz heard these words from the shepherd, he thought: "I will tell him. Perhaps after all he may be able to advise me." And he said: "I will tell you why I am so troubled. The king asked me three questions, which I must answer or lose my neck. I have been thinking about them and cannot find the answer." Then the shepherd said: "What are the three questions? Perhaps I may be able to help you in your great trouble." So Kunz thought: "I will tell him, maybe he is a scholar." And he said: "My dear shepherd, these are the three questions which the king asked me. I must tell him where the sun rises, how far the heavens are from the earth, and what the king is thinking." The shepherd thought it was well to know the answers and said to Kunz: "My dear master, give me your fine clothes, and you put on my poor garments and look after the sheep. I will go to the king and he will think that I am you and will ask me the three questions. Then I shall give him the proper answers and you will be saved from your trouble. Then I shall return here and you will not be in disgrace with your king." Kunz allowed himself to be persuaded, gave the shepherd his good clothes and fine cloak, while he put on the shepherd's rough garments and sat down to look after the sheep, as though he had done it all his life.

When the three days had passed, the shepherd went to the king and said: "Lord king, I have been thinking over the three questions that you asked me." The king said: "Now tell me, where does the sun rise?" The shepherd replied: "The sun rises in the east and sets in the west." The king asked again: "How far are the heavens from the earth?" The shepherd replied: "As far as the earth is from the heavens." Then the king said: "What am I thinking?" The shepherd replied: "My lord king, you are thinking that I am your counselor Kunz, but I am not. I am the shepherd who looks after his flock. My master Kunz was walking in the field one day and saying to himself: 'Who can tell me where the sun rises? Who can tell me how far the heavens are from the earth? Who can tell me what the king has in his mind?' He was walking about all the time and talking in such fashion. So I told him he should give me his good clothes and I would give him my rough clothes; he should look after the sheep and I would, with the help of God, guess the answers to these three questions and save him. He allowed himself to be persuaded, and so he is now out in the field, dressed in my rough clothes and tending the sheep, while I am dressed in his beautiful cloak and his best clothes." When the king heard this, he said to the shepherd: "As you succeeded in persuading Kunz, you shall remain my counselor and Kunz can look after the sheep." Hence the proverb: "You will be left behind as Kunz was left behind to look after the sheep." This is what happened to him. May it go better with us.

[2]

Holy Men

PIOUS AND RIGHTEOUS MEN

INTRODUCTION

The holy man in Jewish folklore is not the one who prays most or fasts most or who mortifies his flesh. The holy man is the righteous man. "And what doth Jehovah require of thee, but to do justly, and to love kindness." (Micah 6.8). "The duty of the heart"—is an exhortation frequent in Jewish devotional literature as a qualification for holiness. But anyone who follows righteousness can be holy, not just the elect. In this connection it is interesting to observe that in Jewish legendary lore "the thirty-six hidden saints," on whose virtue the foundations of the world are supposed to rest, are depicted as unlettered and insignificant men who work at the most humble trades and therefore pass unnoticed among their fellowmen. In keeping with this ideal conception the folk-mind remained ever impatient with the formalistic earmarks of saintliness and with any manifestation of pious humbug or pretension and lampooned them merrily in quip and joke, as in *Saint or Horse*.

Piety too is conceived of in a most unconventional way. To the saintly rabbi in the anecdote, *True Piety*, it did not lie so much in the faithful observance of all the minutiae of religious regulations but in the just and generous treatment of one's fellowman. This concept of holiness and piety was particularly stressed by the *Hasidic* rabbis. For instance, in the story, *God's Drunkard,* we find the holy Rabbi Levi-Yitzchok of Berditchev being outshone in divine grace by Chaim the Watercarrier, an ignorant sot. And the reason for it: God "loves truthfulness above piety and learning."

Because Israel is "a holy people" by tradition, holiness is not considered by the rabbis as a providential gift to God's favorites. All men are God's children. As a religion with a profoundly democratic philosophy Judaism upholds the doctrine that all men are born equal, without any condescension or qualifications. The Rabbis of old did not believe in predestination; they preached the doctrine of Free Will. Man himself was the architect of his destiny by the character of his deeds. God always stood by as a benevolent ally of the righteous. If they suffered and were defeated in life they would be rewarded in the World-to-Come where divine justice reigns. Therefore the declaration by Rabbi Akiba in the *Mishna:* "Everything is foreseen [by God] and Free Will is given." Ben Sira, two hundred years before

Akiba, tersely described this free choice of man to do with his life whatever he wished:

> Poured out before thee are fire and water;
> Stretch out thy hand to what thou desirest.
> (*Book of Sirach*,15.16)

The credo of the pious man in Jewish tradition is his unswerving belief in God's love for him. It is touchingly put by the much-tried Job: "Though He slay me yet will I trust in Him!" It is Rabbi Hillel's dictum though that most pithily summarizes the traditional Jewish attitude towards piety and righteousness: "Do not unto others what you do not wish that others do unto you. That is the whole Torah. Everything else is merely commentary." Hillel, who lived in the time of King Herod in Jerusalem, is widely viewed by historians and scholars as having been the originator of this Golden Rule enunciated later by Jesus: "All things therefore whatsoever ye would that men should do unto you, even so do ye also unto them." (Matt. 7:12) How widely Hillel's teaching was current among the Jews of Palestine in that age can be seen from its inclusion in the Jewish *Book of Tobit:* "And what is displeasing to thyself that do not unto any other." (4:15) That the teachings of Jesus were thoroughly rabbinic in character may be seen in the fact that almost all of the beatitudes in the Sermon on the Mount find their counterparts in the Talmudic literature of that period, almost to the very expressions.

In the folk conception Hillel was the archetype of the ideal man: he was wise and learned, pious and righteous. Therefore, the saying in the Talmud which has been held dear by all the generations of Jews: "Let a man be always humble and patient like Hillel, and not passionate like Shammai." Hillel was the most unsententious of all the rabbinic sages. He spoke the language of the people and taught them ethics. His sayings, which are found in the treatise *Abot* of the *Mishna,* are instinct with humanity and kindness. Celebrated is his counsel: "Be of the disciples of Aaron, loving peace and pursuing peace, loving mankind and bringing them near to the Torah." Perhaps the saying for which he is most revered by the plain folk is his epigram on enlightened self-interest in which the profit of the individual is so intimately bound up with the welfare of society: "If I will not be for myself—who will be? And if I am only for myself—what am I? And if not now—when?"

N. A.

True Piety

RABBI ISRAEL SALANTER was very scrupulous in his observance of all the six hundred and thirteen precepts prescribed by the religious code. It was his custom whenever the Passover holidays came around, to personally supervise the baking of *matzos* in his town. He wished to make sure that it was done according to the time-honored ritual regulations.

On one such occasion, when he was confined by illness, his disciples volunteered to supervise the baking of the *matzos*.

"Instruct us, Rabbi," they said. "Tell us all the important things we have to watch out for."

"My sons, see that the women who bake the *matzos* are well paid," was Rabbi Israel's brief reply.

The Limits of Piety

THE rabbi watched his servant girl panting under the burden of the yoke from which hung two buckets of water. At mealtime, before he sat down to eat with his disciples, he washed his hands using very little water.

"Why are you so economical with the water, Rabbi?" asked one of his disciples.

The rabbi smiled and said: "While it is an act of piety to wash one's hands before meals, I must not be pious at my servant girl's expense."

Rabbi Hillel's Golden Rule

ONCE a heathen came to Rabbi Shammai and said, "I'll gladly accept the Jewish faith, provided you can teach me the entire Torah while standing on one leg."

When Rabbi Shammai heard these insolent words he seized his surveyor's measuring rod and drove the heathen out of his house.

The heathen then went to call on Rabbi Hillel and said, "I'll gladly accept the Jewish faith, provided you can teach me the entire Torah while standing on one leg."

Now just as Shammai was wrathful so Hillel was gentle. He said to the heathen, "*Do not unto others what you do not wish that others do unto you.* That is the whole Torah. Everything else is only commentary. Go and learn!"

Hillel's Patience

A MAN once wagered another that if he succeeded in making Rabbi Hillel angry he would give him four hundred pieces of silver.

On the day preceding the Sabbath the man went to call on Rabbi Hillel. He found him at his ablutions in honor of the Sabbath. So he stood before Hillel's door and called out rudely, "Where is Hillel? Where is Hillel?"

RABBI HILLEL'S GOLDEN RULE: Adapted from the *Agada* in the Talmud.

HILLEL'S PATIENCE: *Ibid.*

Hearing his name called Hillel wrapped himself in a cloth and went out to see who it was.

"What do you wish, my son?" he asked the man.

"I have a question to ask you."

"Ask, my son."

"Why do the people of Babylon have round skulls?"

"My son," answered Hillel, "you have asked a very good question. The Babylonians have round heads because their midwives lack skill."

The man listened and went away. A few minutes later he returned and cried out, "Where is Hillel? Where is Hillel?"

Again Hillel wrapped himself in a cloth and went out to see who it was.

"What do you wish?" he asked.

"I would like to ask you a question."

"Ask, my son."

"Why do the inhabitants of Afriki have broad feet?"

"Because they live in swamps," replied Hillel.

When the man heard this he said, "I have still other questions to put to you, but I'm afraid you'll become impatient."

Hillel sat down and said, "You can ask me all the questions you wish."

"Are you Hillel, the head of the Talmudical College?" asked the man.

"I am."

"In that case may you be the only one of your kind among Jews!"

"Why?"

"Because on account of you I have lost four hundred silver pieces!"

"Far better that you should lose four hundred silver pieces than that I should lose my temper!" answered Hillel.

Three Men and the Torah

WHEN a poor man arrives in the next world and he is asked: "Why didn't you find time to study the Torah?" he is likely to answer, "I was poor and all my time was spent in earning my bread."

So the Heavenly retort is: "Were you a poorer man than Hillel?"

The following story is told about Rabbi Hillel during his student days in Jerusalem: He was a day-laborer then and so poor that he earned only a copper coin for a day's work. Half of this money he gave to the beadle as an entrance fee to the House of Study; he and his family lived on the remaining half.

One day Hillel met with ill luck; he earned nothing. When he came to the House of Study the beadle would not let him in because he could not pay the entrance fee. So Hillel climbed to the roof and lying down over the skylight he strained hard to hear the great teachers Shemaiah and Abtalion expound the Law.

THREE MEN AND THE TORAH: *Ibid.*

It was on a Friday before the arrival of the Sabbath and in mid-winter. But in his eagerness to learn from the great masters Hillel became oblivious to everything. He forgot that his larder at home was bare, forgot to feel the snowflakes as they fell upon him, so that soon they blanketed him entirely.

In this manner he spent the whole evening. On the following morning Rabbi Shemaiah said to Rabbi Abtalion, "Explain to me, brother, why it is so dark in the House of Study today? I did not notice that the sky was overcast."

Looking closely, they noticed the outline of a man lying prone over the skylight. Then they went up to the roof and found Hillel buried under three feet of snow. Even though it was a violation of the Sabbath they carried him down, undressed him, anointed him with oil, and made him sit near the fire. All were of one mind: "On account of such a man one is justified in violating the Sabbath."

When a rich man arrives in the next world and he is rebuked for not devoting himself to the study of the Torah, he usually makes a great many excuses. He explains that he was very rich, was preoccupied with many affairs and never really had the time or the peace of mind for study.

The Heavenly retort to him is: "What! Could it be that you were richer than Rabbi Eleazar ben Harsom?"

The following story is told about Rabbi Eleazar ben Harsom: When his father died he inherited from him one thousand villages and many ships on the sea. Every day, throwing over his shoulder a bag of flour for baking his bread, Rabbi Eleazar would go from town to town and study the Torah.

One day his servants met him on the road but did not recognize him. So they tried to force him to do some work for their master, little realizing that he was their master. Without revealing to them his identity he pleaded, "Please let me go! I must study the Torah."

And they answered, "By the life of our master, Eleazar ben Harsom, we swear that we will not let you go!"

So he paid them ransom money to let him go.

This incident proved so distressing to him that he never again returned home. Ever after he devoted himself night and day to the study of the Torah.

When the wicked man is asked in the next world why he had not found time to study the Torah his answer very likely is, "I was a good-looking young man and the Evil Spirit turned my head."

To him the Heavenly retort is: "Were you better looking than Joseph?"

The following story is told about Joseph: Each day Potiphar's wife, tormented by his beauty, would try to seduce him with her charms and honeyed words. The garments she would put on in the morning in order to find favor in his eyes she would not wear again in the evening.

"Love me!" she pleaded.

"No!" answered Joseph.

"I will cast you into a dungeon!" she threatened.

"God liberates the confined."

"I will bend your proud neck!"

"God straightens those that are crooked."

"I will gouge out your eyes!"

"God opens the eyes of those who do not see."

And Joseph would not be seduced by Zuleika.

Saint or Horse

A YOUNG man once came to a great rabbi and asked him to make him a rabbi.

It was winter time then. The rabbi stood at the window looking out upon the yard while the rabbinical candidate was droning into his ears a glowing account of his piety and learning.

The young man said, "You see, Rabbi, I always go dressed in spotless white like the sages of old. I never drink any alcoholic beverages; only water ever passes my lips. Also, I perform austerities. I have sharp-edged nails inside my shoes to mortify me. Even in the coldest weather, I lie naked in the snow to torment my flesh. Also daily, the *shammes* gives me forty lashes on my bare back to complete my perpetual penance."

And as the young man spoke, a white horse was led into the yard and to the water trough. It drank, and then it rolled in the snow, as horses sometimes do.

"Just look!" cried the rabbi. "That animal, too, is dressed in white. It also drinks nothing but water, has nails in its shoes and rolls naked in the snow. Also, rest assured, it gets its daily ration of forty lashes on the rump from its master. Now, I ask you, is it a saint, or is it a horse?"

The Sin Lies in the Intention

A GREAT scandal stirred up the little Jewish community of a Ukrainian town. Someone had seen their rabbi talking to a pretty woman in the market-place.

"What a blasphemy! And in broad daylight on the street, too!" many people said.

Such things were simply unforgivable in an orthodox God-fearing rabbi! Wasn't he supposed to serve as the spiritual shepherd and upright example for his flock?

When the elders of the congregation heard of this they lectured the rabbi for doing such an unseemly thing in public.

The rabbi listened to them attentively, and, when they had finished, he cried:

"Oh, you pious hypocrites! Isn't it far better to talk with a pretty woman and think of the Almighty than to talk to the Almighty and think of a pretty woman?"

The Prayer That Imposes

THE Rabbi of Ger fell on evil days; he could hardly keep himself and his family alive. So his wife said to him, "Ask God to come to our aid."

"Heaven forbid!" cried the Rabbi. "While I must do God's will—what right have I to ask God to do my will?"

No Virtue in Suffering

RABBI ELEAZAR fell grievously ill. To his bedside came Rabbi Yohanan to comfort him. As he entered he saw the sick man lying in utter darkness. Now Rabbi Yohanan, who was very handsome and whose beauty was as radiant as the sun, uncovered his arm and lo and behold!—the room was filled with light! He looked upon Rabbi Eleazar and saw that he was weeping.

"Why do you weep?" he asked him. "Is it because you feel that you have not studied enough of Holy Lore? Don't grieve! Know that before God it is all the same whether one studies much or little, as long as it is done with pure intention. Perhaps you are grieving because you are poor! Why don't you make peace with your destiny? Very rarely can a man be both rich and learned. Possibly you are grieving because of the anguish your children are causing you! See my anguish then! Behold! Here is a bone of my tenth son whom I have just buried."

"I am not grieving for any of these reasons," replied Rabbi Eleazar. "I am lamenting at the thought that such a beautiful creature as you will have to die some day and rot in the earth!"

"There is indeed much cause in this for weeping," replied Rabbi Yohanan, and he too burst into tears.

Then Rabbi Yohanan again began to comfort Rabbi Eleazar, pointing out that man must reconcile himself to his misfortunes, for God never abandons the good; his reward is in the life-to-be. In conclusion Rabbi Yohanan asked him, "Do you love your sorrow?"

Rabbi Eleazar sighed.

"No," he answered. "I can do without it."

"Give me your hand," said Rabbi Yohanan.

NO VIRTUE IN SUFFERING: Adapted from the *Agada* in the Talmud.

Consolation in Grief

WHEN the son of Rabbi Yohanan ben Zakkai died the master's disciples came to console him.

First came Rabbi Eliezer ben Hyrkanos. Wishing to distract the bereaved father, he asked, "Would you like to listen to my discourse, Rabbi?"

"Speak!" Rabbi Yohanan assented.

So Rabbi Eliezer began: "Adam had a son and he died. Nonetheless, Adam allowed himself to be comforted. We construe this from the fact that Adam and Eve reconciled themselves to their loss and fulfilled their alloted tasks on earth. So you too, Master, must find solace in your bereavement."

"Not enough that I have my own sorrows," cried Rabbi Yohanan reproachfully, "must you remind me of the sorrows of Adam?"

Rabbi Joshua then entered and said, "Will you allow me, Rabbi, to discourse on Holy Lore?"

"Speak," said Rabbi Yohanan.

Rabbi Joshua began: "Job had sons and daughters, but they all died in one day. Nonetheless, he found solace. How do we know that? From the fact that he said: 'God gave and God took, blessed be the name of the Lord!' You too must find comfort."

"Not enough that I have my own grief, must you remind me of Job's grief?" Rabbi Yohanan cried reproachfully.

Rabbi Yose then entered.

"Permit me to say words of comfort to you," he asked.

"Speak," said Rabbi Yohanan.

Rabbi Yose began: "Aaron had two grown sons and both died on the same day. Nonetheless, Aaron allowed himself to be comforted. How do we know that? It is written in the Torah: 'Aaron was silent.' When a man who mourns falls silent it means he has ceased to lament and is consoled. And so, Rabbi, I say: you too must accept solace in your bereavement."

"Not enough that I have my own sorrows," cried Rabbi Yohanan reproachfully, "must you come and remind me of the sorrows of Aaron?"

After Rabbi Yose had left Rabbi Simeon entered.

"Will you allow me, Rabbi, to discourse on Holy Lore?" he asked.

"Speak," said Rabbi Yohanan.

Rabbi Simeon began: "King David had a son and he died. Nonetheless, he permitted himself to be comforted. And how do we know that? It is written in Scripture that he solaced himself with his wife Bathsheba and that she bore him a son whom they named Solomon. Like David, you too must find comfort."

"Not enough that I have my own grief, must you remind me of David's?" cried Rabbi Yohanan.

CONSOLATION IN GRIEF: *Ibid.*

The last to go in to him was Rabbi Eleazar ben Arak.

"Will you allow me, Rabbi, to say words of comfort to you?" he asked.

"Speak," said Rabbi Yohanan.

Rabbi Eleazar began: "Let me tell you a fitting parable. A King had given one of his vassals a valuable object to hold for him. Each day this man would lament: 'Woe is me! When will the King come and take back his possession so that I won't be burdened with such a great responsibility?' The same holds true of you, Rabbi. You had a son who was accomplished and a fine scholar. He left the world unstained, pure from sin. Therefore, you must find comfort in the thought that you have returned unsullied the possession entrusted to your care by the King of Kings."

"You have comforted me, Eleazar, my son!" cried Yohanan.

And he arose and put grief aside.

The Twig of Myrtle

RABBI SAMUEL BAR ISAAC regarded it as an act of virtue to rejoice with a bride and bridegroom. Whenever he came to a wedding he would take a twig of myrtle and dance gaily before the bride and groom.

Once Rabbi Ze'era saw him dance this way and felt ashamed of him.

"Just see how that old fool misbehaves!" he cried.

In time, Rabbi Samuel died. For three hours on end it thundered and lightning rent the heavens. In the midst of it a Celestial Voice cried out, "Woe! Woe! Rabbi Samuel bar Isaac is dead. Rise and pay him the last honors as he deserves!"

As the great throng followed him to his final resting place a column of fire descended from heaven. Miraculously, it was in the shape of a myrtle branch! It stood between the bier of the dead man and the mourners.

Then all agreed that the great honor Heaven bestowed upon Rabbi Samuel was because of his efforts to gladden the hearts of the bride and the bridegroom by dancing before them with a twig of myrtle in his hand.

The Saint and the Penitent

THE Greek invader ruled the Land of Israel with an iron hand, oppressing the Jewish people and desecrating its holy places. Also they condemned to death Rabbi Yose ben Yoezer.

It was on the Sabbath that they led him through the streets of the city to be hanged. The scaffold on which he was to die was carried before him and a great throng followed him. Rabbi Yose suddenly perceived among

THE TWIG OF MYRTLE: *Ibid.*

THE SAINT AND THE PENITENT: Adapted from the *Midrash.*

the multitude his sister's son, Yakim ben Zeroroth. He was riding on a prancing steed. And seeing the look of derision on his face Rabbi Yose's heart grew heavy.

Yakim rode up to him and said mockingly, "Consider, O uncle mine, you saint and God-fearing man, how different are our rewards! God has given me a horse to ride on, and you He has rewarded with a lovely scaffold."

"Your meaning eludes me," Rabbi Yose replied.

Thereupon Yakim ben Zeroroth said, "At all times I have indulged my heart in all its desires and have pampered it with the delights of the flesh. I renounced your Jewish God and His Torah. And behold, I have prospered in all that I have undertaken. It has been otherwise with you, my uncle. You always have been loyal to the precepts of your God's Law, have done only what was good and righteous in His eyes. You denied yourself every pleasure. God therefore loved you and sent His divine grace upon you, saying: 'My son! Great shall be your reward! I shall provide for you a scaffold and a rope for your neck!' "

Tranquil was Rabbi Yose's answer to his nephew: "God has punished me because I am a sinner."

Yakim was filled with wonder. He asked, "How can it be that you, the most upright of men, could have brought upon you God's wrath? Is that why He is sending you to your death? Is there one among all Israel who has served God so devotedly and obeyed all His commandments as you?"

Rabbi Yose answered, "Just think, if even after I have obeyed all His commandments I am being condemned to die, what fate can be in store for those who do not do His will?"

When Yakim heard his uncle's words he was filled with fear, thinking: "If this is the fate that is deserved by my uncle who is God-fearing and upright, what will happen to me who am wicked and a sinner?" Pondering in this wise he was filled with anguish. A faintness seized his limbs and darkness fell upon his eyes.

Rabbi Yose ben Yoezer finally arrived at the place of execution and while the hangmen began to ready the scaffold they entrusted the condemned man to the care of the soldiers.

In the meantime, Yakim ben Zeroroth went away and made for himself a scaffold. To it he tied a rope and beneath it he piled wood and placed a wall of stones around it. Then he set fire to the wood and placed a sharp sword in the middle of it with its point facing upwards. Then he climbed onto the scaffold and placed the noose around his neck. And thus he died!

The fire beneath burst into bright flames and burned the rope on which Yakim hung. Then his body fell upon the sword and was pierced. And as the fires consumed him the wall of stones collapsed and crushed the body underneath them.

As Rabbi Yose sat with bowed head among the soldiers who guarded him he fell into a deep revery, brooding upon the misfortune that had befallen his people at the hands of the foreign tyrant. And as he mused he fell into a deep slumber.

He dreamed that he saw the gates of Paradise open, and there was a rush like the fluttering of wings as the pure souls of the saints entered. Rabbi Yose was filled with rapture and his face shone with a wondrous radiance. His disciples, who surrounded him, looked upon this radiance and exclaimed with awe, "What divine visions our rabbi must be seeing to be filled with such light and rapture!"

At that instant Rabbi Yose felt his soul being separated from his body and it winged its way through the air to the Garden of Eden. As it reached the heavenly gates he saw a spirit so pure that it seemed never to have dwelt in its house of clay. This spirit radiated light and flashed with dazzling beauty. Modestly the soul of Rabbi Yose stood aside and made way for the radiant soul to enter Paradise. And at that instant was heard the singing of the angelic choirs, "Open wide the gates for Yakim ben Zeroroth!"

Rabbi Yose awoke from his slumber and when he saw the disciples standing about him and gazing upon him with wonder, he said, "Know, O my sons, that in my dream it was revealed to me that the penitent Yakim ben Zeroroth entered Paradise one hour before me! And now, bid me farewell, for the hour of my death has arrived!"

The Value of a Good Wife

"HE THAT hath found a virtuous wife, hath a greater treasure than costly pearls."

Such a treasure had the celebrated teacher Rabbi Meir found. He sat during the whole of one Sabbath day in the public school and instructed the people.

During his absence from his house his two sons, both of them of uncommon beauty and enlightened in the Law, died. His wife bore them to her bed-chamber, laid them upon the marriage-bed, and spread a white covering over their bodies.

Towards evening Rabbi Meir came home.

"Where are my beloved sons," he asked, "that I may give them my blessing?"

"They are gone to the school," was the answer.

"I repeatedly looked round the school," he replied, "and I did not see them there."

She reached him a goblet; he praised the Lord at the going out of the Sabbath, drank and again asked, "Where are my sons, that they may drink of the cup of blessing?"

"They will not be far off," she said, and placed food before him that he might eat.

THE VALUE OF A GOOD WIFE: From the Talmud. Translated by Samuel T. Coleridge. In *Hebrew Tales,* by Hyman Hurwitz. Printed for Morrison and Watt. London, 1826.

He was in a gladsome and genial mood, and when he had said grace after the meal, she thus addressed him: "Rabbi, with thy permission I would fain propose to thee one question."

"Ask it, then, my love!" he replied.

"A few days ago a person entrusted some jewels to my custody, and now he demands them again. Should I give them back again?"

"This is a question," said Rabbi Meir, "which my wife should not have thought it necessary to ask. What! Wouldst thou hesitate or be reluctant to restore to everyone his own?"

"No," she replied, "but yet I thought it best not to restore them without acquainting thee therewith."

She then led him to their chamber, and, stepping to the bed, took the white covering off the bodies of their sons.

"Ah, my sons! My sons!" thus loudly lamented the father. "My sons! The light of mine eyes. And the light of my understanding. I was your father, but ye were my teachers in the Law!"

The mother turned away and wept bitterly. At length she took her husband by the hand and said, "Rabbi, didst thou not teach me that we must not be reluctant to restore that which was entrusted to our keeping? See, the Lord gave, the Lord has taken away, and blessed be the name of the Lord!"

"Blessed be the name of the Lord!" echoed Rabbi Meir, "and blessed be His name for thy sake too, for well it is written, 'He that hath found a virtuous wife hath a greater treasure than costly pearls. She openeth her mouth with wisdom, and on her tongue is the instruction of kindness.'"

Man the Peacemaker

WHEN Joshua was building an altar to God the Jews came to him and asked, "Explain to us, our Master Joshua, why God has forbidden the use of iron on stone from which an altar is constructed?"

Joshua explained, "When men sin against God and bring a sacrifice upon His altar and confess their sins, God forgives them and rewards them with long years of peace. This is because the altar is made only to lengthen the life of man and to establish peace between man and God. It is different with iron. From it one fashions swords and spears and all manner of weapons employed to kill, to shorten life and to kindle hatred between man and man, between nation and nation. Therefore God commanded that iron which shortens the life of man be not allowed to touch the stones of the altar which bring him peace and increase his years."

When the people heard Joshua's explanation they were filled with delight and said, "If the stones that see not, hear not and speak not, are so highly prized by God because they make peace between Him and the sons

MAN THE PEACEMAKER: Adapted from the *Midrash*.

of man, how much more prized must man be when he makes peace between
one individual and another, between husband and wife, between nation
and nation!"

His Brother's Keeper

ULLA BAR KOSHAB fled and went into hiding. He had disobeyed the Queen,
therefore he feared her vengeance. For this reason she condemned him to
death.

He finally found asylum with Rabbi Joshua ben Levi in the town of
Ludd. But the Queen's spies discovered his hiding place. They surrounded
the house and said to the Jews, "If you do not deliver to us this man we
will slaughter all the Jews in your town."

Then Rabbi Joshua ben Levi said to Ulla bar Koshab, "I beg you to
forgive me if I deliver you to the Queen's servants. Far better that a
single person should suffer than that an entire populace should be
slaughtered."

Then he went and delivered Ulla to the Queen's spies.

Now in the past, the Prophet Elijah had often miraculously revealed
himself to Rabbi Joshua ben Levi. But, after Rabbi Joshua delivered Ulla
to the Queen's spies, Elijah ceased his visits. Grieved over his continued
absence, Rabbi Joshua fasted for thirty days. Then Elijah came again.

"Why did you desert me?" asked Rabbi Joshua.

"What else did you expect?" cried Elijah. "Should I have anything to
do with a man who delivers an innocent fellow-Jew into the hands of the
heathen?"

"I have only done as the law bids me," Rabbi Joshua said, in justification.
"The *Mishna* teaches us that, when the heathen demand that a single Jew
be delivered to them with the threat of killing all other Jews if this be not
done, then it is right to sacrifice the individual for the entire community."

"The law is as you say," replied Elijah sternly, "but under no circumstances should you have acted as you did. Better that all should perish
than that Jews, with their own hands, should deliver a brother to be murdered by the enemy."

Rabbi Safra's Silence

RABBI SAFRA had some merchandise to sell. When the traders came to buy
he asked ten pieces of gold for it.

"We will give you only five," said the merchants.

HIS BROTHER'S KEEPER: Adapted from the *Agada* in the Talmud.

RABBI SAFRA'S SILENCE: Adapted from the *Midrash*.

When Rabbi Safra refused to sell they went away.

The following morning they returned while the pious man was at prayer. "We have returned to offer you seven gold pieces for your goods," they said.

Because he did not wish to interrupt his prayers, Rabbi Safra did not answer. Thinking he was still dissatisfied with their offer, they finally said, "Very well, then, we will give you the ten gold pieces you're asking."

By this time Rabbi Safra had ended his devotions.

"I could not answer you before," he apologized to them, "because prayer and dross do not mix. Know, however, that before even you spoke I had settled in my mind that I would accept for my merchandise the five gold pieces you offered me yesterday. Therefore, to accept the ten pieces you have offered me now would be to cheat you."

True Pride of Ancestry

ONCE the Rabbi of Belz entertained a poor visiting rabbi with an account of the men of eminence among his ancestors. The poor rabbi remarked with some surprise, "It is hard for me to understand, Rabbi Sholem, how a man of your great understanding could become vainglorious about your ancestors. Isn't it enough for a Jew to be good and pious in his own right?"

Rabbi Sholem was much put out by this rebuke.

"Don't misunderstand me, please," he hastened to explain. "Believe me, I am not proud of my ancestry; the opposite is the case. My reason for dwelling on the eminence of my family is an ethical one. Let us, for instance, examine what our sages prescribe. They urge each one to ask himself: 'When will my achievements equal those of my forefathers?' From this one can readily see that those men with distinguished ancestors are always obliged to feel humble, for they must strive to reach the high goal already set for them. It is different with men whose eminence is greater than that of their fathers. As soon as they achieve fame they develop the vanity of self-made men."

The Scribe and the Rabbi

A PIOUS man in Dinov once ordered a new Torah-scroll for the synagogue. The *sofer*, who was a vain man, went to Rabbi Zevi Elimelech to show off his art.

"*Nu*, Rabbi Zevi Elimelech, how do you like my penmanship?" he asked proudly.

"The penmanship is nothing to get excited about," replied the rabbi thoughtfully, "but ah, what language! What meanings!"

THE SCRIBE AND THE RABBI: Adapted from *Yiddishe Legendes*, by Eliezer Shindler. Ferlag *Grininke Beimelach*. Vilna, 1936.

The Insulting Compliment

RABBI BORUCH of Miedziboz was entertaining an out-of-town scholar on the Sabbath day. Warming up to the occasion the visitor eagerly said, "Rabbi—do expound the Torah for me! I've heard it said you speak so beautifully!"

"May God strike me dumb before I speak beautifully!" snapped Rabbi Boruch.

God's Drunkard

ONCE, Rabbi Levi Yitzchok, "The Compassionate," celebrated the first Seder night with true spiritual fervor. As the feast came to an end the thought occurred to him that, at no time before in his life, had he ever worshipped the Almighty with such love and rapture. And, as he sat thus pleasantly musing, he heard a voice. It sounded sarcastic and rude, and where it came from he could not tell.

"Levi Yitzchok!" mocked the voice. "You are boastful because of the pious way you conducted the Seder service. Know then, that the Seder of Chaim, the Water-Carrier, was infinitely more beautiful than yours!"

The rabbi trembled and called out to his kin and his disciples: "Who is this Chaim, the Water-Carrier?"

"I know him well," said one. "He is an awful sot!"

"Go and fetch him!" commanded the rabbi.

It took his disciples a long time before they could find the house of the water-carrier. They knocked on the door. Chaim's wife came out.

"If you are looking for my husband he is lying dead drunk on his bed!" she said with disgust.

The disciples then lifted the water-carrier and carried him on their backs to the rabbi. After the drunkard had sobered up the rabbi made him sit beside him and he spoke to him as one friend to another.

"Chaim, dear heart," he asked in the gentlest of voices, "did you recite 'Slaves were we in Egypt' last Sabbath day?"

"No, Rabbi," answered Chaim, shamefaced.

"Did you burn the leavened bread before Passover?"

Chaim knitted his brows. For a moment he could not remember. Then the terrible recollection came back to him.

"May the good God have mercy on me, Rabbi!" he exclaimed. "I forgot to burn the leavened bread: I left it lying on the window sill."

"And how did you celebrate the Seder?" inquired Rabbi Levi Yitzchok, growing even more curious.

GOD'S DRUNKARD: Adapted from Priester der Liebe, by Chajim Bloch. Amalthea-Verlag. Wien, 1930.

"I wish to tell the truth," answered Chaim, hanging his head guiltily. "Although I know that it is forbidden to drink brandy during the eight days of Passover, I drank enough tonight to suffice for all eight days. Before I knew it I had dozed off. Then my wife wakened me and gave me an angry talking to.

" 'You sot!' she said. 'Why don't you observe the *Seder* in the decent manner of our forefathers, like all other Jews?'

" 'What do you want of me?' I asked. 'I am only an ignorant man, and the son of an ignorant man. I don't understand anything about all those things. I know only this: That the Jews of old, our ancestors, were taken captive by the gypsies [he meant the Egyptians], but to our luck we have an Almighty who led them out of slavery into freedom. And now, may the Lord pardon me for saying it, we are again slaves. But I know that He will free us some day.'

"So I do ask you, Rabbi: was it my fault that after I ate the *matzos,* the eggs and the other good things, and drank the brandy that I fell asleep?"

At this, Rabbi Levi Yitzchok said to his *shammes,* "Take this good man to his house."

And to his disciples he observed: "God was just in that He preferred Chaim the Water-Carrier's worship to mine, for He loves truthfulness above piety or learning."

Piety in Impiety

THE gentle Rabbi Levi Yitzchok of Berditchev was on his way home from the synagogue on *Tisha Ba'Ab,* the fast day commemorating the destruction of the Temple in Jerusalem. On this solemn day he was filled with the tragic remembrance of Israel's departed glory. As he walked rapt in thought he suddenly came face to face with a member of his flock who was enthusiastically gnawing away at a chicken leg. The rabbi stopped in shocked amazement.

"No doubt you've forgotten that today is *Tisha Ba'Ab,*" he asked, more in sorrow than in anger.

"Not at all!" answered the chicken-leg eater with candor. "What Jew doesn't know that today is *Tisha Ba'Ab?*"

"In that case you must be a sick man and the doctor has forbidden you to fast," ventured the rabbi, solicitously.

"No, Rabbi, I'm quite well, thank you!" answered the man.

Rabbi Levi Yitzchok was overjoyed. Raising his eyes to Heaven he murmured, "Almighty God—just see how upright Your children are! This fine man would rather cry aloud his sins from the housetops than tell a falsehood!"

The Chaste Maid

IN A certain city there lived a maiden. She was chaste and pious and took no pleasure in the vanities of the world.

It so happened that the prince who ruled the city saw her one day and he fell in love with her. On more than one occasion thereafter he sent messengers to her and tried to persuade her to love him. Nevertheless, he failed to bend her to his will. Thereupon, he decided to use violence.

One day he broke into her room followed by his soldiers and he forced her to come with him to his palace.

The maiden cried aloud and lamented. But when she saw that her chaste tears did not move the lustful prince's heart, she asked him, "Please tell me, what is it that you like so much about me?"

He replied: "You have the eyes of a dove; they have taken me captive!"

Hearing this, the maiden said: "Now I see how strong your love for me is! Therefore, I've decided to do your will. Permit me then to go into my private chamber to adorn myself for you."

The prince permitted her to do so and she bolted the door behind her. She then took a knife and gouged out her eyes with it. Groping her way back to the door she opened it and murmured to the prince, "Since you have such great love for my eyes you may have them. Here they are! Do with them what you wish."

Dismayed and shaken the prince stood before her. He let her go home, and she remained pure and chaste as long as she lived.

The Honest Disciple

A CERTAIN rabbi wished to prove the honesty of his disciples, so he asked them the following question: "What would you do if you found a large sum of money?"

"I'd give it back to the one who lost it," said one disciple.

"I don't believe you! You're too glib with your answer," commented the rabbi.

"I'd keep the money if no one saw me find it," said another disciple.

"You're frank, but wicked!" snapped the rabbi.

"To be perfectly truthful with you, Rabbi," said a third disciple, "I'd be greatly tempted to keep it. In that case I'd pray to God that He save me from evil and give me strength to resist it."

The rabbi beamed and exclaimed, "God preserve you! You are the man I'd trust."

THE CHASTE MAID: Adapted from *Tzemach Tzaddik,* by Leone de Modena, Venetian-Jewish preacher, poet and humanist. Venice, 1600.

Hunger Strike

THE beginning of the day's routine for the devout Jew has not varied for generations. He arises, he washes, and before breakfasting he puts on the phylacteries and prays.

But new ideas were abroad, and Moishe the *shammes* disclosed one day to his friend Chaim the *melamed* that Leibel, his eldest son, had refused to put on the phylacteries. Five mornings in a row he had absolutely, irrevocably refused!

"Every morning I ask and every morning he refuses."

"But he'll—God forbid!—starve!" declared Chaim. "How long can he hold out?"

The Worthiest

ONCE there was a great drought in the land. Rabbi Abbahu had a dream in which it was revealed to him from Heaven that a man by the name of Pentakaka was the most favored person to pray for rain.

Rabbi Abbahu awoke and, recalling his dream, was filled with wonder. He knew this Pentakaka as an immoral fellow. His name "Pentakaka" meant in Greek: "The man with the five deadly vices." Reluctantly, Rabbi Abbahu sent for him.

"What is your trade?" he asked him.

"I devote myself to five vices," answered Pentakaka. "I am a procurer of immoral women, I decorate the house of ill fame where they congregate, I beautify them, and dance for them, and play on the pipes."

"Have you ever done a good deed?" Rabbi Abbahu asked him.

Pentakaka told him the following: "Once when I was about to close the house of ill fame I saw a strange woman standing in the corner, weeping bitterly.

" 'Why do you weep?' I asked her.

" 'My husband lies in the debtor's jail,' she told me, 'and I have no money with which to redeem him. I've come to sell my body so that I may be able to liberate him.'

"When I heard this I sold my bed and the bedding and gave the money to the woman, saying, 'Go woman, and free your husband, but do not sell your body to strangers!' "

And Rabbi Abbahu bowed his head before Pentakaka.

THE WORTHIEST: Adapted from the *Agada* in the Talmud.

The Pious Ox Which Refused to Work on the Sabbath and the Example He Set

ONCE upon a time there lived a pious man, who supported himself by means of an ox which he owned. They ploughed together the whole week and on the Sabbath they rested, in accordance with the command of the Lord, blessed be He: "On the Sabbath thou shalt rest, and thy maidservants and thy menservants and thy beasts" (Ex. 20.10).

Now it came to pass that the pious man grew very poor and was compelled to sell his ox to a Gentile, warranting him to be without blemish. The man worked his field with him all the days of the week without discovering any defect. But when the Sabbath came, he took him to the field as usual, but the ox lay down and refused to work, for he had not been accustomed to work on the Sabbath when he was with the Jew, and had rested on that day. The man beat the poor animal very hard, but he would not budge, lay down on the ground and would not get up. When the man saw that the ox had a defect, he went to the Jew and said to him: "You warranted the ox without defect and now he refuses to work, and when I strike him he lies down on the ground. Give me back my money." The poor man was very much upset, for he had spent the money. Then it occurred to him that perhaps the ox still remembered the Sabbath and he asked the man: "Does he always refuse to work?" The man replied: "He works very well all week, but on the Sabbath he refuses to work." When the Sabbath came again, the pious man went with the Gentile to the field and found the ox lying on the ground. The man struck him but he would not rise. Then the pious man addressed the ox and said to him: "As long as you were in my service you were obliged to rest on the Sabbath, for so the Lord God commanded us. But since you are no longer with me but are employed by a Gentile, you are not obliged to rest on the Sabbath, for the Gentile does not keep the Sabbath. Rise, therefore, and do your work so that I may have no further trouble from your master." When the ox heard this, he arose and went to work. When the Gentile saw this, he was greatly astonished and asked the Jew what he had whispered to the ox, so that he might do the same, should the ox again refuse to work. So he told him what he had whispered to the ox. When the Gentile heard this, he began to weep and said: "See, this animal is anxious to keep the Sabbath as commanded by God. How much more should a human being be anxious to observe it!" Thereupon he, together with his whole household, embraced Judaism and became a very pious Jew. He assumed the name R. Hanina and became the rabbi of a town.

THE PIOUS OX WHICH REFUSED TO WORK ON THE SABBATH AND THE EXAMPLE HE SET: Reprinted from the *Ma'aseh Book*, edited by Moses Gaster. With the permission of the copyright owners, The Jewish Publication Society of America. Philadelphia, 1934.

CHARITABLE MEN

INTRODUCTION

The giving of charity is conceived of by Jews as one of the highest forms of piety and righteousness. The philosopher Schopenhauer's thesis in *The Basis of Morality* was that all ethics spring from the compassion aroused in us by the suffering of our fellow beings. However, in the case of the traditional Jewish attitude toward charity, compassion must be linked to social justice. The hypocritical evasion of the fratricide Cain—"Am I my brother's keeper?"—has, in the course of the centuries, been transformed into the affirmative principle of the interdependence of all men and of the moral responsibility of one for all and of all for one.

"The earth is the Lord's, and the fulness thereof," stated the Psalmist simply. The sages of the Talmud elaborated on the meaning of the Scriptural text so that there could remain no loophole of evasion on the part of the egotists: "Thou shalt not say: 'I have no money [to give to the poor],' for all the money belongs to Him as it is written: 'Mine is the silver and Mine is the gold, saith the Lord of Hosts.' " From this the rabbis deduced that God was deeply in debt to the poor since He had apportioned to them but very little of worldly goods. Furthermore, in giving wealth to the rich the Almighty had merely made them His fiscal agents or bankers.

It therefore follows logically that when the poor are made wretched by poverty they have a right to raise their voices to God in complaint as needy creditors because He has neglected to pay them. Thus said Rabbi Judah ben Simon: "The poor man sits and complains to God: 'Why am I different from the rich man? He sleeps in his bed and I sleep here [in the street].' " Therefore, if the rich man refuses to hear this legitimate complaint of the poor it is as if he had transgressed against God Himself, as if he had denied aid to his own kith and kin. The Talmud says with implied rebuke to the heedless: "It is not written, 'the poor man,' but 'thy brother,' to show that both of them are equal."

The Hebrew word for charity is *tzedakah,* which in its traditional meaning signifies "righteousness" and "justice," and not just mere alms-giving which is its vulgarized conception. The practice of *tzedakah* has a variety of overtones as well as outlets of benevolence. Since time immemorial it has been traditional at Jewish funerals for the pious or the charity-collectors to exhort the mourners with the cry: "Charity saves from death!" Charity also brings atonement and remission of sin. But charity must come from the *heart* as well as from the pocket. The unwilling giver, or the one who gives ostentatiously, forfeits his heavenly reward. Maimonides was not the first to formulate the differences between giving and giving. In his *Golden Ladder of Charity* he merely refined the traditional conception of *tzedakah* which rates the gift of the hand without the heart as the lowest form of charity, and the prevention of poverty as the highest act of charity. We thus find in the Talmud the practical admonition for the preservation of the human dignity of the needy: "Lending is greater than alms-giving."

Charity can be expressed in more ways than feeding the hungry or clothing the naked. Ben Sira advises: "Fail not to be with them that weep and mourn with them that mourn." (*Book of Sirach,* 7.34) Tending the sick, helping the crippled, supporting the weak and leading the blind are also acts of charity. So is offering consolation to the afflicted and the bereaved. "Shall not the dew lessen the heat? So is a kind word better than a gift." (*Book of Sirach*, 18.16) Hospitality and assistance to travellers and strangers, such a vital and practical necessity among the peoples of the East, are among the oldest forms of charity. In Jewish legend the Patriarch Abraham practiced this benevolence to the fullest; the wicked men of Sodom, on the other hand, made it a capital crime.

N. A.

The Golden Ladder of Charity

THERE are eight degrees or steps, says Maimonides, in the duty of charity.

The first and lowest degree is to give—but with reluctance or regret. This is the gift of the *hand*, but not of the *heart*.

The second is to give cheerfully, but not proportionately to the distress of the sufferer.

The third is to give cheerfully and proportionately, but not until we are solicited.

The fourth is to give cheerfully, proportionately, and even unsolicited; but to put it in the poor man's hand, thereby exciting in him the painful emotion of shame.

The fifth is to give charity in such a way that the distressed may receive the bounty and know their benefactor, without their being known to him. Such was the conduct of some of our ancestors, who used to tie up money in the hind-corners of their cloaks, so that the poor might take it unperceived.

The sixth, which rises still higher, is to know the objects of our bounty, but remain unknown to them. Such was the conduct of those of our ancestors who used to convey their charitable gifts into poor people's dwellings, taking care that their own persons and names should remain unknown.

The seventh is still more meritorious, namely, to bestow charity in such a way that the benefactor may not know the relieved persons, nor they the name of their benefactor. This was done by our charitable forefathers during the existence of the Temple. For there was in that holy building a place called the *Chamber of Silence or Inostentation;* wherein the good deposited secretly whatever their generous hearts suggested; and from which the most respectable poor families were maintained with equal secrecy.

Lastly, the eighth and most meritorious of all, is to anticipate charity by preventing poverty; namely, to assist the reduced brother, either by a

---

THE GOLDEN LADDER OF CHARITY: From *Hebrew Tales*, by Hyman Hurwitz. Printed for Morrison and Watt. London. 1826 considerable gift, or a loan of money, or by teaching him a trade, or by putting him in the way of business, so that he may earn an honest livelihood; and not be forced to the dreadful alternative of holding up his hand for charity. And to this Scripture alludes when it says, "And if thy brother be waxen poor and fallen in decay with thee, then thou shalt *support* him: *Yea though he be a stranger or a sojourner,* that he may live with thee." *

This is the highest step and the summit of charity's Golden Ladder.

Qualifications for Paradise

THE Gates of Paradise stood open and the procession of the souls of men reached to the Heavenly Tribunal.

First came a rabbi.

"I'm learned in the Law," he said. "Night and day have I pored over the Word of God. I therefore deserve a place in Paradise."

"Just a moment!" called out the Recording Angel. "First we must make an investigation. We've got to find out what was the motive for your study. Did you apply yourself to learning for its own sake? Was it for the sake of honor, or for mercenary reasons?"

Next came a saintly man.

"How I fasted in the life I left behind! I observed all the six hundred and thirteen religious duties scrupulously. I bathed several times a day, and I studied the mysteries of the *Zohar* ceaselessly."

"Just a moment!" cried the Recording Angel. "We first have to make our investigation about the purity of your intentions."

Then a tavern-keeper approached. He said simply, "My door was always open to the homeless and I fed whoever was in need and hungry."

"Open the Gates of Paradise!" cried the Recording Angel. "No investigation is needed."

Only the Dead Are Without Hope

A RICH man once asked, "Of what use to me will be all my labor and of what avail will my great riches be when the day of my death arrives?"

Hearing this, his friends advised him to spend his fortune on charity and doing good for people, and thus his loving kindness would always follow him and protect him in evil times. Also, he would be secure in his future life, for riches do not endure forever and can be lost easily.

---

* Levit. XXV. 35.

ONLY THE DEAD ARE WITHOUT HOPE: Adapted from *The Stories of Rabbi Nissim,* Gaon of Kairwan (11th Century A.D.).

The rich man agreed but swore he would not give charity to anyone except to a man who had already abandoned all hope in life.

One day the rich man went for a walk outside the city. He saw a poor man dressed in rags sitting on a dung heap. The rich man thought: "Here is the very man I've been looking for! He certainly must have abandoned all hope in life! There he sits, tormented by need and waiting for death."

The rich man thereupon handed the poor man one hundred gold pieces.

"Why do you give me so much money?" the poor man asked, amazed. "Why have you chosen me from among the poor in the city for your benevolence?"

The rich man answered, "I have sworn that I would not give charity to anyone but the man who has lost all hope in life."

"Take back your hundred gold pieces!" cried the poor man. "Only a fool or one who denies that there is a God in Heaven can lose hope in life. But I have faith in God and in His Grace and I wait for His help that must come to me any hour, even any minute. Don't you know that God's mercy to all His creatures is infinite? If He wishes He can raise the poor man from the dust, even from a heap of dung! Don't you know that if the Almighty wishes He can make me rich and free me from the destitution I suffer today?"

"Is this how you reward my compassion for you?" the rich man rebuked him. "Have I deserved to be abused thus by you?"

"You are under the impression that you have been good to me," replied the poor man. "It's just the opposite: it is as though you have slain me with your benevolence because only the dead have abandoned all hope in life!"

Paradise Gained?

A PIOUS man asked his rabbi, "What must I do to deserve Paradise?"

The rabbi pondered and replied, "Three things you must observe to earn the everlasting life—you must give alms, care for the sick, and bury the dead."

The man thanked the rabbi and left.

On the way home he met a crippled beggar. At once he recalled the rabbi's words and took the unfortunate man home. He set a lavish dinner before him and praised God that he had with this deed fulfilled the first precept. Unfortunately, the beggar fell sick because he had overeaten. So the pious man put him to bed and gave him a physic. Then he bethought himself of the rabbi's second precept and he rejoiced that he had fulfilled it already.

But during the night the condition of the beggar grew suddenly worse and he died. When morning came the pious man helped prepare him for burial and laid him to rest in the Jewish cemetery. Then, turning his eyes heavenward, he rejoiced, "Praised be the Lord, who has made it so easy for man to enter Paradise!"

The Father of the Poor

ONCE there was a *shammes* in Grodno who was lovingly called "The Father of the Poor." Otherwise he was known by the endearing name of "*Reb* Nochemke." * People loved him because he loved people—as the saying goes: "One heart understands another."

Reb Nochemke was small in stature but he was a great scholar nonetheless. He was modest in his piety and valued kindness to people above learning. At first he did not wish to be a rabbi because he believed it would place him too far apart from people.

"I'll be a *shammes*," he said.

And a *shammes* he became in one of the synagogues of Grodno. He was constantly on the go with the trifling affairs of his calling. He cleaned the synagogue and made the stove in winter. He ran errands for the rabbi and collected money-pledges for the support of his synagogue.

But, in his spare time, *Reb* Nochemke scurried about town gathering alms for the poor. This task was no part of his duties as *shammes;* he did it out of his own free will and with burning eagerness. He had his own group of needy pensioners whom he supported as though he were their loving father and provider. Among them were widows, orphans, the sick, the hungry and the abandoned. He distributed his help so unobtrusively and with such delicacy that no one felt ashamed.

His duties at the synagogue were so numerous that only after it was closed late at night was he free to begin his alms collecting. In the most unseasonable of weather he was constantly seen, a bedraggled little man, trudging determinedly along the muddy or snowbanked roads to the various taverns, inns and winehouses of the town. He chose to frequent these places for he used to say with a wink: "People who live for pleasure are generous with the groschen."

Reb Nochemke would seat himself quietly among the card-players. He would banter them good-humoredly and with merry quips would wheedle out of them a cut of their winnings. It was from these winnings that *Reb* Nochemke fed and clothed his precious flock of the needy.

Late one night he went to sit among a group of card-players. They

---

* *Reb* Nachum Grodner was a famous preacher of Grodno, Lithuania (1811–1879). He was an eminent Talmudist, but his modesty led him to take the post of *shammes* in a synagogue. His acts of brotherly love to the poor and the needy and his untiring devotion on their behalf made him a legendary figure among the poverty-stricken Jewish masses of the Lithuanian ghettos. His preaching was homely and full of folk-wisdom and, although occupying a humble position, he was more beloved and esteemed than the most learned rabbis of his day. In keeping with his folk-character, nobody called him *Reb* Nachum but all used the familiar, endearing "*Reb* Nochemke."—N. A.

had no idea who the odd little man was and paid no attention to him.

"What will you give me for my poor?" he asked them, suddenly.

Everybody laughed, for they did not understand what he was talking about.

"I'll give *you* something, but nothing for your poor!" said one of the card-players, rudely.

And right away he struck *Reb* Nochemke in the mouth with the flat of his hand so that the old *shammes* began to bleed.

To everybody's amazement *Reb* Nochemke took it all good-humoredly, even with a laugh.

"Very well," he said to the ruffian who had struck him, "you've given *me* 'something,' brother—now give me something for the poor."

Touched by *Reb* Nochemke's gentle good-humor, the gambler begged his pardon and gave him ten rubles.

There was nothing that *Reb* Nochemke wouldn't do for his poor.

One day he was told that a rich Jew had arrived in Grodno and was lodging at a certain inn. So, late at night, as was his custom, *Reb* Nochemke went to the inn. But to his distress he found the street door bolted. He knocked again—still no answer. What was he to do? The rich man might decide to leave early in the morning and he might miss him!

Being little and scrawny, *Reb* Nochemke went down on all fours. Then, flattening himself to the ground, he crawled through a narrow opening under the fence of the courtyard of the inn. Immediately a dog began to bark. A servant came out and as soon as he noticed *Reb* Nochemke he raised a hue and cry, "A *goniff*—a *goniff*!"

When they finally caught the "thief" they dragged the rascal into the light. They were struck dumb with amazement when they saw it was *Reb* Nochemke.

"*Reb* Nochemke!" stammered the innkeeper. "What on earth are you doing here? We thought you were a thief!"

"I've come to ask your rich guest for an alms," said the *shammes*.

The innkeeper could not help himself, but had to go and pull the rich man out of bed.

"It's our *Reb* Nochemke who has come for your donation for the poor," he told him, apologetically.

The rich man was very much touched by *Reb* Nochemke's devotion to the poor and he gave him a large sum of money.

Reb Nochemke was a very sick man. He suffered from many serious illnesses. Nonetheless, he was never deterred by them from his labors for the poor even in the worst of weathers.

Late one night, as he was walking along a deserted road, he suffered a heart attack and fell unconscious to the ground. When he came to he began to groan and the sound attracted a passing waggoner who lifted *Reb* Nochemke into his cart and began to drive him home.

On the way *Reb* Nochemke began to feel better.

"Do stop and let me off!" begged *Reb* Nochemke.

"What's the idea, *shammes*?" asked the driver. "You're in no condition to walk, you know."

"I've a lot of people to look after."

"But you're far too sick to go tramping about at this late hour."

"Suppose I were to pay you to drive me through the dark forest at this late hour—would you do it?"

"Of course I would, *shammes*! That's how I make my living. I've a wife and five children to support."

"And, I, my friend, have many more to support," replied *Reb* Nochemke, climbing out of the cart. Then he disappeared into the darkness.

Reb Nochemke took great pains not to hurt the sensibilities of the needy whom he aided, for he was poor himself and only too well understood the pride of the poor.

One day, he was asked to be god-father at a circumcision. Several days before the event he made inquiry and discovered that the father of the infant was in bad financial circumstances and had no money for the celebration. So *Reb* Nochemke went to see him.

"When, my son, are you planning to go to Kovno?" *Reb* Nochemke asked him.

"Why Kovno, *Reb* Nochemke? Who's going to Kovno?" asked the man, astonished.

"I thought that maybe you were going to Kovno," answered *Reb* Nochemke, lamely.

"And what if I was going to Kovno?" inquired the man, curiously.

"Well, if you were going I wanted to ask a favor of you. I owe a man who lives there twenty-five rubles and so I wanted you to pay him for me."

"But *Reb* Nochemke, how do I know when I'll be going to Kovno? I haven't been there for two years."

"There's no particular hurry! The man can wait. Just the same, here are the twenty-five rubles and the next time you do go to Kovno I'll be much obliged to you if you give it to him. On the other hand, should the money come in handy to you in the meantime you're welcome to use it. You can replace it later."

Unsuspectingly, the man took the twenty-five rubles and was glad. He spent the money on the circumcision party and he was not obliged to feel humiliated as he had feared all along.

When *Reb* Nochemke arrived at the circumcision the father said to him anxiously, "You forgot to give me the name and address of the man in Kovno for whom you gave me the money."

"Let me see, now," answered *Reb* Nochemke, as if trying to recall. "No, I'm afraid I can't remember. I have the name and address at home and I'll let you know some other time"

But this other time never came around, for *Reb* Nochemke said he had mislaid the address. After a while, the poor man scraped together the twenty-five rubles and returned them to *Reb* Nochemke.

The Rabbi's Advice

A WEALTHY *Hasid* once came to the great preacher, Rabbi Dov-Ber, and asked him for his blessings.

"Tell me," asked the rabbi, "do you eat well?"

"I live very modestly," answered the rich man, thinking that thereby he would gain the praise of the rabbi. "My meals consist of a dry crust with salt."

The rabbi regarded his petitioner with scorn.

"Why do you stint yourself meat and wine, food appropriate to a man of wealth like you?" he asked. And he continued to speak so harshly to him that the bewildered *Hasid* promised faithfully that in the future he would eat meat and drink wine.

The rabbi's counsel filled the disciples with amazement. And so, when the *Hasid* had gone away, they asked, "What is the meaning of all this, Rabbi? What earthly difference does it make whether this man eats bread and salt or meat and wine?"

Rabbi Dov-Ber smiled and said, "If this rich man lives well and his meals consist of meat and wine—as he can well afford—then at least it will be possible for him to grasp the fact that the poor can dine only on a dry crust with salt. However, when he denies himself all the pleasures of life, even if out of piety, then he will soon begin to think that the poor ought to eat stones."

The Good Job

ONCE there lived a man whose name was Job. He built himself a roomy house that had four entrances, one on each side. He did this, thinking: "When the poor and the hungry come let them quickly find my door."

Whenever a hungry man came Job hastened to bring him food and drink. For these deeds of loving kindness to his fellowmen, God blessed Job: He made him rich and his fame spread throughout the land. Despite his good fortune, Job remained modest and pious as before.

It chanced that a poor man died and left behind him a helpless widow and many orphans. When Job heard of this he said to himself: "I will go to the poor woman to console and help her." At that very instant an angel of Evil rose up before him. But he came in the disguise of one of Job's friends so that the good man did not recognize him for what he really was.

"I've heard," said the angel, "that you wish to comfort the poor widow

THE GOOD JOB: Adapted from the *Agada* in the Talmud.

whose husband has just died. I've hastened here to keep you from going to her."

"Why do you come to mock at me?" asked Job.

"How can you stoop so low as to visit the widow of a poor man!" cried the angel of Evil. "You are the foremost man among your people and its judge, and you must jealously guard the great dignity of your position."

"Hold your peace!" spoke Job sternly. "I will call on this widow none the less. Do you think I am better than God who comforts the widows and the orphans?"

When the angel heard this he departed.

Job went to see the woman; he spoke words of consolation to her and her children. Afterwards he inquired from her neighbors whether her late husband had left her anything, field or vineyard.

"No," they told him, "this man owned only a small field which in recent years gave no yield."

Job decided, therefore, to help the woman.

When the seven days of mourning were ended he went to call on the widow and told her, "When you get ready to cultivate your field, I will send you one of my servants, also a he-ass and a she-ass, to help you."

"Far be it from me to accept aid from a strange man!" she answered him. "God, the father of all orphans, will have mercy on me and my children. He will not abandon us in our need."

"At least let me plant for you a vegetable garden," asked Job.

But this help too she rejected.

When sowing-time arrived the woman sold all her household goods. With the money she rented an ass and cultivated her field. But the results were disappointing; the ground gave forth only thorns and thistles. The poor woman and her children were obliged to go hungry that winter.

When Job heard of her misfortune he sent her grain to last her for a whole year. But she refused to accept it.

"I will hire myself out as a servant," she sent word to Job, "so that I and my children may live by the labor of my own hands."

The widow went to work for another but her wages were far from enough to feed her and her children. So they continued to feel the pangs of hunger.

When Job heard of this his heart grew heavy, and he made a resolve. He let it be known far and wide that the widow was his own blood-relation.

When the people heard of this, they said, "Happy the man who will be lucky enough to marry this woman; he will inherit some of Job's wealth."

And so it happened. A righteous man married the widow, and Job helped him with a lavish hand. The newly wedded couple lived in happiness and peace.

Now it happened that many other men died during that time and a great number of children became orphans. These, too, Job wished to help but when he tried to give them food and clothing and offered to sow their fields, they refused his aid. So Job said to his servants, "Take your tools and cultivate the fields of these unfortunates who don't want to accept my help. Should they try to prevent you, pay no attention to them but go on with your work."

When the servants of Job tried to cultivate their fields the widows and the orphans arose to drive them away.

"Who asked you to cultivate our fields?" they protested.

But Job's servants followed their master's instructions and paid no attention to them. In fact, they were obliged to resist them with force. The inhabitants of the countryside soon heard the news. Then they spoke with bitterness, "What conduct for a pious man like Job! He has seized by violence the fields of helpless orphans! He ignores the rights of the people and does as he pleases! Indeed, he is not pious and good as we always thought, but a wretched hypocrite!"

In this manner Job was slandered and no one esteemed him anymore as they had done hitherto.

But when harvest-time came around, the servants of Job gathered in all the crops and gave them to the orphans. Those who had reviled him before saw how unjust they had been to him, and they were very contrite.

The Good Man's Reward

RABBI ELIEZER, Rabbi Joshua and Rabbi Akiba travelled about each year in the land of Israel to collect money for the poor. Amongst their many and various contributors, none gave more liberally, nor with more cheerfulness, than Aben-judan, who was then in very affluent circumstances.

Fortune however took a turn. A dreadful storm destroyed the fruits of his grounds; a raging pestilence swept away the greater part of his flocks and herds; and his extensive fields and vineyards became the prey of his greedy and inexorable creditors. Of all his vast possessions nothing was left him but one small plot of ground.

Such a sudden reverse of fortune was enough to depress any ordinary mind. But Aben-judan, on whose heart the Divine precepts of his holy religion had been early and deeply imprinted, patiently submitted to his lot.

"The Lord gave," said he, "and the Lord has taken away; let His name be praised forever."

He diligently applied himself to cultivate the only field he had left, and by dint of great labor, and still greater frugality, he contrived to support himself and his family decently, and was, notwithstanding his poverty, cheerful and contented.

The year passed on. One evening, as he was sitting at the door of his miserable hut, to rest from the labor of the day, he perceived the rabbis

---

THE GOOD MAN'S REWARD: From the *Midrash*. In *Hebrew Tales*, by Hyman Hurwitz. Printed for Morrison and Watt. London, 1826.

coming at a distance. It was then that his former greatness and his present deplorable condition at once rushed upon his mind and he felt for the first time the pangs of poverty.

"What was Aben-judan," he exclaimed, "and what is he now?"

Pensive and melancholy, he seated himself in a corner of his hut. His wife perceived the sudden change.

"What ails my beloved?" she asked tenderly. "Art thou not well? Tell me that I may administer to thy relief!"

"Would to God it were in thy power, but the Lord alone can heal the wounds which He inflicts," replied the distressed man. "Dost thou not remember the days of our prosperity, when our corn fed the hungry, our fleece clothed the naked and our oil and wine refreshed the drooping spirit of the afflicted. The orphans came round us and blessed us, and the widow's heart sang for joy. Then did we taste those heavenly pleasures which are the lot of the good and charitable. But now, alas! we cannot relieve the fatherless nor him who wants help, we are ourselves poor and wretched. Seest thou not yonder good men who will come to make the charitable collection? They will call, but what have we to give them?"

"Do not grieve, dear husband," replied his virtuous wife. "We have still one field left. Suppose we sell half of it and give the money for the use of the poor?"

A beam of joy spread over the good man's face. He followed his wife's advice, sold half the field, and when the collectors called he gave them the money. They accepted it and as they departed, said to him, "May the Lord restore thee to thy former prosperity!"

Aben-judan resumed his former spirits, and with them his wonted diligence. He went to plow the small plot of ground still left him.

As he was pursuing his work the foot of the ox that drew the plowshare sank into the ground. In endeavoring to relieve the beast he saw something glittering in the hollow which the foot had made. This excited his attention. He dug the hole deeper and, to his great astonishment and no less joy, found an immense treasure concealed in the very spot.

He took it home and moved from the wretched hovel in which he lived into a very fine house. He repurchased the lands and possessions which his ancestors had left him and which his former distress had obliged him to sell, and he added greatly to them. Nor did he neglect the poor. He again became a father to the fatherless and a blessing to the unfortunate.

The time arrived when the rabbis, as usual, came to make their collection. Not finding Aben-judan in the place where he had lived the year before, they asked some of the inhabitants of the village if they knew what had become of Aben-judan.

"Aben-judan," they exclaimed. "The good and generous Aben-judan! Who is like him in riches, charity and goodness? See you yonder flocks and herds? They belong to Aben-judan. Those vast fields, flourishing vineyards, and beautiful gardens? They belong to Aben-judan. Those fine buildings? They also belong to Aben-judan."

At that moment, the good man happened to pass that way. The wise men greeted him, and asked him how he did.

"Masters," said he, "your prayers have produced much fruit. Come to my house and partake of it. I will make up the deficiency of last year's subscription."

They followed him to his house where, after entertaining them nobly, he gave them a very handsome present for the poor. They accepted it, and taking out the subscription list of the preceding year they showed it to him, saying, "See, though many exceeded thee in their donations, yet we have placed thee at the very top of the list, convinced that the smallness of thy gift at that time arose from want of means, not from want of inclination. It is to men such as you that the wise king alluded when he said: 'A man's gift extendeth his possessions, and leadeth him before the Great'" (Prov. XVIII, 16).

The Charity of the Physician Abba Umna

ABBA UMNA, a Jewish physician, was as much celebrated for his piety and humanity, as for his medical skill.

He made no distinction between rich and poor and was particularly attentive to learned men, from whom he never would accept the least reward for his professional services; he considered them as fellow-laborers, whose functions were still more important than his own, since they were destined to cure the diseases of the mind. Unwilling to deter people from profiting by his medical knowledge, yet not wishing to put anyone to the blush for the smallness of the fee they might be able to give, he had a box fixed in his ante-chamber, into which the patients threw such sums as they thought proper.

His fame spread far and wide. Rabbi Abaye, who then was the chief of the Academy, heard of it; and wishing to know whether everything reported of that benevolent man was true, sent to him two of his disciples who were slightly indisposed. The physician received them kindly, gave them some medicine, and requested them to stay in his house overnight. The offer was readily accepted.

They remained until next morning, when they departed, taking with them a piece of tapestry which had served as a covering to the couch on which they had slept. This they carried to the market-place; and waiting until their kind host had arrived, pretended to offer it for sale, and asked him how much he thought it worth.

Abba Umna mentioned a certain sum.

"Dost thou not think it worth more?" asked the men.

THE CHARITY OF THE PHYSICIAN ABBA UMNA: From the Talmud. In *Hebrew Tales*, by Hyman Hurwitz. Printed for Morrison and Watt. London, 1826.

"No," answered the physician. "This is the very sum I gave for one much like it."

"Why, good man," rejoined the disciples, "this is thine own; we took it from thy house. Now tell us truly, we beseech thee, after missing it hadst thou not a very bad opinion of us?"

"Certainly not," replied the pious man. "Ye know that a son of Israel must not impute evil intentions to anyone, nor judge ill of a neighbor by a single action. And since I was satisfied in my mind that no ill use would be made of it, let it even be so. Sell it, and distribute the money amongst the poor."

The disciples complied with his wishes, left him with admiration and thanks, and increased by their report his well-earned fame.

But the most noble trait in this good man's character was that he never accepted any remuneration from the poor, and even provided them with everything that could, during their illness, contribute to their comfort. And when he had, by his skill and assiduity, restored them to health, he would give them money and say, "Now my children, go and purchase bread and meat; these are the best and only medicines you require."

Expiation

RABBI NAHUM ISH GAMZU was blind in both eyes. He had lost both hands and both feet and his entire body was covered with boils. He was lying prostrate in a house that was at the point of collapsing. In order that the ants might not crawl upon him, the feet of his bed stood in water.

It happened once that his students, worried by the precarious state of his dwelling, wished to carry him to another house. First they wanted to take out the bed on which he lay and afterwards the furniture and household goods. But Rabbi Nahum said to them, "My children, my advice to you is to clear out the furniture first and after that carry me out in my bed. I am certain that as long as I remain here the house will not fall."

The students did as their master bade them and it happened just as he had said: the house collapsed immediately after they had carried him out. The students were filled with amazement.

"Rabbi," they asked, "since you are a man holy enough to cause a miracle why has God punished you so?"

Rabbi Nahum Ish Gamzu answered, "Dear children, I alone am to blame for all my afflictions. Once I was on my way to call on my father-in-law. I brought with me three asses. One was laden with food, another with drink and the third with sweet fruits. On the way a poor man stopped me. 'Give me something to eat, Rabbi!' he pleaded. I was in no hurry and asked him to wait until I had unpacked. But before I had time to do so, the poor man fell dead at my feet. When I saw this I was filled with

EXPIATION: Adapted from the *Agada* in the Talmud.

grief. I cast myself beside his body and cried out: 'My eyes that had no pity on your pleading eyes—may they become blind! My hands that had no compassion for your withered hands, and my feet that were not moved by the sight of your weary feet—may they be severed from my body!'

"And after that I could find no peace until I had said: 'Let my entire body be covered with boils so that I may forever more feel your torment!'"

When the students heard this they raised a great outcry.

"Woe to us that see such afflictions visited upon you!"

"Woe to me it would have been indeed, my sons, if you did not see me in such wretchedness!" replied Rabbi Nahum Ish Gamzu.

Hunger

In the days when King Solomon ruled over Israel there lived in Jerusalem a man who was the richest in all the land. His name was Bavsi. As great as was his wealth he was wicked and a miser. He oppressed his servants and his slaves and made their days bitter with toil from dawn, as soon as the cock crowed, until late in the night. Because he was stingy he did not give them enough food to eat so that they and their children constantly suffered the pangs of hunger.

Finally, he acquired such an evil reputation throughout the land that the saying became popular: "Stingy as Bavsi." Others even said: "Evil as Bavsi." All manner of stories used to be told about his tightfistedness. It was said, for instance, that he had purposely not married in order not to have to support a wife and children. There was also the story that once his brother paid him a visit and dined with him. Accordingly, on that day Bavsi gave no food to his servants and slaves in order to make up for the expense his brother's dinner caused him.

It happened on one occasion that a great famine raged in the land. The wealthy but upright citizens opened their granaries and distributed food among the poor. But not so Bavsi. He kept his granaries well secured and put additional locks upon the doors. He even reduced the food rations of the people of his household. He became a food profiteer, selling for very high prices And so his wealth multiplied in those evil times.

Bavsi's conduct aroused scorn among the people and they muttered angrily against him until their indignation finally reached King Solomon. And when the wise King heard what was being said about Bavsi he grew wroth and fell upon a stratagem. He sent a royal chamberlain to him with an invitation that he sup with him. Bavsi was overwhelmed by such an honor from the King and he rejoiced greatly.

"It seems that I have found great favor in the eyes of the King," he thought vaingloriously. "How my enemies will rage over my good fortune!"

Hunger: Adapted from the *Midrash*.

All day long Bavsi refrained from eating. He wished to arrive hungry at the King's table so that he might consume more of the royal courses.

Upon Bavsi's arrival at the royal palace a chamberlain conducted him ceremoniously into a separate room and said, "The King will sup with you alone tonight. Therefore, I wish to instruct you in the following rules of conduct when you sit down at table with the King. You must do what I bid you, else the King will grow angry. And woe to you if the King should grow angry!"

"I will do as you bid me," answered Bavsi, a little frightened.

"Remember, first of all," admonished the chamberlain, "you must never ask for anything, neither from the King nor from any of the servants. Secondly, no matter what you may see happen you must not ask any questions nor utter any complaint. And lastly, when the King asks you whether you are enjoying the various courses you must outdo yourself in praising them, even if they should not please you. Promise me, therefore, to remember and obey these rules."

"I promise," swore Bavsi, uneasily.

"Very well then," said the chamberlain. "There is still one hour before supper so I will have you wait in another room until I call you."

The chamberlain then conducted Bavsi into a room. There an open door led into the royal kitchens.

As Bavsi waited patiently he saw through the open door the elaborate preparations being made for the King's and his supper. The aromas of the sizzling roasts and the other courses were wafted to his nostrils. And, since he had not eaten all day long, he was very hungry and the smell of the food only teased his appetite. Several times he had to exercise great self-control to keep himself from going into the kitchen so that he might still his hunger. He gritted his teeth and waited for supper.

The time arrived at last. The chamberlain entered and led Bavsi into the royal presence.

"Sit down, my friend," King Solomon said to him affably. "Do not be bashful and eat to your heart's content."

Bavsi seated himself. A servant entered and placed a baked fish on a golden platter before the King. The King commenced to eat and as he ate he exclaimed with rapture, "What fish! How delicious!"

And when the King had done with the fish the servant then placed a dish of fish before Bavsi.

Overjoyed, Bavsi made an eager move towards the fish before him, but at that very instant another servant snatched it from him and carried it off into the kitchens.

Bavsi was on the verge of saying something about it when he suddenly recalled the instructions the chamberlain had given him, and he kept his peace.

A servant then brought for the King a fine broth in a golden bowl. The King drank the broth with relish while Bavsi waited impatiently to be served in turn. When the King had finished his soup the servant, as in the instance of the fish, also brought Bavsi a golden bowl of soup. But no sooner did he make a movement with his hand towards it than another servant quickly snatched it from him. Similarly it happened with the roast and with the other courses.

Bavsi was now beside himself with hunger and indignation. He cast looks of hatred at the servants but he had to remain mute and smiling as he sat facing the King.

To the hungry Bavsi it seemed as if the meal would never come to an end.

"I hope you're enjoying your supper," King Solomon remarked politely.

"I am, indeed, O King! Everything is delicious," the unhappy Bavsi answered.

"I am delighted to hear that," said the King.

"The food has the taste of Paradise in it," cried Bavsi with enthusiasm, recalling further the chamberlain's instructions.

Faint with hunger, the unfortunate guest arose anxious to make his departure. But the King held him back.

"Don't go, my friend!" he said. "Do not part from me so fast. The night is still young. I've commanded my musicians to regale us with fine music."

Reluctantly Bavsi remained.

The musicians entered and played wondrously upon their instruments. But the music only annoyed Bavsi for he could think of nothing but food.

After the musicians had finished, Bavsi once more arose to go.

"Don't go, my friend," said King Solomon. "The hour is too late for you to go home. Sleep this night in the palace."

And Bavsi knew that every word of the King's was a command. So he remained. He did not sleep all night long because of the pangs of hunger. Angrily he began to reflect on the possible meaning of the King's conduct.

"Why did he invite me to a supper which I was not allowed to eat?" he asked himself.

Suddenly it dawned on him that the King had only meant to teach him an object lesson in hunger.

Now, by means of his own experience, he understood the torments of need; he, the wealthy Bavsi, the well-fed one, who had always despised the poor and had laughed at them when they cried that they were hungry.

Abraham the Carpenter of Jerusalem and the Money Buried under a Tree

ONCE upon a time there was a rich man, who lived near Jerusalem. One day a Gentile came to him with an article of value and wanted to borrow

ABRAHAM THE CARPENTER OF JERUSALEM AND THE MONEY BURIED UNDER A TREE: Reprinted from the *Ma'aseh Book*, edited by Moses Gaster. With permission of the copyright owners, The Jewish Publication Society of America. Philadelphia, 1934.

money on it. So he told his wife to go up into the chamber, to open the chest and fetch the money. The good woman went upstairs. But as she opened the chest and wanted to take the money, she heard a voice saying: "Do not touch the money, it is not yours." She was very much frightened, went down and told her husband what had happened to her, and told him to go and fetch the money himself. The man went upstairs to fetch the money, and the voice said again: "Do not touch the money, it is not yours." When the man heard it, he also became very much frightened. Then he recovered himself and said: "If the money is not mine, tell me to whom it belongs." And the voice answered: "If you wish to know, then I tell you that this money belongs to Abraham the carpenter of Jerusalem." Then the good man thought: "If the money does not belong to me, I do not want to have it." And he took all the money and the gold and the silver and the articles of value and the ornaments which he had, cut a hole in the tree which was standing in his garden and put it all in. Then he left, accepting with resignation this misfortune which God had inflicted upon him.

Not long afterwards, there was a great flood, which carried away many houses and trees, including the tree in which all the money had been concealed. A fisherman came along in his boat and, seeing the tree floating on the water, he thought: "That is a very fine tree and very useful for a carpenter. I know a Jewish man in Jerusalem, who is called Abraham the carpenter. I will take it to him and he will pay me well for it." When the fisherman took his fish to Jerusalem on Friday, Abraham the carpenter came to buy fish for the Sabbath. The fisherman said to him: "Abraham, I have a fine log at home, which I took out of the water. I am sure it will be useful to you and you can make many pretty articles out of it." Abraham went home with the fisherman, saw the log, was well pleased with it and had it taken to his house. When he split the tree apart, he found all the rich treasure which the good man had put in. Abraham rejoiced greatly at the wonderful luck which God had granted him.

Not long afterwards, it came to pass that the good man who had put the money in the tree became very poor and had to go about the country begging for alms. One day he said to his wife: "My dear wife, let us go to Jerusalem and see if our money has reached its destination, as the voice said." So they went to Jerusalem, to the house of Abraham the carpenter, pretending that they knew nothing. When they arrived there one Friday, Abraham was busy making a toy for his son. It is customary to put beautiful silver cups on the table, and when these good people saw their own vessels standing on the table, they began to weep. When Abraham's wife saw these poor people crying, she asked them why they were crying, but they would not tell her. Then the good woman said: "Surely, you do not weep for nothing," and she pressed them so long until they told her the whole story, viz. that all those beautiful vessels had belonged to them, and they told her about the money and the voice and about the tree trunk that had been carried away by the waters. And they asked them if it was ail true. "For," they said, "we see all the ornaments and the beautiful things in your possession, as the voice had said." When the woman heard this, she said: "My dear friends, spend your Sabbath in joy. If these things belonged to you, we will give them back to you, for we have, thank God, enough without taking yours." But the poor people replied: "No, we cannot accept it. For if the money had been destined for us, the voice from heaven would not have spoken as it did. We see that the money is intended for you, and we will have none of it. We must have sinned before the Lord." And then they kept silent. The wife told the story to Abraham. Then they made a beautiful cake to give the poor people on their journey. They prepared it with good spices, and put inside, so that no one should know, four hundred gold florins. For Abraham thought: "We will give them this cake to take with them on their journey, and when they open it, they will find the four hundred florins." On Sunday morning they were preparing to leave and bade farewell to Abraham and his wife with tears in their eyes. Abraham wanted to give them money, but they refused. Finally, they gave them the cake and said to them: "Take the cake with you on your journey, it will be useful to you. When you are hungry, break it and refresh your heart." The poor woman did not wish to take the cake either, but Abraham and his wife begged them so hard that they finally accepted it and went away.

On the way they came to a town where they had to pay toll, but they had no money. So they said to the toll-keeper: "We have no money, take this cake for your toll." The man said: "This cake comes at the right moment. I will give it as a present to Abraham the carpenter of Jerusalem on the occasion of his son's wedding, and I will be made welcome there." The toll-keeper took the cake and allowed them to go away in peace. Then he took the cake to Jerusalem and presented it to Abraham, who thus got the cake back with the money. This is the meaning of the verse: "Mine is the silver and Mine is the gold, saith the Lord of hosts" (Hag. 2.8).

The man and the woman died in poverty, because they had never given alms. Therefore God punished them. Therefore he who desires to preserve his money against taint should give much to the poor. Then his wealth will remain. But the converse is also true. If a person does not preserve his money against taint and does not give charity, his wealth will not remain with him, but will pass away with him, as happened to these two people. May God grant us better luck. Amen. Selah.

Adding Insult to Injury

Two charitable men went from house to house collecting alms for their poor neighbor. Finally, they came upon two wealthy men drinking tea. One of them was forthright and bluntly said that he would make no

---

ADDING INSULT TO INJURY: Adapted from the *Parables of the Preacher of Dubno*.

donation. "I don't believe in charity," he declared. The other began to inquire in great detail about the poor man, as to how old he was, whether he had a wife and children, what kind of house they lived in, and similar matters.

The charity collectors were delighted with him, seeing how intensely interested he was in the affairs of the poor man. "Who can tell," they thought hopefully, "this good man might give us a ruble—maybe even five!"

But the poor man proposes and the rich man disposes. After the rich man was through with his thorough questioning, he remarked with disgust, "That man you're gathering alms for is a swindler! He is lazy and a drunkard. I don't give away money to lazy drunkards."

Thereupon the charity collectors arose and said with scorn, "Your friend told us plainly he did not wish to give a donation because he did not believe in charity. Well and good—he has a right to do as he pleases. But how dare you, who never had the intention of giving in the first place, insult and slander an unfortunate poor man!"

MORAL

A wicked man, who does not wish to help the unfortunate, will speak evil of them to cover up his guilty conscience.

The Deserter

IN CZARIST Russia there once lived a Jewish merchant who had made a lot of money by supplying the local military barracks with food. Like most men of this class he was not particularly versed in the Torah, but his piety, none the less, knew no bounds.

When the "ten days of repentance" before Yom Kippur arrived, he nightly went to the synagogue after midnight to recite the *Selichos* prayers. Although he did not understand the meaning of one blessed word of the Hebrew text, he, none the less, prayed with verve and unction. But, tumbling out of bed at such an unearthly hour made both his spirit and flesh sag. After the third night, he complained to the rabbi with an apologetic sigh, "It's hard for me to get up so early every morning—I'm not used to it."

"My friend," answered the rabbi with a laugh, "you have business connections with the Imperial Army so you'll readily understand the point I'm going to make. You know that the army is divided into all kinds of departments and services. There are infantry, cavalry, artillery, sappers, and so on. The soldier in each branch of the service has his own particular function to perform. Now let me ask you—what, for instance, would happen to an infantryman if he deserted his regiment and went to serve in the cavalry? He'd be court-martialed, wouldn't he?"

"Indeed he would," agreed the merchant. "That's a serious breach of discipline. But what's the connection, Rabbi?"

"Know, my friend," answered the rabbi mildly, "that the soldiers of the Lord too are distributed among the various branches of the service. The Torah scholars are the artillerymen; those who do good deeds are the cavalrymen; those who give charity are the infantrymen, and so on. It's very clear that, on account of your money, the Almighty has put you into the charity regiment where you can serve most usefully. You are, therefore, an infantryman of the Lord. Your function is to help the poor, support widows, orphans and destitute scholars. By every rule of discipline you should be home now in bed and comfortably asleep. Instead, I find you have deserted your regiment—the charity regiment—and have joined up with the heavy artillery regiment consisting of Torah scholars. You don't belong here, my friend! Better get back to your own regiment before God, the commander-in-chief, finds out you're missing!"

When Fortune Smiles

WHILE on a journey to a distant town Rabbi Elimelech of Lizhensk and his brother, Rabbi Zisha, stopped at the village of Lodmir. At that time they were unknown and their clothes were shabby. Therefore no one came out to welcome them and extend to them the brotherly "Sholom Aleichem," except a poor tailor whose name was *Reb* Aaron.

Years later, the wheel of fortune turned, and the two rabbis became famed as the jewels of their faith. One day they drove into Lodmir in a fine carriage, drawn by handsome steeds. All the inhabitants poured out of their houses to greet them. The wealthiest member of the community stepped forward and made them a pretty speech of welcome.

"You will confer on me the greatest honor of my life if you will deign to be my guests," he said.

In the crowd Rabbi Elimelech suddenly recognized the poor tailor, *Reb* Aaron, who had befriended him and his brother Zisha when they were unknown.

"My brother and I will be honored," he exclaimed, "if *Reb* Aaron will invite us to his home."

"Rabbi," implored the rich man, "it's unbecoming for men of your eminence to stay in that poor man's wretched hovel! Why—he cannot even feed you!"

"Far sooner would we eat this poor man's black bread and cabbage than your fine roasts!" said Rabbi Elimelech. "When we were poor and unknown and no different than we are now you closed your door on us, and *Reb* Aaron showed us true Jewish hospitality. Now that we come riding in a carriage drawn by handsome horses you are only too honored to welcome us. Clearly then, it's our horses and not us that you are welcoming. In that case, I'm delighted to accept your invitation. Please be good enough to care for our horses while we stay as *Reb* Aaron's guests."

The Rabbi's Only Possession

THE rabbi of the town called on the richest man in the community and urged him to donate a sizeable sum to the orphan asylum. The rich man bluntly turned him down.

"I will sell you my share in Paradise if you will give me the money," said the rabbi.

The rich man agreed. Overjoyed, the rabbi used the money for enlarging the orphan asylum.

When the rabbi's disciples heard of this they stood aghast.

"Rabbi," they remonstrated, "how could you possibly do a thing like that?"

"Two times a day I repeat in my prayers: 'Love thy God with all thy heart, with all thy soul and with all thy possessions.' My sons, I'm only a poor man. What are the possessions with which I can serve God? All that I possess is my share in Paradise, and to serve God's children, His orphans, I am ready to part with even that."

The Rabbi's Gift

ONCE there was a rabbi whose generosity was so great that he was always in deep straits financially. He was never able to resist an appeal for assistance. One day, a poor stranger came to him with a tale of woe. The soft-hearted rabbi was deeply touched. He wanted to give the man some money but found he had none. So he went to his wife's jewel-box and took out her Sabbath ring set with a small diamond, and gave it to the poor man.

Immediately after, the rabbi's wife came in and discovered what her husband had done. She thereupon raised an outcry and sent him posthaste after the man to explain to him that a mistake had been made and that what the rabbi had given him was a gold ring with a genuine diamond in it.

When the rabbi, all out of breath, caught up with the man, he said to him, "Friend, I want you to know that a mistake has been made. The ring I gave you is of gold and is set with a genuine diamond. See, therefore, that the one you sell it to doesn't cheat you."

Generosity Is of the Spirit

ONCE there was a rabbi who was gentle and understanding and tried to practice the Golden Rule of Rabbi Hillel.

One day, a needy man came to him and asked that he lend him ten rubles.

"My wife is sick and I have no money to pay the doctor," he complained bitterly.

Not having any cash with him, the rabbi gave him a silver candlestick. "Go and pawn it for ten rubles," he told the man. "I'll redeem it later myself."

Some time after the rabbi went to redeem his candlestick from the pawnbroker. To his surprise he found that it wasn't ten rubles but twenty-five that the man had drawn against it.

"That man is a swindler, Rabbi!" the pawnbroker indignantly assured him. "The nerve of him—not only doesn't he redeem your candlestick but he borrowed more money than you permitted him!"

"You're wrong," the rabbi answered him, mildly. "This unfortunate man is very modest and considerate. Just think, he needed twenty-five rubles but didn't have the heart to ask me for more than ten!"

When Modesty Is a Vice

A RICH man was questioned by his rabbi. "Do you give much charity?"

"God be praised, Rabbi—I give enough. But I'm a modest man—I don't say much about it."

"Say more about it—and give more!" admonished the rabbi.

Judah Touro Saves the Bunker Hill Monument

ANOTHER Jewish name stands out in the war of 1812, although it gained national recognition some time afterwards and in connection with another event. The building of Bunker Hill Monument was a very ambitious undertaking in the times when it was reared, and the work lagged greatly. Nothing of such magnitude had ever before been attempted in the country. In our day, when government is exalted into a great paternal institution, the thing would be handled in more simple fashion. The public treasury is expected to do everything. The people now are accustomed to go to Congress and get an appropriation when they desire to gratify their patriotism by erecting a monument, but in 1820 public opinion was not so far advanced upon such lines. The people believed that they should commemorate the first great battle of the Revolution by a popular subscription in which each one directly gave his part; and so they embarked upon raising what was then a very large sum of money. After twenty years of struggle the monument was still uncompleted and twenty thousand dollars more were needed. At last, Amos Lawrence, a leading merchant of Boston, offered to give ten thousand dollars if another would give an equal amount.

JUDAH TOURO SAVES THE BUNKER HILL MONUMENT: From *Patriotism of the American Jew*, by Samuel Walker McCall. Plymouth Press, Inc. New York, 1924.

The princely offer was received in cold silence in the financial section of
the neighborhoods such as Boston and New York, from which a favorable
response might have been expected.

But there came a remittance of ten thousand dollars from a remote part
of the country, from Judah Touro, a Jew, of New Orleans, and the completion of the monument was assured. The event was commemorated by a
dinner in Faneuil Hall. Amid the eloquent speeches that were made, a
toast was proposed in lines which recognized the generosity of the two
patriots, but hardly recalls the literary glories of Boston's golden age:

> Amos and Judah, venerated names,
> Patriarch and Prophet press their equal claims;
> Like generous coursers running neck and neck,
> Each aids the cause by giving it a check;
> Christian and Jew, they carry out one plan—
> For though of different faiths, each is in heart a man.*

Touro was born in New England. He migrated to Louisiana where as a
merchant, an importer and exporter, he made a great fortune. When the
war of 1812 moved from the sea and from the North to the Southern field,
he was in the thick of General Jackson's fighting. In the battle of New
Orleans he was almost mortally wounded. Though Touro was wealthy
and lived in a slave state, he owned but a single slave, whom he educated
and made free after giving him a home. He afterwards lived with a friend
who owned slaves, and he made provision for the freedom of all of them.
His philanthropies were country-wide.

MARTYRS

INTRODUCTION

There is no kind of piety in the Jewish traditional conception that equals
that of the martyr, nor does it consider that there is a righteousness or
heroism that can compare with offering one's life in defense of the Jewish
people or *al-Kiddush ha-Shem*, for the Sanctification of the Name. The
martyrology of the Jews, keeping step with their unhappy history, is ex-
ceptionally rich, and legend with its folk-tenderness and emotionalism has
only added poignancy to stark tragedy. There is the same melancholy-
exalted strain running like a *leit-motiv* through all the Jewish martyr tales,
from that about *Miriam and the Seven Little Martyrs* which is chronicled
in the *Fourth Book of Maccabees*, to the martyrdom of Rabbi Amnon in
the Rhineland during the Middle Ages.

In those tragic centuries the Jew's test of loyalty to his identity was
measured by the resistance he offered to apostasy from his faith for which
the irresistible pressures of an entire hostile society had been set in motion.

---

* This doggerel verse won a wide popularity among American Jews and has been
repeatedly quoted since 1820.

The weak and the irresolute could not muster the necessary moral strength for the ordeal, so they sought a dubious safety in conformity. But the overwhelming majority remained loyal to their faith because they lived by principle. They preferred to die a martyr's death. Although the Jewish religious law against suicide and infanticide was implacably stern, the rabbis, none the less, lifted the ban against it in times of supreme trial, for it was morally more endurable to die by one's own innocent hand than to submit to the enemy like a sheep that is led to the slaughter. During the excesses against the Jews at the time of the Crusades, entire communities perished together, with the *Shema* on their lips, as they locked themselves in their synagogues and set fire to them. In the English town of York, for instance, almost the entire Jewish community of five hundred committed suicide rather than accept conversion. Before they died on March 17, 1190, they were addressed by their rabbi, Yom-Tob of Joigny:

"God, whose decisions are inscrutable, desires that we should die for our holy religion. Death is at hand, unless you prefer, for a short span of life, to be unfaithful to your faith. As we must prefer a glorious death to a shameful life, it is advisable that we take our choice of the most honorable and the noblest mode of death. The life which our Creator has given us we will render back to Him with our own hands. This example many pious men and congregations have given us in ancient and modern times."

At these mass suicides, which usually took place in the synagogue, the martyrs recited the Confession before death. Then they sang hymns. Before they helped one another to plunge into the everlasting darkness they recited the special benediction composed for martyrs: "Blessed art Thou, O Lord our God, King of the Universe, who has sanctified us by Thy Commandments and bade us love Thy glorious and awful Name." First mothers killed their children. Then husbands slew their wives. After that the rabbi killed the menfolk. And as they lay in terrible silence about him he raised his voice in the last agonized affirmation of the faith: "Hear, O Israel, the Lord our God, the Lord is One!" And with that he plunged the knife into his own throat.

And so through the centuries there were millions of Jewish martyrs or *Kedoshim*, as they are called in Hebrew. They chose to die singly and in entire communities, killed by their own hand or murdered by the enemy. In the awed estimate of the people they were saints whose memory was never to falter in the grateful recollection of Israel. The widow of every martyr was called upon to honor his memory by never marrying again. The *Kedoshim* and their heroism were commemorated during the Sabbath service for succeeding generations in order that they might serve as an inspiring example in spiritual fortitude to the young.

Folklore based on historical experience is generated but slowly in our sophisticated age. Who can doubt that a vast body of legendary lore, in both song and story, will ultimately emerge from the terrible ordeals which the Jewish people underwent at the hands of the Nazis during World War II? The six million martyrs who were tortured, shot, buried alive, hanged and burned in an orgy of criminal bestiality never before known in history, have left behind them in the scarred memory of their people the raw materials of a staggering martyrology which needs but the passage of time to be transmuted into folklore.

N. A.

The Expiation of Rabbi Amnon

IN THE town of Mayence there once lived a very pious Jew whose name was Rabbi Amnon. He walked in the ways of the Lord and dealt uprightly with all his fellowmen. Therefore, his name became a byword for virtue in Israel and it cast luster upon the entire community.

Rabbi Amnon's fame even reached the ears of the ruler of Mayence who summoned him, and he found favor in his eyes, for Rabbi Amnon's words were full of gentleness and truth. And the Prince was inflamed with a great desire to bring this godly man into the fold of his own faith. He, therefore, spoke beguiling words to him, tried to show him wherein the precepts of his own religion were superior to those of the Jews. He also held before him the promise of great reward and glory if he would but renounce the faith of his fathers.

But Rabbi Amnon remained firm in his faith and to all the beguilements of the Prince he said simply, "Nay!"

Thereupon, the Prince grew exceedingly wroth. "You are as stiff-necked as all your people!" he cried. "Be sure, that I shall break your stubbornness and bend you to my will!"

One day, Rabbi Amnon was summoned once more to the palace of the Prince.

"Accept my faith or die!" cried the Prince.

And a great fear fell upon Rabbi Amnon, and he quaked within him. "Lord," he pleaded, "give me only three days to ponder the matter— then I shall bring you my answer."

"So be it," answered the Prince.

And Rabbi Amnon went away sad at heart. He fasted, and put on sackcloth and ashes and prayed: "O God of my fathers, let me not be led into temptation, for my spirit grows faint with fear!"

When the third day had passed the Prince sat on his throne in his palace waiting for Rabbi Amnon. But he did not appear. And the Prince was filled with astonishment.

"Is not the Jew afraid?" he asked. "Bring him to me quickly that I may judge him because he has defied my will."

The Prince's men-at-arms then came and, laying violent hands on Rabbi Amnon, they led him to their master.

The Rabbi Amnon legend, celebrating the undying loyalty of the individual Jew to his faith, has remained since the Middle Ages dearly beloved among religious Jews the world over. Although by itself it has no historic basis in fact it does reflect, however, the bitter recollection of the persecutions Jews suffered in Europe during the mass-hysteria generated among Christians by the Crusades. No doubt the legend was also inspired by veneration for the New Year's Day prayer it makes reference to: the *U-Nesanneh-Tokef,* which presents a graphic description of the terrors of the Day of Judgment. The legend was first found in the *Mahzor,* or prayer-book, of the Roman rite for the Jewish New Year, printed in 1541. Many subsequent editions also carried the legend, thus disseminating it far and wide in every country where Jews lived. The adaptation given here is from a modern edition of the *Mahzor.*—N. A.

"Jew—how dare you thwart my will?'" cried the Prince. "Why have you broken your promise to bring me your answer after three days?"

And Rabbi Amnon was filled with a great sorrow.

"Alas," he cried, "that in a moment of weakness I should have fallen into sin and have said lying words and promised lying promises! Alas! that to save my life, and yet not deny my faith, I sought the cowardly grace of three days in which to give you my answer. I should have answered you right away: 'Hear O Israel, the Lord our God the Lord is One,' and then perished at your hands!"

The Prince then issued his judgment:

"Because your feet disobeyed me and did not come to me at the bidden time I order that they be severed from your body!"

"Not my feet but my tongue should be torn out, for it betrayed my God!" said Rabbi Amnon.

"Your tongue has uttered the truth and therefore shall not be punished," answered the Prince.

Then he commanded his servants to cut off Rabbi Amnon's feet. And they did as he bade them.

That day was *Rosh Hashanah*, the Jews' sacred New Year's Day. As the prayers of the throng in the synagogue at Mayence were rising to the Throne of Mercy and the prayer-leader was about to begin the recitation of the *Kedushah*, they carried in the dying Rabbi Amnon.

"I ask the permission of the Holy Congregation to recite a prayer I have composed out of my soul's anguish," asked Rabbi Amnon.

The Congregation assented. Then they opened wide the Gates of the Ark and Rabbi Amnon intoned the prayer, *U-Nesanneh-Tokef*. And, when he had uttered the last words, he expired. Then lo and behold! A miracle happened. Before the astonished gaze of the Congregation invisible hands snatched away the body of Rabbi Amnon and no one ever saw it again. Three days later, however, he appeared to Rabbi Kalonymus ben Meshullam in a dream. He made him recite the prayer, *U-Nesanneh-Tokef* with him many times so that he learned it by heart.

"O Kalonymus, my son," pleaded the spirit of the departed martyr, "when you awake from your sleep write this prayer down on paper that it may be made known to all Israel, so that they and all the generations to come may utter it until the day of the Redemption!"

U-NESANNEH-TOKEF

Congregation: We will make mention of the mighty holiness of this day, for it is tremendous and awesome. Thereon is Thy kingdom exalted, and Thy throne established in grace, whereon Thou art seated in truth. Verily, it is Thou who art Judge and Arbitrator, who knowest all, and art witness, writer, sealer, recorder, and teller: Thou callest to mind all things long forgotten by mankind, and dost open the book of records; the acts therein registered proclaim themselves, for it bears every man's signature. The great trumpet is sounded: the still small voice is heard: the angels shudder;

fear and trembling seize them: "Ah!" they cry—"it is the day of Judgment; the heavenly host are to be arraigned in judgment" (for in justice even they are not found sinless before Thee). All who are about to enter into the world now pass before Thee, as a flock of sheep.

Reader: As the shepherd mustereth his flock, and passeth them under his crook, so dost Thou cause to pass, number, appoint, and visit every living soul, limiting the period of life of all creatures, and prescribing their destiny.

[While the ensuing prayer—*Be'Rosh Hashanah Yikusayvin*—follows directly in the synagogue service, it is not an integral part of *U-Nessaneh-Tokef*. However, it touches on the same awesome theme and also resounds with Day of Judgment organ music. Despite its gloomy spirit, it, nonetheless, concludes on the affirmative note of Free Will. Man's fate, it exhorts, although decreed by Heaven, lies in his own power to change by a life of righteousness. Because it represents a powerful tradition in Jewish religious folklore, this prayer is appended here.]

On the First Day of the Year it is inscribed, and on the Last Day of the Year it is inscribed, and on the Fast Day of Atonement, it is sealed and determined, how many shall pass away, and how many be born; who shall live, and who die; whose appointed time is finished, and whose is not; who is to perish by fire, who by water, who by the sword, and who by wild beasts, who by hunger, or who by thirst; who by earthquake, or who by the plague; who by strangling, or who by lapidation; who shall be wandering; who shall remain tranquil, and who be disturbed; who shall reap enjoyment, and who shall be painfully afflicted; who shall get rich, and who become poor; who shall be cast down, and who exalted.

But "Penitence, Prayer, and Charity can avert the evil Decree."

The Prayer of the Ancestors

AND it happened . . . In those dark days of bloody terror the groans of the people rose to the very Throne of God, and the halls of Heaven resounded with lamentation.

"O Jeremiah, Jeremiah! Go and let the ancestors know of your people's grief! Call them forth from their graves that they may raise their voices in sorrow since they have the power to weep and supplicate."

And behold! Following the bidding of the celestial voice, the grief-stricken Prophet wandered along the desolate banks of the Jordan crying aloud:

"O Moses, son of Amram, rise from your grave and look after your flock! In the distant plains of an alien land your people again lives in slavery as it did in your days. Again it is being strangled with the halter of humiliation. Everyone tramples upon it with his feet and fancies he is

THE PRAYER OF THE ANCESTORS: From the Talmud. Translated from the adaptation by Leo Tolstoy.

doing a noble deed. Murderous mobs fall upon the houses of your children, plunder and kill.

"Despair grips the soul of your people and its eyes are full of anguish. O Moses, Moses!"

An outcry of horror and grief rent the breast of Moses, and he hastened to inform the Ancestors. They gathered and sat down upon the Temple ruins . . . The gloom of desolation veiled the heavens. . . .

With tears in his eyes, rent garments and ashes upon his head, Abraham appeared before God and pleaded: "Almighty God! Why have You visited upon my children so much grief and pain?"

And together with Abraham wept and lamented the angels . . . Only the heavens remained mute and the Eternal Judge kept silent. . . .

Again Abraham complained: "Have my children transgressed against You, have they violated Your holy commandments? If so then let the Torah herself appear as accuser against them."

And shimmering in a celestial light the Torah appeared!

"O my daughter!" moaned Abraham. "Recall that when you were scorned by all the nations of the earth, the only ones to elect you were my children. How can you refuse to testify for them in the days of their grief?"

But the Torah kept silent.

"Then let the individual letters of the words in the Torah step forward: let them bear witness against my children!" cried Abraham.

But also the letters of the words in the Torah kept silent.

"Ruler of the Universe!" prayed Abraham. "Remember my devotion to You, and have mercy upon my children. In answer to Your call I left my home, wandered in the wilderness and among desolate mountains, in order to secure for my children a tranquil shelter. You promised it to me . . . You spoke. . . .

"Then recall this, O God, and let Your mercy descend."

But the face of the Almighty remained gloomy and stern.

The Patriarch Isaac now appeared.

"At the command of my father, O Almighty God, I bared my throat to the sacrificial knife upon Mount Moriah. And now, I pray You withdraw the knife from my children's throats and release them from their anguish!"

But the face of the Almighty remained gloomy and stern.

Then Jacob prayed: "All my life I have had nothing but sorrow. My brother Esau incited against me and persecuted me. . . . I endured it all for the sake of my children, so that no one should incite against them, so that no one should persecute them. All my love and tenderness I gave to them, protected them like a bird its fledglings. But now my poor children languish in a distant land and their cruel oppressors fill their lives with terror. Therefore, let Your Word, ring out, O Lord! Redeem them from their sorrow!"

But the face of the Almighty remained gloomy and stern. . . .

Then Moses stepped forward and prayed: "O my God, for forty years, as You had desired, I served as father and shepherd to this people. For forty years I roamed the wilderness like an animal and, when I reached the threshold of the Promised Land, I listened to Your Voice and departed from the world. I believed and hoped that my people was destined to prosper and to be happy. And now . . . Behold! it is scattered, plundered and crushed! And the robbers, they who have done it all, gleefully are sharing their spoil. For how long, O God!"

Then there throbbed the soundless music of Eternity and the heavens were suffused with a great light. And out of the radiance there thundered forth the Voice of God:

"Redemption is nigh!"

Miriam and the Seven Little Martyrs

MIRIAM, the daughter of Tanhum, and her seven sons were taken into captivity and brought before Caesar in Rome.

To the first son Caesar said, "Bow down before the idol!"

"I will not deny the Holy One, praised be He!" replied the boy. "For He has told us: 'I am the Lord thy God.' "

"Kill him!" commanded Caesar.

And they did as he commanded.

Then they led in the second son.

"Bow down before the idol!" ordered Caesar.

"I will not betray my God!" cried the boy. "For He has written: 'Thou shalt have no other gods before Me.' "

Him, too, Caesar ordered slain.

Next came the turn of the third son.

"Bow down before the idol!" ordered Caesar.

The boy answered, "I will not bow before the idol because God has commanded: 'Thou shalt not bow down thyself to them, nor serve them.' "

And they led him out to die like his brothers.

The same happened with the fourth son. He said, "I will not be faithless to my God who has commanded: 'For thou shalt bow down to no other god; for the Lord, whose name is Jealous, is a jealous God.' "

And him too they led away to die.

When the fifth son came before Caesar he cried out, "Shall I abandon my God who has exhorted us: 'Hear, O Israel, the Lord our God, the Lord is One!' "

He too had to die.

MIRIAM AND THE SEVEN LITTLE MARTYRS: Adapted from the Fourth Book of Maccabees, the *Midrash,* and from *The Stories of Rabbi Nissim,* Gaon of Kairwan (11th Century A.D.).

Afterwards they brought the sixth son of Miriam, and Caesar spoke to him in the same manner as he had spoken to his five brothers.

He answered, "I will not turn away from my God, because in His Torah it is written: 'And thou shalt find Him, if thou search after Him with all thy heart and with all thy soul.' "

"Kill him!" cried Caesar.

Finally, they brought the seventh and the youngest son of Miriam.

"Bow down before the idol!" ordered Caesar.

"I will first ask counsel of my mother," the boy answered.

Then he went to his mother and said, "What shall I do, mother?"

And Miriam replied, "Do you wish to stand without while your brothers rest in the radiance of the Almighty? Heed me then: close your ears to this wicked man and remain true to your dear brothers!"

And so the boy returned to Caesar, and Caesar asked, "Will you obey me now?"

"I will not deny my God," cried the boy, "for it is written: 'The Lord thy God is a merciful God; He will not fail thee, neither destroy thee, nor forget the covenant of thy fathers which He swore unto them.' "

"Take heed of my words!" commanded Caesar. "You are only a child and know not what you do. Do as I bid you and I will spare your life. I will cast my ring, upon which is engraved the image of my idol, upon the floor. You must bend down, therefore, and pick it up, so that everyone will think that you have bowed before my god."

"Woe to you, O wicked King!" replied the boy. "If I fear not to face my Maker, the Ruler of the Universe, how much less should I fear you, who are only a man!"

"Then die!" cried Caesar.

And when Miriam saw how they came to put her youngest to death she was filled with a terrible grief.

"Let me kiss him first!" she pleaded.

Caesar granted her wish and she drew the boy into her arms and kissed and fondled him.

"I swear by your life, O Caesar!" she implored. "Slay me first before you slay my child!"

"That I cannot do," answered Caesar, "for your Torah forbids the killing of a mother with her young."

"You hypocrite!" cried Miriam wrathfully. "Have you followed all the precepts of our Torah that only this precept is left for you to observe?"

And Caesar was enraged and cried out, "Let the child be killed instantly!"

But Miriam would not let go of her boy.

"Be not sad and fear not, my child!" she bade him. "You are now going to Paradise to join your dear brothers who have died before you! And when you see our Father Abraham tell him, 'Thus spoke my mother: You, Abraham, must not be vainglorious because you built an altar on which to sacrifice your son Isaac to the Lord—I raised seven altars for

my seven sons. You, Abraham, only *wished* to bring your son as a sacrifice
—I *sacrificed* all my sons. You were only proven—I was bereaved.' "

And, as Miriam spoke thus to her youngest, they killed him in her arms.

She then raised her hands to Heaven and prayed, "My heart exults in
the Eternal, because my children remained faithful to Him in death as in
life! O you enemies and oppressors of Israel—how vain is your arrogance!
Know, that if God punishes us now, it is not because you are mighty, but
because it is His Will. O Lord—I implore you—take my soul from me so
that I may be united with my dear children! Do not abandon me to the
scorn and derision of our enemies, but take me to You!"

And no sooner had she ended her prayer than she sank to the earth and
died.

"Fortunate mother!" cried all of Israel when they heard of it. "Now
she is joined forever with her children!"

"Poor, unfortunate mother!" wailed the angels. "What a sad fate was
her lot!"

And, when the heathen heard of it, they were filled with wonder, and
asked, "What sort of God is this Jewish God for whom His worshippers
are so eager to lay down their lives?"

Their Blood Flowed into the Sea

TROGINUS, THE WICKED, had gone away to war against the Barbarians.
During his absence his wife gave birth to a son. By coincidence it happened that on the day the Prince was born the Jews observed *Tisha Ba' Ab*,
the Fast commemorating the destruction of the Temple by Titus. And so
on this day the Jews touched neither food nor drink, but shed tears of
bereavement and made lamentation.

Again, by an unfortunate coincidence, when the Festival of *Channukah*
arrived the little Prince suddenly sickened and died. All the Jews were
in a quandary.

"Shall we light the *Channukah* candles or not?" they asked of one
another. "Not to light them is to commit a sin. On the other hand, if we
light them we run a great risk, for what will the enemies of the Jews say?
They'll say that on the day when the Prince was born we mourned and
that on the day of his death we made a festival with illuminations!"

In the end, the pious Jews won out with their declaration: "We will light
our *Channukah* candles as we always do. Let those who wish us harm do
their worst!"

Without loss of time, wicked people went to the wife of Troginus to
inform against the Jews.

"See what miscreants the Jews are!" they said. "They went into mourning when your child was born and lighted festival candles when he died."

THEIR BLOOD FLOWED INTO THE SEA: Adapted from the *Agada* in the Talmud.

The wife of Troginus was infuriated. Hastily she dispatched a messenger to her husband.

"Put aside your war against the Barbarians!" she implored him. "Come and conquer the Jews who have revolted against you."

Immediately after he received the letter Troginus embarked for home. He had calculated that the journey would take him ten days. Instead a good wind blew up and brought him to the Holy Land in five days.

When Troginus came to the Jews he found them studying the Torah, which he had forbidden. He heard them recite the passage from *Deuteronomy:* "The Lord will bring a nation against thee from far, from the end of the earth, as the vulture swoopeth down. . . ."

"The vulture, that am I!" cried Troginus. "I had thought to make the journey in ten days, instead I came here in only five."

He then commanded the soldiers to surround the Jews and kill them all.

After the men had been slaughtered he said to the women, "If you do what my soldiers bid you, I will spare your lives. If not, you will all be killed!"

The women replied, "We expect no better end than our husbands have met!"

And so the women were slaughtered and their blood mingled with the blood of their menfolk and flowed into the sea like a river, being carried by the waves as far as Cyprus.

The Martyrdom of Rabbi Hanina

WHEN Rabbi Yose ben Kisma fell sick Rabbi Hanina ben Teradion visited him at his bedside.

"Hanina, my brother," Rabbi Yose asked him, "why do you oppose the Romans? Don't you know that their rule over us is decreed from Heaven? Do you want further proof than that they have burned God's Temple, and have killed all the pious in Israel? Does God punish them for these terrible misdeeds? Of course not! Then it's a sign that the Romans are only doing the Will of God. Now I have heard that you are breaking the laws of the Empire, that you sit in the House of Study and expound the Torah to multitudes in violation of the Imperial decree. Take care that you are not punished with death for your sedition!"

"What does it matter?" Rabbi Hanina answered. "God, who is in Heaven, will show me His mercy."

Rabbi Yose grew angry and reproachfully said, "I am appealing to you with logic—why do you give such a vague answer, as if you expected a miracle to happen? I greatly fear, Hanina, that they will burn you together with the Holy Scrolls!"

Several days later Rabbi Yose died. Because he was in high favor with the Government the great men of Rome attended his funeral and delivered eulogies over his grave.

When they returned from the funeral they found Rabbi Hanina expounding the Torah before a great multitude, so they condemned him to die. They wound about him the Holy Scrolls made of parchment, placed faggots at his feet and set them ablaze. Also they brought bunches of moistened wool which they placed on his breast in order to prolong his agony.

Beholding his torments his daughter, who was near him, cried bitterly, "Is this the Almighty's reward for your devotion to the Torah?"

Rabbi Hanina answered, "How can I feel grief when I'm being burned together with the blessed Scrolls of the Torah? May He Who defends the Torah aginst its traducers also take my part!"

"What do you see, Rabbi?" asked his students, who watched the flames envelope him.

"I see the parchment of the Holy Scrolls burn and its letters fly like sparks in the air."

"Rabbi!" cried his students pityingly, seeing how great were his torments. "Open your mouth so that the fire may enter into you."

Rabbi Hanina then replied, "Far better that my soul should be taken away by Him Who gave it to me than that I myself should injure it!"

When the Roman official who supervised the execution heard Rabbi Hanina's words he was stirred within him mightily.

"Were I to put more faggots on the fire and remove from your breast the bunches of wet wool so that you may die the quicker, will you reward me for this service with a place in your Paradise?" asked the Roman.

"In truth, I will!" replied Rabbi Hanina.

"Then give me your oath!"

And Rabbi Hanina solemnly swore.

The Roman cast more faggots on the fire and the blaze increased. Then he took the bunches of moist wool from his breast. And as Rabbi Hanina was about to give up his soul to God the Roman himself leaped into the flames and was consumed.

A Celestial Voice now sounded: "Know that Rabbi Hanina ben Teradion, together with his executioner, have now entered into the Gates of Paradise!"

The Resignation of the Martyrs

THE Romans condemned to death Rabbi Simeon ben Gamaliel and Rabbi Ishmael ben Elisha. They were then taken into the public square to be executed.

"Why do we deserve such an evil fate?" cried Rabbi Simeon. "Why must we die like common criminals?"

"No man is without sin! There must be a reason for our misfortunes," Rabbi Ishmael explained to him. "It is possible that when we were trial

---

THE RESIGNATION OF THE MARTYRS: *Ibid.*

judges some of our decisions were unjust. Or perhaps some of the witnesses that came before us were perjurers and we did not question them thoroughly enough. That may be why we are forfeiting our lives now. It is also possible that when we went to the bath or dined at home there came clamoring to our doors, widows and orphans who were in distress, and our servants told them that we were too busy to see them. And thus the widows and orphans went away with embittered hearts. Truly, no one may know fully of his sins!"

"I swear by Heaven above," Rabbi Simeon cried, "that such a thing could never have happened with me. I had watchmen who used to sit at my door. When the poor came the watchmen let them into my house, gave them food and drink and said grace with the poor when they had eaten."

"You may have sinned in another way," Rabbi Ishmael continued. "Perhaps you preached in the presence of the great in Israel and you were filled with pride. Know, that too is a sin."

"Hear me Ishmael, my brother!" cried Rabbi Simeon. "I am now reconciled to my fate."

The rabbis were led to the place of execution, and all along the way they behaved with the utmost graciousness to each other.

Rabbi Ishmael pleaded with the executioner: "I am a priest, the son of a High Priest. Therefore it is my privilege to die first. Kill me first, that I may not have to watch the death of my comrade."

And Rabbi Simeon pleaded with the executioner: "I am a *Nasi* and the son of a *Nasi*. Kill me first so that I will not have to see my comrade die."

The executioner said to both: "Draw lots!"

They drew lots and Rabbi Simeon ben Gamaliel was the one designated to die first. The executioner struck off his head with one blow. Rabbi Ishmael then lifted the head in his arms and lamented: "O holy lips! O true lips, lips which poured pearls of truth and wisdom! Behold! Now they have cast you upon the ground, have besmirched you in dust and ashes!"

But before Rabbi Ishmael could even finish these words, the executioner struck off his head.

Rabbi Tanhum Is Thrown to the Lions

THE Emperor once said to Rabbi Tanhum, "Let your people and mine become one nation."

"By your life, O Emperor, what a wonderful plan that is!" cried Rabbi Tanhum. "But inasmuch as we Jews are already circumcised we cannot turn heathen. For this reason let your people be circumcised and be like us."

RABBI TANHUM IS THROWN TO THE LIONS: *Ibid.*

"Well said!" replied the Emperor, ironically. "But he who bests an Emperor in argument deserves to be thrown to the wild beasts."

So they threw Rabbi Tanhum to the wild beasts, but they did him no harm. All who witnessed this marvelled at the miracle. However, among them was a free-thinker who did not believe in miracles. So he derisively explained the incident in this wise, "The wild beasts aren't hungry—that's why they don't eat the Jew."

In order to test the truth of the free-thinker's words the Emperor cast him to the wild beasts.

They devoured him forthwith.

The Power of Prayer

Introduction

The *Agada* of the Talmud relates how once the Roman Emperor Antoninus, who was a philosopher, asked Rabbenu ha-Kodesh: "Give me your opinion: is it right to pray frequently to God?"

"It is not right," answered Rabbenu.

"Why not?"

"One must not become too familiar with God."

But this answer failed to satisfy Antoninus.

Early the following morning Rabbenu again called on the Emperor and, as he entered the room, he cried out: "Peace be with you, O mighty Caesar!"

A little while later he returned and repeated the salutation: "Peace be with you, O mighty Caesar!"

For a third time that morning he returned and cried: "Peace be with you, O mighty Caesar!"

At this Antoninus became angry.

"What is all this mummery?" he asked Rabbenu angrily. "Clearly, you wish to make sport of me!"

"May your ears hear the words of your own mouth!" replied Rabbenu. "O Caesar! If you, who are only a ruler of flesh and blood, take offence when I bore you with my too many greetings, how do you suppose the King of Kings would regard it? Certainly it is wrong to impose too much on God with prayer!"

This legend reflects so trenchantly the thoroughly unpietistic, common sense approach to prayer in rabbinic tradition, the cabalists excepted. Not elaborate prayer but its heartfelt communion is recommended by the Talmudic sages in *The Long and the Short of It*. They called this type of prayer "a service of the heart." It is made even more explicit in the modern anecdote, *Prayer Before Prayer:* "I pray that when I pray it should be with all my heart."

This informal attitude toward prayer is quaintly pointed up by the assertion in the Talmud that God himself prays. He appears to Moses as a *baal-tefilah*, one who leads the congregation in prayer, His face wrapped in His prayer-shawl in order, by His example, to teach all the generations of man both the manner of prayer and its power to change the course of human destiny. And what is God's prayer? "O that My mercy shall prevail over My justice!"

The sages taught: "God longs for the prayer of the pious." And by that they meant that God took no pleasure in punishing men, no matter how justified. He was eager for them to appeal to His attribute of love in order that, by their prayers, they might alter all His retributive decrees. The great Eleventh Century poet of Spain, Abraham ibn Ezra, maintained that, like prophesy, prayer had self-regenerating power; it could make the spirit of man soar into the rarified spheres of godliness.

In Jewish tradition there are many forms of prayer. In earlier primitive times it meant sacrifice. In Hellenistic days one could also pray with healthy productive work which maintains the fabric of the world. "In the handiwork of their craft is their prayer." (*Book of Sirach*, 38.34.) It was also valid to pray with *tzedakah,* the giving of material aid to the needy and extending a helping hand to a fellow-creature in distress.

The East European *Hasidim* of the Eighteenth and Nineteenth Centuries had a poetic conception of prayer. It all lay in the "intention" and, if a man prayed out of a full heart, it did not matter what words he used or whether he used any at all, as in the story *He Whistled for the Glory of God.* In one *Hasidic* legend the pious drover is shown murmuring his halting prayers while he is busy greasing his cart-wheels, and yet God preferred them to the fluent prayers of the holy *tzaddik* in the synagogue. And the reason for this: "What piety! Even when he does such lowly work as greasing his wheels the good carter thinks of God!" Here again we find the overtones of a pantheistic belief that God is everywhere and in everything, as in Rabbi Lebi-Yitzchok's song, *A Dudele,* which is included in the SONGS section. Quite different was the concept of prayer among the cabalists. They took the somewhat mystical erotic view that prayer was a communion as intimate between the worshipper and God as that between the bride and bridegroom.

The three "rainmaker" legends included in this section have a special interest in that they show such a marked similarity to "rainmaker" stories found in the folktales of other peoples. And yet they have a distinctive physiognomy of their own: they convey Jewish ethical values as well as the magical.

Rainmaker stories arose among the Jews from the necessities of their physical surroundings. In olden times, as we know, Palestine had a primitive agricultural economy; there were long spells of dry weather. No doubt there were elements of Nature worship in the ancient rainmaker belief. The prayer for rain and dew, called *Tal* or *Geshem* in Hebrew, represents a survival of this primitive worship. It was an earnest invocation for rainfall because drought meant hunger and death.

The first Jewish rainmakers on record were the prophets Samuel and Elijah who, by the power of their prayer, brought rain. The general view among the Jews of olden times was that drought was visited upon the land as divine punishment for the nation's collective evil-doing. Conversely, national virtue was rewarded by a plentiful rainfall. ". . . and it shall come to pass, if ye shall hearken diligently unto My Commandments which I command you this day, to love the Lord, your God, and to serve Him with all your heart and all your soul, that I will give the rain of your land in its season, the former rain and the latter rain, that thou mayest gather in thy corn, and thy wine, and thine oil." (Deuteronomy 11. 13–14) The rainmakers had to be men of exceptional piety and saintliness for their prayers to exert the necessary power with which to overcome the heavenly decree of drought.

While rainmaking is no longer practiced among the sophisticated Jews of modern times, among the more backward Jews of Asia and Africa it is still in vogue. The magical effect of prayers for rain is still believed in devoutly. For instance, it has been noted that to this day the Jews of Morocco carry on a rainmaking ceremony which no doubt is derived from the agricultural needs of their lives. Four children, symbolizing in themselves innocence and therefore capable of moving God's mercy toward the community, take up a white linen sheet. Each child holds an edge and, as they move through the street where Jews live, they sing out in their Moroccan Arabic: "The sheaf is thirsty; help it O Lord!" The onlookers then pour water into the sheet.*

N. A.

Prayer Before Prayer

ONCE a disciple asked his rabbi, "Tell me, Rabbi, what do you do before you pray?"

"I pray that when I pray it should be with all my heart."

He Whistled for the Glory of God

RABBI ZISHA of Annipole, the brother of "The Seer" Elimelech of Lizhensk, was a devout man. He held himself "small" in spite of his renown and was always fearful that out of vanity he might preen himself as a man of God.

One time he paid a visit to Rabbi Mordecai of Nizchot.

As the hour of midnight approached, he got out of bed and, in a voice

---

* Cited by Raphael Patai in his article, *Control of Rain in Ancient Palestine.* Hebrew Union College Annual, p. 265. Cincinnati, 1939.

HE WHISTLED FOR THE GLORY OF GOD: Adapted from *Priester der Liebe*, by Chajim Bloch. Amalthea-Verlag. Wien, 1930.

There is a remarkable similarity between this legend and the one told by Anatole France in *Le Jongleur de Notre Dame*. In the latter story the jongleur juggles before the Holy Virgin as his homage to her. That Anatole France's charming story is based on an old French legend is well known. However, that it could have traveled from medieval France to late Eighteenth Century Galicia among the Hasidim, is highly problematical. Spontaneous cultural invention of the most remarkable similarity has been known to occur among widely separated peoples.—N. A.

full of anguish, cried out: "God, O my soul! I love You so much, yet I lack the inner power to express it!"

He paced to and fro in his room, repeating these strange, passionate words over and over again with the deepest mortification.

All this while his host, Rabbi Mordecai, stood with a companion behind the door, marveling greatly at what he heard. After a few moments of silence he heard Rabbi Zisha exclaim, "O my Creator! I do not know how to commune with You for my thoughts are confused and my words stumble one upon the other. But dear Lord, I have one insignificant talent —I can whistle. So do let me whistle in order that I may glorify Your Name."

Thereupon the stillness of the night was broken by a rapturous whistling. It was like the song of a bird trilling in the sun. It was like the whisper of the leaves when the wind blows through them. It was like the chant of the Cherubim and the Seraphim winging in joy to the Throne of the Almighty.

When Rabbi Mordecai heard the whistling he began to tremble. "Come!" he cried to his companion. "Let us get away from here before the flames of this holiness consume us!"

The Long and the Short of It

ONCE one of Rabbi Eleazar's students was reading the service at a leisurely pace. At this his fellow students complained, "How he drags out the prayers!"

"Does he pray any longer than Moses, our teacher, whose devotion on Mount Sinai lasted forty days and forty nights?" asked Rabbi Eleazar.

Sometime later another student was officiating at prayer and he, on the contrary, raced through the service like a whirlwind.

"How fast he reads the prayers!" his fellow students complained.

"Is his praying briefer than that of Moses, our Teacher, when he prayed for the recovery of his sister Miriam with the words: 'Heal her, O God.'?"

The Tailor's Prayer

ON THE evening of the Day of Atonement Rabbi Levi Yitzchok of Berditchev, "the poor man's rabbi," asked an illiterate tailor, "Since you couldn't read the prayers today what did you say to God?"

"I said to God," replied the tailor, "Dear God, You want me to repent of my sins, but my sins have been so small! I confess: There have been times when I failed to return to the customers the pieces of left-over cloth. When I could not help it I even ate food that was not kosher. But really

---

THE LONG AND THE SHORT OF IT: Adapted from the *Agada* in the Talmud.

—is that so terrible? Now take Yourself, God! Just examine Your own sins: You have robbed mothers of their babes, and have left helpless babes orphans. So You see that Your sins are much more serious than mine. I'll tell You what, God! Let's make a deal! You forgive me and I'll forgive You."

"Ah, you foolish man!" cried Rabbi Levi Yitzchok. "You let God off too easily! Just think! You were in an excellent position to make Him redeem the whole Jewish people!"

The Drunkard's Prayer

THE rabbi was at the point of death so the Jewish community proclaimed a day of fasting in the town in order to induce the Heavenly Judge to commute the sentence of death.

On that very day, when the entire congregation was gathered in the synagogue for penance and prayer, the town drunkard went to the village tavern for a *schnapps*. When another Jew saw him do this he rebuked him, saying, "Don't you know this is a fast-day and you're not allowed to drink? Why, everybody's at the synagogue praying for the rabbi!"

So the drunkard went to the synagogue and prayed, "Dear God! Please restore our rabbi to good health so that I can have my *schnapps!*"

The rabbi recovered, and it was considered a miracle. He explained it in the following way: "May God Preserve our village drunkard until he is a hundred and twenty years! Know that his prayer was heard by God when yours were not. He put his whole heart and soul into his prayer!"

Hanan Haneheba

HANAN, the son of Honi Ha-M'Aggel's daughter, was a very pious man, but at the same time very modest and meek. For this reason people were wont to call him "Hanan haneheba," which means: "Hanan hides himself in his modesty."

Once there was a drought in the land, and the sages knew that the prayers of the modest Hanan would be answered, but they also knew that the meek Hanan would not pray for rain. What were they to do? At length, they called for some school children, and said to them, "Go to Father Hanan, and ask him to pray to God for rain."

The children went to Hanan, pulled at the tails of his robe, and said, "O father, father, please give us rain."

HANAN HANEHEBA: From *Book of Legends*, by Hyman Goldin. Jordan Publishing Co. New York, 1929. Reprinted by permission of the present copyright holders, Hebrew Publishing Co.

Touched by the pleas of the children, Hanan prayed thus to the Holy One, praised be His Name!—

"Master of the world, cause rain to descend for the sake of these children who do not know the difference between the Father who is able to give rain and the father who is unable to give rain."

Hanan's prayer had the desired effect, and rain descended in abundance upon the earth.

Two Prayers

RABBI HANINA BEN DOSA was on his way home when suddenly a heavy rain began to fall. Thereupon, the sage began to pray, "Lord of the Universe! Everyone else sits comfortably at home while I, Hanina, get drenched to the skin! Is this just?"

Immediately the rain ceased.

When Rabbi Hanina arrived home he prayed again.

"Lord of the Universe! Everyone else is in trouble because the rain stopped and the fields are athirst. Only I, Hanina, sit cozily at home! Is this just?"

Immediately, the rain started again.

The Prudent Rabbi

RABBI ABBA HILKIAH was a grandson of Honi Ha-M'Aggel. Like his grandfather he possessed the power of prayer to make the rain fall. And whenever a drought occurred the rabbis came to ask him to pray for rain.

Once during a great drought the rabbis sent two of their colleagues to him. Not finding him at home they then went into the fields and saw him working there, for Rabbi Hilkiah was only a day laborer. "Peace be to you, Rabbi," they saluted him, but he did not answer, did not even turn his face toward them, but went right on working. He ignored them all the time they were there. However, the rabbis took no offense at his puzzling conduct and waited patiently, without a word, until he would see fit to greet them.

When darkness set in and it was time for Rabbi Abba Hilkiah to return home he gathered a pile of wood and placed it on his shoulder. His coat he slung over the other shoulder. All the way home he carried his shoes in his hand. When he had to ford a stream he put on his shoes. Every time he came to a place where there were sharp thorns he raised his robe until he had passed. On his arrival home his wife came out to welcome him,

TWO PRAYERS: Adapted from the *Agada* in the Talmud.

THE PRUDENT RABBI: *Ibid.*

dressed in all her finery. First to enter the house was his wife, Rabbi Hilkiah followed, and afterwards he permitted the two visiting rabbis to enter.

Rabbi Abba Hilkiah sat down to eat the evening meal, but he did not utter a word of invitation to his visitors to join him. Then he cut up the bread. He handed the elder of his two boys one piece, and to the younger boy he gave two pieces.

At an opportune moment he whispered to his wife:

"I well know that the rabbis have come here about the matter of rain. Let us both go up to the roof to offer our prayers. Maybe God will have compassion on all of us and send us rain. In this way no one will find out that our prayers have had anything to do with it."

Without saying a word to the two rabbis they ascended to the roof. Rabbi Abba Hilkiah stood in one corner, his wife in another, and separately they prayed for rain. Suddenly, a dark cloud appeared in his wife's corner and afterwards spread across the entire heaven. Then it began to rain.

When they came down from the roof Rabbi Abba Hilkiah turned courteously to the rabbis and asked them, "What can I do for you?"

"We came here to ask you to pray for rain."

Rabbi Abba Hilkiah raised his hands to heaven.

"Blessed be the Almighty!" he cried. "He has sent you rain without any need of my praying for it."

"Do not try to conceal it," said the rabbis to Rabbi Abba Hilkiah. "We know for sure that the rain came in answer to your prayers. However, we would like you to explain some puzzling matters to us."

"Ask and I shall answer."

"Why didn't you respond to our greeting when we found you working in the field?"

"I'm a day laborer and it wasn't right of me to waste the time for which I am paid."

"Why did you carry the pile of wood on one shoulder and your coat over the other? Wouldn't it have been more sensible to have cushioned the wood upon the coat so that it would not have rubbed your skin?"

"The coat is not mine, but a borrowed one. It was lent to me to wear and not to place a pile of wood on it."

"Why did you walk barefoot all the way home, putting on your shoes only when you came to the stream?"

"When I walked on the path I could see what I was stepping upon, but in the water where I could not see, I ran the risk of being bitten by a fish or a snake."

"Why did you lift up your robe when you came to where the sharp thorns grew?"

"A scratch on the skin heals quickly, but a tear on a garment is hard to mend."

"Why did your wife put on all her finery when she came out to welcome you?"

"She did this so that my eyes would not stray to another woman."

"Why did your wife enter the house first, you after her, and only then did you admit us?"

"Because I never set eyes on you before and therefore I was discreet."

"When you sat down to eat why didn't you ask us to join you?"

"Because I did not have enough bread for everybody, and knowing that you definitely would have declined my invitation, I did not wish to go through an empty formality."

"Why did you give the younger boy more bread than the older one?"

"Because the older one is home all the time and he can eat whenever he is hungry, but his younger brother is away all day at school."

"Why did a dark cloud appear first over the corner on the roof where your wife stood praying?"

"That was because a woman gives more direct charity than a man. She is always at home, and to him who is hungry she serves cooked food. But the man can give away only small change to the needy."

A Beard and a Prayer

IT HAPPENED at Dunkirk, during the dark days of the war, when the English people were singing, "There'll always be an England," because at the time they weren't sure there would be.

You remember the time. Every ship, boat, and anything that could float was mobilized to save the British trapped at the seaport town. In this Dunkirk there lived an elderly Mr. Nirenberg and he had a beard. Now you see why this story has a beard. Mr. Nirenberg was a pious old Jew— of the ultra-orthodox variety. Mr. Nirenberg was faithful to that commandment—"A razor shall not go over thy head." It was a large, flowing beard, such as one of the prophets of Israel might have worn, or some great savant like Leonardo da Vinci, or perhaps Walt Whitman.

His beard was his pride and also his cross, as it were. Mr. Nirenberg knew that it had long been one of the Nazi sports to pull a Jew's beard. And now the Germans were near Dunkirk. That beard would certainly be fatal to him now. Dunkirk spelled doom to the British. To this man with a beard there certainly would be no hope. He couldn't be identified more definitely as a Jew if he got a megaphone and proclaimed it to the Germans.

Yes, it looked black for Mr. Nirenberg. He stood sadly at the docks and watched the English loading the boats while the German shells were popping all around. He might go up and ask the English to take him with them, but they had not enough boats for their own soldiers. He was not an English Jew. He was a French Jew. The English would feel no particular obligation towards him.

A BEARD AND A PRAYER: From *Bitter Herbs and Honey*, by David Schwartz. Silver Palm Press. New York, 1947.

Yet the English were the only hope of Mr. Nirenberg. He grasped at a straw. He went up to the captain of one of the English boats and asked to be taken with them.

The captain looked at Mr. Nirenberg, looked and thought—thought as much as it was possible to think in all the panic and confusion amid the downpour of German shells.

"Well, I'll tell you what, old man, I'll take you on one condition."

"What is that?" asked Mr. Nirenberg.

"On the condition that on the way over you pray that we reach the coast of England safely."

Mr. Nirenberg's face lit up. "Agreed," he said, and an idea came into his head.

"Captain," he said, "there are a half dozen other Jews in Dunkirk. If you take them along, they will pray too. Won't God be more inclined to hear the prayers of many than of one?"

"All right, bring them here, but do it quickly," said the captain.

Mr. Nirenberg lost no time.

All the Dunkirk Jews went over in that boat, and across the channel these pious Jews, in the ancient tradition of conduct during a great crisis, stood on the deck and chanted the Psalms.

The boat made the crossing in safety.

When they were all safe the captain turned to Mr. Nirenberg. "You know why I took you? It was because of that beard. You look like a godly man with it. And I believe your prayers helped."

And if the captain believed that they did, who shall say that they didn't?

RESISTING TEMPTATION

Nathan with the Halo

THERE once lived a very rich man whose name was Nathan.* He was in love with a woman who was another man's wife. Her name was Hannah and she was very beautiful in face and figure.

The love Nathan bore for Hannah gnawed at him like a fatal illness. At last he fell gravely ill. The doctors said to him:

"There is no cure for you except that you know this woman."

When the teachers of the Law of Moses heard this they cried out:

"Better that this man die than that he break one of the commandments!"

The doctors pleaded: "At least let her come and speak to him!"

---

* The Nathan of this legend is supposedly Nathan de-Zuzitha, the Exilarch (Prince of the Exile) who lived in Babylonia in the first third of the 2nd Century A.D. This legend is adapted from the *Ma'aseh Nissim* by Nissim of Kairwan (11th Century, Tunis), and is also found in later collections of moral tales.

But the teachers said: "That too is not permitted."

And so Nathan's illness became aggravated more and more with time and he wasted away.

It so happened that Hannah's husband, a poor man, was deeply in debt, and, when he could not satisfy his creditors, they threw him into the debtor's prison. Need forced Hannah to do spinning. She worked both day and night and, with the money she earned, she bought bread and brought it to her husband in prison. Unfortunately, his long confinement had made him fall into a deep melancholy; he was so embittered that he prayed for death.

One day he said to Hannah:

"My dear wife, our Torah says that he who saves but one man from death, to his account it will be written that he had kept many of his fellow-men alive. Behold me! I find life unbearable here in prison. Have pity on me! Go to Nathan, the rich man, and beg him to lend you enough money to pay off my creditors and thus save me from death."

And Hannah grew silent and sad. Then she said:

"Surely you have heard that this man Nathan, from whom you wish me to borrow money, is sick for love of me and is at the point of death. Day after day his messengers come bringing me costly gifts of gold and silver, but I refuse to accept them and tell them: 'Go and say to your master that never will he see my face!' And here, from your own lips I hear you bid me to call on him and ask that he lend me money! Were you in your right senses you wouldn't now be asking of me such a frightful thing! But, I'm afraid, your confinement has affected your mind."

And Hannah was filled with righteous anger at her husband and left him abruptly, and she did not visit him for three days.

On the fourth day she reflected deeply on the matter and was filled with compassion for her husband.

"I will go to him and take care of him lest he die!" she cried.

And Hannah went to the prison and stood at her husband's side. When he saw her he said:

"The Lord will surely demand of you an accounting for the injustice you have done to me, and will punish you for it accordingly. Know that it is no secret to me that you wish for my death in order that you may become the rich man Nathan's wife."

When Hannah heard these words she wrung her hands in despair.

"Send me away from you," she cried, "or else give me a letter of divorce to prove I'm no longer your wife! Only then will I go to Nathan."

"Aha! your own words only prove," replied her husband with bitterness, "that it is exactly as I have said—you want to be Nathan's wife!"

At that, Hannah wept loudly. Falling on her face she cried:

"Who has ever heard such evil—who has ever seen such evil! You, my husband, say to me: 'Go and break your marriage vows and act the wanton so that I may be let out of prison!'"

Thereupon, Hannah's husband said:

"Go away and let me be! The Lord will have mercy on me!"

And Hannah went home and brooded upon her grief and upon the grief of her husband. After a little while she again was filled with compassion for him. Then she made her decision.

She went and purified her heart, and prayed.

"I beseech thee, O my Lord—save me! Come to my aid that I may not fall into sin!"

Hannah then went to Nathan's house.

When the rich man's servants saw her, they ran in haste to inform their sick master.

"O master—Hannah stands before the gates!" they cried.

"If what you say is true—I grant you all your freedom!" Nathan exclaimed with joy.

As Hannah entered the courtyard a maid-servant ran to Nathan and cried:

"O master, Hannah is in the courtyard!"

"Also you, I grant freedom," said Nathan joyfully to her.

When Hannah stood before Nathan he raised his eyes to hers and said:

"Whatever you wish, my lady, that I will give to you; whatever you will ask of me that I will do."

And Hannah answered: "I have only one wish—that you lend my husband money so that I may release him from prison. If you will give me the money I can assure you that your deed will be entered into the Heavenly Book of Accounts as a work of justice and mercy."

And Nathan's heart grew soft and he asked his servants to bring him the money and gave it to Hannah. Then he said to her:

"See, I have done as you have asked of me, but you also know that I have fallen sick for love of you. I, therefore, beg you: surrender to my desires and grant me new life."

"I am in your hands and under your roof," replied Hannah. "Here I am powerless to resist you. But I adjure you: this is the hour in which you can win for yourself Life Eternal. Oh guard yourself then, that you do not fritter away for nothing your heavenly recompense! Should you have your will of me I will never again be able to live with my husband. Reflect well before it is too late! For the sake of stilling your momentary lust you will lose so much that is wonderful and good, and the only thing left you will be remorse. What it takes a lifetime of effort in order to be found worthy in the eyes of God you must not throw away in the thoughtlessness of the moment. Listen to my words and stifle your evil urge!"

No sooner had Hannah finished when a great turmoil began to rage in Nathan's breast. He reviled Satan who had taken possession of him. He arose from his couch and prostrated himself face downward to the ground. He then implored God:

"O Lord, put an end to my evil desire! Release me from my passion! Lead me into the path of the righteous! Forgive me my sins and let me atone for them!"

Then Nathan said to Hannah: "Blest are you of God and blest are the words with which you have kept me from sin. Go in peace and may the Lord be with you!"

And Hannah went away rejoicing. With the money Nathan had given her she released her husband from prison. She then told him everything she had said and done. But he did not believe her. In his heart he suspected that Nathan had known her and that she had concealed this from him.

One day, as the great master Rabbi Akiba was looking out of his window, he saw an astonishing sight. A man passed by on horseback and there was a halo about his head that was as dazzling as the sun at noon. Rabbi Akiba thereupon called to one of his students.

"Who is that man on horseback?" he asked.

"Why, that is Nathan who chases after women," answered the student laughingly.

Rabbi Akiba then asked his students:

"Do you see anything strange about that man's head?"

"We see nothing," replied the students.

"Make haste, and bring this man to me!" ordered Rabbi Akiba.

And so they brought Nathan into the master's presence.

"My son," said Rabbi Akiba. "I see a halo about your head. From this I know that you will have a share of the World-to-Come. Tell me, then, what marvellous deed have you done to be found so deserving of Divine Grace?"

Nathan listened with amazement and for a moment was speechless.

"O master," he murmured, "I am but a miserable sinner!"

He then told him of how he had tried so hard to seduce the virtuous wife, Hannah.

Listening to him, Rabbi Akiba was filled with wonder over the strength of his passion and over the even greater strength of his spirit which had conquered it. And so he said:

"My son, you have fulfilled a holy obligation to a fellow-creature. Therefore, God permits the radiance of His light to rest like a crown of grace upon your head. And if it shines so brilliantly on earth, think how much more dazzling its lustre will be in Paradise! Now my son, sit down here beside me and let me teach you the Torah."

This Nathan did, and he sat at the feet of the master who opened wide for him the gates of wisdom. In time Nathan became so learned that he sat at the right hand of the master in the House of Study.

One day, it happened that Hannah's husband was passing by Rabbi Akiba's House of Study and he saw Nathan sitting at the right hand of the master. Thereupon he asked one of the students:

"How did Nathan ever come to such a great distinction?"

And the student told him everything.

And the man was filled with wonder and regret. Now he saw that he should have believed his wife. And all jealousy departed from him like a dark cloud.

He hurried home and, with a contrite spirit, he kissed Hannah.

"Forgive me, my dear wife, for having thought evil of you," he implored her. "Today I saw Nathan sitting at the right hand of the blessed Rabbi Akiba. I then asked and was told all that had happened between you and him. May God increase and multiply your Heavenly reward! All along I've carried the consuming canker of jealousy in my heart, but God in His mercy has at last revealed the truth to me. My burdened spirit is free once more!"

Rabbi Amram's Temptation

ONCE some heathen brought a number of captive Jewish girls to Nehardea. The Jews in the town redeemed them by purchase from the hands of the heathen. The girls were then brought to the house of Rabbi Amram Hasidah, The Holy, to spend the night there. Everybody knew that no more secure place could be found for them than in the home of this saint. Rabbi Amram had the girls led up to the garret and then ordered the ladder removed from there.

During the night, when all were fast asleep, one of the girls came to stand at the garret window. Rabbi Amram looked up and was dazzled by her beauty. He became confused, could not understand what was happening to him. Finally, a mysterious power triumphed over his better judgment, drawing him up to the garret to the captive girl with the luminous face.

Rabbi Amram lifted up the ladder, which was so heavy that usually ten men were required to move it. In that instant of his passion he became so strong that he himself was able to carry it to the garret. He began to climb the ladder, rung by rung. When he had ascended halfway, he regained control of his emotions and cried out, "Fire—fire!"

Hearing his cries the rabbis who lived in the neighborhood came running to help him put out the fire. But when they saw that there was no fire they reproached their colleague:

"We are ashamed of you, Amram!"

"Far better that you should be ashamed of me in this world than that I should be ashamed of myself in the next!" replied Rabbi Amram.

A Real Thanksgiving

MOTKE "the Drunkard" and Fishel "the Guzzler" were in a repentant mood. They swore never to touch a drop again as long as they lived. They shook hands upon it and started for home.

RABBI AMRAM'S TEMPTATION: Adapted from the *Agada* in the Talmud.

On the way they passed the village tavern. Things were merry over there. Snatches of song floated to them through the open windows.

"How jolly it is in the tavern!" sighed Motke.

"I thought we agreed never to set foot again in that accursed place," Fishel reminded him in a chilling voice.

"It's my old weakness that's drawing me there," sighed Motke.

"That's just the way I feel about it," muttered Fishel gloomily.

"I'll tell you," suggested Motke. "Let's close our eyes and run past the inn without looking at it."

"You're right! The temptation is too great," agreed Fishel.

So the two shut their eyes tightly and ran like the wind past the tavern. After a little while they stopped running and opened their eyes.

"Nobody's going to say now that I'm a weakling!" cried Fishel "the Guzzler" exultantly. "I tell you, Motke, it's wonderful to have a strong will. With it you can overcome every temptation. I feel like offering thanksgiving to God for having escaped this danger."

"I tell you what," chirped Motke "the Drunkard," brightly, "how about going into the tavern and offering thanksgiving over a nice glass of *schnapps*?"

The Laying On of Hands

A PRETTY young woman came to the rabbi.

"Bless me, Rabbi!" she implored.

The rabbi spread out his hands over her head and blessed her, but he took care not to touch her head while doing so.

"Why don't you place your hands on my head?" she asked in surprise. "Blessings from a distance aren't as fruitful as blessings from near."

"How do you light the candles on Friday night?" asked the rabbi. "Do you recite the prayer with your hands touching the flame?"

"Of course not—I'd only burn my hands!" answered the young woman.

"Believe me, it's no different with me!" said the rabbi, smiling. "Were I to lay my hands on your head, I might also burn them!"

Satan Is Never Lazy

IT WAS a cold wintry morning, and not a soul could be seen on the street. What was the amazement of the *shammes* when the door opened and the rabbi came in all bundled up!

"Why so early, Rabbi? It's cold enough to freeze one's ears off," he remarked.

"Did you say 'early'?" said the rabbi with a deprecating gesture.

"When I woke up and wanted to dress I suddenly saw the Evil Spirit before me.

" 'Sleep a little bit longer, Rabbi—the cold is so terrible outside!' he argued persuasively.

" 'Be reasonable—I've got to get up and go to the synagogue for morning prayer,' I appealed to him.

" 'Don't be a fool, Rabbi,' said the Evil Spirit to me. 'It's so nice and cozy in bed! Stay a bit longer.'

" 'Impudent fellow!' I cried. 'You weren't too lazy yourself to get out of bed so that you might lead me into temptation, so why should I, a rabbi, sleep like some pampered lazybones?'

"And so what do you think I did? I told him to go to Hell where he belonged. I jumped out of bed quickly, and here I am!"

The Ordeal of Rabbi Mattithiah

RABBI MATTITHIAH BEN HERESH was a very pious man. All his waking hours he spent in the House of Study expounding the Torah. He was as radiant as the sun and his face shone as pure as an angel's. Throughout all the years of his life he had never gazed upon a woman and all his thoughts were chaste.

It chanced one day that Satan suddenly noticed him and exclaimed with resentment:

"Is it possible for such a handsome man to be chaste!"

Then he went to complain to the Almighty, saying:

"What is your opinion of Mattithiah ben Heresh?"

The Almighty answered:

"He is a true saint."

Satan laughed. "Let me entice him into sin!" he implored.

"You will fail in your efforts," answered God. "However, I give you my permission to prove him."

Satan then went and disguised himself as a woman. Such ravishing beauty the world had never gazed upon since Naamah, the sister of Tubal Cain, whose charms seduced the very angels.

Then came the woman and stood before the saint. Rabbi Mattithiah averted his gaze chastely. Then the woman placed herself at his right side. Thereupon Rabbi Mattithiah turned his head to the left.

At this Rabbi Mattithiah became panic-stricken. He thought: "May the Lord protect me! What if I should succumb to the Evil Spirit and be led into sin?"

Rabbi Mattithiah then called one of his students who was in the habit of waiting upon him.

"Bring me fire and nails," he asked him.

THE ORDEAL OF RABBI MATTITHIAH: Adapted from the *Midrash*.

He then placed the nails into the fire until they were red-hot. With them he pierced his eyes so that he might drive the temptation of beauty from them.

When Satan beheld this he began to tremble and fell upon his face in fright. At that very instant the Almighty summoned the Archangel Raphael. "Find Rabbi Mattithiah ben Heresh and heal his eyes!" He commanded.

The Archangel descended to earth and when he appeared before Rabbi Mattithiah the saint asked him:

"Who are you?"

"I am Raphael," answered the Archangel. "God sent me to heal you."

"Go in peace," Rabbi Mattithiah replied, "and let me be!"

And Raphael returned to heaven and told the Almighty that the saint refused to be healed. So the Almighty said to him:

"Return to Rabbi Mattithiah and tell him that I, the Lord of Heaven and Earth, of Righteousness and Justice, promise him that the Evil Spirit will not triumph over him!"

"Heal me then!" cried Rabbi Mattithiah ben Heresh to Raphael.

The Saint Who Sinned

RABBI HAI BAR ASHI used to pray daily to God to protect him against the temptation of sin. Once, when his wife heard him pray thus, she said to herself: "Why is he so afraid of sinning? He is such an old man!" Then she got the notion that she would like to test his virtue.

One day, as he sat in the garden absorbed in his sacred studies, she went and disguised herself. Then she entered the garden and, with wanton air, passed by her husband. She walked to and fro several times so that he finally began to notice her.

"Who are you?" Rabbi Hai asked.

"My name is Haruta," she answered, giving him the name of a famous beauty of the day.

Without loss of time Rabbi Hai tried to coax her into sinning with him

"First bring me that little twig," she asked.

He leaped forward and brought it to her.

Later, when he came home he found his wife building a fire. So overcome was he by his feeling of guilt that he tried to leap into the flames.

"Why do you do this?" she asked, restraining him.

He then told her all that had happened to him that day.

"You have committed no wrong," she comforted him, "because that woman was I."

He was incredulous, so for proof she produced the twig he had given her.

THE SAINT WHO SINNED: Adapted from the *Agada* in the Talmud.

"Nonetheless," he wailed, "I have committed a sin, because I thought you were the beauty Haruta."

For the rest of his life the holy man was tormented by his feeling of guilt, and he died of a broken heart.

The Woman Who Buried Three Husbands

HOMAH, the great grand-daughter of Rabbi Yehuda, was famed for her beauty, but she was also a coquette. She had been married twice and she had seen both of her husbands buried. Each died a short time after he had married her.

It so happened that Rabbi Abbai, who was then getting on in years, fell in love with her. His friends tried to dissuade him from his intention to marry her. They warned him that it was dangerous to marry a woman who had already buried two husbands. But Abbai dismissed their fears as foolish. He married Homah. However, a short while later he too died.

After Homah had become a widow for the third time she went to the House of Judgment to petition Rabbi Raba to give her material assistance.

"Please give me money for food," she asked.

So Rabbi Raba fixed a sum sufficient for her food.

"And now give me money for wine," she added.

Rabbi Raba was surprised.

"I never knew that wine had been drunk in the house of your last husband Abbai."

Homah replied: "I swear by your life, Rabbi, that we used to drink wine from tall goblets, as high as—." And speaking thus she rolled up her sleeve and measured upon her arm the length of the goblets.

The moment she exposed her naked arm a bright radiance filled the room—so beautiful she was!

Her impudence offended Raba, and he angrily left the House of Judgment. And as he went he rejoiced that at home there was waiting for him his true and virtuous wife.

Arriving home, Raba embraced his wife with greater tenderness than was usual with him, so that she was filled with wonder.

"What is the reason for this?" she asked.

"Homah appeared today in the House of Judgment," he answered and lowered his eyes.

Hearing her husband speak thus, Rabbi Raba's wife picked up a large iron key and went out into the street. She found the wanton and ran after her crying, "You've buried three husbands already, do you want to bury a fourth one now?"

And with this cry she followed Homah everywhere she went until she had driven her from the town.

THE WOMAN WHO BURIED THREE HUSBANDS: *Ibid.*

The Foresight of a Good Man

ABOUT a certain nobleman it is related that once he received a gift of magnificent glass tableware. Every piece was most artfully fashioned and lovely to look upon.

The nobleman accepted the glassware with great pleasure, thanked the donor and, in turn, gave him a present even more costly. Later he took the glassware, piece by piece, and shattered it upon the ground. When his servants saw him do this they asked him the reason.

The nobleman answered, "I know my own nature well. I know that I am hot-tempered. I said to myself: 'One of these days one of my servants will accidentally break one of these costly dishes and I will punish him for it.' Far better then, to destroy these dishes beforehand rather than that misfortune may be worked by my hand on another!"

THE FORESIGHT OF A GOOD MAN: From *Tzemach Tzaddik,* by Leone da Modena, Venetian Jewish preacher, poet and humanist. Venice, 1600.

[3]

Miracles

CABALISTS, MYSTICS AND WONDER-WORKERS

INTRODUCTION

Beginning with the Talmudic era, there crept into Jewish thought a persistently mystical and life-denying element. But mysticism never really achieved a dominant position among Jews except for relatively brief periods when, under the stress of persecution, Jewish life became constricted. Then there were those who were eager to escape into the unreal and shadowy world of Cabala.

What is the Cabala? It is not just one book but an entire body of esoteric knowledge which had been created in the course of some two thousand years by those daringly imaginative but sickly minds, the cabalists. They were men disenchanted with life who sought to construct a bridge between "this vale of tears" and God. They were "God-intoxicated" men, dominated by a single drive: "As the hart panteth after the water-brooks, so panteth my soul after Thee, O God!" (Psalm 42.1) To find God, the cabalists renounced the world with all its snares of the senses. They substituted intuition for reason, spirit for flesh, the hidden for the visible, and the unknown for the known.

Cabala, which in Hebrew means "The Received, or Traditional Lore," loftily referred to itself as "The Hidden Wisdom." It represented that kind of knowledge which could be acquired, not by ordinary reason, but by the illumination of the spirit. Therefore, only the spiritually elect, those who were "adepts in Grace," were deemed worthy enough to explore its secret meanings. In short, it was an "aristocratic" body of knowledge like some abstruse higher mathematics; *hoi polloi* had to rest content with Scripture itself.

The history of the Cabala winds along a complicated and uncertain course. It is a strange mystical brew of diverse ingredients, combining Jewish ethics, Zoroastrian dualism, Pythagorean numerology, Neo-Platonic emanations and medieval Christian asceticism. While numerous works collectively constitute the Cabala, the two most prized are the *Sefer Yetzira* (Book of Creation) compiled during the Talmudic era, and the far better known *Zohar* (Splendor) which people sometimes erroneously use interchangeably with Cabala. This second work, ascribed by its first editor, the

175

Spanish mystic Moses Shem-Tob de Leon (1250–1305), to the Galilean *Mishna* writer Simon bar Yohai (Second Century A.D.), became the scriptures of the later cabalists. Next to the Bible itself it was revered above all other sacred Jewish works by its devotees and by awestruck superstitious folk. Because of this the Cabala fell into disrepute among the rationalists. This explains the popular misconception of the Cabala, usually based on inadequate knowledge, as being nothing but a silly hodge-podge of numerological and alphabetical abracadabra, childish beliefs, incantations, and various other kinds of mumbo-jumbo.

Although Jews lived in walled-in isolation in medieval times, they were exposed to the influences of the Christian and Islamic worlds about them. Monasticism, with its rejection of the life of the senses as cardinal sin, left a deep impression on the cabalists of the Middle Ages. They too mortified the flesh in order to subjugate it and, by the power of prayer, strove to break the bonds which kept their spirits earthbound. It was often a pietistic passion close to frenzy that burned like a consuming fire within them, all but destroying the frail human kernel in which the spirit dwelled. A vivid description of this kind of abberated striving can be found in *The Cabalists*, a story by the Yiddish literary master I. L. Peretz, which is included in this section.

It is indeed a paradox of history that the Dark Ages among Jews had never really existed until the latter half of the Sixteenth Century. At the very time when the medieval darkness had sent civilization reeling backwards in Europe, the Jews were probably the most enlightened people in the world. They were the proud inheritors and disseminators not only of their own culture but of the Greek and Arabic civilizations as well. As has so often been pointed out by historians, the Jews were instrumental to a large measure in kindling the bright flame of learning and rationalism in a superstitious feudal society. However, in the twilight years of the Renaissance, while the Christian world was richly developing its sciences, its arts and the humanities, the Jews, yielding to the hammer blows of their enemies, were growing culturally weaker. Superstition, excessive piety and delirious cabalistic dreams proved excellent modes of escape from the unhappy reality of Jewish life. The legends about the Sixteenth Century Cabala masters of Safed in Palestine—Moses Cordovero, Joseph della Reyna, Alkabez, Chayyim Vital, and Isaac Luria, better known as "The Ari"—wove their web of morbid enchantment around Jewish daily thinking and feeling. In addition to harassment from death, hunger, epidemics and persecution, the average Jew now had to endure the terror of a shadowy world haunted by unspeakable demons, specters, ghosts and *dibbukim* (transmigrating souls).

With the rise of the popular mystical sect, the *Hasidim* (The Pious), the Cabala took a new lease on life, but it went through an inner and outer transformation as well. Rabbi Israel Baal-Shem, the founder of *Hasidism*, introduced the Cabala into his mystic cult but without any of its forbidding austerities. He borrowed from it principally the ethical, the poetic and the ecstatic elements.

The legends of the *Hasidim* have a fascinating historical-religious background, unique in all folk-literature. Actually, the time span of their creation was less than two hundred years, for the sect was founded shortly before the middle of the Eighteenth Century. They are more than mere legends; they constitute a genuine body of devotional folk-literature. One of the best ways to worship God, the *Hasidim* believed, was to read and tell the wondrous tales about the *tzaddikim*. The singing of melodies, and the dance, were also considered forms of worship which could serve as substitutes for Torah-study.

The initiator of this social-religious movement, which toward the end of the Nineteenth Century embraced half of all the Jews in Europe, was Israel ben Eliezer, later known as Israel Baal-Shem, or Baal-Shem-Tov (Master of the Good Name). He was born in 1700, either in the Ukraine or in the Carpathian Mountains of Galicia, no one knows where for certain. All his life he revealed a great love for solitude and for nature. He wandered alone through field and forest and communed with God in the poetical-mystical way that was characteristic of him. It was at such times that he spun his visions of the aspiring soul and the redemption of man, which were to become the fundamental doctrines of his sect. Legend has Baal-Shem variously as a *bahelfer*—a religious teacher's assistant—as a synagogue *shammes* in a Galician town, and as a drover in Volhynia. His humble calling exposed him to the ridicule of his middle-class opponents, the *misnagdim*, but it was of tremendous advantage to him in his evangelical labors among the common people, for he spoke the folk-langage and articulated their spiritual hungers and hopes.

The immediate and widespread success of *Hasidism* was due to a variety of historical reasons. One hundred years before there had been the Thirty Years War in which the Jews suffered more than any others and from whose frightful ravages they never fully recovered. In 1648 two cataclysmic events occurred. The first took place during the Cossack uprising against Polish rule, led by the Hetman Bogdan Chmielnicki. In the course of the struggle, terrible barbarities were perpetrated on the Jews. Some three hundred thousand, or about half of the Jewish population in the Ukraine, were massacred. The terrors of the time greatly resembled those initiated against the Jews by the Nazis in our days.

The effect of these mass-atrocities on the Jews of the world was prostrating. Many thought that the end of the world was already at hand, for one of the Jewish Messianic traditions is that, when the suffering of the Jewish people will have reached its most desperate point, God in His mercy will send the Messiah to redeem it.

During the year that the atrocities in the Ukraine occurred, a young Turkish Jew of arresting personality and magnetism, announced himself as the Messiah in the city of Salonika. This was the cabalist Sabbatai Zevi. Because the Jews of his day had the will to believe in a supernatural instrumentality that would save them from further disaster, he came as the answer to their prayers. Messianic hysteria swept like a conflagration over all of European Jewry. Tens of thousands liquidated their worldly affairs and readied themselves for the End of Days.

The result was the only one that could be expected under the circumstances: disillusionment. The psychologically complicated Sabbatai Zevi, after a series of exciting adventures, failed his followers in the end: he embraced Mohammedanism. The Jews of the world were split wide apart over the issue and the so-called "Sabbatian" controversy raged bitterly for more than a hundred years. But the effect of this debacle on the Jewish masses was paralyzing. They grieved and sank into a deep apathy.

However, poverty and persecution continued as usual. Confined in crowded ghettos, deprived of normal outlets for their energies, most Jews sought refuge in cabalistic superstitions and practices. To the Talmudic rationalists of the day religious worship had become ever more formalistic, suffering from a diminishing emotional content. The common folk could find no satisfaction in it, for many could barely read Hebrew and had been taught to recite their prayers parrot-fashion.

It was, therefore, as if in answer to a universal need for a comforter, that Baal-Shem appeared. He went from town to town, preaching an evangel of faith and joy. Laughter, song and the dance he said, were the highest forms of prayer. Love of God he declared more important than formalistic religious worship. To do good among men was better than to observe the minutiae of Law and Ritual. Baal-Shem sanctified all that was humble, that was workaday. But all-fundamental was his central doctrine of love: love of God and love of man. All life was holy, he said. The dry-as-dust, learned Talmudist or rabbi had less of a chance to taste the beatitude of the spirit and the rewards of Paradise than the pure in heart and the humble, even though they might be illiterate.

The evangel of *Hasidism* that Baal-Shem and his disciples preached was therefore as much of a socio-ethical nature as it was religious. It revitalized the Jewish spirit, revived hope, gave the people an affirmative philosophy of life that was warmly emotional, highly ethical, rich in earthiness though very mystical. It was a liveable, workable way of life, regardless of its admitted serious shortcomings.

The Rabbinic authorities, the Talmudic traditionalists, naturally condemned the new sect as heretical. They even pronounced the ban of excommunication against Baal-Shem. But all in vain. *Hasidism* was like a tidal wave sweeping over Galicia, Poland, Hungary, parts of the Ukraine and Lithuania. Nothing could stop it, for it answered an urgent need; the Jewish masses could not survive spiritually without it.

Unfortunately, *Hasidism*, like so many other religious sects, carried within itself the seed of corruption. It was inherent in the very institution of the *Tzaddik*—the Holy Man and Wonder-Worker—who became dynastic and was motivated sometimes by less than spiritual motives. As the intermediary between God's and man's desires, the *Tzaddik* was courted and adulated and offered gifts of money by his worshipping followers. It was but natural that some should have been tempted and thus flung the entire sect into disrepute. This led to a vulgarization of Baal-Shem's exalted teachings. None the less, the spirit of the movement withstood all the corrosions among the plain folk, as the numerous *Hasidic* legends and anecdotes in this collection reveal.

Although *Hasidism*, as a movement, is practically extinct at the present time, isolated circles of *Hasidim* are still to be found, even in New York, Boston, Philadelphia and Chicago. There are also *neo-Hasidim*. These are usually of a sophisticated, intellectual-mystical bent. Professor Martin Buber has been their leader, and at various times has had such influential adherents as Franz Werfel, Marc Chagall, Franz Kafka, Max Brod and Arnold Zweig.

                                                                N. A.

Why Rabbi Israel Laughed Three Times

ONE Friday night Rabbi Israel Baal-Shem, together with all his disciples, ushered in the Sabbath Bride with joyous ecstasy. But immediately after he had recited the benediction he leaned back in his chair and laughed uproariously.

The disciples who sat around him looked on in stunned silence. They were too over-awed by his sanctity to ask him why he laughed so. There was nothing they could see that could have given him cause for such laughter.

A while later he laughed again, and shortly thereafter, he laughed for the third time.

The disciples were filled with amazement. Never before had they seen him do anything like it.

Now it was the custom of Rabbi Israel that after the *Habdalah*, the prayer service that ushered out the departing Sabbath Bride, he would light his long-stemmed pipe. Then his disciple, Rabbi Kitzes, would enter his study and put to him all the questions about matters that had puzzled the disciples.

This time Rabbi Kitzes asked him, "Do tell me, Rabbi, why did you laugh three times yesterday? It must have been for some good reason."

"Have patience, I will soon reveal to you the reason why I laughed," replied Rabbi Israel.

Another Sabbath custom of Rabbi Israel's was that every Sabbath night after the *Habdalah* he would ride out of Miedziboz into the country. This time he ordered his coachman to make ready the large carriage. He took along with him on this journey his closest disciples.

All night long they rode in utter darkness, without knowing where they were going. When morning came they suddenly found themselves in the town of Kozenitz. So they went to call on the head of the community.

The whole town was full of excitement. Everybody talked of nothing but of Rabbi Israel's arrival. Many came to stand at a respectful distance and look upon his holy, radiant face.

After Rabbi Israel had finished the morning service he said to the head of the community, "Send for *Reb* Shabsi, the bookbinder."

"Shabsi, the bookbinder!" cried the elder, hardly believing what he had heard. "What do you want to see that old man for? While we consider him a good man he is not very learned in the Law. It seems to me, Rabbi, that it won't be adding much dignity to a man of your greatness to talk to such a common person. After all, we do have great scholars and cabalists in Kozenitz. Surely you have more in common with them?"

But Rabbi Israel was firm.

WHY RABBI ISRAEL LAUGHED THREE TIMES: Adapted from *Sippuri Tzaddikim* (a collection of wonder stories about Rabbi Israel Baal-Shem and his disciples). Vilna, 1905.

"I have urgent need of *Reb* Shabsi, the bookbinder!" he insisted. "I must talk with him."

So a special messenger was sent to fetch *Reb* Shabsi and his wife.

When they finally arrived Rabbi Israel said to him, "Shabsi, I want you to tell all of us here what you did last night. But you must tell the truth—conceal nothing!"

"I will tell you everything that happened, dear Rabbi," began *Reb* Shabsi. "And, if I have sinned in any way, I trust you will punish me with the right penance.

"Ever since I got married I have earned my livelihood from binding books. I did well at one time. Every Thursday I'd give my wife enough money to make the necessary Sabbath purchases of *chaleh*, fish, meat, wine and wax candles. On Friday morning I closed shop at ten o'clock and went to the synagogue. There I cantillated the Song of Songs and remained all day until after the evening services. That was my custom all along until I grew old.

"Now I no longer have the energy to toil as I did before. I can hardly earn anything. When Thursday arrives my wife can no longer afford to make the necessary Sabbath purchases. There is only one precept that I've been able to follow scrupulously in the days of my decline. At ten o'clock on Friday morning I still close my shop and go to the House of Study.

"Last Friday morning I found I did not have even a groschen to give my wife, and I knew no one from whom I could borrow money, even for *chaleh*. I could not stoop to beg. Never in my life have I asked such help from people. Only in God did I place my trust and, when I saw that God had failed to provide for me the necessities for the Sabbath, I understood that it was just that it should be so.

"I then made up my mind to fast throughout the Sabbath. I had only one fear—that my wife would not be able to contain herself and would tell the neighbors. If she did they would surely give her *chaleh* and other Sabbath foods. So I begged her not to accept any help from anyone, no matter what happened.

"Before I left for the synagogue I told my wife that I planned to come home that Friday night later than usual from the synagogue. I was afraid that I might accidentally meet some neighbor on the way who would be likely to ask me why there were no Sabbath candles burning in my house. So I remained behind in the synagogue until all had gone home—then I left.

"While I was away in the synagogue my old woman tidied up the house in honor of the Sabbath. But, as she was putting things in order, she unexpectedly found an old jacket that she had mislaid for a long time. The jacket had silver buttons overlaid with gold, as was the fashion in olden times. So my wife went and sold the buttons and, for the money, she bought large candles because I had told her that I would be late in coming. She also bought *chaleh,* fish, meat and had some money left besides.

"I returned home from the synagogue quite late. What was my surprise to see large candles burning as I approached my house! I thought: 'Alas, my old woman couldn't hold back from telling her troubles to her neighbors!' When I entered the house I found the table set. There was wine for the benediction, and *chaleh* and all good things. I did not say anything to my wife because I did not wish to mar the Sabbath peace.

"My old woman saw, however, that I was not in a good mood. So, after I had recited the benediction, she said to me, 'Do you remember, Shabsi, how long I've been looking for my old jacket with the silver buttons? Well I found it after you had left for the synagogue. I sold the buttons, and what you see here was bought with the money I got for them.'

"When I heard this my joy was indescribable. I even shed tears and thanked the heavenly Father that we could observe the Sabbath decently without anybody's help. My joy was so great that I arose from the table, took my old woman by the hand and we began to dance. After we had finished the soup we danced once more, and after the sweet *tzimmes,* the dessert, we danced for the third time.

"And so, Holy Rabbi, if you think that by doing this I have sinned, then I beg you to judge me, and what you say I'll do. God alone knows the truth that in dancing my intention was not to display levity but to praise and thank Him for the grace and loving-kindness He has shown me."

And when the old man had finished speaking Rabbi Israel turned to his disciples and said, "Believe me, when *Reb* Shabsi and his old woman laughed and danced with joy all the angels in heaven could not restrain themselves and they too laughed and danced through the celestial halls. And, if the angels of heaven could not restrain themselves, how could I? So I laughed once, twice and three times, just as they did!"

Then Rabbi Israel called to the bookbinder and his wife.

"Come nearer—tell me what you wish! Tell me what your heart most desires. Do you wish to be rich, to live in luxury and honor, or would you rather have a son to comfort you in your old age?"

"Do not mock at us, Holy Rabbi," *Reb* Shabsi answered. "We are both already very old and we never had a child before. Of course, what do we want with riches? We'd rather have a son whom we can love and who will be a comfort to us in our old age."

"Go in peace, then," said Rabbi Israel. "Know that before the year is over you will have a son. I will come to his circumcision and will act as his god-father. You will give him my name, Israel."

And it happened just as Rabbi Israel said. Within a year a child was born to the old bookbinder and his wife. Rabbi Israel was his god-father and he blessed him. As the years passed the boy became the illustrious Preacher of Kozenitz with whose wisdom the whole world became full. He was a saint and a sage, and may his fragrant memory be a blessing to all of us! Amen!

The Water-Spirit

IN OLD Constantine there lived a cousin of the Baal Shem Tov whose name was Reb Shmerl. And Reb Shmerl was a sinner. He committed one sin after another. "What does it matter if I sin twice or sin twenty times?" he said. "At the end of the year I take all my sins and drag them down to the edge of the water. I throw them into the lake, and that is the end of them. And for the new year, I am a clean man." *

So Reb Shmerl lived from year to year. And each year the sea became a little blacker, because of the sins he threw into it, and each year the bundle of sins that he brought down to the edge of the water was greater than that of the year before.

"The lake is close to my house!" he laughed. "I have not far to carry my sins! Let there be a few more in the bundle!"

But his wife said, "It is because of your sinning that God does not send us a son." His wife was a holy woman, a Tsadeket.

Reb Shmerl said, "Do you really think that is so?"

And she said, "Yes."

Then he said, "Well, perhaps it is really so." And he thought no more about it.

And that same year, he committed a sin that was uglier than all the sins

---

THE WATER-SPIRIT: From *The Golden Mountain,* a collection of legends about Baal-Shem, retold by Meyer Levin. Copyright, 1932, by Meyer Levin. New York: Jonathan Cape and Robert Ballou.

* *Tashlich,* the Hebrew for "casting off," is a Jewish religious custom of medieval origin. It was first mentioned in a work by Rabbi Jacob ben Moses Halevi Mölln of Mayence (A.D. 1355–1427). On the afternoon of the first day of Rosh Hashanah the pious Jews in all the countries of the world wend their way to the banks of a river, lake or running stream in which live fish are found. There they recite the verse from the Prophet Micah: "And thou wilt cast all their sins into the depths of the sea."

The cabalists of a later day introduced a new and somewhat bizarre element into the *Tashlich* ceremony. As they uttered the prayer they proceeded to shake out their pockets in order to remove the demons who supposedly hid there. In time this custom degenerated into a meaningless practice of shaking out of all pockets into the water, the stray crumbs, lint and pellets of paper concealed there. This Jews did as a symbolic act of casting off all their sins. Many a time this childish but entirely innocent ceremony was misunderstood only too thoroughly by those Jew-hating elements who were eager to misunderstand. They accused the Jews of throwing poison into the rivers, lakes and wells . . . Many a bloody tragedy to entire Jewish communities resulted from these calumnies.

To say that the *Tashlich* custom was of Jewish origin would be entirely incorrect. There is every proof that it was borrowed from the Christians. No less a personage than the great Florentine poet Petrarch recorded sometime before the middle of the 14th Century that on June 24th of every year, a day which marks the Eve of St. John, the Christians of Cologne marched in procession to the banks of the Rhine where they pronounced certain words and cast herbs into the river in order that the waters might wash away all their bad luck for the ensuing year.—N. A.

he had ever made. This sin was huge and shapeless, it was like a great sponge oozing and dripping with mud. He could hardly find a place to hide it until the end of the year, when he would throw it into the lake. He put it into the basement of his house. But there, the sin seemed to grow larger, to expand, until the basement was not high enough to hold it, and the mud of the sin began to squeeze itself through all the cracks and to ooze into the rooms of the house, and to fill every corner of the house with its damp crawly smell. At last, New Year's day came. Reb Shmerl took hold of the sin in both his arms, and by pulling with all his might managed to squeeze it through the door of the house. He got it out of the house, then he pushed and rolled it down to the lake.

"There!" he said as it sank into the water. "I'm rid of that!"

The lake was angrier than ever. It hissed and shook itself and heaved itself upward trying to hurl the sin back to the shore. Yet all of its rebellion was of no use, for it had been ordained when the waters were created that on New Year's they had to receive into themselves all of the sins of men, and cleanse them. So at last the lake became quiet, and set to work to cleanse the sin. But the deed of Reb Shmerl was not forgotten; the waters waited for vengeance.

Reb Shmerl saw that his hair was becoming grey, and his wife had passed her best years, and still they had no children. At last he said:

"I will go to my cousin Rabbi Israel. They say he performs wonders for every stranger that comes to his door. As for me, I am a member of his family!"

He came to the Baal Shem Tov in Medzibuz and he said, "Cousin, I am growing old, and I would like to have a son to live after me."

Rabbi Israel talked with him for a while, and remembered Shmerl's wife, the holy Tsadeket. At last the Master said, "Go home. I can only promise you that you will have a son."

"But what more did I ask!" said Reb Shmerl; and he began to dance with delight, but the Baal Shem shook his head.

The Baal Shem Tov's promise was fulfilled. Before the year was over, Shmerl's wife gave birth to a strong and beautiful boy. The father was so proud that he said, "I will go at once on another journey to Rabbi Israel, and thank him for what he has done for us."

Then he came again to Medzibuz, and entered the cottage where the Master sat studying. The Master looked up at him, and the Master's eyes were filled with deep compassionate sorrow. When Reb Shmerl looked into the eyes of Rabbi Israel, all his joyous words faded from his lips. He did not know why, but he wanted to weep. Suddenly he was crying like a child.

Then the Baal Shem Tov said to him, "Your son will grow into a strong and happy boy. But on his thirteenth birthday he will go into the water and drown."

Reb Shmerl cried like a woman. He fell on his knees to Rabbi Israel and begged, "Help me."

Everyone knows that the Baal Shem Tov was not fond of weeping. But he remembered that the man's wife was a Tsadeket. Now he lifted up his cousin and said, "The lake is angry with you because of that terrible black sin that you threw into it. There is only one way to save your son. On his thirteenth birthday, he must be kept away from the water."

Reb Shmerl thanked him with all his heart. Reb Shmerl was filled with joy, his tears were forgotten. "That is not difficult at all!" he said. "On his thirteenth birthday, I will keep him away from the water!"

And he was ready to run off on his way back home.

But Rabbi Israel called to him and said, "Do not think it is so easy to remember. You will surely forget the danger that awaits your only son!"

Reb Shmerl said, "How could I forget!"

But the Baal Shem Tov, who saw even then how it would be with Reb Shmerl, said, "Before you go, I will give you a sign that will help you to remember the day. When you awaken on that day, you'll begin to dress yourself, and you'll draw two stockings onto the left foot, and then hunt everywhere for the stocking for your right foot. Warn your household that on the day you cannot find your stocking, something terrible will happen."

Reb Shmerl thanked him and returned to Constantine. And he thought, "What a foolish thing the Rabbi said about the stockings!" So he didn't tell anyone about it.

The boy grew. He was stronger than any of the other boys in old Constantine. He could run faster, and his eyes could see further, and his hands could move more quickly. As for learning, he had only to look upon a page, and he remembered it.

But most of all things, he loved to swim in the water. He would dive to the very bottom of the lake, and there he would swim around, seeking beautiful stones. These he would bring home to his mother.

He learned to stay under the water for many minutes. The fishes would come in and out of his hands, playing with him.

As Reb Shmerl saw his son growing up so strong and big, he forgot all about the gloomy warning of the Baal Shem Tov. By the time thirteen years had passed he did not remember Rabbi Israel's prediction at all. And he prepared to celebrate the Bar Mitzveh of his only son with a great feast.

On the morning of the boy's thirteenth birthday, Reb Shmerl was awakened by the heat of the sun on his face. It was hotter than it had ever been before, he thought. He felt his whole body burning as if it were inside a furnace.

He began to dress himself.

He felt very uncomfortable. He felt he had not slept enough. He was angry because the sun had awakened him. And his head hurt with the heat.

He drew a stocking onto his left foot. And then he stopped to wipe the sweat from his body. And then, without looking what he was doing, he drew his other stocking onto his left foot. Then he looked for the stocking for his right foot. He looked among his clothes, and did not find it. He looked under the bed, and did not find it. He got up, and began to hop around the room, hunting for another stocking. He stumbled into the next room, and blundered all over the house, knocking over chairs, and hurting his knees, and falling, and balancing himself against the wall. And he muttered and cried with anger, because the day was very hot, and he could not find his other stocking.

He shouted and woke his wife.

"What is the matter?" she said.

"Where is my other stocking!" cried Reb Shmerl.

Then his wife arose, to see what was troubling him. He pointed to his leg, and muttered, "Someone has hidden my other stocking! I can't find my other stocking!"

The Tsadeket looked at her husband, and saw that he was wearing two stockings on one foot, for when he went jumping around his stockings had become loosened.

"Look, Shmerl," she laughed, "you have them both on your left foot!"

He looked, and he saw. Then suddenly he remembered the words of Rabbi Israel. And he began to tremble. And he ran to the room where his son slept. The boy was not in his bed.

Reb Shmerl ran to the door. He looked through the doorway, and saw the boy already on his way to the lake.

Reb Shmerl shouted to his son, "Come back!"

But the boy answered, "It's hot! I want to swim in the water!"

"Come back!" cried the father.

But the boy would not come back.

Then, with one foot covered and the other foot bare, Reb Shmerl began to run after his son. The boy ran swiftly. The father saw him nearing the lake.

"Master, help me!" cried the father. And he named the name of Rabbi Israel.

Then the boy tripped over the root of an old tree. Before he could rise to his feet again, his father was at his side.

"Come home with me," said the father.

He led the boy to the house, and placed him in a room, and locked the door.

It became very hot. The boy cried, and beat on the door. "Let me go to the lake!" he screamed. "I want to go to the lake!"

But they would not open the door.

At last he begged them only to let him out of that room, because it was so very hot in there. But they would not let him out of the room. After that, he begged them to give him a pan of water with which to cool his body, but Reb Shmerl was afraid to give him even a glass of water to drink.

And after several hours the boy became worn-out, and weak, and fell to the floor and slept.

Many people went to bathe themselves in the lake that morning. As the sun rose higher, the lake became filled with swimmers. They laughed, and sported in the cool water.

When the sun reached the middle of the sky, and blazed angrily down on the earth, then nearly every soul in old Constantine was bathing in the lake.

At exactly the hottest moment of noon a disturbance began in the water. Ripples grew in circles around a certain spot near the shore, as though a stone had been thrown into the water there. The ripples widened, and became a sworl. And out of the midst of the sworl, a hand appeared, reaching up from the water. Then a second hand appeared. The two hands rose upward, reaching. The full arms appeared, hairy with greenish seaweed. And after the arms came long floating seaweed hair. A head rose from the water, and a neck, and shoulders, and the upper part of a body, all hairy with greenish seaweed. Then the head turned slowly from one side to another, and the arms reached outward, and the eyes looked into the faces of all the bathers.

The mouth moved. The voice was harsh and deep.

"One is missing!" it shouted angrily.

And the head sank back into the sea.

When the sun had gone down, and night had come, the parents opened the room where the boy lay, worn-out, sleeping. They woke him, and gave him wine to drink and dainty things to eat, and they held the feast of his thirteenth birthday.

The Book of Mysteries

WHEN the children of Horodenka ceased to sing, Israel was no longer content to remain in that place. He wandered again, and returned to the town of Okup, where he had been born. There he became the watcher of the synagogue.

The desire for knowledge came into him; and the joy that was given him by flowers and beasts in the forests was no longer sufficient. His mind was afire and thirsty, but his thirst could be quenched only by those waters that had cooled for ages deep in the deepest wells of mystery, and the fire within him was of the sort that burns forever, and does not consume.

The innermost secrets of the Cabbala were for him, and they were only as stars of night against the sun. For to him would be revealed the Secret of Secrets.

The boy lived in the synagogue. But since the time for the revelation of

---

THE BOOK OF MYSTERIES: *Ibid.*

his power was yet far away, he did not show his passion for the Torah to the men of the synagogue. By day, he slept on the benches, pretending to be a clod. But as soon as the last of the scholars blew out his candle and crept on his way toward home, Israel rose, and took the candle into a corner, and lighted it, and all night long he stood and read the Torah.

In another city the Tsadik Rabbi Adam, master of all mysteries, waited the coming of his last day. For in each generation one is chosen to carry throughout his lifetime the candle that is lighted from heaven. And the candle may never be set down. And the soul of the Tsadik may not return to eternal peace in the regions above until another such soul illuminates the earth.

Rabbi Adam was even greater than the Tsadikim who had been before him. For in the possession of Rabbi Adam was the Book that contains the Word of eternal might.

Though Rabbi Adam was not one of the Innocent souls, he had led a life so pure that this Book had been given into his hands. Before him, only six human beings had possessed the knowledge that was in the Book of Adam. The Book was given to the first man, Adam, and it was given to Abraham, to Joseph, to Joshua ben Nun, and to Solomon. And the seventh to whom it was given was the Tsadik, Rabbi Adam.

This is how he came to receive the Book.

When he had learned all Torah, and all Cabbala, he had not been content, but had searched day and night for the innermost secret of power. When he knew all the learning that there was among men, he said, "Man does not know." And he had begged of the angels.

One night Rabbi Adam arose from his sleep. He walked into a wilderness. Before him stood a mountain, and in the side of the mountain was a cave. And that was one mouth of the cave, whose other mouth was in the Holy Land. It was the cave of the Machpelah, where Abraham lies buried.

Rabbi Adam went deep into the cave, and there he found the Book.

All of his life Rabbi Adam had guarded the secret of knowledge. Gazing into it, he had grown old, and he had come to see with the grave eyes of one who sees to the end of things.

And when he saw himself growing old, he began to ask, "What will become of my wisdom?"

Then he rose, and looked to the Lord and said, "To whom, Almighty God, shall I leave the Book of Wisdom? Give me a son, that I may teach him."

He was given a son. His son grew, and became learned in the Torah. The rabbi taught his son all that there was in the Torah. And he said, "My son learns well." He began to teach his son the Cabbala. His son was sharp in understanding. But when the boy had learned the secrets of the Cabbala, he asked no more. Then the old heart of Rabbi Adam was weary and yearned for death. "My son is not the one," he said.

Night after night Rabbi Adam prayed to the Almighty that he might be relieved of the burden of knowledge. And one night the word came to him, saying, "Give the Book into the hands of Rabbi Israel, son of Eleazer, who lives in Okup."

Rabbi Adam was thankful, for now he might give over his burden, and die. He said to his son, "Here is one book in which I have not read with you."

His son asked, "Was I not worthy?"

"You are not the predestined vessel," said Rabbi Adam. "You would break with the heat of the fluid."

Then he said to his son, "Seek out Rabbi Israel, in the city of Okup, for these leaves belong to him. And if he will be favourable toward you and receive you as his servant and instruct you in his Torah, then count yourself happy. For, my son, you must know that it is your fate to be the squire who gives into the hands of his knight the sword that has been tempered and sharpened by hundreds of divine spirits that now lie silent under the earth."

Soon Rabbi Adam died. His son did not think of himself, but thought only of fulfilling the mission his father had given into his charge. He deserted the city of his birth and, taking with him the leaves of the Book, went in search of that Rabbi Israel of whom his father had spoken.

The son of Rabbi Adam came to the town of Okup. He wished to keep secret the true reason of his coming, so he said, "I am seeking a bride. I would marry, and live my life here." The people of the town were delighted, and felt greatly honoured because the son of the Tsadik, Rabbi Adam, had chosen to live among them.

Every day he went to the synagogue. There he encountered scholars, and holy men, and rabbis. He asked their names of them. But he did not meet with any one called Rabbi Israel, son of Rabbi Eleazer.

Often, when all the others had gone from the synagogue, Rabbi Adam's son remained studying the Torah. Then he noticed that the boy who served in the synagogue also remained there, he saw that the eyes of the boy were bright with inner knowledge, and that his face was strained with unworldly happiness.

Rabbi Adam's son went to the elders of the house of prayer and said to them, "Let me have a separate room in which to study. Perhaps I shall want to sleep there sometimes when I study late into the night. Then give me the boy Israel as a servant."

"Why has he chosen the boy Israel, who is a clod?" the elders asked.

Then they remembered that Israel was the son of Rabbi Eleazer. "He has chosen him to honour the memory of his father, Eleazer, who was a very holy man," they said.

When the boy came to serve him, the son of Rabbi Adam asked, "What is your name?"

"Israel, son of Eleazer."

The master watched the boy, and soon came to feel certain that this was indeed the Rabbi Israel whom he sought.

One night he remained late in the synagogue. He lay down on a bench, and pretended to be asleep. He opened his eyes a little, and he saw how the boy Israel arose and took a candle and lighted it, and covered the light, standing in a corner and studying the Torah. For many hours the boy remained motionless in an intensity of study that the rabbi had known only in his father, the Tsadik Rabbi Adam.

All night long the boy studied. And when the sunrise embraced his candle flame, he slipped down upon the bench, and slept.

Then the rabbi arose and took a leaf from the holy book his father had given him, and placed the leaf on the breast of Israel.

Soon the boy stirred, and sleeping reached his hand toward the page of writing. He held the page before his eyes, and opened his eyes and read. As he read, he rose. He bent over the page of mysteries, and studied it, and his whole face was aflame, his eyes glowed as if they had pierced into the heart of the earth, and his hands burned as if they lay against the heart of the earth.

When full day came, the boy fell powerless upon the bench, and slept.

The rabbi sat by him and watched over him until he awoke again. Then the rabbi placed his hand upon the boy's hand that held the leaf out of the book. The rabbi took the other pages of the book, and gave them to him, saying: "Know, that I place in your hands the infinite wisdom that God gave forth on Mount Sinai. The words that are in this book have been entrusted only in the hearts of the chosen of the chosen. When no soul on earth was worthy to contain its wisdom, this book lay hidden from man. For centuries it was buried in unreachable depths. But always there came the time for its uncovering, again it was brought to light, again lost. My father was the last of the great souls to whom it was entrusted. I was not found worthy of retaining it, and through my hands my father transmits this book to your hands. I beg of you, Rabbi Israel, allow me to be your servant, let me be as the air about you, absorbing your holy words, that otherwise would be lost in nothingness."

Israel answered, "Let it be so. We will go out of the city, and give ourselves over to the study of this book."

The son of Rabbi Adam went with Israel to live in a house that stood outside of the town. There, day and night, they were absorbed in the study of the pages that contained the words of all the mysteries.

Israel was as one who feeds on honey and walks on golden clouds. His soul swelled with tranquil joy, and his heart was filled with the peace of understanding. Often, he went with the leaves of the book into the forest, and there, the words of the book were as the words spoken to him by the flowers and by the beasts.

But the son of Rabbi Adam was eaten by that upon which he fed, and yet his hunger grew ever more insatiable. The grander the visions that opened before him, the greater was the cavern within himself. And he was afraid, as one who stands on a great height and looks downward.

Each day, his eyes sank deeper, and became more red.

Rabbi Israel, seeing the illness that was come into his companion, said to him, "What is it that consumes you? What is it that you desire?"

Then the son of Rabbi Adam said, "Only one thing can give me rest. All that has been revealed to me has set me flaming with a single curiosity, and each new mystery that is solved before me only causes a greater chaos in my mind, and a greater hunger in my heart."

"What is the one thing that you desire?"

"Reveal the Word to me!"

"The Word is inviolate!" cried Rabbi Israel.

But the son of Rabbi Adam fell on his knees and cried, "Until I see the end of all wisdom, I cannot come to rest! Call down the highest of powers, the Giver of the Torah Himself, force Him to come down to us, otherwise I am lost!"

Then the Master shrank from him. He said, "The hour has not yet come for His descent to earth."

His companion was silent. He never pleaded with Israel again.

But each day Rabbi Israel saw his face become darker, and his body become more feeble. The hands were weak, and could hardly turn a leaf.

Rabbi Israel was torn with pity for his companion.

At last he said, "Is it still your wish that we name the Giver of the Torah, and call Him to earth once more?"

The son of Rabbi Adam remained silent. But he lifted his eyes to the eyes of Rabbi Israel. They were as the eyes of the dead come to life.

"Then we must purify our souls, that they may reach the uttermost power of will."

On Friday, the two rabbis went to the mikweh, where they bathed in the spring of holy water. From Sabbath to Sabbath they fasted, and when they reached the height of their fast they went again to the mikweh, and purified themselves in the bath.

On the second Friday night they stood in their house of prayer. They called upon their own souls and said, "Are you pure?" Their souls answered, "We have been purified."

Then Rabbi Israel raised his hands into the darkness, and cried out the terrible Name.

The son of Rabbi Adam raised his arms aloft, and his feeble lips moved as he repeated the unknowable Word.

But in the instant that the word left those lips, Israel touched him and said, "My brother, you have made an error! Your command was wrongly uttered, it has been caught by the wind, it has been carried to the Lord of Fire! We are in the hands of death."

"I am lost," said the son of Rabbi Adam, "for I am not pure."

"Only one way is left to us," cried Rabbi Israel. "We must watch until day comes. If one of us closes an eyelid, the evil one will seize him, he is lost."

Then they began to watch. They stood guard over their souls. With their eyes open they watched. And the hours passed. They stood in prayer, and the hours passed.

But as dawn came, the son of Rabbi Adam, enfeebled by his week of purification, and by the long struggle against the darkness of night, wavered, his head nodded, and sank upon the table.

Rabbi Israel reached out his arm to raise him. But in that moment an unseen thing sped from the mouth of Rabbi Adam's son, and a flame devoured his heart, and his body sank to the ground.

The Trial of Rabbi Gershon

RABBI GERSHON of Kuth would not believe in the power of his brother-in-law. He said, "Rabbi Israel is nothing but a lime-burner come out of the mountains. He couldn't even earn a living as a tavernkeeper."

Once he went to Medzibuz to visit his sister. And he thought, "Let me see the wonder-working of this brother-in-law of mine." So he remained over the Sabbath.

On Friday afternoon he saw Rabbi Israel prepare for the Mincha prayer. "But it is still very early," said Rabbi Gershon. Nevertheless, the Master began to pray. And when Rabbi Israel came to say the benediction he remained standing motionless on his feet for four whole hours. Perspiration was upon his forehead, and his face was in an agony of labour. But at last he made an end to his prayer.

"Why did you take four hours to say the benedictions?" asked Rabbi Gershon.

"Stay until next Sabbath," said Rabbi Israel, "and I shall teach you how to say the benedictions as I say them."

Now, the truth was that when the Master said the benedictions on the eve of Sabbath, he first uttered the Word of the Will, that sundered the bonds of all dead and living souls. Then myriads of dead souls came rushing toward him out of their eternal wandering in nothingness, and begged him to put them in his prayers, so that his prayers might at last carry them into heaven.

When he uttered the words "Quicken the Dead!" he was always surrounded by these innumerable exiled souls, and it was the labour of carrying these souls into heaven that occupied him for so many hours. But at this labour he worked unceasingly, lifting the dead souls onto the wings of his powerful prayers, and sending them into heaven, until he heard the Daughter of the Voice call "Holy! Holy!" Then he knew that no more

---

THE TRIAL OF RABBI GERSHON: *Ibid.*

souls could be admitted into heaven on that day, and he made an end to his prayer.

On the following Friday afternoon the Baal Shem Tov said to his brother-in-law Rabbi Gershon, "I will tell you a word to utter before you begin the Mincha prayer. Then you will understand why I remain so many hours over the benedictions." And he whispered the secret Word of the Will to Rabbi Gershon.

Rabbi Gershon repeated the Word, and began to say Mincha.

But Rabbi Israel himself did not begin to pray. He stood and toyed with his tobacco pouch, and fingered the alms-box, and waited. He waited until Rabbi Gershon came to the words "Quicken the Dead!"

And in that instant there came a terrible rush of souls, thousands upon thousands of dead souls came flying to crowd weeping and shrieking and begging around the praying Rabbi Gershon. And Rabbi Gershon fainted with fright.

When the Baal Shem Tov had taken care of his brother-in-law, he set himself to say the benedictions, and helped those thousands of souls into heaven.

Baal-Shem and the Demon

RABBI ISRAEL BAAL-SHEM, the Master of the Ineffable Name, very much wanted to go on a pilgrimage to Jerusalem, but it was ordained from Heaven that he should not do so.

One day a demon, disguised as a man, said to him, "I know how great is your desire to journey to the Holy Land. I know for certain that once you get there God will reveal Himself to you, just as He did to the Prophets. Ah—what a blessing it is to behold the beauties of the Land of Israel! Each grain of sand, each pebble you tread upon there is holy. If you wish to go there I will reveal to you a wonderful secret. God has shown me an underground cave by means of which you can leave Miedziboz and quickly and safely reach the Holy Land."

Rabbi Israel Baal-Shem was filled with rapture when he heard this. In his excitement he failed to look closely at the stranger. Had he but done so he would have recognized that it was not a man but a demon. Instead, he hastened eagerly after him into the cave.

All day long they walked in the cave and the farther they went the darker it became.

"How much farther is it?" asked Rabbi Israel, out of breath. "I'm very tired—I'd like to rest awhile."

"Have patience," answered his guide. "Very soon we'll be in the Land of Israel. We only have to walk across the log that lies across the deep quicksands over there."

BAAL-SHEM AND THE DEMON: Adapted from a Yiddish groschen chapbook.

And, as he said this, he stepped upon the log. All he waited for was for Rabbi Israel to follow him so that he might push him into the quicksands where he would perish. Only one more instant and Rabbi Israel would have been lost for Eternity. But just as he raised his foot to place it on the log the Prophet Elijah suddenly appeared. He seized hold of his hands firmly and drew him back.

In that instant Rabbi Israel understood that his guide was a demon who had wished to mislead him and rob him of his portion of Paradise. So he intoned an incantation against him. Uttering cries of terror the demon vanished.

Elijah the Prophet then led Rabbi Israel out of the cave and brought him safely home to Miedziboz.

The Poor Wayfarer

THE great wonder-working saint, Rabbi Meier Primishlaner, blessings on his name, once related the following story:

"When I was a young man I had an irresistible desire to see Elijah the Prophet, and so I pleaded with my father to show him to me. My father replied, 'If you study the Torah with unceasing devotion you'll become worthy of seeing him.'

"I, therefore, applied myself ardently to my studies, pored over the sacred books by night and by day for four weeks. Then I went to my father and told him, 'I've done what you asked me to do, but, I assure you, the Prophet Elijah has failed to reveal himself.'

"So my father replied, 'Don't you be so impatient! If you deserve it he'll surely reveal himself to you.'

"One night, as I sat at my desk in my father's House of Study, a poor man came in. He was dusty from the road and dressed in tatters, one patch laid on the other. Moreover, he had a very ugly face. On his bent back he carried a heavy pack. As he began to put his pack down I restrained him. 'Don't you do this!' I rebuked him angrily. 'What do you take this holy place to be—a tavern?'

" 'I'm very tired!' the wayfarer pleaded. 'Let me rest here awhile, then I'll look for lodgings.'

" 'It's no use,' I told him, 'you can't rest here! My father doesn't like all kinds of tramps to come and settle themselves here with their dusty packs.'

"So the stranger sighed, lifted his pack to his shoulders, and went away.

"No sooner had he gone, than my father came in.

" 'Well, have you seen the Prophet Elijah?' he asked me.

" 'No, not yet,' I replied sadly.

" 'Was nobody here today?" he further asked.

THE POOR WAYFARER: Adapted from *Sefer Gevurath Israel*. Warsaw, 1924.

" 'Yes,' I said. 'A poor wayfarer carrying a heavy pack was here just before.'

" 'Did you say *sholom aleichem* to him?'

" 'That I didn't.'

" 'Why didn't you? Didn't you know it was Elijah? Now I'm afraid it's too late!'

"Ever since," said Rabbi Meier Primishlaner, concluding his story, "I've taken upon myself the sacred obligation to say *sholom aleichem* with a full heart to every man, no matter who he is, or how he looks, or what his station in life may be."

The Cabbalists

IN BAD times the finest merchandise loses its value, even the *Torah*—which is the best *Schoirah*. And thus of the big *Yeshiva* of Lashtshivo, there remained only the principal, Reb Yekel, and one of his students.

THE CABBALISTS: From *Bontshe the Silent*, by I. L. Peretz. Translated from the Yiddish by Angelo S. Rappoport. Stanley Paul & Co., Ltd. London, 1927.

The *yeshiva-bocher*, the Talmudic college student, was a traditional type in Jewish life. There was an unbroken continuity in the pattern of his values for almost twenty-five hundred years. The ideals of learning that animated him in the time of Rabbi Hillel during King Herod's reign were handed down like a precious legacy from generation to generation to our own days. To the *yeshiva-bocher* the study of the Torah was not merely an intellectual pursuit but a religious-ethical way of life. He was deliberately conditioned by his teachers to avoid the snares of riches and pleasure, and single-mindedly to devote his waking hours to study and to strivings of self-perfection. The Talmud itself vividly describes his hard lot in ancient times: "A morsel of bread with salt you must eat, and water by measure you must drink. You must sleep upon the ground, and live a life of trouble, the while you toil in the Torah."

Beginning with the Middle-Ages the ordeals of the student and scholar increased, rather than diminished. The material circumstances of Jewish life, strangulated by ghetto hopelessness and lack of economic opportunity, made the tribulations of the *yeshiva-bocherim* well-nigh intolerable. Sons of poor parents, who made excessive sacrifices to keep them at their studies, and having no trade or calling to help support themselves by their own efforts, they were frequently reduced to pauperism. For that reason it was considered to be an act of supreme merit *(mitzvoh)* for Jews to contribute to the support of these scholarly youths who constituted the most talented element in the community. This support, however, because of the widespread penury of the Jewish population, proved inadequate, to say the least.

From necessity the institution of *essen teg* ("eating days") arose. The unfortunate youth, struggling with his own pride, would be invited to make a circuit of a number of the kitchens of the pious and the well-to-do in the town, receiving his humble fare for one day a week in each of them. Often he was given only the table-leavings and he would suffer the pangs of hunger. He would sleep on the unyielding wooden benches in the House of Study with nothing but his threadbare *kapote* to cover him on cold winter nights. The song *Mykomashmalon* (which is in the SONGS section of this book) has superbly caught the hopelessness and gloom of the *yeshiva-bocher's* existence.

There were, of course, a few bright prospects in store for the *yeshiva-bocher*. One was that eventually his piety and learning would lead him to the respected rabbinate.

The principal is an old, lean Jew, with a long unkempt beard and extinguished eyes. Lemech, his favourite pupil, is a tall, slight, pale-faced youth, with black curly locks, sparkling, dark-rimmed eyes, dry lips, and an emaciated throat, showing the pointed Adam's apple. Both the principal and his pupil are wearing tattered garments showing their naked breasts, as they are too poor to buy shirts. With great difficulty the principal is dragging on his feet a pair of peasant's boots, whilst the student, with stockingless feet, is shuffling along in a pair of sabots much too big for him. The two alone had remained of all the inmates of the once famous *Yeshiva*.

Since the impoverished townspeople had begun to send less and less food to the *Yeshiva* and to offer fewer *days* to the students, the latter had made tracks for other towns. Reb Yekel, however, was resolved to die and be buried at Lashtshivo, whilst his favourite pupil was anxious to close his beloved master's eyes.

Both now very frequently suffer the pangs of hunger. And when you take insufficient nourishment your nights are often sleepless, and after a good many hungry days and sleepless nights you begin to feel an inclination to study the *Cabbala*. If you are already forced to lie awake at night and go hungry during the day, then why not at least derive some benefit from such a life? At least avail yourself of your long fasts and mortifications of the body to force open the gates of the invisible world and get a glimpse of all the mysteries it contains, of angels and spirits.

And thus the two had been studying the *Cabbala* for some time. They are now seated at a long table in the empty lecture-room. Other Jews had already finished their mid-day meal, but for these two it was still before breakfast! They are, however, quite used to it. His eyes half-shut, the principal is talking, whilst the pupil, his head leaning on both his hands, is listening.

"There are," the principal is saying, "four degrees of perfection. One man knows only a small portion, another a half, whilst a third knows an entire melody. The *Rebbe,* of blessed memory, knew, for instance, an entire melody. And I," he added sadly, "I have only been vouchsafed the grace of knowing but a small piece, a very small piece, just as big as——"

He was also buoyed up by the hope that he might possibly become a communal dignitary of ecclesiastical status, such as *dayyan* or a *shochet*. At the very worst he could be a humble *melamed* and, for all the poverty of that calling, he would at least have the satisfaction of teaching the word of God to children. Better yet, the outstanding *yeshiva-bocherim* were in great demand as sons-in-laws by the well-to-do. Under such favorable circumstances the young scholar would live on *kest* (he, his wife, and the family they might raise would be supported by his wife's father for several years or even permanently). This would enable him to devote most of his time to his Torah studies.

No other people has given rise to a type quite like the *yeshiva-bocher*. Jewish folklore has created a rich body of literature in which he figures, usually as the unworldly idealistic *schlimazl*. He is portrayed as being partly comical and partly pathetic, a bewildered misfit unable to adjust himself to a hurly-burly life in which his virtues prove his biggest stumbling-block.—N. A.

He measured a tiny portion of his lean and emaciated finger, and continued:

"There are melodies which require words. That is the lowest degree.
There is also a higher degree; it is a melody that requires no words, it is
sung without words—as a pure melody. But even this melody requires a
voice and lips to express itself. And the lips, you understand me, are
appertaining to *matter*. The voice itself, though a nobler and higher form
of matter, is still material in its essence. We may say that the voice is standing on the border-line between matter and spirit. Anyhow, the melody
which is still dependent upon voice and lips is not yet pure, not yet entirely
pure, not real spirit.

"The true, highest melody, however, is that which is sung without any
voice. It resounds in the interior of man, is vibrating in his heart and in
all his limbs.

"And that is how we are to understand the words of King David, when
he says in his Psalms: 'All my bones are praising the Lord.' The melody
should vibrate in the marrow of our bones, and such is the most beautiful
song of praise addressed to the Lord, blessed be His name. For such a
melody has not been invented by a being of flesh and blood; it is a portion
of that melody with which the Lord once created the Universe; it is a
part of the soul which He has breathed into His creation. It is thus that
the heavenly hosts are singing——"

The sudden arrival of a ragged fellow, a carrier, his loins girt with a
cord, interrupted the lecture. Entering the room, the messenger placed a
dish of gruel soup and a piece of bread upon the table before the *Rosh-
Yeshiva* and said in a rough voice, "Reb Tevel sends this food for the *Rosh-
Yeshiva*." Turning to the door, he added: "I will come later to fetch the
dish."

Torn away from the celestial harmonies by the sound of the fellow's
voice, the principal slowly and painfully rose from his seat and dragged
his feet in their heavy boots to the water basin near the door, where he
performed the ritual ablution of his hands. He continued to talk all the
time, but with less enthusiasm, whilst the pupil was following him with
shining, dreamy eyes, and straining his ears.

"I have not even been found worthy," said the principal sadly, "to know
the degree at which this can be attained, nor do I know through which of
the celestial gates it enters. You see," he added with a smile, "I know well
enough the necessary mortifications and prayers, and I will communicate
them to you even to-day."

The eyes of the student are almost starting out of their sockets, and his
mouth is wide open; he is literally swallowing every word his master is
uttering. But the master interrupts himself. He performs the ritual ablution of his hands, dries them, and recites the prescribed benediction; he
then returns to the table and breaking off a piece of bread, recites with
trembling lips the prescribed blessing. His shaking hands now seize the
dish, and the moist vapour covers his emaciated face. He puts down the

dish upon the table, takes the spoon into his right hand, whilst warming his left at the edge of the dish; all the time he is munching in his toothless mouth the morsel of bread over which he had said a blessing.

When his face and hands were warm enough, he wrinkled his brow and extending his thin, blue lips, began to blow. The pupil was staring at him all the time. But when the trembling lips of the old man were stretching out to meet the first spoonful of soup, something squeezed the young man's heart. Covering his face with his hands, he seemed to have shrivelled up.

A few minutes had scarcely elapsed when another man came in, also carrying a basin full of gruel soup and a piece of bread.

"Reb Yoissef sends the student his breakfast," he said.

The student never removed his hands from his face. Putting down his own spoon, the principal rose and went up to him. For a moment he looked down at the boy with eyes full of pride and love; then touching his shoulder, he said in a friendly and affectionate voice, "They have brought you food."

Slowly and unwillingly the student removed his hands from his face. He seemed to have grown paler still, and his dark-rimmed eyes were burning with an even more mysterious fire.

"I know, Rabbi," he said, "but I am not going to eat to-day."

"Are you going to fast the fourth day?" asked the *Rosh-Yeshiva*, greatly surprised. "And without me?" he added in a somewhat hurt tone.

"It is a particular fast-day," replied the student. "I am fasting to-day for penance."

"What are you talking about? Why must you do penance?"

"Yes, Rabbi, I must do penance, because a while ago, when you had just started to eat, I transgressed the commandment which says, 'Thou shalt not covet——' "

Late in the night the student woke up his master. The two were sleeping side by side on benches in the old lecture-hall.

"*Rebbe, Rebbe!*" called the student in a feeble voice.

"What is the matter?" The *Rosh-Yeshiva* woke with a start.

"Just now, I have been upon the highest summit."

"How's that?" asked the principal, not yet quite awake.

"There was a melody, and it has been singing in me."

The principal sat up.

"How's that? How's that?"

"I don't know it myself, *Rebbe*," answered the student in an almost inaudible voice. "As I could not find sleep I plunged myself into your lecture. I was anxious at any cost to learn that melody. Unable, however, to succeed, I was greatly grieved and began to weep. Everything in me was weeping, all my members were weeping before the Creator of the Universe. I recited the prayers and formulas you taught me; strange to say, not with my lips, but deep down in my heart. And suddenly I was dazzled by a great light. I closed my eyes, yet I could not shut out the light around me, a powerful dazzling light."

"That's it," said the old man leaning over.

"And in the midst of the strange light I felt so strong, so light-hearted. It seemed to me as if I had no weight, as if my body had lost its heaviness and that I could fly."

"That's right; that's right."

"And then I felt so merry, so happy and lively. My face remained motionless, my lips never stirred, and yet I laughed. I laughed so joyously, so heartily, so frankly and happily."

"That's it; that's it. That is right, in the intensest joy——"

"Then something began to hum in me, as if it were the beginning of a melody."

The *Rosh-Yeshiva* jumped up from his bench and stood up by his pupil's side.

"And then? And then?"

"Then I heard how it was singing in me."

"And what did you feel? What? What? Tell me!"

"I felt as if all my senses were closed and stopped; and there was something singing in me, just as it should be, without either words or tunes, only so——"

"How? How?"

"No, I can't say. At first I knew, then the song became——"

"What did the song become? What——?"

"A sort of music, as if there had been a violin in me, or as if Yoineh, the musician, was sitting in my heart and playing one of the tunes he plays at the *Rebbe's* table. But it sounded much more beautiful, nobler and sadder, more spiritual; and all this was voiceless and tuneless, mere spirit."

"You lucky man——!"

"And now it is all gone," said the pupil, growing very sad. "My senses have again woke up, and I am so tired, so terribly tired that I. . . . *Rebbe!*" the student suddenly cried, beating his breast. "*Rebbe,* recite with me the confession of the dying. They have come to fetch me; they require a new choir-boy in the celestial choir. There is a white-winged angel— *Rebbe—Rebbe—Shmah Yisroel, Shmah——*"

Everybody in the town wished to die such a death, but the *Rosh-Yeshiva* found that it was not enough.

"Another few fast-days," he said, "and he would have died quite a different death. He would have died by a Divine Kiss."

The Rabbi Who Wished to Abolish Death

IT CHANCED once that a great calamity almost befell the Angel of Death.

THE RABBI WHO WISHED TO ABOLISH DEATH: Adapted from the *Agada* in the Talmud. Henry Wadsworth Longfellow retold this Talmudic tale in the poem, *The Legend of Rabbi Ben Levi,* in *Tales of a Wayside Inn.*

He came pretty near losing the knife with which he severs the life of man.

When Rabbi Joshua ben Levi was at the point of death the Angel of Death came to see him.

"Show me first my place in Paradise," pleaded Rabbi Joshua. "That will make it easier for me to depart from this life."

"Come, I will show you," answered the Angel of Death.

And so they ascended to the celestial regions.

On the way, Rabbi Joshua said to the Angel of Death, "Do give me your knife. I am afraid that you will frighten me with it while we are on the way."

The Angel of Death felt pity for him and gave him his knife.

When they at last arrived in Paradise the Angel of Death showed Rabbi Joshua the place reserved for him. A great yearning then seized Rabbi Joshua and he sprang forward within the Gates. But the Angel of Death seized hold of him by the skirts of his garment and tried to pull him back.

Having the knife in his possession Rabbi Joshua refused to budge from his place.

"I swear I will not leave Paradise!" he cried.

Thereupon, a great tumult was heard among the angels. It seemed very much as if death was about to be abolished from the world and people would be able to live forever, like the angels.

The Angel of Death stood in a great quandary. "What to do now?" he wondered.

The holy man had solemnly sworn that he would not leave Paradise, and who could violate the oath of such a man? So the Angel of Death went to complain to God Himself. And God said, "I decree that Rabbi Joshua must return to earth. His time has not come yet."

The Angel of Death came again to Rabbi Joshua and demanded in a terrible voice, "Give me back my knife!"

"I will not give it back to you!" cried Rabbi Joshua. "I want to abolish Death forever!"

Suddenly the Voice of God was heard sternly commanding, "Return the knife, Joshua! Man must continue to die!"

Asking for the Impossible

IN THE days of Rabbi Isaac Luria, or as he was better known, *Ari Hakodesh,* "the Holy Lion," there lived in a certain country a king whose feet rested heavily on the necks of the Jews in his kingdom.

One day, he issued a royal proclamation ordering the Jews to raise for him an enormous sum of money in a very short time. Should they fail to carry out his command fully he threatened to drive them out of his kingdom.

ASKING FOR THE IMPOSSIBLE: Adapted from *Maaseh Nissim Shel-ha-Ari* (Story of the Miracles of the *Ari*). 1720.

When the Jews read the king's proclamation they rent their garments, strewed ashes upon their heads and went into mourning. Fervently they prayed to God to intercede for them and rescue them from certain disaster. For the Jews were very poor. Where could they get the money the king asked for? In their extremity they thought of "the Holy Lion." So they sent two messengers to him in Safed where he lived.

Blessed with fair winds the ship that carried the two messengers arrived safely in the Land of Israel. They journeyed by caravan to Safed without rest and reached the city late Friday, just before the holy Sabbath was ushered in.

Without loss of time they called on the Master of the Cabala. They found him attired in spotless white robes and surrounded by worshipful disciples. His face shone as radiantly as the springtime sun and he had the appearance of an angel of God.

"What brings you to Safed?" he asked the two messengers.

They answered: "We have come to ask for your intercession with God in order that we may not perish from the earth."

And they told him of the mortal danger they and all their brethren in the distant kingdom were in.

When they had spoken the Seer replied, "It is a sin to desecrate the peace of the Sabbath with sad thoughts. Remain with me until tomorrow night, then you will depart. Banish all fear and be carefree, for God never abandons the righteous."

When the following evening came and Rabbi Isaac Luria had finished blessing the departing Sabbath-Bride, he turned to his disciples and to the two messengers and said:

"Take with you a long rope and follow me."

So they all did as he bade them and followed him into the fields. At last he stopped before a deep pit and commanded:

"Lower the rope into the bottom of this pit and hold fast to the end."

The disciples and the messengers did as he told them.

"Now pull with all your might!" he ordered.

Filled with wonder they pulled on the rope and felt a great weight below. When they had drawn the object to the surface they were startled to see that it was a magnificent couch. They could hardly believe their own eyes at what they saw: on it lay a king fast asleep.

Rabbi Isaac went up to the sleeper and shook him, crying, "Are you the hard-hearted ruler who so cruelly oppresses the Jews in his kingdom?"

"I am," answered the king, quaking in every limb.

"Get up, then!" sternly commanded the holy man.

The king got out of bed; his face was full of fear. Rabbi Isaac then handed him a dipper that had no bottom and said, "Empty the well with this dipper. I expect you to be through with your task before dawn."

When the king saw that this dipper had no bottom he wailed, "Even were I to live a thousand years I wouldn't be able to empty the well with this useless dipper!"

Score with

New Method
CLEANERS
LAUNDERERS

Call 37-222

CANASTA TALLY

BONUS					
POINTS					
TOTAL					
BONUS					
POINTS					
TOTAL					
BONUS					
POINTS					
TOTAL					
BONUS					
POINTS					
TOTAL					

Good Appearance Pays

"Since you recognize that what I've asked you to do is impossible to accomplish—why then do you ask the impossible of the poor Jews in your kingdom?"

The king lowered his eyes and murmured, "You are right—I will withdraw my command. Only spare my life!"

"You must guarantee your assurance to me with your signet-ring," answered Rabbi Isaac.

And the king did as he was asked.

The following morning, when the king awoke from his sleep, he thought he had dreamt it all.

"What a frightful dream that was!" he shuddered. "Dreams are nothing but lies."

And he dismissed the matter from his mind.

When the day finally came for the Jews to bring the required sum of money the two messengers came before the king. They showed him his rescinding order with his signature. He recognized his seal and said, "It is my signature."

Then he gave them presents and let them depart in peace.

Rashi and Godfrey of Bouillon

IN THE days of the great scholar, Rabbi Solomon ben Isaac (Rashi), there lived in France the famous Godfrey de Bouillon. He was a brave man and a hero in battle, but he was also a destructive, cruel man. The repute of Rabbi Solomon's wisdom was spread over the land and also reached the ears of Godfrey. The prince tried his utmost to draw Rabbi Solomon into his service but to no avail; the scholar refused to leave his home.

Angered by the rabbi's stubbornness, Godfrey, accompanied by his men-at-arms, hastened to the town where the rabbi lived. He came before the House of Study and found all the doors wide open. The holy books lay open on the rabbi's desk yet he was nowhere to be seen.

"Solomon, Solomon!" Godfrey cried out in a loud voice.

The scholar replied, "What do you want of me, my lord?"

But, wondrous to relate, although Godfrey could hear his voice he could not see him.

"Where are you?" he asked him.

"I am right here," Rabbi Solomon replied.

"Why don't you reveal yourself in the flesh?"

"I am afraid of you."

"Don't fear me," Godfrey begged him. "I promise to do you no harm."

Hearing these words, Rabbi Solomon made himself visible before Godfrey.

RASHI AND GODFREY OF BOUILLON: Adapted from *Shalshelet ha-Cabala* (Chain of the Cabala), by Gedaliah ben Yachya (1515–87).

"Now you have convinced me of your wisdom about which I have heard so much," said Godfrey. "I am going to tell you of the great plans I have made. My wish is to conquer Jerusalem from the Saracens. I have at my command two hundred large ships and one hundred thousand horsemen. There are also seven thousand horsemen in Akron who are ready to join my standard. With these forces I expect to crush the Saracens who are expert in the art of war. Therefore tell me, what do you think of my outlook for victory and don't be afraid to speak your mind."

Rabbi Solomon answered, "You will conquer Jerusalem but will rule over it only three days. On the fourth day the Saracens will rout you, and you will escape with only three horsemen."

Hearing this Godfrey of Bouillon was very angry.

"Beware, Jew!" he cried. "Should I return with four horsemen I will throw your carcass to the dogs and kill all Jews in the kingdom."

In the end it happened exactly as Rabbi Solomon foretold, but with one important exception: Godfrey of Bouillon returned, not with three but with four horsemen. He therefore gloated over the prospect of revenging himself on the scholar.

As Godfrey reached the town where Rabbi Solomon lived, a stone fell from the lintel of the gate and killed one of the four horsemen and his mount. At this Godfrey was filled with fear; he understood now, that with his great wisdom Rabbi Solomon had foreseen everything. Therefore, he went in search of him in order that he might do him homage.

But in the meantime the scholar had gone to join his forefathers and Godfrey grieved after him.

Rabbi Amram's Rhine Journey

THE teacher Rabbi Amram left his home town of Mayence for Cologne. There he opened a Talmudic college.

As the years passed and he grew old and infirm he saw that he no longer had the required strength to return to the town of his birth. Therefore, he instructed his students that, upon his death, they were to carry his body to Mayence and there bury it beside the graves of his forefathers. The students remarked that such a journey was charged with great danger for them.

RABBI AMRAM'S RHINE JOURNEY: *Ibid.*

The medieval Amram legend is undoubtedly an analogue of the legend about St. Emmeram. The Seventh Century German saint, upon his death in Munich, had been placed in an unattended barge and the tide, with incredible speed, carried it from the Isar River up the Danube to the town of Regensburg. In commemoration of this miracle, Emmeram was canonized and a church, bearing his name, was erected outside the town. The transformation of the name Emmeram to Amram was not a too difficult matter to effect. It is also significant to note that in several Jewish versions, Amram is referred to as "Rabbi Amram of Regensburg." But, except for the legend, nothing is known of him bearing on his historicity.—N. A.

To this Rabbi Amram answered, "Purify my body after I die. Lay it in a coffin and then place the coffin in a small boat. Let the boat loose and it will drift with the tide up the River Rhine. In this way it will reach its right destination."

The time came at last when the soul departed from Rabbi Amram and his students went to fulfill their promise. They placed his coffin in a boat and set it adrift on the stream.

When the river-boatmen saw the strange bark with the coffin they understood that it carried a holy man whom they were duty-bound to lay in a grave in their town. So they stretched out their hands to pull the boat in, but, to their astonishment, the vessel glided backwards out of their reach. In this they saw the hand of God so they went to report the incident to the authorities.

When news of this got abroad multitudes came swarming to the river edge to see the extraordinary sight. Among them were also several Jews.

Once more the river-boatmen tried to lay their hands on the boat, but again the tiny craft glided away from them. It floated for a little distance until it reached the spot where the Jews stood.

Seeing this the authorities said to them, "Get into the boat and put an end to this mystery."

The Jews reached out their hands and the boat swiftly glided towards them. They climbed into it and pried open the lid of the coffin. There they saw the body of the sage and on it lay a scroll with Hebrew writing. It read: "Dear brothers and friends, members of the Holy Community of Mayence: I come to you from Cologne where I departed this life. I beg of you—bury me near where my forefathers lie."

At this the Jews went into mourning. They drew the coffin from the boat and placed it beside the bank of the Rhine. But the Christian burghers of Mayence wouldn't permit the coffin of the holy man to remain in the hands of the Jews, so they drove them away. They then tried to carry away the dead man in order to give him proper burial, but they could not lift the coffin. So they placed watchmen to guard it and on the very spot they erected a chapel which they henceforth called the Chapel of Amram.

In vain the Jews implored the authorities to return to them the body of Rabbi Amram.

Every night thereafter the spirit of Rabbi Amram appeared to his former students in Mayence in a dream.

"Bury me where my forefathers lie!" he begged them.

The students held counsel with one another in order that they might do their departed rabbi's urgent bidding.

One dark night they went and cut down the body of a criminal that hung on a tree outside the town. They drew Rabbi Amram's shroud on him and laid him in his place in the coffin. The holy man they bore to the Jewish cemetery and laid him to eternal rest according to the rites and customs of the Jews.

The Hidden Saint

IN THE holy city of Safed lived one of the *Lamed-Vav-Tzaddikim* * one of the thirty-six secret saints. He was very poor, but he shared his crust with those who were even poorer than he. Yet he wished to disguise his virtue so that no one might say he was good and cause him to fall into the error of self-righteousness.

As the Passover holidays came near this meek saint fell gravely ill and was no longer able to earn his crust. His wife and children now suffered hunger. There seemed no chance at all that they would have the money to buy *matzos* and wine. And, since they were proud, no one knew of their plight. But the saint consoled his household, "Have faith in God —He raises up the fallen!"

No one in Safed knew of the holy man's trials except Rabbi Isaac Luria, "The Holy Lion," the Master of the secret wisdom of the Cabala. He took off his white garments of sanctity and put on a wayfarer's dusty clothes. With wanderer's staff in hand and a knapsack on his back he went forth to aid the hidden saint.

For a while he passed to and fro before the hidden saint's dwelling. Finally, when the good man came out, he saw standing before him a dusty traveller.

"*Sholom aleichem!*" the traveller greeted him.

"*Aleichem sholom!*" answered the saint. "Are you looking for someone?"

"No, but I'm in trouble," sighed the stranger. "I have no place to spend the holy Passover."

"I've nothing to give you, but you're welcome to stay with me," answered the saint.

The traveller was grateful and rejoiced in his good fortune.

THE HIDDEN SAINT: Adapted from a Yiddish groschen chapbook.

* The thirty-six hidden saints, referred to in Hebrew as *Lamed-Vav-Tzaddikim* and in Yiddish as *Lamedvovniks*. This widely-held belief among pious Jews is based on the opinion stated by Rabbi Abaye in the Talmud: "There are in the world not less than thirty-six righteous persons in every generation upon whom the *Shekhina* [God's radiance] rests." This became a popular theme for folk-legends among the Sixteenth and Seventeenth Century cabalists and, beginning in the second half of the Eighteenth Century, with the *Hasidim* of Eastern Europe as well.

The *lamedvovniks* are described by legend as being so modest and upright that they invariably conceal their virtue behind a mask of boorishness, poverty and ignorance. They live humbly and unobtrusively and, following the example of the Talmudic sages and saints of Israel, they earn their livelihood by the sweat of their brow, as tailors, shoemakers, blacksmiths, etc. The Jews in whose midst they live never suspect their true identity, and whenever this is accidentally exposed, the *lamedvovniks* rudely deny it. However, when danger threatens the Jewish people, the *lamedvovnik* emerges from his self-imposed concealment and, by the cabalistic powers he possesses, averts the threatened misfortune to the discomfiture of all of Israel's plotting enemies. That accomplished, he returns once more to his humble anonymity, but elsewhere, in a Jewish community where he is unknown.—N. A.

"Here are a hundred *dinar*," he said to the saint. "Prepare the Passover feast!"

"What is your name?" asked the hidden saint in amazement.

"Rabbi Nissim they call me," the stranger replied.

On the first night of Passover the saint sat down to read the *Seder* service that tells of the liberation of the Jews from their bondage in Egypt, but he would not begin without the stranger who had not returned yet from the synagogue. He waited and waited, but in vain. Rabbi Nissim seemed to have disappeared. Suddenly, in a flash of illumination, the identity of the stranger became clear to him. No doubt the good Lord had sent an angel from Heaven to help him in his need!

Yet, neither he nor any one else knew that this Rabbi Nissim (Miracles) was none other than *The Holy Lion*, the *Ari* himself.

MESSIAH STORIES

INTRODUCTION

There is no agreement in Jewish tradition as to when and where the Messiah will come. One belief is that when men grow hopelessly bad that will be the time to expect his coming. Another belief is that he will come only when misfortune will rise up and sweep over Israel like the sea at flood-tide. Still another view is that the Son of David will come to that generation which will repent of its evil ways and become thoroughly righteous.

Once, two sages of the Talmud, Rabbi Hai the Great and Rabbi Simeon ben Halafta, were travelling all night in the valley of Arbal. As the first rays of the sun shot over the rim of the horizon Rabbi Hai was filled with rapture. "Rabbi," he cried to his companion, "this will be the way the Jewish Redemption will come, like the rising sun, gradually, slowly, until it will appear in the sky in all its dazzling radiance."

The longing for the Messiah's coming was the golden dream of the Jewish people through the ages. The greater its suffering, the more unendurable its persecution—the more compelling became its escape drive to the mysticism of the Cabala. Where it could not cope with the problems of life by ordinary means its desperation led it to reach out to the super-natural, like day-dreaming children. By invoking the magical yet ever elusive powers supposed to reside in the hidden wisdom of the Cabala, they hoped to bring an end to their Exile and to their suffering. To hasten the coming of the Messiah and the Redemption of Israel became, therefore, the single-minded objective of all cabalists, including some of the Eighteenth Century *Hasidic tzaddikim*.

The Messiah quest of the Cabalists is nowhere as strikingly projected as in the legend of Joseph della Reyna. It is the Golden Legend of the cabalists and is imbued with a lofty altruism. Considered in relation to the spirit and the culture of the times, the cabalists, by and large, were men of selfless and pure intention. To hasten the Redemption they were ready to offer every personal sacrifice, even to the extent of life itself.

Of all the legends of the cabalists that of Joseph della Reyna is the most dramatic. For many generations it has stirred the imagination and emotions of the Jewish folk-mind, for it articulates its ages-old longing for the Messiah. The Messianic tradition is the most fundamental and pervasive in Jewish religious thought. It poignantly reflects the frustration of the life-force of a whole people for many centuries. To the discerning reader it soon becomes clear that, behind all the medieval magical trappings of the legend of Joseph della Reyna, so natural to a superstitious age, there shines forth a moving ethical doctrine that is imbued with a compassion and a selfless love for mankind.

N. A.

Joseph della Reyna Storms Heaven

SEEING that there were in Jerusalem so many pious men who sought God and loved truth, Rabbi Joseph della Reyna came to a firm decision:

"It is high time to force the coming of the Messiah!"

He knew full well that it would not be an easy thing to accomplish. None the less, he remained hopeful that where others had failed he would succeed.

Among his disciples there were five who were pure in heart and in intention. They were cabalists who had delved deeply into the secret truths of the *Zohar*. Night and day they sat with Rabbi Joseph over their sacred studies. It was to them that he revealed all the hidden wisdom of this world and the next. Together they would grieve and lament over the Exile of the *Shekhina* * and over the sorrows of the Jewish people in dispersion.

Once, as they sat studying the Cabala with deep inner rapture, Rabbi Joseph paused and said to the five disciples, "Know, that I have given much thought about you and have gone through great inner searching about myself. The Lord has blessed us with wisdom and knowledge. We have acquired a greater mastery of the Cabala than have all those who have come before us. To us have been revealed all the innermost secrets of the Torah. By its power we are capable of performing the greatest wonders. For these reasons I have come to the conclusion that it is our duty to use these exceptional powers for great ends. We are able to accomplish something that will be sure to create a tremendous stir on earth and in heaven.

"My beloved sons, it is our sacred duty to drive all evil from the world, to hasten the coming of the Messiah, to redeem the Jewish people and to bring back the Holy *Shekhina* from its long Exile.

"Don't think I have arrived at my decision lightly. I have concerned myself with this matter for a long time and have drawn up my plans in

---

JOSEPH DELLA REYNA STORMS HEAVEN: Adapted from a Yiddish groschen chapbook.
* God's radiance, or emanation, a neo-Platonic concept.

detail. But because it is difficult for one individual to accomplish such a tremendous task I therefore require your help."

The five disciples answered as with one voice, "Holy Rabbi! We are eager to do everything necessary in order to help you in this great work. We know that God, blessed be His Name, is with you, and we hope that you will succeed in achieving your goal."

When Rabbi Joseph della Reyna heard this he rejoiced greatly and said to them, "We must now make ready for our holy task. Go, therefore, and bathe, put on clean raiment, and for three days and three nights thereafter you must keep your bodies and souls pure and holy. After that you will prepare food and drink to last a long time. On the third day we will go forth into the wilderness. We cannot return until we have successfully carried out our mission."

The disciples then went about making their preparations with great inner trembling. Their spirits, too, were filled with a sacred flame and longing to accomplish their task. So they bathed and made themselves clean. They put on white raiment and renounced all worldly interests. They preserved their bodies and their thoughts in purity and holiness. They also prepared ample provisions for the long journey.

On the third day they came to Rabbi Joseph della Reyna. When they arrived they found Rabbi Joseph in deep thought; a dazzling radiance streamed from his face. He was praying with such deep ecstasy that his soul seemed to have risen aloft from this world of sin. It soared upwards into the highest regions of Heaven.

When Rabbi Joseph saw his disciples he greeted them with the tenderness of a father.

"Come to me, my beloved disciples," he said. "You have done what I have asked of you. You are now worthy of helping me in my sacred task. God, blessed be He, will most assuredly show us the way. He will help us reach our goal by the power of His Holy Name."

"Amen!" the disciples answered fervently.

Their souls became intertwined with his and rose up from the sinful world, winging their way to the pure celestial regions.

Rabbi Joseph also had completed his preparations. Besides food and drink, he took along with him a writing quill and parchment.

"Let us go!" he said to his disciples.

And then they started out on their quest.

At last they came to Meron and prayed at the grave of Rabbi Simeon ben Yohai, the teacher of all cabalists, the author of the *Zohar*.

They spent three days and three nights there. They neither ate nor slept but delved into the mysteries of the *Zohar* and sent up flaming prayers to God.

On the third day, when dawn began to break, Rabbi Joseph suddenly ended his vigil and fell asleep. This filled his disciples with alarm. Could it be that the master's spirit was blemished with weakness? But they held their peace and did not say a word.

As Rabbi Joseph slept he dreamed that Rabbi Simeon ben Yohai and his son Eleazer came and reproved him: "How rash of you to have undertaken such a terrifying task as this! Be forewarned: you will fail miserably in your attempt! You will be beset by insuperable difficulties and dangers. You cannot emerge out of this alive and, having failed, your souls will be condemned to everlasting purgatory. However, since you are resolute in your decision, let us caution you to be discreet in your speech and in your actions, so that those evil spirits who wish to do you harm may not have any power over you."

"Almighty God, blessed be His Name, knows my pure intention," replied Rabbi Joseph. "He knows full well that what I am doing is not for my selfish ends but for the good of all the Jews and of all mankind. Therefore, He will help me achieve my goal in order that I may sanctify His Name among all the peoples of the earth."

The souls of Rabbi Simeon ben Yohai and his son Eleazer then gave their blessings to Rabbi Joseph.

"May God help and keep you wherever you may turn!" they prayed.

Rabbi Joseph awoke and told his disciples what he had dreamed. They then understood that he had fallen asleep by the Will of God, and that it was not due to weakness of spirit.

Then they arose and continued on their way.

Not far from Tiberias they came to a large forest and remained there all day. They tasted neither food nor drink for they wished to purify their bodies and spirits from earthly taint.

The beauty of the forest enveloped them. Cool green trees wafted their fragrance everywhere. The birds sat in the branches trilling their songs of joy to the Creator. But Rabbi Joseph and his disciples neither saw nor heard them out of fear that sensuous thoughts might snare them away from their sacred mission.

All day long they delved into the profoundest mysteries of Cabala, studied the sacred formulae, calculated *gematriot* * and drew mystic designs of God's ten emanations, the *Sefirot*.

This they did for two days and neither ate nor drank, all the time remaining apart from the earth and from its pleasures. Thirty-three times a day they purified their bodies in the Sea of Galilee and each time they repeated the holy formulae and incantations.

At the end of each day they broke their fast. But they tasted neither fish nor flesh. They ate only bread and water, but not too much of that, only enough to keep alive.

On the afternoon of the third day Rabbi Joseph and his disciples recited

---

* Cabalistic cryptographs which give, instead of the intended words, their numerical value. According to cabalistic theory, the twenty-two letters of the Hebrew alphabet possess dynamic and supernatural powers. Since the essence of things is number, the cabalist seeks the reduction of everything—objects, names, even ideas—to number.

the *Mincha* prayers with great fervor and, as they stood silently pronouncing the eighteen benedictions, their thoughts dwelled with utmost concentration on the secret mysteries of the Cabala.

Rabbi Joseph della Reyna then prayed by himself. He invoked all the angels and seraphim to come to his aid. By the power of the Cabala he invoked the Prophet Elijah to make his appearance before him.

"O Elijah," he exhorted. "Come to me and teach me how I should behave so that I may carry through the plan I have undertaken!"

No sooner had he finished praying than Elijah appeared.

"Tell me what it is you wish and I will teach it to you," he promised.

"Forgive me, Holy Prophet, for troubling you," Rabbi Joseph replied. "Believe me, it is not for my own glory and not for that of my ancestors but for the glory of God, blessed be His Name, and of His people and of His Holy Torah. I believe I deserve your help. Show me the way I can triumph over Satan and his hosts. Show me how I can make holiness triumph over evil and thus bring redemption to all mankind."

Elijah the Prophet grew sad.

"I wish to warn you," he said, "that you have taken upon yourself a task that no human being can accomplish. In order to vanquish Satan and his demons you and your disciples must become holier and purer than you are. I might say that to triumph over Satan you will have to become like the very angels. Your aim, of course, is an exalted one and, should you succeed, you will be the happiest man on earth for you will have brought redemption to the whole world. Nevertheless, I warn you that you are attempting something beyond your human strength. Take my advice —abandon your plan!"

Thereupon Rabbi Joseph began to weep.

"Dear Prophet of God," he pleaded. "How can I give up what I have started? Do not abandon me now! It is too late for me to turn back. I have sworn before God that I will not rest until I have driven Satan from the earth and have brought Messiah, the Redeemer of the Jewish people and of all peoples. I will not rest until I have restored the *Shekhina* to the glory it possessed when the Temple still stood in Jerusalem. For these ends I am eager to sacrifice my life. Know that I will not let you go until you help me and show me the right path to follow and the right course to take."

As the Prophet Elijah looked upon Rabbi Joseph della Reyna he was filled with a great compassion for him.

"Dry your tears, dear son," he said. "I will help you in whatever way I can to fulfill your task. You and your disciples must continue fasting for twenty-one days, nor must you touch any impure thing. When you break your fast at night eat only a morsel of bread, just enough to keep alive. In addition, you must bathe twenty-one times in the Sea of Galilee so that you become pure and holy like the angels. And, when the twenty-one days are up, you must enter into a fast which will last three days and three nights. At the end of the third day you must recite the *Mincha* prayers wearing *talith* and *tefillin*. After that you must recite the verse: 'Flaming angels surround the Holy One, blessed be He!' After that you must invoke the Angel Sandalfon by means of cabalistic formulae. Thereupon, he and his angel hosts will appear immediately.

"Be prepared with strong spices for the coming of these angels, so that they might revive you from the terror into which you will fall when you perceive the holy fire and the mighty whirlwind which will come in the wake of the Heavenly Host. Remember, when they appear you must fall upon your faces and recite the verse: 'Praised be His Name whose glorious kingdom is forever and ever!'

"After that the mighty Angel Sandalfon will reveal himself to you. You must then ask him what you should do in order to drive the spirit of evil from the world.

"If you do as I bid, and provided Almighty God wills it so, then you will be able to bring the Redemption for all the world."

After having blessed Rabbi Joseph and his disciples the Prophet Elijah vanished.

And Rabbi Joseph della Reyna and his five disciples did all that the Prophet Elijah had told them. When their fasting, vigils, prayers and austerities were over, a terrifying tumult arose in Heaven. The Angel Sandalfon with his host of seraphim swept down upon the earth amidst a whirlwind and with a pillar of flame before them. Seeing them, Rabbi Joseph and his disciples became faint with fear and fell upon their faces. But they smelled the strong spices and their energies returned.

Then they cried out: "Praised be His Name whose glorious kingdom is forever and ever!" Only then did they dare to look upon the angels clothed in flame and splendor.

The Angel Sandalfon now spoke and his voice sounded like the low muttering of thunder, "O sinful mortals! Where did you get the strength and the insolence to cause such a turmoil in all the Seven Heavens? How dare you trouble me and the Hosts of Heaven to descend to the sinful earth? I bid you desist from this madness!"

So great was the terror of Rabbi Joseph that he lost the power of speech. Finally he fortified his spirit and replied, "Holy Angel Sandalfon! Believe me, I have not done this for my glory but for the glory of the Creator, blessed be His Name, for the glory of the Holy Torah, for the glory of the grandchildren of Abraham, Isaac and Jacob! Forgive me my insolence, for I could not help myself.

"I could no longer look on the suffering of my people in Exile. I could no longer stand by watching our enemies trampling us underfoot in the dust. My only aim is to drive away the impure demons who defile the world, who dim the holy flame of our faith. I wish to return the *Shekhina* to the ancient luster it had when the Temple still stood in Jerusalem. Let God be my witness that my intention is pure and my course upright!

"Therefore, O Holy Angel, I beg you to help me! Show me the right path, teach me the right course, so that I can bring the Messiah, the Redeemer, down on earth!"

The Angel Sandalfon was filled with compassion as he looked upon Rabbi Joseph della Reyna.

"May God be with you until you reach your goal!" he cried. "Rest assured that all angels in Heaven are in agreement that the Messiah should come and bring the Redemption for the Jewish people who suffer in Exile. Yet I must warn you that you have undertaken a very difficult task, for Satan and the demons have untold power. Even we, the angels, cannot vanquish them. Only if God Himself stands by you will you be able to achieve your aim. But how can you expect God to support you unless He believes that the right time has come for the Messiah?

"Again I must warn you: your path is full of folly. Should you fail you might make matters even worse, you might hand the victory to Satan and he will become more arrogant and do greater evil than hitherto to mankind."

Rabbi Joseph's heart overflowed with bitterness. Alas! Even the mighty Angel Sandalfon would not help him!

In the meantime, the five disciples lay prostrate upon the ground, their faces hidden in terror.

"Rise up—rise up!" cried Rabbi Joseph. "Unite with me in prayer! Perhaps all together we will able to soften the hearts of the angels and they will agree to help us in our great work."

Once again Rabbi Joseph della Reyna pleaded with the Angel Sandalfon, "Help me, show me the right way!"

Sadly the Angel Sandalfon replied, "If I have come to you it is because you forced me by pronouncing the Ineffable Name, but alas, I cannot help you! I myself do not know the means by which you can triumph over Satan and the demons. My one duty is to guard the way along which the prayers of the righteous mount to Heaven and to bring them before the Throne of God. I have no power over Satan and do not know whether I can pit my strength against his.

"However, if you are so desperately determined to achieve your goal you must call upon the Angel Metatron and his hosts. They have been assigned by God to prevent Satan from growing stronger. Yet, I doubt very much whether you will be able to bring this great angel down to you. He resides in the Seventh Heaven right next to the Heavenly Throne. Therefore, not every prayer can penetrate up to him. Even should he hear you, I doubt whether you and your disciples will be able to survive the terror of his presence. Know that he appears as a pillar of fire and that his face is more dazzling than the sun. Therefore, I beg of you: abandon your plan, for it is madness!"

Still Rabbi Joseph would not submit.

"I know," said he brokenly, "that I am weak and insignificant. I know that it is impudence on my part to dare talk with angels and to contradict them. But I hope that the Ruler of the World, reading my heart, will not spurn my prayer and will aid me in the work that I have undertaken. O Angel of the World, help me! Tell me how I can bring the Angel Metatron down to earth."

"Since you insist," replied the Angel Sandalfon, "you and your disciples must do the following: You must fast forty more days and purify yourself twenty-one times each day in the Sea of Galilee. You must study Cabala and say your prayers incessantly. Both by day and by night must you purify your thoughts. You must eat still less than you have hitherto, and live on spices alone. After that you must recite the Ineffable Name formed by seventy-two letters and call upon Metatron, the Angel of this mystic name, to appear before you."

The Angel Sandalfon then gave Rabbi Joseph and his disciples his blessing, "May your spirits be strong and survive the terror of Metatron's presence!"

Then, followed by his hosts of Angels, he mounted to Heaven in a whirl-wind.

The stubbornness of Rabbi Joseph della Reyna aroused all the angels in Heaven. Nothing was spoken of but his daring attempt to bring the Messiah down to earth. The Messiah himself was hopeful that soon he would have to descend on his white horse to the children of man.

Even his horse began to chafe and paw, eager to be let out of the Heavenly stable. Also, the Prophet Elijah took out his great *shofar* and began to practice on it, for he would be the one to announce the coming of the Messiah with a mighty blast.

When Satan got wind of the news he trembled at the danger that was threatening him. At the time when all the angels and seraphim in Heaven were rejoicing, he sat gnashing his teeth in the bottom-most regions of the lowest *Gehenna*. He then took counsel with his wife Lilith who upbraided him for doing nothing while their very existence was being threatened. Thereupon, Satan hurried off to press his complaints before God.

"The Angels are playing me a trick!" he cried. "They wish to make an end of me before my time has come! How, O Lord, can Messiah come when there are so many sinners among the Jews? As for this stubborn fool, Joseph della Reyna, give me permission to do with him what is just."

But God denied him his request, for the prayers that Rabbi Joseph and his disciples had intoned, their days and nights of fasting, their sacred reflection and austerities, stood around them like a fortified wall. Therefore, Satan had no power over them.

Yet Satan could not be silenced. God told him that, although his arguments were just, it still lay within God's power to hasten the Redemption.

even before the appointed day, if He but wished it. Moreover, if the Jews possessed such a saint as Rabbi Joseph della Reyna they were indeed worthy of the Messiah's quick coming.

"However," added God, "should Joseph della Reyna stray from righteousness by even the thickness of a hair, I will give you the power to bring his plan to naught!"

When Rabbi Joseph della Reyna told his disciples what the Angel Sandalfon had counselled him to do, they answered with one voice, "We will do whatever you require of us!"

They then left Tiberias and went up to a mountain fastness. They found a cave and made their home in it. Here they performed their austerities and vigils for forty days and forty nights, just as the Angel Sandalfon had said. Finally, they became released from all the tentacles of this sinful world and reached the highest degree of sanctity and virtue.

When the forty days were over they went farther into the wilderness and purified themselves in Lake Kishon. Then they recited the *Mincha* prayers with great fervor. After that they clasped hands and formed a mystic circle. They prayed that God might give them the necessary strength to survive the terror of the fiery presence of the Angel Metatron and of his angelic host.

Finally, Rabbi Joseph pronounced the Ineffable Name of God formed of seventy-two letters.

Thereupon, the earth became convulsed and trembled. Lightning and thunder rent the heavens and a whirlwind came.

Rabbi Joseph and his disciples stood firm, clasping hands in the mystic circle. They smelled strong spices to fortify their spirits and intoned prayers.

The Angel Metatron appeared, surrounded by his host of angels and seraphim.

"O sinful man!" cried the angels. "O puny creature of flesh and blood, wretched as a worm! How dare you storm the Heavens with your prayers and oblige the angels to come to earth?"

Rabbi Joseph and his students were filled with terror. Summoning up all his courage, Rabbi Joseph spoke at last.

"Holy angels, help me! Give me the strength to talk to you!"

The Angel Metatron then drew near and touched Rabbi Joseph, whereupon he lost all fear and spoke. "Believe me, I have no evil intention. All I want is to bring the Messiah in order to end the Exile of the Jewish people. Therefore, teach me how to vanquish Satan and his evil power."

The Angel Metatron became stern.

"Foolish man!" he cried. "All your efforts are in vain! Know that Satan is all powerful. He is fortified by a great wall of the sins of the Jewish people. How can you expect to break through where others have failed? Only when God wills that the Messiah should come will He come. Therefore, abandon your plan!"

But Rabbi Joseph was stubborn.

"Almighty God has helped me thus far and I've remained among the living," he said. "Therefore, I will not turn back!"

When the Angel Metatron saw that Rabbi Joseph could not be moved in his determination he was filled with compassion for him. He then advised him what to do.

He revealed to him all the mystic formulae, all the incantations and the Ineffable Name. With their aid, he said, Rabbi Joseph would succeed in capturing Satan and Lilith and thus drive all evil from the world. With that accomplished, the Messiah would surely come!

He also had him engrave on a metal plate the Ineffable Name and taught him how to use it. He warned him especially to guard himself against the weakness of pity towards evil after he had made captive Satan and Lilith. Under no circumstance was he to give them any food or any spices to smell. If he did, all his efforts would be wasted. He would thus only expose himself to the revenge of Satan.

When the Angel Metatron and his host had departed, Rabbi Joseph and his disciples began making preparations for their battle with the Evil One.

Rabbi Joseph della Reyna and his five disciples went up on Mount Sheir. On the way they met many wild dogs. These, they very well knew, were demons that Satan had sent in order to confuse and frighten them. But Rabbi Joseph pronounced an incantation and they vanished.

As they continued on their way they came to a snow-capped mountain that seemed to pierce the very Heavens. They then pronounced mystic formulae that the angels had taught them and the mountain vanished.

On the third day they came to a turbulent sea. Here too they recited mystic formulae and the ocean dried up before their very eyes.

Further on they found their way obstructed by an iron wall which reached to the sky. Behind it stood Satan, lying in wait for them. Rabbi Joseph took a knife on which was engraved one of the mystic names of God and with it he ripped the wall asunder.

They then ascended a towering mountain from the top of which they heard the loud barking of dogs. When they finally reached the summit Rabbi Joseph saw a hut. As he tried to enter, two frightfully big dogs sprang at his throat. Rabbi Joseph recognized them to be Satan and Lilith, so he quickly raised before them the metal plate with the Ineffable Name engraved upon it. Thereupon, they lost their evil power and slunk away.

The five disciples then bound the dogs with ropes on which were tied little metal amulets engraved with the mystic names of God. Immediately, the dogs were transformed. They took on the appearance of humans except that they had wings and fiery eyes.

"Do give us something to eat," they whined.

But Rabbi Joseph recalled the Angel Metatron's warning against falling prey to the weakness of pity towards evil. So he gave them no food.

Rabbi Joseph and his disciples were now filled with indescribable bliss. At last, at last, they had succeeded in capturing Satan and Lilith! Now they would be able to bring Messiah down to earth!

"Let us hurry!" impatiently cried Rabbi Joseph della Reyna to his disciples. "We are already nearing our goal! Soon the Gates of Heaven will open wide for us and the Holy Messiah will come forth to welcome us!"

All this time Satan and Lilith were moaning in heartbreaking voices, "Help us! Give us something to eat! We're dying of hunger!"

Still Rabbi Joseph della Reyna hardened his heart against them.

When they saw that they could not swerve him Satan and Lilith asked wheedlingly, "At least give us a smell of your spices or we perish!"

Now Rabbi Joseph was a compassionate man. He could not endure the sight of suffering in man or beast. Having triumphed over Satan and Lilith he thought he could now safely show a small measure of magnanimity towards them. He therefore gave them some of the strong spices to smell.

Immediately, tongues of searing flame shot from their nostrils. All their former strength returned to them. They tore away their bonds and summoned to their aid hosts of shrieking demons and devils.

Two of the disciples instantly died of terror. Two of them went out of their minds and wandered away. Only Rabbi Joseph and one disciple remained.

A terrible wailing was now heard in Heaven and the angels went into mourning. The Messiah wept and led his white horse back into its Heavenly stall. Also the Prophet Elijah grieved and hid the great *shofar* of the Redemption. Then the voice of the Almighty sounded:

"Pay heed, O Joseph della Reyna! No human has the power to end the Exile! I alone, God, will hasten the Redemption of the Jewish people when the right time comes!"

The Messiah Came to Town

PERIODICALLY Rabbi Elijah, the Vilna Gaon, wished to do penance. So he went into "exile," wandered forth on foot disguised as a poor man. He carried a stick and wore the traditional beggar's sack so that no one knew who he was.

Once, when his period of "exile" was completed, Rabbi Elijah turned his face toward Vilna again. Footsore and weary he trudged the road back. At last a peasant, who was passing by in his wagon, gave him a lift to town. The peasant was slightly drunk and drowsy.

"Here, Jew, drive!" he said.

Rabbi Elijah took the reins and drove into Vilna while the peasant lay down to sleep in the back of the wagon.

As he drove through the streets the Jews recognized him. Everyone was filled with wonder, for they had never seen the likes of it since the day they were born. There, in the driver's seat and dressed in tatters like the commonest beggar, sat the "Crown of Israel," the greatest Jew on earth!

One Jew ran into the synagogue.

"The Messiah is coming! The Messiah is coming!" he cried jubilantly.

The people excitedly ran out of the synagogues, out of their shops and houses, and into the street in order to see the wonder of wonders.

"Where is the Messiah?" they asked the man.

"See for yourself!" he cried. "There's the Vilna Gaon! If the Vilna Gaon in beggar's rags is driving a wagon, who is worthy enough to be his passenger? It can be none other than the Messiah!"

Why the Messiah Doesn't Come

ONCE there was a poor man who, may God spare us all a like fate, did not have a groschen to his soul. Nevertheless, he sat night and day studying the Torah with pure intention, as God has bidden.

One Friday morning, when his wife discovered that they did not have the wherewithal to buy the necessities for celebrating the Holy Sabbath, she drove him out of the house.

"Go to the marketplace!" she cried bitterly. "Look around—maybe you can earn a few kopeks so that the children and I will not have to starve on God's holy day!"

Lost in gloomy thoughts the poor man made his way to the marketplace.

"Alas!" he mused, "what a sad fate is mine! Instead of devoting my time to the study of the Torah I must now worry about groschen and kopeks!"

As he walked with downcast eyes he suddenly heard a voice near him say, "Sholom aleichem!"

"Aleichem sholom!" answered he. And, looking up, he saw an old man with a long gray beard and a wonderfully holy face.

"Who are you?" asked the poor man, overawed.

"I'm the Messiah!" answered the old man. "I see you are sad. Confide your trouble to me!"

And the poor man told him of his great need and of his grief in being diverted by base cares from his study of the Torah.

"Cease your lamentation!" said Messiah. "Let me give you this sack—it's a marvellous little sack! Whatever you desire the sack will give you.

WHY THE MESSIAH DOESN'T COME: Adapted from a Yiddish groschen chapbook.

All you have to do is to put your hand into it and draw forth whatever your heart desires. The little sack has also another virtue. Should anyone wish to hurt you—all you have to do is to call out: 'Swallow him, little sack!' And, believe me, it will do exactly as you say."

Overjoyed, the poor man took the little sack, thanked Messiah in a heartfelt way, and returned home to his unhappy wife and children.

From that day on the wheel of fortune turned for him. He thrived and he prospered and was wanting for nothing of all the goods of the earth. He lived in honor and tranquility. He saw his children and his children's children grow up and marry happily, and sorrow shunned his threshold.

Unfortunately, like most men who grow rich, he forgot the manner in which his prosperity came to him, forgot to do good with it, to serve his fellowmen, to feed the poor and clothe the orphans. He even gave up his study of the Torah.

As he lay dying, he called his heirs to his bedside and said to them, "Give me my magic little sack. It will save me from the Angel of Death."

His heirs did as he had asked them.

When the Angel of Death rose up before him, he asked, "What is your name?"

"I will not tell you!" the dying man cried. "Leave me in peace!"

But the Angel of Death would not leave him. Again and again he repeated, "What is your name?"

When the dying man saw that he could not resist him any longer, he picked up his little sack and said, "Little sack, little sack! Swallow the Angel of Death!"

Immediately, the Angel of Death disappeared into the little sack.

In the meantime, on the Throne of Mercy sat the Celestial Judge impatiently waiting for the Angel of Death to arrive with his daily catch of souls.

Angered by his tardiness, God sent the angels Gabriel and Michael down to earth.

"Go," said He, "and find out what's keeping the Angel of Death."

When the angels came to the man they asked him, "Where is the Angel of Death?"

He did not answer. Again and again they asked him the question. When he saw that he could not stand up against them any longer he picked up his little sack and cried, "Little sack, little sack! Swallow the angel Michael!"

And lo and behold! Michael disappeared into the little sack.

When the angel Gabriel saw this he fled and returned to Heaven.

As Gabriel reported to God what had happened to him the Messiah suddenly recalled how he had given the little magic sack to a poor man he had once met.

"Lord," said the Messiah to God, "give me leave to go down and find this man."

So the Messiah descended to earth and went in search of the man. When

he found him he asked him sternly, "What is the meaning of your conduct? Explain yourself!"

"You too!" cried the man angrily, not recognizing the Messiah. "How
many more of you will come down to browbeat me?"

"Why, don't you know who I am?" began the Messiah.

But before even he could finish what he had begun to say, the man picked
up his magic little sack and cried, "Little sack, little sack! Swallow this
one too!"

And the Messiah also disappeared into the little sack.

And now, dear friends, do you want to know why the Messiah doesn't
come?

SKEPTICS AND SCOFFERS

INTRODUCTION

The awed belief in the supernatural powers of the cabalists and in the
wonder-working feats of the *Hasidic Tzaddikim* was far from being unani-
mous among the Jewish masses. These mystics always found a determined
and powerful opposition arrayed against them in the Talmudic rationalists.
The *Hasidim* especially had to contend with a dangerous enemy—one that
fought with the devastating weapon of ridicule. The opponents of the
Hasidim were known as *Misnagdim*. They were a gay set of rogues who
created an entire humorous literature with their sly, tongue-in-the-cheek
scoffing against the wonder-working rabbis, and most of all against their
gullible, worshipful disciples. These quips and jokes received wide currency among the people and added a great deal to the merriment of Jewish
community life which stood so badly in need of diversion. And if any proof
is needed of the extraordinary capacity Jews have for telling jokes at their
own expense it is furnished by the novel fact that these anti-*Hasidic* jokes
were almost as popular among the *Hasidim* themselves as among the *Misnagdim*. Of course, the *Hasidim* found a convenient way of avoiding embarrassment. They always assumed that the scoffing was being directed
against fanatics, to which category of *Hasidim* they themselves, of course,
did not belong!

                                                                    N. A.

Conclusive Proof

A WONDER-WORKING rabbi, accompanied by his disciples, once went on
a journey. Late at night he came to a wayside inn. He knocked on the
door and asked to be let in, but the innkeeper refused to get out of bed
as it was a cold night. Full of holy wrath, the rabbi cried, "Wicked fellow!
I hereby decree that your inn shall burn down tomorrow!"

Frightened out of his wits, the innkeeper got out of bed and let the rabbi
and his disciples in. He treated them with the utmost hospitality and set
a feast before them. Mollified by the innkeeper's eagerness to please, the
rabbi cried, "I now decree that your house shall not burn down tomorrow!"

And, miracles and wonders! It happened exactly as the rabbi said!
The rabbi's disciples themselves witnessed this miracle. They saw with
their own eyes that the inn did not burn down the next day!

The Right Kind of Judge

A VILLAGER once came to see the rabbi in a big town and said to him,
"Rabbi, I come from a nearby village. I want to bring a lawsuit against
God. My reason for it is this. I had a wife and, in addition, ten thousand
rubles. What did God do? First he took away the ten thousand rubles and,
afterwards, my wife too. I ask you: what would it have mattered to God
if He had done the reverse? Had He taken away my wife first I would
have remained a widower with ten thousand rubles. In that case it would
have been easy for me to have married a woman with a ten thousand ruble
dowry. After that, had God wanted to take from me the ten thousand
rubles, I still would have had left a wife and ten thousand rubles."

"Tell me, my friend," asked the rabbi a bit puzzled at all this, "why did
you come to me with your suit and not to the rabbi in your village?"

"I'll be perfectly frank with you," replied the villager. "I couldn't trust
such a matter to our rabbi because I know what a God-fearing man he is
and he would give Him the decision. On the other hand, I know you have
no fear of God and so, at least I'll have half a chance with you."

Leave It to the Rabbi

A JEWISH innkeeper, who held the concession from a Jew-hating Polish
nobleman, was in great despair. His landlord treated him with savage
cruelty. Whenever he couldn't make his annual payment he even beat him
and drove his wife and children into the wintry night. At his wit's end, he
decided to ride to town to see the rabbi and get his counsel.

"Advise me, Rabbi," he begged him. "Save my life! I no longer know
what to do. That Haman of a landlord is fast driving me into my grave.
I can see only one solution to my trouble, and one only: that by your
wonder-working powers you bring about his death."

"Ah! That's a very difficult thing to do, my son," the rabbi replied
discouragingly. "Besides, you just can't go and kill a man as easily as
all that! After all, aren't Jews called 'Sons of the Compassionate'? Even
your landlord is a human being, just like you and me."

"*He* a human being?" snorted the petitioner, with indignation. "He's a torturer, Rabbi, a wild beast! He'd as soon kill me as take a pinch of snuff."

The rabbi agreed with a sigh and retired into his private study to hold communion with God. When he emerged, he said to the innkeeper, "Go home now! Your persecutor is dead."

Rejoicing greatly over this miraculous piece of news, the innkeeper started for home. But on the way he was suddenly filled with misgiving. "Was it wise of me to ask the rabbi to bring about the death of my landlord," he asked himself. "What will I have gained by it? When his son and heir, who is in Paris now, hears of his father's death he will hurry home to take over the estate. In that case, it will be worse for me for he is even more wicked than his father. Then it will surely be the end of me!"

So he turned his cart around and, whipping up his horse, returned to the rabbi.

"Rabbi!" he cried. "I shouldn't have asked you to make the landlord die. I've done wrong—a terrible wrong! If he's as wicked as Haman, his son is like the Angel of Death. Now I'm sorry for the whole business!"

The rabbi threw up his hands in exasperation.

"What do you want me to do now—resurrect him?" he asked, bitingly. Then he relented and said, "Believe me, it's a very difficult matter, but I'll see what I can do."

The rabbi again went into his private study to commune with God. When he came out he said cheerfully to the innkeeper, "You may go home now—your landlord is alive again."

Murmuring a prayer of thanksgiving, the innkeeper climbed into his cart and drove home. When he got there, what was his delight to see his landlord walking about hale and hearty and real as life, just as if nothing at all had happened to him!

Deduction

A DISCIPLE came to his rabbi. His wife was gravely ill at home and therefore he begged the holy man to pray for her.

"Go home and stop worrying," the rabbi told him.

Several days later the disciple came again, lamenting tearfully, "Oh Rabbi, my wife is dead!"

"That cannot be," insisted the rabbi heatedly. "I myself tore the slaughterer's knife from the hand of the Angel of Death!"

"I don't know about that, Rabbi, but my wife is dead!" wailed the bereaved husband.

"In that case," sighed the rabbi, "nothing else could have happened but that the Angel of Death strangled her with his bare hands!"

Realistic Miracles

A DISCIPLE was bragging about his wonder-working rabbi:

"When my rabbi climbs on a bench he can see with his luminous eyes to the very ends of the earth!"

"What's the idea of your rabbi having to get on a bench if he can see that far?" he was asked.

"My rabbi, I'd like you to know, wants his miracles to look realistic," answered the disciple proudly.

A Believer's Truth

A DISCIPLE of a wonder-working rabbi once was boasting of the supernatural feats of his master.

"Every night," he stated, "my rabbi transforms himself into the Prophet Elijah!"

"How do you know that?" asked a skeptic.

"Why the rabbi himself told it to me!"

"The rabbi could have told you a lie!"

"How dare you say such a thing about my rabbi!" raged the disciple. "Do you think for one moment that a man who can transform himself into the Prophet Elijah every night has the need to tell a lie?"

Miracles

Two disciples were bragging about the relative merits of their wonder-working rabbis. One said, "Once my rabbi was travelling on the road when suddenly the sky became overcast. It began to thunder and to lighten and a heavy rain fell—a real deluge. What does my rabbi do? He lifts up his eyes to Heaven, spreads out his hands in prayer and immediately a miracle happens! To the right, darkness and a downpour— to the left, darkness and a downpour. But in the middle, a clear sky and the sun shining!"

"Call that a miracle?" sneered the other disciple. "Let me tell you what happened to my rabbi.

"Once he was riding in a wagon to a nearby village. It was on a Friday. He remained longer there than he had intended and, on his way back, he found that night was falling. What was to be done? He couldn't very well spend the Sabbath in the middle of the field, could he? So he lifted his eyes to Heaven, spread out his hands to right and left, and immediately a miracle took place! To the right of him stretched the Sabbath, to the left of him stretched the Sabbath—but in the middle was Friday!"

The Farseeing Rabbi

THE rabbi of Odessa was deep in prayer one day when, interrupting himself with a wail, he announced that the rabbi of Warsaw had just died. Accordingly, the entire Odessa congregation went into mourning in his honor.

A few days later, some Jews from Warsaw arrived in Odessa. Asked for details of the sad event, they declared their rabbi was in the best of health.

"What a spectacle your rabbi made of himself," one of them said, "seeing our rabbi die in Warsaw, when as a matter of fact our rabbi was—and still is—living!"

"What of it?" answered the undaunted disciple of Odessa. "Isn't it marvelous enough that our rabbi can see all the way from Odessa to Warsaw?"

Pipe-Dreams

THE holy rabbi died. All his disciples who loved him wished to obtain a memento of him. One of the disciples had fixed his heart upon the rabbi's long-stem pipe with the beautifully painted porcelain bowl.

"It will cost you a hundred rubles," the rabbi's wife told him.

"It's a lot of money for me," said the disciple with some hesitation. "However, let me try it out and we'll see about it later."

So the rabbi's wife gave him the pipe and he lit it.

And what do you suppose happened?

No sooner had he taken the first draw when it seemed to him as if all the seven gates of Heaven opened wide for him and he saw what even the prophet Ezekiel hadn't seen there!

With trembling hands he counted out the hundred rubles and, overjoyed, hastened home with his purchase.

No sooner did he arrive home than he eagerly lit the pipe once more. He gave one mighty draw.

And what do you suppose happened?

Nothing!

Nothing?

Yes, nothing!

Pell-mell the disciple ran off with his pipe to see the new rabbi. He blurted out to him the whole story in a breathless voice.

"My son," said the new rabbi, smiling into his beard, "the whole matter is as clear as day. When the pipe still belonged to the rabbi, and you smoked it, you saw just what the rabbi saw when he smoked it. But, no sooner did it become yours when it turned into just a plain, everyday pipe, and you saw what you always see!"

The Gulden Test

AN ATHEIST once came to see a wonder-working rabbi.

"*Sholom aleichem*, Rabbi," said the atheist.

"*Aleichem sholom*," answered the rabbi.

The atheist took a gulden and handed it to him. The rabbi pocketed it without a word.

"No doubt you've come to see me about something," he said. "Maybe your wife is childless and you want me to pray for her?"

"No, Rabbi, I'm not married," replied the atheist.

Thereupon, he gave the rabbi another gulden. Again the rabbi pocketed the gulden without a word.

"But there must be something you wish to ask me," he said. "Possibly you've committed a sin and you'd like me to intercede with God for you."

"No, Rabbi, I don't know of any sin I've committed," replied the atheist.

And again he gave the rabbi a gulden and again the rabbi pocketed it without a word.

"Maybe business is bad and you want me to bless you?" asked the rabbi, hopefully.

"No, Rabbi, this has been a prosperous year for me," replied the atheist.

Once more the atheist gave him a gulden.

"What do you want of me, anyway?" asked the rabbi, a little perplexed.

"Nothing, just nothing," replied the atheist. "I merely wished to see how long a man can go on taking money for nothing!"

A Fool Asks Too Many Questions

ON THE fast day of *Tisha Ba'Ab* a sick Jew went to see the rabbi in order to get his permission to eat, for he was afraid his health would suffer if he didn't. But, as he entered the rabbi's house, he was struck dumb with amazement when he saw the rabbi enjoying a hearty lunch.

"Rabbi," he faltered, not at all sure of himself, "I'm a sick man—do I have to fast today?"

"What a question!" replied the rabbi, his mouth full of roast duck. "Of course you do!"

For a moment the petitioner stood in bewilderment, not knowing whether he was coming or going. Finally, he scraped up sufficient courage to ask, "Pardon my impertinence, Rabbi, but how can you order me to fast when you yourself are eating?"

"I wasn't fool enough to ask the rabbi," replied the rabbi with a grin and went on with his lunch.

[4]

Fighters and Strong Men

INTRODUCTION

The fighter, as we have already observed, was not idealized as a hero by Jewish tradition and folklore. We have but the most fragmentary allusions of the most primitive kind to Jewish warriors in the *Midrash* and in later sources of folklore. Nevertheless, there did arise some outstanding fighters because Jews led an autonomous national existence in ancient days in Palestine, kept up military establishments, and waged many wars.

There was, for instance, the strong man Samson who fought the Philistines. He possessed such magical strength that, legend tells us, he could rub two mountains together as if they were two pebbles. Then there was Deborah, the Jewish Joan of Arc. Her hymn of victory in the Bible has the wild martial strain in character with some primitive tribal chieftainess. And of course there is the legend of the battle between David and Goliath in which the Jewish hero proves himself to be more brave and nimble-witted than doughty as a warrior. Clearly enough, the folklorists of the *Midrash*, raised in a contemplative, anti-militaristic spirit, vastly preferred brain over brawn, and scorned to retell the gory tales about Jewish fighters and strong men of ancient days.

However, we do find revealed in *Midrashic* Jewish folklore a somewhat different attitude toward those warriors who fought for their people's freedom. The stirring tales about the Maccabees, Judith of Bethulia, and Bar Kochba have been prime favorites of the Jewish people throughout the many centuries. They have not been revered merely as folktales but have been considered a means of rekindling the national heroic spirit among the Jews in the days of their oppression and decline.

In the centuries following the destruction of the Jewish state in A.D. 70, the martial spirit, except for its brief upsurge under Bar Kochba, naturally grew dim among the Jews. Being scattered and persecuted wherever they lived, Jews were not allowed to be soldiers or even to fight for their country, except in some isolated Asiatic and North African regions.

The first opportunity Jews had to fight openly on equal terms with Gentiles was in the American Revolution. Yet it was not a warlike spirit that animated them to take up arms but a love of liberty and a desire to participate in the creation of a democratic society in the New World. Dr. Benjamin Rush of Philadelphia, a signer of the Declaration of Independence, remarked: ". . . . in the Colonies all the Jews are Whigs." This, of course, was an enthusiastic overstatement for, like so many of their non-Jewish countrymen, there were also among the Jews some Tories who fought with the British.

As we can see from the remarkable account about Berek Yoselovich and the Jewish regiment that so stoutly defended Praga against the Russians in 1794, they were inspired to fight for the freedom of their country by the gallant example set them by the American Jewish patriots who fought in the War of Independence in 1776. No doubt, with these precedents of Jewish valor in mind, Louis Napoleon organized two battalions of Dutch Jews to fight for France in 1807. And in 1830, when again the Poles raised the standard of revolt against Russia, the Jew, Sini Hernisch, petitioned the Polish leaders to approve the formation of a Jewish regiment to fight for the Fatherland. When the Commander-in-chief, General Chlopitcki, read the petition he made the scornful marginal notation: "It is not fitting that Jewish blood should mingle with noble Polish blood." However, the General quickly reconsidered the whole matter when the news reached him that a great Russian Army was marching on Poland. Berek Yoselovich's son, Yossel Berkovitch, organized a Jewish regiment of 850 Jewish youths, just as his father had done in 1794. But it was not permitted to function as a separate unit. Instead it was incorporated into the national guard in Warsaw that was under the command of General Ostrovsky. Because they wore beards the Jewish militiamen became known as "The Beardlings." They prayed twice daily, ate only kosher food, and rested on the Sabbath. Nonetheless, they distinguished themselves in battle with such acts of bravery that General Ostrovsky was prompted to state publicly: "The spectacle of the Jewish militiamen and their sacrifices for Poland must have convinced everyone how much we have sinned against the Jews."

Since those days Jews have fought in every war that has plagued Europe and the Americas. In all instances they proved themselves neither better nor worse as fighters than any other group of their fellow countrymen.

Yet there were instances in World War II in which the fighting courage of the Jew was displayed to a degree almost without parallel in modern military history. These were the desperate last-ditch stands of defenseless, untrained and poorly armed Jewish men and women—the young and the old, the well and the sick, and even the children—when they entered into an obviously suicidal struggle against the organized might of the Nazis. Heroic in the extreme were the tragic battles fought by these civilian fighters in the ghettos of Warsaw, Vilna, Minsk, Lodz, Cracow, Byalistok, and many other places. Immured in their ghettos, they fought savagely against the enemy until they were slain. Most memorable of all, Maccabean in its grandeur and in the pure flame of its sacrifice, was the Battle of the Warsaw Ghetto, a moving eye-witness account of which (already touched with the legendary) is included in this section. As in the case of the recent Jewish martyrology that arose in the death camps of Hitler, it is yet too early for these heroic incidents of Jewish valor to be transmuted by the Jewish folk-fancy into popular legend, as undoubtedly will be done in the years to come.

It is but natural that a people, that had been as cruelly prevented from developing its physical strength as have the Jews, should take an immoderate pride in its strong men as a form of psychological over-compensation.

To be sure, the majority of Jews still hold to their ancient traditional values in which the arts of civilization are vastly preferred to the feats of brute strength. Just the same, a more robust, and certainly more balanced, attitude toward physical strength and sports has been adopted by the modern Jew. In the late Eighteenth and early Nineteenth Centuries the Jews in the English-speaking world glowed with pride over the galaxy of great Jewish boxers that, incredibly enough, arose in the small Jewish community of London. There were among them such prize-fighters as Daniel Mendoza, called "The Father of the Art of Boxing," Dutch Sam Elias, the originator of the "upper-cut," and the bruisers Bildoon and Belasco, two stalwart pupils of Mendoza. The modern American Jew has taken equal pride in such heroes of Fistiana as Battling Kid Levinsky, Tony Pastor, Benny Leonard and Barney Ross.

Significantly enough, from a psychological standpoint, the all-Jewish soccer team of Vienna, which remained the unchallenged world champion in that sport during the 1920's, went by the Hebrew name of *Hakoah* (Strength). In addition to their enthusiasm for the sport in which they excelled, the members of *Hakoah* were anxious to restore in the eyes of the world the faded glory of the Jews' physical prowess of ancient days. This was also the avowed aim of Houdini, the greatest magician of our time, and of Zisha Breitbart, the modern Samson of Poland. Both were painfully self-conscious of the excessive intellectuality of the Jew. As Breitbart strained to perform the incredible feat of lying prone and raising above his head a huge platform on which stood a team of horses, he had the theatre orchestra play *Kol Nidre*, the most revered of Jewish chants, in order to derive from it the necessary fighting courage to complete his stunt. As he expressed it ingenuously: "I perform this feat of strength for the honor of the Jewish people."

N. A.

Judah, "The Hammer"

Not since Alexander of Macedonia had there arisen a king like Antiochus IV. He ruled over the land of Syria with a heavy hand and the kings of many lands paid him yearly tribute. He built to himself a monument—a mighty city which he named Antioch. But the more power he had the more he wanted; he was filled with an insatiable hunger to fill the whole world with his glory.

"I will conquer the world, like Alexander of Macedonia!" he boasted.

And so foolish was his pride that he called himself Epiphanes, which in Greek means "The Manifest God"; for like the Roman Caesars he wished

JUDAH, "THE HAMMER": Adapted from the Talmud, the *Midrash*, the *Antiquities of the Jews* by Josephus, *The Scroll of Antiochus*, and the *First Book of Maccabees*.

that all men worship him as a deity. But the Jews had another name for him. They called him "Antiochus the madman." And to show their opinion of him they quoted Scripture, saying "Antiochus 'is a root bearing gall and wormwood.' "

Now it happened that in the twenty-third year of his reign (168 B.C.) which was two hundred and thirteen years after the rebuilding of the Temple by Ezra the Scribe, Antiochus turned his face wrathfully toward Jerusalem, and he said to his generals:

"I can no longer endure the Jews that dwell in the land of Israel. I know that in their hearts they hate me and hope for my destruction. They are not like us. They do not sacrifice to our gods, nor do they observe our laws, but speak scornfully of them. Therefore, I have sworn that I will bring them low and put the yoke upon their necks."

And Antiochus sent a great host against the Jews. They sacked Jerusalem and they massacred its people, and yet there was no one to stand up against them, for the chief men of the nation remained cowed and silent and failed to rally the people. The Greeks broke into the Temple, and robbed it of its treasure. Many Jews fled to Alexandria, and others to Babylonia, to Persia and to other distant lands. Whomever the Greek soldiers chose they killed. Women and children they sold in all the slave-markets of the world. The walls of Jerusalem they tore down and made desolate its houses and streets.

Antiochus had said to his generals: "Abolish the Torah and all the academies where it is taught from the land of the Jews! Punish with death all those who observe the Jewish customs. I decree that they no longer may circumcise their male infants and that they may not observe their dietary laws. Compel them to violate the Sabbath, to bow before our gods, and bring their sacrifices to them upon our altars. And send my servants throughout the land to see that this be done."

And the generals did as Antiochus told them. They went throughout the entire land of Israel and they pulled down the synagogues and the houses of study. They defiled and destroyed the Torah scrolls, and slew all who murmured against them. And there were many martyrs who died to sanctify His name and their blood was on the head of Antiochus.

Not long after that the heathen priests of Antiochus consecrated the Temple to their chief god Zeus and they raised a great statue of him upon the altar in the sanctuary. In his honor they sacrificed a pig upon the altar and sprinkled its unclean blood in the sanctuary.

And when the people of Israel heard of this they shuddered with horror, but they dared not murmur aloud as their lives would be forfeit. So they fled Jerusalem in great numbers until Zion was a deserted city.

Now it chanced that Apelles, a Greek official, came to the village of Modin, which is not far from Jerusalem, to carry out the decree of Antiochus. He raised an altar to the Greek gods and commanded the Jews to sacrifice a swine upon it. Among those who gathered was Mattathias, an old priest of the Hasmonean clan, and his five sons, Yohanan, Simon,

Judah, Eleazar and Jonathan. When Mattathias heard what abomination Apelles wished the Jews to perform he said to them:

"O my brothers, let all the nations of the provinces that are subject to King Antiochus obey him if they choose, even to the extent of betraying the religion of their forefathers. But we swear we shall not leave the path of our religion to go either to the right or to the left."

With these words he smote Apelles the Greek, and he slew him.

Then Mattathias cried out to the Jews: "Take up arms! Whoever is for God and His holy Law let him follow me!"

He and his five sons, and many others of the sect of the Hasidim, or the Pious, fled into the hills. In the darkness they would descend on the Greek garrisons and, although few in number and ill-armed, they slew many, for they were fierce with the hatred of the enemy and aflame with a love for their people and their God.

The time came at last for Mattathias to die, for he was very old. And so he called his five sons together and said:

"O my sons! I must now depart from you. And so, I wish to appoint a leader over you and over our army. I therefore choose you, Judah my son, to succeed me, for your wisdom and heroic deeds are comparable to Judah, the son of Jacob. Even as he was likened to a lion, so are you, and may our enemies tremble when they feel your strength. Serve God with all your heart and soul and bring redemption to Israel."

Saying this, Mattathias died, and Judah was general in his stead. So invincible was he in battle, so merciless in pursuit of the enemy, that the Jews called him Makbi (Maccabeus), which in Aramaic means "hammer," for he struck at the Greeks mightily like a hammer, blow upon blow.

And the example of Judah set the hearts of his people aflame. They found new hope and new courage and many flocked to him in the fastnesses of the hills and took up arms and fought with him against the Greeks. For they saw that he was wise and a great leader of men and understood the art of war. Also his four brothers, Yohanan, Simon, Eleazar and Jonathan, were great warriors. They too led the people to victory and performed acts of valor. And when those who had fled heard the reports of all this they took heart and returned to the land of Israel, for they too wished to share in the glory of the sacred struggle.

When King Antiochus heard of this he grew very wrathful and sent army after army to punish the Jews. But Judah Maccabeus swooped down upon them unexpectedly from the hills, fierce as a mountain lion, and crushed them all.

Again King Antiochus summoned his generals and said: "Have you heard what Judah Maccabeus has done to me? He has destroyed all my armies and killed their generals. An end must come to this!"

And so he sent his most cunning generals, Ptolemy, Nicanor, and Gorgias, with a Greek host of forty thousand foot-soldiers and seven thousand horsemen, as well as many thousands of Syrian auxiliaries. And they paused at the city of Emmaus which lies in the plain. There they pitched their camp and waited to give battle to Judah. So confident were they of victory that they brought with them Phoenician slave merchants carrying chains with which to bind the captives.

When the Jews beheld the assembled hosts of the enemy and saw how more numerous they were than their own forces they were struck with fear. Seeing this, Judah said to them:

"Terrible indeed is the might of the Greeks, but more terrible is the vengeance of the Lord when He strikes at the wicked! Fear not the enemy even though they are many and we are but few. Know that God is with us, even though we are weak, and our righteous cause will triumph over their greater numbers. Therefore, gird your spirits and' strengthen your hearts and be as men of valor."

And so, as was his custom before battle, Judah put on sack-cloth and poured ashes on his head like the veriest penitent. He fasted and sent his supplications winging to God. He also confessed his sins. And his men did as he did. Then they no longer were afraid.

After that Judah arose and said to his assembled host: "If there are any among you who are afraid, withdraw then from the battlefield! Also the newly married and those who have but recently acquired riches, let them depart for they will fight in a cowardly manner, being full of regret for what they have left behind."

When these were gone Judah drew up his forces in the ancient order of battle of the Jews. He appointed over them captains of thousands, and of hundreds and of tens. Then he spoke to them as follows:

"O my fellow-Jews! Let us fight manfully for the liberty of our people and the honor of our Torah. Should we lose the battle, we shall all be slain, and our wives and children will be sold into slavery. Therefore, we must be victorious. Thus we will regain the liberties our enemies have taken from us, and we will be restored to our blessed way of life. Fear not O Jacob, for the God who led us out of bondage in Egypt will not abandon us!"

That night, the Greek General Gorgias left the main part of his army at Emmaus and came with five thousand foot-soldiers and one thousand horsemen to fall upon Judah in the darkness. But Judah encompassed his plan. Now, he felt, he could deal better with his enemies since their forces were divided. Therefore, Judah purposely left many fires burning in his camp in order to deceive and confuse Gorgias, and then he and his army departed.

He marched all night long and arrived before the town of Emmaus where was the camp of the enemy. Judah observed that the Greeks were well and skillfully fortified in their camp and that their numbers were many times greater than his for he had come with only three thousand men. But he took heart knowing that they were fast asleep and did not expect him to attack.

And when the moment came to strike Judah commanded the trumpeters to sound the call to battle. When the Greeks heard it they were astonished and dismayed for they were certain Gorgias had destroyed the Jews. Judah and his men then fell upon the enemy who ran hither and thither in confusion and terror. And they slew many of those that resisted them to the number of three thousand. The rest they pursued as far as Gedarah, Ashdod and Jamnia.

Now Gorgias, who had gone in search of Judah and had not found him in his camp, was exceedingly puzzled. So he hastened back to the camp of the Greeks at Emmaus. When he came there and saw what had happened he and his men turned in fright and fled.

Yet for all the defeats inflicted on his armies Antiochus would not rest. The next year he sent against Judea another host, this time of sixty thousand foot-soldiers and five thousand horsemen under his greatest general, Lysias. Judah met him in the hill country of Beth-Sur with only ten thousand men and yet he routed him and slew a great multitude of Greeks.

Now Lysias was a prudent man. He marked well the spirit of the Jews, for he saw that they would rather die than lose their liberty and worship any but their own God, and that Judah inspired them with a heroism and a desperation in fighting that was more than human. Therefore he gathered the remnants of his army and by forced marches returned to Antioch.

This time King Antiochus felt fear in his heart and he fled to the sea provinces of his kingdom. But wherever he went the people rose up in revolt against him, and mocked at him saying: "Coward! Runaway!" Whereupon Antiochus, out of humiliation, cast himself into the sea and was drowned.

Upon the departure of the enemy Judah assembled the people in Jerusalem and he said to them:

"Let us go up to the House of God and purify it, for it has been wickedly profaned!"

And after they had carefully purified the Temple and cast out all the idols and their altars, they brought in new vessels: the seven-branched golden *Menorah*, the table of show-bread, and the altar of incense. They also pulled down the altar for burnt-offerings, which had been profaned, and built a new one in its place.

And so, on the twenty-fifth day of the month of *Kislev*, Judah rededicated the Temple. He lighted the lamps of the *Menorah* and offered incense and burnt offerings upon the altar. However, when they wished to light the lamps they went in search of pure olive oil but they found none except one small vessel of unprofaned oil which had been closed with the seal of the High Priest in the ancient days of the Prophet Samuel. The vessel contained oil sufficient for one day only. Yet a miracle happened. The oil burned for eight days until new holy oil could be prepared.

And, in commemoration of the rededication of the Temple, Judah Maccabeus decreed that on the twenty-fifth day of *Kislev* of each year the Jews were to celebrate the Festival of Lights, or *Channukah*, for eight days. They were to burn lights during this period, adding a new light each

night, and sing songs of praise (*Hallel*) to celebrate the triumph of
Israel in the struggle for its freedom.

Judith and Holofernes

THE Greek General Holofernes was besieging the town of Bethulia. He
ordered destroyed all the wells and springs nearby so that, by means of
the torments of thirst, he might force the Jews to surrender.

The inhabitants of Bethulia then began to despair for they felt that
they could hold out no longer against the enemy. Therefore they clamored
to the commander of the city's armed forces that he surrender.

"Wait only five more days, my brothers," the commander pleaded with
them. "Maybe help will come in the meantime from our fellow-Jews.
A long time ago I sent urgent messages for aid to Jerusalem but the
soldiers of Holofernes are guarding all the roads and it was hard for my
couriers to get through. If, however, aid does not arrive within five days
we will hand the city over to the enemy."

At that time there lived in Bethulia a widow by the name of Judith. The
loss of her husband had left her grief-stricken. She loved him so that for
the honor of his soul she fasted every weekday and tasted food only on the
Sabbath, on the Holy Days, and at the time of the new moon.

Judith was very beautiful, rich and pious. When she heard that it was
the intention of the commander of the city to surrender it in five days she
was infuriated. She went to him and to the elders and said:

"The thing you plan is unthinkable! Why do you wish to wait only five
days longer? Isn't it always easier to wait for God's help than to perish
at the hands of the enemy? Wait then, no matter how long it takes for
aid to come. I know it must come!"

"You are right!" answered the commander. "But what can I do when
the people clamor that I surrender? I have taken an oath before them and
I must keep it. But you, O pious Judith, pray for us, pray for rain to fill
our dry cisterns."

Judith thought awhile, then she spoke:

"Meet me at the city gates tonight. I will be there with my maid. Then
she and I will go to the camp of the enemy. There I will do what I have
decided upon. May God bless my plan with success! Don't ask me what
it is. Wait until I have the enemy in my power."

Then they said: "Go in peace."

In the evening Judith said her prayers. Then she laid aside her garments
of mourning and, in their stead, put on festive attire. She adorned herself
in her finery and her jewels and took along wine, cheese, oil, bread and figs.
Accompanied by her maid she then set forth on her journey.

JUDITH AND HOLOFERNES: Adapted from the apocryphal work, *The Book of Judith,*
and from other sources.

At the city gates she was awaited by the commander and the elders. They blessed her and offered prayers that her plan might meet with success. Then they parted from her.

After Judith had walked for some distance she was stopped by the Greek soldiers.

"Who are you?" they asked her.

"I am a Jewess," she answered. "I have fled from my people because I'm convinced that our city will soon fall. Therefore, lead me to your general; I wish to help him."

"You have done well," answered the soldiers. "Our general will receive you gladly."

Then they led Judith to him.

As soon as she saw him she fell on her knees before him, but he asked her to rise.

"Have no fear, my daughter," he reassured her. "Tell me why you have fled from your people."

"We no longer have any water, my Lord, and soon there won't be any bread either," replied Judith. "Things have reached such a pass that the Jews have decided to eat those animals that are forbidden to them by their Law. Once they do that God's wrath will fall on them and they will be delivered into your hands. Because I know this well I fled in time. My advice to you, therefore: Attack and take the city immediately! It is the right time, for God does not help a sinful people."

"But how will I know the day on which the inhabitants of Bethulia sin by eating forbidden flesh?" asked Holofernes.

"Every night I will leave your camp, my Lord, and will go to Bethulia and speak to the people I know. That way I'll discover the exact day and will let you know immediately."

Holofernes agreed. He assigned a tent to her and had food and drink served to her. But she did not touch any of it.

"Why don't you eat?" the general asked her.

"Even though I have left my people, my Lord, I remain true to my God. I eat only food which is permitted, and that I've taken along with me."

"What will you do when you have eaten up all your food?"

"By that time God will have completed His work and the city of Bethulia will rest in your hands."

So Judith remained in the camp of Holofernes. When evening came she would go out of the camp to pray to God that He stand by her. This she did for three days. On the fourth day Holofernes ordered that a banquet be prepared to which only Judith was invited.

"Taste for once some of my food," Holofernes urged her.

"I will do so, my Lord," she answered, "if you first will taste some of my food."

She gave him some cheese to eat, and immediately he became thirsty. So she gave him some wine to quench his thirst. He liked its flavor and continued drinking.

"What excellent wine!" he exclaimed. "Give me more!"

And Judith gave him as much wine as he asked for. Soon he became drunk, stretched himself out on his couch and fell asleep.

Judith was waiting with impatience for this very moment. Quickly she ran and locked the door. She took the sword of Holofernes from the wall and smote him with it. Then she hurried out, again locked the door, and called for her maid. The two then returned to Bethulia.

"Open the gates! Open the gates!" she cried to the watchmen of the city when she was yet at a distance. "We are saved! God has helped us!"

Quickly the watchmen hurried to the elders who ordered that the gates be opened. The people streamed out. They lit torches, turning night into day.

Judith then told them everything she had done.

"Glory to God!" cried the people. "Praise the Lord, praised be He forever!"

"Glory to Judith! Glory to her noble deed!" cried the commander. "She has liberated the city—she has saved our lives!"

"Amen!" cried the people.

When morning came, the people, upon the advice of Judith, went forth to meet the enemy. When the Greeks caught sight of the approaching Jews they ran to waken Holofernes. His servant opened his door. Dismayed, he ran out again and called the other generals. When they saw what had happened they were filled with fear. The news soon spread among the Greek soldiers and panic seized them. They all milled about shouting.

Nobody knew what to do, nor was there anyone to take command. The Jews profited by this confusion and smote the enemy.

When news of the victory reached Jerusalem the women of the city went forth to gaze upon Judith. They sang and danced before her and praised her exceedingly. Judith then took some olive branches and gave them to her maidens. Out of them they wove a crown for her and set it upon her head. They raised their voices in songs of jubilation and their rejoicing mounted to the Heavens.

The spoils from the enemy that were brought to Judith she would not take for herself but dedicated them to God and the needy.

Judith died at the age of one hundred and five years and all Israel mourned her passing.

Bar Kochba, "The Star"

DESOLATE lay Zion, in ruins moldered Jerusalem; the Temple was but a heap of stones. Where once stood the sanctuary now grew weeds, and jackals howled in the Temple court where once David the Psalmist and his

---

BAR KOCHBA. "THE STAR": Adapted from the Talmud, the *Midrash,* and other sources.

vast choir of Levites plucked the harp strings and raised their voices in songs of praise to the Eternal. Sixty years had passed since Titus the Roman sacked the Temple and led the Jewish captives in triumph to Rome. There were few now alive who could remember the beauty of the Temple. Yet all, young and old, still grieved over the desolation of Israel, but for their sorrow they could find no consolation. Their Roman masters oppressed them sorely, afflicted their lives with humiliations without number. Worst of all was Tinnius Rufus, the Roman governor of Judea. He mocked at their suffering with the frank cruelty of the conqueror.

Thereupon the Jews raised an outcry to Heaven: "For how long, O Lord, will the Roman legions stamp on the neck of Judah? For how long, O Lord, will the Roman eagle dig its sharp claws into our flesh?"

Yet they did not abandon hope. Still too weak to strike back, they brooded in silence and secretly prayed for the day of vengeance.

But there was one who could not wait, who could not rest, who could not resign himself to silence. That was Rabbi Akiba, "The Crown of the Torah," he who expounded the Law to hushed multitudes. Aged as he was, he went on a hazardous long journey into all the far lands of the Dispersion, wherever Jews lived, in search of one worthy enough to lead a holy rebellion against Roman tyranny. And he exhorted his brethren in Babylonia, in Egypt, in Arabia and other lands, "Return to the land of your forefathers! The rising against the enemy of our people is not far off!"

One day there came to Rabbi Akiba a man of radiant beauty and great strength.

"My name is Simeon bar Kosiba," he said. "I have heard the cries of my people and have come to lead them out of the Roman bondage. Give me your blessing, O Akiba!"

And Akiba saw that this man's spirit was like flame and that his words were like sparks falling on kindling wood. He marvelled greatly, and his heart was filled with gladness. He then spoke the words of Scripture:

"There shall come a Star (Kochba) out of Jacob and a Sceptre shall rise out of Israel and shall smite the corners of Moab and destroy all the children of Sheth." (Numbers 24:17)

Thereupon, Akiba renamed him Bar Kochba in order that in this wise he might fulfill the Scriptural passage concerning the coming of the Messiah. Then, turning to the multitude, Akiba cried out with rapture: "Behold! King Messiah!"

There were twenty-four thousand disciples who were ready to follow Akiba in life. And when they heard Bar Kochba's voice they were prepared to follow him even in death for the sake of Zion and Israel. So they cried with one voice: "Surely this is King Messiah who has come to break our bonds and lift the yoke of tyranny from us. Lead us, Bar Kochba!"

"The time has not come yet!" he replied.

And he told them to prepare secretly for the uprising: "Beat your plowshares into swords and not your swords into plowshares, as the Prophet bade you. Hide them and wait!"

Now the Emperor Hadrian in Rome sent word to Tinnius Rufus in Judea: "Turn Jerusalem into a great Roman city, and it shall be the capitol of all my provinces in the East. Let it be called Aelia Capitolina. And where the Temple of the Jews formerly stood let there be raised a temple to the glory of our god, Jupiter Capitolinus."

Tinnius Rufus did as his master bade him, and he began to build a Roman city and a temple to the Roman god.

When Bar Kochba beheld these abominations he was filled with wrath. "The time has come!" he cried.

Thereupon, thousands upon thousands of Jewish youths, foremost among them the disciples of Akiba, dug up the arms they had hidden. They gathered around Bar Kochba and swore a solemn oath with him that they would not rest until the enemy had been driven from the land of Israel.

Thereafter, by ship and by caravan, across treacherous deserts and stormy seas, from every land of exile in which Jews suffered and dreamed of the redemption of their people, came great multitudes of Jews to join Bar Kochba's army. Also thousands of heathen flocked to him from neighboring countries, even from distant Parthia. They said: "If the Jews regain their liberty, we too will be free, for then the tyranny of Rome will have been broken."

When Bar Kochba had gathered the great multitude of his soldiers he said to them:

"Know, O my brothers, that the enemy is mighty. They are well armed and well trained; we have poor arms and are not trained for war. Our valor is our greatest weapon. Therefore, I have chosen to test each man of you. Who will come foward and cut off one of his fingers as proof that he is unafraid?"

Thereupon two hundred thousand of his men came forward and cut off each his own finger, thus proving their firmness of spirit.

When the sages heard of this they were dismayed.

"Why do you wish to make cripples out of this great multitude?" they rebuked him.

"Do you know a better way to test their courage?" asked Bar Kochba.

So the rabbis counselled him: "Let every one of your soldiers, while riding on horseback, show his strength by tearing up a cedar with his hands."

Bar Kochba readily agreed to their counsel, and thus he proved two hundred thousand more soldiers without any injury to them.

This took place in the sixty-first year after the destruction of Jerusalem by Titus.

And Bar Kochba began to harass the enemy on every side. He attacked the Roman garrisons when they least expected it and destroyed them. And, before any Roman force could be sent against them, he and his men escaped into the hills and hid in the caves.

Finally Bar Kochba met in open battle the Roman legion led by Tinnius Rufus. So wise was Bar Kochba as a leader, so fierce the hatred of his men for the Romans, so ardent their love of Zion and their people, that they flung themselves upon their enemies and won the victory.

When the Emperor Hadrian in Rome first heard of the revolt in Judea he laughed. "What fools! Do they expect to overthrow the power of Rome?" But when he heard of the many victories of the Jews he became alarmed. "What if the Jews succeed in their revolt?" he said to himself. "That will put heart into all rebellious people in my provinces."

And so Hadrian commanded Publius Marcellus, the Proconsul of Syria, to march at once with his legions to the aid of Tinnius Rufus. But he too was defeated in battle by Bar Kochba who, in one year's time, captured from the Romans fifty strongholds and nine hundred and eighty-five towns and villages.

Thoroughly frightened, the Emperor Hadrian called for his greatest general, Julius Severus. "Take four mighty legions and bring me back Bar Kochba alive, and tied to your chariot wheel!"

And Severus marched against the rebels in the land of Israel.

Now Severus was a cunning general. He said to himself: "Where those Roman generals who came before me failed I will succeed. They were impatient; I will be patient. They fought open battles; I will triumph by starving the Jews."

Severus then slowly and cunningly laid his plans. He cut off, one by one, the sources of Bar Kochba's supplies. The Heavens too seemed to be against the Jews, for a severe drought settled on the land. Thus the crops were burnt and Bar Kochba's soldiers had little food. One by one the Romans choked up the wells of the Jews. They turned aside the rivers and streams so that the Jews had to suffer the torments of thirst as well as of hunger.

Also one by one the patient Severus gained back each stronghold held by Bar Kochba.

Now it happened that Bar Kochba had retreated with all the remnants of his army into the fortified city of Bethar. There the Romans laid siege for one whole year; no food could reach the defenders. When Bar Kochba saw his soldiers dying of hunger and thirst and the enemy drawing ever closer to the walls of the city, he cried out in sorrow: "O Lord, since you do not help us, at least do not help our enemies!"

The Romans finally broke through the gates and poured through a breach in the walls into the city. Bar Kochba knew that the end had come, whereupon he called to his men in a mighty voice: "Better death as free men, than life as slaves under the Romans!"

With these words he flung himself into battle. None could withstand him and he slew many of the enemy. And all the Jews followed his example and fought until they could fight no more, and were slain.

Now Julius Severus remembered Hadrian's words, how he had commanded him to return to Rome in triumph with Bar Kochba tied to his chariot wheel. So he offered a large reward for his capture. A greedy Samaritan had chanced upon the body of Bar Kochba as it lay in death upon the wall, bleeding from a hundred wounds. He cut off the head and, eager for the reward, hastened with it to the Roman general.

When Severus saw Bar Kochba's head he cried out in rage to the Samaritan: "Fool! I wanted Bar Kochba alive—not his head!"

And Severus could no longer take any pleasure in his victory.

INTRODUCTORY NOTE TO *Berek Yoselovich*

After he had fought for American freedom in the Revolutionary War, the Polish General Tadeusz Kosciusko returned to his native land where he organized a popular uprising of his people against their overlords, the Russian Czar and the King of Prussia. He issued his call for the rebellion in late summer of 1794. The best elements of the population joined his army of liberation. The Jews of Poland, too, became inflamed by the ardent spirit of the times for liberty, although they were hemmed in by numerous and harsh discriminations. A certain Jewish trader and business broker, Berek (Berke) Yoselovich, and an obscure colleague, Joseph Aronovitch, sought and received Kosciusko's permission to raise a regiment of Jewish volunteers for a light cavalry unit.

Until that time the idea of allowing Jews to serve as soldiers would have appeared insane in Europe, notwithstanding that hundreds of American Jews had fought, many with distinction and gallantry, in the American War of the Revolution. In Poland, as elsewhere in Europe, except in France where the Revolution of 1789 had bestowed equal rights on the Jews of the country, Jews did not enjoy the status of citizenship, and therefore did not have the right to fight for their country. Kosciusko's authorization accordingly set a daring and historically significant precedent. A genuine republican, together with all liberal-minded men of his time he believed in the equal status of all men as their natural right.

Kosciusko appointed Berek Yoselovich as commander of the Jewish regiment. The latter then gathered money among the Jews in the ghetto of Warsaw with which to buy arms for his men, each one of whom was expected to bring his own horse.

On October 1, 1794, Berek issued his call for volunteers written in the Yiddish language:

"Pay heed, O children of Israel! All Jews who have God in their hearts and who want to help in the war for the Fatherland should gird themselves with courage because the hour has struck at last. Love for the Fatherland commands you to produce fresh healthy blood in the place of the blood that poisonous snakes have sucked out of your veins. This is made easy for us because our God-sent leader, Tadeusz Kosciusko, has, out of the great goodness of his heart, occupied himself with the organization of a Jewish regiment. And why shouldn't we, the most oppressed people in the world, take up arms to help free our Fatherland? Why shouldn't we, by participating in the struggle, help achieve liberty which ever after we will enjoy with all others?

"Let none of you think that I am trying to mislead you, or that, God forbid, I wish to lead you to your death. No, dear brothers! I have placed my faith in God and I fervently believe that the hour has come at last to defeat the enemy because it is the will of Almighty God. All we need is unity and courage among us, and then God will surely be with us. You will see for yourselves that in moments of greatest danger I will go ahead of you and all you need do is to follow me.

"It has been my great fortune to become the commander of a Jewish regiment, therefore, with all the means at your command, you must help me liberate our oppressed Poland! Let us fight for our Fatherland, so long as we have a drop of blood in our veins. And, even if we ourselves won't be blessed to be here to enjoy the fruits of liberation, yet we will have achieved it for our children so that they may be able to live in peace and not be forced to wander over the face of the earth like wild hunted animals.

"Awake, dear brothers! Be like lions and leopards and, with God's help, we will drive the enemy from our land!"

Five hundred volunteers promptly stepped forward. In the main they were tailors, butchers, waggoners and blacksmiths. General Kosciusko contributed an initial three thousand gulden. The greater part of the funds required was contributed by the Jews of Warsaw.

Throughout the brief war of the Rebellion, Berek and his men displayed great gallantry and self-sacrifice. Kosciusko assigned to them the most dangerous positions to defend. When the celebrated Russian General Suvarov assaulted Praga outside of Warsaw on November 4, 1794, Berek's regiment occupied an advance position against the Russians' overwhelming attack.

During this time the Jewish regiment held religious services morning and evening. The men observed every ritual regulation of their religion, eating only the kosher food that the Jews of Praga brought them. On the Sabbath day that Suvarov ordered a hundred cannon into position against the fortification which the regiment was defending, so pious were the men that Berek asked the rabbi of Praga for special permission to fight that day. And when the battle began, the Jews of Praga were no longer able to bring them kosher food, so that throughout all the fierce fighting during the last tragic hours the men had to go without food.

Wave after wave of seasoned Russian veterans swept against the position defended by Berek's regiment, but his men stood firm and refused to give ground. As the sun went down almost all of them lay dead at their posts. Colonel Berek himself fought with extraordinary bravery throughout the engagement and, when at last he saw that all was lost, he rallied the last twenty Jewish survivors and fought his way out with them through the enemy lines.

When Suvarov's men captured Praga they carried out a bloody massacre among the Jews. At the height of the killing a philanthropic Jew by the name of Schmul Zbitkover, who had some influence with the Russians because he had served them as a commissary agent, performed deeds of unusual loving kindness towards his unfortunate fellow-Jews, about which a touching legend has come down to us. That day he had placed in his courtyard two barrels; one was full of gold pieces, the other, of silver pieces. Then he let it be known among the Russian soldiers that whoever would bring him a live Jew he would reward with a gold coin. To the soldier who would bring him a dead Jew, so that he could bury him according to the rites of Israel, he promised a silver piece. When the greedy pogromists heard of the offer they promptly stopped their slaughter of the Jews whom, both dead and living, they brought to Schmul to collect their gold or silver coins. By the time the two barrels had been emptied Suvarov ordered the massacre to halt.

Berek Yoselovich was killed during the Napoleonic War on May 5, 1809 at the battle of Kotzk while leading a spirited attack of an infantry regiment against the Austrian hussars. His almost legendary deeds on the battlefields of Poland in the cause of freedom are still recounted in several patriotic Polish folksongs.—N. A.

Berek Yoselovich

THE VAN was not moving. Along the road hobbled an old man on a crutch, with a pack on his back.

"Good morning! Take a Jew along with you into town!"

The passengers made room for him in the van. Someone asked him: "Are you from Kotzk?"

"Almost," replied the old man, smiling. "That is to say, I was born in Praga. But I've been living in Kotzk for forty years."

"How old are you, grandfather?" asked a young man, tugging at his sleeve.

"Is it important for you to know?" asked the old man, in an offended tone. Then his voice became softer. "I'll tell you: I don't know myself. I served under Berek, before Praga; I was sixteen at the time, and that is a while since. It was in 1790. Well, figure it out for yourself." The old man smiled, showing his two sole remaining teeth, which looked like a pair of shovels.

"Then you're almost eighty," cried another.

"That's a bad guess, uncle," said the old man, smiling again. "I'm older than that."

"Of course you are," interjected Samuel. "He is more than eighty."

"The young man is right," said the old man, nodding. "On the first day of Pentecost I became eighty-one."

The horses had reached the highroad, tugged hard at the van, and bore it forward with a merry clatter. The van creaked, the ungreased axles ground with a scraping squeak that set the teeth on edge.

Mordecai looked admiringly at the Jew who had taken part in the battle of Praga, and felt somehow related to him. He edged closer to the old man and was at a loss, out of sheer embarrassment, what to ask him first. More than once Mordecai had heard his father tell that their relative, Shmuel Zbitkover, in those days had paid a Cossack a silver ruble for a dead Jew and a five ruble gold piece for a living one.

"Did you really serve under Berek Yoselovich?" asked a Hasid, who

BEREK YOSELOVICH: From *In Polish Woods,* by Joseph Opastoshu. Translated from the Yiddish by Isaac Goldberg. Reprinted with the permission of the copyright owners, The Jewish Publication Society of America. Philadelphia, 1938.

all this time had been lying upon his bundle, and now suddenly sat up, rubbing his eyes. "With the same fellow who lies buried just outside of Kotzk?"

"Yes, the very same," answered the old man, taking out a horn snuff-box, inhaling a generous pinch, making a wry face, sneezing into his beard, and passing the snuff-box to his companions. "The very same. I served under Berek Yoselovich."

"And there was really a slaughter, eh?" asked a Hasid, as he polished his velvet cap. "They say it was fearful . . . In fact, they say that the whole Jewish regiment was wiped out . . ."

"True, true," said the old man, pointing to his crutch. "That's where I lost my foot."

"So, indeed! Ay, ay!" exclaimed several Hasidim, looking at the crutch as if now it had a deeper meaning.

The old man mused a while, then sighed:

"Ah, that was years ago . . . years ago . . ."

"And was he really—I mean Berek," asked the Hasid with the velvet cap again, "such a great general? Then he must have had brains! Army strategy—that's no trifle! That's a difficult subject!"

"He was an infidel," offered somebody. "He publicly desecrated the Sabbath!"

"You're unworthy of pronouncing his name," raged the old man. "Who are you, anyway? Better worry about your own sins!"

"He waged battle on the very Day of Atonement," said another Hasid.

"So he did!" retorted the old man, almost raising his crutch in anger, as if squaring off for a set-to with the Hasid. "But Reb Meir permitted it If you don't know what you're talking about, keep your mouth shut!"

"No quarreling, no quarreling," admonished Samuel, calming the old man.

"Who's quarreling?" yelled the octogenarian, in a voice louder than ever. "I detest it when a man opens his mouth and doesn't know what he's talking about!"

Mordecai brought forth a flask of sweet brandy, and offered it to the old man, who in one swallow drained it of more than half its contents. Now he was warmed up and felt more lively.

"How did he talk with you—Berek, I mean. In Yiddish?" asked Mordecai.

"What a question! How, then? Yiddish, of course!" answered the old man, smiling. "I remember it as clearly as if I saw him before me now. There he sat on his white steed, looking like an emperor. And he had a pair of moustaches that was the envy of more than one Pole. Without exaggeration, those moustaches reached to his shoulders."

"Were there elderly Jews in the regiment, too?" asked Mordecai.

"Elderly?" The old Jew closed his eyes, thought for a while, as if he hadn't quite understood the question. "There were few older men; mostly youngsters. But our regiment was as good as the best of them. Even the

Uhlans gave way and couldn't stand up against the enemy's fire, while we Jews lay for more than a month in the old cemetery, behind the breastworks, and let the Russians smell our powder. We didn't allow them to advance. And if we'd have got reinforcements that time, even a single regiment"—the old man's voice was softer now, as if he were telling a secret—"Warsaw would have remained in our hands. We didn't leave the trenches even on Yom Kippur. Reb Meir absolved us. I remember clearly that after *Kol Nidre* the sky was full of stars, it was a bright night; yes, the stars were thick as chicken-pox. None of us closed an eye. We sat in groups around small fires. Chatted, discussed Jewish learning, and expected any moment that the enemy would storm our redoubts. Berek was with us, too, going from one group to another, with a pleasant word for everyone, a joke, and wherever he appeared things got livelier. I tell you, he was a gem of a fellow! Where was I, now? Yes. The enemy was sure that Jews would not battle on Yom Kippur, so he began his attack at daybreak. Well, children, how can I describe the scene? The air was aflame. It rained fire . . . But we weren't silent, either. Every time the enemy came rushing at us from out of the woods, it looked as if the woods themselves were on the move. It was an awful sight to see. And as the enemy approached our position, our cannons mowed them down like grass under a scythe. This kept up till the day was well advanced, and Berek ran from one redoubt to the other. That morning three horses were shot under him, and every time he shouted 'Fire!' the cannons replied with such a thunderous din that our very ear-drums quivered. The enemy drew nearer. The wooden houses of the Jews caught fire, so there we were, fire behind us, fire in front of us. But we stood there as one man until the very last minute, and when the enemy came pouring into the trenches, we did not retreat. We fought over every inch of soil, and blood flowed like water. Do you understand? There were ten Russians to every Jew. They came swarming out of the forest like locusts. And now Berek gave the signal for retreat. Out of all the regiment there were some ten of us left. Not one of us surrendered. It was during the retreat that I got a bullet in the leg."

"They say that Shmuel Zbitkover," began one of the listeners.

"Did I know Shmuel Zbitkover? Ha, ha ha! There was an angel for you!" interrupted the old man. "Why, when the Cossacks entered Praga, they made such a massacre—Heaven protect us and deliver us! If it hadn't been for Shmuel Zbitkover, who knows whether a Jew would have been left alive in Praga? He sent out couriers—Reb Shmuel, I mean—and announced that every Cossack would receive a silver ruble for every dead Jew and for every living Jew a five ruble gold piece. So you understand that they brought him more living Jews . . ."

The old man was silent, and then, out of habit, felt for his crutch; he sighed and bowed his head.

"And what became of Berek?" asked Samuel. "Did he remain in Poland?"

"He would have been a fool to do so," said the old man, smiling. "That selfsame day he left the country. Why, if he had remained in Praga a moment longer, they would have strung him up! It was all planned, down to the smallest detail. And behind it all, you must know, there were men of brains!"

"But he did return—I mean Berek," interrupted an elderly Hasid.

"Take your time, uncle," said the old man, motioning the man to hold his tongue. "Don't catch your fish before you spread the net! What was I about to tell you? Yes. For a while nothing was heard of him—of Berek, I mean—as if he had been drowned. Later, people said that he had become Napoleon's adjutant, was capturing one country after another, and everybody, even the Christians, believed that he would recapture Poland. And now, gentlemen, let us forget Berek and return to my foot. You may listen to the whole story. I lay in the hospital for a good part of the winter. The wound festered and festered, and there was no improvement. In short, why should I drag out the tale? They amputated my foot from the ankle. I don't have to tell you what suffering I went through—there I was, a cripple, not a groschen to my name, and here was Passover coming around. There was nothing else to do but to take a wallet and go begging. But there's a God in heaven, who sends the healing before the wound is inflicted. The very day that I was supposed to leave the hospital, in came an absolute stranger, asked my name, left with me a purse of some two hundred gulden, and before you could look around he was gone. Later I learned that a Jewish magnate had sent the sum to every Jew of Berek's regiment who had been left alive. In those years, understand, two hundred gulden was a fortune. And surely enough, they were soon trying to match me off with a girl from Kotzk—with Shloime the Bath-man's youngest daughter. In short—why drag it out?—I married her. After the marriage, my father-in-law, who was a smart fellow, says to me, 'Simhe, if you'll take my advice, you'll become a barber. If a stranger can make a living at it, certainly you should be able to. A little shearing, a little bleeding—no worry, with God's help you'll do a good business.' In those days, understand, every man of standing had his hair cut once a month, and was bled at the same time. The whole pleasure cost a trifle, ha, ha, ha! In short—I've forgotten what I was talking about. Where was I? So I became a barber. During the early days I had a hard time of it. Our children—may you be spared that misfortune—didn't live. But that's not my point. To make a long story short, things didn't happen as fast as I tell them. Once I was sent for by someone beyond Lukov—some village there. A renter had suffered a shock and would have nobody bleed him save me. At that time it was a difficult journey. Kotzk, understand, belonged to the Austrians and Lukov to the Russians. Such a journey, in fact, meant that you took your life in your hands. But I wasn't afraid; I knew that nobody would harm me, a cripple. In short, I bled the fellow, he improved, and as I was leaving the town, whom should I meet but Berek? He hadn't changed a bit. The same moustaches, the same cut on his forehead. He had a different hat, that was all—a bearskin fur cap. I jumped down from my wagon, shouldered my crutch, as in the good old days, brought my hand to my peak, in salute, greeted him as Colonel so-and-so, with his full title . . . What shall I say? You won't believe me! He embraced me, and tears came to his eyes. He asked how I was doing, and reminded me how we lay behind the redoubt. He simply wouldn't let me go. I had to accept a drink from him, and I give you my word that if he had told me then and there that he needed me, I'd have left my wife and children and joined him. Before we separated, I said to him, 'Colonel, the Austrian Uhlans are pressing us hard.' And he answered, 'Have patience. We'll soon have Poland back again.' Who could have dreamt, at that time, that such a sorry end was in store for him? In short, I don't know to this day just how it all befell. I believe that the enemy must have outwitted him, and the moment he marched into the market-place with his few soldiers, they blocked the turnpike and opened fire directly. As for retreating, you understand, that was out of the question. It was a devil of a fix, so he started to hack his way out with his sword. Jewish storekeepers, who happened to be on the market-place, told me that he sliced off heads the way you slice off cabbage. And if his horse hadn't fallen under him, he would have come through safely. And do you know what? There on his feet, he defended himself, clutching his sword tightly, till a Uhlan stole up behind him and laid him low with a pike-blow over the head. And when Berek lay at last in a pool of blood, the Uhlans took their vengeance, and cut him into strips. Soon a Polish detachment came up, routed the Austrians out of Kotzk and buried Berek with full military honors at the very entrance to the city . . . Here we are, at the very grave!"

The Last Twelve Hours of Hymie Epstein

"IN WAR I guess the best go first," says Maj. Bert Zeef, of Grand Rapids. "That kid was the best."

This is the last twelve hours of Hymie Epstein's life as Zeef tells it.

"We were sent out to carry rations to one of our units, cut off in the forest ahead of us. They had several dead and a number of wounded.

"Epstein was a medical aide. Medical aides are forbidden by the Geneva Convention to bear arms. Casualties among their ranks have been as high or higher than among the fighting troops because when the Japs wound a man with sniping they do not finish him off but wait for the medical aide man to come and then get both.

"The Japs must have heard us creeping along because they moved a machine gun across our line of crawl. Then they got another there and

THE LAST TWELVE HOURS OF HYMIE EPSTEIN: From *Jews in American Wars*, by J. George Fredman and Louis A. Falk. Copyright, 1942, by J. George Fredman and Louis A. Falk. Jewish War Veterans of the U. S. New York.

had the two converging lanes of fire directed upon our mudholes. Then
they sent snipers around the sides so that they could pick us off where we
were if we stopped moving. But we had to stop because it was getting
dark and we could not see where we were going. Then they opened fire
on us.

"Epstein, a small, slight youngster from Omaha, Neb., was lying at the
major's side about three feet away to the right. Suddenly, a man about
eight feet ahead was hit in the neck by a machine gun bullet.

"Both Epstein and myself saw him get it. But the Japs knew we were
all there and kept their fire right in that spot. I would not order anyone
to go out into that fire to get that man. It was just throwing one life after
another.

"But this little Jewish kid crawls right from the mud to the wounded
man. Epstein got out his sulfanilimide powder and bandages and, lying
on his back, bound the wounded man's neck. Then he crawled back with
bullets all around him.

"Just before darkness came down another man was hit in the head.
Without any hesitation out crawled that kid again with his packet. He
got to the man, rolled him over and, lying on his back, bound up his head.
I could not understand how he ever got back that time. The Japs simply
poured fire around him. But he did get back."

All that night, the Americans hugged the mud as low as possible, while
Japanese machine-gunners and snipers systematically worked over the
ground where they lay. Zeef continued:

"You could hear the men talking all night. 'Did you see what little
Epstein did?' they would say. Word had gone the whole length of the line
in whispers. Then at dawn the Japs began to get more accurate with their
fire. A man over on the left was hit, and word came that a medic was
needed. Epstein crawled down the line. Five minutes later, word was
passed up the line that he was dead.

"How they had finally got him was this way:

"There was a badly wounded guy out there with fire all around him.
Epstein went out and got him fixed. Then the Japs put in everything they
had. Epstein could have crawled back but he chose to stick. He stayed
a little too long.

"What I will always remember was the wounded man when he dragged
himself in. It's not often you hear a soldier crying and he was a tough
baby himself. He kept saying between sobs, 'Somebody's gotta go out
there and take care of Epstein! Epstein's bleeding to death. Somebody's
quick gotta go out and get Epstein.' Of course he was delirious. We
could see that Epstein was already dead. But even in delirium and with
his wound that guy felt worse about Epstein than about himself.

"We buried this man the next night, and we buried Epstein by day
as we pulled back through the forest. You never know who is going to be a
good soldier and who isn't. But when they are handing honors around,
you can give mine to little Hymie Epstein and that goes for all of us."

The Battle of the Warsaw Ghetto

THE battle of Warsaw Ghetto lasted for forty-two days and nights, beginning on the first Seder Night, April 19, 1943 and ending a week before Shevuoth. On that first night all of the forty thousand Jews still left in the ghetto after the wholesale deportations and massacres, went out to fight with weapons in their hands. On the forty-second day of the uprising only one four-story building stood in the ghetto as a fort from which fluttered the blue-and-white flag. It held out against the siege of the Nazis for eight hours. A fierce battle was fought for every floor of the building separately until, by midnight, it fell into the hands of the enemy.

On the first Seder Night, about midnight, German soldiers entered the ghetto and began throwing a cordon around a street from which they were to take away Jews as in previous mass-deportations. Formerly the Germans had been accustomed to see Jews allow themselves to be led to slaughter without resistance, and a few dozen Nazi soldiers would be enough to carry out the deportation of thousands of Jews. But in Warsaw, in January 1943, the Jewish youth, mostly the Zionists, had already offered resistance and many young Jews were killed. In order to overawe the Jews, the Nazis on the first night of the Passover arrived in six tanks. On reaching the main street the Germans were met by an intense fusillade on all sides when the ghetto fighters opened fire on their tanks. The Nazis tried to flee, but they did not leave the ghetto alive and died in the flames of their own exploded tanks.

It was then that the signal was given for the general uprising in the ghetto. Jewish houses were covered with proclamations and announcements of the uprising in which "the Jews will fight to the last drop of blood."

The leaders went out into the streets and organized the fight. Every able bodied man and woman was given weapons. The youth took up positions as sentinels on the streets. The larger houses were converted into forts where large groups of fighters were concentrated. Every street was assigned a command and equipped with an arsenal. The fighters took up positions at the gates and windows of the buildings, with weapons in their hands. On the same night trenches were dug in the streets for a battle with the enemy and cellars were dug for shelter. The whole ghetto was made into one large fortress and every house into a citadel. The children were charged with the grave task of acting as messengers among the fighters in different streets. They were also to bring food to the fighters. The children performed their part in the uprising at the peril of their lives, often under

---

THE BATTLE OF THE WARSAW GHETTO: From *The Extermination of 500,000 Jews in the Warsaw Ghetto*. Published by the American Council of Warsaw Jews and American Friends of Polish Jews. New York, 1944.

An eyewitness account of the heroic resistance of the Jews to the Germans in the fierce uprising which lasted 42 days until the last man fell with the Jewish flag in his arms. This report, received by the World Jewish Congress, is reprinted with their permission.

a rain of bullets. The old people, men and women whose number in the ghetto was small, took over the work in the kitchens of preparing food for the fighters. Everything was fully organized on the first night. Not a minute was to be lost. The situation was very grave. It was known that soon a fierce struggle was to break out for which it was necessary to be well prepared.

Early in the morning a special detachment of the fighters surrounded the German workshops where Jews were employed and the German arsenals. From these the Jews took the German uniforms which Jewish workers had been finishing or repairing. Thus special squads were formed of fighters wearing German uniforms. Jews also entered German stores and seized large transports of foodstuffs which they later distributed among the fighters in the ghetto.

In the morning the banners of revolt were hung out from the windows, the blue-and-white waving side by side with the Polish colors. The German and Lithuanian police which used to escort the Jews to their daily labor, this time came to the ghetto, but did not leave it. The ghetto appeared deserted and desolate, and no human being was to be seen on the streets. Everyone was in some building ready for battle. The German soldiers who came in as usual to supervise the Jewish workers in the German workshops, were not given a chance to leave. Soon all Warsaw knew that the ghetto had proclaimed a general uprising.

At noon of the first day of Passover the ghetto became a battlefield. Motorized military detachments, fully armed, appeared on the streets of Warsaw headed for the gate of the ghetto, ten tanks leading the procession. A cordon was thrown around the non-Jewish section by German military forces who brought up machine-guns. Many Poles were arrested, suspected of complicity in the preparations for the uprising in the ghetto and of planning to help the Jewish fighters. It was strictly forbidden to leave the non-Jewish section or to enter it.

By noontime the first shots were heard and soon there was an enormous fusillade. Thick flames and smoke shot up from the ghetto and fires broke out on both sides. The battle lasted far into the night. The Germans were now convinced that they were faced by an organized rebellion of the whole ghetto which was ready to fight to the last drop of blood. They were fired on from every house in the ghetto they tried to approach. Late in the evening the Germans abandoned tanks and machine-guns which had been put out of commission. The gates of the ghetto were blown up, the houses on the outskirts of the ghetto were burned down, after being vacated by the fighters.

In the evening an order was issued by the leaders of the uprising to cease fire. The surviving Germans were surrounded and taken prisoner. In the evening the battlefield was quiet, but flames and pillars of smoke were rising on all sides. The Jews were forbidden by their leaders to leave the houses and their defense positions. The guard was reinforced.

That night and the whole of the next day passed without any clash. It was evident that the Germans were preparing to quell the uprising in the shortest possible time before it could cross the borders of the ghetto and before the central military authorities had learned of it. The third night was therefore spent by the Jews in preparing the defense. Detachments of Jews went out at night attacking the arsenals of the Gestapo, killing the guards and seizing the weapons. All night long German trucks were loaded with ammunition and arms and taken into the ghetto. Whatever was left of the arsenals was blown up and burned down.

The next day it became known throughout Warsaw that the German arsenals had been seized and blown up and that dozens of Gestapo agents had fallen into the hands of the Jews. Large transports of arms had secretly been brought into the ghetto some time earlier when the task of watching the ghetto was assigned to the Polish police who cooperated in preparing for the uprising. Bombs, machine-guns and anti-tank cannon hidden under potatoes had been brought in on hundreds of trucks sent in by the secret Polish military organization.

On the third night the six thousand young Jewish workers of the so-called "Small Ghetto" who worked for the German army, joined the revolt. Their position in comparison with that of the 40,000 in the large ghetto was a privileged one and they were in no danger of deportation. But when they learned of the uprising, they set fire to their "Small Ghetto" and went over to the fighters.

The ensuing few days passed without clashes with the Germans. There was a conflict between the Gestapo and the German military authorities about the methods of quelling the uprising. The military authorities interpreted the revolt as directed against the Gestapo because of its brutal treatment of the Jews and rejected the Gestapo pleas for assistance, waiting for instructions from Berlin. The Gestapo, in the meantime, did not dare take any steps on its own.

On the seventh night the leaders of the uprising received a plea from the prisoners in the Pawiak jail: "Save us and we will fight with you!" The jail contained several thousand prisoners, mostly Jews and Poles, but also deserters from the German army. The Jewish leaders sent in the following reply: "Every one of you is important to us, we will do everything to free you." On the next day, the eighth day of the uprising, 500 Jews dressed in German uniforms left the ghetto for the Pawiak jail which was guarded by German soldiers. At night the Jews opened fire. In the confusion of the dark one could not tell which of the men in German uniform was a Jew and which was a German guard. The Jews entered the jail bringing with them German uniforms for the prisoners and taking them out by groups disguised as German soldiers. By morning they were all out of jail. All of them, including the German deserters from the front lines, went over to the fighters in the ghetto, organized in separate detachments.

The liberation of the Pawiak prisoners encouraged the fighters in the ghetto and evoked enthusiasm among the Polish youth in Warsaw as well as among those young Jews who were living outside the ghetto by virtue of their "Aryan" documents. Many young Poles volunteered to fight in the ghetto. Some partisans hiding in the woods also joined. Every one was getting ready for a great battle.

It became known that instructions had come from Berlin to destroy the ghetto completely. Large detachments of Storm Troopers arrived from Galicia and the German forces in Warsaw were increased. On the night before the great offensive for which the Germans were making intensive preparations, they issued an ultimatum to the Jews that unless the struggle was discontinued and the German prisoners given up, the whole ghetto would be wiped out. The Jews replied that they were ready to give up the captured Germans on conditions that for each German prisoner ten Jews were delivered by the Germans. There were a large number of German captives in the ghetto at the time.

The next morning the Germans opened the great battle. The ghetto was surrounded on all sides by tanks and cannon which subjected it to enormous fire. The Germans were determined to bombard the ghetto until it surrendered. In this, however, they failed. The German tanks and cannon were showered by bullets and bombs from the houses and streets of the ghetto. The special suicide squad of the Jews broke through the lines and wrought ruin among the enemy. Disguised in German uniforms they crawled under the German tanks and blew them up with hand grenades, losing their own lives in the fire which killed the Germans. Such was the havoc wrought by this method that the Germans were careful not to place groups of cannon behind tanks. Thus passed the day of the desperate battle. The Germans realized that they would not be able to vanquish the ghetto without heavy sacrifice. Hundreds of German soldiers lost their lives and splinters of German tanks and guns were mingled with the debris of ruined houses at the gates of the ghetto.

The German command then issued an order to have the whole ghetto blown up by incendiary bombs. A night of inferno then descended on the ghetto. All night incendiary bombs rained on it and fires broke out in many places. Houses came crashing down and among their ruins were heard the cries of wounded men, women and children. Many brave fighters perished among those ruins.

In the morning the ghetto stood in a sea of flames. The survivors, numbering some 30,000, began reorganizing for defense. The houses on the outskirts were vacated and the arms taken to the centre of the ghetto. Also the food which could still be saved was taken away. Special squads of the fighters fortified themselves again in the remaining buildings. When the enemy again attacked in the morning, he was confronted by stiff and desperate resistance at every step, near every building. The battle lasted all day long, and the Germans had to fight for hours before capturing a single house, even if it was but a ruin. In the evening the Germans managed to penetrate deeper into the ghetto and to capture a few of the taller buildings.

After the Night of Inferno and the ensuing battles on the following morning the leaders of the ghetto saw that the end was near unless new methods of warfare could be devised. They tried to reach an understanding with the Polish Underground and suggested that the non-Jewish population of the city rise against the Germans thus forcing the Germans to fight on both sides. But the Poles replied that the time had not yet come for a general uprising on their part. Under these circumstances the fighters of the ghetto abandoned their defense tactics for acts of terror and revenge. Groups of fighters went out of the ghetto, attacking and killing German soldiers. The Jewish heroes fought the Germans until they themselves were killed. Others fled to the woods and joined the Polish guerrillas. Many perished on the road, fighting German soldiers. Many others surrendered to the Germans, having hand grenades hidden in their clothes with which they later killed their guards, losing their own lives in the explosions.

After a few more days of fighting the Germans realized that they would have to contest every house in the ghetto. Every building now became an even more fortified stronghold. Whenever Germans appeared in front of a house they were fired on from the windows, from the garrets, from the roof, until they managed to blow up the house, and its heroic defenders perished in its ruins. In the last house were gathered all those who had survived and were still carrying on the fight. During the last few days the situation was horrible. There was hardly any food left and water could not be brought in because it was impossible to go out on the street. The Nazis committed terrible atrocities, bringing captured Jews and hanging them on the posts of the ghetto and otherwise exceeding their own record for brutality in all the years of their occupation.

On the forty-second day of the uprising there was only one four-story building left in the center of the ghetto over which the blue-and-white flag waved. For eight hours a battle raged over that house and by midnight the Germans captured it. Every floor, every step was hotly contested. When all defenders at the gates fell, the Germans entered the building, encountering the fierce resistance of those on the ground floor. When the first floor was taken, the second floor was contested just as desperately, and so on from floor to floor. The blue-and-white banner held by a young *halutz* was carried by the survivors from floor to floor. Late at night it fluttered from the top story where a desperate struggle was still going on.

When the shooting was over a crash was heard. The young *halutz* hurled himself down wrapped in the blue-and-white flag which he had guarded for forty-two days and nights. The flag was red with the blood of the martyr, the last fighter of the ghetto, who ended his life in this heroic manner.

The next morning the Germans "triumphantly" announced that the ghetto of Warsaw no longer existed. Thousands of German soldiers paid for that "victory" with their lives. The heroes of the ghetto fought and died like saintly martyrs.

Daniel Mendoza, Father of the Art of Boxing

I was born on the fifth day of July, 1764, in the parish of Aldgate, London. My parents, who were of the Jewish persuasion, were by no means in affluent circumstances; they might however be considered as in the middling class of society: and though their family was large, they contrived to bestow a tolerable education on all their children. They justly conceived this to be an object of the highest importance, as it concerned their future welfare in life, and therefore used every effort in their power to accomplish it.

I was accordingly sent at a very early age to a Jewish school, where I remained some years, and was instructed in English grammar, writing, arithmetic, and those branches of education which are usually taught in schools; I was also instructed in the Hebrew language, in which, before I quitted school, I made considerable progress.

Being blessed with a robust and vigorous constitution, and enjoying excellent health and spirits, I engaged at this early period of my life in several contests with boys considerably older than myself, till I at length attained such a reputation for courage, activity and strength, that none would venture to contend with me, and I was acknowledged by all of them to be their master.

Whenever I returned home with a black eye, or any external mark of violence, my father never failed to inquire strictly into the cause, and would reprove me severely when it appeared I had involved myself wantonly in a quarrel; but on the other hand, if he found I had acted only in self-defense, or from any justifiable motive, he would freely forgive me, and declare he would never exert his paternal authority to prevent me from standing in my own defence, when unjustly assailed, being well aware that courage is not only useful, but almost indispensably necessary to carry us through life.

In justice to the memory of my father, I must mention that perhaps no man had a clearer notion of the difference between true and false courage than himself; he would often declare how gratified he felt in seeing resolution and fortitude displayed upon proper occasions; though at the same

DANIEL MENDOZA, FATHER OF THE ART OF BOXING: From *Memoirs of the Life of D. Mendoza,* in the London edition of 1828. Cited in *Memoirs of My People,* by Leo W. Schwarz. Copyright, 1943, by Leo W. Schwarz. Farrar & Rinehart. New York.
The master-tailor, Francis Place, a Gentile contemporary of Daniel Mendoza, wrote that in the years following the Naturalization Law of 1753 anti-Jewish feeling was rampant in London: "I then saw the Jews being chased, whistled at, beaten, their beards plucked and spat at in the public street without any passerby or officer of the law coming to their aid. . . . Dogs were not treated so shabbily as some Jews were. One circumstance above all others brought the mistreatment of Jews to an end. In the year 1787 the Jew, Daniel Mendoza, became a famous boxer. He opened a school where he taught the art of boxing as a science. This sport spread rapidly among young Jews. . . . It was no longer wholesome to molest a Jew if he did not happen to be an old man. . . ."—From an unpublished ms. in the British Museum Library, cited by Fritz Heymann in *Der Chevalier von Geldern.*

time no one could hold the character of a bravado, or quarrelsome man, in greater abhorrence. His observations on this subject I have often reflected on, and I trust they will never be effaced from my memory. . . .

Feeling the utmost aversion to a life of idleness, and unwilling to become an incumbrance on my father, I gladly availed myself of the first opportunity of employment that offered and therefore entered into the service of a fruiterer and greengrocer in our neighborhood, from whom and whose family I experienced, during my stay with them, very kind and liberal treatment. I was here frequently drawn into contests with the butcher and others in the neighborhood, who, on account of my mistress' being of the Jewish religion, were frequently disposed to insult her. In a short time, however, I became the terror of these gentry, and when they found that young as I was, I was always ready to come forward in her defense, they forbore to molest her.

My next situation in life was with a tea dealer, in whose service I fought the first pitched battle that attracted the attention of the public. This was in the year 1780; I was then only sixteen years of age, and the occasion of my fighting arose from the following circumstance.

A porter who had been sent to our house with a load, upon my offering him the price of a pint of porter as a gratuity for himself, rejected the offer in a contemptuous manner, and made a demand of double the money. At this moment my master entered the shop and, remonstrating with him on the impropriety of his behavior, the fellow became still more abusive and challenged him to fight. Upon which I turned him into the street and told him that since he was so desirous of fighting, I was at his service, and that I felt myself fully competent to punish him for his insolence, and was willing to give him instant proof of it, if he pleased. He accepted my challenge with great eagerness, and most probably flattered himself with the hopes of gaining an easy victory over a youth (being himself a stout athletic man in the prime of life).

A ring being consequently formed in the street, we immediately set to and, after a severe contest of about three quarters of an hour, my antagonist confessed himself unable to stand longer against me, and gave in. Upon this occasion Mr. Richard Humphreys, whom I shall frequently have occasion to mention in the course of these memoirs, was my second.

This battle which first brought me into public notice, laid the foundation of the fame I afterwards enjoyed; the spirit and resolution I displayed throughout a contest with an antagonist of such superior strength, excited the general applause of the spectators (many of whom were intimately acquainted with me) and became the general subject of conversation in the neighborhood for some time after.

Shortly after this one of my friends called upon me and informed me that, having witnessed such uncommon exertion on my part in the last contest, he had matched me to fight a man in the Mile End Road, on the ensuing Saturday (being a leisure day with us); I had never before fought for money, and felt some reluctance to a battle of that sort on the present occasion; however, as my friend had made the match, I was unwilling to disappoint him, and therefore resolved to use my utmost exertions in his favor.

Accordingly, at the time appointed, I met my opponent, and here again had to contend against superior strength; but, after a contest which lasted near an hour, had the satisfaction once more to come off victorious.

Mr. Humphreys was likewise my second on this occasion; and when some of the spectators called out to him to direct me where to strike, I well recollect hearing him reply, "There is no need of it, the lad knows more than us all."

Though the success of these two battles had gained me great repute for courage, as well as for skill and activity, I had not then any intention of devoting my future life to the practice of pugilism, nor of quitting the situation in which I was engaged; but, on my return to my master on the Monday following, he expressed great displeasure at my having fought the last battle, and immediately discharged me from his service.

Shortly after I was dismissed from the service of the tea dealer, I was invited to join some friends in celebrating a Jewish festival and we accordingly agreed, by way of frolic, to disguise ourselves and represent a party of sailors, in which I was to bear the part of the lieutenant. This frolic, however, which seemed likely to produce a great deal of merriment and diversion, had a very unpleasant termination; for, happening to meet with a press gang, I and two of my friends were actually made prisoners by them, and it was not without considerable difficulty that we procured our release; this however we effected after two days confinement. . . .

Soon after this I entered into the service of a tobacconist, who resided in the neighborhood of Whitechapel. I was engaged by him chiefly for the purpose of traveling with samples of the various articles he sold, and to procure orders for him, etc., and having been sent into Kent on some business of this sort, was drawn into a pugilistic contest from the following circumstance.

Walking on the road near Chatham Barracks, part of a regiment of soldiers happened to pass (I believe the 25th, but am not certain), when one of the sergeants accosted me in a very rude manner, and ordered me in a peremptory tone to get out of the way, and upon my remonstrating with him on his uncivil behavior, struck me a severe blow with his halbert; feeling my indignation roused to the highest pitch at this treatment, I could not refrain from offering to fight him on the spot, and he readily accepted my challenge. At this moment a party of sailors happened to come up who, having inquired into the cause of this contest, assured me of their determination of seeing fair play.

We accordingly stripped and set to, and after fighting for nearly an hour, I had the satisfaction of coming off completely victorious, and of inflicting a severe and deserved punishment on my antagonist, in revenge for the ill treatment I had borne from him.

One of the officers of the regiment who, in the first instance, seemed rather inclined to take the part of my opponent, was so much gratified at witnessing what he was pleased to term an uncommon instance of spirit and resolution in a youth, that he immediately presented me with five guineas, and afterwards exerted his influence, with effect, in procuring orders for my employer.

As for the behavior of the sailors, it was so truly noble and generous and made so deep an impression on my mind, that I cannot forbear relating it. These gallant sons of Neptune watched every turn of the battle with the most anxious solicitude, and when it terminated in my favor, expressed their congratulations at my success in the most friendly manner, and cheered me with loud and repeated acclamations. They afterwards carried me with them in triumph to Gravesend, a distance of eight miles. And as the bags which I had out with me containing the different samples of merchandise were, in the course of the affray, thrown down and trampled on, it became necessary for me to return to town for a fresh supply, and I accordingly came up with them on the same boat.

On my return, my master expressed his surprise at seeing me again so soon, but on my relating the cause, and giving him an account of the battle, he expressed the greatest satisfaction at my conduct, and told me that so far from being inclined to blame me for my behavior, he thought I deserved the highest commendation for having acted as I had done.

I returned almost immediately afterwards to Chatham, and transacted the business on which I was sent before, and was prevented in the manner I have just related.

On my return to town, I was induced, at the request of some of my acquaintances, to engage in a pugilistic contest for five guineas, with a man who had signalized himself in many instances, and who the most sanguine of my friends expected would prove a formidable opponent.

Having mentioned the subject to my master, and requested his permission to fight, he very readily granted it, and was afterwards present at the battle.

On this occasion the friends of my opponent were so confident of his success, on account of the evident superiority he possessed in size and strength, and the reputation he had already acquired, that they offered bets of five to one in his favor. Notwithstanding which, however, when I engaged with him, I had the satisfaction of having my exertions crowned with success, after a hard contest of an hour and a quarter.

I was about this time induced to quit the service of the tobacconist upon the prospect of a situation of more emolument; the remuneration I received from him was very trifling and inadequate to procure me many little enjoyments I wished for; I therefore eagerly embraced an offer that was made me of a situation in which I was to receive a guinea per week and my board, which I at that time could not fail of considering a most liberal remuneration for my services, more especially upon being given to understand that my employment would be to assist in conveying different sorts of merchandise from the coast to various places to be disposed of, and that I was to be furnished with an excellent horse for that purpose.

As the application was made to me from a quarter that I had always considered as respectable, I had not the least suspicion of there being anything illegal or improper in the concern; but immediately upon my engaging in it, I was informed that I was hired for the purpose of escorting smuggled property, and was likewise told that I should be expected to guard and protect (even at the hazard of my life) whatever might happen to be entrusted to my care, against any seizures that might be attempted to be made thereon.

This certainly was most unwelcome intelligence to me. I am not aware of ever having wanted resolution and courage upon proper occasions, but was not desperate enough to disregard entirely the consequences of such a dangerous profession, and having learnt that one of our party had, but a few weeks previous to this, lost his life in an affray with some revenue officers, I quitted my employment in disgust, having remained therein only four or five days.

Shortly after my return to town, I was induced to engage in another pugilistic contest: for being present one day in company with a young man at a fight at Kentish Town, my friend happened to be grossly insulted by a man, whom I challenged in consequence, and we accordingly set to, when after a contest of about half an hour, he was forced to give in, being so severely beaten as to be scarcely able to stand and, indeed, he was obliged to be carried off the field. . . .

I had now so completely established my reputation for a thorough knowledge of the theory and practice of the art of pugilism, that my friends as well as myself were desirous that, instead of seeking fresh contests, I should avail myself of the fame I had already acquired, and make such a use of my skill as would enable me to derive from thence a regular and liberal income; and being now applied to by several gentlemen to teach the art of self-defense, I was induced, in consequence of the number of such applications, to open a school for that purpose in Chapel Court, behind the Royal Exchange . . .

[Mendoza subsequently engaged in several spirited bouts with Humphreys, in the ring and outside of it. The most celebrated of these was the one fought at Doncaster. The following is a contemporary newspaper account of it as cited in *Pugilistica*, by H. D. Miles. Vol. I, pp. 75–76. London, 1906.—N. A.]

"September 29, 1790, is rendered memorable in the annals of pugilism by the well-fought third battle between the celebrated pugilists Humphries and Mendoza.

"An inn-yard at Doncaster was pitched upon as the spot for the decision of the contest. The time (the Sellinger and Cup week), and the place were capitally chosen. The ground was bounded on two sides by the backs of houses, at one end by the inn, at the other by a strong palisade, behind which ran the river Don. Upwards of 500 tickets at half-a-guinea were sold, and the persons admitted. But the Yorkshire 'tykes' of humbler means were not to be baffled; and a 'cute ferryman having brought over some hundreds at sixpence a-head, the crowd outside soon demolished the paling, stout as it was, and an immense concourse got in. The spectators seated around the stage, however, prevented any inconvenience or interruption of the principal performers.

"At about half-past ten Humphries made his appearance, immediately followed by Mendoza; the former mounted the stage, which was about four feet high, and twenty-four square, with astonishing agility, evidently in high spirits. Mendoza also seemed equally alert and devoid of apprehension. Ward seconded Humphries, and Jackson was his bottle-holder; Colonel Hamilton being chosen by him as his umpire. Tom Johnson was second to Mendoza, and his bottle-holder Butcher. Sir Thomas Apreece, who was umpire for Mendoza on his last battle with Humphries, at Stilton, was also chosen on this occasion, and Mr. Harvey Aston was mutually agreed upon as the third umpire, should any altercation arise during the combat, and a difference of opinion arise between the Colonel and Sir Thomas with respect to its decision.

"Everything being thus arranged, the combatants began to strip. Odds were laid five to four in favour of Mendoza, and readily accepted by Humphries's friends, who considered that although perhaps it might be impossible for him to beat the Jew by carrying on the fight regularly and in a scientific style, yet, by his impetuous exertions at the commencement, would be able to overcome his antagonist, and bear away the palm."

THE FIGHT

ROUND 1.—The onset of Humphries was bold and astonishingly vigorous, but was repelled by Mendoza with equal force; they mutually closed, struggled, and both fell.

2.—The same vigorous spirit was manifested on both sides, but Humphries struck the most blows, though apparently without overpowering Mendoza.

3.—This round was fought with much caution on both sides, each being equally careful of giving or receiving a blow; what passed, however, were in Mendoza's favour, and it terminated by his giving Humphries a knockdown blow.

4.—They engaged, but only for a few moments.

5.—Humphries aimed a severe blow at Mendoza's stomach, which he dexterously stopped, and struck him in the face; this blow, however, Humphries returned, but at the same time fell.

"A number of rounds after this took place, but in every one of them Mendoza evidently had the advantage, and odds had risen forty to five, and ten to one in his favour; Humphries continually fell, sometimes in consequence of blows, but more frequently from a policy often used in boxing, which perhaps may be considered fair; several times he sunk without a blow, which conduct, although contrary to the articles of agreement, was passed unnoticed, as his general manners placed him above the suspicion of cowardice. For although he had undoubtedly the worst throughout the battle, he fought with great resolution, and even when his friends, perceiving him conquered, and one eye perfectly closed, persuaded him to yield, he solicited to fight a little longer. Notwithstanding all this display of excellent bottom, he was again obliged to acknowledge the ascendency of the Israelite.

"Mendoza was very much cut about the left side of his head, his left eye and ear being much mutilated, and he had received a severe cut in the ribs on the right side by a projectile left-handed blow of his antagonist.

"Humphries had several hits which drew blood under his left arm; his right eye was closed early in the battle, and he had a severe cut over his left. He had a wound clear as a razor cut by the left side of his nose by a straight-forward springing blow of Mendoza's. The same hit also split his upper lip. He was carried through the crowd on the shoulders of his friends, who conveyed him in a post-chaise out of the town. Mendoza walked on the race-ground on the Town Moor for some time after the combat, 'the observed of all observers.' "

SONG.*
ON THE BATTLE FOUGHT BETWEEN
HUMPHREYS AND MENDOZA.
AT
Stillton in Huntingdonshire

O my DICKY, my DICKY, and O my DICKY my dear,
Such a wonderful DICKY is not to be found far nor near;
For DICKY was up, up, up, and DICKY was down, down, down,
And DICKY was backwards and forwards, and DICKY was round, round, round.
    O my DICKY, &c.

My DICKY was all the delight of half the genteels in the town;
Their tables were scarcely compleat, unless my DICKY sat down;
So very polite, so genteel, such a soft complaisant modest face,
What a damnable shame to be spoil'd by a curst little Jew from Duke's Place!
    O my DICKY, &c.

My DICKY he went to the school, that was kept by this DANNY MENDOZA,
And swore if the Jew would not fight, he would ring his Mosaical nose, Sir,
His friends exclaimed, go it, my DICKY, my terrible! give him a derry;
You've only to sport your position, and quickly the Levite will sherry.
    O my DICKY, &c.

Elate with false pride and conceit, superciliously prone to his ruin,
He haughtily stalk'd on the spot, which was turf'd for his utter undoing;
While the Jew's humble bow seem'd to please, my DICKY's eyes flash'd vivid fire;
He contemptuously viewed his opponent, as DAVID was viewed by GOLIAH.
    O my DICKY, &c.

---

*A contemporary song, cited by Fritz Heymann in *Der Chevalier von Geldern.*

Now Fortune, the whimsical goddess, resolving to open men's eyes;
To draw from their senses the screen, and excite just contempt and surprise,
Produced to their view, this great hero, who promis'd MENDOZA to beat,
When he proved but a boasting impostor, his promises all a mere cheat.

For DICKY, he stopt with his head,
   Was hit through his guard ev'ry round, Sir,
Was fonder of falling than fighting,
   And therefore gave out on the ground, Sir.

Houdini the Magician

HOUDINI, whom Old World mystics would have regarded as a particularly well-versed cabalist, was the son of an American Rabbi not at all devoted to mystic lore. To a member of the staff of *The American Hebrew,* a few weeks before his death (on Oct. 31, 1926) he recalled:

"Soon after I left home, under pressure of a great *wanderlust,* my folks moved from Appleton to Chicago, where father continued as a (Hebrew) teacher. And here's something few ever heard me tell about. I taught Hebrew myself, assisting my father in teaching beginners *Aleph-Bess.* A few years later we moved to New York, where conditions were so precarious for a while that father had to sell some of his finest Hebrew books. It was in New York also that I attained *Bar Mitzvah,* the memory of which I still cherish. As I recall, it was the Rev. Dr. Bernard Drachman who confirmed me and who learned my identity in after years."

Doubtless it was the influence of the circus side-show that came to Appleton, Wis. that induced the three sons of Rabbi Mayer Weiss, to embark upon the magician "business." One of the rabbi's sons, Harry Weiss, who took the name of "Houdini," acquired international celebrity.

That side of Harry Weiss Houdini's career which was least known was his interest in Jewish affairs and philanthropies. He helped to organize the Rabbis' Sons Theatrical Benevolent Association, which includes in its membership Al Jolson, Irving Berlin, the Howard Brothers, and other stars of equal magnitude, and which has rendered admirable service by organizing and performing at volunteer entertainments for patriotic and philanthropic movements. Pride in their Jewish origin and the manifestation of the very Jewish spirit of "help thy brother" prompted these generous showmen to come together to the aid of humanity through their own distinctive gifts.

For over a quarter of a century—from Maine to California, from London to Moscow—Harry Houdini astonished and thrilled the world by the apparent ease with which he overcame seemingly insuperable physical difficulties. Padlocked and nailed into a packing case, he was

HOUDINI THE MAGICIAN: From *Close-Up of Houdini, Master Magician,* by Franklin Gordon. *The American Hebrew,* Nov. 12, 1926. New York.

lowered into the depths of the sea, to appear at the surface, free and un-manacled, in less than two minutes. In 1907 he was riveted into a large, hot water boiler, by the employees of the Maine Boiler Works, of Toledo, Ohio, and escaped without so much as leaving a trace of his exit. To the general public, Houdini was known as a strong man, illusionist, possessed with some weird, natural or supernatural force. . . .

What was the real nature of Houdini's marvellous powers? The wizard once said: "That I cannot tell you. When I was a young man on my first visit to New York, broke and hungry, I offered to exhibit my 'tricks' and explain their nature to four of the biggest newspapers in town for the sum of twenty dollars. Everyone turned me down. The secret will go with me to my grave. If it were anything in the nature of a contribution to science, anything that might help humanity, I would assuredly disclose it, but it is not. The secret is peculiar to myself and it is improbable that there will be another individual in several generations so oddly constituted. For one thing, I was born with an inordinate physical strength."

Zisha Breitbart, the World's Strongest Man

IT SEEMS an anomaly to have a Jew hailed the strongest man in the world. But that is what they say of Sigmund Breitbart, regarded as the superman of physical prowess and perfection. Echoes of the remarkable feats of strength exhibited by this modern Samson have reached us from time to time and of his successful appearances in the theatres of Vienna, London and other European capitals. Recently he made his debut at the Orpheum Theatre in Brooklyn; thence he will travel over the Keith Circuit, appearing at the Palace Theatre in New York during the week commencing December 3.

The youngest son of a mighty blacksmith in the little Polish village where he was born, Breitbart exhibited remarkable power even as a child. His only toys were the horseshoes and nails around his father's shop. While he never had occasion to tear a lion's mouth apart or carry off the gates of Gaza like Samson of old, or strangle a huge serpent with his hands as Hercules did, there is no telling what Sigmund Breitbart might do in an emergency. Today he can twist an iron bar, snap a steel beam or bite in two a thick metal chain as easily as the average man can break a match or bite an apple. Moreover, he can put a piece of leather in his mouth, hitch

ZISHA BREITBART, THE WORLD'S STRONGEST MAN: From *Breitbart, Modern Samson. The American Hebrew*, Sept. 28, 1923. New York.

"Sigmund Breitbart of Vienna, who played with drayhorses and bit iron chains apart, succumbed to blood poisoning induced by a scratched finger. . . . The Titans of history and legend have rarely attained advanced age. Perhaps it is a natural reluctance to see the hero go down before the march of Time. . . . How long would Samson have lived if he had not gone philandering in Philistia?"—From "Strength and Longevity," an editorial in the *N. Y. Times*, October 16, 1925.

himself to a truck loaded with people and draw it casually around the block.

Breitbart has many pseudonyms. He is known as the Iron King, the Polish Apollo, the Modern Samson, the Superman of Strength. But the remarkable thing about Breitbart is that there is little in his general appearance to indicate the possession of such prodigious strength. True, he is tall and fairly heavy, but his face is that of a thinking human being, unlike one who lives by brute strength alone. He looks like the average well-set athletic young man. In general appearance he somewhat resembles Valentino, the idol of the screen, or perhaps Houdini, the Jewish handcuff king.

Breitbart's hobby is a library of some two thousand volumes on the history of the Golden Age in Rome. Referring to the Roman Coliseum, which he considers his favorite spot in all the world, Breitbart told the interviewer: "I'd take a furnished room there any time. When I was a little boy working in my father's blacksmith shop in Lodz, Poland, I used to love to read about the Roman emperors and generals, and the things they did. I was especially interested in the tortures they tried on people. I would try to devise the same instruments and try them on myself, and most of the time I could stand them without much pain and without suffering any real injury."

Sigmund Breitbart comes from a Jewish family long noted for its strength. To judge from such examples of physical strength and dexterity as the European Breitbart, and the display of muscular agility by American Jews like Benny Leonard and Harry Houdini, it looks as if a sturdier Jew is now in the making. The poor, despised Ghetto type with bent shoulders and hollow chest is rapidly passing. The Jews of today can point with pride to Sigmund Breitbart as the ideal presentment of their people from a physical standpoint just as Einstein typifies the Jewish ideal in the world of the intellect.

"I WANT TO BE SAMSON" *

Once I said to my elder brother:

"You know what? I want to be another Samson."

My brother looked at me as if I were crazy. He was only a year older than I, but he was a child of an entirely different cut.

"You're crazy!" said my brother. "Samson lived in the land of Israel, there can be no Samson today."

"Just the same, I'm going to be another Samson," I argued stubbornly. "I'll prove to you that I can knock down a fortress with my bare hands. You know well enough that I am a Samson and you'll have to stop making fun of me."

---

* Translated from *Zisha Breitbart, Der Moderner Shimshon Hagibor* (The Modern Samson, the Strong Man), an autobiography in Yiddish. Ferlag Hagvira. New York, 1925.

"But where will you get some Philistines?" he asked me. "And even if you will get them they'll burn out your eyes."

That stumped me. Really! How in the world was I to get some Philistines? The thought of having my eyes burned out didn't trouble me. After all—if one is a Samson one should be prepared for such a thing. Ah, but Philistines—where was I to find Philistines? Without them the whole business was off.

Day after day I dreamed about Samson. I let my hair grow long, drank no wine—not because I was a Nazirite like Samson, but because we were so poor there was never any wine in our house—not even for the Sabbath cup of benediction. Just the same, I had the certainty that I was in every way like Samson. I used to blow the bellows in my father's smithy and every time that the flames mounted and the sparks began to fly I saw in my mind's eye how Samson put the foxes' tails on fire and let them loose in the fields of the Philistines. Of course I didn't know how to rend apart a lion because I never saw a lion except on the curtain of the Holy Ark in the synagogue, and there it had the wings of an eagle. However, in an alley not far from where we lived there was an anti-Semite who owned an enormous vicious dog. I made up my mind that I would tear that animal limb from limb and thus prove to every doubter that I was the strong man Samson.

One day I gathered some small boys of my age and we started for the Jew-hater's house. I was going to show them that, since I was Samson, I would rip that dog apart.

As soon as the dog saw us approach he began to thrash about, gnashed his teeth and howled. My companions stood frightened but I hastened forward unconcerned. That dog could spot a Jew a mile off and thereupon started to growl; he never attacked Gentiles, only Jews. You can well imagine how he felt when he sniffed the presence of an entire gang of Jews. True, we were only mites of Jews—but for his purposes we were fully Jews. *Nu, nu,* did he dance and leap about joyfully! His owner stood by and had great pleasure from his dog's rage.

"Children!" I cried to the boys—"Have no fear! I am with you and I am the strong man Samson, and I will tear this lion to pieces!"

In my eyes that dog was no dog, but a real lion. In my fantasy I saw myself in the forest of Judaea where I came face to face with a lion and tore him in two. The other little boys became infected with my courage and they followed me.

No sooner did we get close when the dog leaped at us like an honest-to-goodness lion. The boys began to shriek in terror. At that moment I truly felt like a strong man. I knew that it was my duty to save the boys and so, with the cry of *"Shema Yisroel!* (Hear, O Israel—The Lord our God, the Lord is One)" I grappled with the dog. A fierce life-and-death struggle took place. He was a lot bigger than I and tried to get his jaws into me, but every time he opened his mouth I pounded at him with my fists and he let out a piteous howl.

The battle lasted fully five minutes until the beast lay stretched out before me bleeding from many wounds. He was hardly breathing. His owner, who watched the fight from a distance, had been certain that I would wind up a sorry mess and so he stood by smiling with great pleasure. But later, when he saw his dog lying on the ground with blood streaming from him he raised a great outcry and seized a gun. When we saw him do that we fled. Just the same, that was the end of that dog, and we never had any trouble again from that quarter.

"Zisha, the blacksmith's son, is Samson!" the Jewish children used to boast about me thereafter. "Zisha, the blacksmith's son, has torn apart a lion! Wait and see—he'll yet conquer the Philistines. . . ."

Did I need more proof that I was a genuine Samson? Yes, I did! If I was Samson I had to stand between the pillars of the Philistines' temple as they stood praying in it and bring it down on their heads. But there was the rub. Where was I to lay my hands on some Philistines? And God only knew if there were any more Philistines on earth! I used to sit with a far-away look at my prayer-desk in the synagogue and create Philistines out of the thin air. I was certain they could be found somewhere but where exactly I didn't know.

One day I approached a very old Jew with a flowing gray beard and beetling eyebrows as he sat poring over his *Mishna* in the synagogue. He looked old enough to know.

"Where can I find the Philistines who gouged out Samson's eyes?" I asked him.

"What on earth do you need Philistines for?" he shot back at me, his thick eyebrows quivering with laughter.

"I need them badly," I answered. "I am the strong man, Samson, and I want to throw down their temple."

"Oh, I see!" laughed the old man. "So you are Samson! Well, well. Know then that there are no more Philistines in the world. God let them perish because they behaved wickedly toward the Jews. And God will also punish in the same way all those nations that are harming Jews today, rest assured."

When I heard that there were no more Philistines in the world I grew heavy-hearted. I don't know whether I would have grieved more had I been informed that my entire family had died of the pestilence. Believe me, it was no joke. Without any Philistines how could I be a Samson? And how could I knock down their temple?

That day I lost my appetite and went about moping miserably: "There are no Philistines. . . . God destroyed them all because they were wicked toward the Jews. . . . No Philistines . . . no Samson!"

One day I observed that the synagogue was supported by wooden posts. As I looked at them they suddenly became transformed in my eyes into stone pillars and I resolved that I must knock them down. At that there took place a bitter struggle within me—between the Evil Spirit and the Good Spirit. The Evil Spirit whispered to me.

"Listen, Zisha, don't worry yourself over it and go ahead and knock down those pillars! Aren't you Samson? No one will believe you are until you knock down those pillars."

The Good Spirit, on the other hand, argued: "Don't be a fool, Zisha. These are no pillars—only posts. Without their support the synagogue would cave in. What the devil do you want to do—knock down the synagogue? A fine Samson you'll be then to knock down a house of God where Jews pray and study the Torah."

For two interminable weeks I walked about in a daze, in me raging a battle between good and evil. My eyes looked feverish; I became emaciated. But one evening I no longer could hold out and I entered the synagogue. I took firm hold of a post and tried to wrench it loose. I must have looked insane, for a number of Jews ran up to me and seized hold of my arms.

"Crazy boy!" they shouted. "What are you trying to do—knock down the synagogue?"

At that I came to and was filled with horror. I let go of the post and fled.

PART THREE
The Human Comedy

Introduction

There is a saying in the Talmud: "You may know a man by three things —by his wine-cup, by his anger, and by his purse. Some say: also by his laughter." The folk-philosophy of Jewish humor is revealingly expressed in many sayings. For instance, there is the optimistic counsel in Yiddish: "Does your heart ache? Laugh it off!" Among the sectarian *Hasidim*, for whom laughter and other modes of conviviality were considered forms of prayer, the telling of jokes was held in great esteem. "The *Rebbe* has ordered everybody to be merry!" is a well-known *Hasidic* saying. The same idea underlies the following anecdote:

The famous Rabbi Zevi Elimelech of Dinov had a son, Dovidl, who was himself a *Hasidic* rabbi and had many ardent disciples. On every Sabbath and also on Holy Days, Rabbi Dovidl refrained from the time-honored custom of expounding the Torah as he sat in the midst of his disciples. Instead, he diverted them with merry tales and jokes, and everybody, even the graybeards, would laugh heartily.

Once, Rabbi Yichezkel Halberstam was paying him a visit, and he was amazed at Rabbi Dovidl's odd carryings-on.

"Who ever heard," he began indignantly, "that a *tzaddik* and his disciples should behave in such an outrageous way? A fine thing indeed to celebrate God's Sabbath with nonsense, funny stories and jests! Really, Rabbi Dovidl, you ought to feel ashamed of yourself! Come now—expound a bit of Torah for us!"

"Torah!" exclaimed Rabbi Dovidl. "And what do you suppose I've been expounding all this time? Believe me, Rabbi, there's God's holy truth in all stories and jests!"

The average Jew cannot carry on a conversation without trying to illuminate it with a story or joke. In fact, the need for this is sometimes too compulsive. It has even given rise to a Jewish witticism in paraphrase of its Talmudic original: "Who is a hero? He who suppresses the urge to tell a joke."

Jews are skillful at joke-making because they are also virtuosi in the art of pathos. They have been tempered by necessity to take life passionately —with gaiety as well as with sober earnestness. This dual capacity for weeping and laughing at the same time, from which was coined the Yiddish expression, "laughter through tears," has had its origin in the chaos of life. The harmony of light and shadow is always at work; the same experiences which have made the Jew realistic and thoughtful have also exposed to his ironic eye the foolishness and incongruities of the Human Comedy. It is one of the wholesome defense mechanisms by which he is enabled to keep a balanced outlook.

Like every thoughtful tragedian, from Dionysus down, he has taught himself how to laugh. Perhaps most important of all, he has learned how to laugh at himself. This has made it easier for him to take himself and his troubles less seriously and thus help remove the sting from an unjust fate. Gentiles too have recognized this talent of sophisticated irony in the Jew. In discussing the humor of Max Beerbohm, James Gibbons Huneker remarked: ". . . he has that delightful ironic touch which is Hebraic. It abounds in Hebraic literature."

Jewish jokes and witticisms, as those in this compilation will bear out, are not just "fun-loving" and laugh-provoking; they are frequently bitten with the acid of satire, and are permeated by a philosophy of gentle ruefulness which is a commentary on the limitations inherent in life and mankind. We find these same elements in Don Quixote and Sancho Panza and in Sholom Aleichem's droll but tragic Tevye and Menachem Mendel.

The psychologic trait of self-irony in Jews, for which Heine was celebrated, led Freud to remark in *Wit and Its Relation to the Unconscious:* "This determination of self-criticism may make clear why it is that a number of the most excellent jokes . . . should have sprung into existence from the soil of Jewish national life. There are stories which were invented by Jews themselves and which are directed by Jewish peculiarities . . . I do not know whether one often finds a people that makes so merry unreservedly over its own shortcomings."

One outstanding feature of Jewish humor is its preoccupation with characterization and its relative unconcern with mechanical word-play. Human beings are not viewed *en masse* by the Jewish folk-mind in jokes and tales but are highly individualized, probed into psychologically and rounded out with all their peculiarities and foibles. By this means they cease being just amusing mannikins but become instinct with life. Everybody is thus able to recognize his own common humanity with theirs. Probably no other folklore can parade such a large variety of distinctive humorous characters as the Jewish.

Jewish humor is seldom savage or cruel, but genial, tongue-in-cheek and philosophic. To be sure, it holds up to ridicule stupidity, boorishness, avarice, hypocrisy and humbug. It gleefully exposes smug ignorance and the hollow pride of caste. Yet it is rarely marked by self-righteousness. By and large it reveals a tolerance of human frailties.

Certainly not all Jewish jokes are funny. As with all humor, they require a critical and selective approach. A large body of so-called "Jewish dialect jokes" are not Jewish at all, but the confections of anti-Semites who delight in ridiculing and slandering the Jews. About this type of joke Freud has said: "The Jewish jokes made up by non-Jews are nearly all brutal buffooneries in which the wit is spoiled by the fact that the Jew appears as a comic figure to a stranger. The Jewish jokes which originate with Jews admit this, but they know their merits as well as their real shortcomings."

The overtones of satire, irony and quip we hear even in the Old Testament. For example, there is the gay mockery of the Prophet Elijah as he listens to the idol-worshipping soothsayers of Baal, invoking their god morning, noon and night: "O Baal, hear us!" To this the rational-minded Elijah remarks tauntingly: "Cry ye louder, for he is a god; he is perhaps talking or walking, or he is on a journey, or peradventure he sleepeth and must be awaked."

We also find satire and irony in the Prophets, especially in the writings of Amos and Isaiah. With matchless skill they lay bare the weaknesses and the follies of their contemporaries. They satirize the hypocrite, the miser, the skinflint, the profligate, the coquette, the self-satisfied and the self-righteous. It is from this acid portraiture that much of Jewish folklore found its inspiration and themes. The fables, parables, anecdotes and sayings in the Talmud and *Midrash*, as the reader of this book will find out for himself, were rich in those very characteristics with which we associate Jewish humor today.

Laughter is a universal bond that draws all men closer. Jewish humor contains every variety of laughter: bitter and sweet and also bitter-sweet laughter; ironic, scornful and rapier-like laughter; gentle, world-weary laughter; tongue-in-cheek, skeptical and wry laughter; wise laughter turned deprecatingly against oneself. And not least, the turbulent and lusty laughter of the earth earthy, the infectious belly-laughter which shakes body, mind and emotions—an affirmation of the will-to-joy.

The liveliness and the many-sidedness of Jewish humor make it possible for everyone to find in it that which will suit his taste. It is a treasury in which lies stored up three thousand years of a people's laughter. Its variety recalls the words of Bar-Hebraeus, the Thirteenth Century Syrian-Jewish folklorist, in his introduction to his *Laughable Stories:* "And let this book be a devoted friend to the reader, whether he be Muslim, or Jew, or Aramean, or a man belonging to a foreign country and nation. And let the man who is learned, I mean to say the man who hath a bright understanding, and the man that babbleth conceitedly even though he drive everyone mad, and also every other man, choose what is best for himself. And let each pluck the flowers that please him. In this way the book will succeed in bringing together the things which are alike, each to the other."

N. A.

【1】

Droll Characters

SCHNORRERS AND BEGGARS

INTRODUCTION

It was but inevitable that the widespread poverty among the Jews of Europe should have given rise to a class of beggars and panhandlers. They possessed all the traits usually associated with their type, and practiced the proverbial skulduggery of beggars among all peoples. There were lynx-eyed "blind" men, "mutes" who were eloquent with abuse, fleetfooted "cripples" and "dying" *nebiches* with the appetite of a healthy horse. There are innumerable stories about beggars in Jewish folklore which merrily describe their duplicities in obtaining alms.

Apart from them was a certain type of beggar who stood entirely in a class by himself. This was the *schnorrer*. Although he had his counterpart among other peoples since he was the product of the same material necessity, nevertheless, he was cast in a distinctive mold. It might be well to point out that the psychologic makeup of the *schnorrer*, or for that matter of any other Jewish type, was not due to anything innately peculiar to the character of the Jewish people, but was due rather to the peculiar conditions with which Jewish life was burdened for so many centuries.

What were the characteristics of the *schnorrer?* He disdained to stretch out his hand for alms like an ordinary beggar. He did not solicit aid—he demanded it. In fact, he considered it his divine right. Unlike the whining, obsequious beggar, he recoiled from demeaning himself, this by no means from the compunctions of a sensitive soul, but from sheer arrogance and vanity. Since he was obliged to live by his wits he, understandably enough, developed all the facile improvisations of an adventurer. To reach his objective, he considered all means fair. Tact and self-restraint were not his strong points; they would only prove practical stumbling-blocks to the practice of his "profession." Next to his adroitness in fleecing the philanthropic sheep was his *chutzpah*, his unmitigated impudence. He would terrorize his prey by the sheer daring of his importunities, leaving him both speechless and wilted, with no desire to continue the unequal combat.

Schnorring was no mean art. Duplicity and *chutzpah* were not enough; one also had to be trigger-intelligent, imaginative, persuasive—in short, a salesman to the gullible of one's crying poverty. Many men of this type were even learned; for Torah-scholarship was another dart in the quiver of *schnorring* persuasiveness. It often required the superficial glitter and respectability of the *schnorrer's* Torah-learning to make a kind-hearted Jew, steeped in the bookish traditions of his people, feel that it was a privilege to be mulcted.

It was with first-hand knowledge of this type of rogue that Israel Zangwill created his literary tour-de-force, *The King of Schnorrers*. When the smug patron of the story, Joseph Grobstock, complains plaintively to the "King of the Schnorrers": ". . . have I not given freely of my hardearned gold?" the implacable *schnorrer* retorts scornfully: "For your own diversion! But what says the Midrash? 'There is a wheel rolling in the world—not he who is rich today is rich tomorrow, but this one He brings up and this one He brings down, as is said in the seventy-fifth Psalm. Therefore lift not up your horn on high, nor speak with a stiff neck.' "

Wit was another talent a successful *schnorrer* had to possess. He had to be good at repartée, at telling jokes, at proving agreeably diverting to his rich "client." This helped him greatly in maneuvering with lightningfast timing. Imperceptibly he would spin a spider-web around the unwary rich fly who, like Joseph Grobstock, found it hard to disentangle himself.

Often, the sheer originality of the *schnorrer's* stratagems, and his lively wit during the course of their execution, would mollify his victim after he had caught his breath. If the latter had a sense of humor he would feel amply rewarded for the fleecing.

While morose rogues were given a wide berth, gay rogues—such as talented *schnorrers*—were even welcomed by some. *Schnorrer* stories abound by the hundreds in Jewish folklore. They are invariably gay with impudent mirth and have brought enormous diversion to the folk.

N. A.

The King of Schnorrers

IN THE days when Lord George Gordon became a Jew, and was suspected of insanity; when, out of respect for the prophecies, England denied her Jews every civic right except that of paying taxes; when the *Gentleman's Magazine* had ill words for the infidel alien; when Jewish marriages were invalid and bequests for Hebrew colleges void; when a prophet prophesying Primrose Day would have been set in the stocks, though Pitt inclined his private ear to Benjamin Goldsmid's views on the foreign loans—in those days, when Tevele Schiff was Rabbi in Israel, and Dr. de Falk, the Master of the Tetragrammaton, saint and Cabbalistic conjuror, flourished in Wellclose Square, and the composer of "The Death of Nelson" was a choirboy in the Great Synagogue; Joseph Grobstock, pillar of the same, emerged one afternoon into the spring sunshine at the fag-end of the departing

---

THE KING OF SCHNORRERS: From *The King of Schnorrers*, by Israel Zangwill. New York: The Macmillan Company, 1893. With the permission of the present copyright owners, The Jewish Publication Society of America.

stream of worshippers. In his hand was a large canvas bag, and in his eye a twinkle.

There had been a special service of prayer and thanksgiving for the happy restoration of his Majesty's health, and the cantor had interceded tunefully with Providence on behalf of Royal George and "our most amiable Queen, Charlotte." The congregation was large and fashionable—far more so than when only a heavenly sovereign was concerned—and so the court-yard was thronged with a string of *Schnorrers* (beggars), awaiting the exit of the audience, much as the vestibule of the opera-house is lined by footmen.

They were a motley crew, with tangled beards and long hair that fell in curls, if not the curls of the period; but the gabardines of the German Ghettoes had been in most cases exchanged for the knee-breeches and many-buttoned jacket of the Londoner. When the clothes one has brought from the Continent wear out, one must needs adopt the attire of one's superiors, or be reduced to buying. Many bore staves, and had their loins girded up with coloured handkerchiefs, as though ready at any moment to return from the Captivity. Their woebegone air was achieved almost entirely by not washing—it owed little to nature, to adventitious aids in the shape of deformities. The merest sprinkling boasted of physical afflictions, and none exposed sores like the lazars of Italy or contortions like the cripples of Constantinople. Such crude methods are eschewed in the fine art of *schnorring*. A green shade might denote weakness of sight, but the stone-blind man bore no braggart placard—his infirmity was an old established concern well known to the public, and conferring upon the proprietor a definite status in the community. He was no anonymous atom, such as drifts blindly through Christendom, vagrant and apologetic. Rarest of all sights in this pageantry of Jewish pauperdom was the hollow trouser-leg or the empty sleeve, or the wooden limb fulfilling either and pushing out a proclamatory peg.

When the pack of *Schnorrers* caught sight of Joseph Grobstock, they fell upon him full-cry, blessing him. He, nothing surprised, brushed pompously through the benedictions, though the twinkle in his eye became a roguish gleam. Outside the iron gates, where the throng was thickest, and where some elegant chariots that had brought worshippers from distant Hackney were preparing to start, he came to a standstill, surrounded by clamouring *Schnorrers*, and dipped his hand slowly and ceremoniously into the bag. There was a moment of breathless expectation among the beggars, and Joseph Grobstock had a moment of exquisite consciousness of importance, as he stood there swelling in the sunshine. There was no middle class to speak of in the eighteenth-century Jewry; the world was divided into rich and poor, and the rich were very, very rich, and the poor very, very poor, so that everyone knew his station. Joseph Grobstock was satisfied with that in which it had pleased God to place him. He was a jovial, heavy-jowled creature, whose clean-shaven chin was doubling, and he was habited like a person of the first respectability in a beautiful blue body-coat

with a row of big yellow buttons. The frilled shirt front, high collar of
the very newest fashion, and copious white neckerchief showed off the
massive fleshiness of the red throat. His hat was of the Quaker pattern,
and his head did not fail of the periwig and the pigtail, the latter being
heretical in name only.

What Joseph Grobstock drew from the bag was a small white-paper
packet, and his sense of humour led him to place it in the hand furthest
from his nose; for it was a broad humour, not a subtle. It enabled him to
extract pleasure from seeing a fellow-mortal's hat rollick in the wind, but
did little to alleviate the chase for his own. His jokes clapped you on the
back, they did not tickle delicately.

Such was the man who now became the complacent cynosure of all eyes,
even of those that had no appeal in them, as soon as the principle of his
eleemosynary operations had broken on the crowd. The first *Schnorrer*,
feverishly tearing open his package, had found a florin, and, as by elec-
tricity, all except the blind beggar were aware that Joseph Grobstock was
distributing florins. The distributor partook of the general consciousness,
and his lips twitched. Silently he dipped again into the bag, and, selecting
the hand nearest, put a second white package into it. A wave of joy
brightened the grimy face, to change instantly to one of horror.

"You have made a mistake—you have given me a penny!" cried the
beggar.

"Keep it for your honesty," replied Joseph Grobstock imperturbably, and
affected not to enjoy the laughter of the rest. The third mendicant ceased
laughing when he discovered that fold on fold of paper sheltered a tiny
sixpence. It was now obvious that the great man was distributing prize-
packets, and the excitement of the piebald crowd grew momently. Grobstock went on dipping, lynx-eyed against second applications. One of the
few pieces of gold in the lucky-bag fell to the solitary lame man, who
danced in his joy on his sound leg, while the poor blind man pocketed his
half-penny, unconscious of ill-fortune, and merely wondering why the
coin came swathed in paper.

By this time Grobstock could control his face no longer, and the last
episodes of the lottery were played to the accompaniment of a broad grin.
Keen and complex was his enjoyment. There was not only the general
surprise at this novel feat of alms; there were the special surprises of
detail written on face after face, as it flashed or fell or frowned in congruity
with the contents of the envelope, and for undercurrent a delicious hubbub
of interjections and benedictions, a stretching and withdrawing of palms,
and a swift shifting of figures, that made the scene a farrago of excitements.
So that the broad grin was one of gratification as well as of amusement,
and part of the gratification sprang from a real kindliness of heart—for
Grobstock was an easy-going man with whom the world had gone easy.
The *Schnorrers* were exhausted before the packets, but the philanthropist
was in no anxiety to be rid of the remnant. Closing the mouth of the considerably lightened bag and clutching it tightly by the throat, and recom-

posing his face to gravity, he moved slowly down the street like a stately treasure-ship flecked by the sunlight. His way led towards Goodman's Fields, where his mansion was situated, and he knew that the fine weather would bring out *Schnorrers* enough. And, indeed, he had not gone many paces before he met a figure he did not remember having seen before.

Leaning against a post at the head of the narrow passage which led to Bevis Marks was a tall, black-bearded, turbaned personage, a first glance at whom showed him of the true tribe. Mechanically Joseph Grobstock's hand went to the lucky-bag, and he drew out a neatly-folded packet and tendered it to the stranger.

The stranger received the gift graciously, and opened it gravely, the philanthropist loitering awkwardly to mark the issue. Suddenly the dark face became a thunder-cloud, the eyes flashed lightning.

"An evil spirit in your ancestors' bones!" hissed the stranger, from between his flashing teeth. "Did you come here to insult me?"

"Pardon, a thousand pardons!" stammered the magnate, wholly taken aback. "I fancied you were a—a—a—poor man."

"And, therefore, you came to insult me!"

"No, no, I thought to help you," murmured Grobstock, turning from red to scarlet. Was it possible he had foisted his charity upon an undeserving millionaire? No! Through all the clouds of his own confusion and the recipient's anger, the figure of a *Schnorrer* loomed too plain for mistake. None but a *Schnorrer* would wear a home-made turban, issue of a black cap crossed with a white kerchief; none but a *Schnorrer* would unbutton the first nine buttons of his waistcoat, or, if this relaxation were due to the warmth of the weather, counteract it by wearing an over-garment, especially one as heavy as a blanket, with buttons the size of compasses and flaps reaching nearly to his shoe-buckles, even though its length were only congruous with that of his undercoat, which already reached the bottoms of his knee-breeches. Finally, who but a *Schnorrer* would wear this overcoat cloak-wise, with dangling sleeves, full of armless suggestion from a side view? Quite apart from the shabbiness of the snuff-coloured fabric, it was amply evident that the wearer did not dress by rule or measure. Yet the disproportions of his attire did but enhance the picturesqueness of a personality that would be striking even in a bath, though it was not likely to be seen there. The beard was jet black, sweeping and unkempt, and ran up his cheeks to meet the raven hair, so that the vivid face was framed in black; it was a long, tapering face with sanguine lips gleaming at the heart of a black bush; the eyes were large and lambent, set in deep sockets under black arching eyebrows; the nose was long and Coptic; the brow low but broad, with straggling wisps of hair protruding from beneath the turban. His right hand grasped a plain ashen staff.

Worthy Joseph Grobstock found the figure of the mendicant only too impressive; he shrank uneasily before the indignant eyes.

"I meant to help you," he repeated.

"And this is how one helps a brother in Israel?" said the *Schnorrer*, throwing the paper contemptuously into the philanthropist's face. It struck him on the bridge of the nose, but impinged so mildly that he felt at once what was the matter. The packet was empty—the *Schnorrer* had drawn a blank; the only one the good-natured man had put into the bag.

The *Schnorrer's* audacity sobered Joseph Grobstock completely; it might have angered him to chastise the fellow, but it did not. His better nature prevailed; he began to feel shamefaced, fumbled sheepishly in his pocket for a crown; then hesitated, as fearing this peace-offering would not altogether suffice with so rare a spirit, and that he owed the stranger more than silver—an apology to wit. He proceeded honestly to pay it, but with a maladroit manner, as one unaccustomed to the currency.

"You are an impertinent rascal," he said, "but I daresay you feel hurt. Let me assure you I did not know there was nothing in the packet. I did not, indeed."

"Then your steward has robbed me!" exclaimed the *Schnorrer* excitedly. "You let him make up the packets, and he has stolen my money—the thief, the transgressor, thrice-cursed who robs the poor."

"You don't understand," interrupted the magnate meekly. "I made up the packets myself."

"Then, why do you say you did not know what was in them? Go, you mock my misery!"

"Nay, hear me out!" urged Grobstock desperately. "In some I placed gold, in the greater number silver, in a few copper, in one alone—nothing. That is the one you have drawn. It is your misfortune."

"*My* misfortune!" echoed the *Schnorrer* scornfully. "It is *your* misfortune—I did not even draw it. The Holy One, blessed be He, has punished you for your heartless jesting with the poor—making a sport for yourself of their misfortunes, even as the Philistines sported with Samson. The good deed you might have put to your account by a gratuity to me, God has taken from you. He has declared you unworthy of achieving righteousness through me. Go your way, murderer!"

"Murderer!" repeated the philanthropist, bewildered by this harsh view of his action.

"Yes, murderer! Stands it not in the Talmud that he who shames another is as one who spills his blood? And have you not put me to shame —if anyone had witnessed your almsgiving, would he not have laughed in my beard?"

The pillar of the Synagogue felt as if his paunch were shrinking.

"But the others—" he murmured deprecatingly. "I have not shed their blood—have I not given freely of my hard-earned gold?"

"For your own diversion," retorted the *Schnorrer* implacably. "But what says the Midrash? There is a wheel rolling in the world—not he who is rich to-day is rich to-morrow, but this one He brings up, and this one He brings down, as is said in the seventy-fifth Psalm. Therefore, lift not up your horn on high, nor speak with a stiff neck."

He towered above the unhappy capitalist, like an ancient prophet denouncing a swollen monarch. The poor man put his hand involuntarily to his high collar as if to explain away his apparent arrogance, but in reality because he was not breathing easily under the *Schnorrer's* attack.

"You are an uncharitable man," he panted hotly, driven to a line of defence he had not anticipated. "I did it not from wantonness, but from faith in Heaven. I know well that God sits turning a wheel—therefore I did not presume to turn it myself. Did I not let Providence select who should have the silver and who the gold, who the copper and who the emptiness? Besides, God alone knows who really needs my assistance— I have made Him my almoner; I have cast my burden on the Lord."

"Epicurean!" shrieked the *Schnorrer*. "Blasphemer! Is it thus you would palter with the sacred texts? Do you forget what the next verse says: 'Bloodthirsty and deceitful men shall not live out half their days'? Shame on you—you a *Gabbai* (treasurer) of the Great Synagogue. You see I know you, Joseph Grobstock. Has not the beadle of your Synagogue boasted to me that you have given him a guinea for brushing your spatterdashes? Would you think of offering *him* a packet? Nay, it is the poor that are trodden on—they whose merits are in excess of those of beadles. But the Lord will find others to take up his loans—for he who hath pity on the poor lendeth to the Lord. You are no true son of Israel."

The *Schnorrer's* tirade was long enough to allow Grobstock to recover his dignity and his breath.

"If you really knew me, you would know that the Lord is considerably in my debt," he rejoined quietly. "When next you would discuss me, speak with the Psalms-men, not the beadle. Never have I neglected the needy. Even now, though you have been insolent and uncharitable, I am ready to befriend you if you are in want."

"If I am in want!" repeated the *Schnorrer* scornfully. "Is there anything I do not want?"

"You are married?"

"You correct me—wife and children are the only things I do *not* lack."

"No pauper does," quoth Grobstock, with a twinkle of restored humour.

"No," assented the *Schnorrer* sternly. "The poor man has the fear of Heaven. He obeys the Law and the Commandments. He marries while he is young—and his spouse is not cursed with barrenness. It is the rich man who transgresses the Judgment, who delays to come under the Canopy."

"Ah! well, here is a guinea—in the name of my wife," broke in Grobstock laughingly. "Or stay—since you do not brush spatterdashes—here is another."

"In the name of my wife," rejoined the *Schnorrer* with dignity, "I thank you."

"Thank me in your own name," said Grobstock. "I mean tell it me."

"I am Manasseh Bueno Barzillai Azevedo da Costa," he answered simply.

"A Sephardi!" * exclaimed the philanthropist.

---

* A Spanish Jew.

"Is it not written on my face, even as it is written on yours that you are a Tedesco? * It is the first time that I have taken gold from one of your lineage."

"Oh, indeed!" murmured Grobstock, beginning to feel small again.

"Yes—are we not far richer than your community? What need have I to take the good deeds away from my own people—they have too few opportunities for beneficence as it is, being so many of them wealthy; brokers and West India merchants, and—"

"But I, too, am a financier, and an East India Director," Grobstock reminded him.

"Maybe; but your community is yet young and struggling—your rich men are as the good men in Sodom for multitude. You are the immigrants of yesterday—refugees from the Ghettoes of Russia and Poland and Germany. But we, as you are aware, have been established here for generations; in the Peninsula our ancestors graced the courts of kings, and controlled the purse-strings of princes; in Holland we held the empery of trade. Ours have been the poets and scholars in Israel. You cannot expect that we should recognise your rabble, which prejudices us in the eyes of England. We made the name of Jew honourable; you degrade it. You are as the mixed multitude which came up with our forefathers out of Egypt."

"Nonsense!" said Grobstock sharply. "All Israel are brethren."

"Esau was the brother of Israel," answered Manasseh sententiously. "But you will excuse me if I go a-marketing, it is such a pleasure to handle gold." There was a note of wistful pathos in the latter remark which took off the edge of the former, and touched Joseph with compunction for bandying words with a hungry man whose loved ones were probably starving patiently at home.

"Certainly, haste away," he said kindly.

"I shall see you again," said Manasseh, with a valedictory wave of his hand, and digging his staff into the cobblestones he journeyed forwards without bestowing a single backward glance upon his benefactor.

Grobstock's road took him to Petticoat Lane in the wake of Manasseh. He had no intention of following him, but did not see why he should change his route for fear of the *Schnorrer*, more especially as Manasseh did not look back. By this time he had become conscious again of the bag he carried, but he had no heart to proceed with the fun. He felt conscience stricken, and had recourse to his pockets instead in his progress through the narrow jostling market-street, where he scarcely ever bought anything personally save fish and good deeds. He was a connoisseur in both. To-day he picked up many a good deed cheap, paying pennies for articles he did not take away—shoe-latchets and cane-strings, barley-sugar and butter-cakes. Suddenly, through a chink in an opaque mass of human beings, he caught sight of a small attractive salmon on a fishmonger's slab. His eye glittered, his

---

* A German Jew.

chops watered. He elbowed his way to the vendor, whose eye caught a corresponding gleam, and whose finger went to his hat in respectful greeting.

"Good afternoon, Jonathan," said Grobstock jovially, "I'll take that salmon there—how much?"

"Pardon me," said a voice in the crowd, "I am just bargaining for it." Grobstock started. It was the voice of Manasseh.

"Stop that nonsense, da Costa," responded the fishmonger. "You know you won't give me my price. It is the only one I have left," he added, half for the benefit of Grobstock. "I couldn't let it go under a couple of guineas."

"Here's your money," cried Manasseh with passionate contempt, and sent two golden coins spinning musically upon the slab.

In the crowd sensation, in Grobstock's breast astonishment, indignation, and bitterness. He was struck momentarily dumb. His face purpled. The scales of the salmon shone like a celestial vision that was fading from him by his own stupidity.

"I'll take that salmon, Jonathan," he repeated, spluttering. "Three guineas."

"Pardon me," repeated Manasseh, "it is too late. This is not an auction." He seized the fish by the tail.

Grobstock turned upon him, goaded to the point of apoplexy. "You!" he cried. "You—you—rogue! How dare you buy salmon!"

"Rogue yourself!" retorted Manasseh. "Would you have me steal salmon?"

"You have stolen my money, knave, rascal!"

"Murderer! Shedder of blood! Did you not give me the money as a free-will offering, for the good of your wife's soul? I call on you before all these witnesses to confess yourself a slanderer!"

"Slanderer, indeed! I repeat, you are a knave and a jackanapes. You —a pauper—a beggar—with a wife and children. How can you have the face to go and spend two guineas—two whole guineas—all you have in the world—on a mere luxury like salmon?"

Manasseh elevated his arched eyebrows.

"If I do not buy salmon when I have two guineas," he answered quietly, "when shall I buy salmon? As you say, it is a luxury; very dear. It is only on rare occasions like this that my means run to it." There was a dignified pathos about the rebuke that mollified the magnate. He felt that there was reason in the beggar's point of view—though it was a point to which he would never himself have risen, unaided. But righteous anger still simmered in him; he felt vaguely that there was something to be said in reply, though he also felt that even if he knew what it was, it would have to be said in a lower key to correspond with Manasseh's transition from the high pitch of the opening passages. Not finding the requisite repartee he was silent.

"In the name of my wife," went on Manasseh, swinging the salmon by the tail, "I ask you to clear my good name which you have bespattered in the presence of my very tradesmen. Again I call upon you to confess before these witnesses that you gave me the money yourself in charity. Come! Do you deny it?"

"No, I don't deny it," murmured Grobstock, unable to understand why he appeared to himself like a whipped cur, or how what should have been a boast had been transformed into an apology to a beggar.

"In the name of my wife, I thank you," said Manasseh. "She loves salmon, and fries with unction. And now, since you have no further use for that bag of yours, I will relieve you of its burden by taking my salmon home in it." He took the canvas bag from the limp grasp of the astonished Tedesco, and dropped the fish in. The head protruded, surveying the scene with a cold, glassy, ironical eye.

"Good afternoon all," said the *Schnorrer* courteously.

"One moment," called out the philanthropist, when he found his tongue. "The bag is not empty—there are a number of packets still left in it."

"So much the better!" said Manasseh soothingly. "You will be saved from the temptation to continue shedding the blood of the poor, and I shall be saved from spending *all* your bounty upon salmon—an extravagance you were right to deplore."

"But—but!" began Grobstock.

"No—no 'buts,' " protested Manasseh, waving his bag deprecatingly. "You were right. You admitted you were wrong before; shall I be less magnanimous now? In the presence of all these witnesses I acknowledge the justice of your rebuke. I ought not to have wasted two guineas on one fish. It was not worth it. Come over here, and I will tell you something." He walked out of earshot of the bystanders, turning down a side alley opposite the stall, and beckoned with his salmon bag. The East India Director had no course but to obey. He would probably have followed him in any case, to have it out with him, but now he had a humiliating sense of being at the *Schnorrer's* beck and call.

"Well, what more have you to say?" he demanded gruffly.

"I wish to save you money in future," said the beggar in low, confidential tones. "That Jonathan is a son of the separation! The salmon is not worth two guineas—no, on my soul! If you had not come up I should have got it for twenty-five shillings. Jonathan stuck on the price when he thought you would buy. I trust you will not let me be the loser by your arrival, and that if I should find less than seventeen shillings in the bag you will make it up to me."

The bewildered financier felt his grievance disappearing as by sleight of hand.

Manasseh added winningly: "I know you are a gentleman, capable of behaving as finely as any Sephardi."

This handsome compliment completed the *Schnorrer's* victory, which was sealed by his saying, "And so I should not like you to have it on your soul that you had done a poor man out of a few shillings."

Grobstock could only remark meekly: "You will find more than seventeen shillings in the bag."

"Ah, why were you born a Tedesco!" cried Manasseh ecstatically. "Do you know what I have a mind to do? To come and be your Sabbath-guest! Yes, I will take supper with you next Friday, and we will welcome the Bride —the holy Sabbath—together! Never before have I sat at the table of a Tedesco—but you—you are a man after my own heart. Your soul is a son of Spain. Next Friday at six—do not forget."

"But—but I do not have Sabbath-guests," faltered Grobstock.

"Not have Sabbath-guests! No, no, I will not believe you are of the sons of Belial, whose table is spread only for the rich, who do not proclaim your equality with the poor even once a week. It is your fine nature that would hide its benefactions. Do not I, Manasseh Bueno Barzillai Azevedo da Costa, have at my Sabbath-table every week Yankelé ben Yitzchok—a Pole? And if I have a Tedesco at my table, why should I draw the line there? Why should I not permit you, a Tedesco, to return the hospitality to me, a Sephardi? At six, then! I know your house well—it is an elegant building that does credit to your taste—do not be uneasy—I shall not fail to be punctual. *A Dios!*"

This time he waved his stick fraternally, and stalked down a turning. For an instant Grobstock stood glued to the spot, crushed by a sense of the inevitable. Then a horrible thought occurred to him.

Easy-going man as he was, he might put up with the visitation of Manasseh. But then he had a wife, and, what was worse, a livery servant. How could he expect a livery servant to tolerate such a guest? He might fly from the town on Friday evening, but that would necessitate troublesome explanations. And Manasseh would come again the next Friday. That was certain. Manasseh would be like grim death—his coming, though it might be postponed, was inevitable. Oh, it was too terrible. At all costs he must revoke the invitation. Placed between Scylla and Charybdis, between Manasseh and his manservant, he felt he could sooner face the former.

"Da Costa!" he called in agony. "Da Costa!"

The *Schnorrer* turned, and then Grobstock found he was mistaken in imagining he preferred to face da Costa.

"You called me?" enquired the beggar.

"Ye—e—s," faltered the East India Director, and stood paralysed.

"What can I do for you?" said Manasseh graciously.

"Would you mind—very much—if I—if I asked you—"

"Not to come," was in his throat, but stuck there.

"If you asked me—" said Manasseh encouragingly.

"To accept some of my clothes," flashed Grobstock, with a sudden inspiration. After all, Manasseh was a fine figure of a man. If he could get him to doff those musty garments of his he might almost pass him off as a prince of the blood, foreign by his beard—at any rate he could be certain of making him acceptable to the livery servant. He breathed freely again at this happy solution of the situation.

"Your cast-off clothes?" asked Manasseh. Grobstock was not sure whether the tone was supercilious or eager. He hastened to explain. "No, not quite that. Second-hand things I am still wearing. My old clothes were already given away at Passover to Simeon the Psalms-man. These are comparatively new."

"Then I would beg you to excuse me," said Manasseh, with a stately wave of the bag.

"Oh, but why not?" murmured Grobstock, his blood running cold again.

"I cannot," said Manasseh, shaking his head.

"But they will just about fit you," pleaded the philanthropist.

"That makes it all the more absurd for you to give them to Simeon the Psalms-man," said Manasseh sternly. "Still, since he is your clothes-receiver, I could not think of interfering with his office. It is not etiquette. I am surprised you should ask me if I should mind. Of course I should mind—I should mind very much."

"But he is not my clothes-receiver," protested Grobstock. "Last Passover was the first time I gave them to him, because my cousin, Hyman Rosenstein, who used to have them, has died."

"But surely he considers himself your cousin's heir," said Manasseh. "He expects all your old clothes henceforth."

"No. I gave him no such promise."

Mannesseh hesitated.

"In that case," repeated Grobstock breathlessly.

"On condition that I am to have the appointment permanently, of course."

"Of course," echoed Grobstock eagerly.

"Because you see," Manasseh condescended to explain, "it hurts one's reputation to lose a client."

"Yes, yes, naturally," said Grobstock soothingly. "I quite understand." Then, feeling himself slipping into future embarrassments, he added timidly, "Of course they will not always be so good as the first lot, because—"

"Say no more," Manasseh interrupted reassuringly, "I will come at once and fetch them."

"No. I will send them," cried Grobstock, horrified afresh.

"I could not dream of permitting it. What! Shall I put you to all that trouble which should rightly be mine? I will go at once—the matter shall be settled without delay, I promise you; as it is written, 'I made haste and delayed not!' Follow me!" Grobstock suppressed a groan. Here had all his manœuvring landed him in a worse plight than ever. He would have to present Manasseh to the livery servant without even that clean face which might not unreasonably have been expected for the Sabbath. Despite the text quoted by the erudite *Schnorrer*, he strove to put off the evil hour.

"Had you not better take the salmon home to your wife first?" said he.

"My duty is to enable you to complete your good deed at once. My wife is unaware of the salmon. She is in no suspense."

Even as the *Schnorrer* spake it flashed upon Grobstock that Manasseh was more presentable with the salmon than without it—in fact, that the salmon was the salvation of the situation. When Grobstock bought fish he often hired a man to carry home the spoil. Manasseh would have all the air of such a loafer. Who would suspect that the fish and even the bag belonged to the porter, though purchased with the gentleman's money? Grobstock silently thanked Providence for the ingenious way in which it had contrived to save his self-respect. As a mere fish-carrier Manasseh would attract no second glance from the household; once safely in, it would be comparatively easy to smuggle him out, and when he did come on Friday night it would be in the metamorphosing glories of a body-coat, with his unspeakable undergarment turned into a shirt and his turban knocked into a cocked hat.

They emerged into Aldgate, and then turned down Leman Street, a fashionable quarter, and so into Great Prescott Street. At the critical street corner Grobstock's composure began to desert him: he took out his handsomely ornamented snuff-box and administered to himself a mighty pinch. It did him good, and he walked on and was well nigh arrived at his own door when Manasseh suddenly caught him by a coat button.

"Stand still a second," he cried imperatively.

"What is it?" murmured Grobstock, in alarm.

"You have spilt snuff all down your coat front," Mannasseh replied severely. "Hold the bag a moment while I brush it off."

Joseph obeyed, and Manasseh scrupulously removed every particle with such patience that Grobstock's was exhausted.

"Thank you," he said at last, as politely as he could. "That will do."

"No, it will not do," replied Manasseh. "I cannot have my coat spoiled. By the time it comes to me it will be a mass of stains if I don't look after it."

"Oh, is that why you took so much trouble?" said Grobstock, with an uneasy laugh.

"Why else? Do you take me for a beadle, a brusher of gaiters?" enquired Manasseh haughtily. "There now! that is the cleanest I can get it. You would escape these droppings if you held your snuff-box so—" Manasseh gently took the snuff-box and began to explain, walking on a few paces.

"Ah, we are at home!" he cried, breaking off the object-lesson suddenly. He pushed open the gate, ran up the steps of the mansion and knocked thunderously, then snuffed himself magnificently from the bejewelled snuff-box.

Behind came Joseph Grobstock, slouching limply, and carrying Manasseh da Costa's fish.

Bagel-and-Lox

A RICH man was so much moved by a poor man's ghastly appearance that he took pity on him and impulsively gave him half a dollar. An hour later, what was the amazement of the rich man to see the poor man gorging himself on *bagel* and *lox* in a local dairy restaurant!

"You've got some nerve!" cried the rich man, angrily. "Did I give you fifty cents for *bagel* and *lox*?"

"What an unreasonable person!" replied the poor man. "Before, I didn't have fifty cents, so I couldn't afford to eat *bagel* and *lox*. Now that God has helped me and you've given me the fifty cents you forbid me to eat *bagel* and *lox*! So tell me, wise guy, *when can I eat bagel and lox*?"

They Got the Itch

As a rich merchant of Lemberg was looking out of the window one day he saw a strange sight. A shabby-looking man was rubbing his back against the picket-fence. It was clear, the poor fellow had an itch. So the rich man called him into his house and listened to his tale of woe.

"I haven't had a bath for months," complained the unfortunate man, "I haven't on one stitch of underwear, and I'm so hungry I could eat nails!"

The rich man was moved to tears by the man's desperate plight. So he dined and wined him, gave him underwear, and, in addition, ten kreutzer for the steambath. Then he sent him away with God's blessings.

The news of the rich man's loving kindness swept through Lemberg like wildfire. That very day two *schnorrers* took their position against his picket fence and, with woeful cries, fell to rubbing their backs vigorously against it. Attracted by their cries, the rich man went to the window and, when he saw what the two rogues were up to, he got very angry.

"Out of my sight, you shameless *schnorrers*!" he cried. "Stop rubbing your filthy backs against my picket fence!"

"Why did you help the man with the itch before and why do you refuse to help us now?" they asked reproachfully. "Tell us, in what way is he better than we? We too have the itch."

"Is it my duty to relieve every man of his itch?" cried the rich man, outraged. "If I helped the man with the itch before it was because he had no one to scratch his poor back for him. As for you—you louts—you are two. Go ahead—scratch each other's backs!"

On the Minsk-Pinsk Line

Once a poor Jew had to go to Pinsk from Minsk. As he had no money he got on the train without a ticket. At the first stop the conductor took him by the scruff of his neck, kicked him in his rear end and threw him off the train.

The man got up, brushed the dust off his clothes and boarded the next train to Pinsk. This time, too, the conductor kicked him in his rear end and threw him off at the next station.

For the third time he boarded a train and, as the conductor appeared, a man sitting next to him inquired, "How far are you going, uncle?"

"That depends! If my backside holds out, I'm going to Pinsk!"

The Schnorrer and the Farmer

A CITY *schnorrer* once came to a poor farmer and asked for a night's lodging.

"You are indeed welcome," said the farmer and he treated the *schnorrer* with the traditional Jewish hospitality shown to penniless strangers. His wife fed him well and gave him a comfortable bed to sleep in.

The *schnorrer* was so pleased with his host that in the morning he said to him, "I like it here so much—perhaps you will let me stay until to-morrow."

"You are welcome to stay," answered the polite farmer, but not as heartily as the day before.

That day the farmer's wife fed the stranger, but a little less lavishly. He felt the growing coldness toward him but paid no attention to it.

The following morning he decided he would stay another day, but this time he did not ask for permission, for he was afraid it might be refused. So he stayed on and, as the farmer and his wife were polite, they said nothing to him about it. But the meals they served him grew skimpier.

"What kind of hospitality is this?" suddenly cried the *schnorrer* angrily. "Do you want me to starve to death?"

The farmer felt abashed and began to apologize. "Believe me, it isn't from stinginess! We're poor people and we've hardly enough food for ourselves. If you stay another day we'll simply have nothing more to eat."

"Good God!" exclaimed the *schnorrer*. "Had I only known this I wouldn't have accepted your hospitality in the first place. Please forgive me! I'll leave tomorrow morning. Be so good as to wake me bright and early."

At dawn the farmer came and woke him.

"It's time to get up," he said. "The cock has already crowed."

"What!" cried the *schnorrer*, overjoyed. "You still have a cock? Then I can stay another day!"

One Blind Look Was Enough

A BLIND beggar stood on Essex Street in New York's East Side holding out his little tin cup.

"Help a blind man!" he whined piteously.

An old Jewish woman hobbled by.

"*Nebich*—a poor blind man!" she commiserated, and gave him a dime.

The beggar was enraptured.

"As soon as I took the first look at you I knew you had a kind heart!" he exclaimed.

Price Is No Object

THE woman of the house took pity on a Jewish beggar and invited him on the Sabbath day to eat *gefillte fish*. She placed a platter of black bread and white *chaleh* on the table. She noticed however that the beggar was gorging himself on the *chaleh* which was more expensive, but didn't touch the black bread at all.

"Why do you eat only *chaleh* and not black bread?" she asked with some irritation.

"I like *chaleh* better," he said.

"My friend, *chaleh* is very dear."

"Believe me, auntie, it's worth it!"

A Sure Cure

A *schnorrer* came to a large city and went to see a rich man for an alms. But the servants would not let him in for the rich man lay gravely ill.

"I know a sure cure for the sick man," the *schnorrer* insisted.

And so they let him in.

"I have a sure cure for you," said the *schnorrer* when he was taken to the sick man's bedside. "But I want to be well rewarded for it."

"What's your cure?" asked the rich man.

"Move to Kolomea right away!"

"What's so good about Kolomea? Are there big doctors there?"

"No, not at all. But you see, I come from Kolomea and, in the memory of the oldest inhabitant there, no rich man has ever died in Kolomea!"

Every Expert to His Own Field

A CERTAIN *schnorrer* attempted to gain Rothschild's ear, only to meet with rebuff. The beggar at last determined to create a bit of turmoil, this being one of the time-honored techniques when all appears to be lost.

So the *schnorrer* set up a commotion in the foyer of the Rothschild establishment, shrieking at the top of his voice, "My family is starving to death, and the Baron refuses to see me."

The baron, driven to distraction by the racket, came out. "Very well," he declared philosophically. "I'm defeated. Here are twenty thalers. And may I add a bit of advice. If you hadn't made so much noise, you'd have got forty."

"Sir," said the *schnorrer*, pocketing the money, "you are a banker; do I give you banking advice? I'm a *schnorrer*; don't give me *schnorring* advice."

No Credit

THE *schnorrer* made his usual request modestly, firmly, with dignity.

"But I haven't a cent in the house right now. Come back tomorrow," said the householder.

"Ah, my friend," said the *schnorrer*, "if only you knew what a fortune I have lost by giving credit."

Cause and Effect

Two beggars came to the house of the richest but most tight-fisted man in town. Before going in to ask him for alms they talked the matter over.

"You better go in alone," said one. "Only last week I went to see him and he wouldn't give me anything because he said he didn't like the way I asked. He doesn't know you, so you'd better go."

The other beggar agreed and went in to see the miser.

It wasn't long before he came out flushed and angry, his clothes ruffled.

"You idiot!" he raged at his partner. "The idea of sending me in to see that dog!"

"Why, what did he do to you?"

"Do to me! Why he wanted to throw me out!"

"How do you know he wanted to throw you out?"

"If he didn't want to, why did he do it?"

He Spared No Expense

DR. LEVINE, the great specialist, had just finished examining Blum the *schnorrer*.

"What is the cost?" asked the patient.

"Twenty-five dollars."

"Twenty-five dollars! It's too much! I ain't got it!"

"Too much? All right, fifteen dollars."

"Fifteen dollars That's out of the question!"

"Out of the question? Make it five dollars."

"Five dollars! Who has five dollars? I'm a poor man!"

The doctor had had enough. "If five dollars is too much, how much have you?"

"I have nothing."

The doctor was now angry. "If you have nothing, how do you have the nerve to come to so expensive a specialist as myself?"

"For my health," shouted Blum, beating his breast with the strength of the righteous, "*nothing* is too expensive!"

A Local Reputation

A STRANGE *schnorrer* had just received so warm a welcome that he was touched.

"Your welcome is a heart-warming thing," he said to the rich miser, "but how do you know that I come from another city?"

"Because you came to me," said the miser. "Anybody from this town would know better."

What Can You Expect for a Kopek?

"I'M A poor man," whined the *schnorrer* piteously when he went to call on a prosperous merchant. "Give me an alms!"

"What *chutzpah*!" raged the merchant. "A man like you with the strong arms of an ox certainly has no right to go around *schnorring*!"

"What would you want me to do, uncle?" sneered the *schnorrer*. "Cut off both of my arms for the miserable kopek you might give me?"

The Fire-Victim

CONFLAGRATION swept the little town. Row after row of houses were reduced to ashes. The communal treasury opened to aid the victims. Among them showed up a poor man whose little house had been left untouched by the fire.

"What kind of trickery is this?" one of the town officials asked him angrily. "Did you suffer from the fire?"

"Did I suffer!" replied the poor man. "Believe me, I was scared to death!"

No Faith

A CERTAIN *schnorrer*, finishing a square meal in a restaurant, had just settled down to manipulation of his toothpick when the proprietor asked for payment.

"I'll tell you what," said the *schnorrer*, suddenly inspired, "I'll go out and beg what I owe, and the minute I reach that sum, I'll come back and pay up."

"Very fine," said the restaurateur, "but how do I know you'll keep your word?"

"Come on along," said the *schnorrer*, "and watch."

"What, me, a respectable restaurant owner, let myself be seen with a filthy *schnorrer*? Not on your life!"

"All right," said the *schnorrer*, calmly, "I'll wait here. You go out and beg."

She Acquired a Taste for It

ONCE a respectable widow fell in love with a beggar who went from house to house asking for alms.

"I will marry you," he told her, "only on one condition. For a whole year after our wedding night you will have to go begging with me. After that, I promise to find another occupation."

"But everybody knows me in this town! I'll die of shame if I go begging alms," she pleaded.

"No matter—we'll go to another town where nobody will know you," he answered.

So the widow married the beggar and for a whole year they went from door to door begging for alms. On the day that the year was up the beggar said to his wife, "At four o'clock it will be exactly one year since our marriage."

But his wife seemed to show no interest.

Later, as the clock struck four, the beggar exclaimed with joy, "The time is up at last! We are through now with begging forever."

"Let's finish this row of houses first," she coaxed.

The Schnorrer-in-Law

EVERY Friday evening for years, the *schnorrer* had appeared at the rich man's house for the Sabbath meal. But one Friday, a young stranger appeared with him.

The host, put out by this, asked, "Who is this?"

"Oh," replied the *schnorrer* tolerantly, "I suppose I should have told you. It's my new son-in-law. You see, I promised to give him board for the first year!"

The Honest Deceiver

A POOR man, with no source of livelihood, was badly in need of a new coat. As there was nothing else that he could do, he went from house to house begging for alms. When he had saved up a neat pile of copper coins he went to a clothing merchant and begged that he give him a coat as an alms. The shopkeeper took pity on him and gave him a coat. But no sooner did

---

THE HONEST DECEIVER: Adapted from the *Parables of the Preacher of Dubno*.

the poor man get the coat when he drew forth his bag of copper coins and gave it to the merchant, saying, "There you have your money!"

The shopkeeper was astounded.

"I don't understand," he said. "First you asked me to give you the coat as an alms, and now you are paying me for it!"

The poor man answered, "The money I have given you are the alms I have collected, and you know what people throw at a poor man. One gives a flattened kopek, another a broken three-groschen piece, and still another a bent half-gulden that's no longer recognizable. If I had come to you at first and showed you my coins you would have said: 'Take away your junk! I can't sell you a coat for that!' But since you've given me the coat for nothing, and I'm an honest man, I'm sure you'll take my coins now."

WAGS AND WITS

INTRODUCTION

Like every other people the Jews were mirthfully entertained by their wits and wags, pranksters and scalawags. It was a normal expression of folk-life. There were a great number of such droll characters among Jews. Many were nameless, but others were real persons, like Shmerl Shnitkover, Yossel Marshalik, *Reb* Shloime Ludmirer, Mordchi Kharkover, Motke Chabad, Sheike Feifer and Froyim Greidinger. Some of the anecdotes in which they figured are still current but, by and large, their pranks and jests are no longer associated with their names and have been assimilated into the large body of anonymous Jewish humor. And often, where attribution does occur, it is of very doubtful authenticity; the same stories and jokes have been variously ascribed to several of them. They have very often served conveniently as personality-pegs on which to hang a popular story or jest.

Gay as all these wags were, none of them could compare with Hershel Ostropolier, for he was a man of comic originality. He belongs to the merry company of Nasreddin and Tyl Eulenspiegel. Like them he was a folk-jester whose crackling wit and droll pranks shook the Yiddish-speaking world with laughter. Like them too Hershel was no mythical character— a product of the folk fancy. On the contrary, it was Hershel who began the process of creating folklore about himself. If he has had such an enormous vogue to this very day, it is because his drolleries represent the sanity of laughter among Jews.

Hershel was endowed with an unusual capacity for self-irony, a rueful comicality in facing disaster, and a philosophy of disenchantment unmarred by a shred of defeatism. From the countless stories circulating about him for the past one hundred and fifty years emerges the portrait of a remarkably clear and uninvolved character. He was an impish likeable *schlimazl* whose misfortunes did not, by any means, arise from his own personal character weaknesses but rather from the illogic of the topsy-turvy world he lived in.

Born in Balta, in the Ukraine, during the second half of the Eighteenth Century, Hershel was condemned by pauperized parents and by the lack of opportunity so general in the ghetto to a life without a trade or calling. Whatever he put his hand to went askew. But because he was a dynamic individual, blessed with a nimble intelligence and an indestructible optimism, he and his family managed to subsist by his wits as well as by his wit.

For a number of years during the period 1770–1810, when Rabbi Boruch reigned as the hereditary *Hasidic tzaddik* of Miedziboz, Hershel served as his "court" jester. The rabbi, who was the dynastic successor of his grandfather, Rabbi Israel Baal-Shem, the founder of the *Hasidic* movement, was utterly unlike his saintly ancestor. He was a vain self-indulged man who lived as lavishly as the Polish *Pans* on the income of the "redemption fees" he collected from his worshipping followers. Because he suffered from melancholia, and also because he wished to ape the landed Polish nobility, he decided to acquire a jester. So he grandly hired the down-at-the-heels Hershel from Ostropolia to drive his gloom away with merry quips and capers.

It goes without saying that, although Rabbi Boruch was diverted by Hershel's clowning, he didn't like him a bit. How could he? Hershel was not particular upon whom he played his pranks. He struck at Rabbi Boruch's most vulnerable weaknesses, and it must have hurt. Nor in truth can it be said that Hershel was charmed by Rabbi Boruch. In fact, there is every evidence that he disliked him heartily, as would any man of sensibility if he were obliged to play the mountebank to a stingy and parasitical nonentity whose entire stock-in-trade lay in his *yiches*, in his illustrious ancestry. Tradition has it that Hershel Ostropolier could boast more Torah-learning than his rabbinical master and on occasion would successfully expose his ignorant pretensions before the *Hasidim*.

N. A.

He Worried Fast

ONCE there was a rabbi who was most unusual in one respect: he was a prosperous merchant on the side. It chanced that because of misjudgment he staked all his money on a certain business deal and almost overnight became a poor man. His disciples, hearing of this, hastened to his house in order to comfort him for they expected to find him broken in spirit. To their astonishment they found him serenely absorbed in his studies.

"Holy Rabbi!" they stammered incredulously. "We cannot understand . . . don't you worry at all?"

"Certainly I worry," said the rabbi, "but you see God has blessed me with a quick brain. The worrying that others do in a month I can do in an hour!"

The Choice

THE little Jewish jester was overcome with grief. His world was at an end! For a long time he had served the Caliph at Bagdad and his Court, keeping them amused whenever they called upon him. But in a moment of thoughtlessness he had displeased his ruler who ordered that he be put to death.

"However," said the Caliph, "in consideration of the merry jests you've told me all these years, I will let you choose how you are to die."

"O most generous Caliph," replied the jester, "if it's all the same to you, I choose death by old age!"

Mutual Introduction

A JEW was walking on the Bismarck Platz in Berlin when unintentionally he brushed against a Prussian officer.

"Swine!" roared the officer.

"Cohen!" replied the Jew with a stiff bow.

Tit for Tat

ONCE I was a rabbiner. A rabbiner, not a rabbi. That is, I was called rabbi—but a rabbi of the crown.

To old-country Jews I don't have to explain what a rabbi of the crown is. They know the breed. What are his great responsibilities? He fills out birth certificates, officiates at circumcisions, performs marriages, grants divorces. He gets his share from the living and the dead. In the synagogue he has a place of honor, and when the congregation rises, he is the first to stand. On legal holidays he appears in a stovepipe hat and holds forth in his best Russian: *"Gospoda Prihozhane!"* To take it for granted that among our people a rabbiner is well loved—let's not say any more. Say rather than we put up with him, as we do a government inspector or a deputy sheriff. And yet he is chosen from among the people, that is, every three years a proclamation is sent us: *"Na Osnavania Predpisania . . ."* Or, as we would say: "Your Lord, the Governor, orders you to come together in the synagogue, poor little Jews, and pick out a rabbiner for yourselves . . ."

Then the campaign begins. Candidates, hot discussions, brandy, and maybe even a bribe or two. After which come charges and countercharges, the elections are annulled, and we are ordered to hold new elections. Again the proclamations: *"Na Osnavania Predpisania . . ."* Again candidates,

TIT FOR TAT: From *The Old Country*, by Sholom Aleichem. Translated by Julius and Frances Butwin. Copyright, 1946, by Crown Publishers. New York.

discussions, party organizations, brandy, a bribe or two . . . That was the life!

Well, there I was—a rabbiner in a small town in the province of Poltava. But I was anxious to be a modern one. I wanted to serve the public. So I dropped the formalities of my position and began to mingle with the people—as we say: to stick my head into the community pot. I got busy with the *Talmud Torah*, the charity fund, interpreted a law, settled disputes or just gave plain advice.

The love of settling disputes, helping people out, or advising them, I inherited from my father and my uncles. They—may they rest in peace— also enjoyed being bothered all the time with other people's business. There are two kinds of people in the world: those that you can't bother at all, and others whom you can bother all the time. You can climb right on their heads—naturally not in one jump, but gradually. First you climb into their laps, then on to their shoulders, then their heads—and after that you can jump up and down on their heads and stamp on their hearts with your heavy boots—as long as you want to.

I was that kind, and without boasting I can tell you that I had plenty of ardent followers and plain hangers-on who weren't ashamed to come every day and fill my head with their clamoring and sit around till late at night. They never refused a glass of tea, or cigarettes. Newspapers and books they took without asking. In short, I was a regular fellow.

Well, there came a day . . . The door opened, and in walked the very foremost men of the town, the sparkling best, the very cream of the city. Four householders—men of affairs—you could almost say: real men of substance. And who were these men? Three of them were the *Troika*— that was what we called them in our town because they were together all the time—partners in whatever business any one of them was in. They always fought, they were always suspicious of each other, and watched everything the others did, and still they never separated—working always on this principle: if the business is a good one and there is profit to be made, why shouldn't I have a lick at the bone too? And on the other hand, if it should end in disaster—you'll be buried along with me, and lie with me deep in the earth. And what does God do? He brings together the three partners with a fourth one. They operate together a little less than a year and end up in a brawl. That is why they're here.

What had happened? "Since God created thieves, swindlers and crooks, you never saw a thief, swindler or crook like this one." That is the way the three old partners described the fourth one to me. And he, the fourth, said the same about them. Exactly the same, word for word. And who was this fourth one? He was the quiet little man, a little innocent-looking fellow, with thick, dark eyebrows under which a pair of shrewd, ironic, little eyes watched everything you did. Everyone called him Nachman Lekach.

His real name was Nachman Noss'n, but everybody called him Nachman Lekach, because as you know, *Noss'n* is the Hebrew for "he gave," and *Lekach* means "he took," and in all the time we knew him, no one had ever seen him give anything to anyone—while at taking no one was better.

Where were we? Oh, yes . . . So they came to the rabbiner with the complaints, to see if he could find a way of straightening out their tangled accounts. "Whatever you decide, Rabbi, and whatever you decree, and whatever you say, will be final."

That is how the three old partners said it, and the fourth, Reb Nachman, nodded with that innocent look on his face to indicate that he too left it all up to me: "For the reason," his eyes said, "that I know that I have done no wrong." And he sat down in a corner, folded his arms across his chest like an old woman, fixed his shrewd, ironic, little eyes on me, and waited to see what his partners would have to say. And when they had all laid out their complaints and charges, presented all their evidence, said all they had to say, he got up, patted down his thick eyebrows, and not looking at the others at all, only at me, with those deep, deep, shrewd little eyes of his, he proceeded to demolish their claims and charges—so completely, that it looked as if they were the thieves, swindlers and crooks—the three partners of his—and he, Nachman Lekach, was a man of virtue and piety, the little chicken that is slaughtered before *Yom Kippur* to atone for our sins—a sacrificial lamb. "And every word that you heard them say is a complete lie, it never was and never could be. It's simply out of the question." And he proved with evidence, arguments and supporting data that everything he said was true and holy, as if Moses himself had said it.

All the time he was talking, the others, the *Troika,* could hardly sit in their chairs. Every moment one or another of them jumped up, clutched his head—or his heart: "Of all things! How can a man talk like that! Such lies and falsehoods!" It was almost impossible to calm them down, to keep them from tearing at the fourth one's beard. As for me—the rabbiner—it was hard, very hard to crawl out from this horrible tangle, because by now it was clear that I had a fine band to deal with, all four of them swindlers, thieves and crooks, and informers to boot, and all four of them deserving a severe punishment. But what? At last this idea occurred to me, and I said to them:

"Are you ready, my friends? I am prepared to hand down my decision. My mind is made up. But I won't disclose what I have to say until each of you has deposited twenty-five *rubles*—to prove that you will act upon the decision I am about to hand down."

"With the greatest of pleasure," the three spoke out at once, and Nachman Lekach nodded his head, and all four reached into their pockets, and each one counted out his twenty-five on the table. I gathered up the money, locked it up in a drawer, and then I gave them my decision in these words:

"Having heard the complaints and the arguments of both parties, and having examined your accounts and studied your evidence, I find according to my understanding and deep conviction, that all four of you are in the wrong, and not only in the wrong, but that it is a shame and a scandal for Jewish people to conduct themselves in such a manner—to falsify accounts, perjure yourselves and even act as informers. Therefore I have decided that since we have a *Talmud Torah* in our town with many children who have neither clothes nor shoes, and whose parents have nothing with which to pay their tuition, and since there has been no help at all from you gentlemen (to get a few pennies from you one has to reach down into your very gizzards) therefore it is my decision that this hundred *rubles* of yours shall go to the *Talmud Torah*, and as for you, gentlemen, you can go home, in good health, and thanks for your contribution. The poor children will now have some shoes and socks and shirts and pants, and I'm sure they'll pray to God for you and your children. Amen."

Having heard the sentence, the three old partners—the *Troika*—looked from one to the other—flushed, unable to speak. A decision like this they had not anticipated. The only one who could say a word was Reb Nachman Lekach. He got up, patted down his thick eyebrows, held out a hand, and looking at me with his ironic little eyes, said this:

"I thank you, Rabbi Rabbiner, in behalf of all four of us, for the wise decision which you have just made known. Such a judgment could have been made by no one since King Solomon himself. There is only one thing that you forgot to say, Rabbi Rabbiner, and that is: what is your fee for this wise and just decision?"

"I beg your pardon," I tell him. "You've come to the wrong address. I am not one of those rabbiners who tax the living and the dead." That is the way I answered him, like a real gentleman. And this was his reply:

"If that's the case, then you are not only a sage and a Rabbi among men, you're an honest man besides. So, if you would care to listen, I'd like to tell you a story. Say that we will pay you for your pains at least with a story."

"Good enough. Even with two stories."

"In that case, sit down, Rabbi Rabbiner, and let us have your cigarette case. I'll tell you an interesting story, a true one, too, something that happened to me. What happened to others I don't like to talk about."

And we lit our cigarettes, sat down around the table, and Reb Nachman spread out his thick eyebrows, and looking at me with his shrewd, smiling, little eyes, he slowly began to tell his true story of what had once happened to him himself.

All this happened to me a long time ago. I was still a young man and I was living not far from here, in a village near the railroad. I traded in this and that, I had a small tavern, made a living. A Rothschild I didn't become, but bread we had, and in time there were about ten Jewish families living close by—because, as you know, if one of us makes a living, others come around. They think you're shoveling up gold . . . But that isn't the point. What I was getting at was that right in the midst of the busy season one year, when things were moving and traffic was heavy, my wife had to go and have a baby—our boy—our first son. What do you say to that? "Congratulations! Congratulations everybody!" But that isn't all. You have to have a *bris*, the circumcision. I dropped every-thing, went into town, bought all the good things I could find, and came back with the *Mohel* with all his instruments, and for good measure I also brought the *shammes* of the synagogue. I thought that with these two holy men and myself and the neighbors we'd have the ten men that we needed, with one to spare. But what does God do? He has one of my neighbors get sick—he is sick in bed and can't come to the *bris*, you can't carry him. And another has to pack up and go off to the city. He can't wait another day! And here I am without the ten men. Go do something. Here it is—Friday! Of all days, my wife has to pick Friday to have the *bris*—the day before the Sabbath. The *Mohel* is frantic—he has to go back right away. The *shammes* is actually in tears. "What did you ever drag us off here for?" they both want to know. And what can I do?

All I can think of is to run off to the railroad station. Who knows—so many people come through every day—maybe God will send some one. And that's just what happened. I come running up to the station—the agent has just called out that a train is about to leave. I look around—a little roly-poly man carrying a huge traveling bag comes flying by, all sweating and out of breath, straight toward the lunch counter. He looks over the dishes—what is there a good Jew can take in a country railroad station? A piece of herring—an egg. Poor fellow—you could see his mouth was watering. I grab him by the sleeve. "Uncle, are you looking for some-thing to eat?" I ask him, and the look he gives me says: "How did you know that?" I keep on talking: "May you live to be a hundred—God him-self must have sent you." He still doesn't understand, so I proceed: "Do you want to earn the blessings of eternity—and at the same time eat a beef roast that will melt in your mouth, with a fresh, white loaf right out of the oven?" He still looks at me as if I'm crazy. "Who are you? What do you want?"

So I tell him the whole story—what a misfortune had overtaken us: here we are, all ready for the *bris*, the *Mohel* is waiting, the food is ready—and such food!—and we need a tenth man! "What's that got to do with me?" he asks, and I tell him: "What's that got to do with you? Why—everything depends on you—you're the tenth man! I beg you—come with me. You will earn all the rewards of heaven—and have a delicious dinner in the bargain!" "Are you crazy," he asks me, "or are you just out of your head? My train is leaving in a few minutes, and it's Friday afternoon—almost sundown. Do you know what that means? In a few more hours the Sabbath will catch up with me, and I'll be stranded." "So what!" I tell him. "So you'll take the next train. And in the meantime you'll earn eternal life—and taste a soup, with fresh dumplings, that only my wife can make . . ."

Well, why make the story long? I had my way. The roast and the hot soup with fresh dumplings did their work. You could see my customer lick-ing his lips. So I grab the traveling bag and I lead him home, and we go through with the *bris*. It was a real pleasure! You could smell the roast all over the house, it had so much garlic in it. A roast like that, with fresh warm twist, is a delicacy from heaven. And when you consider that we had some fresh dill pickles, and a bottle of beer, and some cognac before the meal and cherry cider after the meal—you can imagine the state our guest was in! His cheeks shone and his forehead glistened. But what then? Before we knew it the afternoon was gone. My guest jumps up, he looks around, sees what time it is, and almost has a stroke! He reaches for his traveling bag: "Where is it?" I say to him, "What's your hurry? In the first place, do you think we'll let you run off like that—before the Sabbath? And in the second place—who are you to leave on a journey an hour or two before the Sabbath? And if you're going to get caught out in the country somewhere, you might just as well stay here with us."

He groans and he sighs. How could I do a thing like that to him—keep him so late? What did I have against him? Why hadn't I reminded him earlier? He doesn't stop bothering me. So I say to him: "In the first place, did I have to tell you that it was Friday afternoon? Didn't you know it yourself? And in the second place, how do you know—maybe it's the way God wanted it? Maybe He wanted you to stay here for the Sabbath so you could taste some of my wife's fish? I can guarantee you, that as long as you've eaten fish, you haven't eaten fish like my wife's fish—not even in a dream!" Well, that ended the argument. We said our evening prayers, had a glass of wine, and my wife brings the fish to the table. My guest's nostrils swell out, a new light shines in his eyes and he goes after that fish as if he hadn't eaten a thing all day. He can't get over it. He praises it to the skies. He fills a glass with brandy and drinks a toast to the fish. And then comes the soup, a specially rich Sabbath soup with noodles. And he likes that, too, and the *tzimmes* also, and the meat that goes with the *tzimmes,* a nice, fat piece of brisket. I'm telling you, he just sat there licking his fingers! When we're finishing the last course he turns to me: "Do you know what I'll tell you? Now that it's all over, I'm really glad that I stayed over for *Shabbes.* It's been a long time since I've enjoyed a Sabbath as I've enjoyed this one." "If that's how you feel, I'm happy," I tell him. "But wait. This is only a sample. Wait till tomorrow. Then you'll see what my wife can do."

And so it was. The next day, after services, we sit down at the table. Well, you should have seen the spread. First the appetizers: crisp wafers and chopped herring, and onions and chicken fat, with radishes and chopped liver and eggs and *gribbenes.* And after that the cold fish and the meat from yesterday's *tzimmes,* and then the jellied neat's foot, or *fisnoga* as you call it, with thin slices of garlic, and after that the potato *cholent* with the *kugel* that had been in the oven all night—and you know what that smells like when you take it out of the oven and take the cover off the pot. And what it tastes like. Our visitor could not find words to praise it. So I tell him: "This is still nothing. Wait until you have tasted our *borsht* tonight, then you'll know what good food is." At that he laughs out loud—a friendly laugh, it is true—and says to me: "Yes, but how far do you think I'll be from here by the time your *borsht* is ready?" So I laugh even louder than he does, and say: "You can forget that right now! Do you think you'll be going off tonight?"

And so it was. As soon as the lights were lit and we had a glass of wine to start off the new week, my friend begins to pack his things again. So I call out to him: "Are you crazy? Do you think we'll let you go off, the Lord knows where, at night? And besides, where's your train?" "What?" he yells at me. "No train? Why, you're murdering me! You know I have to leave!" But I say, "May this be the greatest misfortune in your life. Your train will come, if all is well, around dawn tomorrow. In the meantime I hope your appetite and digestion are good, because I can smell the *borsht* already! All I ask," I say, "is just tell me the truth. Tell me if you've ever touched a *borsht* like this before. But I want the absolute truth!" What's the use of talking—he had to admit it: never before in all his life had he tasted a *borsht* like this. Never. He even started to ask how you made the *borsht*, what you put into it, and how long you cooked it. Everything. And I say: "Don't worry about that! Here, taste this wine and tell me what you think of *it*. After all, you're an expert. But the truth! Remember—nothing but the truth! Because if there is anything I hate, it's flattery . . ."

So we took a glass, and then another glass, and we went to bed. And what do you think happened? My traveler overslept, and missed the early morning train. When he wakes up he boils over! He jumps on me like a murderer. Wasn't it up to me, out of fairness and decency, to wake him up in time? Because of me he's going to have to take a loss, a heavy loss— he doesn't even know himself how heavy. It was all my fault. I ruined him. I! . . . So I let him talk. I listen, quietly, and when he's all through, I say: "Tell me yourself, aren't you a queer sort of person? In the first place, what's your hurry? What are you rushing for? How long is a person's life altogether? Does he have to spoil that little with rushing and hurrying? And in the second place, have you forgotten that today is the third day since the *bris*? Doesn't that mean a thing to you? Where we come from, on the third day we're in the habit of putting on a feast better than the one at the *bris* itself. The third day—it's something to celebrate! You're not going to spoil the celebration, are you?"

What can he do? He can't control himself any more, and he starts laughing—a hysterical laugh. "What good does it do to talk?" he says. "You're a real leech!" "Just as you say," I tell him, "but after all, you're a visitor, aren't you?"

At the dinner table, after we've had a drink or two, I call out to him: "Look," I say, "it may not be proper—after all, we're Jews—to talk about milk and such things while we're eating meat, but I'd like to know your honest opinion: what do you think of *kreplach* with cheese?" He looks at me with distrust. "How did we get around to that?" he asks. "Just like this," I explain to him. "I'd like to have you try the cheese *kreplach* that my wife makes—because tonight, you see, we're going to have a dairy supper . . ." This is too much for him, and he comes right back at me with, "Not this time! You're trying to keep me here another day, I can see that. But you can't do it. It isn't right! It isn't right!" And from the way he fusses and fumes it's easy to see that I won't have to coax him too long, or fight with him either, because what is he but a man with an appetite, who has only one philosophy, which he practices at the table? So I say this to him: "I give you my word of honor, and if that isn't enough, I'll give you my hand as well—here, shake—that tomorrow I'll wake you up in time for the earliest train. I promise it, even if the world turns upside down. If I don't, may I—you know what!" At this he softens and says to me: "Remember, we're shaking hands on that!" And I: "A promise is a promise." And my wife makes a dairy supper—how can I describe it to you? With such *kreplach* that my traveler has to admit that it was all true: he has a wife too, and she makes *kreplach* too, but how can you compare hers with these? It's like night to day!

And I kept my word, because a promise is a promise. I woke him when it was still dark, and started the *samovar*. He finished packing and began to say goodbye to me and the rest of the household in a very handsome, friendly style. You could see he was a gentleman. But I interrupt him: "We'll say goodbye a little later. First, we have to settle up." "What do you mean—settle up?" "Settle up," I say, "means to add up the figures. That's what I'm going to do now. I'll add them up, let you know what it comes to, and you will be so kind as to pay me."

His face flames red. "Pay you?" he shouts. "Pay you for what?" "For what?" I repeat. "You want to know for what? For everything. The food, the drink, the lodging." This time he becomes white—not red—and he says to me: "I don't understand you at all. You came and invited me to the *bris*. You stopped me at the train. You took my bag away from me. You promised me eternal life." "That's right," I interrupt him. "That's right. But what's one thing got to do with the other? When you came to the *bris* you earned your reward in heaven. But food and drink and lodging —do I have to give you these things for nothing? After all, you're a businessman, aren't you? You should understand that fish costs money, and that the wine you drank was the very best, and the beer, too, and the cherry cider. And you remember how you praised the *tzimmes* and the puddings and the *borsht*. You remember how you licked your fingers. And the cheese *kreplach* smelled pretty good to you, too. Now, I'm glad you enjoyed these things: I don't begrudge you that in the least. But certainly you wouldn't expect that just because you earned a reward in heaven, and enjoyed yourself in the bargain, that *I* should pay for it?" My traveling friend was really sweating; he looked as if he'd have a stroke. He began to throw himself around, yell, scream, call for help. "This is Sodom!" he cried. "Worse than Sodom! It's the worst outrage the world has ever heard of! How much do you want?" Calmly I took a piece of paper and a pencil and began to add it up. I itemized everything, I gave him an inventory of everything he ate, of every hour he spent in my place. All in all it added up to something like thirty-odd *rubles* and some *kopeks* —I don't remember it exactly.

When he saw the total, my good man went green and yellow, his hands shook, and his eyes almost popped out, and again he let out a yell, louder than before. "What did I fall into—a nest of thieves? Isn't there a single human being here? Is there a God anywhere?" So I say to him, "Look, sir, do you know what? Do you know what you're yelling about? Do you have to eat your heart out? Here is my suggestion: let's ride into town together—it's not far from here—and we'll find some people—there's a rabbiner there—let's ask the rabbi. And we'll abide by what he says." When he heard me talk like that, he quieted down a little. And—don't worry—we hired a horse and wagon, climbed in, and rode off to town, the two of us, and went straight to the rabbi.

When we got to the rabbi's house, we found him just finishing his morning prayers. He folded up his prayer shawl and put his phylacteries away, "Good morning," we said to him, and he: "What's the news today?" The news? My friend tears loose and lets him have the whole story—everything from A to Z. He doesn't leave a word out. He tells how he stopped at the station, and so on and so on, and when he's through he whips out the bill I had given him and hands it to the rabbi. And when the rabbi had heard everything, he says: "Having heard one side I should now like to hear the other." And turning to me, he asks, "What do you have to say to all that?" I answer: "Everything he says is true. There's not a word I can add. Only one thing I'd like to have him tell you—on his word of honor: did he eat the fish, and did he drink the beer and cognac and the cider, and did he smack his lips over the *borsht* that my wife made?" At this the man becomes almost frantic, he jumps and he thrashes about like an apoplectic. The rabbi begs him not to boil like that, not to be so angry, because anger is a grave sin. And he asks him again about the fish and the *borsht* and the *kreplach,* and if it was true that he had drunk not only the wine, but beer and cognac and cider as well. Then the rabbi puts on his spectacles, looks the bill over from top to bottom, checks every line, and finds it correct! Thirty-odd *rubles* and some *kopeks,* and he makes his judgment brief: he tells the man to pay the whole thing, and for the wagon back and forth, and a judgment fee for the rabbi himself. . . .

The man stumbles out of the rabbi's house looking as if he'd been in a steam bath too long, takes out his purse, pulls out two twenty-fives and snaps at me: "Give me the change." "What change?" I ask, and he says: "For the thirty you charged me—for that bill you gave me." "Bill? What bill? What thirty are you talking about? What do you think I am, a highwayman? Do you expect me to take money from you? I see a man at the railroad station, a total stranger; I take his bag away from him, and drag him off almost by force to our own *bris,* and spend a wonderful *Shabbes* with him. So am I going to charge him for the favor he did me, and for the pleasure I had?" Now he looks at me as if I really am crazy,

and says: "Then why did you carry on like this? Why did you drag me
to the rabbi?" "Why this? Why that?" I say to him. "You're a queer
sort of person, you are! I wanted to show you what kind of man our rabbi
was, that's all. . . ."

When he finished the story, my litigant, Reb Nachman Lekach, got up
with a flourish, and the other three partners followed him. They buttoned
their coats and prepared to leave. But I held them off. I passed the
cigarettes around again, and said to the story-teller:

"So you told me a story about a rabbi. Now maybe you'll be so kind
as to let me tell you a story—also about a rabbi, but a much shorter story
than the one you told."

And without waiting for a yes or no, I started right in, and made it brief:

This happened, I began, not so long ago, and in a large city, on *Yom
Kippur* eve. A stranger falls into the town—a businessman, a traveler,
who goes here and there, everywhere, sells merchandise, collects money . . .
On this day he comes into the city, walks up and down in front of the
synagogue, holding his sides with both hands, asks everybody he sees
where he can find the rabbi. "What do you want the rabbi for?" people
ask. "What business is that of yours?" he wants to know. So they don't
tell him. And he asks one man, he asks another: "Can you tell me where the
rabbi lives?" "What do you want the rabbi for?" "What do you care?"
This one and that one, till finally he gets the answer, finds the rabbi's house,
goes in, still holding his sides with both hands. He calls the rabbi aside,
shuts the door, and says, "Rabbi, this is my story. I am a traveling man,
and I have money with me, quite a pile. It's not my money. It belongs
to my clients—first to God and then to my clients. It's *Yom Kippur* eve.
I can't carry money with me on *Yom Kippur*, and I'm afraid to leave it at
my lodgings. A sum like that! So do me a favor—take it, put it away in
your strong box till tomorrow night, after *Yom Kippur*."

And without waiting, the man unbuttons his vest and draws out one
pack after another, crisp and clean, the real red, crackling, hundred *ruble*
notes!

Seeing how much there was, the rabbi said to him: "I beg your pardon.
You don't know me, you don't know who I am." "What do you mean, I
don't know who you are? You're a rabbi, aren't you?" "Yes, I'm a rabbi.
But I don't know *you*—who you are or what you are." They bargain back
and forth. The traveler: "You're a rabbi." The rabbi: "I don't know
who you are." And time does not stand still. It's almost *Yom Kippur*!
Finally the rabbi agrees to take the money. The only thing is, who should
be the witnesses? You can't trust just anyone in a matter like that.

So the rabbi sends for the leading townspeople, the very cream, rich and
respectable citizens, and says to them: "This is what I called you for. This
man has money with him, a tidy sum, not his own, but first God's and then
his clients'. He wants me to keep it for him till after *Yom Kippur*. There-

fore I want you to be witnesses, to see how much he leaves with me, so that later—you understand?" And the rabbi took the trouble to count it all over three times before the eyes of the townspeople, wrapped the notes in a kerchief, sealed the kerchief with wax, and stamped his initials on the seal. He passed this from one man to the other, saying, "Now look. Here is my signature, and remember, you're the witnesses." The kerchief with the money in it he handed over to his wife, had her lock it in a chest, and hide the keys where no one could find them. And he himself, the rabbi, went to *shul*, and prayed and fasted as it was ordained, lived through *Yom Kippur*, came home, had a bite to eat, looked up, and there was the traveler. "Good evening, Rabbi." "Good evening. Sit down. What can I do for you?" "Nothing. I came for my package." "What package?" "The money." "What money?" "The money I left with you to keep for me." "You gave *me* money to keep for you? When was that?"

The traveler laughs out loud. He thinks the rabbi is joking with him. The rabbi asks: "What are you laughing at?" And the man says: "It's the first time I met a rabbi who liked to play tricks." At this the rabbi is insulted. No one, he pointed out, had ever called him a trickster before. "Tell me, my good man, what do you want here?"

When he heard these words, the stranger felt his heart stop. "Why, Rabbi, in the name of all that's holy, do you want to kill me? Didn't I give you all my money? That is, not mine, but first God's and then my clients'? I'll remind you, you wrapped it in a kerchief, sealed it with wax, locked it in your wife's chest, hid the key where no one could find it. And here is better proof: there were witnesses, the leading citizens of the city!" And he goes ahead and calls them all off by name. In the midst of it a cold sweat breaks out on his forehead, he feels faint, and asks for a glass of water.

The rabbi sends the *shammes* off to the men the traveler had named— the leading citizens, the flower of the community. They come running from all directions. "What's the matter? What happened?" "A misfortune. A plot! A millstone around our necks! He insists that he brought a pile of money to me yesterday, to keep over *Yom Kippur*, and that you were witnesses to the act."

The householders look at each other, as if to say: "Here is where we get a nice bone to lick!" And they fall on the traveler: how could he do a thing like that? He ought to be ashamed of himself! Thinking up an ugly plot like that against their rabbi!

When he saw what was happening, his arms and legs went limp, he just about fainted. But the rabbi got up, went to the chest, took out the kerchief and handed it to him.

"What's the matter with you! Here! Here is your money! Take it and count it, see if it's right, here in front of your witnesses. The seal, as you see, is untouched. The wax is whole, just as it ought to be."

The traveler felt as if a new soul had been installed in his body. His hands trembled and tears stood in his eyes.

"Why did you have to do it, Rabbi? Why did you have to play this trick on me? A trick like this."

"I just wanted to show you—the kind—of—leading citizens—we have in our town."

The Jew and the Caliph

ONCE there was a Caliph of Arabia who hated Jews. So he issued the following decree: "Every Jew who enters my kingdom must be halted by the guards and ordered to tell something about himself. If he lies—he is to be shot. If he tells the truth—he is to be hanged."

By this stratagem the Caliph hoped to exterminate all the Jews in Arabia.

One day a Jew came. When the Caliph's servants commanded him to tell something about himself he said, "I am going to be shot today."

The guards were confused by his words, so they brought the matter to their royal master's attention.

"H-m-m!" cogitated the wily Caliph. "This is indeed a difficult matter! If I were to shoot the Jew it would imply that he told the truth. In that case the law is that he should be hanged; so I cannot shoot him. On the other hand, if I had him hanged it would imply that he told a lie, and for that the law provides shooting; so I cannot hang him."

And so they let the Jew go.

When a Scholar Takes to Drink

A TALMUDIC scholar a souse? An unheard of thing! Yet there was such a scholar. Once a friend rebuked him.

"Don't you know that our sages condemned drunkenness?"

"Do you need to tell me that?" retorted the scholar. "Of course I know! I'm not drinking to get drunk, but to drown my sorrows!"

"Have you succeeded in drowning them?" the friend asked.

"No, I'm afraid not," the scholar answered grimly. "You see, my sorrows are very spiteful. The more I drink the better swimmers they become!"

Drinking Logic

AN OLD Jew was arrested for drunkenness and taken before a magistrate.

The magistrate was taken aback. "How," he asked sympathetically, "did this happen?"

"Nothing happened," answered the prisoner. "I'm not drunk at all."

"Now see here, uncle," said the judge, "it's perfectly obvious that something happened to put you in this state. Come, tell me in your own words."

"It is really very simple," began the old man. "I took one drink. There are many Biblical authorities for such conduct. One drink, anyone may take. Now this drink made me a new man. Naturally, the new man was entitled to a drink. So he had a drink. Then we were two. As all the world knows, when two Jews get together, it is permissible for them to have a drink. By this time we were joyous. And on a joyous occasion, one *must* drink!"

A Time for Everything

YUDEL the waggoner, having banished the bad taste of a long, hard journey with a dose of brandy, was immersed in a plate of *borsht*.

"Yudel," his neighbor Yankel yelled into the kitchen, "something terrible has happened!"

The waggoner continued to eat with intense concentration.

"Yudel, you idiot," cried Yankel, "prepare yourself for bad news. Something terrible, I tell you, has happened!"

Still Yudel ate, unperturbed.

"Yudel," Yankel persisted, "you poor man. Your wife has just died!"

The news had no apparent effect.

"How can you eat so calmly?" Yankel rebuked him. "It isn't natural."

"Make no mistake!" The waggoner looked up from his plate for a moment. "When I finish this *borsht, will I give a yell!*"

You're as Old as You Feel

A FORTY-YEAR-OLD man married a girl of twenty. It caused a sensation in their social circle. Once, when someone indelicately referred to the difference in their ages, he replied, "It's really not so bad. When she looks at me she feels ten years older, and when I look at her I feel ten years younger. So what's wrong—we're both thirty!"

Free Analysis

STEPHEN S. WISE once told this story about himself. He was in Vienna and called on Sigmund Freud. In the course of the conversation, Freud asked Wise whom he considered to be the four greatest Jews in the world.

FREE ANALYSIS: From *Bitter Herbs and Honey,* by David Schwartz. Silver Palm Press. New York, 1947.

"Well," replied Wise, "I would put you and Einstein as the first two and Brandeis and, I think, Weizmann as the last two."

"But what about yourself, Dr. Wise?" countered Freud.

"Oh—no—no—no—no!" replied Wise, gesticulating very emphatically.

"It seems to me you protest too much," remarked Freud.

"So you see," said Dr. Wise telling of the incident, "I got a free psycho-analysis."

The Injection

DR. CHAIM WEIZMANN, the Zionist leader, is famed as a story-teller. He tells of his visit to Dr. Paul Ehrlich, discoverer of 606. Weizmann sought to interest Ehrlich in Zionism.

For an hour Weizmann argued with Ehrlich in the latter's laboratory.

At the end of that period of time, Ehrlich turned to Weizmann. "Listen, Dr. Weizmann," he said, "you have taken a whole hour of my time. Do you know there are princes and nobles, great and famous men, waiting to get a few moments of my time?"

"Yes," said Dr. Weizmann, "but they are coming to get an injection from you and I have come to give you an injection."

Mazel Tov!

"I HAVE come to report," said Tevye the carpenter to the secretary of the burial society, "that my wife has died, and I wish the sum required for her burial."

"But how can that be?" asked the official. "We buried your wife two years ago."

"Oh, that was my first wife," said Tevye, "and now my second wife, too, has died."

"Excuse me," said the secretary, "I didn't know you had remarried. *Mazel tov!*"

Wrong Order

ON AN unbearably hot day, at the very door of a soda fountain, an elderly Jew fainted away.

People rushed to his side crying, "Water! Water! A man has fainted! Water!"

Feebly the old man raised his head, and corrected the bystanders: "A malted!"

THE INJECTION: *Ibid.*

The Foresighted Traveller

A WEARY traveller, alone in a train compartment enjoying a few hours of relaxation, was accosted by a stranger with the customary *"Sholom aleichem."*

Instead of the usual *"Aleichem sholom,"* in reply, this traveller sat up and began wearily: "Listen closely, my friend. I'm from Byalistok, and I'm on my way to Warsaw. I'm in the wholesale grocery business, but it's really, I assure you, a small business. My last name is Cohen. My first name is Moishe. I have one son, about to be *Bar Mitzvah,* and two daughters, both lovely, one married and the other engaged to be married. I don't smoke, I don't drink, I have no hobbies, and I stay out of politics. I hope I haven't forgotten anything but if I have, please don't stand on ceremony. Ask me now, because I'm dead tired and I'm going to take a nap!"

Dramatic Criticism

MRS. GOLDSTEIN could never induce her husband to enter a theatre.

He had an excuse always for staying home, or for joining his cronies at gin rummy or pinochle.

But at last Mrs. Goldstein's patience was exhausted. "This time," she proclaimed, "you go with me, or I'll give you reason to regret it."

So Mr. Goldstein permitted himself to be dragged to the drama. He squirmed and fidgeted through the evening, while his wife responded appropriately to the play.

"What do you say now?" she asked, triumphantly, when the lights went up.

"It stinks," was the laconic reply.

"What do you mean it stinks?" she asked.

"I'll tell you," said Mr. Goldstein, disgust finally breaking through his restraint. "In the theatre it's always the same—a man and a woman . . . Now when he wants, she doesn't want . . . And when she wants, he doesn't want . . . And when they both want, down comes the curtain!"

Logic

LATE one winter night, Shloimke and Rivke had gone to bed. Suddenly Rivke's voice, sleepy but insistent, broke the silence.

"Shloimke, please close the window . . . it's cold outside."

To which Shloimke answered, *"Nu* . . . and if I close the window, will it be warm outside?"

Courtesy to a Customer

A DOG dashed into the village butcher shop and ran off with a chunk of meat between his teeth. Thereupon, the butcher grabbed his meat cleaver and, brandishing it, ran after the thief.

"What's happened?" a neighbor inquired as he ran.

"A dog has run off with a chunk of meat!"

"So why the cleaver?" called the neighbor after him. "Do you have to chop the meat up for him?"

Why Noodles Are Noodles

ONCE, someone asked Motke Chabad, the wag, "Tell me, Motke, you're a smart fellow—why do they call noodles 'noodles'?"

Motke answered without hesitation, "What a question to ask! They're long like noodles, aren't they? They're soft like noodles, aren't they? And they taste like noodles, don't they? So why shouldn't they be called noodles?"

Deadly Poison

MOTKE CHABAD once came to an inn. He was ravenously hungry but all the innkeeper's wife could give him was some chopped chicken liver with a slice of white radish. Needless to say, he didn't sleep all night.

In the morning the innkeeper's wife asked him, "Motke—you're a man of the world and get around a lot—so tell me: what's a good poison with which to get rid of the rats in this inn?"

"Why do you ask me?" retorted Motke. "Give them some of your chopped liver and I guarantee you'll never see them again!"

The Big Blow

FROYIM GREIDINGER, the Galician prankster, was on his way home one Friday night. It was past midnight when he passed the house of his pious grandparents. To his surprise he saw that they were still up, the Sabbath candles burning brightly, so he went in.

"Why aren't you asleep?" he asked. "It's past midnight."

His grandparents looked dejected.

"We can't go to sleep on account of the candles," his grandfather explained. "If we let them burn themselves out the house may catch fire, and we can't snuff them out because it's the holy Sabbath. Nor is there a peasant around to blow them out."

For a moment Froyim was lost in thought.

"Tell me grandpa, when is *Purim*?" asked Froyim standing in front of one of the candles.

He spoke in a very loud voice and, when he came to the letter *P* in *Purim* he puffed out his cheeks and bellowed. The candle went out instantly.

Then, standing in front of the second candle, Froyim asked, "And when is Passover?"

When he came to the letter *P* in Passover he again puffed out his cheeks and bellowed. The second candle also went out. Then turning with a grin to his grandparents, Froyim said, "Now you can go to bed. Thank God none of us had to violate the Sabbath!"

The Sacrifice Was Too Great

FROYIM GREIDINGER went into an inn and ordered supper. When the meat course was put before him he saw a tiny bit of roast. At this he burst into loud wailing. The startled innkeeper ran up to him and cried, "What is it—what has happened?"

"Happened!" wept Froyim. "To think that just because of this little morsel of meat a great big ox had to be killed!"

HERSHEL OSTROPOLIER

Hershel's Conflict

ONCE, on a Thursday, Hershel Ostropolier came to his rabbi to ask from him money for the Sabbath. It had been definitely agreed that the rabbi was to pay him weekly wages. Had he not imported Hershel from Ostropolia to Miedziboz to serve as his jester in order to help him drive away his depression? But the rabbi, who was ill-natured and tight-fisted, was reluctant to pay him his wages. Hershel had to resort to all kinds of stratagems to collect from him. Many a time, he and his wife and children were forced to go hungry, did not have the wherewithal to observe the Sabbath with decency.

"What do you think—money grows on trees?" the rabbi said at first. Afterwards, when he saw that Hershel was determined, he put on a cheerful face and said to him, "If you'll tell me a good story I'll try and find for you a couple of gulden to buy food for the Sabbath."

Hershel almost burned up on hearing these words. He lusted for revenge! He thought the matter over and finally told the rabbi the following story:

"Two weeks ago, not having any money with which to buy food for the

Sabbath, I began to worry. From whence will come my aid? And as I walked along the deserted road I suddenly saw rising before me, right out of the ground, the Evil Spirit himself!

" 'Why do you look so worried, Hershel?' he asked me.

" 'Why should I be jolly?' I replied. 'It's Thursday already and my wife hasn't a broken kopek to go to market with.'

"When the Evil Spirit heard this he laughed.

" 'What a fool!' he leered at me. 'Why don't you go to the rabbi's house and, when no one is looking, steal from his table a silver spoon so you'll spend a nice Sabbath?'

"So I did as he said. And believe me, I had a pleasant Sabbath! A week ago Thursday I again didn't have anything for the Sabbath. Again I decided to go to the rabbi's house for a silver spoon. But on the way there, I met with the Good Spirit who buttonholed me.

" 'Where is a Jew going, Hershel?' he asked.

"I cringed.

" 'I'm on my way to the rabbi's house to steal a silver spoon so that I'll be able to buy food for the Sabbath,' I replied.

"Hearing this, the Good Spirit began to preach at me.

" 'How can you do such an awful thing, Hershel?' he demanded. 'The very idea should make you tremble like a leaf! Surely, a man of your learning knows the difference between good and evil! It is specifically mentioned in the Ten Commandments: 'Thou shalt not steal.'

" 'Nonsense!' I replied. 'Granted I do know that to steal a silver spoon from the rabbi is a sin, but what can I do when the rabbi, who employs me as his jester, doesn't pay me my weekly wages?'

" 'Follow my advice,' said the Good Spirit, 'don't steal and God will surely come to your aid.'

"Believe me, Rabbi, the Good Spirit stuck to me like a leech and wouldn't let go of me until I agreed to follow his advice. I returned to my shanty and observed the Sabbath in a way, may it not be said of my worst enemy, O Lord!

"Now, Rabbi, today is again Thursday and, as usual, I expect to get no money from you, so my Sabbath will again be ruined. I walked about racking my poor brains—whose advice should I follow—that of the Good Spirit, or that of the Evil Spirit? And, as I was struggling within myself, who should appear if not the Good Spirit!

" 'You see, Hershel!' he cried, triumphantly. 'A man has got to be honest! You saw for yourself how it was possible for you to celebrate the Sabbath without wicked thievery!'

" 'Indeed I did,' I answered him tartly. 'And what a wretched Sabbath it was too! My family and I were so famished we were almost ready to collapse, although it was hardly a hair's difference from what we usually feel every day in the week. No, my good brother, rest assured I shan't repeat that mistake twice. This coming week, praise God, I'll again follow the Evil Spirit's advice!'

"The Good Spirit almost jumped out of his shoes.

" 'Once and for all, Hershel, don't you dare steal!' he cried.

"That, Rabbi, was about the last straw! I was going to show him up, so I said to the Good Spirit, 'If you are such a saint, why don't you go to the Rabbi and tell him he should pay me my wages so I can celebrate God's Sabbath together with all other Jews?'

"So what do you think the Good Spirit answered?

" 'Believe me, Hershel,' he assured me with tears in his eyes. 'Gladly would I do you this little favor, but I swear before God that I don't know the rabbi at all. In fact, I've never even crossed his threshold in all these many years!' "

Hershel's Revenge on the Women

As soon as Hershel Ostropolier went to serve Rabbi Boruch of Miedziboz as his jester, he met with a hostile stare from the rabbi's wife. She found all sorts of petty pretexts to abuse him. Once, when he tried to defend himself, she turned her back on him insultingly and shut him up with the retort, "Your excuses are making me deaf—you're raising such a racket with them!"

Hershel smarted under the abuse and lay low. Someday, he vowed, he'd avenge the insult.

Some time soon after, the rabbi's wife said to Hershel, "Send your wife to me; it's high time we got to know each other."

"With pleasure," answered Hershel eagerly. "She'll regard it as a very great honor, believe me. But I must warn you—may it not happen to a dog—she's deaf as a wall! If you want her to hear you you've got to shout."

"I understand, I understand," the rabbi's wife assured him commiseratingly. "Never fear, I'll manage. Just have her come to see me."

When Hershel came home he said to his wife, that illustrious shrew, "The rabbi's wife told me she would like to get acquainted with you. But, I've got to warn you betimes: she's stone deaf. If you want her to hear you you've got to shout."

"I understand," said Hershel's wife knowingly, and went to see the rabbi's wife.

When the two women met they both began to shout and scream at each other, ever louder and louder. Their cries even reached into the rabbi's study where he was closeted with his disciples. Frightened out of his wits, the rabbi dashed into his wife's room, the disciples close at his heels. What the rabbi saw was something he never forgot. Both women were at the point of collapse. Their voices were hoarse, and their cries sounded more like croaks.

"What's the meaning of this?" cried the rabbi in astonishment. "Why are you shouting this way?"

"Hershel's wife is deaf," gasped his wife. "I had to yell so she could hear me."

"And why do you shout?" asked the rabbi of Hershel's wife.

"What else should I do—your wife is stone deaf!" croaked Hershel's wife, her tongue hanging out.

"My wife stone deaf? You're crazy, woman!" cried the rabbi, beside himself with rage. "Who told you that?"

"Why Hershel did!"

All this while Hershel stood near the rabbi enjoying himself tremendously.

"Impudent fellow!" roared the rabbi. "Explain yourself instantly. What kind of a prank is this anyway?"

"I am innocent, Rabbi," pleaded Hershel.

"All right, so it's my fault!" said the rabbi sarcastically.

"Blame your wife, Rabbi," urged Hershel. "The other day she was angry at me for some reason. I was entirely innocent."

Then, addressing the rabbi's wife, Hershel continued, "Do you remember that when I tried to explain you turned your back on me and said: 'You're raising such a racket with your excuses they're making me deaf!' Well, what did you expect—I shouldn't believe you? Why should I have doubted you? Also, was it wrong of me to give due warning to my wife? If she spoke in a low voice you wouldn't have heard a thing. Besides, wouldn't it have been highly inconsiderate of her to do so?"

"But why did you tell me your wife was deaf?" rasped the rabbi's wife in a hoarse voice.

"What a foolish question!" retorted Hershel. "Imagine, if after only a few months I made you deaf with my excuses, how deaf do you think I've made my wife after being married twenty years to her? Don't either of you say I didn't warn you!"

Reciprocity

HERSHEL OSTROPOLIER was asked once, "Is it true, Hershel, what people say—that you beat your wife with a stick and she clouts you over the head with a rolling-pin?"

"That's not altogether true," answered Hershel. "Sometimes we change over."

How Hershel Almost Became a Bigamist

HERSHEL OSTROPOLIER's wife was nagging him to death.

"You're a ne'er-do-well!" she cried. "You're a *schlimazl* and a fool, only you think you're smart. If you didn't speak so impudently to the rabbi and to the *gabbai* and to all the rich men of the town we wouldn't be so badly off."

When Hershel heard this he grew angry.

"You're a nice one to preach at me!" he said bitterly. "Why you've caused me more trouble than if you were ten good-for-nothing relatives!"

"What on earth are you jabbering about?" asked his wife.

"Listen to this story and you'll know," began Hershel. "Years ago, when I was still young and handsome, shortly after we had married, I was making a journey on foot. I never was more tired and hungry than I was that day. On the way I met another poor traveller.

" 'Uncle,' I asked him, 'do you know if there's a Jewish settlement nearby where some kindhearted person will take pity on a footsore traveller and give him something to eat and a place to sleep?'

" 'Indeed I do,' replied the man. 'Not far from here lives a Jewish tenant-farmer. He is stuffed with money like a Passover goose, but he won't give a poor man a teaspoonful of water. The only person welcome in his house is a marriage-broker because his daughter is an ugly old maid, and he would like to see her married at all costs.'

"When I heard this I went to call on the miser. I introduced myself, not as a marriage-broker but as a virtuous young man in search of a bride. Would you believe it, after being wined and dined in his house for several days, he proposed that I become his son-in-law!

"To make a long story short, I consented."

"You miserable wretch!" interrupted Hershel's wife. "How could you have done a wicked thing like that with me being your wife then?"

"Easy, easy!" cautioned Hershel. "Just listen patiently to the end of my story.

"A day was fixed for the wedding to take place—in several weeks. In the meantime, I lived in luxury, tasted everything from honey to vinegar, and, when the wedding day arrived, there was nothing left to do but to break down and tell the truth. So I said to my bride's father, 'Listen, father dear, since today is my wedding day, it is my duty to tell you everything about my family so that later on you shouldn't have any grievances against me.'

" 'I am listening,' he said.

" 'I have a brother,' I began, 'and he is an immoral fellow.'

" 'What difference does it make?' he answered, cold-bloodedly.

" 'My sister-in-law is unfaithful to her husband.'

" 'If your brother doesn't bother me, why should your sister-in-law?'

" 'I have two good-for-nothing uncles.'

" 'That should be my biggest worry.'

" 'I have a sister and she has an illegitimate child.'

" 'What? An illegitimate child! Bad, bad! But what can we do about it?'

" 'I assure you that in my family there are drunks, cardplayers and libertines without number.'

"At this my bride's father broke into a smile.

" 'What has that got to do with you?' he asked. 'All we have to do is to take out the cow and burn the barn.'

"I saw I was in a desperate position, so I finally said, 'But dear father, I have a wife!'

"When he heard this he became livid with rage. He seized me by the scruff of my neck and threw me out.

"I ask you—say yourself: doesn't that prove that you are worse than all the ten good-for-nothings in my family rolled in one?"

Hershel as Coachman

HERSHEL's wife clamored: "Money! Money!"

"I have no money," he pleaded.

"You can tell that to your grandmother!" she retorted. "All I know is that the children are hungry."

When Hershel heard this he became serious and arose from his chair.

"Go to our next-door neighbor and borrow a whip," he said sternly to his oldest boy.

Hearing this, his wife began to tremble.

"God have mercy!" she thought with dismay. "Now he's going to give me a whipping!"

But this was farthest from Hershel's mind. When his boy brought him the whip he went into the market-place and cracked it loudly in the air.

"I'm taking people to Letitshev for half fare!" he shouted.

"What a bargain!" people thought, and in a wink there were eager customers.

Hershel collected money from them and gave it to his boy.

"Run home and give it to your mother," he said.

"Where are the horses?" inquired his passengers as they followed him down the road.

"Come along and don't worry!" Hershel told them. "I'll take you right into Letitshev."

So they followed him without further questions.

They had already left the town, but still no horses. In the distance they saw the bridge. "No doubt the horses are at the bridge," they thought. But when they reached the bridge there still were no horses. By this time they had already covered half the distance. So they thought to themselves: "Very well, this man is a swindler, but what good will it do us to turn back now?"

Finally, they reached Letitshev.

"Return us our money, you thief!" they demanded of Hershel. "You fooled us!"

"I fooled you?" laughed Hershel scornfully. "Answer me, did I or did I not promise to take you to Letitshev?"

"Yes, but ride there, not walk!"

"Pfui!" snorted Hershel. "Did I ever say a word about horses?"

The passengers looked at one another dumbfounded, and since there was nothing they could do about it they spat out in contempt and went away.

When Hershel got home his wife met him at the door, beaming.

"I can't understand, Hershel," she said. "You had a whip, but where on earth did you get the horses?"

"Don't ask foolish questions!" Hershel laughed. "What do I need horses for? You know the saying: 'If you crack a whip you can always find some horses.'"

The Poor Cow

ONE Sabbath afternoon Hershel Ostropolier stood at the window in the rabbi's study looking outside.

"Rabbi," he suddenly asked, "if one sees a cow drowning on the Sabbath —must one save her or let her drown?"

"Of course you can't save her! It's not allowed! What are you looking at anyway?"

"Nothing! A cow fell into the lake."

"What can one do?" sighed the rabbi. "The Torah forbids it!"

"Just look!" cried Hershel. "*Ai-ai-ai!* Now the water is going over her head! It's a pity on the poor dumb animal!"

"What can one do?"

"So you say, Rabbi, nothing can be done for her?"

"What concern is it of yours anyway?"

"Now I can no longer see the poor cow . . . she's gone under . . . drowned! A pity—a great pity!"

"What's the matter with you, Hershel! Why are you lamenting so?"

"You'll be sorry, Rabbi! I tell you—you'll be sorry!"

"Why, in God's name?"

"It's your cow, Rabbi!"

Advance on Account

AS THE Sabbath was approaching and Hershel Ostropolier did not have even a broken kopek with which to buy *chaleh,* fish and chicken, he became desperate. So he went to the head of the communal treasury and raised an outcry.

"*Gewalt,* Jews!" he cried. "A terrible misfortune has fallen on my head! My wife has just died! But where, tell me, will I get money for a shroud and a coffin?"

With words of sympathy and regret for his great loss the elders of the community gave him ten rubles.

Later on, when they came to Hershel's house in order to do the good woman the last honors, what was their amazement when they saw her alive and gorging herself on some delicious roast chicken. Immediately they raised an outcry.

"Hypocrite! Deceiver!" they cried. "To play on our heart-strings like that, only to swindle ten rubles out of us! Was that a nice thing to do?"

"Don't get excited!" Hershel soothed them. "What difference does it make to you? I just took an advance from you—sooner or later you'll have the beauty!"

A Perfect Fit

HERSHEL's coat was falling to pieces. It was a disgrace, he felt, to show himself in it before decent people. But what was he to do? He didn't have a broken kopek. Somehow he had gotten wind of the fact that his wife had hidden a little pile, a few groschen at a time.

Hershel began to daydream. . . .

"If I could only get that money out of her," he said to himself, "I'd have a new coat made."

Shortly after, he climbed up the ladder to the garret. And, as his wife was below, she was surprised to hear Hershel talking angrily to someone.

"With whom are you talking, Hershel?" she called up to him.

"With whom do you think? With Destitution, of course," Hershel roared down from the garret.

"How on earth did he get up there?"

"He says he got sick and tired of our dingy rooms and so, for a change, he's come up to the garret."

"What does he want of you?"

"The Devil take him! He wants a new coat. He says if I'll order a new coat for him he'll move out of our house and never come back."

When Hershel climbed down from the garret his wife said to him, "It would pay to make Destitution a new coat if we can get rid of him that way."

"You're a smart one!" jeered Hershel. "If money grew on trees we could make a sweet pudding of it!"

"I've put by a couple of groschen," confessed Hershel's wife. "Here is the money, buy Destitution a coat, and then we'll tell him to go and break his hands and feet!"

As Hershel started to leave the house his wife called him back.

"You've forgotten to take Destitution's measure!"

Hershel nodded and went up again to the garret. When he came down he said, "I don't have to take his measure. He and I are like two peas in a pod—not a hair's difference."

Hershel went to a tailor who took his measure for a new coat. When it was completed he put it on, and under no circumstances would he take it off.

"Why don't you take the coat off, Hershel?" pleaded his wife. "If Destitution finds out that you are wearing his coat he'll get mighty angry and he'll give it to us in the neck."

"You're right," said Hershel, and, taking off his coat, he went up to the garret.

After a little while he returned with the coat.

"Why didn't you give him the coat?" his wife reproached him.

"It's no use!" said Hershel, downcast. "The coat doesn't fit him."

"I thought you said there wasn't a hair's difference between your measure and his."

"True!" replied Hershel. "But that was before we spent money on his new coat. Now that we've spent it we're poorer and Destitution has grown bigger!"

A Tooth for a Tooth

IN THE town was an upstart rich man—an ignoramus and a boor. He had an only daughter who had nothing to recommend her except her father's money. Whatever match was proposed for her the father would turn down.

"My daughter will marry only a man of good family!" he said haughtily.

One day, made desperate by need, Hershel Ostropolier came to him with a proposition.

"The youth I'm proposing for your daughter is a gem," he told the rich man. "He's handsome, he's learned in the Torah, and he has a fine character."

"Who is he?" asked the rich man, beaming with anticipation.

"Shmul, the cobbler's son," answered Hershel.

"You lout!" roared the rich man. "How dare you propose such a match for my daughter! Out of my house this minute!"

And he took Hershel by the scruff of his neck and the seat of his pants and threw him out of the house.

Several days later, who should call on the same rich man but Hershel!

"You here again?" shouted the rich man angrily. "I told you not to show your face again here!"

"Don't be angry," began Hershel, mollifyingly. "I have a first-class match for your daughter this time."

The rich man became curious.

"Really?" he asked. "Who is it now?"

"None other but the rabbi's son."

The rich man leaped to his feet with delight.

"Wonderful! This is really unexpected!" he murmured. "But tell me Hershel, my dear friend, were you already at the rabbi's? Did you talk to him about the matter yet?"

"What a question: 'Was I there?' Of course I already spoke to the rabbi about it."

"Tell me! What did he say?" inquired the rich man eagerly.

"What did he say? He said just what you said to me the other day! 'You lout! How dare you propose such a match for my son! Out of my house this minute!' And he took me by the scruff of my neck and the seat of my pants and threw me out!"

What Hershel's Father Did

ONCE Hershel Ostropolier stopped at an inn to spend the night. There were no other guests at the time. The innkeeper was away and only his wife was there to receive Hershel.

"I'm half dead with hunger," Hershel told her. "Do give me something to eat."

Looking at his shabby clothes the woman thought to herself, "This man is a tramp. Why take a chance and feed him?"

"I'm very sorry, my good man, but there isn't a drop of food in the house."

"What? No food?" cried Hershel, jumping up.

For a moment he stood deep in thought. Then he muttered, "In that case, I'm afraid I'll have to do just what my father did!"

When the innkeeper's wife heard this she grew alarmed.

"What did your father do?" she asked, all a-tremble.

"Never mind, my father did what he did!" said Hershel, ominously.

"What in heaven's name could this man's father have done?" the innkeeper's wife wondered. "It's a bad business, me all alone with him in the house. Who can tell—his father may have been a murderer, and if he threatens to do what his father did—good God . . . !"

Without a word she set the table and served Hershel all manner of good things. Hershel was so hungry he ate like a wolf. When he had finished he smacked his lips and said, "I haven't eaten such a good dinner since Passover!"

Seeing that the stranger was in a good mood the woman asked timidly, "Be so good and tell me—what was it that your father did!"

"Oh, my father?" replied Hershel innocently. "Whenever my father didn't have any supper he went to bed without it."

Gilding the Lily

"HERSHEL," said a rich man to the celebrated pauper-wag, "if you'll tell me a lie without thinking, I'll give you one ruble."

"What do you mean one ruble—you just said two!"

When Hershel Eats——

IN A certain village lived a rich man. He was stingy and hardhearted, but he was also clever and knew how to conceal his corruption. Those who didn't know him even got the impression that he was kind-hearted. On the Sabbath he would invite some poor traveller to his table, but woe to the unwary victim who fell into his clutches!

As a mark of honor he would place the wretch at the head of the table. Then the cat-and-mouse play began. He would ply the stranger with innumerable questions so that out of politeness he'd have to answer them. This gave him no opportunity to eat. In the meantime his host was enjoying both his food and his own cunning. To add insult to injury, when practically nothing was left on the table the host would turn with solicitude to his guest and upbraid him gently, "Why didn't you eat? Why did you talk so much?"

What was the poor man to do? He had to thank his host like a hypocrite and go to bed hungry.

Once it chanced that Hershel Ostropolier arrived in this village. Hearing of the queer ways of this rich man and his tricks, he decided to take revenge on him for all the poor unfortunates he had maltreated.

When Friday night arrived Hershel asked the *shammes* of the synagogue to arrange that he be invited to this rich man's house as his Sabbath guest. The *shammes* even tried to dissuade him from the step.

"Take my word for it," he said, "this rich man is wicked."

But Hershel insisted. So the *shammes* made the necessary arrangements for his visit.

After the Friday night service in the synagogue Hershel went home with the rich man. When they sat down to supper his host seated him in the place of honor, introduced him to the members of his household and showed him marked attention. After they all had recited the blessings over the wine the servant brought in a tureen of fish. Its aroma made the already hungry Hershel even hungrier.

The head of the household first stuck his fork into a fine portion of *gefillte fish* and put it on his plate. Then, as if absent-minded, he didn't pass the tureen to Hershel but kept it near himself. He fell into a revery.

"From where do you come, uncle?" he asked.

"From Vishnitz," answered Hershel, mentioning a name at random.

"From Vishnitz? Then surely you must know Shaiah the miller! How is he? What's he doing?"

"Shaiah the miller?" echoed Hershel. "He died."

Thereupon, without any further ceremony, Hershel extended his arm across the table and stuck his fork into a large portion of fish which he put on his plate. He fell to and ate with zest.

But his host was flabbergasted at what Hershel had told him. He turned pale and put down his fork.

"Did you hear, Malke?" he cried incredulously to his wife. "My old friend Shaiah is dead! Why didn't his wife let me know? I wonder what will happen to his fortune—he must have left a nice little pile! But tell me—how is Velvel?"

"Which Velvel?"

"Why Shaiah's eldest son, you know, the one who runs the inn in Vishnitz."

"Oh, you mean Velvel who runs the inn? He died too!" said Hershel in a matter-of-fact voice, spearing another piece of fish.

"Velvel died?" cried the rich man incredulously. "Did you hear, Malke—Velvel died! Woe is me. He owes me five hundred rubles! But tell me how is Velvel's partner, Yoshe the vintner? Is he running the inn now?"

"No!" sighed Hershel, chewing away at the fish. "He also died."

"What! Yoshe the vintner is also dead! Woe is us, Malke! My money is lost!"

And as the rich man continued to rave and get excited Hershel went on eating calmly, smiling into his beard.

"Uncle," the rich man finally ventured with trepidation, "maybe you know what Shaiah's brother, Avrum the dry-goods merchant, is doing?"

"What Avrum?" asked Hershel innocently, almost choking on a mouthful of delicious white *chaleh.*

"Why, don't you know—Avrum the dry-goods merchant! He lives near the lake, in the big white house!"

"Oh, he? I knew him well," answered Hershel. "He's dead too!"

"Have you gone out of your head, uncle?" shrieked the rich man in an unearthly voice, jumping up from his chair. "Surely, you don't mean to tell me that everybody in Vishnitz died?"

"My dear friend," drawled Hershel in his nasal way, "when I eat, everybody is as good as dead for me! But say, my good host, you've been so busy talking you've forgotten to eat! Know what? Your *gefillte fish* is really first rate!"

Hershel as Wine-Doctor

AT A time when the grape crop failed, the wine dealer of the town began to skin his customers alive. "I don't need any customers!" he said haughtily. "I can afford to wait for my price!"

Because of his attitude the townfolk had to go without wine, and so they thirsted for revenge.

"Just you wait!" Hershel Ostropolier said to them. "I'll teach this wretch such a lesson that he'll remember his grandmother!"

Hershel borrowed some good clothes in order to look respectable and, accompanied by the young men of the town, he went to call on the wine-seller. His companions waited outside as he entered.

"Good morning!" began Hershel. "Allow me to introduce myself. I am a well-known wine-maker from Lemberg. I can make good wine out of bad and better wine out of good."

The wine-seller was overjoyed.

"Are you staying long in town?"

"No, just passing through. I wanted to see how the wine business was in these parts."

"I'll be much obliged to you, young man, if you'll teach me how to improve my wine."

"With the greatest of pleasure!" answered Hershel. "Take me down to your cellar and I'll teach you."

So they went down into the wine-cellar. Out of his travelling bag Hershel took a drill and bored a hole in one barrel. He stuck his finger in the hole, then moistened his lips with it.

"Not bad," he wagged his head, judiciously, like an expert. "Be so good as to put your finger into this hole while I taste the wine in the next barrel."

The wine-seller did as he was told.

Hershel then bored a hole in the next barrel, tasted the wine and smacked his lips.

"Not bad!" he said judiciously. "Please be good enough to stop up this hole with a finger of your other hand."

The wine-seller did as he was told. And, when he had both hands thus occupied, Hershel called to his companions. Realizing that he had been trapped the profiteer became livid with rage.

"You rogue!" he cried. "I'll have you thrown into prison for this!"

"Just see how well he holds on to his wine," said Hershel gleefully. "We'll let him hold on this way all night, just to teach him not to be such a pig!"

The Feast

HERSHEL OSTROPOLIER found himself travelling in a stage coach with a company of *Hasidim*. These were upstart rich men who had a lot of fun making sport of Hershel. He didn't enjoy their fun at all, but held his peace, thinking: "Just you wait, you rascals! My name isn't Hershel for nothing! Make sport of me to your hearts' content—you'll pay for it dearly."

"Hershel!" one of the company suddenly called out. "You owe us a feast!"

"I owe you a feast? What miracle has happened?"

"You were appointed jester to the rabbi some time ago, and we haven't yet had a chance to drink on it."

"A feast, a feast!" cried the others.

"I haven't any money."

"Sell your fine clothes then. Pawn your wife's pearls! But make a feast for us."

"But my wife has no pearls."

"What do you mean, your wife has no pearls! Buy them for her and then pawn them!"

Seeing that he was in a hole Hershel agreed reluctantly, saying, "You're right! I owe you a feast and I'll pay up."

So they continued on their journey. Towards noon they came to an inn. The *Hasidim* were hungry and wanted to stop there. But Hershel didn't want to go in with them.

"I owe the innkeeper some money," he said. "And I can't pay him now."

The *Hasidim* laughed and gave him the following instructions, "You, Hershel, ride ahead with the carriage. We'll eat and rest awhile and later on we'll catch up with you at the inn in the next village."

Hershel did as they suggested, and in three hours' time he reached the next inn. Before entering he took his Sabbath gabardine out of his travelling bag. Looking important, he went up to the innkeeper, extended his hand with a loud *"Sholom aleichem!"* and said, "Know that in a short while a large carriage will arrive with a company of rich people. They sent me ahead to give you the message—that you should prepare the finest *gefillte fish*, the fattest geese, and the most expensive wines. Prepare everything with generosity. There's absolutely no question about money! Only hurry, because they'll soon be here."

"And what, if I may ask, is the reason for this celebration?" asked the innkeeper.

Hershel answered without hesitation, "Several days ago, while passing through the forest, they were waylaid by a gang of robbers. But they came out of the business unscathed. Therefore, they're making this feast in thanksgiving."

The innkeeper told his wife the good news, and in a wink everybody became feverishly busy, cooking, scouring and cleaning as one would, expecting important guests. Hershel requested that the place be brightened festively. So they lit many candles.

When the *Hasidim* neared the inn they saw Hershel running towards them. At first they were frightened.

"Why do you run all out of breath, Hershel?" they asked. "What has happened?"

"God is good!"

"What! Have you found a treasure?"

"You wanted a feast, didn't you? Well, the good Lord has arranged it. There, in that inn, they've already been celebrating for a week. Every Jewish traveller who passes by is obliged to stop here and feast with the innkeeper without paying one kopek."

"The innkeeper is crazy!" the *Hasidim* agreed among themselves.

"Why is he crazy?" protested Hershel. "There's a whole story to it. A week ago a gang of robbers waylaid the innkeeper as he was passing through a dark forest. Because he escaped without a scratch the innkeeper is celebrating this way in thanksgiving to God. It would be a sin, believe me, to let such a fine feast get away from us! Remember though, don't mention a word about money! You'll only embarrass the innkeeper."

This story pleased the *Hasidim* so they drew up before the inn and entered.

Everybody could see that Hershel had told the whole truth. The inn was beautifully illuminated as though for a feast. The tables were set with all good things. The innkeeper and his wife were dressed in their Sabbath best. Without hesitation the *Hasidim* seated themselves and began to make merry. The innkeeper almost crawled out of his skin to please his guests. The *Hasidim* gorged themselves. They sang and they even danced in a circle.

Thus the night passed.

Just at the point of daybreak the door of the inn was thrown wide open and the driver of the carriage in which the *Hasidim* had come stormed in.

"It's high time to leave!" he announced. "And I'm not going to wait a minute longer!"

When Hershel heard this he stole out of the inn. Barely able to stand on their legs, the *Hasidim* staggered out and began to climb into the carriage. Seeing this, the innkeeper ran up and held on to the horses.

"I won't let you go until you pay me!" he cried.

Everybody began to shout at the same time, and no one knew what anybody was saying. The shock of the news almost sobered up the *Hasidim*. Blazing with anger they said to the innkeeper, "How dare you demand payment of us? Hershel distinctly told us that you were inviting every passerby to a feast of thanksgiving because you were saved from a gang of robbers in the woods last week."

"That's a lie!" raged the innkeeper. "Hershel told me distinctly that it was *you* who escaped unscathed from a gang of robbers and that's why you were sending him with a message to me that I should prepare a feast of thanksgiving *for you*. A fine bunch of robbers you are yourselves, you pious hypocrites! On my word as a Jew, if you don't pay up immediately I'll have you arrested and sent to prison!"

And the *Hasidim* paid.

The Way to Die

HERSHEL OSTROPOLIER, the famous jester, died as he had lived—with a joke on his lips.

When Rabbi Boruch and his disciples stood around Hershel's bed and listened to him making sport of everything and everybody they were filled with wonder.

"Haven't you done enough ridiculing in your life without having to do so on your deathbed?" the rabbi rebuked him sternly. "Aren't you afraid of Hell?"

"Never fear," replied the dying Hershel, "I'll joke myself out of there, too!"

"For instance?" asked the rabbi.

"If the Angel of Death asks me whether I devoted my days and nights to the study of the Torah, I'll answer: 'If you think I'm not a scholar don't make me your son-in-law.' If he asks me what my name is—I'll tell him: 'Getzel.' Naturally, he'll get angry. 'What's the idea, your name is Hershel!' So I'll tell him: 'Since you know, why do you ask?' And if he asks me: 'What have you accomplished in life? Have you mended anything that was wrong in the world?' I'll answer: 'Mended? Surely, I mended— I mended my socks, my shirt, my pants. . . .'"

A little later, when the members of the Burial Society arrived, Hershel said to them with his dying breath, "Remember, my friends, when you lift me up to lay me in my coffin be sure not to hold me under the arm-pits. I've always been very ticklish there!"

And so, with a smile on his lips, Hershel breathed his last.

FOOLS AND SIMPLETONS

INTRODUCTION

Laughing at the absurdities of fools is one of the oldest diversions of mankind. There is within all of us a deep-seated psychological drive to achieve self-elevation by means of disparaging others whom we are pleased to consider less bright than ourselves. A fool, of course, is always the other fellow, never ourselves.

There are a great number of ancient and modern Jewish sayings that refer disdainfully to fools: "It is better to hear the rebuke of the wise than for a man to hear the song of fools. . . . For as the crackling of thorns under a pot, so is the laughter of a fool. . . . A fool's voice is known by a multitude of words. . . . It is better to lose to a wise man than to win from a fool. . . . Never show half-finished work to a fool."

However, there is still another tradition about fools. It, on the contrary, is not scornful but understanding and compassionate, and springs from the ethical values of the folk who keep in mind the admonition of the Prophet

Jeremiah: "Let not the wise man glory in his wisdom." This attitude is derived from the precept of humility taught in Israel since the days of the Prophets and the sages. This is trenchantly pointed in the saying: "All wise people act foolishly sometimes."

There is a whimsical little story in the Talmud about a man who had left a will stipulating: "My son shall not receive his inheritance until he becomes foolish." The rabbinical judges were confounded by this clause. What on earth could it mean? So they decided to call on the astute Rabbi Joshua ben Korha (2nd Century A.D.) in order to ask his advice in the matter.

When they entered the rabbi's house they drew back in amazement. There, on the floor, crawling on all fours was Rabbi Joshua! With a cord in his mouth and his little son astride him, he was playing the time-honored game of "horsie."

When Rabbi Joshua regained his dignity and listened to the rabbis' question about the will he could not contain his mirth: "My Masters," he laughed, "I have given you a concrete illustration of your case. Know that everyone becomes foolish as soon as he has children!"

During the Middle Ages, when "The Fool in Christ" became a cherished belief of the Christian mystics, the Jews did not remain unaffected by it. There are stories about the *Lamed-Vav-Tzaddikim*, the Thirty-Six Hidden Saints, that carry this theme in modified form and in characteristic Jewish garb. There is a striking similarity between them and the Christian tales about saintly fools, and even with modern literary treatments of these folk-tales, such as Tolstoy's moral stories about "holy fools" and the "holy simpleton" tale, *Fra Giovanni,* by Anatole France.

There is no body of humorous folk-literature more widely disseminated among Yiddish-speaking Jews than the stories about the fools (or "sages" as they are scoffingly called) of Chelm. There are, of course, fools and fools, but in the Jewish folk-fancy the fools of Chelm represent the *ne plus ultra* in simpletons. They have even entered into the Yiddish language. When a Jew refers to a pretentious foolish person, likely as not he will say of him ironically: "Just look at him—a regular *Chelmer chochem.*"

What is Chelm? It is a real town in Poland, like Gotham in England and Schildburg in Germany. These three towns have one thing in common —for some unaccountable reason they were elected in irreverent folklore to serve as the centers of all innocent stupidity. The historical origin of the foolish stories about the inhabitants of all three places is closely linked. Which of them came first chronologically is like debating which came first —the chicken or the egg. However, we do know one fact, that the tales about the fools of Schildburg were translated in 1597 from the German into Yiddish, and enjoyed enormous popularity in central and eastern Europe.

Whether there already existed before that time a body of humorous Yiddish stories about the fools of Chelm, we have no way of knowing. It is reasonable, though, to conjecture that, prior to that time, there must have been in circulation among Jews many jokes about fools but there was no unifying peg on which to hang them. Conceivably, the Schildburger tales may have served as a model for the adoption of Chelm as a town of Jewish fools. Since then many a story about fools has conveniently been ascribed to the inhabitants of Chelm.

The Chelm stories have their own flavor and coloration, differing considerably from the Schildburg and Gotham stories. They not only have Jewish settings and, to some extent, are an index to Jewish character, customs and manners, but they also possess many facets of Jewish irony and wit. Unquestionably, they constitute an original body of folk-humor.

                                                                    N. A.

What Makes a Fool

A FOOL went to the rabbi and said: "I know I'm a fool, Rabbi, but I don't know what to do about it. Please advise me what to do."

"Ah, my son!" exclaimed the rabbi, in a complimentary way. "If you know you're a fool, then you surely are no fool!"

"Then why does everybody say I'm a fool?" complained the man.

The rabbi regarded him thoughtfully for a moment.

"If you yourself don't understand that you're a fool," he chided him, "but only listen to what people say, then you surely *are* a fool!"

Some of the Nicest People

A JEW came to his rabbi to lodge a complaint against other members of the congregation.

"Rabbi," he asked plaintively, "do you think it right of them to call me a fool?"

The rabbi listened with sympathy.

"Why get upset by such a trifle!" he consoled him. "Do you think fools are so very different from other people? Believe me, some of the nicest people I've ever known were fools. Why, even a fine, intelligent man like you could be one!"

The Blessings of a Good Memory

THE "town fool" once came to the *shammes* in the synagogue with a complaint. Everywhere he went the roughnecks were making sport of him, playing pranks on him, making his life miserable.

"What shall I do?" he wailed.

"Take my advice," said the *shammes*, very much aroused. "When one of those hooligans starts up with you again grab a big stone and slam him over the head."

"That's all right on the street, *Shammes*, but there are no stones in the bathhouse."

"In the bathhouse you grab up a tub of hot water and scald him with it."

"But in the synagogue there are neither stones nor hot water."

"All right, in the synagogue you grab up a brass candlestick and you knock him over the head."

"That's all right for weekdays, *Shammes*, but what am I going to do on the Sabbath when I'm not allowed to touch or lift a candlestick?"

"Very well, on the Sabbath all you have to do is to give him a good kick in his 'I beg-your-pardon,' so that sparks will fly out of his eyes."

"It's easy for you, *Shammes* to give me such good advice. You have a good memory—you remember everything. But take me—I've got a poor memory. Just think of all I've got to remember. When in the street—a rock over the head; when in the bath—scald him with hot water; when in the synagogue on weekdays—over the head with a candlestick; on the Sabbath—a good kick in his 'I beg-your-pardon.' Believe me, *Shammes*, if I were clever enough to remember all these complicated things—would I have to come to you for advice?"

Paying Three Times

A KING once said to his slave: "Go to market and buy me a fish!"

The slave went and bought a fish, but the fish stank.

"I swear by your life," cried the King, "that I will not forgive you for your stupidity, unless you accept one of three punishments: either you eat the fish yourself, or you pay me back what it cost, or you let me give you a hundred lashes!"

"I will eat the fish," said the slave.

But he had no sooner begun to eat when he felt nauseated.

"Better give me the hundred lashes!" he begged the King.

So they began to count the lashes one by one. When they had counted fifty the slave felt that he was near death.

"Better let me pay for the fish!" he cried.

What did the slave profit from it all? He ate the rotten fish, he got fifty lashes, and, in the end, he paid!

Why Waste Money?

ONCE there was a nitwit, and he could not be trusted with anything from here to there. Naturally, he was a source of grief to his parents. But what could they do, poor people—he was their own flesh and blood!

One day his mother said to him, "Motkele, my son, here is a ruble! Go

PAYING THREE TIMES: Adapted from the *Midrash*.

to market and buy a hen for me. But remember, hold tight to the ruble and don't lose it."

Motkele promised faithfully and went to market. But on his return his mother almost fainted. Motkele had brought back a jug filled with water!

"Motkele, my son, what on earth have you done?" she cried. "Didn't I ask you to buy a hen? What's this water for?"

"Don't be angry with me, mother!" pleaded Motkele. "Let me tell you what happened. I went to market to buy a hen, as you told me to. When I asked the poultry woman to sell me a hen she said: 'I want you to know that this is no mere hen—it's heavenly chicken-fat!' When I heard her praise chicken-fat so I knew that chicken-fat must be better than a hen, so I went to buy chicken-fat. I asked the butcher for some chicken-fat. He said to me: 'This is no mere chicken-fat—it's as clear as oil!' I understood then that oil must be better than chicken-fat. So I went into a shop and asked for oil, and the shopkeeper said: 'This is no mere oil! You can see it's pure as water!' When I heard that water was better than oil, I said to myself: 'What's the use of wasting a good ruble?' So I got the pitcher and filled it with pure water, and here I am!"

Philosophy with Noodles

ONCE a proposal of marriage was brought to a young man who was simple-minded. Poor fellow! He had no idea how to behave in the company of others. And so, in order to save him from embarrassment, his father, who was a man of the world, cautioned him as follows:

"When you visit the bride for the first time you no doubt will not know what to talk to her about. Therefore, if you want to make a good impression on her, here's my advice. First, begin talking about love. Then you can touch on family affairs. You can wind up with a little philosophy."

The groom nodded gravely and replied that he understood perfectly well how he was to behave. Then, with his father's blessings, he went off to make his first call on his intended.

At first he felt great constraint because the girl's parents were present, but when they left from motives of delicacy, he relaxed somewhat. Then, remembering his father's counsel, he suddenly asked the girl, "Do you love noodles?"

"Sure," she answered in surprise. "Why shouldn't I love noodles?"

After a moment of silence, he continued, "Do you have a brother?"

"No, I have no brother."

The groom rejoiced—he had safely weathered his father's first two instructions, had talked about love and family matters. Now he still had to philosophize a bit.

"*Kaleh*," he asked, furrowing his brow, "if you had a brother, would he have loved noodles?"

The Dissertation

THE rabbi was wearily drilling his stupid rich pupil in the art of giving a Talmudic dissertation.

"Divide your lecture in three parts," he told him. "The first part is the Scriptural text or the *Posek*, the second part is the question or the *Kashe*, and the third part is the answer or the *Teretz*. But don't mix them up and don't put the cart before the horse."

Since the pupil still looked bewildered, the Rabbi began giving him illustrations:

"The *Posek* says: 'It is dark and slippery, and the Avenging Angel pursues?' So the *Kashe* is: 'Why doesn't the Avenging Angel slip and fall?' So the *Teretz* is: 'He isn't the Avenging Angel for nothing.'

"To give you another example—the *Posek* says: 'Noah had three sons, Sem, Ham and Japhet.' So the *Kashe* is: 'What was their father's name?' So the answer is: 'His name was Noah.'

"To give you still another example—the *Posek* says: 'And Joseph knew his brethren, but they did not know him!' So the *Kashe* is: 'How did it happen that they did not recognize their own brother?' So the answer is: 'Before he had no beard, but later he grew a beard.'

"Now, do you understand how to construct a dissertation?" concluded the rabbi hopefully. "You see, it's all very logical."

"I understand," answered the youth confidently.

The following Sabbath he arose in the synagogue, went up to the preacher's rostrum, and began to expound Torah:

"The *Posek* says: 'It is dark and slippery and the Avenging Angel pursues.' So the *Kashe* is: 'What was his father's name?' So the *Teretz* is: 'Before he had no beard, but later he grew a beard.'"

Surplus

IN ANY Jewish village of old Russia a Gentile could earn small sums on the Sabbath and holy days by performing certain duties for orthodox Jews that were forbidden to them by their religion.

On a train, Yoshke the *luftmensch*, from a tiny village, was sitting next to a Jew from Kharkov.

In the course of the inevitable conversation Yoshke stated with pride, "Our town is quite a town. We have five hundred Jews and fifty Gentiles. How big is your town?"

"In our town we have a hundred thousand Jews," said the man from Kharkov bluntly.

Yoshke was overwhelmed. "Unbelievable!" he said. "How many Gentiles have you?"

"About a million."

"A million! What do you need so many Gentiles for?"

If It Were Anyone Else

"Doctor, I need help," complained a patient. "I talk to myself."

"Do you suffer pain?" asked the doctor.

"No, no pain."

"Well," said the doctor, "then go home, don't worry. Millions of people talk to themselves. . . ."

"But, doctor," cried the patient, "you don't know what a *nudnik* I am!"

It's Terrible

In a hot, dusty train unequipped with the luxury of water an old Jew sat opposite a stranger in the cramped seats.

"*Oy*," said the old man for about the ninetieth time, "am I thirsty!"

The stranger twitched with irritation.

"What a terrible thirst I have!" the old man repeated hoarsely.

Again the stranger's nerves tensed.

"*Oy*, am I thirsty!" again exclaimed the old man.

Just then the train stopped at a station. The stranger hastened into the station, obtained a cup of water, and returned. Thrusting it at the old man he cried, "Here, drink!"

"Thank you," said the old man, and drank.

As the train started up again the stranger settled back to enjoy the peace. But in a moment the quiet was shattered by a mighty sigh.

"*Oy*, did I have a thirst!"

Making It Easy

Every afternoon Herr Gutman went to play pinochle with several cronies at the Café Schlagobers in Vienna. One afternoon, as he sat playing, he suddenly fell forward; he had died from a stroke.

His cronies decided to send the dead man's bosom companion, Herr Lubin, to break the news to the poor widow.

"*Guten Tag*, Herr Lubin," Frau Gutman greeted her unexpected visitor. "How are things?"

"How should they be? Fine."

"Have you seen my husband?"

"I have."

"In the Café, no doubt?"

"Where else?"

"No doubt he played pinochle?"

"What else?"

"I wouldn't be surprised if he lost all his money!"

"Who else's money would he lose?"

"What! He lost his money? May he be struck dead, the good-for-nothing!"

"You see, Frau Gutman," cried Herr Lubin, overjoyed. "That's just what I've come to see you about!"

THE WISDOM OF CHELM

The Mistake

THE rabbi of Chelm and one of his Talmud students were spending the night at the inn. The student asked the servant to wake him at dawn because he was to take an early train. The servant did so. Not wishing to wake the rabbi, the student groped in the dark for his clothes and, in his haste, he put on the long rabbinical gabardine. He hurried to the station, and, as he entered the train, he was struck dumb with amazement as he looked at himself in the compartment mirror.

"What an idiot that servant is!" he cried angrily. "I asked him to wake me, instead he went and woke the rabbi!"

The Golden Shoes

THE citizens of Chelm met in council and decided that for a community like theirs, so renowned for its wisdom, it was only fitting that it should have a Chief Sage. So they elected a Chief Sage. But to their dismay, nobody seemed to pay any attention to him when he walked out on the street, for he looked like any other ordinary Chelm citizen.

So they bought him a pair of golden shoes.

"Now everybody will know that he is the Chief Sage!" they said.

The first day the Chief Sage put on his golden shoes a deep mud lay on the streets. In no time at all the mud covered the shoes and it was impossible to see that they were golden. Therefore nobody knew it was the Chief Sage. No attention was paid to him.

The Chief Sage did not like to be ignored that way so he went to complain to the Council of Sages.

"If I don't get some respect quickly I'll resign!" he threatened.

"You're perfectly right!" the Council agreed. "We're going to do something drastic about it! The dignity of our Chief Sage must be protected!"

They therefore ordered for him a pair of fine leather shoes to wear over the golden shoes. True enough, when the Chief Sage went out upon the street the leather shoes protected the golden shoes from the mud, but since no one got a glimmer of the golden shoes, how could they tell it was the Chief Sage? So again they paid no attention to him.

"It is an outrage!" cried the Chief Sage. "What's the use of being Chief Sage if everybody ignores you?"

"You're right—absolutely right!" agreed the Council. "Trust us—we'll do everything to protect your dignity."

So they ordered from the shoemaker a new pair of leather shoes for the Chief Sage. These were to have holes in them. In this way they would protect the golden shoes against the mud, and at the same time would reveal them. Everybody would thus be able to recognize the Chief Sage.

Unfortunately, this plan, too, miscarried. The mud went through the holes and mired the golden shoes as well as the leather shoes. Therefore, since nobody had any inkling that it was the Chief Sage they paid no attention to him, as usual.

"This is an outrage!" cried the Chief Sage. "I'm humiliated, and soon I won't be able to show my face on the street!"

"When you are mortified we are mortified too!" the Council consoled him. "Never fear, we shall do something about it."

Thereupon, they stuffed the holes in his leather shoes with straw. True, the straw prevented the mud from entering the shoes but the old trouble was still there—nobody could get a glimmer of the golden shoes. And again the Chief Sage passed ignored. This was the last straw!

So the sages of Chelm went into solemn council, once for all to settle the matter. And, after long and heated deliberation, they emerged triumphantly with a solution.

"Henceforth," they told the Chief Sage, "you will walk out on the street wearing ordinary leather shoes, but, in order that everybody might know that you are the Chief Sage, you will wear the golden shoes one on each hand!"

The Chelm Goat Mystery

THE rabbi of Chelm once fell gravely sick. While he could work wonders for others, he refused to use his supernatural powers for himself—such a saint he was! So they had to do the next best thing and call the doctor.

The doctor examined the holy man and shook his head.

"Bad, bad!" he muttered to the *rebbitzen*. "There's only one thing that can help him—a steady supply of fresh goat's milk. But for this you've got to own a goat. My advice to you is: buy a goat."

So the *rebbitzen* asked two of the rabbi's disciples to go to the next village and buy a good nanny goat at a reasonable price.

"Trust us!" cried the disciples. "We'll bring you the best goat in goat-land!"

So they went to the next village and bought a white nanny goat.

THE CHELM GOAT MYSTERY: A brilliant literary treatment of this folktale has been given by the Yiddish humorist Sholom Aleichem in his story: *The Enchanted Tailor*. An English translation of it has been made by Julius and Frances Butwin in *The Old Country*, by Sholom Aleichem. Crown Publishers. New York, 1946.

"Are you sure it's a good nanny goat?" the disciples asked the dealer, just to make sure.

"Is it a good nanny goat?" cried the dealer offended. "Why, it gushes milk like a fountain!"

Delighted with their purchase, the disciples started for home, leading the goat by a rope.

"With such an animal the rabbi will surely get well!" they rejoiced.

On the way they came to an inn. Already in high spirits the disciples said, "Let's drink to the health of our rabbi and his nanny goat!"

So, after tying their goat to a post in the stable, they went into the inn and ordered some drinks.

Made talkative by the *schnapps* they began to boast before the innkeeper.

"Some goat we've just bought for our rabbi! It's positively the best goat in goatland—it gushes milk like a fountain! There isn't another like it in Chelm!"

"You don't say so!" replied the innkeeper with amazement.

Now this innkeeper was an irreverent rogue; he had a hearty dislike for wonder-working rabbis as well as for all the people of Chelm. Therefore, he plotted a mischievous prank against the rabbi's disciples. While they were merrily celebrating, he quietly slipped out into the stable. He untied the wonderful white nanny-goat they had bought and in its place he tied his own white billy-goat.

When the disciples had sobered up a bit they paid the innkeeper, untied their goat, and continued on their homeward journey.

They arrived in Chelm toward nightfall. In their eagerness to show off their purchase they ran to the rabbi's house, with the goat galloping behind them and a crowd of curious children trotting after the goat. When they reached the rabbi's house the disciples called, "*Rebbitzen,* quick, come out and look at the wonderful goat we bought for you!"

"Really a fine goat!" said the *rebbitzen,* judiciously. "The question is, does she give a lot of milk?"

"Don't ask—just milk her and you'll see for yourself!" said the disciples, beaming.

The *rebbitzen* went for a stool and a pot and sat down to milk. She tried and tried but no milk came.

"May such a misfortune happen to my enemies!" she burst out angrily. "What kind of a goat did you buy? She doesn't give a drop!"

"Don't be so hasty, *rebbitzen,*" they implored her. "The Torah says specifically: 'Everything has to be done with knowledge and with understanding.' Since you have never owned a goat before let's call in a goat expert."

So they called in a goat expert, who took one look at the goat and he cried out in surprise, "This is no nanny-goat! This is a billy-goat!"

The disciples grew bitter.

"That enemy of Israel!" they cried, referring to the dealer in goats.

"Tomorrow we'll take this wretched beast back to him and tell him a thing or two for this swindle."

Early the next morning the disciples, boiling with anger, started out with the goat. Again they passed the wayside inn.

"Let's go in and cheer ourselves up with a drink," one suggested. "After all, we don't have to make ourselves miserable on account of a flea-bitten goat!"

So, after tying the goat in the stable, they went into the inn and ordered drinks.

"What kind of a swindle do you suppose that dog of a goat dealer put over on us?" they said to the innkeeper. "Gave us a billy instead of a nanny!"

"Tsk, tsk!" exclaimed the innkeeper commiseratingly. "The trouble with you scholars is that you're so unworldly. You believe everything you're told. Why don't you keep your eyes open when you buy something?"

To drown their humiliation the disciples drank heavily and, while they were at it, the innkeeper went quietly into the stable, removed his own billy and in its place he tied the nanny that he had taken from the disciples the day before.

Through with their drinking, the disciples untied their goat and departed.

"Enemy of Israel!" they called out with rage when they saw the goat-dealer. "Don't think you can swindle honest folk so easily!"

"What's wrong, what's wrong?" murmured the dealer in confusion.

"What's wrong? You said you sold us a nanny! And what do you suppose we found when we got home—a billy!"

"I swear, you're crazy!" cried the dealer as he took but one look at the goat.

"Malke!" he called to his wife. "Just milk this nanny for these fine scholars!"

The woman brought a stool and a pot and began to milk the goat. The disciples stood by, their eyes popping out of their heads. There, right before their very eyes, the goat was streaming milk like a fountain, just as the dealer had told them she would!

"*Nu, schlemihls,* are you satisfied now?" he asked scornfully.

Muttering their apologies the rabbi's disciples took their goat and started for home.

Elated, they burst into song. When they passed the inn again one said, "Now we should really celebrate! Our goat is some gusher!"

Into the inn they went and ordered a big bottle of *schnapps* and, while they were drinking to the health of the rabbi and the goat, sure enough that rascal of an innkeeper stole away and once more exchanged the goats.

Unsuspectingly the happy disciples returned home. But the same thing happened this time as before. When the *rebbitzen* sat down to milk the goat she discovered it was a billy!

"There's witchcraft in this!" cried the disciples horrified. "With our own eyes we saw the dealer's wife milk this goat. We must tell the whole story to the rabbi!"

Breathlessly they went to the sick rabbi and told him all that had happened.

"It's clear to me that the dealer is a swindler," was the rabbi's judicious opinion. "There's only one thing left for you to do. Return immediately to the dealer with the goat and summon him to Rabbi Shmul in his town. Demand a signed document from the rabbi that the goat you finally leave with is a nanny and not a billy."

The following day, bright and early, the disciples started out again with the goat. As they had done every time before they went into the inn to cheer themselves up. When he heard their story the innkeeper said, "You're a bunch of *schlemihls*! If your goat dealer had played a trick on me like that I'd have broken every bone in his body!"

"Never fear!" promised the disciples. "We'll fix him so he'll see his dead grandmother!"

And, while they were drinking to give themselves courage for the final encounter with the goat-dealer, the sly innkeeper again exchanged the goats. The disciples left in high spirits to call on the dealer.

"Swindler!" they cried. "Do you expect us to spend the rest of our lives travelling from Chelm to your cursed village with this miserable animal? Here's your goat. Now show us, before we make you join your dead grandmother, how much milk you can squeeze out of your gusher!"

Without a word the dealer sat down and milked the animal.

The disciples looked on stunned. They could hardly believe their eyes. The milk was pouring into the pot in a foaming stream.

"To your rabbi! Take us to your rabbi!" they now demanded. "We want a document from him that this is a genuine nanny!"

The goat-dealer shrugged his shoulders disdainfully and went with them to the rabbi who carefully examined the goat and pronounced it a nanny. He gave them a signed and sealed document attesting to that effect.

Now the disciples were certain that all their troubles were over, so they started for home in a merry mood. To crown their triumph they again went into the inn for a round of drinks. Once more the innkeeper exchanged the goats.

When the disciples reached the rabbi's house, they cried joyfully, "*Rebbitzen!* Just come out and see! It's a genuine nanny this time. Here you have Rabbi Shmul's written word for it!"

Eagerly the *rebbitzen* ran for her pot and stool and sat down to milk the goat. With a cry she leaped up and screamed, "Numskulls! Lunatics! What sort of game do you think you're playing with me?"

She then made them go with her to the rabbi's room.

"Here you have Rabbi Shmul's document!" cried the disciples in bewilderment. "Tell us, what does all this mean? Do you perhaps see the Evil Eye in it, Rabbi?"

"Bring me my spectacles!" ordered the rabbi.

They brought him his spectacles. He put them on and carefully read Rabbi Shmul's document.

For a long time the rabbi sat deliberating, his brow furrowed, his eyes far away. Then he spoke, "This is my opinion: Rabbi Shmul is a wise and upright man. He never writes anything that is not true. If he tells us that the goat is a nanny you can rest assured that it is not a billy. Now, you will ask: how is it that the goat he tells us is a nanny turns out to be a billy? The answer is very simple: true, the goat he examined and testified to was a nanny. But such is the confounded luck of us Chelm *schlimazls* that, by the time a nanny goat finally reaches our town, it's sure to turn into a billy!"

Innocence and Arithmetic

A YOUNG scholar of Chelm, innocent in the ways of earthly matters, was stunned one morning when his wife gave birth. Pell-mell he ran to the rabbi.

"Rabbi," he blurted out, "an extraordinary thing has happened! Please explain it to me! My wife has just given birth although we have been married only three months! How can this be? Everybody knows it takes nine months for a baby to be born!"

The rabbi, a world-renowned sage, put on his silver-rimmed spectacles and furrowed his brow reflectively.

"My son," he said, "I see you haven't the slightest idea about such matters, nor can you make the simplest calculation. Let me ask you: Have you lived with your wife three months?"

"Yes."

"Has she lived with you three months?"

"Yes."

"Together—have you lived three months?"

"Yes."

"What's the total then—three months plus three plus three?"

"Nine months, Rabbi!"

"Then why do you come to bother me with your foolish questions!"

By the Beard of His Mother

A YOUNG man from Chelm, who was studying to be a sage, felt very much troubled in mind. So he went to the Chief Sage and asked him, "Perhaps you can tell me why no hair is growing on my chin? Now it couldn't be heredity—or could it? Take my father—you know what a fine thick beard he has."

The Chief Sage reflectively stroked his beard for a while and then his face lit up.

"Perhaps you take after your mother!" he suggested.

"That must be it, since my mother has no beard!" cried the youth with admiration. "What a sage you are!"

The Great Chelm Controversy

ALTHOUGH the Jews of Chelm loved their rabbi, he remained aloof from the populace, as a wonder-working rabbi should. They hardly ever saw him. That's why nobody knew for certain whether he had a head or not.

One day the rabbi disappeared and all the people of Chelm went searching for him. They looked high and low, but found no trace of the rabbi. Finally, one searching party found a headless body in the woods. So the sages were sent for. They examined the body carefully, reflected and reflected. Then up spoke the Chief Sage, "This is indeed very puzzling! If the rabbi had a head, then it's clear that this is not his body."

"On the other hand," another sage took exception, "if the rabbi didn't have a head then it's certain, as my name is Shabsi, that this *is* his body!"

"We must clear up this point!" insisted the Chief Sage. "Let us question the *shammes* who always waited on the rabbi."

So they called the *shammes*.

"*Reb* Todros," they asked, "do you know whether our rabbi had a head?"

Reb Todros knitted his forehead. He thought and he thought and finally he said, "God preserve us all! I don't know what to tell you. You know what kind of a man our rabbi was. He was always wrapped up in his prayer-shawl, like the saint he was. Therefore, I never saw anything of him but his feet. How should I know whether this is his body?"

"Let the bathman be questioned now," ordered the Chief Sage.

So the bathman stepped forward.

"Tell us, my good man, do you know whether our rabbi had a head?" he was asked.

The bathman shook his head doubtfully.

"For the life of me I can't tell whether our rabbi had a head or not! The only time I ever saw him was in the steam-bath where he would lie sweating on the topmost bench. When I scourged him with birch-twigs I could only see his backside. So how do you expect me to know whether this is our rabbi?"

"This is bad! A very knotty problem indeed!" cried the sages.

"Let us call on the *rebbitzen*!" suggested the Chief Sage. "She should know!"

"An excellent idea!" echoed his colleagues, and they went to see the rabbi's wife.

They found her drenched in tears.

"What a saint my dear husband was!" she lamented. "As a wonder-working rabbi there wasn't his like in the whole world. He himself told me his soul went up to heaven every night!"

"We know, we know all that!" the Chief Sage interrupted her impatiently. "What we would like to know is whether he had a head or not."

"A head, did you say?" asked the *rebbitzen*, drying her tears. "Now let me think! The only thing I'm certain of is that he had a nose because he used to take snuff. But whether he had a head or not only the Lord knows!"

And so what do you think happened? All Chelm became divided into two hostile camps; one maintained heatedly that the rabbi did have a head—the other just as heatedly argued that he didn't.

Now, I ask you *Reb* Jew, what's your opinion?

Superfluous

"WHICH is more important, the sun or the moon?" a citizen of Chelm asked his rabbi.

"The moon, of course," replied the rabbi. "It shines at night, when it is needed. The sun shines only during the day, when there is no need of it at all!"

Wet Logic

A SAGE of Chelm went bathing in the lake and almost drowned. When he raised an outcry other swimmers came to his rescue. As he was helped out of the water he took a solemn oath: "I swear never to go into the water again until I learn how to swim!"

Can This Be I?

A MAN of Chelm, having concluded that people could be distinguished from one another only by their clothing, began to fear lest one day he be lost in the bathhouse, where all are naked and therefore indistinguishable one from the other. To guard against such a risk he tied a string around his leg.

Unfortunately the string came loose, and he lost it. Another man of Chelm found it and, perhaps disturbed by the same fear, fastened it around his own leg.

The first man noticed the second as both were emerging to dress. "Woe is me," he cried, "if this fellow is me, who am I?"

The Columbus of Chelm

IN THE town of Chelm there lived a man whose name was *Reb* Selig. He was a sage, but a restless one. He had the wanderlust in his blood and always dreamed of seeing the world. But, since he was a sage, he was poor, so he could never afford to travel abroad like the rich merchants in the town.

One day, a Chelm merchant returned from a visit to Warsaw. That day, and every day thereafter for a week, one could hear nothing else talked about in Chelm except the wonders of Warsaw that the merchant had described so vividly. No one listened more raptly than *Reb* Selig.

From that time on he walked about like one possessed, filled with only one desire: to see Warsaw. He could neither eat nor sleep nor find rest for himself. His wife was perplexed; she didn't know what had come over her Selig.

One morning he arose and said to her with a faraway look in his eyes, "I've got to go to Warsaw!"

"What for?"

"I hear it's a wonderful city!"

"But you have no money."

"I'll walk."

"But you'll wear out your shoes."

"I'll walk barefoot and carry them in my hand."

"You've gone out of your mind, Selig!"

"I've got to see Warsaw!" *Reb* Selig insisted.

So he put some bread and cheese in a knapsack and threw it over his shoulder. He took up his oak stick and, with his shoes in his hands, he started out for the great city.

Reb Selig hastened along borne on wings. He didn't mind at all that he was barefoot and that the sharp pebbles pricked the soles of his feet. He sang all the way and was filled with joy thinking that soon his eyes would feast on the wonders of Warsaw.

When the sun stood high in the sky *Reb* Selig began to feel the pangs of hunger. He sat down in the shade of a tree at a fork of the road. He ate his noonday meal of bread and cheese. Then, feeling drowsy, he decided to take a short nap in order to refresh himself. But before doing that, he wanted to make sure that he would continue on the right road when he awoke.

"Now, let me see," he said to himself. "I'm at the fork of two roads; one goes to Warsaw and the other goes back to Chelm. I must make sure to take the one to Warsaw and not the one back to Chelm."

So he took his shoes and placed them on the road with the toes facing Warsaw. "When I awake I'll be sure to take the right road," he thought.

Pleased with his cleverness he stretched his length on the grass and went to sleep.

Ai, what a sleep that was! It was the sleep of the blessed, like that of the Patriarch Jacob when he saw angels in his dream! And while *Reb* Selig slept so soundly, so sweetly, a peasant came jogging along in his cart. When the peasant saw the pair of shoes in the road he said to himself: "What luck! Here's a pair of shoes sitting like orphans in the road!"

So he stopped his horse, climbed off the cart and picked up the shoes.

"The black cholera take them!" he murmured. "They're not shoes— they're so full of holes they're sieves!"

So he dropped the shoes, but, in dropping them, they fell with the toes facing Chelm.

After a while *Reb* Selig awoke. Recalling where he was he jumped up, eager to continue on his journey.

"How clever of me," he gloated, "to have had the foresight to place my shoes with their toes pointing toward Warsaw. Now I just can't go wrong!"

And he continued on his journey.

Soon he came in sight of the city. Selig hastened his footsteps. As he passed through the streets he couldn't help marvelling at the strange appearance of things, at the houses, the streets and the people.

"As I live and breathe!" he cried. "Warsaw isn't as big as I expected it to be. Why it looks exactly like Chelm, like two peas in a pod!"

He continued on his way and, as he passed the bathhouse, a man sitting at the door greeted him amiably with a *"Sholom aleichem!"* Selig responded with a hearty, *"Aleichem sholom!"*

"As my name is Selig," he muttered to himself, "this man looks like Fishel the bathman way back in Chelm, and the bathhouse looks like ours, too! What can it all mean?"

Soon he came to the synagogue.

"This is an exact copy of ours in Chelm!" he thought in surprise.

Out of force of habit he went inside.

What he saw there made his hair stand on end.

"If I didn't know that I was in Warsaw I could swear that the people here are all my fellow townsmen!" he muttered to himself.

And, as he stood gaping, the *shammes,* hurrying by, elbowed him aside and stepped on his corns.

"Out of my way!" he cried.

"As there's a God in Heaven," Selig said to himself not believing his own senses, "this *shammes* not only looks like our *shammes* in Chelm but he even talks and acts like him! Strange, very strange."

Reb Selig left the synagogue full of bewilderment.

"What can all this mean?" he asked himself, anxiously. He was so wrapped up in his thoughts that he did not realize where he was going. Suddenly he looked up and found himself walking on a very familiar street.

"So help me God!" he cried. "Why this looks like my own street! So this is Warsaw? What a disappointment! Did I have to go to all this trouble to come here only to see a street that looks exactly like my own?"

In front of a house that also looked like his own he saw some children rolling hickory nuts into a hole.

"May I break hands and feet if that is not my Moishele playing there!"

At that very moment a woman stuck her head out of a window and cried: "Selig, why do you stand there right in the middle of the street with your mouth open like an idiot? Come in—dinner is ready!"

Selig marvelled: He could have sworn the woman was like a twin sister of his wife, Leah! Spoke exactly the same way too! Besides, had she not called him Selig? Indeed, he had to get to the bottom of it all. So he went inside and pretended he was her husband Selig.

Sure enough, the house was furnished just like his own! He sat down to dinner. Just as he had expected—the roast was burnt, the same way his wife Leah burned it.

"The only conclusion I can come to," finally decided *Reb* Selig, "is that Warsaw is *exactly* like Chelm, down to the last detail. True, this is a house that looks like my own, a woman like my wife and a little boy like my Moishele, and her husband's name is Selig. But I *know* very well that they are not mine!"

So *Reb* Selig sat thoughtfully at table and began to feel very homesick for his own little family in Chelm.

"What bothers me though," he decided finally, "is whether the Warsaw Selig that lives in this house is also exactly like me. I know already that his name is Selig and that he looks like me. The question is: who and where is he?"

And so *Reb* Selig, provided he's still living, is waiting to this very day, with characteristic Chelm patience, for the arrival of the other Selig—the Selig of Warsaw.

To such lengths do the sages of Chelm go in order to establish the truth!

Food Out of the Horse's Mouth

A MERCHANT from Chelm drove to market in a neighboring town.

"What are you selling?" asked a prospective customer.

Bending over confidentially, the merchant whispered in his ear: "Oats."

"Oats?" the customer asked in astonishment. "What the devil's the secret then?"

"Sh-sh!" cautioned the merchant of Chelm. "Not so loud! I don't want the horse to know!"

A Sage Question

A SAGE was examining a horse in the marketplace of Chelm.

"This is a wonderful horse!" the horse-dealer went into raptures. "He gallops like the wind! Imagine, if you leave Chelm with him at three in the morning you'd get to Lublin at six!"

The sage looked doubtful.

"What on earth will I do in Lublin so early in the morning?" he asked, scratching his head.

Chelm Justice

A GREAT calamity befell Chelm one day. The town cobbler murdered one of his customers. So he was brought before the judge who sentenced him to die by hanging.

When the verdict was read a townsman arose and cried out, "If your Honor pleases—you have sentenced to death the town cobbler! He's the only one we've got. If you hang him who will mend our shoes?"

"Who? Who?" cried all the people of Chelm with one voice.

The judge nodded in agreement and reconsidered his verdict.

"Good people of Chelm," he said, "what you say is true. Since we have only one cobbler it would be a great wrong against the community to let him die. As there are two roofers in the town let one of them be hanged instead!"

Pure Science

Two sages of Chelm got involved in a deep philosophical argument.

"Since you're so wise," said one, sarcastically, "try to answer this question: Why is it that when a slice of buttered bread falls to the ground, it's bound to fall on the buttered side?"

But as the other sage was a bit of a scientist he decided to disprove this theory by a practical experiment. He went and buttered a slice of bread. Then he dropped it.

"There you are!" he cried triumphantly. "The bread, as you see, hasn't fallen on its buttered side at all. So where is your theory now?"

"Ho-ho!" laughed the other, derisively. "You think you're smart! You buttered the bread on the wrong side!"

Overcoming Messiah

ITZIK the landowner, a leading citizen of Chelm, startled his wife, Chashe, by storming into the house with the news that the Messiah was coming—was at that very moment only a few hours' journey from Chelm.

But the news dismayed Itzik somewhat. "I have only recently built this home, and have invested our funds in cattle, and besides, I have just finished sowing our crops!"

Chashe calmed him, declaring philosophically, "Don't worry! Think of

the trials and tribulations our people have met and survived—the bondage
in Egypt, the wickedness of Haman, the persecutions and pogroms without
end. All of these the good Lord has helped us overcome, and with just a
little more help from Him, we will overcome the Messiah, too!"

The Umbrella

Two sages of Chelm went out for a walk. One carried an umbrella, the
other didn't. Suddenly, it began to rain.

"Open your umbrella, quick!" suggested the one without an umbrella.

"It won't help," answered the other.

"What do you mean, it won't help? It will protect us from the rain."

"It's no use, the umbrella is as full of holes as a sieve."

"Then why did you take it along in the first place?"

"I didn't think it would rain."

Excavation in Chelm

THE citizens of Chelm were digging a foundation for a new synagogue
when one of them suddenly paused in his labors, rested on his spade, and
began to stroke his beard. "What are we going to do," he asked of no one
in particular, "with all this earth we're digging up?"

"I never thought of that," said another. "What, indeed, are we going
to do with it?"

"Ah, I know," the first went on, "we will make a pit, and into it we'll
put all this earth we're digging up for our synagogue."

"But wait a minute," said the other, "that doesn't solve it at all! What
will we do with the earth from the pit?"

"I'll tell you what," said the first, "we'll dig another pit, twice as big as
the first, and into it we'll shovel all the earth we're digging now, and all
the earth from the first pit!"

Whereupon, both went back to their digging.

The Worriers of Chelm

THE people of Chelm were worriers. So they called a meeting to do something about the problem of worry. A motion was duly made and seconded
to the effect that Yossel, the cobbler, be retained by the community as a
whole, to do its worrying, and that his fee be one ruble per week.

The motion was about to carry, all speeches having been for the affirmative, when one sage propounded the fatal question: "If Yossel earned a
ruble a week, what would he have to worry about?"

The Safeguard

To THE scandal of Chelm the poor box was stolen from the synagogue. So it was unanimously resolved that a new poor box be prepared, and suspended from the ceiling of the synagogue entrance hall, but so close to the ceiling that no thief would ever be able to reach it. Satisfied that a crisis had been averted, the people dispersed congratulating each other on a sage decision.

But soon the *shammes* raised a new problem. "It is true," he declared, "that the new box is safe from thieves, but it is out of reach also of the charitable! No one at all can reach it!"

But no problem was too discouraging for the wisdom of Chelm. It was promptly decreed that a ladder be built, reaching to the poor box, so that the charitable might get to it, and that, lest any pious citizen be hurt, the ladder be permanently and immovably fastened to both floor and ceiling!

The Discreet Shammes

A MAN died suddenly in Chelm while doing business in the market-place. So the rabbi sent the *shammes* to the dead man's wife.

"Be careful," he cautioned him, "and break the news to her as gently as possible!"

The *shammes* knocked. A woman came to the door.

"Does the widow Rachel live here?" he asked.

"I'm Rachel, and I live here," replied the woman, "but I'm no widow."

"Ha! Ha!" laughed the *shammes*, triumphantly. "How much do you want to bet you are?"

A Riddle

ONCE on a visit to Berditchev a certain sage of Chelm joined a circle of kibbitzers around the synagogue stove while waiting for the services to begin. Seeing a stranger, the *shammes* tried to entertain him, so he put to him the following riddle: "Who is it—he's my father's son, yet he's not my brother?"

The sage of Chelm racked his brains for the answer but in vain.

"I give up!" he said finally. "Now tell me—who is it?"

"Why, it's me!" replied the *shammes*, triumphantly.

The sage of Chelm was amazed by the cleverness of the riddle and when he returned home he lost no time in assembling all the other sages.

"My masters," he began gravely, stroking his long gray beard reflectively,

"I am going to put to you a riddle and see if you can answer it. Who is it—he's my father's son, yet he's not my brother?"

The sages of Chelm were greatly perplexed. They thought and thought and finally said: "We give up! Tell us! Who is it?"

"He's the *shammes* in the Berditchev synagogue!" the sage announced triumphantly.

Taxes

Two sages of Chelm were tangled up in deep argument.

"What I would like to know," asked one, "is why the Czar has to collect from me a ruble for taxes. Hasn't he got a mint of his own? Surely he can make as many rubles as he likes."

"What a silly argument for a sage!" his colleague mocked at him. "Now take a Jew: every time he does a good deed he creates an angel. So you will ask: why on earth does God need your good deed in order to add one more angel to the millions of angels that are already in Heaven? Surely, He's fully capable Himself of creating as many angels as He likes! Then why doesn't He do so? Simply because He prefers *your* angel. The same thing is true about taxes. Of course the Czar can make as many rubles as he likes; but, you see, he prefers to take *your* ruble!"

The Affair of the Rolling Trunk

A *melamed* once lived on top of the hill on Synagogue Street in Chelm, and he was a great *schlimazl*. Everything turned for him, as the saying goes, "buttered side down." It was therefore with a nagging envy that he watched the rich people of Chelm having all the good things in life, while he, poor *schlimazl*, had to dine daily on a dry crust of bread and an onion.

One day, he said wistfully to his wife, "Leah-Zoshe, my heart, I can no longer endure bread and onion; it's already crawling out of my gullet. It's about time we had a little pleasure, just like the rich. Let's put money by for a cake, the kind we tasted at the wedding of the rabbi's daughter, full of honey and delicious raisins and almonds."

The idea pleased Leah-Zoshe no end. "Good—I have a plan!" she said eagerly. "You know my grandmother's large trunk with the four wheels up in the garret. Let's make a little hole in it. Every Friday afternoon before you go to the *mikveh* you drop in a kopek. I will do the same before I light the Sabbath candles. In that way, by the time *Shevuos* comes around, we'll have enough money to make a cake that will melt in your mouth."

On the first Friday the *melamed* and his wife dutifully dropped into the trunk a kopek each. But when the second Friday came around the *melamed*, who was a profound scholar, thought the matter over in this wise. "Fool that I am! What's the earthly use of dropping in kopek after kopek in this trunk? Surely Leah-Zoshe, that faithful old soul, will keep dropping in kopeks regularly so that we'll soon have money for a wonderful cake without my contributions. I can use the money for other things."

So the *melamed* stopped his contributions.

Now Leah-Zoshe was so smart she could even have been a *rebbitzen*. "If God gave you a head, Leah-Zoshe, use it!" she admonished herself. "After all I'm only a poor *yiddena!* Must I bother my head with kopeks? That's a man's job! I have enough trouble as it is to make ends meet on the ten rubles a month that *schlimazl* gives me for household expenses. There are important things for which I can use my kopeks. In any case what do we need so many kopeks for? The kopeks Mendel drops in will be enough, I'm sure."

So she too stopped her contributions.

Several days before *Shevuos* Mendel the *melamed* and Leah-Zoshe his wife decided it was time to open the trunk and take out all the kopeks.

"*Ai,* what a cake that'll be!" exclaimed Mendel rapturously. "It will have all the tastes of the Garden of Eden!" And Mendel sighed contentedly and smacked his lips as if he had already eaten the cake.

With great ceremony Mendel unlocked the trunk. Carefully he lifted the lid and peered inside.

"*Gewalt!*" he cried, turning pale. "We're robbed!"

Leah-Zoshe quickly stuck her head into the trunk and exclaimed, "*Tateniu!* They left us only two kopeks, the rascals!"

Then suddenly a dark thought clouded her mind. "*Schlimazl,*" she cried, "tell me the truth! Did you drop more than one kopek into the trunk?"

"What do you take me for, a fool?" retorted Mendel. "Of course not. I figured your kopeks would be enough. Now that you have mentioned it, my fine shrew, what happened to your kopeks?"

"My kopeks? What do you mean, *my kopeks?* If you were honest enough to put in yours we wouldn't have needed mine."

At this both became inflamed with anger at each other and they set to with a right good will so that their cries could be heard all the way down Synagogue Street. In the scuffle, Mendel lost his balance and fell into the trunk, pulling Leah-Zoshe with him.

And before you could say "Constantinople" the lid had snapped shut on them! However, in their frantic struggle to get out they set the trunk in motion on its four wheels. The door of their little cottage being open, for it was a balmy day, the trunk rolled through the doorway with the greatest of ease and down the hill into Synagogue Street.

"*Gewalt! Gewalt!*" Unearthly voices issued from the trunk as it rolled toward the synagogue.

Women shrieked, children bawled and all the dogs of Chelm ran barking madly after it.

"It surely must be a demon!" commented the Chief Sage as the trunk whirled by him and he heard the muffled cries inside it.

The trunk's wild journey came suddenly to an end in front of the synagogue. By this time all of Chelm had gathered around it, gaping with curiosity.

"Fetch Berl the locksmith!" ordered the Chief Sage in a voice of authority. "All together we'll drive this demon out!"

And so, after chanting appropriate incantations, the lock was pried open by Berl the locksmith and, more dead than alive, out peered Mendel the *melamed* and his wife Leah-Zoshe.

"Heaven preserve us, look who's here!" the people of Chelm cried.

The runaway trunk had so frightened the people of Chelm that in response to the general clamor, the Chief Sage was obliged to call a special meeting of all the sages of Chelm.

After long and judicious deliberation they resolved that never again must such an unseemly thing happen in their town. To make their decision effective and binding forever upon all future generations of Chelmites they passed the following laws:

1. That every door in Chelm had to be provided with a high threshold.
2. That no *melamed* could ever live on Synagogue Street.
3. That henceforth no trunk could have any wheels.

The Secret of Growing

Two sages of Chelm sat around the synagogue stove on a cold winter day. They debated heatedly over the following question: at which end does a human being grow?

"What a question!" cried one. "Any fool knows that a man grows from his feet up."

"Give me proof," demanded the other.

"Several years ago I bought myself a pair of pants but they were so long that they trailed on the ground. Now look at them—see how short they've gotten. There's your proof."

"It's just the other way around," maintained the other. "Anyone with eyes in his head can see that man grows from the head. Why, just yesterday I watched a regiment of soldiers on parade and it was clear as daylight that at the bottom of their feet they all were the same; they differed in size only at the top!"

SCHLEMIHLS AND SCHLIMAZLS

INTRODUCTION

Out of the poverty of European ghetto life arose two folktypes—the *schlemihl* and the *schlimazl*. True, they had their counterparts in the misfits and the maladjusted of all peoples, but who could compare with them in the extent and intensity of their almost comic wretchedness?

The words *schlemihl* and *schlimazl* are rarely applied according to their precise meanings. Almost always they are used interchangeably. This, of course, is not altogether without reason—the two types did have an affinity; they both had their origin in the same economic swamp of ghetto-stagnation. Also their end product was identical—failure!

What actually is a *schlemihl*? The etymology of the word is very much in doubt. Outside of Yiddish, the first mention of the word is in the title of Chamisso's famous story of *Peter Schlemihl* (1813), the man who sold his shadow. The Bible mentions a Shelumiel who was a prince of the tribe of Simon. But there is nothing to associate him with a *schlemihl*. A theory about the *schlemihl*, one not to be taken too seriously, is built upon the folk story of probable medieval origin concerning a certain Schlumiel who went off on a journey for more than a year. Upon his return he is aghast to discover that his wife has just given birth; but the rabbinical authorities by a very liberal interpretation of the laws of nature convince him that he is no cuckold.

In the Jewish folk-mind, however, the *schlemihl* is conceived of as an awkward, bungling fellow, plagued not only with "butter-fingers," but with absolutely no skill in coping with any situation in life. He is forever getting in his own and everybody else's way and spoils everything he attempts. A comic-strip portrayal of the *schlemihl* on the American scene was *Moishe Kapoir* (Moses Upside-Down). He regaled readers of a Yiddish newspaper in the early 1920's and proved so popular that his name even entered into the language.

What is a *schlimazl*? He is a first cousin to the *schlemihl*. No matter what he too puts his hand to turns out wrong, but not because he lacks ability or intelligence but because he simply has no luck; the cards of an intensely competitive life are stacked against him. In fact, that is the probable meaning of the word *schlimazl*: *schlim* being the German word for "bad"—*mazl* the Hebrew word for "luck."

To put it succinctly, a wit has made the following neat distinction between these two types: "A *schlemihl* is a man who spills a bowl of hot soup on a *schlimazl*."

In the Twelfth Century a *schlimazel* of genius, the poet Abraham ibn Ezra, (of whom Robert Browning has written) laughed at his own misfortunes with mirthful irony:

If I sold shrouds,
No one would die.
If I sold lamps,

Then, in the sky
The sun, for spite,
Would shine by night.

How the *schlemihl* or *schlimazl* managed to survive was a minor miracle. He seemed to draw his livelihood, such as it was, from the very air. That is what led Max Nordau, a well-known Jewish figure at the turn of the century, to coin the word *luftmensch* (air-man).

As identifiable types, *schlemihls* and *schlimazls* must have sprung into being with the first drastic economic discriminations against Jews by the Byzantine emperors, beginning with Justinian (530–560) who froze the social and economic restrictions against the Jews into ruthless Roman law. The Imperial Code bristled with a great number of prohibitions—"the Jews shall not" and "the Jews must not," features which thereafter entered into almost all legal codes in European countries down to the Nuremberg Laws of Hitler. As one writer has remarked: "It reduced men, who through the generations had loved to live by the work of their hands, to the necessity of living by the exercise of their wits."

In the course of time the *schlemihl* and the *schlimazl* became typed in folklore and acquired traditional physiognomies that were half-ludicrous and half-pathetic. In order to survive, they had to be eternally hopeful, untiringly enterprising, and yet—by the very nature of circumstance and their personalities they were pathetic flops. The many anxieties of their family life, the uncertainties of their sustenance which became a daily harassment, brought a haunted apologetic look into their eyes. Sholom Aleichem drew endless amusement out of the misadventures of his irrepressible, daydreaming *schlimazls,* Tevye the Dairyman and Menachem Mendel. If he made merry over them it was only with the compassionate intention of minimizing their own troubles for thousands of other Tevyes and Menachem Mendels struggling for survival.

In the Russian and Polish ghettos, not only the unemployed scholar, but the petty shopkeeper, the occasional trader, and the man without a trade as well, were driven to pursue the elusive firefly of many occupations, and usually starved on all of them.

This particularly held true during the Nineteenth Century when, by Imperial ukase, there took place many mass-expulsions of Jews from the small towns and villages into the already overcrowded city ghettos. Keen as competition was before in those places, it now became even more feverish and desperate. Count Pahlen reported to the Czar in 1888: "About ninety per cent of the whole Jewish population form a mass of people that are entirely unprovided for . . . a mass that lives from hand to mouth amidst poverty."

There is a type of *schlemihl* in Jewish folklore who stands by himself. He is the henpecked husband. Because there were so many *schlemihls* in Jewish life there was naturally a superfluity of henpecked husbands. In Bible times the shrew was considered as a divine punishment "which shall fall to the lot of the sinner." There is the proverb: "It is better to dwell in the wilderness, than with a contentious and angry woman." An unknown, but probably long-suffering Talmudic sage, became downright bitter about it: "Life is not worth living for a husband who has a domineering wife."

Of course there were some gentle and unembittered souls among henpecked husbands who endured their marital martyrdom with philosophical resignation. They tried hard to read into their misfortune some hidden blessings. The sage Rabbi Hiyya, for instance, had a quarrelsome and shrewish wife. He tried to turn her wrath from him with gifts. Whenever he saw some pretty trinket that he thought would charm her, he would

buy it, put it in his turban, and hasten home with it to surprise her.
"Isn't she a shrew, continually pecking at you?" he was asked once.

Rabbi Hiyya replied: "Taking care of our children and saving us from
sin is sufficient for us to be tender to our wives, regardless of their dispositions."

N. A.

The Master

A MAN was married to a shrew who ordered him around the livelong day.
Once, when she had several women friends calling on her, she wanted to
show off before them what absolute control she had over her husband.

"*Schlemihl*," she ordered, "get under that table!"

Without a word the man crawled under the table.

"Now, *schlemihl*, come out!" she again commanded.

"I won't, I won't!" he defied her angrily. "I'll show you that I'm still
master in this house!"

The Henpecked Rabbi

RABBI JACOB ISAAC of Lublin had a shrewish wife. She constantly nagged
him but, as he practiced great self-restraint, he suffered in silence. At last
one day, when his patience had worn thin, he retorted to her with a few
sharp words. When his disciple, Rabbi Bunam, heard this he was filled
with amazement.

"What suddenly made you talk back to your wife, Rabbi?" he asked.

"It would have been cruel not to answer her," replied Rabbi Jacob Isaac.
"What irritated her more than anything else was the fact that I did not
respond to her nagging."

Bagel Troubles

BUSINESS was going from bad to worse for the baker of *bagel*. He began
to lose his appetite and he worried so much that he could not fall asleep.

One night, as he and his wife lay in bed, he asked, "Sarah, are you
asleep?"

"If I were asleep would I hear you?"

"It looks bad, Sarah. The *bagel* business will be our ruin yet."

"What's the trouble?"

"There's no profit in *bagel*. If I make the hole big—my, what a lot of
dough it takes to go around that hole!"

"*Nu*, so you make the hole small."

"It's easy for you to say!" snorted the husband. "If I make the hole
small what a lot of dough it takes to fill the *bagel*!"

Poor Man's Luck

A RABBI was asked to explain why it was that everything was permitted the rich but not the poor.

"Is there a separate Torah for the rich and another for the poor?"

"It's all a matter of luck," answered the rabbi. "Moses came down from Mt. Sinai and found that the Jews had fashioned a golden calf. He got so angry about it that he went and shattered the Ten Commandments. The Tables of the Law, as you know, were made of the most precious gems. When the multitude saw Moses break them they leaped forward to pick up the valuable pieces that fell in every direction. Now who do you think had all the luck in the world? The rich, of course! They picked up all the pieces on which was written—*Thou shalt*. The poor, on the other hand, who have been *schlimazls* ever since the beginning of Creation, had no luck at all. All they could pick up in the scramble were little bits of the Tables on which was written the word *not*. So there!"

The Rebbe and the Rebbitzen

ONCE there was a young rabbi, but he was a great *schlemihl* and never got anywhere despite his learning.

One day, a new rabbi was being chosen for the principal synagogue in town. Our *schlemihl* too was a candidate for the post.

"Since you are such a *schlemihl* leave the whole matter to me!" his wife told him.

So he let her do all the wirepulling and soliciting of influential votes for him.

Finally, with his wife's and God's help, he was elected to the post.

His new dignity turned the rabbi's head. He began to speak grandly to his wife and tried to lay down the law for her in everything. Finally they quarreled.

"To the whole town you may be the rabbi of the Great Synagogue," she lashed out at him, "but to me you're only the same old *schlemihl*! You think that because you're the *rebbe* I'm the *rebbitzen*. Believe me, it's the other way around. Everybody in town, except you, knows that you're the *rebbe* because I'm the *rebbitzen*!"

Two Possibilities

A POOR *melamed* made up his mind he was going to get a cow, for he had many children and he could not afford to buy milk for all of them. So he tried hard to convince his wife that his idea was sound.

"Believe me," he urged with enthusiasm, "it would even be worthwhile to pawn everything we've got in order to buy a cow!"

But his wife was more cautious than he, so she asked, "What guarantee do you have that the cow you'll buy will give milk?"

"What a silly question to ask!" replied the teacher heatedly. "In any case there are two possibilities! If the cow gives milk—it will be fine! On the other hand—if the cow does not give milk—— What do you mean if the cow does not give milk! How is it possible that the cow will not give milk?"

To Avert Disaster

". . . But you've just *got* to give me some money!" insisted the *schlimazl*.

"Why so?" demanded the rich man.

"Because if you don't, I'll . . . I'll go into the hat business!"

"So what?"

"What do you mean, so what? If a man with my luck goes into the hat business, every baby in this country from that day on will be born without a head!"

Poor Fish

A fish dealer in a Jewish neighborhood in the Bronx once put out a sign, reading: "Fresh fish sold here."

A customer came in and asked in surprise, "Why did you put the word 'fresh' on your sign? It's understood your fish are fresh—or do they stink?"

"Of course not!" agreed the fish dealer, and hurriedly he painted out the word "fresh."

A little while later another customer came in and commented, "What for do you need the word 'here' on your sign? Where else could you be selling your fish?"

"You're right!" agreed the fish dealer, and he painted out the word "here."

Later, another customer complained, " 'Sold'! What do you mean, 'sold'? Surely you're not giving away any of your fish!"

"Indeed not!" agreed the fish dealer, and he went and painted out the word "sold."

Finally, an old lady wearing a kerchief hobbled in. She saw the sign, and croaked in a high thin voice, " 'Fish'? You don't need to advertise your fish! Believe me, you can smell them a mile away!"

The fish dealer heaved a deep sigh, picked up his brush and painted out the word "fish."

A Jewish Highwayman

ONCE there was a poor Jew who had a wife and six children but no source of income. His wife scolded him all day long for being a *schlemihl* and his children cried all the time because they were hungry. And so, with a troubled spirit, he sat down to think.

Suddenly a terrible thought occurred to him! He was going to be a highwayman, a wicked, throat-slitting highwayman! He had often heard tales of such men, how with the greatest of ease they acquired large sums of money. Not that he had ever seen any or knew how they went about their business. But he was not going to stand his wife's nagging anymore! He would show her what kind of a *schlemihl* he was!

So early one morning he put on a large sack over his clothes, stuck a hatchet in his belt, took along his *tallis* and *tefillin* and went into the forest.

He hid behind a tree and from there kept a sharp lookout. He waited and waited. But what poor Jew has luck? The morning passed and then the afternoon, and still not a solitary person came in sight. Finally the sun began to set and the shadows of night fell. Seeing this the highwayman grew uneasy.

"*Nu*, what can I do now?" he thought. "It's time to say the *Mincha* prayer."

So he started to pray. But no sooner had he started the eighteen benedictions and was reciting: "Look but upon our affliction, and fight our fight, and redeem us speedily for the sake of Thy Name," when he suddenly saw a Jew coming towards him. Silently he motioned to him to wait until he had finished the prayer. Politely, and with a pious man's regard for another's devotions, the stranger waited.

Having finished the recitation of the eighteenth benediction with a resounding "Amen!" the highwayman ran up to the stranger and, drawing his hatchet, he cried, "Your money or your life!"

The stranger regarded him with amazement.

"What are you—crazy or just a nit-wit?" he inquired.

"I am a highwayman!" answered the highwayman sternly. "And if you won't give me all your money right away I'm going to kill you in cold blood!"

"See here," pleaded the stranger seeing that he was in earnest, "I am a Jew, a destitute man! I am a father and a husband! Where do you suppose a man like me would get money from? Surely you don't want to make my children orphans and my wife a widow! Who will provide for them? With me dead they'll perish of hunger!"

The highwayman listened attentively and nodded his head.

"*Nebich!*" he thought. "A poor man, a father and a husband!"

"You're right!" he said aloud. "It would indeed be a pity to kill you. Very well then, so I won't kill you—but do give me a ruble."

"A ruble!" cried the stranger, getting red in the face with anger. "Who do you take me for—Rothschild?"

"Well then give me ten kopeks."

"Ten kopeks! Are you crazy? Why should I give you ten kopeks? Even a rich man doesn't give an alms of ten kopeks at one smack."

"In that case, give me a cigarette."

"A cigarette! I don't smoke."

"*Nu,*" sighed the highwayman wearily, "let me have a pinch of snuff."

"Oh, a pinch of snuff! Why didn't you say so in the first place?"

So the stranger opened his snuff-box and graciously offered it to the highwayman.

The highwayman took a pinch of snuff and sneezed: "A-choo!"

"*Gesundheit!*" said the stranger heartily.

Then the stranger took a pinch of snuff and sneezed: "A-choo!"

"*Gesundheit!*" echoed the highwayman politely.

They sneezed so heartily that the forest reverberated with the sound. Then they shook hands and said goodnight.

Two Songs for Three Hundred Rubles

A RICH man once lived in a small town. He had an only daughter, and he looked around to see if he could find a suitable husband for her. Finally, he approved of a young Talmudic scholar. He promised him a dowry of three hundred rubles and *kest* for three years.

Agreed!

So they drew up the engagement contract and, soon after, the marriage took place.

After the wedding, the newlyweds made their home, as agreed upon, with the young wife's parents. From that day on the young Talmud scholar devoted himself undisturbed to his sacred studies.

Three years thus passed, and they sped by so swiftly the young couple hardly noticed it. At last the time came for the scholar to shift for himself. His wife now began to reproach him.

"How long must we eat my father's bread? It's high time that you began to think of earning some money!"

"What shall I do?" asked the Talmudist anxiously.

"Since my father has a horse and cart," she answered, "he has agreed to give them to you. You now can ride out into the country to buy and sell merchandise."

"A good idea!" he replied, but without much enthusiasm.

He then hitched his father-in-law's horse to the cart and, taking along the three hundred rubles dowry owed him, he started out on his journey to seek his fortune.

TWO SONGS FOR THREE HUNDRED RUBLES: Adapted from *Folks Meiselach in Anekdoten mit Nigunnim,* by Shmul Lehman. In *Archiv far Yiddisher Sprachwissenschaft, Literaturforschung in Etnologie.* Edited by Noach Prilutzki and Shmul Lehman. Warsaw, 1926–33.

As he drove out of the town and followed the road through the fields he met a shepherd grazing his sheep. The young peasant was singing a lovely little tune:

When the scholar heard this tune he was enchanted. He said to himself: "If I bought this tune from the shepherd I could sell it to our town cantor for at least three times the price I'll probably have to pay for it. That'll bring me a handsome profit and the cantor's gratitude besides."

So he climbed out of the wagon and, going up to the shepherd, asked him:

"How much do you want for your tune, shepherd?"

"A hundred and fifty rubles," replied the shepherd, amused.

Without a moment's hesitation the scholar counted out a hundred and fifty rubles and the shepherd taught him the tune. Then he climbed back into his cart, picked up the reins, and cried: *"Vee-aw!"* And as he rattled away he raised his voice lustily in song:

He rode and he rode until he met another shepherd who, as he stood grazing his sheep, played a sweet tune upon his reed. The scholar stopped his cart and listened raptly:

The scholar said to himself: "What an enchanting tune this is! If I piece it together with the other tune I bought for one hundred and fifty rubles I'll earn a pretty kopek, I'll wager!"

And without further reflection he went over to the shepherd and asked: "How much do you want for your tune?"

"I want one hundred and fifty rubles," answered the shepherd laughingly.

"One hundred and fifty rubles!" exclaimed the Talmudist, alarmed.

And to himself he said: "If I give him my remaining one hundred and fifty rubles there'll be nothing left of my wife's dowry! In that case, what will I have to show when I return home?"

But how could he possibly resist the shepherd's delightful tune? It trembled on his lips to be sung. It was too much of a treasure to let slip through his fingers. Eagerly he counted out to the shepherd the remaining money and, in return, learned the tune from him. Then he got into his cart and turned his horse towards home. Cracking his whip he cried: "*Vee-aw!*"

Above the rattle of the cart-wheels and the pounding of the horse's hooves the scholar sang:

He reached town when the day was beginning to break. He drove straightway to the house of Berish, the tailor. "I'll ask Berish, the tailor, to sew my two tunes together with thread and needle," he thought. "Then I'll go to the town cantor and sell them to him for a large sum."

The scholar knocked on Berish's window.

"Open up, *Reb* Berish!" he called to him.

"Who's knocking?" asked the tailor sleepily.

"It's me, Moishe."

"What do you want?"

"I want you to do some piecing together for me."

"What have you got?"

In answer the scholar threw his head back, closed his eyes rapturously, and sang:

"Is that it?" asked the tailor astonished.

"No, *Reb* Berish, there's some more."

"What is?"

"Just wait and see," answered the Talmudist. And again he sang:

Reb Berish laughed heartily, shrugged his shoulders, then measured the two tunes. First he heated his pressing-iron. Then he cut, trimmed, stitched and pressed the two tunes together. The scholar paid him several groschen for his pains, and then he got into his cart and hurried home.

It was still very early when he drew up before his father-in-law's house. He suspected his wife was still asleep.

"Wake up, Surele!" he called softly to her, knocking on the door.

"Who is it?" asked Surele, frightened.

"It's only me, your husband Moishe!" he answered reassuringly. "I've just got back!"

Surele tumbled out of bed and ran out to see what sort of merchandise her husband had bought. She looked into every corner of the cart, but there was not a sign of anything.

"Where's the merchandise?" she asked.

"What's the difference? I have it!"

"What do you have?"

In answer to her question the Talmudist smiled significantly and sang:

"Is that what you've bought?" she asked in amazement.

"No, my wife, this isn't all! There's still more."

"More what?"

Her husband chuckled softly to himself and sang further:

Hearing this, the scholar's wife ran in terror to her father.

"Oy tateniu, father dear!" she wailed. "Just see what a crazy husband you've given me! I've simply got to divorce him! Imagine, he took the three hundred rubles you gave me for a dowry and he traded them for two worthless little tunes!"

When her father heard this he ran quickly to the rabbi who sent his *shammes* to fetch the scholar and his wife for the divorce hearing.

"You got three hundred rubles for a dowry—what have you done with the money?" demanded the rabbi sternly.

"*Rebbiniu,* crown of my life!" pleaded the scholar. "I've bought fine merchandise with the money!"

"What sort of merchandise?"

"With a look of triumph the scholar threw his head back and began to sing:

"Is that the merchandise?" asked the rabbi, amazed.

"No, rabbi my life—there's still some more!" the scholar joyfully assured him.

"Some more of what?" muttered the rabbi.

"Just wait and you'll hear!" answered the scholar.

And closing his eyes rapturously he sang further:

When he got through singing the rabbi shook his head and sighed.

"I grant you a divorce," he said briefly to the wife.

A Lesson for Henpecked Husbands

KING SOLOMON once gave an audience to a wealthy Jewish farmer, and received from him a costly present. To show his appreciation of the gift, the king offered to bestow upon the farmer any favour he might ask. But,

---

A LESSON FOR HENPECKED HUSBANDS: From the *Prince and the Dervish* by Abraham ben Chasdai Barcelona, circa 1230. In J. Chotzner's *Hebrew Humor and Other Essays.* Luzac & Co. London, 1905.

to the king's surprise, the farmer asked the favour of being taught by the king to understand the secret language spoken by the farmyard animals. After some hesitation the king granted his request, but he warned him not to divulge the secret to anybody under the penalty of immediate death.

Now, it so happened that the farmer had a shrew for a wife, and, wishing to live in peace with her, allowed himself to be ruled by her in all domestic affairs. One day, while occupied in the farmyard, he overheard a conversation between an ox and an ass, which amused him so much that he burst out laughing.

At that moment his wife appeared, and insisted on being told the joke. He begged her not to press him to disclose a secret, on the keeping of which his very life depended. But she remained obdurate. Seeing that there was no way out of the difficulty, he told her that he would fulfil her desire in a few days, but that he had in the meantime to settle his worldly affairs, before going to meet his inevitable and premature death. To this she agreed.

Next day, while again standing in the farmyard, he heard his dog rebuking the cock for crowing as loudly as ever, though he was aware of his master's approaching death. But the cock said that since the master was a coward and a fool, he did not deserve to be pitied by anybody.

"Let him," said the cock, "take a lesson from me, and his life will certainly be saved. There are in the farmyard a number of hens, who all obey me implicitly, as they know very well that any case of disobedience on their part would be attended with a well-deserved punishment. Now, our master has only *one* wife to deal with, and if he is idiotic enough to allow her to rule over him, he must bear the consequences."

When the farmer heard the cock's wise remarks he regained courage, and presently meeting his wife, he told her that he refused to let her know his secret, and that he was fully determined to be and to remain the ruler in his own house from that time forward.

These words had the desired effect, and from that day forth he lived with his wife in harmony and undisturbed peace.

Definition

A POOR man, a *schlimazl*, once came to the rabbi.

"Advise me, Rabbi—what shall I do?" he complained. "Whatever I put my hand to fails. If I sell umbrellas—it doesn't rain. And if I sell shrouds—nobody dies. What trade shall I take up?"

"Take my advice, my son, and become a baker," said the rabbi. "If you become a baker you'll at least have bread in the house."

"True," answered the hard-bitten *schlimazl*, "but what will happen if I don't have money to buy flour?"

"You won't be a baker then," said the rabbi.

The Two-Faced Goat

A POOR teacher of Scripture, after much deprivation, had succeeded in putting by enough money to purchase a goat so that he would have a steady supply of milk.

Once, when a fair was being held in town, he went there to buy a goat. Because he knew very little about animals they palmed off a billy-goat on him. When he discovered the deception he shrugged his shoulders with resignation. "Too late to argue about it! A billy-goat, that's also something!" he said to himself. He would hold the fellow until the next fair. Then with God's help, he'd exchange him for a nanny-goat that would give milk.

One day a plague struck all the nanny-goats in town, and they fell like flies. So the teacher rejoiced that he had a billy-goat and not a nanny-goat like the others.

But who should know God's designs beforehand? The teacher's billy-goat too sickened and died.

Then the teacher of Scripture wailed: "Oh you billy-goat! When it had to do with milk you were a billy-goat, but when it had to do with dying you became a nanny-goat!"

Willing But Not Able

MIRIAM-HANNAH, the wife of *Reb* Nissen the scribe, once sent her husband to market to buy a milch cow.

When Miriam-Hannah saw the cow at her door she grabbed a pail and ran out to milk her but it wasn't long before she returned to the house, blazing with fury, her pail empty.

"May the devil take both you and the cow—you old goat!" she shrilled.

"What's the matter?" mumbled *Reb* Nissen, turning pale as a sheet.

"You ask yet? Your precious cow doesn't want to give me one drop of milk!"

"Maybe you don't know how. Let me try!"

So *Reb* Nissen took up the pail and went outside to woo the cow.

It didn't take long before he returned with empty pail in hand.

"You ought to be ashamed of yourself, Miriam-Hannah," he rebuked her sternly. "How could you say the cow doesn't want to give any milk? Believe me—to give she wants, but, poor thing, she can't!"

X Marks the Spot

SHMUL the tailor came to America from a little Russian town. He didn't know how to read or write but he opened a clothing shop in New York and he began to prosper. In time he went to the bank to open a checking account. Not knowing how to write, he signed two crosses on the bank documents in lieu of his name.

As time went on he prospered still more. He sold his cloak-and-suit business and began to manufacture textiles. So he went to the bank and opened up a new account. This time he signed all the bank documents with three crosses.

"Why three crosses?" asked the bank president. "You've always signed with two."

"Oh, you know how women are, fancy-shmancy," he muttered apologetically. "My wife wants me to take on a middle name!"

Marriages Are Made in Heaven

FOR many years the meek rabbi endured the nagging of his shrewish wife with resignation. Everyone marvelled greatly over his self-control. One day a friend of his said to him:

"It's simply not human to be as patient as you are! If I were in your place I'd divorce your wife—she's the scandal of the whole town."

The rabbi sighed wearily and murmured:

"It must be God's will."

"Nonsense!" protested his friend. "Surely you don't mean to tell me that it is God's will to punish a holy man like you!"

"Far be it from me to question the justice of God's will," gently answered the rabbi. "My own common sense tells me that it is wise. What if my wife had been married instead to an impatient man? Why, he would have divorced her and ruined her life forever after! Therefore, you see that God must have known what he was doing when he gave her to me who can tolerate her nagging."

An Absent-Minded Fellow

ONCE there was a gentle Talmud scholar, but in his wife's eyes he was only a *schlemihl*. He always lost things—never found anything.

One Friday afternoon, he came home from the steambath. His wife was startled to see that he was without a shirt.

"Where is your shirt, my fine *schlemihl*?"

"Oh, the shirt? Somebody must have changed his for mine at the bath by mistake!"

"But where is his? I can see you haven't got yours."

"Tsk, tsk!" reflected the teacher. "The man must have been an absent-minded fellow—he forgot to leave me his!"

A Prayer and a Deal

ONCE there was a poor man, a *schlemihl*. He was so unhappy that he took pleasure in day-dreaming.

One day he uttered the following prayer:

"Dear God—give me ten thousand dollars for the New Year. I'll tell you what—I'll make a deal with you. I swear to give five thousand dollars of this amount for charity, the other half let me keep. You say you have doubts about my honorable intentions?—then give me the five thousand dollars I ask for myself and the other five thousand dollars *you* give to charity yourself."

Vice Is Also an Art

THE rabbi was disappointed in his son-in-law.

"What a simpleton our son-in-law is!" he complained to his wife. "He doesn't know the first thing about drink and cards."

"Is that a misfortune?" asked his wife wonderingly. "May all sons-in-law be as ignorant about such things! So again, what is the misfortune?"

"The misfortune is," lamented the rabbi, "that not knowing how to drink, he drinks nevertheless, and not knowing how to play cards, he insists on playing them!"

IGNORAMUSES AND PRETENDERS

From What Einstein Makes a Living

BENNY's old grandfather, a grey-bearded patriarch from Poland, was very much puzzled by all the newspaper talk about Einstein and his theory of relativity.

"Tell me, Benny," he finally asked with curiosity one day when his grandson returned home from college. "Who is this Einstein and what is all this relativity business about?"

"Einstein is the greatest living scientist," began Benny enthusiastically, a little uneasy about his own knowledge of the matter. "Relativity is—well, it's hard to explain. Let's put it this way: if a man's sweetheart sits on his knee, an hour feels like a minute. On the other hand, if the same man sits on a hot stove, a minute feels like an hour. That's the theory of relativity!" concluded Benny triumphantly.

Grandpa looked shocked. For a minute he kept stunned silence, an expression of incredulity in his eyes. Then he muttered into his beard: "America *goniff*!

"Tell me, Benny," he finally asked "and from this your Einstein makes a living?"

One Use for Scholarship

ONE day a stranger came into the House of Study; no one had ever seen him before. Without a word he made his way to the shelves where the books of sacred lore were stored. He began to pull out one huge tome after another, folios of the Talmud, the commentaries of Rashi, Ibn Ezra and the *Rambam*.

At the time, the House of Study was full of scholars. They watched the man at his work with incredulity.

"What a learned scholar he must be!" whispered one, awestruck.

"Never in my life have I seen a scholar use so many authorities at one time!" said another.

Methodically, the stranger piled up his big books. Then, to everybody's amazement, he climbed on top of them and reached for a hard cheese he had hidden on the very top shelf.

The Truth about Falsehood

NO MAN was imposed upon by rabbinical careerists as much as the kind-hearted Rabbi Elijah, the Vilna Gaon.

One day, a pretentious Talmudic scholar asked him for a testimonial for a learned treatise he was about to publish. Rabbi Elijah couldn't say "no," as much as he wanted to do so, and wrote a half-hearted testimonial. Although he had plenty of room he signed his name at the very bottom of the page.

"Why do you sign your name so far from your testimonial, Rabbi?" asked the scholar.

Rabbi Elijah smiled ruefully and answered:

"Scripture commands us: 'Get thee at a distance from falsehood!'"

A Violation of Nature

ONCE there was a pretentious scholar who lost no opportunity to sing his own praises and to push his own wares.

One day, having finished a commentary on the Book of Psalms, he came to the Vilna Gaon for a testimonial. The great Rabbi Elijah read it and, when he had finished, said firmly, "I'm sorry, but I cannot give you a testimonial."

"Why?"

"It reverses the natural order of things."

"How so?" inquired the pretender, flattered at the thought that his ideas were daringly original.

"The natural order is to make paper out of rags," replied the Vilna Gaon. "But you, my friend, have reversed the process—you have made a rag out of paper!"

It Takes More than Brains

CONGRATULATIONS were showered on Kaplan. His number 49 had won the top prize in the lottery.

"Say, Kaplan," asked Goldstein, "how did you happen to pick number 49?"

"I saw it in a dream. Six sevens appeared and danced before my eyes. Six times seven is 49, and that's all there was to it."

"But, six times seven is 42, *not* 49."

"Hah? . . . All right, so *you* be the mathematician!"

The Diagnosis

A STRANGER came to town and called on a rich *apikoiros*.

"I'm a rabbi and a scholar and I am very sick. Please give me a donation," he asked.

Unimpressed with the man's appearance, the freethinker, who was also a bit of a scholar, began to feel his visitor's intellectual pulse.

"Tell me, my dear Rabbi, are you familiar with the Rambam's * *Guide to the Perplexed*?"

"Am I familiar with it! I studied it when I was thirteen!" replied his visitor.

"Have you ever studied Rabbi Tolstoi's Talmudic commentary, *Resurrection*?"

"What a question!" the stranger replied airily. "I know it by heart! I studied it when I was a youth at the *Yeshiva*."

"My friend," remarked the freethinker with a smile, "in my opinion you're not so much a sick scholar as a healthy ignoramus!"

---

* The popular name for Moses ben Maimon (Maimonides), great philosopher and physician during the Jewish Golden Age in Spain.

What Does It Matter?

ONE day, complaining of a stomach ache, Tevye visited a doctor. After due deliberation, with solemnity, the doctor informed him that he had cancer.

"Cancer, shmancer," said Tevye, gaily, "as long as I'm healthy!"

Philosophy

FOR a long time Levy and Bernstein sat over their teacups, saying nothing. At last Levy broke the silence. "You know, Bernstein," he said, "life is like a glass of tea."

"Life is like a glass of tea . . . why?" asked Bernstein.

"How should I know," said Levy, "am I a philosopher?"

Note to Obstetricians

ALTHOUGH he himself had been deprived of the opportunity for an education, the wealthy Mr. Levine sent his only daughter to a "finishing" school in Paris.

Upon her return to Cleveland she married and, in due course of time, was taken to the maternity hospital.

When her obstetrician came to find out how she was doing she moaned languorously: *"Mon dieu! Mon dieu!"*

"Doctor, doctor—quick, she's giving birth!" gasped her father in alarm.

The doctor indifferently shook his head and answered: "Not yet! Not yet!"

An hour later, when the daughter heard the doctor coming, she wailed elegantly: *"Sauvez moi, Docteur!"*

"Doctor, doctor—quick, she's giving birth!" cried Mr. Levine wringing his hands frantically.

"Not yet," replied the doctor, looking bored.

A few minutes later a piercing shriek rang through the hospital corridors. *"Oy, gewalt, Mama!"*

"She's giving birth now!" said the doctor to Mr. Levine as he hurried into the daughter's room.

The Dachshund

THE great Russian landowner summoned his Jewish business-agent and said to him:

"Here are twenty-five rubles—I want you to buy me a dachshund!"

"May it please Your Excellency," urged the agent, "but how is it possible to buy a good dachshund for such a small sum? Take my advice, give me fifty rubles and I'll buy you a dachshund that *will be* a dachshund!"

"Good!" agreed the landowner. "Here are twenty-five more rubles— but make sure it's a first class dachshund!"

"You can rest easy on that, Your Excellency," the agent assured him. And as he was about to leave he hesitated and asked apologetically:

"A thousand pardons, Your Excellency, but what *is* a dachshund?"

[2]

Rogues and Sinners

TRICKSTERS AND ROGUES

INTRODUCTION

Tricksters and rogues, and all other men who live by cunning and deceit, are treated with almost condescending pity in the folk tales of the Jews. This attitude is not difficult to explain about a people one of whose cardinal religious beliefs is in God's justice, and in its corollary—that divine retribution must always follow the evil that men do. Sooner or later, the ethical-minded Jew maintains, it must catch up with the rascal and lay him low—if not in this life, most certainly in the World-to-Come.

Scripture is full of comfort to the righteous when they bitterly complain against the worldly good-fortune of rogues, and, conversely, against the frequent bedevilment on earth of the righteous. "Fret not thyself because of evil-doers," the Psalmist consoles the good man, "neither be thou envious against the workers of iniquity. For they shall soon be cut down like the grass and wither as a green herb." (Psalm 37.1, 2.) The Book of Proverbs also offers the balm of solace to the suffering men of virtue. It sees the good-fortune of the wicked as being only deceptive and ephemeral. "Whoso diggeth a pit shall fall therein: and he that rolleth a stone it will return upon him." (Proverbs 26.27)

According to Jewish folk-belief, the first evil men in the world were those who lived in Sodom and Gomorrah in the days of the Patriarch Abraham. Both the Bible and the Talmud tell of God's wrath against the inhabitants of those cities of sin. Because of their wickedness, He vowed to destroy them root and stem but, upon Abraham's compassionate intercession, He agreed to spare Sodom provided ten good men could be found there. But, when Abraham failed to find even that modest number, God descended upon the city in His wrath and destroyed it and all its wicked inhabitants with fire and brimstone.

In time, the Men of Sodom began to personify the genius of evil to the Jewish folk. And thus we find many ancient Rabbinic tales in which their wicked traits and diabolical cleverness are graphically described for the edification of all posterity in order that it be forewarned betimes and thereby avoid the terrible fate of those unheeding evil-doers.

N. A.

The Thief Who Was Too Clever

A MERCHANT went on a distant journey to buy goods. He carried five hundred gold pieces in a bag. When he arrived at his destination he began to get worried. He said to himself: "I'm a stranger here and I don't know a soul. If I carry the money on me I may be robbed. Better that I conceal it until I'm ready to make my purchases."

With this thought in mind the merchant went to an unfrequented place. He looked cautiously about him and, convinced that no one was looking, he dug a hole and concealed his money in it. However, he did not know that there was an opening in the wall of a house nearby and that someone had seen him hide his money.

No sooner had the merchant left than the man who saw him bury the bag of gold came out of his house and dug it up.

Several days passed. The merchant was now ready to pay for the goods he had bought. He therefore went to the spot where he had buried his money. When he saw that it had been stolen he was filled with despair.

"What will I do now?" he lamented. "From whom can I claim my money? No one saw me bury it."

Troubled, the merchant began to look around him and soon discovered the opening in the wall. He began to suspect that the owner of that house was the likely thief. So he went to him and said:

"I've heard it said that you're a wise man and can give me good advice. I came here to buy merchandise and I brought with me two bags of gold. One was filled with five hundred gold pieces; the other with eight hundred pieces. Since I'm a stranger here and don't know a soul, I decided to conceal the bag with the five hundred gold pieces in a hole in the ground. I still carry around with me the bag with the eight hundred gold pieces, but I find it a great burden. Please advise me what to do; shall I keep it with me, shall I bury it in the same hole with the other gold, or shall I look for another hiding place for it? Possibly you might know of an honest man in town to whose care I could entrust it."

The man thought for a moment and replied with cunning:

"Take my advice. Don't entrust your money to anyone because it is possible that he might even deny that you ever gave it to him. Also, I counsel you not to look for a new hiding place but to bury your gold in the same hole with the other bag."

The thief reasoned this way: "It's clear that this poor fool doesn't know yet that the bag with the five hundred gold pieces is missing. Therefore, the best way to get his second bag is to return the first bag to its place, because, if I don't do that, he will be afraid to bury the second bag there. In that way I'll get both bags."

The merchant was fully aware that the thief would follow such a course. Therefore, he said to him:

THE THIEF WHO WAS TOO CLEVER: Adapted from the *Midrash*.

"Thank you for your good advice. I will do as you bid me and will bury the gold after dark tonight."

No sooner had the merchant left him than the thief went in great haste to put the first bag of gold back in its place. The merchant, who was hiding nearby, quickly dug up his money and joyfully walked away.

You Can't Fool God

Two sisters, twins, lived in a certain town. They looked so much alike that when they were together no one could tell them apart. Although both sisters were married, one of the two was a wanton and made a cuckold of her husband.

One day on a pretext this wanton told her husband that she had to go to another town. Instead she had a secret meeting with a lover. Upon her return her husband became very suspicious and, being exceedingly troubled by his doubts, he demanded that she go with him to the High Priest so that he might prove her with the bitter waters. If the bitter waters she drank did not harm her, it would be divine proof of her innocence. On the other hand, should she be guilty, she would die from the drink.

The woman had no alternative and was forced to go with her husband to the High Priest for the ordeal. On the way they passed the house where her twin sister lived. With pretended innocence she said to her husband:

"I beg you, my husband, let me go for a moment into the house of my sister while you wait for me here."

The sinful woman went into her sister's house and said to her:

"Help me, sister! My husband is outside waiting to take me to the High Priest to put me through the ordeal of the bitter waters. Now listen to me: There is something you can do for me. We both look alike, and if you put on my clothes my husband won't know the difference. I know I'm a sinful woman and the bitter waters will kill me. But you are innocent and the waters cannot harm you. Go in my place and you will save my life!"

And so the good sister changed garments with the faithless one and went out to the waiting husband. Unsuspectingly, he led her into the house of the High Priest. There she drank the bitter waters and passed through the ordeal without harm.

"I pronounce this woman innocent!" cried the High Priest. "You have misjudged her," he rebuked the husband.

Overjoyed, the man went home with his wife. On the way they passed the sister's house.

"Do wait for me here for one moment," begged the woman, "while I tell my sister that I have safely passed through the ordeal."

YOU CAN'T FOOL GOD: *Ibid.*

The happy husband agreed. As she entered, the wanton sister ran to greet her with tears of gratitude in her eyes.

"You have saved my life!" she cried, embracing and showering kisses on her.

But as she kissed her sister she inhaled from her mouth the aroma of the bitter herbs and they entered into her body. With a moan she fell to the floor, dead, her body swollen, her belly split.

The Wise Rogue

A MAN once caught stealing was ordered by the king to be hanged. On the way to the gallows he said to the governor that he knew a wonderful secret and it would be a pity to allow it to die with him and he would like to disclose it to the king. He would put a seed of a pomegranate in the ground and through the secret taught to him by his father he would make it grow and bear fruit overnight. The thief was brought before the king and on the morrow the king, accompanied by the high officers of state, came to the place where the thief was waiting for them. There the thief dug a hole and said, "This seed must only be put in the ground by a man who has never stolen or taken anything which did not belong to him. I being a thief cannot do it." So he turned to the Vizier who, frightened, said that in his younger days he had retained something which did not belong to him. The treasurer said that dealing with such large sums, he might have entered too much or too little and even the king owned that he had kept a necklace of his father's. The thief then said, "You are all mighty and powerful and want nothing and yet you cannot plant the seed, whilst I who have stolen a little because I was starving am to be hanged." The king, pleased with the ruse of the thief, pardoned him.

The Fate of a Disloyal Friend

Two timid students were on their way home from the Talmudic College for the holidays. When night fell they stopped in a certain village. It was before Passover and it was still cold. When they entered the village inn, hungry and chilled to the bone, they found there several officers in the midst of carousing.

"I can give you nothing to eat," the innkeeper told them. "The officers have devoured everything. They haven't left even a crumb of black bread. However, if you wish you can sleep in the kitchen."

THE WISE ROGUE: From *The Exempla of the Rabbis,* by Moses Gaster. The Asia Publishing Co. London and Leipzig, 1924.

THE FATE OF A DISLOYAL FRIEND: Adapted from the *Parables of the Preacher of Dubno.*

Thankful for this small favor the students went into the kitchen. One slept on the warm ledge over the oven; the other on a hard bench. Suddenly the door burst open and two drunken officers staggered in. When they saw the young Talmudist on the bench they decided to have a little sport with him, so they pummeled him good and proper. The student was afraid to make a sound, although he came very close to crying out with pain. Then he heard the officers say: "Let's call the others in so they can have a little fun, too."

Then they left the kitchen.

In haste the student got off the bench and began to shake his comrade who was sleeping soundly on the oven ledge.

"Get up! You've had a good warming up already, so don't be selfish, and let me sleep awhile on the ledge, too."

His comrade didn't think the request was unreasonable, so he changed places.

No sooner had they settled down again when six officers entered, led by the first two.

"Why should we trounce the same wretched fellow," said one of the two officers compassionately. "Over there, on the ledge, lies his friend. Let's give him his share."

And they did as they said.

MORAL

One does not always prosper by changing places. One may even stumble upon worse luck.

A Sodom Trick

WHENEVER a rich man came to Sodom, the inhabitants would put their heads together and plot to rob him of his possessions.

Once, when a rich merchant arrived in town a wicked man went to call on him carrying a flagon of fragrant oil that cost much money. He said to the unsuspecting stranger, "This flagon I have here is very precious, and I'm afraid that thieves will steal it. Therefore, do me a favor and keep it secure among your own treasures."

"Gladly!" answered the rich man, and he took the flagon and hid it among his own valuables.

Late that night, the wicked man of Sodom came stealthily with his friends. The smell of the fragrant oil led them to where the stranger's treasure was hidden. Then they made off with it.

A SODOM TRICK: Adapted from the *Agada* in the Talmud.

Justice in Sodom

THERE were four judges in Sodom. Their names were: Liar, Falsifier, Bribe-taker and Swindler.

Whenever an inhabitant of Sodom came to the judges and complained: "That wicked man has gone and cut my ass's ears off!" the judges would say: "Give your ass to that man, and, as punishment, let him feed the ass until its ears grow back again!"

Sodom's Bed for Strangers

THE inhabitants of Sodom constructed a wonderful bed for the reception of strangers. If the stranger was too tall, they amputated his legs to fit the bed. If he was too short, they stretched him until they tore off a limb or two.

Once, when Eleazar came for a visit, they invited him to lie on the bed.

He replied evasively: "Ever since my dear mother died I've taken a vow never to sleep in a bed again."

Charity in Sodom

THE people of Sodom practiced charity in their own hypocritical way. Whenever a poor stranger used to ask for alms everyone would give him a gold piece on which was engraved the name of the donor.

However, there was a town law that no stranger could buy food, so in time he'd die of hunger. Afterwards, each man sorrowfully would come and take back his gold piece.

Example in Sodom

THE rogues of Sodom had an odd custom. The man who owned a cow was obliged to graze all the town's cattle for one day; he who had none was made to graze them for two days.

Now there was a youth of Sodom, an orphan, who lived with his poor

---

JUSTICE IN SODOM: *Ibid.*

SODOM'S BED FOR STRANGERS: *Ibid.*
There is the identical tale in Greek mythology of Procrustes the Stretcher and his iron bedstead.

CHARITY IN SODOM: *Ibid.*

EXAMPLE IN SODOM: *Ibid.*

mother. He owned no animal at all. But, following the custom, he was forced to graze all the cattle for two days.

Enraged by this injustice, the orphan went and killed all the cattle in Sodom. Then he said to the inhabitants, "Let him who owned one cow come and take one hide. Let him who had none, come and take two hides."

"What kind of calculation is that?" cried the inhabitants.

"Don't blame me! You yourselves set the example for me," answered the youth.

Cunning Against Greed

ONCE there was a cunning man who came to his rich neighbor and asked him to lend him a silver spoon. The rich man gave it to him. A few days later, the borrower returned the spoon and with it a small spoon.

"What is that for?" the rich man asked. "I lent you only one spoon."

"Your spoon," the borrower replied, "gave birth to this little spoon, so I have brought you back both mother and child, because both belong to you."

Although what the man said sounded foolish, the rich man, who was avaricious, accepted both spoons.

A while later the cunning man again came to his rich neighbor and asked that he lend him a large silver goblet. The rich man did so. Several days later the borrower returned the goblet and with it a little goblet.

"Your goblet," he told him, "gave birth to this little goblet. I'm returning them because both belong to you."

After a while the cunning man paid a visit to his rich neighbor for the third time and said to him: "Would you mind lending me your gold watch?"

"With pleasure!" answered the rich neighbor, thinking to himself that it would be returned to him together with a small watch. So he gave him his watch which was set with diamonds.

One day passed, and another, and still another, but the borrower failed to show up with the watch. The rich man became impatient and went to the house of his neighbor to make inquiry.

"What about my watch?" he asked.

The cunning borrower heaved a deep sigh.

"Alas!" he said. "I am sorry to tell you that your watch is *nebich* dead! I had to get rid of it."

"Dead? What do you mean dead?" cried the rich man angrily. "How can a watch die?"

"If a spoon can bear little spoons," answered the cunning man, "and if a goblet can bear little goblets, why should it surprise you that a watch can die?"

CUNNING AGAINST GREED: Adapted from the *Parables of the Preacher of Dubno.*

The Way Tailors Figure

A MAN bought some material and went to see a tailor.

"Have I enough goods for a suit?" he asked.

The tailor measured the material carefully and said, "No. It'll never do. There just isn't enough material."

So the man went to see another tailor. He too measured the goods carefully.

"There's enough material," he said.

He took the measurements and told the customer the suit would be ready in two weeks' time.

When the man called for his suit, what was his amazement to see that the tailor's little boy was wearing a suit made out of the same stuff as his own.

"See here," he asked the tailor, "can you tell me why the tailor across the street told me there wasn't enough material, and yet not only have you made me a suit out of it but have had enough left to make a suit for your little boy?"

"Well," replied the tailor, "you see, for me the material was enough because I've only one boy—but for the other tailor it would never do. He's got two boys!"

He Was Underpaid

ONCE there was a tailor in Galicia and, although he sewed clothes for the entire population of the town, he himself walked about in tatters. He even would appear this way in synagogue on the Sabbath day to the mortification of all, particularly of the *gabbai*.

"Isn't it a disgrace that you, a respectable tailor, should go around dressed in rags?" the *gabbai* reproached him one day.

"What can I do? I'm a poor man and I've got to work all the time to make a living," replied the tailor piteously. "Where do you think I'll find the time to work on my own clothes?"

"Here are two gulden," said the *gabbai*. "Imagine I am one of your customers and I am paying you to fix your own coat."

"Agreed!" cried the tailor with alacrity and he pocketed the two gulden.

However, on the following Sabbath, when the tailor again came to the synagogue, the warden noticed with annoyance that he was still wearing the same ragged coat.

"What sort of behavior is this?" cried the *gabbai* angrily, feeling he had been imposed upon. "Didn't I give you two gulden last week to mend your own coat? Anybody can see you haven't even touched it!"

"What am I to do?" the tailor apologized. "When I got home and examined my coat I realized that I'd be losing money on the job if I did it for two gulden!"

The Penitents

Two students of the Talmud came woebegone to their rabbi and wailed:
"Rabbi, we've committed a sin!"

"What have you done?"

"We looked with lust upon a woman!"

"God preserve you!" cried the rabbi. "You've indeed committed a
terrible sin!"

"We wish to do penance, Rabbi!"

"In that case, I order you to put peas into your shoes and walk about
that way for a week. Then perhaps you'll remember not to commit such a
sin again."

The two penitents went away and did as the rabbi told them. Several
days later they met on the street. One was hobbling painfully and looked
haggard, but the other one was calm and smiling. So the hobbler said to
his friend reproachfully, "Is this the way you do penance? I see you
haven't followed the rabbi's orders. You didn't put peas in your shoes!"

"Of course I did!" insisted the other. "But I cooked them first!"

One Shot Too Many

WHEN the Passover holidays were drawing near, a Jewish carpenter, who
had been working in Gomel, was on his way home to his little village with
three months' wages in his pocket. As he was passing through a dark
forest he suddenly found himself looking into the muzzle of a robber's
gun.

"Hand over your money or I'll shoot!" roared an evil-looking bandit.
What could the poor man do? He gave him his money.

As the robber was stuffing the money into his pockets his victim pleaded
with him:

"See! It's just before Passover. The money you took from me was to
have bought *matzos*, wine, chickens and new clothes for my wife and children. Do you think my wife will believe me when I go home and tell her
that a robber in the forest took my money?"

"That's your affair!" growled the bandit.

"At any rate, can't you help me a bit, make everything look real so that
my wife will believe me?"

"What do you want me to do?"

"Put a bullet through my cap."

The robber laughed, threw the poor fellow's cap into the air and shot
through it as it came down.

"Fine!" rejoiced the Jew. "Now fire into my coat."

The robber sent a bullet through a corner of his coat.

"Once more," pleaded the Jew, holding up the other corner for him.

"No more bullets," grunted the bandit.

"In that case, my fine fellow, to the devil with you!" cried the Jew, overjoyed. And he pummelled the rascal so hard that he didn't leave one whole bone in his body. Then, taking back his money, he continued joyfully on his way home.

The Clever Thief

IN A certain village they once caught a thief. So they laid hold of him and beat him black and blue.

At this he raised a great outcry.

"Do with me what you like! Beat me, hang me, shoot me—but for God's sake, don't throw me over the fence!"

When the villagers saw how scared he was of being thrown over the fence, they thought: "No doubt something terrible awaits him there!" So they threw him over the fence, crying: "Served the rascal right!"

When the thief found himself on the other side of the fence he laughed heartily and ran away.

Very Very Antique

A MAN, who had a passion for old things, went into an antique shop and asked the owner to show him some rare objects. The shopkeeper showed him an old watch.

"My friend, here you see a watch that's one of the seven wonders of creation. Most certainly you know that the *Rambam* (Maimonides) was a famous doctor? Well, this was his watch. He used to look at it as he felt the pulse of his patients and he brought it with him after a visit to America."

"What are you talking about?" marvelled the customer. "How could the *Rambam* ever have been in America? When he lived no one had even heard of America!"

"Precisely!" said the antique dealer. "That's the wonder of it. That's what makes the watch so valuable!"

New Management

OTTO KAHN, the well-known financier, was one day driving through the lower East Side of New York when he saw a large sign reading: "Samuel Kahn, cousin of Otto Kahn." He immediately called up his lawyer, instructing him to have the sign changed, sparing no expense. A few days later, Kahn drove by the place again. The offending sign had been changed. It read: "Samuel Kahn, formerly cousin of Otto Kahn."

Thank God

"THANKS be to God," the thief reflected, "for jailing and punishing thieves and pickpockets. If it weren't for that, my profession would be so over-crowded that a poor thief like me could never earn a living."

The Ways of a Rogue

A THIEF cast a longing eye on a cow that belonged to a peasant.

One night, he knocked on the peasant's door and said piteously, "I'm a poor traveller—let me spend the night here!"

The peasant was kind-hearted and gave him a night's lodging.

Hours later, while the peasant was fast asleep, the thief went into the barn and stole the cow. He led it deep into the woods, tied it to a tree, and then returned to the peasant's house.

Early in the morning, when the peasant arose, he found the barn-door open and the cow gone. He looked high and low but could not find it.

Then a suspicion occurred to him. "Maybe the stranger took it!" He hurried into the house but he found the stranger sound asleep. He shook him so that he awoke.

"What is the matter?" asked the thief, innocently.

"Someone has stolen my cow!" said the peasant.

"You poor man!" exclaimed the thief, pityingly.

Later, when it was safe to do so, the thief made his departure.

He went into the woods, untied the cow, and then sold it to a peasant in the next village. But, as he left, he stole this peasant's horse and returned to the first peasant with it.

"I've come back to tell you," he told him, "that, as God is my witness, I saw your cow in a peasant's barn in the next village!"

Then, very casually, he offered to sell him the horse cheap. The peasant bought it and the thief went away for the second time.

The peasant then mounted the horse he had bought and rode off to the next village to claim his cow.

Sure enough, he found her tied in a stall in the other peasant's barn.

"Thief!" cried the first peasant. "You stole my cow!"

"Thief yourself!" cried the second peasant. "You stole my horse!"

"You're a liar—I bought the horse!"

"Liar yourself—I bought the cow!"

And before you could pronounce Con-stant-i-no-ple they were rolling on the ground, pummeling each other, while the thief was on his way gleefully rattling the money in his pockets and whistling a gay tune.

Professional Pride

THE rabbi's fur hat was stolen. The whole town was stunned by the news. It was generally agreed that a professional thief must have been the perpetrator of the crime. So the rabbi sent for a man who was known as the leader of all the thieves in town.

"What do you think—will you be able to get back my fur cap?" asked the rabbi.

"Well, that depends," mused the thief. "In the event that one of my disciples stole it, I promise I can get it back for you. But if one of your own disciples stole it, then, Rabbi, you had better forget about it!"

Honor among Thieves

Two beggars, one blind and the other a cripple, came to a Jewish tenant-farmer and said they were hungry. The farmer's wife placed a large bowl of cherries before them.

"You take one and I take one, but always wait for your turn," admonished the blind man with cunning for he was afraid that his partner would try to cheat him.

"Agreed," said the cripple readily.

Then they both attacked the cherries with relish.

For several minutes neither of them spoke, being too intent on devouring the cherries. Suddenly, the blind beggar caught the wrist of the cripple and raised an outcry: "Liar! Thief!"

"How dare you call me such names!" protested the crippled beggar indignantly.

"What else should I call you—you wretch!" rasped the blind man. "Here am I behaving like a gentleman and taking only two cherries at a time but just because I'm blind must you take advantage of me and steal four at a time?"

"How in the world do you know I took four?" the cripple asked startled.

"What else could it be?" shot back his blind companion. "If for five minutes you didn't say 'boo!' while I ate two cherries at a time it became perfectly clear to me that you were cheating and taking at least four at a time!"

LIARS AND BRAGGARTS

INTRODUCTION

In Rabbinical lore there were four classes of evil-doers who would be denied the joys of the World-to-Come. They were the hypocrites, tale-bearers, scoffers and liars. However, the Jewish folk-attitude toward liars, as reflected in its tales and sayings, was a great deal more tolerant. The liar, who is deceitful because of corrupt aims, is, of course, considered a rogue. Yet there are liars, and also braggarts, who are recognized as being quite harmless, who tell untruths or exaggerate, not out of malice and evil intention, but out of sheer perverseness and imaginativeness, or because of some childish compulsion. About such liars and braggarts, humorous Jewish lore makes merry. "A liar should have a good memory," it advises good-naturedly.

N. A.

The Strategists

Two rival Jewish merchants met in a railway station.

"Where are you going?" asked one.

"To Pinsk."

"Ahah!" said the other, "you tell me you are going to Pinsk because you think I'll figure you are going to Minsk. But I happen to know you *are* going to Pinsk. So what's the idea of lying?"

Total Destruction

A POOR man, whose house had burnt down, trudged from town to town collecting alms with which to rebuild his house.

"Have you written proof that your house was burnt down?" he was asked.

"Oh, the proof!" wailed the poor man. "That too, *nebich*, was destroyed in the big fire!"

Veracity

A POOR Jewish farmer called on his more affluent neighbor to borrow his donkey.

"I'm sorry, neighbor," said the well-to-do farmer, "but my donkey is over in the pasture now."

At that very moment the hee-haw of a donkey was heard coming from the stable.

"What a foolish excuse to give me!" said the poor farmer angrily. "Why, your donkey has just brayed in its stall!"

The well-to-do farmer became offended.

"Whom would you rather believe," he asked with dignity, "the braying donkey or me?"

A Knotty Problem

Two poor Jews came to the rabbi with a complaint. They both clutched at the same five zloty note.

"It's mine!" cried one.

"It's mine!" bellowed the other.

"What proof have you got?" the rabbi asked.

Both hung their heads.

The rabbi was puzzled. It was an impossible case to settle.

"Excuse me for a moment," said he, taking the note and going into the adjoining room where his wife was sitting. He made sure, however, to leave the door ajar so that his voice could be heard by the two litigants.

"I certainly have a knotty problem there!" said the rabbi to his wife in a loud voice. "Each of those two men claims the five zloty note, but neither can prove that it is rightfully his. Funny though, they don't know that one of the corners of the note is torn off!"

The rabbi then returned to the two men.

"Rabbi!" cried one joyfully. "I just realized that I can prove that the note is mine!"

"Excellent!" said the rabbi. "What's your proof?"

"The note is torn in one of the corners."

"Torn in one of the corners!" the rabbi exclaimed with pretended surprise. "Look, there is no tear on this note! Clearly then it's not yours. It must belong to your friend!"

And he handed the note to the other.

The Birds That Turned to Stone

KING SOLOMON, the wisest of mankind, understood the language of the birds in the air, the beasts in the forest, the fowl in the barnyard and the fish in the sea. One day he sat at the entrance to his palace on the Temple

---

THE BIRDS THAT TURNED TO STONE: Reprinted from *Legends of Palestine*, by Zev Vilnay. With the permission of the copyright owners, The Jewish Publication Society of America. Philadelphia, 1932.

Mount, delighting in the bright sky and clear daylight. Before him two cooing birds caressed each other, twittering merrily.

As the King looked up he heard one bird say to his spouse, "Who is this man seated here?" And she answered, "This is the King whose name and fame fill the world." Then the bird answered in mocking pride, "And do they call even him mighty? How is his power sufficient for all these palaces and fortresses? Did I so desire I could overthrow them in a second by fluttering one wing."

His spouse encouraged him, saying, "Do so and show your valor and power, if you have the strength to carry out your words." And Solomon, listening to the conversation in astonishment signed to the bird to approach and asked him the cause of his overweening pride.

Terrified, the trembling bird answered the august King, "Let my Lord the King grant me forgiveness out of his loving-kindness and goodness of heart. I am naught but a poor powerless bird who can do him no evil. All that I said was only to please my wife and raise myself in her esteem." And Solomon laughed to himself and sent the bird back to his spouse.

She, meanwhile, stood on the roof and could not contain herself, waiting for her mate to return and tell her why the King had sent for him. When he came back she asked excitedly, "What did the King want?"

And his chest swelling with pride, he answered, "The King heard my words and entreated me not to bring destruction upon his court and not to carry out my purpose."

When Solomon heard this he grew wroth with the brazen bird and changed them both into stone slabs, to warn others to refrain from vain bragging and empty boasting, and to teach women folk not to incite their chosen ones in their vanity to undertake foolish and foolhardy deeds.

If nowadays you gaze at the southern wall of the Mosque of Omar, which rises on the site of Solomon's Temple, you will see a marble slab set in a black border; it is veined through with red in the likeness of two birds, and these are the birds that Solomon turned to stone.

Miracles and Wonders

Two disciples of rival camps were bragging about their respective wonder-working rabbis.

"Take my rabbi," began one disciple, "his like has not been seen in the world before. He can do such wonders that would raise your hair on end were you just to hear about them. The other day, when he unexpectedly brought home some dinner-guests, the *rebbitzen* told him: 'I've only one fish in the pot!' But do you think my rabbi was upset? Not at all! 'Look again in the pot,' he told her. She looked—and what do you suppose she found? *Five fish!*"

"Don't brag!" chided the other disciple. "How can your rabbi compare to mine? The other day he sat down to play cards with the *rebbitzen*. She had four queens. So what do you suppose my rabbi did? Very casually he laid his cards on the table. He had *five kings!*"

"What sort of grandmother's tale are you telling me!" protested the other disciple indignantly. "You know very well there are only four kings!"

"I'll tell you what then," answered the other, "let's make a deal. You take out one fish from your *rebbitzen's* pot and I'll take a king away from my rabbi's cards!"

Misers and Stingy Men

The Great Experiment

Once there was a miser who was very clever at thinking up original ideas.

One day he decided that his horse was eating too much oats.

"He'll eat me out of my house!" he wailed.

So he decided to cut down on his horse's feed, but not too drastically, a little bit each day. In this way, he thought, the creature would get accustomed to eating less.

As time went on, although the horse got thinner and thinner, the miser was overjoyed to see that it did easily with less food. Naturally, he thought he was a very smart man and went about bragging of his discovery. But one fine day, what does his obliging horse do but stretch itself out and die!

As the miser looked down on the dead horse he muttered:

"A pity! What a pity! Just when I had almost got him trained not to eat at all that stupid ass had to go ahead and die!"

The Sweating Will

The town miser, who had never given a groschen in his life to the poor, fell gravely ill. He was wracked with fever but he could not perspire. It was absolutely necessary for him to perspire if he was to live. And so the doctor tried, by all homeopathic means, to induce him to sweat, but to no avail.

Frightened, the miser called for the rabbi. He confessed and he drew up a will in which he left a large sum for charity.

"Write it down, Rabbi! Write it down!" he cried. "It's for the good of my soul!"

And the rabbi wrote down everything the miser told him, when suddenly the miser gave an unearthly cry: "Hold on, Rabbi, I'm sweating!"

The Orphan

A RICH man, who was a miser, was once asked to give a donation to buy *matzos* for the poor. He gave a trifling sum to the committee.

"Your son, who is a poor man, has given more generously than you," he was told ironically.

"How can you compare me to my son?" he replied. "He has a father who's a rich man. I have no father at all."

He Got His Ruble Back

A RICH man, who had been stingy all his life, suddenly sickened and died.

As his spirit floated down into the other world the demons seized hold of him by his hands and feet and whirled him down to Hell.

At this he began to shriek: "Help! Let me go! I belong in Paradise and not in Hell!"

"Only people who have done good on earth go to Heaven," the imps teased him.

"But I have one good deed to my credit," wailed the spirit.

"What is that?" they asked him.

"Twenty years ago I gave a ruble to a poor man. I swear I did! Look into your account book and you'll see it's entered to my credit."

The demons, not knowing what to do with him, sent a messenger post-haste to consult God in the matter.

"Return his ruble to the wretch," commanded God angrily, "and send him straight to the Devil!"

The Miser

THE ailing miser needed the aid of a specialist. Yet the fees appalled him: $25 for a first visit and $10 for subsequent visits. Still, it was life or death, and besides, he had an inspiration.

As he entered the doctor's inner office the miser exclaimed, "Well, doctor, here I am *again*."

The doctor examined the patient with great thoroughness, then said, "And as for the treatment . . . just continue . . . the same as before."

Who Counts?

THE guests were bidding their hosts farewell. "And I want to tell you, Mrs. Liebowitz," Mrs. Ginsberg concluded, "your cookies were so *tasty*, I ate four."

"You ate five," Mrs. Liebowitz corrected, "but who counts?"

A Sure Sign

ONCE a miser died. Even when the deceased was being prepared for burial his wife did not cry. But no sooner had the funeral procession started and the charity-collectors began to rattle their tin boxes, crying: "Charity saves from death!" when the wife burst into bitter weeping.

"Up till now you didn't cry—why do you carry on so now?" her son rebuked her.

"Why shouldn't I cry?" wailed the widow. "Now that I see that your father doesn't run away when the charity-collectors come around I'm definitely convinced he is dead!"

SINNERS

INTRODUCTION

The sinner is dealt with almost gently in Jewish belief and in folklore. This is due to the ages-old cultivation among Jews of a scorn for self-righteousness. The pious man says about an evildoer, even if he himself has been victimized by him: "Let God judge him." Or, if in anger he should speak harshly of him, he hastens to add: "May God not punish me for the words." Besides, it is regarded wrong of anyone to imagine that he himself is without sin: "There is not a just man upon earth that doeth good and sinneth not." (Ecclesiastes 7.20)

There is a layer of mellow humanism in Jewish thought, secular as well as religious, which shrinks from harsh strictures against the misconduct of others. "Live and let live," is its benign attitude. This springs, no doubt, from a practical realism which starts out with the fundamental recognition that men are not angels and that everybody has his weaknesses and limitations. After all, sinning is a matter of degree—everybody sins, from the holy rabbi down to the tavern roisterer!

In Jewish folk-humor the sinner gets a merry ribbing—but no more. Frequently, however, as in the delightful stories, *Saint and Sinner* by the Preacher of Dubno, and in *Heavenly Justice,* he is contrasted with scoffing hilarity to the overpious saint. Suprisingly enough, he gets the better end of the treatment here. And this, not because he is considered an admirable character. Far from it. He serves merely as a convenient pretext to shoot a barbed arrow at the holier-than-thou men who expect heavenly rewards for their virtue. As such, these jokes about sinners and saints have served as an excellent corrective in Jewish life, for they preach the doctrine of the Golden Mean and warn against fanaticism.

N. A.

Saint and Sinner

A RICH man, who was a profligate, a souse and a lecher, died in a certain town. The entire community mourned his death and followed his hearse to his last resting place. What a wailing, what a lamentation, was heard as his coffin was lowered into the grave! In the recollection of the oldest inhabitant no rabbi or sage had ever departed this life amidst such general sorrow.

It chanced that on the following day another rich man died in the town. He was just the opposite of the first in character and manner of living. He was ascetic and dined on practically nothing but dry bread and turnips. He had been pious all the days of his life and sat all the time in the House of Study poring over the Talmud. Nonetheless, no one except his own family mourned his death. His funeral passed almost unnoticed, and he was laid to rest in the presence of only a handful.

A stranger, who happened to be visiting in the town at the time, was filled with wonder, and asked:

"Explain to me the riddle of this town's strange behavior. It honors a profligate yet ignores a saint!"

To this one of the townsmen replied:

"Know that the rich man who was buried yesterday, although he was a profligate and a drunkard, was the leading benefactor of the town. He was easy-going and merry, and loved all the good things in life. Practically everybody in this town profited from him. He'd buy wine from one, chickens from another, geese from a third, and cheese from a fourth. And, being kindhearted, he'd pay well. That's why he is missed and we mourn after him. But what earthly use was that other one, the saint, to anybody? He lived on bread and turnips and no one ever made a kopek on him. Believe me, no one will miss him!"

Heavenly Justice

A SAINT and a sinner died on the same day, and both appeared before the Heavenly Judgment Seat to hear their reward or punishment.

First the saint was called up.

"What reward, in your opinion, do you deserve?" the Heavenly Judge asked him.

"I deserve Paradise," he said confidently.

The angels laughed.

"What makes you think you're so deserving?" the saint was asked.

"I always lived uprightly," answered the saint. "I studied the Torah night and day. I faithfully observed all the six hundred and thirteen regulations of piety. Furthermore, I renounced as evil all the pleasures of life,

---

SAINT AND SINNER: Adapted from the *Parables of the Preacher of Dubno.*

lived with my ugly wife for fifty years and never was unfaithful to her."

"Truly a *tzaddik*!" cried the angels rapturously.

"Just a moment!" called out the Accusing Angel. "I wish to call a witness who will disprove this *tzaddik's* hypocritical claims!"

Thereupon, he called the soul of a tiny flea to the witness-stand.

"Tell the Court what this man did to you," the Accusing Angel demanded of him.

The flea then spoke:

"One day, as I was taking a nap in his ear, what does this brute do but stretch out his huge hairy hand and crush me to death."

"When did that happen?" asked the Accusing Angel.

"On a Sabbath."

Triumphantly the Accusing Angel turned to the Court.

"Did the Court hear that?" he cried. "This '*tzaddik*' killed a defenceless little creature, God's own creation, and on the holy Sabbath, too!"

The angels began to murmur angrily amongst themselves.

"This is really a serious matter!" the Heavenly Tribunal declared. "We cannot decide this case right away so the judgment will have to wait until the coming of the Messiah. Until that time, it is decreed that the accused *tzaddik* and the witness flea shall both be confined in the same cell."

And they led the *tzaddik* away.

Then tremblingly, the sinner came forward to be judged.

"Tell us, what in your own opinion do you deserve?" the Heavenly Tribunal asked him.

The sinner burst into sobs and wailed:

"God's justice has at last caught up with me! I've no doubt that the fiery caldrons of all the purgatories are already boiling for me—and serves me right too! There isn't a vice that I didn't practice, a sin that I didn't commit, a holy precept I didn't violate. I robbed widows and orphans, stole from the charity-box, slandered all my neighbors and lusted after strange women. But I'm fully reconciled to my fate—pronounce your punishment and let us be done with it!"

"What a wretch!" cried the angels in horror. "He deserves a place in the bottommost purgatory!"

"Just a moment!" cried the angelic counsel for the defendant. "I wish to call a witness with whose testimony I will prove that not only was this man not the villain that he has painted himself but is in fact a saint, a noble creature!"

And he called to the witness stand the soul of a charming young widow.

"You tell your story," he bade her.

"One day," she began, "while I was all alone a fire broke out in the house. Soon the flames enveloped it and I was in danger of being burned alive, when this good man, hearing my cries for help, broke through the flames and rescued me!"

The angels were amazed. "He's not such a bad sort, after all!" they murmured.

"This is a very baffling case!" declared the Heavenly Tribunal. "Judgment is therefore postponed until the coming of the Messiah. In the meantime, we order that both accused and his witness be confined in one cell and wait for the first blast from the *shofar* of Redemption!"

Consolation to the Pious

IN A certain town a woman died. So they buried her. But the following morning, what was the amazement of the town folk when they discovered that the woman had been cast out of her grave!

"The earth has rejected her!" lamented the pious women of the town. So they went to the rabbi to hear his opinion.

The rabbi searched among all his holy books and found the explanation.

"The wretched woman neglected to bake her *chaleh* according to our ancient rites," he said.

"What shall we do with her?" asked the women.

"Pile up wood and burn her!" ordered the rabbi.

But when they threw the body into the flames the fire would not consume it.

"What is wrong now?" wailed the women.

"The wretch!" stormed the rabbi. "She neglected to light the Sabbath candles as our Holy Law bids! Therefore the fire won't have her either."

"What shall we do now?" asked the women.

"Cast the body into the river!" ordered the rabbi.

So the women took large stones and tied them to the corpse and threw it into the river. But the water rejected it and cast it out upon the shore.

"The wretch!" raged the rabbi. "She neglected to bathe regularly in the *mikveh* according to our ancient rites. Therefore the water doesn't want her, either."

When the women heard what the rabbi said they broke into loud lamentation.

"Hush! You silly women!" the rabbi admonished them. "What are you wailing about? Surely you're all pious women! You've observed all the commandments and regulations when you baked the *chaleh,* lit the Sabbath candles and bathed in the *mikveh.* Take my word for it, you'll not suffer the fate of this miserable woman! The earth will hold you, the fire will consume you, and the water will accept you!"

Filial Love

A RICH man, having confidence in his son, gave him all his property in his lifetime. After awhile the son commenced to neglect his father, ill-treating him and sending him away to be among the beggars.

One day the old man, clad in tatters, met his grandson and asked him to beg his father to let him have a mantle to cover himself, as it was so cold.

After much begging the father sent his son up to the loft and told him to fetch a certain mantle which was hanging on a hook. Whilst on the loft the boy took a knife and cut the mantle in half.

The father, wondering what the boy was doing all that time, went to find out. The son told him that he had been busy cutting the mantle in half and added that he would give his grandfather one half and keep the other half for his own father when he grew old.

The man was greatly surprised at this reply and, recognizing the wickedness of his action, took his father back and treated him with all honour.

Relativity

YOSHKE the Drunkard died. Members of the Burial Society came and prepared him for his final rest. When the body was lowered into the grave not one pious man had a good word to say for the wretch with which to send him off into the life everlasting.

Just as the grave-digger lifted his spade to cover the coffin with earth a compassionate old Jew cried out:

"Just a moment! How can we let the dead depart from this life without a good word from those of us who knew him? Believe me, he was not as bad as you think! I myself know that he has a son in New York who is a thousand times worse a guzzler than he ever was!"

The members of the Burial Society heaved a sigh of relief.

"What a pious man he was!" they exclaimed heartily.

When Prayer Is No Help

A SAINT and a sinner were once fellow passengers on an ocean voyage. Suddenly a storm broke. The ship seemed in danger of sinking. Thereupon all the crew and the passengers began to pray.

"Save us, O Lord!" cried the sinner.

"Sh-sh!" warned the saint. "Don't let God know you are here or it will be the end of all of us!"

FILIAL LOVE: From *The Exempla of the Rabbis*, by Moses Gaster. The Asia Publishing Co. London and Leipzig, 1924.

The Martyr

SAMMY was sent to the saloon to look for his father, an habitual drunkard. There he lay on the floor, drunk. Looking up, seeing the boy, he called thickly, "Come here, Sammy, have a drink."

"Oh, no, Papa!" said the child.

"Come here, I say," said the father, angrily. Raising himself, he grabbed the boy and forced a liquor glass to his lips.

Sammy sputtered and choked. "Oh, Papa! It's terrible. It tastes like gall!"

"What do you think—it tastes like honey to me?"

The Way to Live and Die

A MAN came to the rabbi and said, "Help me, Rabbi! I am old and a sinner and I would very much like to die like a good, upright Jew."

"Why do you worry about dying like an upright Jew?" asked the rabbi. "Better live like one, and you'll die like one!"

Absent-Minded

A GROUP of young miscreants were caught redhanded breaking the Sabbath peace. They were smoking, playing cards and doing other things forbidden on the Sabbath.

On the following day, when they were brought up on charges before the rabbi, he sternly demanded an explanation of them.

The first said: "Rabbi, I was absent-minded; I forgot that it was the Sabbath."

"That could be," said the rabbi, stroking his beard reflectively. "You are forgiven!"

The second said: "I also was absent-minded; I forgot that one mustn't gamble on the Sabbath."

"That could be," said the rabbi, stroking his beard reflectively. "You are forgiven!"

Then the turn came for the owner of the house in which the young men had been found desecrating the Sabbath.

"And what is your excuse?" asked the rabbi. "Were you absent-minded, too?"

"Indeed I was, Rabbi," answered the man regretfully.

"What did you forget?"

"I forgot to pull the curtains down!" said the man.

God Made a Good Choice

ON SIMCHAS TORAH, the day of "The Rejoicing of the Torah," which marks the completion of the reading of the Five Books of Moses, the synagogue in the little Hungarian town was filled with gaiety. Clasping a Torah Scroll crowned with silver ornaments in his arms, a man was dancing rapturously before the Holy Ark. Everybody knew him as one ignorant in matters of Torah and altogether lax in its observance.

"What's all your rejoicing about?" a wag asked in surprise. "Do you love the Torah so? Why, everybody knows you are a Sabbath-breaker and that you violate every religious precept!"

"I have every good reason to rejoice that the dear God gave us the Torah," the man replied. "What if He had given the Torah to the police? It would certainly have gone bad with us! We'd have to observe all the six hundred and thirteen precepts, and like it too!"

From Bad to Worse

As THE rabbi sat deep in thought, a youth came before him and said:

"Rabbi, I want to confess—I'm guilty of a great sin. I failed to say grace one day last month."

"Tsk-tsk!" murmured the Rabbi. "How can any Jew eat without saying grace?"

"How could I say grace, Rabbi, when I hadn't washed my hands?"

"*Oy vey!*" wailed the Rabbi. "How can a Jew swallow a mouthful without first washing his hands?"

"But you see, Rabbi, the food was not kosher."

"Not kosher! How can a Jew eat food that's not kosher?"

"But Rabbi, how in the world could it be kosher; it was in the house of a Gentile?"

"What! You miserable apostate! How could you eat in the house of a Gentile?"

"But Rabbi, no Jew was willing to feed me!"

"That's a wicked lie!" cried the Rabbi. "Who has ever heard of a Jew refusing food to anybody who is hungry?"

"But Rabbi," argued the youth, "it was the Day of Atonement!"

[3]

Traditional Types

INTRODUCTION

An entire gallery of distinctive traditional types has been created by the volatile forces in Jewish life. They are all to be met with in folklore, many of them in colorful humorous garb. Though different from one another, every type had an organic unity with the rest, because all emerged from the same social-cultural environment. The confined ghetto of bygone days, in which Jews led their own semi-autonomous existence, was an entertaining as well as a tragic microcosm.

The Jew, an adept at the Wise King's teaching to do everything in its own season, found time to scoff as well as to revere, to be skeptical as well as to extoll. This was not done from caprice or malice, but rather out of good-humored raillery, prompted by a recognition that the noblest and the wisest also have their comic and foolish sides. Therefore, all life passed in review before the folk-humorist who was no respecter of persons or of the degree of their eminence. Everybody without exception was a candidate for the butt of his jokes: preachers and rabbis, scholars and teachers, sextons and charity collectors, cantors and marriage brokers, waiters and innkeepers, doctors and patients, tailors and butchers, shopkeepers and peddlers, rich men, poor men, philanthropists and misers. In short, it was the procession of the whole Jewish people, a motley array of characters in all of their complex laugh-provoking relationships.

Take the *hazzan*, the synagogue cantor. He often is as vain of himself and his art as any operatic tenor, a prey to all the tantrums and exhibitionism of the artistic temperament. Yet he has his special characteristics due probably to the peculiar role he plays in the congregation. More often than not he serves as a cause of contention among its members. Either he is idolized and hero-worshipped as a nightingale of God, or he serves as the butt of the sarcastic jokes of his deriders.

It is well known that there are among Jews many passionate music lovers. There is hardly one among the pious who doesn't think of himself as a bit

386

of a sagacious musical critic in matters of the cantorial art. He is avid in discussing and analyzing all the technical faults of a cantor, ready to point out his inferior musicianship or his lack of understanding of the text in his interpretation. And just like an Italian opera enthusiast, who performs a musical autopsy on a singer, the cantorial connoisseur too contrasts his victim's failings with the virtues of more favored cantors. However, because there are more cantors there are also more carping musical critics among Jews.

The cantor himself does not always enjoy the congregational civil war over him. Being sensitive, like any other artist, he takes offence easily. He is ready to hand in his resignation upon the slightest provocation. In fact, many cantors never let the synagogue grass grow under their feet, but are constantly on the lookout for other posts; the cantorial pasture always looks greener elsewhere.

It was the great poverty of the Jews in Europe that made them regard the few Jewish millionaires with awe, and sometimes even with incredulity. Because of the isolation of ghetto life a Rothschild or a Montefiore was largely a legendary creature to them. They tried to reconstruct in imagination the sort of world in which these rich men lived. And out of this fantasy came a number of stories in which, with studied innocence and sly banter, was depicted the life of luxury they were supposed to lead—the way they did business, dispensed charity and ran their households.

It was only natural that the many philanthropies of the Rothschilds and the Brodskys should have attracted to them, like flies to honey, all the *schnorrers* in creation. There are, accordingly, many anecdotes about Rothschild's encounters with these buzzards. Now, of course, when Jews said "Rothschild" it wasn't necessarily any particular member of that large family they had in mind; it was a generic name for all Jewish millionaires.

Perhaps the wittiest of all these anecdotes are those which describe the pity of the poor for the pleasures of the rich, as in *Montefiore's Buttons* and *Rich Man's Folly*. In this connection it is interesting to point out that it was this same humorous pity for the rich which led to the adoption by East Side Jewish folklore of John D. Rockefeller. "Poor Rockefeller!" the Yiddish folksay runs commiseratingly. "He's the richest man in the world and just look at him—all he can eat is crackers and milk!"

Perhaps peculiar to the American scene alone is the old-time Jewish restaurant waiter. You never see him flatter or kowtow to his customers. He is proud of his independence and, because of the jealousy with which he guards it, he frequently acts with defensive gruffness. To a genial, submissive customer he acts like a protector, a patron, even like a father—advising, warning, lecturing and scolding. He tells him what's good and what's bad for his health, what to choose on the menu and what to avoid like the plague.

But woe to the arrogant high-and-mighty customer! He not only browbeats him but shrivels him with scorn. And if he provokes him too much he tells him straight up and down to go to another restaurant—or to the devil! In fact, a customer rash enough to offend a Jewish waiter is liable to remember the encounter with lingering indigestion, and that not so much from the food he ate, but from the near apoplexy brought on by the excitement of the collision. Yes, the old-time Jewish waiter is an upstanding mettlesome fellow, and it is these traits of his which are mirthfully recorded in anecdote.

N. A.

CANTORS

Carping Critics

THE congregation advertised for a cantor. A candidate appeared and on the following Sabbath he held forth.

When the congregation met later to discuss his qualifications the membership was split wide open on the issue.

"He croaks like a frog!" contended one group.

"He sings with feeling!" countered the others.

They argued so long and excitedly about the matter that the rabbi, who all along had held aloof from the controversy, was drawn in as mediator.

"My sons," began the rabbi, in a soothing voice. "What is all this dispute about? Our holy Torah requires a cantor to be pious, a fairly good scholar, mature in age, of praiseworthy character, and lastly—to have a melodious voice. Just let us examine the qualifications of this candidate. Are we all agreed that he's pious, a fairly good scholar, mature in age, and that he has a praiseworthy character?"

"Yes, Rabbi!" answered the congregation.

"In that case, what is all the fuss about?" asked the rabbi. "The only difference of opinion is whether he has a good voice or not, and surely you won't let a little matter like that deprive the man of the job!"

The Corpse Won't Disappear

THE town had nothing but bad luck. Everytime they got a new cantor he was sure before long to find himself a better post elsewhere.

On one occasion, after a great deal of effort and expense, they succeeded in engaging a new cantor. This time they wanted to make sure that he would not leave them. They decided to ask him for a ten-year contract. They then went to see the rabbi in order to talk the matter over with him.

"Before you go to the trouble of drawing up a contract," said the rabbi, "let me tell you a story.

"The old cemetery in a certain town in Galicia got so overcrowded that the congregation bought ground for a new cemetery. But, since everyone in town was superstitious, no one wanted to be the first to be buried there.

The elders of the congregation were greatly troubled. What were they to do? After much debate they finally let it be known that the first Jew who was willing to be buried in the new cemetery would not only get free burial but a hundred gulden in addition.

"It so happened that the town had its own official ne'er-do-well, a sot who rolled in all the ditches. Although he had no virtue to boast of particularly, nevertheless he tried to be as pious as other folk. When Passover came around he said to his wife, 'Feigele, my heart, I'll get into bed and pretend I'm dead. Then you must go to the elders and tell them I'm dead. Also tell them that my last wish was that I be buried in the new cemetery. In that event they'll give you a hundred gulden and we'll be rich. You'll then have enough money to buy *matzos,* wine, meat, clothes and what not.'

" 'I always said you have a head on your shoulders!' exclaimed his wife with shining eyes.

"So the sot got into bed and lay like a dead man. His wife ran quickly to the elders.

" 'My dear husband, that holy saint, is dead!' she wailed. 'His last request was that he be buried in the new cemetery.'

"When the elders heard this they were overjoyed. At last the ice would be broken! So they spoke words of comfort to the poor 'widow' and gave her a hundred shiny gulden. She then hurried home and laid 'the corpse' on the floor, covered him with a sheet, and placed candles at his feet.

"Later, two pious members of the Burial Society came. They laid the body on a bier and carried it off with them to the cemetery.

"On the way, they became very thirsty and stopped at an inn to take a *schnapps.* While they lingered pleasantly over their drink 'the corpse' disentangled itself from its shroud and went home.

The two men finally came out feeling high and cheerful. They lifted the bier and, marvelling over how light the body had become, they bore it to the cemetery. It was only when they began to lay the body in the grave that they made the sad discovery that it was gone.

They felt thoroughly frightened by their extraordinary experience and, for the life of them, could not explain what had happened. So, in order to save themselves from embarrassing questions, they pretended that nothing was wrong. They buried the shroud and quietly went home.

"Not long after another poor man died, and the same two members of the Burial Society went to give him the last honors. Again they stopped for a *schnapps* at the inn. 'This time,' one said wisely, 'we'll tie the corpse securely with ropes so it won't get away from us.'

" 'Idiot!' retorted the other. 'How can he run away? It's the other corpse who was alive we should have tied! This one here is as dead as a post and won't move until the Messiah comes!' "

Then the rabbi concluded: "Why do you need a contract with this cantor? Rest assured he won't run away and you don't need to tie him up for ten years—for believe me, he's no cantor!"

The Rump-Test of Vocal Art

AN ELDERLY, corpulent cantor, whose voice was already cracking, was considering two offers: one for the synagogue of the horsedealers, the other for the synagogue of the butchers. After much deliberation, he accepted the vacant post at the butchers' synagogue.

"Why have you chosen the butchers' and not the horsedealers' synagogue?" he was asked.

"I'll tell you," replied the worldly wise cantor. "You know how horsedealers are—they have a habit of looking their merchandise in the mouth. I'm afraid of that; you see, I'm too old. But take the butchers—what's their main interest? They principally examine the rumps of their merchandise. I'll surely pass their test!"

Musical Criticism

THE man had no voice but he insisted on being a cantor. Besides having a voice like a rip-saw, he was ignorant of the liturgy and tangled up the whole service.

One day, when he got through singing the service, a quiet little man came up to him.

"A difficult calling ours—not so, Cantor?" he sighed.

"Are you too a cantor?"

"Lord preserve me, no! I'm a shoemaker."

No Trick to It

Two members of the congregation were discussing the new cantor.

"Ah," said one, "what wonderful singing!"

"What's so wonderful about it?" said the other. "If I had his voice, I'd sing just as well!"

The Tune and the Words

FOR a long time the cantor and the *gabbai*, the treasurer of the congregation, had carried on a bitter feud.

One day, feeling especially aroused, the cantor said publicly, "If you ask me, the *gabbai* is nothing but a *goniff*! He digs his hand into the treasury and then puts it into his own pocket."

When the *gabbai* heard this he complained to the rabbi.

"How dare you spread such a slander against an honest man?" the rabbi rebuked the cantor. "You knew your charge was false, so why did you say

it? The least you can do now is to get up in the synagogue on the Sabbath
and make a public apology to the *gabbai*."

"What do you want me to say?"

"You must get up and say 'The *gabbai* is no *goniff*.' "

"Very well."

"No, I want to hear it now, right from your own lips!"

The cantor sighed, and, reconciling himself to his unpleasant task, said
in a low matter-of-fact: "The *gabbai* is no *goniff*."

"That's not the way!" said the rabbi angrily. "You must speak the words
in a loud ringing voice so that everybody in the synagogue can hear you!"

"Listen, Rabbi," replied the cantor with exasperation, "when it comes
to the Torah—you're the expert. But in such matters as tone and voice—
I'm the specialist!"

A Cantor After Seventy

WHEN God created the world he first made animals and, after that, man.

After he had created the dog the dog asked God, "What must I do in
the world?"

And God answered, "You will have a master who will beat you if you
will not obey him. You'll chew on bones and bark at the moon."

"How long will I live?"

"Seventy years."

"What?" cried the dog. "Lead a dog's life for seventy years! Fifteen
is enough!"

"Fifteen years it shall be!" agreed God graciously.

Next, God created a horse.

"What must I do in the world?" the horse asked.

And God answered, "You will pull a load and get a good whipping for
your trouble."

"How long will I live?"

"Seventy years."

"What?" cried the horse. "Lead a horse's life for seventy years?
Twenty-five is enough!"

"Twenty-five years it shall be!" agreed God graciously.

Having created all the animals, God next made a cantor.

"What must I do in the world?" asked the cantor.

And God answered, "You will have to sing at all weddings and circumcision parties. When you chant the service in the synagogue the members
of the congregation will be in raptures. Your life will be an endless
pleasure."

"How long will I live?"

"Seventy years."

"Seventy years! Why that's too little!" cried the cantor. "Almighty
God! Grant me many more years beyond my allotted seventy."

"You shall have more years if you wish it," agreed God graciously.

But where could God find for him the years beyond three-score and ten? He could only give it to him from the years allotted to the dogs and the horse. Therefore, good friend, if you listen to a cantor who is above seventy years old, don't be surprised if he howls like a dog, and if you eat with him don't be surprised if he gorges like a horse!

PREACHERS AND RABBIS

Letter of Recommendation

THE post of rabbi was vacant in a Bronx congregation. A rabbi, who had but recently given up a pulpit in Brooklyn, applied. The president of the Bronx congregation did the usual routine thing: he wrote a letter of inquiry about the rabbi to the Brooklyn congregation. Shortly after, he got the following answer:

"Our former rabbi can easily be compared to Moses, to Shakespeare, to Demosthenes and to God the Father."

The Bronx congregation was impressed and delighted with this glowing praise and so they appointed the Brooklyn rabbi to their pulpit. But it did not take long for them to discover that their new rabbi was no genius. So, in a huff, the president wrote a sizzling letter to the Brooklyn congregation upbraiding it for the deception and demanding an explanation. Several days later they got the following reply:

"Why do you call us names? Who has deceived you? We wrote you as we did for the following reason:

"Our former rabbi can be compared to Moses because, like him, he knows no English; to Shakespeare because, like him, he knows no Yiddish; to Demosthenes because, like him, he speaks as if he has pebbles rolling in his mouth; and to God the Father because, like Him, our former rabbi is positively not human."

He Preached Too Sweetly

A RABBI once held forth so sweetly on a drowsy Sabbath afternoon in the synagogue that he lulled his audience to sleep. To wake them he suddenly began to cry, "Fire—fire!"

The members of the congregation awoke in terror.

"Where's the fire—where . . . where?" they gasped.

"In Hell!" thundered the preacher. "There's a fiery furnace waiting there for those damned souls who in this life choose to sleep while their rabbi preaches!"

Fair Solution

THE rabbi was walking along the road when he met a fat rich man who was smoking.

"Why do you smoke? It's an awful vice!" he rebuked him.

"I smoke to help me digest my dinner; I overate," apologized the fat rich man.

Further on the rabbi met a thin poor man who also was smoking.

"Why do you smoke? Don't you know it's a terrible vice?" the rabbi lectured him severely.

"I smoke to drive away the pangs of hunger," murmured the thin poor man apologetically.

"Lord of the World!" cried the rabbi, lifting his eyes to heaven. "Where is Your Justice? If only the fat rich man would give the poor thin man some of his dinner both of them would be healthier and happier, and neither of them would have to smoke!"

The Merits of Not Preaching

RABBI LEVI YITZCHOK of Berditchev disliked travelling preachers so much that when they came to town he refused to give them his permission to deliver their fire-and-brimstone sermons.

One day, the Preacher of Dubno came to his town. Naturally he could not say no to the most celebrated preacher of the day. When the preacher held forth in the synagogue Rabbi Levi Yitzchok himself came to hear him.

"How did you like my preaching?" asked the Preacher of Dubno afterwards.

"Splendid! Splendid!" beamed Rabbi Levi Yitzchok, pumping his hand. "But how can you compare the merits of preaching to *not* preaching?"

The Obedient Congregation

A YOUNG, inexperienced rabbi called on an aged colleague for advice.

"Take the heads of this congregation, for instance," said the old rabbi. "They are pious and God-fearing. I never have any trouble with them. They always do what I tell them."

"What makes you so sure that they do?" the young rabbi asked.

The old rabbi laughed. "You see, I'm careful not to ask them to do what I know they won't do!"

He Did the Best He Could

WHEN Czar Nicholas I issued his decree obliging all able-bodied Jews to bear arms, the Jews of a little Russian town went to their rabbi and implored him to intercede with God for them.

"Once our sons go into the army they'll stop being Jews!" they wailed.

The rabbi fasted and prayed and, when he was through, he called the Jews of the town together and said, "My prayers have been heard. God will surely tell the Czar to withdraw his decree."

But, when the recruiting officers of the Czar arrived and snatched away even the little Jewish boys of six and seven, the Jews of the town descended angrily upon the rabbi.

"Didn't you tell us that God would have the Czar withdraw his decree!" they shouted.

"Indeed, I did!" the rabbi admitted. "And believe me, God *did* tell that Haman to withdraw his decree. But is it my fault if that dog doesn't want to obey God?"

ROTHSCHILD AND OTHER RICH MEN

His Bad Luck Held

A PETITIONER once came to see the great banker Rothschild in Vienna.

"I've been having a lot of bad luck all my life," he complained.

"What is your profession?" asked the banker politely.

"I'm a musician. I played for years in the Philharmonic Orchestra but ever since it was disbanded I haven't been able to get any employment."

"Too bad, too bad," murmured Rothschild commiseratingly. "What sort of instrument do you play, anyway?"

"I play the bassoon."

"The bassoon!" echoed Rothschild, his face lighting up. "That's wonderful! You must have heard how much I love good music. In fact, I have a surprise for you—I own a bassoon! I'm simply crazy about the bassoon; it's my favorite orchestral instrument! Come, my friend, let's go into the music room and you'll play me something on the bassoon."

"What was I telling you, Herr Baron?" wailed the petitioner. "I've never had anything but bad luck in my life. Of all instruments I might have mentioned I had to go and pick a bassoon!"

Discovery at 7 A.M.

THE banker Baron de Rothschild of Paris was a hard taskmaster to his clerks. Once, he called them together and said, "It's about time that you all came into the counting house early. From now on you have to report to work at seven A.M. To set you all an example in punctuality I will do the same. And what I, Rothschild, can do all of you can do!"

Then up spoke a thin frightened little clerk, "Monsieur le Baron, it may be all right for you to come in an hour earlier. That way you have the pleasure of discovering one hour earlier each day that you are the mighty Baron de Rothschild. But take me, for instance, Jacques Velvel-Shmul—when I come in an hour earlier what do I discover? I discover, Monsieur le Baron, one hour earlier than usual that I am the clerk, Jacques Velvel-Shmul, whose salary is seventy-five francs a month—woe is me!"

Whose Money?

THE famous Viennese Jewish wit and author, Saphir, was a protégé of Baron Rothschild, for he could never make a living out of his writing. His dependence on the largesse of the banker embittered him no end.

One day, when he came for his annual stipend, Rothschild spoke to him in a bantering tone of voice: "Ah, Saphir, I see you've come for your money!"

"For *my* money, Baron?" retorted Saphir ironically. "You mean—for *your* money."

Living de Luxe

IN THE Jewish cemetery at Frankfort-Am-Main lies the magnificent grave of *Reb* Amshel Rothschild, the founder of the famous banking family.

One day a poor man from Galicia came to see the grave and stood marvelling at the tombstone's beauty and costliness.

"Tsk-tsk, that's what I call living!" he murmured to himself in rapture.

The Good Life

THE two poor Talmudic students couldn't fall asleep that night in the synagogue. The benches were so hard—their stomachs so empty!

"Tell me," began one student idly, just to drive away the time, "how often do you think the rabbi changes his shirt?"

"Oh, I should guess about twice a week," speculatively answered the other student.

"And the landowner of this village?"

"Three times a week."

"The Count?"

"Five times a week."

"The Czar?"

"Every day."

"How about Rothschild?"

"Oh, Rothschild! Why he pulls on, pulls off, pulls on again, pulls off again—all day long. That's what I call living!"

Rothschild's Poverty

BERNSTEIN the *schnorrer* was passing Rothschild's house one day when Epstein the *schnorrer* was bodily thrown out of it.

"What happened to you," asked Bernstein, when his colleague had picked himself up.

"They claimed in there," said Epstein, "that they kicked me out because I was making too much noise, but they can't fool me! Things are bad with Rothschild; I just saw, in that big parlor, his two girls playing on one piano!"

The Rights of Schnorrers

FOR several years two brothers had presented themselves at the home of Rothschild once a month and each had been given 100 marks. Then, one died, so the survivor made the usual call alone.

The keeper of the Rothschild funds handed him the usual 100 marks.

"But you've made a mistake!" the *schnorrer* protested. "I should get 200 marks, 100 for my brother."

"No," said the treasurer, "your brother is dead. This is your hundred."

"What do you mean?" The *schnorrer* drew himself up indignantly. "Am *I* my brother's heir . . . or is Rothschild?"

Montefiore's Buttons

"THEY say that when Sir Moses Montefiore was received by the Czar he wore a fancy dress-coat on which the buttons, all ten of them, were of gold and each one was studded with a diamond worth five thousand rubles!

"Now I ask you—aren't the rich first-class idiots? What on earth makes them do silly things like that? Take me, for instance. On my Sabbath gabardine I have three buttons. All three of them together are worth half a groschen. Should I lose one—so what? It's like losing a chick-pea. But imagine that Montefiore—how he must fuss and take care and keep watch over his precious buttons! Should he lose one—goodbye to five thousand smackers! Tell me your honest opinion, do you think he sleeps nights? *Ach!* the pleasures of the rich!"

The Price of a Millionaire

WHEN the millionaire Brodsky came to a small Ukrainian town all the inhabitants poured out into the streets to welcome him. With official pomp he was led to the inn where he ordered two eggs for breakfast. When he had finished, the innkeeper asked him for twenty rubles. Brodsky was astonished.

"Are eggs so rare in these parts? he asked.

"No, but Brodskys are!" was the quick answer.

The Devoted Friend

THE two met in a train-compartment on the way to the Czech capital and they engaged in casual conversation.

"Do you happen to know Moritz Weintraub?"

"Do *I* know Moritz Weintraub? Of course I know Moritz!"

"What sort of man is he?"

"Must you ask? He's as stubborn as a mule. One who didn't know him could easily get the idea that he was really somebody. But it takes somebody a lot cleverer than Moritzchen to fool *me!*"

"What do you know about him?"

"Huh! What *I* know about him? What I know about him! What will you say for instance, if I tell you that he borrows money which he never returns? Have you any idea how many times he has bankrupted? *Three times!* He beats his wife. He violates the Sabbath. He even eats on *Yom Kippur!*"

"But how do you know all those things about him?"

"What do you mean 'how do I know?'—Moritzchen is my very best friend!"

The One to Call the Tune

NATHANSON, the wealthy millinery supply wholesaler, lay dying. He motioned to his wife to come nearer to his bedside.

"Leah, I neglected to draw up a will," he began in a weak voice. "Listen carefully to what I'm going to tell you:

"First of all, I'm leaving the business to Irving."

"You're making a mistake," protested his wife tearfully. "Irving has only one thing on his brain—horses. He'll surely ruin the business! I think you'd do better if you left it to Max; he's serious minded and steady."

"Good—let it be Max then," sighed the dying man resignedly.

"Our summer house in the Catskills I leave to Rachel," Nathanson continued.

"Rachel!" exclaimed his wife. "What does Rachel need our summer home for? Her husband is rich enough. It would be better if you gave it to Julia who is poor."

"Very well," sighed her husband. "Let Julia have it. Now, as for the car, I leave it to Benny."

"Benny?" asked his wife in surprise. "What does Benny need your car for? Hasn't he got one already? Believe me, Louie could make much better use of it!"

At this a look of exasperation came into the dying man's face. Collecting his ebbing strength he cried, "Listen, Leah! Who's dying around here—you or I?"

True Grief

AT THE funeral of the richest man in town a great many mourners turned out to pay their last respects to the dead. Among the multitude was a poor man who heaved deep sighs as he followed the hearse.

"Are you a close relation of the deceased," someone asked him commiseratingly.

"I'm no relation at all!" he replied.

"Then why do you weep?"

"That's why."

Steam-Bath Soliloquy

"BELIEVE me, uncle, it's a topsy-turvy world! The rich merchants have all the money in the world, yet they're the ones who are being stuffed with credit and goods, but the poor little shopkeeper who never has a broken groschen in his till, he's got to pay cash for everything! If there was justice in the world wouldn't they arrange things just the opposite? The rich merchant who has plenty of money would be forced to pay cash and the little shopkeeper who hasn't a groschen would get plenty of credit. Would that be so terrible? Under my plan, suppose the poor shopkeeper cannot afford to pay his bills. So what? The rich merchant who extends him the credit will therefore lose money and will probably become poor, too. Where's the tragedy? Once he's a poor man he'll be entitled to unlimited credit. So what's there to worry about for anyone?"

Rich Man's Folly

A POOR man ran home in haste and told his wife breathlessly, "I've just been to see the richest man in town and I found him at dinner eating *blintzes.* As I stood there and smelled their delicious fragrance, the juices in me began to work. Those *blintzes* certainly must taste wonderful! Believe me when rich men eat something, it's *something*."

Then the poor man sighed longingly. "Oh, if I could only taste *blintzes* just once!"

"But how can I make *blintzes*? I need eggs for that," answered his wife.

"Do without the eggs," her husband advised.

"And I'll need cream."

"Well, you'll have to do without the cream."

"And you think sugar doesn't cost any money?"

"You'll have to do without sugar, then."

The wife then set to work and made the *blintzes,* but without eggs, cream and sugar. With a judicious air the husband started to eat them, chewed them slowly and carefully. Then suddenly a look of bewilderment came into his face. "Let me tell you Sarah," he murmured, "for the life of me, I can't see what those rich people see in *blintzes!*"

A Man of Affairs

A MAN, reputedly wealthy, went walking down the street with a youth whom a *shadchan* had brought to meet his daughter.

"See that man?" boastfully remarked the prospective father-in-law pointing out a passer-by. "I owe him a thousand rubles."

When they had walked a little further he stopped again and said, "See that man with the cane? I owe him three thousand rubles."

A little further on he stopped again and said, "Notice that man in the brown gabardine. I owe him five thousand rubles. No mean sum, eh?"

"Why do you tell me what you owe?" exclaimed the young man impatiently. "Better tell me what you've got!"

"But what I owe is all I've got!" murmured the man, heaving a deep sigh.

Credit Too Good

KOGAN borrowed a hundred rubles from Katz, promising to repay him in a week. And he did, much to Katz's surprise.

A few days later, again needing funds, Kogan borrowed another hundred rubles, again agreeing to pay it back in a week. Once more he kept his word.

Not long after, Kogan asked for another hundred, but this time Katz said, "Enough's enough! Twice already you've fooled me! Three times would be too much to expect!"

A Father with Foresight

ONCE there was a rich man who owned a factory and other business establishments. In addition, he was the proprietor of the only wine-house in town. He had two sons and heirs: one was respectable and well-behaved, the other was a roisterer and spendthrift.

A time came when the rich man felt that he was reaching his end. So he drew up a will in which he left his factory and all his other properties to his profligate son. To his good and upright son he left only the wine-house.

When his friends heard of this they reproached him, saying, "How did you come to do such a silly thing? Why are you leaving the bulk of your wealth to that good-for-nothing sot who will only waste the wealth you accumulated with the effort of a lifetime?"

"Believe me," said the rich man, "I have carefully considered the matter. Were I to leave the wine-house to my good-for-nothing son there's no doubt that he'd drink it all away in no time with his boon companions. In the end, his creditors would take it away from him. Therefore, in order to prevent this situation from arising, I have left the wine-house to my sober, well-behaved son, and my other possessions to his brother. You see it's all very simple! Because my wine-shop is the only one in town, it is certain that my profligate son will go to drink there with his bad companions. I have no doubt that he will thus fritter away the factory and everything else. In that case it will be my good son who, in the long run, will not only have the wine-shop but will also acquire the rest of my wealth."

TAILORS

Out of Style

THE tailoring business was so bad that Feitelberg said to his partner, "Only the Messiah could help us."

"How could even the Messiah help us?" asked the partner in despair.

"Why," said Feitelberg, "he'd bring back the dead, and naturally they'd need new clothes."

"But some of the dead are tailors," the partner observed gloomily.

"So what?" asked Feitelberg. "They wouldn't have a chance! How many would know this year's styles?"

A FATHER WITH FORESIGHT: Adapted from the *Parables of the Preacher of Dubno.*

Both from Minsk

A CZARIST police inspector, glittering in his gold-braid uniform, was walking through the streets of Moscow when he passed an anemic little Jewish tailor who failed to doff his cap.

"Here, Jew!" he roared angrily and seized the unlucky tailor by the scruff of his neck and shook him until his teeth rattled. "What do you mean by passing me without removing your cap! I won't be surprised if you haven't even a residence permit! Quick, tell me—where do you come from?"

"From Minsk," stammered the Jew.

"Now, what about your hat?" rasped the police inspector, kicking him in the shins.

"Also from Minsk," stuttered the tailor.

Napoleon and the Jewish Tailor

WHILE the Emperor Napoleon was retreating from Russia he passed through a Jewish village as he fled before the enemy. Seeing that all avenues of escape were cut off he dashed into a house in which lived a Jewish tailor.

In a tremulous voice he pleaded with the tailor, "Hide me quick! If the Russians find me they'll kill me!"

Although the little tailor had no idea who the stranger was he was moved by pity for a fellow-creature. So he said to the Emperor, "Get under the featherbed and lie still!"

Napoleon got into bed and the tailor piled on him one featherbed, and another, and then still another.

It wasn't long before the door burst open and two Russian soldiers with spears in their hands rushed in.

"Is there anybody hiding here?" they asked.

"Who would be foolish enough to hide in my house?" the tailor answered.

The soldiers pried into every corner but found no one. As they were leaving, just to make sure, they stuck their spears several times through the featherbeds.

When the door had finally closed on them Napoleon crawled out from under the pile of featherbeds. He looked deathly pale and was covered with perspiration. Then turning to the tailor he said, "I want you to know, my dear noble friend, that I am the Emperor Napoleon. Because you have saved me from certain death you can ask me three favors. No matter what they are I will grant them to you."

NAPOLEON AND THE JEWISH TAILOR: Translated and adapted from *Royte Pomerantsen,* a collection of Jewish folk humor, by Immanuel Olsvanger. By permission of Schocken Books. New York, 1947.

The little tailor thought for a while, then he said, "Your Majesty, the roof of my house has been leaking for the past two years but I've never had any money to fix it. Would you be so kind and have it fixed for me?"

"Blockhead!" exclaimed Napoleon impatiently. "Is that the greatest favor you can ask of an Emperor? But never mind—I'll see that your roof is fixed! Now you can make your second wish, but make sure this time that it's something substantial."

The little tailor scratched his head. He was really perplexed. What on earth could he ask for? His face suddenly brightened.

"Some months ago, Your Majesty," he began, "another tailor opened his shop across the way and he is ruining my business! Would it be too much trouble for you to ask him to find himself another location?"

"What a fool!" cried Napoleon disdainfully. "Very well, my friend—I'll ask your competitor to go to the devil! Now you must try and think of something that's *really* important. Keep in mind though that this is positively the last favor I'll grant you!"

The tailor knitted his brows and thought and thought. Suddenly an impish look came into his eyes.

"Begging your pardon, Emperor," he asked with burning curiosity, "but I'd very much like to know how you felt while the Russian soldiers were poking their spears through the featherbeds!"

"Imbecile!" cried Napoleon beside himself with rage. "How dare you put such a question to an Emperor? For your insolence I'll have you shot at dawn!"

So said, so done. He called in three French soldiers who placed the little tailor in irons and led him away to the guardhouse.

That night the tailor could not sleep. He wept and quaked, quaked and wept. Then he recited the prayer of confession and made his peace with God.

Promptly at dawn he was taken out of his cell and tied to a tree. A firing squad drew up opposite him and aimed their muskets at him. Near by stood an officer with watch in hand waiting to give the signal to fire. He lifted his hand and began to count: "One—two—thr—" But before he could even complete the word, the Emperor's aide-de-camp dashed up on horseback, crying, "Stop! Don't shoot!"

Then he went up to the tailor and said to him, "His Majesty, the Emperor, gives you his gracious pardon. He also has asked me to give you this note."

The tailor heaved a deep sigh and began to read, "You wanted to know," wrote Napoleon, "how I felt under the featherbed in your house. Well, now you know."

Scholars and Scripture Teachers

Etiquette Among Scholars

A RICH man once invited two hungry scholars to tea. They came, sat down at the table and began to discuss Torah, for what other pastime do Jews have? As they got themselves well tangled up in Talmudical argument, the hostess entered and placed before them glasses of tea with lemon. Then she brought in a platter with two cookies. It so happened that one cookie was somewhat larger than the other. Understanding etiquette very well, neither of the two scholars wished to be the first to reach for the cookies.

One said gallantly, "You first, *Reb* Yankel."

"No, no! Help yourself first, *Reb* Isaac!" urged *Reb* Yankel with equal delicacy.

Finally, after much aimless feinting, *Reb* Yankel suddenly reached out and took a cookie—but he chose the larger one.

Reb Isaac looked on dumbfounded.

"How is it, *Reb* Yankel," he chided him in an injured tone of voice, "that a scholar like you should be so utterly without table manners? How could anybody be so rude as to grab for himself the bigger portion and leave the smaller one to another?"

"*Nu*, and what would you have done in my place?" asked *Reb* Yankel.

"What do you mean what would I have done? As a man who knows etiquette I most certainly would have taken the smaller cookie."

"Well, that's what you got," answered *Reb* Yankel sweetly. "So what are you getting excited about?"

Goal Achieved

A CERTAIN *melamed* was in the habit of snatching a quiet drink while his students droned on. But in the course of time this became known and he lost all his pupils.

A friend, moved by the teacher's sad situation, tried to induce him to reform. "Look, Chatzkl," he pleaded, "if only you'd give up drinking, you'd have all your pupils back. Come on, try and give it up!"

"You're a fool!" the *melamed* replied. "Here for years I've been teaching so I'd be able to drink . . . and you suggest I stop drinking, so I'll be able to teach!"

Strictly Kosher

THE teacher of Scripture in a little Polish town got sick and tired of his drudgery and of suffering cold and hunger. He decided to become a robber.

One day, he took a knife from the kitchen and went into the woods. Hiding behind a tree he lay in ambush for passersby. At last he saw a rich lumber dealer of the town trudging along unsuspectingly. Without a word, he threw himself upon him and raised his knife as if to stab him. Suddenly he seemed to recall something and let the knife drop to the ground.

"It's your luck," he muttered. "I just remembered that this is a *milchig* knife!"

Potatoes

A POOR Talmud student was making the rounds from one householder to another. Each one, out of the goodness of his heart and as an act of piety, gave him food and lodging for several days. In one of these homes, however, he was treated with ill-grace and in a perfunctory manner. Three times daily they gave him only one dish to eat—potatoes.

One day, when he saw the platter of potatoes being placed before him, he shuddered and asked his host, "Tell me, please, what is the benediction that is said over potatoes?"

"What a question to ask!" exclaimed his host. "You're a Talmud student, aren't you? Why, even the most ignorant man knows that you say: 'Blessed are the fruits of the earth,' over everything which comes out of the soil."

"That may be so," retorted the Talmud student, "but what should I say when the potatoes are coming out of my ears?"

MERCHANTS, SHOPKEEPERS, PEDDLERS

To Save Time

ON THE express train to Lublin, a young man stopped at the seat of an obviously prosperous merchant.

"Can you tell me the time?" he said.

The merchant looked at him and replied: "Go to hell!"

"What? Why, what's the matter with you! I ask you a civil question, in a properly civil way, and you give me such an outrageous, rude answer! What's the idea?"

The merchant looked at him, sighed wearily, and said, "Very well. Sit down and I'll tell you. You ask me a question. I have to give you an answer, no? You start a conversation with me—about the weather, politics, business. One thing leads to another. It turns out you're a Jew—I'm a Jew. I live in Lublin—you're a stranger. Out of hospitality, I ask you to my home for dinner. You meet my daughter. She's a beautiful girl— you're a handsome young man. So you go out together a few times—and you fall in love. Finally you come to ask for my daughter's hand in marriage. So why go to all that trouble. Let me tell you right now, young man, I won't let my daughter marry anyone who doesn't even own a watch!"

A Tradesman's Revenge

SEVERAL merchants sat at a table in an Odessa restaurant absorbed in conversation about business affairs. Every once in a while a peddler came up to them and pestered them to buy something from him.

"I have fine handkerchiefs, and scarves that are beauties, and coin purses that are A-1," he called out in a raucous voice.

Out of patience with him, one of the merchants said, "What do you say to this pest! I'd like to play a trick on him that he'll never forget."

And, turning to the peddler, he asked, "Do you have any suspenders, uncle? But they must be A-1."

"What a question!" cried the peddler with an offended air. "Do I have A-1 suspenders!" And quickly he fished out a pair of suspenders. "You asked for A-1, but, believe me, these are A-1 A-1."

"How much?"

"Two rubles."

Without a word the merchant paid the two rubles and the peddler walked away with a dazed look on his face.

"What was the idea?" asked a colleague of the merchant who had bought the suspenders. "Why did you immediately pay him what he asked?"

"Never fear, I've struck home," replied the merchant with glee. "He'll eat his heart out now because he didn't ask for three rubles."

A Kindness

A CERTAIN merchant was notorious for not paying his bills, so his good friend Abrams was astonished one day to find him haggling endlessly over a deal. He took the merchant aside.

"Look," he said, "I can't understand you. You know you won't ever pay this man anyway, so why do you bargain so brutally?"

"Listen," said the merchant, "he's a nice guy, and I want to keep down his losses!"

The Rich Uncle

ONCE there was a retired New York merchant who owned a large summer home in the Catskill Mountains. He had a kind heart and because of that his summers became a nightmare for him. With the appearance of the crocuses and with the first liquid notes of the robin all his poor relations from Brownsville, East New York, Midwood and West Bronx descended upon him in the country in force. They never gave him a moment's peace or privacy until the leaves began to turn. Then they returned to New York.

One day, as he sat gloomily regarding a young third cousin-in-law upon whom a thousand hints had been wasted, he sighed and said, "There is little likelihood, is there, that you'll ever come on another visit here?"

"What a thing to say!" protested the young man with heat. "Why, you are the prince of hosts! Why shouldn't I come again?"

"How can you come again if you never go away?" moaned his host plaintively.

He Should Worry

SAM SCHNEIDER, the candy-store keeper, owed one hundred dollars to his acquaintance Friedman. He could no longer postpone paying it for Friedman had served him with an ultimatum: "You either pay me tomorrow or I'll sue you!" But what could Schneider do? You can't squeeze money out of a stone! Therefore, that night he couldn't fall asleep and he walked to and fro and then fro and to.

"Why don't you go to sleep, Sam?" his wife called sleepily to him.

"Who can sleep?" muttered Schneider, dejectedly. "I owe Friedman a hundred dollars, and God knows when I'll be able to pay it back!"

"So why do you have to be so foolish, Sam?" chided his wife. "Come to bed—let Friedman walk the floor!"

How Near—How Far?

THE agent was showing a summer *datcha* to the prospective buyer, a wealthy merchant from the city.

"Just look at this wonderful house! Where else could you get a *datcha* so near the Dnieper River at this low price? See for yourself; it practically stands on the river bank."

"So what?" answered the merchant with an icy indifference. "What'll I get out of the Dnieper River?"

"How can you say a thing like that?" argued the agent with warmth. "The Dnieper is a wonderful river! From the balcony of this *datcha* you'll get a fine view of it. Your laundress will be able to do her washing at the river edge; you and your wife can bathe there, and your children can fish and row on it."

"That's all well and good so far as it goes," answered the merchant. "But what if the Dnieper overflows and carries my house away?"

"Nonsense!" quickly shot back the agent. "How can you say a thing like that? Just see how far away this house is from the Dnieper!"

The Fly in the Ointment

THE little storekeeper and his wife were in seventh heaven. Their only son, Irving, was home from college—graduated with a degree, and he had agreed to help his old man and make a real business out of the store.

"First," he said, "we'll get an accountant and set up a proper system. You've got things in terrible shape here. When bills come in you just stick them on a spindle and don't make any other record of it. Every few days you take some cash out of the drawer, take some bills off the spindle and pay them without any proper bookkeeping entry. That's no good; but the accountant will change everything, don't worry."

"I won't," said the little storekeeper.

But a few weeks later his wife could see that something really serious was bothering him. His nights were sleepless, and during the day he walked about restlessly.

"Jacob," asked his wife, "tell me what is it? Something is worrying you."

"No, no. I can't tell you."

"What do you mean, you can't. Twenty-five years we've been married and now we should have secrets from each other!"

"Well, all right. Rebecca, the accountant says we are bankrupt. I don't know what to do. I think of this, maybe that, but it's no use. I don't know what to do."

"Jacob," said Rebecca, "listen! We've always had enough to eat, yes? We've always had a good roof over our heads, yes? We've managed to send our boy to college, yes? And where did the money come from, if not the store? The store is the same, we're the same, the customers are the same. Only the accountant is different. It's all very simple. Send away the accountant!"

Production Worries

FRIEDMAN the clothier was distressed at the haggardness of his partner Weinberg, who suffered from insomnia. "I'll bet you," he said to him, "you never tried the commonest remedy, after all your specialists."

"What's this commonest remedy?"

"Counting sheep."

"All right," said the sick man. "What can I lose? Tonight I'll give it a try."

But next morning Weinberg was more haggard than ever. "Did you do like you said?" Friedman eagerly asked.

"Sure I did," said Weinberg wearily. "But something terrible happened. I counted sheep up to 50,000. Then I sheared the sheep, and in a little while I made up 50,000 overcoats. Then all of a sudden a problem came up, and I was tearing my hair all night: *where could I get 50,000 linings?*"

Nickeleh-Pickeleh

AN OLD Jewish woman on Essex Street stuck her hand into the brine of a pickle barrel and fished out a large pickle.

"How much is this pickle?" she asked.

"A nickel," answered the dealer.

"A nickel is too much," she said and put the pickle back into the barrel. She fished in the barrel again and came up with a little pickle.

"How much is this little *pickleh*?" she asked in a tender voice.

"That *pickleh*?" answered the shop-keeper, just as tenderly. "Only a nickeleh!"

Too Late

A JUNK peddler on the East Side died. His widow collected two thousand dollars insurance.

"What miserable luck!" she complained. "For forty years we lived in poverty and now that God has made us rich, Sol had to go and die!"

Doctors and Patients

Kreplach

A Jewish mother was much distressed over the problem of her young son who was afraid to eat the popular dish known as *kreplach*. She took the boy to a psychiatrist for consultation. After hearing the case, the doctor said, "Now, madam, this is very simple. Take the boy home, take him out into the kitchen, and show him the ingredients that go into the dish. And then, show him how *kreplach* are made. This should probably eliminate the condition."

Hopefully the mother followed his advice. On the kitchen table she put out a small square of dough beside which was a small mound of prepared chopped meat. "Now," she said, "there's nothing here you should mind." The lad beamed and nodded encouragingly. The mother then put the meat in the center of the dough and folded over one corner. The boy smiled and all seemed to be going well. She folded over the second corner and the third. The boy was nodding and the experiment seemed to be progressing most favorably. Then she folded over the fourth and final corner; whereupon the boy groaned and muttered, *"Oi, kreplach!"*

A Calculation

Two Galicians went to live in Vienna. After some time they met on the street.

"How are you making out in Vienna?" one asked with a sigh.

"One step removed from the grave," answered the other bitterly. "How about you?"

"Not so bad! Why should I complain? I'm making a living. After all, can a Jew ask for more? But I have been sick of late. Why, do you know that in the last three months I've spent 400 gulden on doctors and medicines!"

"Ach!" exclaimed the other with a homesick sigh. "Back in Galicia you could have been sick on that money for at least six years."

One of the Diseases of Mankind

Dr. Isaac Hourwich, the noted Yiddish scholar, had a goatee and he looked exactly like Russian-Jewish doctors are expected to look.

One day, an old Jewish woman came to see him.

"Doctor," she complained, "I suffer the tortures of hell from my rheumatism. Would you please—"

"I'm sorry," Dr. Hourwich interrupted her, "but you've made a mistake, my dear woman. I'm only a Doctor of Philosophy."

"Tell me, doctor," she murmured, "what kind of sickness is 'philosophy'?"

How to Collect Dues

IN THE great, gay days of Vienna a certain physician determined to slough off his Jewish origin in an effort to achieve the maximum social distinction.

Into the hospital where he served as clinical professor of dermatology there came one day a little Jew, bearded, wearing a greenish derby hat, a rusty alpaca coat, and carrying a battered briefcase. "I wish to see Professor Mannheimer," he proclaimed.

"Impossible," said the attendant curtly.

"What do you mean 'impossible'? I'll wait," said the little man. He sat down on a bench in the reception room, and waited, all day long. For several days thereafter he came and waited all day.

On the fifth day, a new attendant decided to help the little old man. "I'll give you a tip," he said. "Professor Mannheimer gives a clinical lecture tomorrow, and he uses people as examples of diseases while he lectures. The only chance you have of ever seeing him is to join the line of these people. They pass through that corridor, over there, exactly at three o'clock. But you've got to undress."

"*Nu,*" said the old man, "if I have to undress, I have to undress."

So the next day, at three, the old man, naked except for his hat, his briefcase still clutched in one hand, brought up the end of the line. In a moment, with the half-dozen other "specimens," he found himself in the amphitheatre. The professor entered, and began his lecture.

Pointing with a long professorial staff at the first of the poor souls, he said, "Here, gentlemen, we have a perfect case of dermatitis. . . ." And, after a lengthy description of the symptoms, he thanked the "specimen" and waved his pointer to the next in line.

"This," he declared, "is tertiary syphilis . . . note this symptom . . . note that . . ." And again, he waved to the next case.

Finally the great professor stood face to face with the little old man. He looked the "specimen" over from head to foot, wiped his own spectacles and then, thoroughly puzzled, asked, "What's the matter with *you*?"

"What's the matter with *me*!" echoed the little man. "What's the matter with *you*, Professor Mannheimer? For four years, you haven't paid one cent of your dues to the Jewish charities!"

Insomnia

OLD man Epstein suffered from insomnia. His family had tried dozens of doctors, and scores of home remedies, to no avail. Finally a great specialist was recommended, a neurologist reported never to fail. He was forthwith sent for.

Arriving at the house, the great doctor said to the son, "You wait here, while your father and I have a few moments together." And the doctor entered the old man's room.

"It's all very simple," said the doctor when they were alone. "Just follow me. Do everything I do."

And the great neurologist raised both arms aloft. So did Epstein. Then he lowered his arms and breathed deeply. Epstein followed suit. The physician raised his arms sideways, did three quick knee-bending maneuvers, put his hands on his hips, and then executed five or six more calisthenic operations. Epstein followed faithfully.

Suddenly, panting a little from these rigorous exercises, the doctor fixed little Epstein with a commanding eye, and declared soothingly, "Now . . . you will go . . . to sleep!" He pointed to the bed.

The doctor then strode from the room, and summoned the younger man. "You may go in to your father, now," he said. "You'll find him fast asleep."

Happily, the son tiptoed to his father's bedside, put his lips near the old man's ear, and whispered, "Papa, it's me. You're sleeping?"

Very cautiously, old man Epstein opened one eye, and asked, "That *meshuggener* . . . he's still here?"

WAITERS AND RESTAURANTS

The Customer Is Always Right

A CUSTOMER in a Jewish restaurant in New York gave his order to the waiter.

"I want some roast duck."

"I'm sorry—we have no roast duck today—only roast goose."

"Ask the boss."

The waiter went to the boss.

"Mr. Weintraub wants roast duck."

"Tell him we have no roast duck today—only roast goose."

"I told him so, but he insists on having roast duck."

The boss sighed and said, "All right, if Weintraub insists, he insists! Ask the cook to cut off a portion of roast duck from the roast goose."

Service

THE restaurant was crowded. Waiters scurried everywhere. A line of standees awaited tables. The noise was overpowering.

As a waiter whizzed past one table, a customer looked up and asked, "Waiter—what time is it?"

He got a quick answer. "I'm not your waiter."

A Fishy Conversation

A CUSTOMER came into a restaurant in Kharkov, ordered a fish, and when it was brought, bent over the fish as if it were a friend, apparently talking to it. The manager, observing this, came over to the table.

"What," he asked the diner, "are you doing?"

"Oh, just conversing with this fish."

"Conversing with this fish?" The manager was astounded. "And what were you saying to it?"

"I asked him where he was from. And he said the Dnieper."

"The Dnieper, eh?" The manager determined to see this through. "Then what did you say?"

"I asked what was new on the Dnieper."

"And he answered?"

"He was terribly sorry, but he'd left there so long ago, he wouldn't know."

Noodle Soup

A MAN went into a Jewish restaurant on Second Avenue and ordered a table d'hote dinner. He started off his meal with soup. After the first spoonful he made a wry face.

"Waiter!" he called out. "This cabbage soup isn't sour enough!"

"Who told you it was cabbage soup?" retorted the waiter. "This is noodle soup, mister!"

"Oh, so it's noodles!" sighed the customer apologetically. "Well, for noodle soup it's sour enough!"

Oysters for Atonement

ON HIS way to *shul* on *Yom Kippur*, the Day of Atonement, holiest of fast days, a Jew spied his partner at a table in the very window of a sea-food restaurant. Storming into the restaurant, he planted himself at his partner's elbow.

"How can you do such a thing?" he bellowed. "How on this day of all days can you sit here and eat oysters?"

"What's the matter?" asked the culprit. "There's no 'R' in *Yom Kippur*?"

MATCHMAKERS

INTRODUCTION

Matchmaking, practiced among many peoples, has had a venerable history among Jews. It had an honorable tradition for countless generations, and served a socially useful purpose besides. It received serious discussion as far back as the Talmudic tractate, *Baba Kama*. But then, unlike modern times, it was not regarded as a business but as a pious practice to be carried on for the love of God, the perpetuation of the Jewish family, and the increase of Israel. As a distinctive calling, matchmaking was already in existence among European Jews during the Twelfth Century. The *shadchan* was even then a clearly recognizable personage. In fact, he was an important Jewish communal functionary, who collected his modest fees prescribed by rabbinical decisions and by the legal statutes of the realm.

It was the Crusades which spurred the growth of Jewish matchmaking throughout Europe. Wholesale massacres, persecutions, and the constant flights of Jews hither and thither before their enemies, made normal social life impossible. In such circumstances, the *shadchan* became a pillar of national survival, an important instrumentality for the preservation of the Jewish people.

He was among those brave souls who devoted themselves to the vital task of establishing and preserving contact among the scattered remnants of Israel. It was a labor of devotion on his part, involving many risks to life and limb as he traveled through hostile territory from town to town and province to province.

No mere hucksters or business "agents" were permitted by the Jewish communities to devote themselves to the "sacred" union of youth. Only high-minded rabbis and scholars were chosen. It is interesting to note that such celebrated scholars and rabbis as Levi of Mayence, Jacob Molir and Leona da Modena were *shadchonim;* and they were honored for this work by their communities.

In time, with the growth and permanency of Jewish settlements in ghetto-towns, the traditional integrity of the *shadchan* began to waver. By the time of the Jewish "Dark Ages," which began at the end of the Sixteenth Century, there were already *mussar* (moralistic) writings in which the *shadchan* was roasted over the coals for his venality and gross misrepresentations. With pointed sarcasm he was reminded that, in olden times, only unselfish scholars and great rabbis were privileged to practice his profession.

One of the principal reasons for the decline in the moral stature of the matchmakers was the fact that usually men with unstable backgrounds and occupations were tempted into its uncertain undertakings. The peculiar persuasive and social talents required drew toward it, and even stimulated, the development of a unique type. It would be an understatement to say that the *shadchan* became the Jewish counterpart of Figaro. Even more than he, the *shadchan* was a perpetual chatterbox, lively and impudent by turn, good-natured with raillery and guileless with malice.

The *shadchan* is a classic type in the great portrait gallery of Jewish folklore and in the works of fiction writers as well. He is drawn vividly and in broad satiric lines, dressed up in all the fine plumage of his humbug, talkativeness, and genius for euphemistically glossing over the physical and character defects of his clients. Yet, with it all, he is touched with a certain comic pathos which belongs to the *schlimazl*, a trait Figaro did not possess.

N. A.

The Unreasonable Young Man

AN OLD marriage broker once came to a young man proposing a match with an ugly girl. The young man, who knew the girl, looked at the broker as if he had gone out of his mind.

"What's the idea of making sport of me?" he asked him indignantly.

"You're wrong!" the broker assured him. "You know I don't like to joke. I mean it very seriously. What are your objections to the girl anyway?"

"Objections? Why she's blind!"

"You call that a fault? In my opinion it's a virtue. You'll be free to do whatever you please."

"But she's also a mute!"

"For a woman that's a virtue. You'll never hear a sour word from her."

"But she's also deaf!"

"Can you think of anything better? You'll be able to abuse her to your heart's content and she won't hear you."

"But she's also lame!"

"Call that a fault? You'll be able to run after other women and she won't be able to follow you."

"But she's also hunchbacked!"

"Really, I cannot understand you!" cried the marriage broker in exasperation. "Can't you tolerate even one fault in the girl you plan to marry?"

Happiness, Ready-to-Wear

THE young man was indignant.

"What sort of a match are you proposing to me, anyway?" he rebuked the *shadchan*. "Why, this woman is the mother of three children!"

"So what if she is?" countered the *shadchan*. "Believe me, it's a lot better so. Suppose you were to marry a girl and you both decided to have children. What inconvenience you'd have to go through to have three children! Three pregnancies, and all the fuss that goes with them. What a waste of time, energy and expense, of doctors, nurses, hospitals and medicines! After each birth your wife would have to convalesce, no? You even may have to send her to the country to recuperate. Since you work in town you'll both be cruelly separated. What sort of a dog's life will you lead then? You'll have to eat in rotten restaurants and spoil your digestion. And you'll have to look after your kids while your wife is away. This way, if you'll marry the widow with the three children I'm proposing, it'll be a ready-made job. She's all through with the bother. Three nice children, all custom-made, and their mother is in the pink of condition, thank you! My friend, if you don't grab this proposition you're a fool!"

The Art of Exaggeration

ONCE there was a marriage broker who felt he was getting old and unable to get around any more as much as he used to. He therefore hired a young assistant who knew nothing about the business. He had to start from scratch with him.

"Know, young man," said the marriage broker, "that the most important thing in matchmaking is exaggeration. You must lay it on thick!"

"I fully understand," answered the assistant brightly.

One day the master took his assistant along on a matchmaking visit to a rich man who had an only son.

"Remember what I told you!" the marriage broker warned his assistant. "Above all things, be enthusiastic and don't hesitate to lay it on."

When they came to the rich man the broker began:

"I've just the right girl for your son! She comes of a good family."

"Good family!" exclaimed his assistant rapturously. "Why, they're descendants of the Vilna Gaon!"

"And they are rich too," the broker went on.

"What do you mean 'rich'?" interrupted his assistant. "They're millionaires!"

"As for the girl, she's as pretty as a doll!" gushed the broker.

"A doll!" snorted his assistant with scorn. "Why, she's a raving beauty!"

At this the broker threw a dubious look at his assistant.

"To tell the truth," he faltered, "she has just a trifling little handicap— she has a tiny wart on her back."

"What do you mean, a tiny wart!" enthused his assistant. "Why, she has a regular hump!"

The Aristocrat

SHORTLY after the Bolshevik Revolution, a *shadchan* called on a lady client in Minsk.

"How much dowry have you?" he asked delicately.

"Two thousand rubles."

The *shadchan* then took out his little black book and said, "Well now, let see! H-mm. For two thousand rubles I can give you a doctor."

"No, I don't want a doctor."

"Maybe you'd like a rabbi?"

"No, no rabbi."

"How about a cantor?"

"No, no cantor."

"Then what is it you want?"

"I want a worker."

"A worker? You're a smart one! For two thousand rubles you think you can get a worker?"

The Over-Enthusiastic Shadchan

A *shadchan* once came to a young man and said, "Young man, I have a girl for you—pure gold!"

"Thank you very much," answered the young man politely, "but I don't want to get married."

"Don't want to get married!" cried the *shadchan* incredulously. "Who ever heard of such a thing? How can a Jew live without a wife?"

"What do I need a wife for?" retorted the young man irritably.

"*Ai-ai!* That's bad!" sighed the *shadchan,* sadly shaking his head. "You talk like a child. You simply have no idea how good it is to have a wife! Without one, my dear friend, you can't know the meaning of life. Bachelors are always depressed; they feel as lonely as a stone in the wilderness. But with a wife—and believe me I know what I'm talking about for I have a wife of my own (may God keep her in health and vigor!)—with a wife, life is a joy without end.

"Imagine for a moment—you get up in the morning and your wife places before you a steaming cup of coffee. Then, while you are away for morning prayer or on business in the market-place, she makes ready a delicious breakfast—the same as my wife does (may God preserve her to one hundred and twenty years!). Later, when you return, you eat together, alone and at the same table. Everything is so cosy, so pleasant! Just think

---

THE OVER-ENTHUSIASTIC SHADCHAN: Translated and adapted from *Royte Pomerantsen,* a collection of Jewish folk humor, by Immanuel Olsvanger. By permission of Schocken Books. New York. 1947.

of it—you eat every meal the same way, three times a day, seven days a week, and every day of your life!

"Then on Friday, before the Holy Sabbath arrives, she dusts and cleans and scours until everything is spick and span. She polishes the large silver candlesticks that your mother-in-law gave you for a wedding-gift, until you can almost see your face in them. She then places them on the table, and, saying a prayer, she lights the candles, as a pious Jewish daughter should. When you return from evening prayer in the synagogue you chant the benediction over excellent wine in a silver goblet. And think of it! There, opposite you, sits your loving wife looking up at you smiling with her dear eyes, just as my wife (God bless her!) does on such occasions.

"After supper, you both sit down to chat comfortably. You first talk of this and of that. Then your wife (what a clever little head she has on her shoulders!) begins to tell you one witty story after another. You listen as she prattles so sweetly, so charmingly, just as my wife does. And so she goes on talking while you listen—and she talks . . . and she talks . . . and talks . . . and talks . . . *Oy,* can she talk! She's driving me crazy with her talk!"

The Truth Will Out

A MARRIAGE broker had taken a young man on a visit to a prospect. As they left the house the broker said triumphantly, "Didn't I tell you what a wonderful family they were, and how rich? Did you notice the quality of the silverware on the table? Pure sterling!"

"Y-e-s," grudgingly conceded the young man. "But don't you think it's possible that in order to make a good impression on me they borrowed the silverware?"

"*Ach,* what nonsense!" cried the broker with exasperation. "Who'd lend any silverware to those thieves?"

What a Life!

"WHAT was the idea of fooling me that way?" a prospective bridegroom bitterly reproached his *shadchan.*

"What do you mean, I fooled you?" indignantly replied the broker. "What did I say that wasn't so? Isn't the girl a beauty? Doesn't she embroider nicely? Doesn't she sing like a canary?"

"Ye-es," grudgingly conceded the groom. "The girl is all right, as far as that goes. But she comes from a terrible family! That's where you lied to me: you told me her father was dead, but the girl herself tells me he's been in jail for ten years."

"*Nu*—I ask you? Do you call that living?" asked the *shadchan.*

Speak Up

"You faker, you swindler!" hissed the prospective bridegroom, taking the *shadchan* aside. "Why did you ever get me into this? The girl's old, she's homely, she lisps, she squints—"

"You don't have to whisper," interrupted the *shadchan*, "she's deaf, too!"

Only Sometimes

The boy and girl went for a stroll. The boy said to his *shadchan* when next they met, "But she limps!"

"Only when she walks," agreed the *shadchan*.

In Haste

To my honored, beloved and respected friend, Sholom Aleichem:

I want to begin by informing you that I am still—Bless the Lord—among the living, and that I hope to hear the same from you, Amen. Next I want to tell you that, with God's help, I am now a king; that is, I have come home to Kasrilevka to spend the Passover with my wife and children, my father-in-law and mother-in-law, and with all my loved ones. And at Passover, as we all know, a Jew surrounded by his family is always a king. If only briefly, I hasten to inform you of all this, my dear, true friend. For a detailed account there is no time. It is Passover Eve, and on this day we must all do everything in great haste, standing on one foot. As it is written, "For *in haste* didst thou come forth out of the Land of Egypt."

But what to write of first, I hardly know myself. It seems to me that before anything else I ought to thank you and praise you for the good advice you gave me, to try my hand at matchmaking. Believe me, I shall never, never forget what you have done for me. You led me forth from the Land of Bondage, from the Gehenna of Yehupetz; you freed me from the desolate occupation of a commission salesman, and lifted me to a noble, respected profession. And for this I am obligated to praise and exalt you, to bless and adorn your name, as you well deserve.

It is true that thus far I have not succeeded in negotiating a single match, but I have made a beginning. Things are stirring, and once things begin to stir there is always the possibility and the hope that with God's help something may come of it. Especially in view of the fact that I do not work alone. I operate in partnership with other matchmakers, the best matchmakers in the world. As a result of these connections I now have a reputa-

IN HASTE: From *The Old Country*, by Sholom Aleichem. Translated by Julius and Frances Butwin. Copyright, 1946, by Crown Publishers. New York.

tion of my own. Wherever I come and introduce myself, Menachem-Mendel from Yehupetz, I am invited to sit down, I am given tea with preserves, I am treated like an honored guest. They introduce me to the daughter of the house, and the daughter shows me what she can do. She turns to her governess and begins to speak French with her. Words come pouring like peas out of a sack, and the mother sits gazing at her daughter proudly, as though to say, "What do you think of her? She speaks well, doesn't she?"

And listening to these girls, I have picked up some French myself and I can understand quite a bit of the language. For instance, if someone says to me, *"Parlez-vous Français?"* ("How are you feeling these days?") I say, *"Merci, bonjour."* ("Not bad, praise the Lord.")

Then, after she has given a demonstration of her French, they have her sit down at the pianola to play something—overtures and adagios and finales—so beautiful that it penetrates to the very depth of one's soul! In the meantime the parents ask me to stay for supper and I let them talk me into it. Why not? . . . At the table they serve me the best portions of meat and feed me *tzimmes* even on weekdays. Afterwards, I strike up a conversation with the daughter. "What," I ask, "is your heart's desire—a lawyer, an engineer, a doctor?" "Naturally," she says, "a doctor." And once more she starts jabbering in French with the governess, and at this point the mother has an opportunity to display her daughter's handiwork. "Her embroidery and her knitting are a feast to the eye," she says, "and her kindness, her goodness, her consideration for others—there is no one like her! And quiet—like a dove. And bright—as the day . . ."

And the father, in his turn, traces his pedigree for me. He tells me what a fine family he comes from, and his wife as well. He tells me who his grandfather was, and his great-grandfather, and all his wife's connections. Every one of them of the finest. Rich people, millionaires, famous and celebrated all over the world. "There is not a single common person in our whole family," he assures me. "And not one pauper," his wife adds. "Not a single workingman," he says. "No tailors and no cobblers," she adds. "You'll find no fakes or frauds among us," he tells me. "Or apostates either, I can assure you," she puts in.

In the doorway, when I'm ready to leave and they wish me a good journey, I sigh and let them know how expensive it is to travel these days. Every step costs money. And if he is not obtuse he knows what I mean, and gives me at least enough for expenses . . .

I tell you, my dear friend, that matchmaking is not at all such a bad profession—especially if God ever intercedes and you actually conclude a match! So far, as I have told you, I have not succeeded in marrying anyone off. I have had no luck. At the start everything looks auspicious. It could hardly be better. It was a match predestined since the Six Days of Creation. But at the last moment everything goes wrong. In this case the youth does not care for the maiden; in the other, the girl thinks the groom is too old. This one has too fine a pedigree; that one does not have enough money.

This one wants the moon on a platter; that one doesn't know what he wants. There is plenty of trouble connected with it, and heartaches, and indigestion, I can assure you.

Right now I am on the verge of arranging a couple of matches—naturally with a few partners—which, if the Lord has mercy and they go through, will be something for the whole world to talk about. Both parties come from the wealthiest and finest and oldest families—there is none like them. And the girls are both the greatest beauties. You can't find their equal anywhere. Both are well-educated, gifted, kind, bright, quiet, modest—all the virtues you can think of. And what do I have to offer them? Real merchandise! One—a doctor from Odessa. But he wants no less than thirty thousand *rubles* dowry, and he has a right to it, because according to the practice that he says he has, he should be worth much more. I have another from Byelotzerkiev—a rare find! A bargain at twenty thousand! And another in Yehupetz—only he doesn't want to get married. And a whole flock of young little doctors who are only too anxious to get married.

Besides these I have a pack of lawyers and attorneys and justices at fifteen thousand and ten thousand, and smaller lawyers—young ones just hatched—that you can have for six thousand or five thousand, or even less. On top of that I have a couple of engineers who are already earning a living, and a few engineers still looking for work. And that is not all. I have an assortment of miscellaneous clients, elderly men, relics of past campaigns from Tetrevitz, from Makarevka, from Yampola and from Strishtch, without diplomas, but fine enough specimens, distinguished, skilled, intelligent. In short, there are plenty to pick from. The only trouble is that if the gentleman wants the lady, the lady does not want the gentleman. If the girl is willing, the man is not. Perhaps then you will ask why the man who does not want girl number one will not take number two, and vice versa? I thought of that myself, but it doesn't seem to work. Do you know why? Because strangers are always mixing in. They may be good people. They mean no harm. But they spoil everything. And meanwhile letters are flying back and forth. I send telegrams and receive telegrams every day. The whole world rocks and rolls!

And in the midst of it all, Passover gets in the way, like a bone in the throat, blocking everything. I think it over. My fortune won't run away from me. The merchandise I deal in is not so perishable. Why shouldn't I take a few days off and go to see my family in Kasrilevka? It's been so long since I've been there. It is not fair to my wife and children to be away from them so long. It does not look good to others, and it is even embarrassing to myself. So, to make it short, I have come home for Passover, and that is where I am writing you this letter from.

[4]

Humorous Anecdotes and Jests

The Tune's the Thing

ONE day a rich man received a letter from his son who was studying in another city. Being occupied, he asked his secretary to read it to him. The secretary, who was in a bad mood, read in a disagreeable petulant voice, "Father! Send me some money right away. I need a new pair of shoes and a coat."

When the father heard what his son had written, he cried out, "That impudent lout! How dare he write in such a disrespectful manner to his own father! He won't get one kopek from me!"

A little later, when the secretary had gone away, his wife entered.

"Just see what kind of letter our precious son writes!" the aggrieved father remarked, handing his wife the letter.

When she saw her son's handwriting her mother's heart melted, and she began to read the letter aloud in the tender, supplicating voice she used at prayer, "Father! Send me some money right away. I need a new pair of shoes and a coat."

"Well! That's different!" cried the father. "Now he's asking like a gentleman! I'll send him the money right away."

Züsskind the Tailor

THE Bishop of Salzburg issued a decree that on a certain day the Jews of the principality were to present their champion to hold a dispute with a certain Christian scholar who was a great Bible authority and theologian. The dispute was to take place in the Cathedral Square before the entire populace. Whichever of the two opponents was bested in argument was to lose his life.

A great terror fell upon the Jews when they heard of this. They rent

THE TUNE'S THE THING: Adapted from the *Parables of the Preacher of Dubno.*

their garments and fasted. The Rabbinical Council issued a call that whoever wished to engage in the disputation with the Christian scholar should report to the Chief Rabbi.

But only Züsskind the Tailor showed up.

The communal leaders were filled with consternation. Was this the man to represent them against the most learned priest in the land? But what was there to be done? No one else had come forward for everyone knew it spelled certain death, and here was the town tailor, ready to sacrifice his life for the good of all and for the sanctification of His Name!

The appointed day for the disputation arrived. The populace assembled in the Cathedral Square according to the Bishop's decree. The Bishop then asked the Jewish champion to step forward and begin the disputation.

Said Züsskind the Tailor to the Christian scholar: "If you are such an authority on Jewish lore, then tell me: what is the meaning of the Hebrew words *Lo Idati?*" *

"I don't know," answered the scholar, readily.

"Aha!" cried the tailor exultantly. "Let me put the question to you again: What does *Lo Idati* mean?"

"I don't know!" answered the scholar, this time with some exasperation.

When the Bishop heard the scholar's apparent admission of ignorance for the second time he ordered that the disputation be halted. They then quickly hanged the scholar and the Jews returned home with songs of thanksgiving on their lips. They conducted the tailor in triumph to the rabbi.

"Tell me," asked the rabbi, "how did you hit upon such a clever plan to best the scholar?"

"I'll tell you, Rabbi," replied the tailor. "I looked into the Yiddish translation of the Torah because I do not know any Hebrew, and it said about *Lo Idati:* 'I don't know.' So I figured—if the holy Yiddish Bible translation admits 'I don't know' how can this enemy of Israel know! And, as you see, I judged right."

The Power of a Lie

IN THE town of Tarnopol lived a man by the name of *Reb* Feivel. One day, as he sat in his house deeply absorbed in his Talmud, he heard a loud noise outside. When he went to the window he saw a lot of little pranksters. "Up to some new piece of mischief, no doubt," he thought.

"Children, run quickly to the synagogue," he cried, leaning out and improvising the first story that occurred to him. "You'll see there a sea monster, and what a monster! It's a creature with five feet, three eyes, and a beard like that of a goat, only it's green!"

And sure enough the children scampered off and *Reb* Feivel returned

---

* It means: "I don't know."

to his studies. He smiled into his beard as he thought of the trick he had played on those little rascals.

It wasn't long before his studies were interrupted again, this time by running footsteps. When he went to the window he saw several Jews running.

"Where are you running?" he called out.

"To the synagogue!" answered the Jews. "Haven't you heard? There's a sea monster there—a creature with five legs, three eyes, and a beard like that of a goat, only it's green!"

Reb Feivel laughed with glee, thinking of the trick he had played, and sat down again to his Talmud.

But no sooner had he begun to concentrate when suddenly he heard a dinning tumult outside. And what did he see? A great crowd of men, women and children, all running toward the synagogue.

"What's up?" he cried, sticking his head out of the window.

"What a question! Why, don't you know?" they answered. "Right in front of the synagogue there's a sea monster. It's a creature with five legs, three eyes, and a beard like that of a goat, only it's green!"

And as the crowd hurried by Reb Feivel suddenly noticed that the rabbi himself was among them.

"Lord of the world!" he exclaimed. "If the rabbi himself is running with them surely there must be something happening. Where there's smoke there's fire!"

Without further thought Reb Feivel grabbed his hat, left his house, and also began running.

"Who can tell?" he muttered to himself as he ran, all out of breath, toward the synagogue.

The Merchant from Brisk

A MERCHANT from Brisk ordered a consignment of dry-goods from Lodz. A week later he received the following letter: "We regret we cannot fill this order until full payment has been made on the last one."

The merchant sent his reply: "Please cancel the new order. I cannot wait that long."

Interference

WHILE walking on the street a man felt a stinging blow on his back. He turned around and saw a stranger.

"Hoodlum!" he yelled. "How dare you strike me?"

"Excuse me," apologized the other. "I made a mistake. I could have sworn you were Mendel!"

"And what if I was Mendel?" retorted the other. "Was that a nice thing to do?"

"See here," cried the stranger angrily. "What's the idea of sticking up for Mendel when you don't even know him? Let Mendel take care of himself."

The Biggest Favor

ONE day, while Hitler was horseback riding in a Berlin park, his mount became frightened and ran wild.

"Help! Help!" cried the Fuehrer.

A passerby leaped forward, caught the reins of the runaway horse, and brought it to a standstill.

"My good man," said Hitler gratefully. "Do you know who I am? I am your Fuehrer! And who are you?"

"I am Israel Kohn, a Jew," answered his rescuer, all a-tremble.

Hitler looked startled for a moment. Then he said, "You may be a Jew but you're a brave man! You've saved my life and I want to reward you! Just tell me what favor you'd like me to do for you."

"Favor!" muttered Israel Kohn, despondently. "The biggest favor you can do for me is not to breathe a word about this to a soul!"

Secret Strategy

DURING the first World War a Jewish soldier greatly distinguished himself by the large number of prisoners he took. Late at night, when all firing had ceased and everything was still, he would cautiously crawl over the top into No Man's Land. Before long he would return, followed by a number of prisoners. He did this with baffling regularity all night long until dawn broke. No one could understand how he managed it, and he wouldn't divulge his secret even to his superior officers.

When the General of his division heard of it he ordered him up for questioning.

"My boy," he said sternly, "out with your secret! If you can take prisoners that easily it's your duty to tell us how so we can teach others."

"General," the young soldier confessed, embarrassed, "my method is not according to the Army Manual. I do simply this. Late at night I crawl to the nearest enemy trench. Then I call out in Yiddish: 'Jews, wherever you are! We need a *minyan* of ten men for reciting the *Kaddish* prayer over a dead comrade.' Immediately, Jews come piling over the top from the German trenches and I lead them back to camp."

Mother-in-Law Relativity

"HELLO, Mrs. Levine! How are you?"

"Fine and dandy!"

"And how's your daughter Shirley?"

"God bless her, she's fine! What a wonderful husband she has! He doesn't let her put her hand in cold water all day long! She lies in bed until twelve and then her maid serves her breakfast in bed. At three she goes shopping in Saks Fifth Avenue and at five she has cocktails at the Ritz. And dresses just like a movie star! What do you say to such *mazel*?"

"And how's your son? I hear he's married."

"Yes, he's married! Poor boy—he has no *mazel*. He's married to one of those fancy-shmancy girls. What do you think she does all day long? She doesn't do a thing! The good-for-nothing! She sleeps until noon. Then she has to have her breakfast brought to her in bed. And do you think she takes care of her home? No! She has to shop all afternoon and waste her husband's hard-earned money on dresses like a movie star. How do you think she winds up the day? Guzzling cocktails! Call that a wife?"

All Agents Are Alike

ONCE there was an old couple. They did poorly, and even suffered hunger. At last, driven by desperation, the old man said to his wife, "Malke, let's write God a letter."

So they sat down and wrote God a letter, imploring Him for help. They signed it, sealed it carefully, and wrote the name of God on the envelope.

"How do you suppose we can mail this letter?" the old woman asked in perplexity.

"God is everywhere," her pious husband replied. "Our letter is bound to reach Him any way we send it."

So he went outside and threw it into the wind which whirled it away down the street.

It happened that at that very moment a charitable rich man was out walking and the wind blew the letter towards him. He picked it up out of curiosity, read it, and was touched by the trusting innocence of the old couple as much as by their sad plight. He resolved to help them.

A little later he knocked on their door.

"Does *Reb* Nute live here?" he asked.

"I am *Reb* Nute," replied the old man.

The rich man beamed at him.

"In that case, I've some business to transact with you," he said. "I want you to know that God received your letter a few minutes ago. As I am

His personal agent in White Russia He gave me a hundred rubles for you."

"What do you say to that, Malke?" exclaimed the old man with joy. "You see, God did get our letter!"

The old couple took the money and showered their blessings on God's agent in White Russia.

When they were alone again the old man's face became clouded.

"What's wrong now?" his wife asked him.

"I've a suspicion, Malke," answered the old man thoughtfully, "that that agent wasn't altogether honest; he was a little too smooth. Well, you know how agents are! Likely as not God probably gave him two hundred rubles for us but that swindler must have taken off fifty percent as his commission!"

All About the Elephant

A PROFESSOR of zoology at Harvard some years ago asked his graduate students, among whom were several foreigners, to write papers on the elephant.

A German student wrote: "An Introduction to the Bibliography for the Study of the Elephant."

A French student wrote: "The Love-Life of the Elephant."

An English student wrote: "Elephant Hunting."

An American student wrote: "Breeding Bigger and Better Elephants."

There was also a Jewish student in the class. He wrote: "The Elephant and the Jewish Problem."

Babe Ruth and the Jewish Question

A LITTLE Jewish boy on the East Side of New York came home from school and with great excitement told his patriarchal grandfather: "Grandpa! Imagine! Babe Ruth hit three homers today!"

"Tell me," asked the old man, "what this Babe Ruth did—is it good for the Jews?"

Foolish Woman!

WHEN Rabbi Elimelech of Lizhensk sat at table with his disciples, a Jew from Lublin began to tell the following story:

"The other day, near my town, they fished a drowned man out of the lake. No one knew who he was but, after several days, an old woman showed up and identified the body as that of her husband.

" 'Have you any signs by which you can identify him?' our rabbi asked her.

" 'Of course I have!' replied the old woman. 'I have two signs. My husband was very ticklish; he stammered, too!' "

At this point Rabbi Elimelech and his disciples laughed heartily, but loudest of all laughed the rabbi's *shammes*.

The rabbi was curious to know his reason for laughing so uproariously.

"Tell me, *shammes*, what makes you laugh so?" he asked him.

"Hah, hah, hah!" roared the *shammes*, doubling up with laughter. "What a fool that woman was! Did she think her husband was the only person in the world who was ticklish and who stammered?"

The Captain

HE HAD always been a simple and unassuming man until he suddenly became rich. Looking around he noticed that the very rich owned yachts. Clearly, to own a yacht was a badge of wealth. So why shouldn't he own a yacht too? He therefore bought himself one and appropriately rigged himself out in a fancy "captain's" uniform.

For the first trip he invited his old father and mother from the Bronx. They seemed impressed but slightly dubious of his new glory.

"What do you say to me now, mama?" cried her son proudly, pointing to his new uniform. "I'm a regular captain now!"

His old mother smiled indulgently and murmured, "That's fine, that's fine!"

"But mama," protested her son, looking a little hurt, "you don't seem very enthusiastic about it."

"Listen, Benny dear," replied his mother, "by papa you're a captain, by me you're a captain, by you you're a captain—but, believe me, by a *captain* you're no captain!"

Ready for Everything

A TALMUD student was sleeping in a strange house. At night he was awakened by a noise, so he cried out: "Scat! Scat! *Gewalt! Gewalt! Shema Yisroel! Shema Yisroel!*"

"What's the meaning of your gibberish?" his host called out to him in surprise.

"Very simple," explained the Talmud student. "I wish to cover all eventualities. If it was a cat—'scat! scat!' would drive it away. If it was a thief—'*gewalt! gewalt!*' would frighten him off. If it was a ghost— then '*Shema Yisroel!*' would protect me."

Sermon Without End

ON AND on the preacher droned. It seemed as though he would never end his sermon. He was so carried away by his own eloquence that he became unaware of his audience. They yawned and twisted restlessly in their seats.

With eyes closed the preacher was describing in attractive detail the joys the pious would find in Paradise. He therefore did not notice the members of the congregation tiptoeing out one by one.

When the last one had departed the *shammes* walked up to the preacher and tugging at his sleeve, he said, "Rabbi, here's the key to the synagogue. When you get through, do you mind locking up?"

Also a Minyan-Man

"WHAT is your business?" asked the judge of the witness, a little bearded old Jew.

"I'm a *minyan*-man."

"What's that?" asked the judge.

"When there are nine persons in the synagogue and I join them they are ten," answered the old man.

"What kind of talk is that?" snapped the judge, impatiently. "When there are nine persons, and *I* join them, there are also ten."

A look of delight appeared on the old Jew's face. Bending over towards the judge he asked in a confidential whisper, "Also a Jew?"

When Your Life Is in Danger

A JEWISH merchant once came on matters of business to the estate of a Polish landowner in the country. He found the landowner at breakfast. On the table were hot cutlets and a bottle of wine. The host politely asked the merchant to take a seat at the table and urged him to eat a pork chop. The Jew thanked him but declined.

"Don't you like pork chops?"

"On the contrary, I would like them very much but they're forbidden to us Jews."

The landowner laughed. "I know, I know," said he, "you call them *tref*."

After that he poured him a glass of wine. Again the Jew declined with thanks. That, too, was forbidden.

Out of patience, the landowner exclaimed, "Your God certainly is a hard-hearted one! He puts upon your shoulders a burden too heavy to carry. Tell me what, for instance, would you do if you got lost in a forest, had nothing to eat for several days, and began to feel that you were about to collapse from hunger? Suppose somebody came along and handed you food that was *tref*—would you eat it?"

"That's entirely another matter," answered the Jew. "Our Law makes provision for emergencies where human life and health are at stake."

Suddenly, the landowner jumped to his feet. He glared murderously at the Jew and, whipping out a revolver, pointed it at him, crying, "Drink this wine, or I shoot!"

Before you could say *Bim* the Jew had downed the wine in one gulp. Still pointing the revolver at him, the landowner poured him a second glass. Before you could say *Bam* the Jew had gulped it down.

Putting down the revolver, the landowner said smiling to the Jew, "Don't be angry with me, I beg you, I was only joking. Assure me you're not angry."

"Why shouldn't I be angry—I have every right to be angry," retorted the Jew. "You should have started your joke a little earlier, when you first got around to the pork chops!"

They Misled the Gendarme

WHEN the Czar had issued the infamous May Laws against the Jews in 1881, three Jews in a little Ukrainian town gave vent to their indignation.

"He is an idot, a nitwit!" jeered one.

"He guzzles vodka like a swine!" sneered another.

"Not only that, but he's a thief! He collects taxes and puts them in his own pocket!" raged the third.

No sooner had he said this than a gendarme appeared as though he had sprung out of the ground.

"Seditious Jews!" he roared angrily. "Just wait—you'll pay dearly for insulting our Holy Czar! Come with me—you're under arrest!"

So the three Jews, trembling with fear, went with the gendarme to the police station.

"How dare you insult our beloved Czar?" shrieked the commissioner of police.

"Who was talking about the Czar?" replied the Jews innocently. "We were talking about Kaiser Wilhelm, that enemy of Israel!"

The police commissioner softened.

"Oh, in that case—be more careful the way you talk next time. How was the gendarme to know? When you said 'idiot . . . drunkard . . . thief' . . . he naturally thought you meant the Czar."

Very Understandable

A PREACHER once came to a village and held forth in the synagogue on the Sabbath afternoon. A great crowd turned out to hear him. In the village lived a man who was a bit of a scholar. Seeing that everybody was going to hear the preacher, he went too.

The following morning the preacher met this man on the street.

"How did you like my sermon?" he asked him.

"All I can tell you is that I could not fall asleep after I heard you preach."

"Did my preaching have such an effect on you?"

"Not at all, only when I sleep during the day I can't close an eye at night!"

Commentary

Two old men sat silently over their glasses of tea for what might have been, or at any rate seemed, hours. At last, one spoke: *"Oy, veh!"*

The other said: "You're telling me!"

Comfort

"WHAT s news, Mr. Goldstein? What does your son write from Detroit?"

"Ai! Thank you for asking. Believe me—it's bitter. His wife died recently. She was *nebich* a young woman, a mother of three children, the prettiest little doves you've ever seen! But now, blessed be His name, he has only two left—the third fell sick and died. And his business is going to the devil! He had a house, but it burned down. Burglars looted his little shop so that nothing remains of any value. In one word—he has been left *nebich* without a shirt on his back. It's a bitter misfortune! But let me tell you—*does he write a letter in Hebrew! Ai!* It's a pleasure to read—I'm telling you!"

Cold Hospitality

A RICH man was annoyed because every time he sat down to dinner the door opened and in came a certain *schnorrer*. What was the rich man to do? He had to invite him to dinner.

One night at the usual dinner hour when his steady customer called again, the rich man suddenly asked him, "Do you like cold noodles?"

"Oh, I love cold noodles!" replied the *schnorrer*, enthusiastically.

"Fine!" snapped the host. "Come back tomorrow night for them. They're hot just now."

Conversation Piece

"How are you?"
  "Mm-mm."
  "I mean, how is business?"
  "Tsk-tsk!"
  "And how's your wife?"
  "Eh-eh!"
  "And your children?"
  "Nn-nn!"
  "Well, good-bye! It certainly was good to see you. Believe me—there's nothing like a good heart-to-heart talk with a friend to get your troubles off your chest!"

The Botanist

MOE and Abe, associates in the dress business, took their vacation together at an expensive hotel in the Catskills.

As soon as they were settled in their room, the cards were out and play was begun. Gin rummy continued until dinner. Then Moe noted the beauties of the lounge, soft rugs, polished floors, chairs and tables.

"What dopes we are!" he proclaimed to Abe. "We're paying $25 a day and just sitting up in a lousy room. Tomorrow we play here."

And so they did. But late in the afternoon Moe glanced up from his hand and noticed the porch, with comfortable wicker furniture.

"Look," he said, "we're cooped up in here for $25 a day when there's a beautiful porch. Tomorrow we play there."

And so they did. But as the sun was sinking, Moe looked over the rail and saw the beautiful rolling, shaded lawns.

"Look," he said, "grass! Here we are, sitting on a porch and there's all that beautiful grass."

"All right," said Abe, indifferently, "tomorrow we'll play on the grass."

At the end of the next day's play on the grass, Abe noticed a little pink flower close by.

"Look, Moe," he said, "a flower, a beautiful flower."

"You're right," Moe agreed, "it's a beautiful flower. What kind of flower do you think it is?"

"How should *I* know," said Abe, "am I a milliner?"

Lines Crossed

A JEWISH housewife in the Bronx answered the telephone and was astounded to hear an almost unintelligibly British accent say, "This is

Mrs. Astor's secret'ry. She wishes to confirm her luncheon engagement with Mrs. Vanderbilt at the Colony today. Is that correct?"

"*Oy*, mister!" gasped the housewife, almost breathless. "Have you got a wrong number!"

Stop Me If . . .

AN old Jew, seated at the end of a sparsely filled subway car, was making strange and elaborate gestures and grimaces, interspersed with laughter and deprecatory hand wavings.

A fellow passenger, overcome with curiosity approached the old man, asking, "Is something wrong? Is there anything I can do?"

"No, no!" said the gesturer, "thank God, I'm all right. But when I travel I have the habit of passing the time telling myself stories."

"Well," said the other, "why do you make such faces and gestures, as if you were in pain?"

"Oh, that!" said the old man. "Every time I start a new story I have to tell myself that I've heard it before."

A Livelihood

LEVINE bought a diamond and emerald ring for his wife. At lunch he showed it to his friend, Siegel.

"What did you pay for it?" asked Siegel.

"Five hundred dollars."

"I like it," said Siegel. "I'll give you seven hundred, that's $200 profit for you."

So it was done. But the next day Levine regretted it. His wife would have liked it. He went to Siegel and offered to buy it back for $800.

Siegel sold. After all, it was a quick $100 profit. But he had become attached to the ring and phoned Levine, later, saying, "Look, if you'll sell it back to me I'll give you a thousand for it." So it was again Siegel's. And Levine joyously pocketed the extra $200.

Before Siegel could present it to his own wife, his partner, Berman, saw it and offered $1500. The ring changed hands.

The next day, Levine again sought the ring, offering Siegel $1200.

"I've sold it to Berman for $1500," Siegel explained.

"You idiot," cried Levine. "How could you do such a thing! From that ring we were both making such a nice living!"

A Full Accounting

WHEN Mr. Berg came home his wife accosted him. "Sam, give me five dollars."

"What happened to the five dollars I gave you this morning?"

"Do you want me to give you an accounting?"

"Yes," said Mr. Berg.

"All right," said his wife. "A dollar here and a dollar there is two dollars."

"Yes."

"And before you turn around is another two dollars."

"Yes."

"And the last dollar—I won't tell you!"

Mother Love

A MOTHER tenderly guided her four-year-old Sarale down Second Avenue. As they crossed 14th Street, the child sneezed.

"God bless you, my sweet!" breathed Mama, patting the child's head.

As they crossed 13th Street, the child sneezed again.

"Ah, may your health be a thing of wonder, my jewel," Mama sweetly sighed.

At 12th Street, the child sneezed again and once more Mama patted her head and uttered a fervent *"Gesundheit!"*

At 11th Street, little Sarale sneezed again, and received a smart slap in the face. "Go to the devil!" cried Mama. "You're catching another cold!"

What a Pity

PERHAPS the young man had not set foot in a synagogue for a long time. He seemed ill at ease. An old man thought he would try to help the stranger.

It proved to be quite simple: the young man's wife had given birth to a girl and he couldn't decide after whom to name her.

"My son," said the patriarch, "it is the custom of our people to name children after departed members of the family . . . for instance, your father, your mother, your brother, your sister, or your grandmother or grandfather."

"But they're all alive," said the young father.

"Oh, that's too bad," said the helpful soul.

Initiative

A JEW was engaged once to drive a bus on a lower East Side line in New York. As he handed in his receipts at the end of the first day he looked plainly discouraged. They amounted to less than ten dollars.

The following day he started out on his route early in the morning but somehow he eluded the inspectors. Very much puzzled they tried to find out what had become of him and his bus.

Finally, towards nightfall, the new bus driver appeared at the terminal grinning happily. With a flourish he handed the cashier one hundred and nine dollars.

"What's this? What's this?" the cashier exclaimed in amazement. "We never had so much money made on that run before. How did you do it?"

"Very simple," answered the driver. "I said to myself: 'What's the use of wasting my time on this God-forsaken route where there are hardly any passengers?' I'm not such a fool! I turned my bus into 14th Street and, believe me, it's a gold mine over there!"

No Admittance

ONE of the synagogue's chief means of obtaining revenue is the sale of seats for the high Holy Days. This is always done in advance since the carrying and handling of money on these days is forbidden to orthodox Jews. For the same reason, it is customary to employ non-Jews as keepers of the gate.

One *Yom Kippur,* a ticket-taker at a Brooklyn house of worship was confronted by a Jew with no ticket who pleaded to be allowed to enter.

"No ticket, no admission," the guard said, firmly.

"But I've got to see my partner, Liebowitz, in the fourth row," insisted the man. "It's urgent."

"For the last time," said the guard, "I'm telling you, no ticket, no admission to this synagogue!"

"But it's a business matter," persisted the man. "I'll just be a minute. I swear to you . . . just a minute."

"Well, if it's a business matter," said the guard, finally weakening, "I'll let you in for a minute. . . . But remember—no praying!"

Whose Drawers?

DURING his first visit to America, Israel Zangwill, the noted Anglo-Jewish writer, was the guest of Jacob Schiff, the banker-philanthropist. To his dismay, Zangwill found the weather in New York too balmy for his heavy English woolies. Schiff, a conservative banker of the old school, promptly lent him a pair of his own jean underdrawers, the kind with tapes around the ankles.

Blithely Zangwill strolled down Fifth Avenue, basking in the fine afternoon sunshine, completely unaware that the tapes on his underwear had gotten loose and were trailing on the ground.

As he passed a corner a policeman called out to him, "Hey, Mister, the strings of your drawers are hanging out!"

For a moment Zangwill was taken aback.

"You're mistaken," he finally replied, recovering from his embarrassment, "they're not *my* drawers, they're Mr. Jacob Schiff's drawers."

Shortcut

FELD and Bein met on the street. "*Sholom aleichem*," said Feld, politely. "Go to hell," said Bein.

"Look," Feld said indignantly, "I speak nicely to you and you tell me to go to hell. What's the idea?"

"I'll tell you," said Bein. "If I answered you politely you would ask where am I going, and I would tell you I'm going to the 8th Street baths.

"You would tell me I'm crazy, the Avenue A baths are better, and I would say *you're* crazy, the 8th Street baths are better, and you would call me a damn fool and I would tell you to go to hell.

"This way it's simpler. I tell you right away go to hell, and it's finished."

A Matter of Degree

As THEY were driving by Calvary Cemetery, Goldman suddenly turned to Meyerson, saying, "If you don't mind, I want to stop here so I can visit a grave."

"But it's a *goyish* cemetery!" Myerson said, surprised.

"Just the same," said Goldman, "I want to go in."

So they went in and walked until they arrived at a family plot marked "Reilly." At its entrance was a block of granite bearing the names:

> James Joseph Reilly
> Francis Xavier Reilly
> John James Reilly
> Mary Martha Reilly
> William John Reilly
> Rebeccah Reilly

Pointing to the last name, Goldman said, "This was my daughter."

"Your daughter?" exclaimed Meyerson dismayed. "She might as well be dead!"

Retorts

Rabbinical Limits

THE saintly rabbi was deep in his devotions, praying with his face turned to the wall. Suddenly, a practical joker came up to him from behind and smacked him on his backside. Startled, the rabbi turned around.

"Oh, Rabbi!" cried the joker, his teeth chattering with fright. "The truth is . . . your back was turned . . . I didn't recognize you . . . I thought it was somebody else . . . Please forgive me . . . I didn't mean to . . ."

"Never mind!" the rabbi interrupted him. "There's no harm done—I'm no rabbi in my rear end."

Montefiore and the Anti-Semite

ONCE the great Baron Montefiore of London visited the Emperor of Austria. At dinner, one of the Imperial Ministers, who was an anti-Semite, gave an account of his travels in equatorial Africa.

"I didn't see one pig or Jew there," he remarked maliciously to the champion of the Jews.

"In that case," answered Montefiore, "it would be advisable that Your Excellency and I go there."

Animated Conversation

SHOLOM ALEICHEM, the celebrated Yiddish writer, was once seen by a friend talking to himself on the street.

"For heaven's sake," cried the friend, "do you realize you're talking to yourself?"

"And what if I do?" retorted Sholom Aleichem. "When at last I've found a clever person to talk to—do you have to butt in?"

The Snob

IN A certain town there lived two brothers. One was a rabbi—the other was a thief. The rabbi was ashamed of his brother and always gave him a wide berth. One day, as the two met by accident on the street, the rabbi deliberately snubbed his brother. This enraged the thief who reproached him:

"What makes you so stuck up? If I were stuck up I'd have reason—
my brother is a rabbi! But you have a brother who is a thief, so why do
you put on airs!"

Pessimist and Optimist

THE eminent German-Jewish physician and philosopher, Marcus Hertz,
used to go calling on his patients in a carriage which bore his monogram
M.H. on the door.

"Why do you have such a suggestive monogram on your carriage?" his
friend Heinrich Heine, the poet, chided him. "Don't you know that in
Hebrew *M.H.* stands for the *Malech Hamoves* (The Angel of Death)?"

"*Ach,* Heine, what a pessimist you are!" laughed the old doctor. "Don't
you know that in Hebrew *M.H.* also stands for *Mechayai Hameissim* (to
give life to the dead)."

Why Not?

THE prosecutor began to cross-examine the witness: "Do you know the
accused?"

"How should I know him?"

"Did he ever try to borrow money from you?"

"Why should he borrow money from me?"

Out of patience, the judge asked the witness, "Why do you answer
every question of the prosecutor with another question?"

"Why not?"

Proper Distinctions

THE Jewish communal official was summoned to court as a witness in a
case.

"*Shochet* Levy!" called out the Polish judge.

"I beg your pardon, Your Honor—my name is not *Shochet* Levy," the
witness demurred. "I am Levy, the communal official."

But the judge was obstinate.

"In my records," he persisted, "I read that, among other things, you
are also a slaughterer. I, therefore, am justified in calling you '*Shochet*
Levy.'"

"Your Honor," replied the witness with dignity, "when I stand before
the court I'm *Pan* Levy. When I stand before my congregation and
conduct the service I'm Cantor Levy and, when I stand before an ox,
I'm *Shochet* Levy."

Evil to Him . . .

A TRAVELLING charity collector was invited by a hospitable villager to spend the night. Before the stranger went off to the synagogue for evening prayer, his host noticed with surprise that he clamped a padlock on the box in which he kept his money. Offended by this, his host went and put his own padlock on the box.

When the charity collector saw the unfamiliar padlock on his box he was chagrined and asked his host, "What's the idea of putting a padlock on my box?"

"What do you mean 'padlock'? There are two padlocks!"

"One of them is mine."

"Why did you put it on?"

"W-e-l-l! You know how things are . . . I'm away from home . . . among strangers . . . one has to be careful! Things could be taken out of my box!"

"You're absolutely right!" answered his host. "I feel the same way about it. You know how it is . . . a stranger in the house . . . valuable things around . . . one has to be careful! Things could be put into your box."

Essential Trade

WHILE patrolling the streets of Saint Petersburg two Czarist policemen arrested a Jew who had no residence permit. When the Jew came before the inspector he defended his right to live in the capital on the grounds that he was an essential worker. Not wishing to take the responsibility of a decision on himself the inspector referred the matter to the Governor of the city.

"What is this trade of yours that's so essential?" the Governor asked the Jew when he was brought before him.

"I make ink!" modestly answered the Jew.

"What's so essential about that?" asked the Governor contemptuously. "Why, even I could make ink if I wanted to!"

"That's fine!" beamed the Jew. "In that case, your Excellency has the right to live in Saint Petersburg too!"

The Henpecked Husband

A HENPECKED husband came to the rabbi to ask for a divorce.

"How can you, a pious man, think of such a thing!" the rabbi rebuked him sternly. "Don't you know what the Talmud says. 'When a man divorces his wife not only the angels but the very stones weep!'"

"Listen, Rabbi," replied the dissatisfied husband, "if the angels and the stones want to weep, let them. I want to rejoice!"

BITTER JESTS

INTRODUCTION

The bitter jests of the Jews are dipped in the gall and wormwood of their experience. Since the Book of Proverbs, the Jewish folk have been saying: "Even in laughter the heart is sorrowful, and the end of that mirth is heaviness." This type of humor, of course, is not unique to the Jews, but among them, however, it has acquired deep undertones that stamp it with originality. Jewish bitter jests exude a certain cosmic irony. They show the rational intelligence of the Jew staggered by the cruel incongruities of his enemies' conduct.

Most of the themes of these bitter jests treat of the luckless fate of the Jews. Their mirth has a sardonic bite as it contemplates the bizarre helplessness of their position in a hostile world. An anonymous Cervantes must have conceived the story, *The Life of a Jew* (see JEWISH SALT, page 17), which makes bitterly merry over some of the so-called "protectors" of the Jews who, out of a pretended solicitude for them, inflict on them as much harm as their worst enemies. The ruefulness of the Jew in the face of the violation of every civilized value, is sharply drawn in the anecdote, *The Independent Chicken*, which describes an unequal encounter with Nazi storm-troopers. The helpless victim tries to joke himself out of his fix, but his humor rings absurd in his own ears, so outraged is his intelligence.

Where else could there have arisen such grim jests as *God's Mercy* and *They Shoot First* but out of the special conditions of Jewish life? They are timeless in their application, for the incidents they relate might easily have occurred in almost any age in the Jewish past. The story of *Hitler's Circus*, for instance, which has run through innumerable variants, could just as well have held true in Roman days when, to amuse the "master-race," live Jews were thrown to the lions in the circus.

N. A.

The Independent Chicken

A JEW, carrying a chicken under his arm, was walking along the street in Frankfort-am-Main. He was stopped by a Nazi storm trooper who demanded, "Where are you going, Jew?"

"To the store, to buy my chicken some food."

"And what will you feed this chicken?"

"Corn."

"Corn, eh? Germans go hungry while you, Jew, feed your chicken on German corn!" So saying, the trooper beat the Jew, then went on his way.

A few minutes later another trooper stopped the Jew. "Where are you going, dog?"

"To the store, to buy my chicken some food."

"Food, eh? What kind?"

"Some wheat, maybe."

"Wheat! Germans are starving and you give your Jewish chicken wheat!" And he beat him severely.

The poor, battered Jew continued on his way and was challenged by yet another trooper. "Where are you going?"

"To get my chicken something to eat."

"So! And what will you feed this chicken?"

"Listen," said the Jew, desperately, "I don't know. I'll give him a couple of *pfennigs* and he'll buy what he likes!"

Applied Psychology

IN A little Southern town where the Klan was riding again, a Jewish tailor had the temerity to open his little shop on the main street. To drive him out of town the Kleagle of the Klan set a gang of little ragamuffins to annoy him.

Day after day they stood at the entrance of his shop.

"Jew! Jew!" they hooted at him.

The situation looked serious for the tailor. He took the matter so much to heart that he began to brood and spent sleepless nights over it. Finally, out of desperation, he cooked up a plan.

The following day, when the little hoodlums came to jeer at him, he came to the door and said to them, "From today on any boy who calls me 'Jew' will get a dime from me."

Then he put his hand in his pocket and gave each boy a dime.

Delighted with their booty the boys came back the following day and began to shrill: "Jew! Jew!"

The tailor came out smiling. He put his hand in his pocket and gave each of the boys a nickel, saying, "A dime is too much—I can afford only a nickel today."

The boys went away satisfied because, after all, a nickel was money too.

However, when they returned the next day to hoot at him the tailor gave them only a penny each.

"Why do we get only a penny today?" they yelled.

"That's all I can afford today."

"But two days ago you gave us a dime, and yesterday we got a nickel. It's not fair, mister!"

"Take it or leave it. That's all you're going to get!"
"Do you think we're going to call you 'Jew' for one lousy penny?"
"So don't!"
And they didn't.

Handicapped

AN OLD patriarchal Jew from a small Polish town was on his way to
Warsaw. Opposite him in the train sat a Jew-hating "Pilsudski Colonel"
with his dog.

The officer openly showed his contempt for the old Jew. Whenever he
spoke to his dog he called him "Yankel." But the Jew said nothing.
Finally, it got under his skin.

"What a pity that the poor dog has a Jewish name!" he muttered.

"Why so?" asked the Colonel.

"With such a name as 'Yankel' he just has no chance!" replied the
Jew. "It's a real handicap. Without it—who knows? He could even
become a colonel in Pilsudski's army!"

God's Mercy

A GREAT calamity threatened the little Ukrainian village. Shortly before
the Passover holidays a young peasant girl had been found murdered.
Those who hated the Jews quickly took advantage of the unhappy incident
and went about among the peasants, inflaming them with the slander that
the Jews had killed the girl in order to use her Christian blood for making
matzos. The fury of the peasants knew no bounds.

A report spread like wildfire throughout the village that a pogrom was
in the offing.

Dismayed by the news the pious ran to the synagogue. They rent their
garments, and prostrated themselves before the Holy Ark. As they were
sending up their prayers for divine intercession, the shammes ran in breathlessly.

"Brothers—brothers!" he gasped. "I have wonderful news for you!
We've just discovered, God be praised, that the murdered girl was Jewish!"

They Shoot First

A TRAVELING circus once came to a Jewish town. It had all kinds of performing animals, among them a bear. One day the bear broke out of its
cage. Thereupon, the chief of police issued an order that the bear should
be shot on sight.

The news that the bear was on the loose frightened the inhabitants of the town. One Jew said to another, "I'm leaving town!"

"What for?"

"What do you mean 'what for'? Haven't you heard the police chief's order to shoot the bear on sight?"

"Well, you're no bear."

"That's what you say! Before you know it some Jew will be shot. Only afterwards they'll find out he's no bear. . . ."

Rabbi Mendel's Comparison

RABBI MENDEL of Libavitch frequently went to St. Petersburg to plead the cause of the Jews at the Court of the Czar. On one of those visits he was taken to task by one of the Imperial Ministers.

"How do you explain, Rabbi," asked the Minister mockingly, "that your Talmud is full of the grossest exaggerations? Can you think of anything more preposterous than the story about the dying whale who leaped out of the sea and laid waste to sixty towns?"

Rabbi Mendel smiled and answered, "Not so long ago, Your Excellency, you yourself dipped your pen in ink once and signed a decree driving out all the Jews from six hundred towns. Now, just imagine, what might a future historian write about this event? He might say: 'With one drop of ink on his pen His Excellency drowned all the Jews in six hundred Russian towns.' Would that be a gross exaggeration?"

Sedition Saved Him

A JEW was drowning in the Dnieper River. He cried for help. Two Czarist policemen ran up. When they saw it was a Jew, they said, "Let the Jew drown!"

When the man saw his strength was ebbing he shouted with all his might, "Down with the Czar!"

Hearing such seditious words, the policemen plunged in, pulled him out, and arrested him.

Hitler's Circus

A CIRCUS came to a Bavarian town shortly after Hitler decreed the Nuremberg laws against the Jews. Posters were pasted up all over the town announcing the various attractions but stressing the main feature which was to consist of a man dressed in the skin of a lion who would enter the cage of a tiger to wrestle with him.

The circus had advertised for a man to do this dangerous job, but the only applicant to show up was a Jew with the degrading yellow badge on his arm.

"Why, you're a Jew!" exclaimed the manager in amazement.

"Who else but a Jew would accept such a job?" replied the applicant bitterly. "No one will give me any employment because of my race."

"Aren't you afraid?" the manager asked with a laugh. "This is dangerous—you may be killed by the tiger!"

"Yes, I know, but it doesn't matter," replied the Jew wearily. "I have to take this chance for my starving family."

And so the Jew was hired.

On the day of the opening a great crowd turned out to see the main feature; it promised to be very exciting indeed. The circus was filled to the tent-top.

When the main feature came on the Jew appeared. He was trembling in every limb and, before the very eyes of the spectators, he put on a lion's skin. Then, roaring like a real lion and crawling on all-fours, he opened the tiger's cage and dashed in. As he came face to face with the terrible tiger and looked into his cruel green eyes he was frantic with fear.

"It's all over with me now," he said to himself and he cried out in an unearthly voice the creed Jews recite in the face of death:

"*Shema Yisroel!* Hear O Israel!—"

"*Adonoy Elohenu adonoy echod!* The Lord our God, the Lord is One," fervently finished the tiger.

"Why you scared me out of my wits—I thought you were a real tiger!" the lion rebuked him.

"Listen, uncle," snorted the tiger. "What makes you think you're the only Jew in Germany trying to make a living?"

Wasted Protection

GOTTLIEB, the proprietor of a little candy-store, had his money deposited in a savings bank. When business began going badly he went to the bank, drew his last $73.19 and had his account closed. As he walked out with reluctant steps, feeling sad and let down by the world, he saw the armed guard at the door. Impulsively he walked up to him and said, "My friend, for my part you can go home—there's nothing to guard anymore!"

Pity

LITTLE Mary McHale liked the boy who sat next to her in school and talked of him incessantly to her mother. "What is he?" she asked, one day.

"Why, he's an American, of course, just like you," said the mother.

"I know that," answered Mary, "but what else is he?"

"Oh," said her mother, "that! Why, he's a Jew."

"So young," mused little Mary, "and already a Jew . . ."

PART FOUR
Tales and Legends

〖 1 〗

Biblical Sidelights

INTRODUCTION

Jewish religious lore was never fully frozen into canon. It was in a constant state of organic growth and left room for further elaboration and interpretive deepening. This dynamic purpose was served by the vast literature of the *Midrash*. The *Midrash* attempted to penetrate into the spirit of the Bible by revealing its inner meanings which were not in literal evidence in the text. The Talmud describes the expository method of the *Midrash* as: "A hammer which awakens the slumbering sparks in the rock." This it tried to do, as we have already noted, by means of legends, parables, myths, fables and ethical sayings.

This body of folklore came into being because the masses of the people found the Scriptural text insufficient for their understanding. The folk were eager for deeper and more interior explanations of the characters and incidents recorded in the Bible. This need may be seen from the fact that the voluminous literature of the *Midrash* was in continuous growth until about the time of the Crusades.

The mass-mind had a natural inclination to seek a personal identity with its national heroes. This resulted in a remarkable individualization in the *Midrash* writings of all outstanding Biblical worthies from Adam down to Jonah and his whale. It goes without saying that the *Midrash* hardly wields the same religious authority as Scripture. Nonetheless, its very vivid characterizations of Bible personages, with its added wealth of details and incidents, have in many ways superseded the Scripture versions in the folk-fancy. It is both the nature and the power of folklore that the people themselves serve as the recreators of that which they are taught.

Not always does the *Midrash* legend follow closely the Bible text. Frequently the unknown folk poet finds in some general situation indicated in Scripture, a convenient pretext for his narrative creations. Thus God's fashioning of the world as recounted in Genesis gave him the opportunity to weave such exquisite allegories as *The Secret of Power* [see JEWISH SALT, page 19] and *The First Tear*. With its celebrated informality the *Midrash* even offers leeway for banter. A folk-humorist, who wished to make merry over certain failings allegedly peculiar to women, even com-

446

posed a tongue-in-cheek "takeoff" on the Bible text which deals with God's creation of Eve out of one of Adam's ribs.

In the entire history of the Jewish people there was no personality that left its stamp on the Jewish consciousness as indelibly as Moses. The folk regarded him not only as its greatest hero, its supreme prophet, its law-giver and its ruler, but also as its teacher. That is why for three thousand years Jews have referred to him as *Mosheh Rabbenu* (Moses, Our Teacher). The love and veneration of the people for him in every generation knew no bounds. Jews were drawn to him by those ties of intimacy created by the need of a weak and persecuted people for a protector-father. For them he possessed all the intellectual and moral qualities required for such a role. He it was who had led them out of the Land of Bondage; he had stilled their hunger and quenched their thirst during the forty years of wandering in the wilderness; and he had shielded them against God's wrath when they offended Him with their misdeeds.

Of all the stirring Moses legends in the *Midrash,* that which describes his solitary death on the summit of Mount Pisgah has lain closest to the hearts of the people. The Bible account of it troubled them. They found it hard to understand why, after having suffered and battled all his life on their and God's behalf, he should have been condemned by the Divine Will to die at the very gates of the Promised Land. The moral question for many became challenging: was there no reward for virtue? If Moses, the most righteous man who ever lived, was denied the just attainment of his strivings, how could they, sinners and backsliders all, ever hope for forgiveness and the peace of the World-to-Come?

Out of these troubled gropings of the Jewish folk-mind, out of its compelling need to reconcile divine justice with the limitations of life, emerged the *Midrash, Petirat Mosheh,* The Death of Moses.

The Prophet Elijah has been the subject of a greater number of legends than any other Bible hero. In the totality of all these legends, naïve in character as they may appear, he is built up into a highly individualized personality—partly human, partly divine. His principal mission, as it appears in most of these legends, is to counsel and protect the common folk in times of trouble. In short, he is an invisible household friend.

Elijah is pictured in legend as being gentle, benign and tolerant of human failings. To the poor he gives material help, to the sorrowful he gives comfort. Like a devoted shepherd he watches over the sheep that have gone astray, pleading their cause before God with the fervor of a father petitioning for his children.

Much of Rabbinic and later legend about Elijah is based upon the *Agada* belief that he did not die like other mortals but was "translated" to Heaven while still alive, swept aloft in a chariot of fire by a whirlwind.

Because the Prophet Malachi foretold that God would send Elijah as a forerunner of the Messiah before "the great and dreadful day," he has been associated in the Jewish folk-mind with the mysterious designs of Providence. And, added to the fact of his miraculous "translation" for which he is called, in the *Agada,* "The Bird of Heaven," popular fancy has assigned to him a unique role—to be guide and helper to the souls of men in the World-to-Come. The folk conception sees him as a benevolent friend standing at the crossroads of Paradise and Hell. The souls of the pious he escorts to their appointed places in Paradise; those of the sinners, out of compassion for their torments, he conducts out of Hell for their "day of rest" on the Sabbath and returns them forthwith at the close of the Sabbath.

Because of Elijah's "translation" to Heaven the folk-mind considers that he never really died and will remain immortal. Cabalistic literature endows him with supernatural attributes as an angel of the highest rank. Thus he can move about among men on earth in time, space and eternity, taking on human shape whenever he chooses. His disguises, of course, are protean because his humility obliges him to dispense his benevolence incognito. It is only after Elijah has departed that his true identity is discovered.

In cabalistic and *Hasidic* folklore, Elijah is delineated as the eternally wandering Jew who never finds rest from the missions of mercy he has to perform. This conception, of course, has no connection with the well-known medieval legend of the Wandering Jew which is anti-Semitic in character. Jewish folk-fancy pictures Elijah with all the loving details of informality. He is a plain Jew, shabbily dressed, with a wanderer's sack slung over his shoulder, trudging along his solitary way, dusty and footsore. In this humble guise, legend usually has him appear before the afflicted, the needy and the sorely beset to help them in their distress. Probably from this popular visualization of Elijah, as the anonymous doer of good hiding behind the humility of his plainness, emerged the mysterious figures of the *Lamed-Vav-Tzaddikim*, the Thirty-Six Hidden Saints.

As an intimate friend, though usually invisible, the plain folk have always accorded Elijah a hearty welcome by means of a quaint symbolism. During the rite of circumcision, for instance, Elijah serves as the "Angel of the Convenant." Therefore, in his honor, the most comfortable chair in the household is reserved for him and is placed at the right hand of the *sandek*, or godfather. This is designated as "Elijah's Chair." In orthodox homes it also is the custom during the *Seder* home service on Passover Eve to pour a cup of wine for him and for the youngest child to open the door in order "to let Elijah in." Symbolically he thus spends this most convivial of all Jewish festivals in the bosom of every family.

King Solomon (*Shelomo Ha-Melech*) too occupies a foremost position in legendary lore. His wisdom, which became proverbial, marked him for the hero-as-sage in many *Midrashic* legends.

The Solomonic folklore literature is very considerable. This is not only because of the material splendor which characterized Solomon's reign—which legend magnified a thousand-fold—but principally because most Jews revered wisdom. Tradition has it, of course, that King Solomon was the author of many wisdom books: the *Song of Songs, Ecclesiastes* and the *Book of Proverbs* in the Old Testament, and of the pseudoepigraphic works: the *Psalms of Solomon, The Testament of Solomon* and *The Wisdom of Solomon*. The Rabbinic writers of those days sometimes wrote anonymously or they modestly hid their individuality under the name and prestige of King Solomon.

King Solomon was fabled to be so wise that he could read the guilt or the innocence of those he judged merely by looking into their faces. He was also considered to be one of the prophets upon whom the *Shekhina* or Divine Radiance dwelled. When the *Shekhina* descended upon him, legend has it, he was inspired to write the *Song of Songs, Ecclesiastes,* and the *Book of Proverbs.*

Because he had chosen the pursuit of wisdom for his goal, the folk believed that God had rewarded him with the splendor of power and great riches. He also gave him dominion over the upper world of angels, over the nether world of spirits and demons, over all the earth and its inhabitants, including beasts and reptiles, birds and fishes. During the forty years of his reign, some of the laws of nature were miraculously reversed: for instance, the full moon never waned. All living creatures obeyed his command, the eagle especially serving as his messenger and principal means of conveyance. When he built the Temple, reputed by legend to have been the most beautiful structure the world had ever seen, angels and demons helped him in the task. He hewed the immense stones which went into its construction by means of the magical worm, the *Shamir* [see *King Solomon and the Worm:* DEMON TALES, page 594].

It is indeed curious that only in later *Midrashic* legends was Solomon hero-worshipped. In earlier folklore he was held up to righteous scorn for having negated by his conduct the wisdom he affected. With one solitary exception, the sages used him as a springboard for their ethical preachments. They charged he was no wise man at all, for only a fool would be so concerned with accumulating a thousand wives, owning innumerable horses and hoarding untold gold and silver to no good purpose. Moreover, they castigated him for being overweeningly proud of his wisdom. Of *Ecclesiastes,* they said it could hardly be considered a sacred work because it represented only the wisdom of Solomon.

Profoundly impressed with the danger both to man's spirit and to society of the misuse of power and riches, the *Midrash* spun a great number of tales concerning the punishments God meted out to Solomon for his arrogance. The *Story of the Ant* dwells with superb philosophical irony on the empty pride of "wisdom" and power. It humbles the sage Solomon when he vaingloriously brags: "Behold, there is none like me in the world, for the Holy One hath given me wisdom and understanding, and knowledge and discernment, and hath made me ruler over all His creations."

The royal sage's vanity and misconduct finally bring down upon his head God's vengeance. First he is deprived of his dominion over the inhabitants of the upper world, then over the demons and the spirits, then over the creatures of the earth, and, lastly, over Israel. At the end he loses even his bed, and all that is left to him is a beggar's staff. It is Ashmodai, the king of the demons, whom God then appoints to be the Avenging Angel to drive Solomon off his throne and to put the crown of Israel upon his own head. But, since repentance and a contrite heart are fundamental to religious belief among Jews, Solomon became worthy again after he had fully expiated for his transgressions.

Vivid in the recollection of the Jewish folk is their memory of the Prophet Jeremiah. Next to Moses they revere him most, conceive him in terms of moral grandeur. In the *Agada* Jeremiah and Moses are often linked together as having experienced the same trials. A *Midrash* says: "As Moses was a prophet for forty years, so was Jeremiah; as Moses prophesied concerning Judah and Benjamin, so did Jeremiah; as Moses' own tribe (the Levites under Korah) rose up against him, so did Jeremiah's tribe revolt against him; Moses was cast into the water, Jeremiah into a pit . . . ; Moses reprimanded the people in discourse, so did Jeremiah."

The Jewish folk revered Jeremiah not only for his prophetic writings and the *Book of Lamentations* which is credited to him by tradition, but because of his selfless labors on behalf of his people. Moreover *Midrashic* legend is steeped in a national consciousness of guilt toward him. This is because Jews believed that, while he had devoted his life to his people and was persecuted on their account, *they* had not heeded his pleas and warnings to return to righteousness. Thus, because of their many transgressions, God had punished them. The Babylonian invader, Nebuchadnezzar, served as God's instrument of retribution, and he destroyed the Temple that Solomon had built and led the Children of Israel into captivity.

The Sorrow of Jeremiah undoubtedly represents the most elegiac of all Jewish legends. The folk-mind indentifies itself emotionally with the Prophet Jeremiah's sorrowful reflections and with their people's historic misfortunes. The legend gives utterance to a national grief perhaps unmatched in all folklore.

N. A.

The Mightiest Thing on Earth

God created ten mighty things in the world.
A rock is mighty, yet iron can break it.
Iron is mighty, yet fire can make it soft.
Fire is mighty, yet water can quench it.
Water is mighty, yet the clouds can carry it.
The cloud is mighty, yet the wind can disperse it.
Wind is mighty, yet man can endure it.
Man is mighty, yet fear can break him.
Fear is mighty, yet wine can drown it.
Wine is mighty, yet sleep can dissipate it.
Sleep is mighty, yet death is mightier.

THE MIGHTIEST THING ON EARTH: Adapted from the *Agada* in the Talmud.

The Making of Adam

WHEN the Creator wished to make man he consulted with the ministering angels beforehand, and said unto them: "We will make a man in our image."

The angels asked: "What is man that Thou shouldst remember him, and what is his purpose?"

"He will do justice," said the Lord.

And the ministering angels were divided into groups.

Some said: "Let not man be created."

But others said: "Let him be created."

Forgiveness said: "Let him be created, for he will be generous and benevolent."

Peace objected and said: "Let him not be created, for he will constantly wage wars."

Justice said: "Let him be created, for he will bring justice into the world."

Truth said: "Let him not be created, for he will be a liar."

The Creator then hurled Truth from Heaven to earth, and, in spite of the protests of the angels, man was created.

"His knowledge," said the Creator, "will excel yours, and tomorrow you will see his wisdom."

The Creator then gathered all kinds of beasts before the ministering angels, the wild and the tame beasts, as well as the birds, and the fowls of the air, and asked the ministering angels to name them, but they could not.

"Now you will see the wisdom of man," spake the Creator. "I will ask him and he will tell their names."

All the beasts and fowls of the air were then led before man, and when asked he at once replied: "This is an ox, the other an ass, yonder a horse and a camel."

"And what is your own name?"

"I" replied man, "should be called Adam because I have been created from *adama* or earth."

Mother Eve

WHEN the Almighty wished to create Eve He did not know from which part of Adam's body He should fashion her.

THE MAKING OF ADAM: From *Myths and Legends of Ancient Israel,* by Angelo S. Rappoport. The Gresham Publishing Co. Ltd. London, 1928. Reprinted by permission of the present copyright holders, Messrs. Blackie & Son Ltd., Glasgow.

MOTHER EVE: Adapted from the *Midrash.*

"I won't create her from his head," He said, "so that she should not be conceited.

"I won't create her from his eye, so that she should not be curious.

"I won't create her from his ear, so that she should not listen to gossip.

"I won't create her from his tongue, so that she should not be a chatterbox.

"I won't create her from his heart, so that she should not be jealous.

"I won't create her from his hand, so that she should not be grasping.

"I won't create her from his foot, so that she should not be a gadabout.

"Instead, I will fashion her from an invisible part of man, so that even when he stands naked it cannot be seen."

Then God created Eve from one of Adam's ribs, saying: "Be thou a modest and chaste woman!"

None the less, God's excellent plan miscarried. Woman is conceited, curious, a gossip, a chatterbox, is jealous, grasping and a gadabout.

The First Tear

AFTER Adam and Eve had been banished from the Garden of Eden, God saw that they were penitent and took their fall very much to heart. And as He is a Compassionate Father He said to them gently:

"Unfortunate children! I have punished you for your sin and have driven you out of the Garden of Eden where you were living without care and in great well-being. Now you are about to enter into a world of sorrow and trouble the like of which staggers the imagination. However, I want you to know that My benevolence and My love for you will never end. I know that you will meet with a lot of tribulation in the world and that it will embitter your lives. For that reason I give you out of My heavenly treasure this priceless pearl. Look! It is a tear! And when grief overtakes you and your heart aches so that you are not able to endure it, and great anguish grips your soul, then there will fall from your eyes this tiny tear. Your burden will grow lighter then."

When Adam and Eve heard these words sorrow overcame them. Tears welled up in their eyes, rolled down their cheeks and fell to earth.

And it was these tears of anguish that first moistened the earth. Adam and Eve left them as a precious inheritance to their children. And since then, whenever a human being is in great trouble and his heart aches and his spirit is oppressed then the tears begin to flow from his eyes, and lo! the gloom is lifted.

THE FIRST TEAR: *Ibid,*

Falsehood and Wickedness

AFTER Noah had completed the building of the ark, the animals were gathered together near it by the angels appointed over them. They came in pairs, and Noah stood at the door of the ark to see that each one entered with its mate. As soon as the waters of the flood rose upon the surface of the earth, the children of men hid themselves in their homes for safety. All traffic and business ceased, for the angel of death was abroad. This state of affairs caused Falsehood to realize that henceforth there was no chance of her plying her trade. Was it not quite evident that the ever-increasing waters of the flood would soon sweep away the wicked folk who had rebelled against their Heavenly Creator? Where should Falsehood betake herself for safety?

Forthwith she hastened to the ark, but its door was shut. What was to be done?

Falsehood knocked at the door with trembling hand. Noah opened the window of the ark, and put out his head to see who was knocking. It was a strange creature before the door. Noah had never seen her before, because he was a righteous man who never told lies.

"What dost thou want?" he cried.

"Let me go in, please," she replied.

"Gladly," cried Noah, "would I admit thee if thy mate were with thee, for only pairs are admitted here."

In grief and disappointment Falsehood went away. She had not gone a few yards before she met her old friend Wickedness, who was now out of employment.

"Whence cometh thou, dear friend Falsehood?" asked Wickedness.

"I come," said Falsehood, "from old father Noah. Just listen. I asked him to let me come into the ark, but he refused unless I complied with his rules."

"What does he require?" asked Wickedness.

"The good old man stipulated that I must have a mate, because all the creatures admitted into the ark are in pairs," Falsehood replied.

"Now, dear friend, is this the truth?" queried Wickedness with a merry twinkle in his evil eye.

"Of course it is the truth, on my word of honour," rejoined Falsehood. "Come now," she added, "wilt thou be my mate? Are we not just fit to be joined together, two honest and poor creatures?"

"If I agree," said Wickedness, "what wilt thou give me in return?"

Falsehood thought awhile and with a cunning look at her friend she exclaimed, "I faithfully promise to give to thee all that I earn in the ark. Have no fear, I shall do excellent business even there, because I feel very fit and energetic."

Wickedness agreed to the terms immediately, and there and then a

FALSEHOOD AND WICKEDNESS: From the *Midrash*. In *Jewish Fairy Tales*, selected and translated by Gerald Friedlander. Robert Scott. London, 1917.

proper agreement was drawn up, and duly signed and sealed. Without
further delay they both hastened to Noah, who readily admitted the happy
pair.

Falsehood soon began to be very busy and earned good money. She
often thought of her agreement with Wickedness with regret, as she
realized that she alone did all the business. She even said to him one day,
"Look here, how easily I can carry on my trade singlehanded!"

Wickedness merely reminded her of the agreement, and day by day he
wrote down in his ledger the sum total of the day's takings.

At the end of the year, for the flood lasted twelve months, they came
out of the ark. Falsehood brought home much treasure, but Wickedness
came with her and claimed the whole of the hard-earned fortune. Thereupon Falsehood said to herself, "I will ask my mate to give me some of
my earnings."

She approached Wickedness and in a gentle voice said, "Dearest friend,
please give me a share of what I have so honestly earned, for I alone did
all the work."

Wickedness looked at her in contempt and with harsh voice cried aloud,
"Thy share is nought, O cheat! Did we not solemnly agree that I was to
take everything which thou shouldest earn? How could I break our
agreement? Would this not be a very wicked thing to do, now would it
not?"

Falsehood held her peace and went away, well knowing that she had
been foiled in her attempt to cheat her friend Wickedness.

True indeed is the proverb: "Falsehood begets much, but Wickedness
taketh all that away."

The Four Cups

NOAH was working with a will to break the hard clods, for the purpose of
planting the grape. Suddenly Satan appeared before him and asked,
"What art thou planting here?"

"It's a vineyard I am planting," answered Noah.

"And what fruit will it bring forth?"

"The grape which gives joy to man and gladdens his heart."

"Then let us work together," said Satan.

Noah consented.

Thereupon Satan brought a lamb, slaughtered it and poured its blood
over the clods of earth. He then caught a lion, slaughtered it and again
poured out the blood, drenching the soil with it. Noah looked and wondered. Satan thereupon caught an ape, slew it and poured the blood upon

THE FOUR CUPS: From *Myths and Legends of Ancient Israel*, by Angelo S. Rappoport. The Gresham Publishing Co. Ltd. London, 1928. Reprinted by permission of
the present copyright holders, Messrs. Blackie & Son Ltd., Glasgow.

the clods of earth. At last he brought a pig, slaughtered it and fertilized the ground with its blood. And thereby Satan wished to indicate to Noah the following lesson:

After tasting the juice of the grape—drinking the first cup of wine— man becomes as mild and soft-spirited as a lamb. After the second cup, he becomes courageous as a lion, boasts of his power, and of his might. After the third cup, he becomes intoxicated, dances, leaps, and gambols like an ape, making a fool of himself; but when he has drunk four or more cups, he is like a pig, bestial, filthy and degraded; he is like a hog that wallows in mud.

Abraham and the Idols

TERAH, the father of Abraham, was himself an idol worshipper; he even carried on a substantial trade in idols.

One day he had to leave home and left his shop full of idols in charge of his son Abraham who was then very young.

Soon an idol worshipper came in and wished to buy an idol.

"How old are you?" asked Abraham.

"Fifty years," answered the idolator.

"What! An old man like you bows down before a mere image that was just finished yesterday! Think it over."

The seeds of Truth were thus planted in the heart of the idolator.

Another time, again while his father Terah was away, a woman came and placed before the idols in the shop a bowl of flour as a sacrificial offering. No sooner had the woman left when Abraham picked up a stick and broke all the idols. Only one, the largest, did he spare. In the hand of this one Abraham then stuck the stick.

Upon his return Terah saw the destruction Abraham had wrought among the idols. He flung himself upon him, crying, "Who did this?"

"Just listen father and be amazed!" replied Abraham serenely. "A woman came and brought a full bowl of flour for an offering. I placed the bowl at the feet of the idols. Immediately, a murderous battle broke out among them. Each of the idols said the flour was meant for him. While they all squabbled and pulled, the largest of them, determined to create order, picked up a stick and . . . See for yourself—he killed them all!"

"You ne'er-do-well!" cried Abraham's father. "How can you say the idols squabbled and pulled when they can neither speak nor understand?"

"Father, father!" replied Abraham, "the holy truth lies in your words!"

ABRAHAM AND THE IDOLS: From the Talmud. Translated from the adaptation by Leo Tolstoy.

Abraham Before Nimrod

THE report reached Nimrod's ears that Abraham was mocking the idols, so he ordered that the boy be brought before him.

Nimrod turned his gaze on him and said imperiously, "Here is fire; worship it!"

"My Lord," answered Abraham fearlessly, "wouldn't it be better to worship water since it can put out the fire?"

"Let it be as you say: worship water!"

"Shall I do an injustice to the clouds which give the earth all its water?"

"Very well then: worship the clouds!"

"But how can the clouds compare with the winds who have the power to scatter them?"

"Then worship the wind!"

"The wind? What will He who directs the fire, water, clouds and wind say to that? . . . O you blind man! Don't you perceive the mighty Hand that guides the world?"

The King was abashed and, turning away, left young Abraham in peace.

God Protects the Heathen Too

ONCE, as the Patriarch Abraham sat at the entrance of his tent, he saw an old tired man approach. Abraham arose and ran forward to bid him welcome. He begged him to enter his tent and rest, but the old man declined the invitation and said, "No, thank you! I will take my rest under a tree."

But, after Abraham continued to press him with his hospitable attentions the old man allowed himself to be persuaded and entered the tent.

Abraham placed before him goat's milk and butter and baked for him fresh cakes. The stranger ate until he was satisfied. Then Abraham said to him, "Now praise the Lord, the God of Heaven and earth, Who gives bread to all His creatures!"

"I do not know your God," replied the old man coldly. "I will only praise the god that my hands have fashioned!"

Then Abraham spoke to the old man, told him of God's greatness and loving kindness. He tried to convince him that his idols were senseless things who could neither help nor save anyone. He urged him therefore to abandon them and put his faith in the one true God and thank Him for His gracious acts that He did for him every day. But to all of Abraham's fervent pleas the old man answered indignantly, "How dare you talk to me this way, trying to turn me away from my gods! You and I have nothing in common, so do not impose on me any further with your words, because I will not heed them!"

ABRAHAM BEFORE NIMROD: *Ibid.*

GOD PROTECTS THE HEATHEN TOO: Adapted from the *Midrash.*

At this Abraham grew very angry and cried out, "Old man, leave my tent!"

Without a word the old man departed and he was swallowed up by the dark night and the desert.

When the Almighty saw this He grew very wrathful and appeared before Abraham.

"Where is the man who came to you this night?" He asked sternly.

"The old man was stubborn," replied Abraham. "I tried to persuade him that if he believed in You everything would be well with him. He refused to heed my words so I grew angry and drove him out of my tent."

Then spoke God: "Have you considered what you have done? Reflect for one moment: Here am I, the God of all Creation—and yet have I endured the unbelief of this old man for so many years. I clothed and fed him and supplied all his needs. But when he came to you for just one night you dispensed with all duties of hospitality and compassion and drove him into the wilderness!"

Then Abraham fell upon his face and prayed to God that He forgive him his sin.

"I will not forgive you," said God, "unless you first ask forgiveness from the heathen to whom you have done evil!"

Swiftly, Abraham ran out of his tent and into the desert and after much searching found the old man. Then he fell at his feet and wept and begged for his forgiveness. The old man was moved by Abraham's pleas and he forgave him.

Again God revealed Himself to Abraham and said, "Because you have done what is righteous in My eyes I will never forget My covenant with your posterity. When they sin I will punish them, but never will I sever My covenant with them!"

Moses the Shepherd

ONE day, while Moses was grazing his flock, he noticed that a little goat had strayed away, so he ran after it for fear that it would get lost and die of hunger and thirst in the wilderness.

Suddenly, from a distance, Moses saw the little goat stop and drink eagerly from a spring. Then he understood that the little animal was thirsty and for that reason had left the flock. When Moses came nigh it he said, "My dear little goatkin! Had I known that you were only thirsty I would not have run after you."

When the little goat had quenched its thirst, Moses placed it upon his shoulders and carried it all the way back to the flock. "The little goat is weak and young," he thought compassionately, "therefore I must carry it."

When God saw what Moses had done He was greatly pleased and said

MOSES THE SHEPHERD: *Ibid.*

to him, "Deep is your compassion, O Moses! Because of your kindness to this little animal you will be the leader of My people Israel, and are destined to serve as their devoted shepherd."

The Love of Moses for His People

WHEN Moses was twenty years old Pharaoh elevated him and showered honors upon him. He had him dressed in kingly raiment and he gave him a precious jewel to wear in his headdress. He gave him slaves to serve him and to carry his weapons wherever he went. And Moses was highly esteemed and honored throughout the land.

One day Moses went out to see his brothers, the Jews, who were building the cities of Pithom and Rameses. And when he saw the heavy labor that the Egyptians laid upon them, the mortar and bricks that they made and their bent backs—he burst into weeping.

"Far better that I were dead!" he cried, "than to see the terrible suffering and the heavy toil of my people!"

Then Moses arose and left his slaves, who followed him bearing his weapons, and he went to the Jews that he might help them and lighten their toil. He placed his shoulder under the heavy burdens that they carried. He helped the very young and the weak to haul the mortar and bricks and he comforted them, put courage into their hearts, and gave them hope for better times to come.

And when God saw this He rejoiced and said to Moses, "Because you have done what is good in My eyes, and you have renounced your pleasures in the house of Pharaoh in order to help My people Israel, and because you had compassion on them like a brother, a day will come when I will spurn all heaven and earth and will come and speak to you face to face."

Israel Undying

MOSES was grazing his flock deep in the wilderness and far from the habitation of men. Once, when he came to Mount Horab, he saw a thorn bush. It looked ugly and forbidding. It was stunted and its branches were full of briars. As he gazed upon it Moses mused bitterly: "To this thorn bush in the wilderness, O my people of Israel, can you be likened! You are as lowly and all who see you shun you!"

And as he stood thus lost in sorrowful thought about the suffering of his people, suddenly he saw that the bush was enveloped in flame. Startled, Moses cried out: "To this thorn bush have I compared my people Israel, when alas—out of it must spring forth a flame to consume it! O my Lord God, must my people perish?"

THE LOVE OF MOSES FOR HIS PEOPLE: *Ibid.*

ISRAEL UNDYING: *Ibid.*

And when Moses saw how the thorn bush burned and yet was not consumed his sorrow vanished and he was filled with exceeding joy. Then he heard the Voice saying: "Even as the thorn bush is not consumed by the flame, so will the Jewish people endure. All the fires of hate that will be kindled against it will be put out, and no evil and misfortune will be able to destroy it!"

The Crossing of the Red Sea

GOD spake to Moses, saying, "Why dost thou stand here praying? My children's prayer has anticipated thine. For thee there is naught to do but lift up thy rod and stretch out thine hand over the sea, and divide it." . . .

Moses spoke to the sea as God had bidden him, but it replied, "I will not do according to thy words, for thou art only a man born of woman, and, besides, I am three days older than thou, O man, for I was brought forth on the third day of creation, and thou on the sixth." Moses lost no time, but carried back to God the words the sea had spoken, and the Lord said: ". . . Lift up thy rod, and stretch out thine hand over the sea, and divide it."

Thereupon Moses raised up his rod—the rod that had been created at the very beginning of the world, on which were graven in plain letters the great and exalted Name, the names of the ten plagues inflicted upon the Egyptians, and the names of the three Fathers, the six Mothers, and the twelve tribes of Jacob. This rod he lifted up, and stretched it out over the sea.

The sea, however, continued in its perverseness, and Moses entreated God to give His command direct to it. But God refused, saying: "Were I to command the sea to divide, it would never again return to its former estate. Therefore, do thou convey My order to it, that it be not drained dry forever. But I will let a semblance of My strength accompany thee, and that will compel its obedience." When the sea saw the Strength of God at the right hand of Moses, it spoke to the earth, saying, "Make hollow places for me, that I may hide myself therein before the Lord of all created things, blessed be He." Noticing the terror of the sea, Moses said to it: "For a whole day I spoke to thee at the bidding of the Holy One, who desired thee to divide, but thou didst refuse to pay heed to my words; even when I showed thee my rod, thou didst remain obdurate. What hath happened now that thou skippest hence?" The sea replied, "I am fleeing, not before thee, but before the Lord of all created things, that His Name be magnified in all the earth." And the waters of the Red Sea divided, and not they alone, but all the water in heaven and on earth, in whatever vessel it was, in cisterns, in wells, in caves, in casks, in pitchers, in drinking

THE CROSSING OF THE RED SEA: Reprinted from *The Legends of the Jews*, by Louis Ginzberg. With the permission of the copyright owners, The Jewish Publication Society of America. Philadelphia, 1913.

cups, and in glasses, and none of these waters returned to their former estate until Israel had passed through the sea on dry land. . . .

God caused the sea to go back by a strong east wind, the wind He always makes use of when He chastises the nations. The same east wind had brought the deluge; it had laid the tower of Babel in ruins; it was to cause the destruction of Samaria, Jerusalem, and Tyre and it will, in future, be the instrument for castigating Rome drunken with pleasure; and likewise the sinners in Gehenna are punished by means of this east wind. All night long God made it to blow over the sea. To prevent the enemy from inflicting harm upon the Israelites, He enveloped the Egyptians in profound darkness, so impenetrable it could be felt, and none could move or change his posture. He that sat when it fell could not arise from his place, and he that stood could not sit down. Nevertheless, the Egyptians could see that the Israelites were surrounded by bright light, and were enjoying a banquet where they stood, and when they tried to speed darts and arrows against them, the missiles were caught up by the cloud and by the angels hovering between the two camps, and no harm came to Israel.

On the morning after the eventful night, though the sea was not yet made dry land, the Israelites, full of trust in God, were ready to cast themselves into its waters. The tribes contended with one another for the honor of being the first to jump. Without awaiting the outcome of the wordy strife, the tribe of Benjamin sprang in, and the princes of Judah were so incensed at having been deprived of pre-eminence in danger that they pelted the Benjamites with stones. God knew that the Judæans and the Benjamites were animated by a praiseworthy purpose. The ones like the others desired but to magnify the Name of God, and He rewarded both tribes: in Benjamin's allotment the Shekinah took up her residence, and the royalty of Israel was conferred upon Judah.

When God saw the two tribes in the waves of the sea, He called upon Moses, and said: "My beloved are in danger of drowning, and thou standest by and prayest. Bid Israel go forward, and thou lift up thy rod over the sea, and divide it." Thus it happened, and Israel passed through the sea with its waters cleft in twain.

The dividing of the sea was but the first of ten miracles connected with the passage of the Israelites through it. The others were that the waters united in a vault above their heads; twelve paths opened up, one for each of the tribes; the water became as transparent as glass, and each tribe could see the others; the soil underfoot was dry, but it changed into clay when the Egyptians stepped upon it; the walls of water were transformed into rocks, against which the Egyptians were thrown and dashed to death, while before the Israelites they crumbled away into bits. Through the brackish sea flowed a stream of soft water, at which the Israelites could slake their thirst; and, finally, the tenth wonder was, that this drinking water was congealed in the heart of the sea as soon as they had satisfied their need.

And there were other miracles, besides. The sea yielded the Israelites whatever their hearts desired. If a child cried as it lay in the arms of its mother, she needed but to stretch out her hand and pluck an apple or some other fruit and quiet it. The waters were piled up to the height of sixteen hundred miles, and they could be seen by all the nations of the earth. . . .

Wonderful as were the miracles connected with the rescue of the Israelites from the waters of the sea, those performed when the Egyptians were drowned were no less remarkable. First of all God felt called upon to defend Israel's cause before Uzza, the Angel of the Egyptians, who would not allow his people to perish in the waters of the sea. He appeared on the spot at the very moment when God wanted to drown the Egyptians, and he spake: "O Lord of the world! Thou art called just and upright, and before Thee there is no wrong, no forgetting, no respecting of persons. Why, then, dost Thou desire to make my children perish in the sea? Canst Thou say that my children drowned or slew a single one of Thine? If it be on account of the rigorous slavery that my children imposed upon Israel, then consider that Thy children have received their wages, in that they took their silver and golden vessels from them."

Then God convoked all the members of His celestial family, and He spake to the angel hosts: "Judge ye in truth between Me and yonder Uzza, the Angel of the Egyptians. At the first I brought a famine upon his people, and I appointed My friend Joseph over them, who saved them through his sagacity, and they all became his slaves. Then My children went down into their land as strangers, in consequence of the famine, and they made the children of Israel to serve with rigor in all manner of hard work there is in the world. They groaned on account of their bitter service, and their cry rose up to Me, and I sent Moses and Aaron, My faithful messengers, to Pharaoh. When they came before the king of Egypt, they spake to him, 'Thus said the Lord, the God of Israel, Let My people go, that they may hold a feast unto Me in the wilderness.' In the presence of the kings of the East and of the West, that sinner began to boast, saying: 'Who is the Lord, that I should hearken unto His voice, to let Israel go? Why comes He not before me, like all the kings of the world, and why doth He not bring me a present like the others? This God of whom you speak, I know Him not at all. Wait and let me search my lists, and see whether I can find His Name.' But his servants said, 'We have heard that He is the son of the wise, the son of ancient kings.' Then Pharaoh asked My messengers, 'What are the works of this God?' and they replied, 'He is the God of gods, the Lord of lords, who created the heaven and the earth.' But Pharaoh doubted their words, and said, 'There is no God in all the world that can accomplish such works beside me, for I made myself, and I made the Nile river.' Because he denied Me thus, I sent ten plagues upon him, and he was compelled to let My children go. Yet, in spite of all, he did not leave off from his wicked ways, and he tried to bring them back under his bondage. Now, seeing all that hath happened to him, and that he will not acknowledge Me as God and Lord, does he not deserve to be drowned in the sea with his host?"

The celestial family called out when the Lord had ended His defense, "Thou hast every right to drown him in the sea!"

Uzza heard their verdict, and he said: "O Lord of all worlds! I know that my people deserve the punishment Thou hast decreed, but may it please Thee to deal with them according to Thy attribute of mercy, and take pity upon the work of Thy hands, for Thy tender mercies are over all Thy works!"

Almost the Lord had yielded to Uzza's entreaties, when Michael gave a sign to Gabriel that made him fly to Egypt swiftly and fetch thence a brick for which a Hebrew child had been used as mortar. Holding this incriminating object in his hand, Gabriel stepped into the presence of God, and said: "O Lord of the world! Wilt Thou have compassion with the accursed nation that has slaughtered Thy children so cruelly?" Then the Lord turned Himself away from His attribute of mercy, and seating Himself upon His throne of justice He resolved to drown the Egyptians in the sea.

The first upon whom judgment was executed was the Angel of Egypt—Uzza was thrown into the sea. A similar fate overtook Rahab, the Angel of the Sea, with his hosts. Rahab had made intercession before God in behalf of the Egyptians. He had said: "Why shouldst Thou drown the Egyptians? Let it suffice the Israelites that Thou hast saved them out of the hand of their masters." At that God dealt Rahab and his army a blow, under which they staggered and fell dead, and then He cast their corpses in the sea, whence its unpleasant odor.

At the moment when the last of the Israelites stepped out of the bed of the sea, the first of the Egyptians set foot into it, but in the same instant the waters surged back into their wonted place, and all the Egyptians perished.

But drowning was not the only punishment decreed upon them by God. He undertook a thoroughgoing campaign against them. When Pharaoh was preparing to persecute the Israelites, he asked his army which of the saddle beasts was the swiftest runner, that one he would use, and they said: "There is none swifter than thy piebald mare, whose like is to be found nowhere in the world." Accordingly, Pharaoh mounted the mare, and pursued after the Israelites seaward. And while Pharaoh was inquiring of his army as to the swiftest animal to mount, God was questioning the angels as to the swiftest creature to use to the detriment of Pharaoh. And the angels answered: "O Lord of the world! All things are Thine, and all are Thine handiwork. Thou knowest well, and it is manifest before Thee, that among all Thy creatures there is none so quick as the wind that comes from under the throne of Thy glory," and the Lord flew swiftly upon the wings of the wind.

The angels now advanced to support the Lord in His war against the Egyptians. Some brought swords, some arrows, and some spears. But God warded them off, saying, "Away! I need no help!" The arrows sped by Pharaoh against the children of Israel were answered by the Lord with fiery darts directed against the Egyptians. Pharaoh's army advanced with gleaming swords, and the Lord sent out lightnings that discomfited the Egyptians. Pharaoh hurled missiles, and the Lord discharged hailstones and coals of fire against him. With trumpets, sackbuts, and horns the Egyptians made their assault, and the Lord thundered in the heavens, and the Most High uttered His voice. In vain the Egyptians marched forward in orderly battle array; the Lord deprived them of their standards, and they were thrown into wild confusion. To lure them into the water, the Lord caused fiery steeds to swim out upon the sea, and the horses of the Egyptians followed them, each with a rider upon his back.

Now the Egyptians tried to flee to their land in their chariots drawn by she-mules. As they had treated the children of Israel in a way contrary to nature, so the Lord treated them now. Not the she-mules pulled the chariots, but the chariots, though fire from heaven had consumed their wheels, dragged the men and the beasts into the water. The chariots were laden with silver, gold, and all sorts of costly things, which the river Pishon, as it flows forth from Paradise, carries down into the Gihon. Thence the treasures floated into the Red Sea, and by its waters they were tossed into the chariots of the Egyptians. It was the wish of God that these treasures should come into the possession of Israel, and for this reason He caused the chariots to roll down into the sea, and the sea in turn to cast them out upon the opposite shore, at the feet of the Israelites.

And the Lord fought against the Egyptians also with the pillar of cloud and the pillar of fire. The former made the soil miry, and the mire was heated to the boiling point by the latter, so that the hoofs of the horses dropped from their feet, and they could not budge from the spot.

The anguish and the torture that God brought upon the Egyptians at the Red Sea caused them by far more excruciating pain than the plagues they had endured in Egypt, for at the sea He delivered them into the hands of the Angels of Destruction, who tormented them pitilessly. Had God not endowed the Egyptians with a double portion of strength, they could not have stood the pain a single moment.

The last judgment executed upon the Egyptians corresponded to the wicked designs harbored against Israel by the three different parties among them when they set out in pursuit of their liberated slaves. The first party had said, "We will bring Israel back to Egypt"; the second had said, "We will strip them bare," and the third had said, "We will slay them all." The Lord blew upon the first with His breath, and the sea covered them; the second party He shook into the sea, and the third He pitched into the depths of the abyss. He tossed them about as lentils are shaken up and down in a saucepan; the upper ones are made to fall to the bottom, the lower ones fly to the top. This was the experience of the Egyptians. And worse still, first the rider and his beast were whisked high up in the air, and then the two together, the rider sitting upon the back of the beast, were hurled to the bottom of the sea.

The Egyptians endeavored to save themselves from the sea by conjuring charms, for they were great magicians. Of the ten measures of magic allotted to the world, they had taken nine for themselves. And, indeed, they succeeded for the moment; they escaped out of the sea. But immediately the sea said to itself, "How can I allow the pledge entrusted to me by God to be taken from me?" And the water rushed after the Egyptians, and dragged back every man of them.

Among the Egyptians were the two arch-magicians Jannes and Jambres. They made wings for themselves, with which they flew up to heaven. They also said to Pharaoh: "If God Himself hath done this thing, we can effect naught. But if this work has been put into the hands of His angels, then we will shake His lieutenants into the sea." They proceeded at once to use their magic contrivances, whereby they dragged the angels down. These cried up to God: "Save us, O God, for the waters are come in unto our soul! Speak Thy word that will cause the magicians to drown in the mighty waters." And Gabriel cried to God, "By the greatness of Thy glory dash Thy adversaries to pieces." Hereupon God bade Michael go and execute judgment upon the two magicians. The archangel seized hold of Jannes and Jambres by the locks of their hair, and he shattered them against the surface of the water.

Thus all the Egyptians were drowned. Only one was spared—Pharaoh himself. When the children of Israel raised their voices to sing a song of praise to God at the shores of the Red Sea, Pharaoh heard it as he was jostled hither and thither by the billows, and he pointed his finger heavenward, and called out: "I believe in Thee, O God! Thou art righteous, and I and My people are wicked, and I acknowledge now that there is no god in the world beside Thee." Without a moment's delay, Gabriel descended and laid an iron chain about Pharaoh's neck, and holding him securely, he addressed him thus: "Villain! Yesterday thou didst say, 'Who is the Lord that I should hearken to His voice?' and now thou sayest, 'The Lord is righteous.'" With that he let him drop into the depths of the sea, and there he tortured him for fifty days, to make the power of God known to him. At the end of the time he installed him as king of the great city of Nineveh, and after the lapse of many centuries, when Jonah came to Nineveh, and prophesied the overthrow of the city on account of the evil done by the people, it was Pharaoh who, seized by fear and terror, covered himself with sackcloth, and sat in ashes, and with his own mouth made proclamation and published this decree through Nineveh: "Let neither man nor beast, herd nor flock, taste anything; let them not feed nor drink water; for I know there is no god beside Him in all the world, all His words are truth, and all His judgments are true and faithful."

Pharaoh never died, and never will die. He always stands at the portal of hell, and when the kings of the nations enter, he makes the power of God known to them at once, in these words: "O ye fools! Why have ye not learnt knowledge from me? I denied the Lord God, and He brought ten plagues upon me, sent me to the bottom of the sea, kept me there for fifty days, released me then, and brought me up. Thus I could not but believe in Him."

The Widow and the Law

KORAH was a great scoffer. He used to gather the Children of Israel around him and abuse our teacher Moses and his brother Aaron and the multitude of the laws they established.

One day he told them the following story:

"In my neighborhood there lived a poor widow and her two daughters. She owned a field that she had inherited from her husband. When she began to plow Moses said to her, 'Thou shalt not plow with ox and ass together.'

"When she began to sow Moses said to her, 'Thou shalt not sow thy field with two kinds of seed.'

"When the time for cutting the wheat and making sheaves arrived Moses again came to her and said, 'You must leave "gleanings," "the poor man's sheath," and the "corner." '

"When the widow got ready to thresh the wheat, he said to her, 'Yield up the priest's share and the first and second tithes.'

"The poor woman did as she was told and gave Moses whatever he asked. But seeing that she got nothing out of her wheat she sold the field and with the money bought two sheep. She expected a great deal from them—she'd make clothing from their wool and the little sheep would supply her with mutton.

"But no sooner did the sheep bear their young when Aaron the high priest came and said, 'Give me the first-born, for Moses decreed that all the firstlings belong to the priests.'

"The widow thereupon obeyed the law and gave away the first-born.

"When shearing time came Aaron again came and said to her, 'Give me the first shearing, for that too belongs to the priest.'

"Out of patience, the widow cried out, 'I can no longer endure this! I shall slaughter these animals, eat their meat, and bring an end to all this!'

"But no sooner had she slaughtered them when Aaron said to her, 'According to the Law you must give me the neck, the cheeks and the belly.'

" 'What!' exclaimed the widow. 'Is it possible that I'm still not rid of you? In that case neither you nor I are going to have any of it. By my life, I shall consecrate it!'

" 'If you consecrate it,' replied Aaron, 'then it belongs altogether to me, for the Lord hath said: "Everything consecrated in Israel shall be thine." '

"So he took the sheep and went away and left the widow weeping."

WIDOW AND THE LAW: Adapted from the *Midrash*.

Manna

As a reward for Abraham's readiness, in answer to the summons to sacrifice Isaac, when he said, "Here am I," God promised manna to the descendants of Abraham with the same words, "Here am I." In the same way, during their wanderings through the wilderness, God repaid the descendants of Abraham for what their ancestor had done by the angels who visited him. He himself had fetched bread for them, and likewise God Himself caused bread to rain from heaven; he himself ran before them on their way, and likewise God moved before Israel; he had water fetched for them, and likewise God, through Moses, caused water to flow from the rock; he bade them seek shade under the tree, and likewise God had a cloud spread over Israel. Then God spoke to Moses: "I will immediately reveal Myself without delay; mindful of the services of Abraham, Isaac, and Jacob, 'I will rain bread from My treasure in heaven for you; and the people shall go out and gather a certain rate every day.' "

There were good reasons for not exceeding a day's ration in the daily downpour of manna. First, that they might be spared the need of carrying it on their wanderings; secondly, that they might daily receive it hot; and, lastly, that they might day by day depend upon God's aid, and in this way exercise themselves in faith.

While the people were still abed, God fulfilled their desire, and rained down manna for them. For this food had been created on the second day of creation, and ground by the angels, it later descended for the wanderers in the wilderness. The mills are stationed in the third heaven, where manna is constantly being ground for the future use of the pious; for in the future world manna will be set before them. Manna deserves its name, "bread of the angels," not only because it is prepared by them, but because those who partake of it become equal to the angels in strength, and, furthermore, like them, have no need of easing themselves, as manna is entirely dissolved in the body. Not until they sinned, did they have to ease themselves like ordinary mortals.

Manna also showed its heavenly origin in the miraculous flavor it possessed. There was no need of cooking or baking it, nor did it require any other preparation, and still it contained the flavor of every conceivable dish. One had only to desire a certain dish, and no sooner had he thought of it, than manna had the flavor of the dish desired. The same food had a different taste to every one who partook of it, according to his age; to the little children it tasted like milk, to the strong youths like bread, to the old men like honey, to the sick like barley steeped in oil and honey.

As miraculous as the taste of manna was its descent from heaven. First came a north wind to sweep the floor of the desert; then a rain to wash it

MANNA: Reprinted from *The Legends of the Jews*, by Louis Ginzberg. With the permission of the copyright owners, The Jewish Publication Society of America. Philadelphia, 1913.

quite clean; then dew descended upon it, which was congealed into a solid substance by the wind, that it might serve as a table for the heaven-descending manna, and this frozen dew glistened and sparkled like gold. But, that no insects or vermin might settle on the manna, the frozen dew formed not only a tablecloth, but also a cover for the manna, so that it lay enclosed there as in a casket, protected from soiling or pollution above and below.

With an easy mind every individual might perform his morning prayer in his house and recite the Shema, then betake himself to the entrance of his tent, and gather manna for himself and all his family. The gathering of manna caused little trouble, and those among the people who were too lazy to perform even the slightest work, went out while manna fell, so that it fell straight into their hands. The manna lasted until the fourth hour of the day, when it melted; but even the melted manna was not wasted, for out of it formed the rivers, from which the pious will drink in the hereafter. The heathen even then attempted to drink out of these streams, but the manna that tasted so deliciously to the Jews, had a quite bitter taste in the mouth of the heathen. Only indirectly could they partake of the enjoyment of manna: They used to catch the animals that drank of the melted manna, and even in this form it was so delicious that the heathen cried, "Happy is the people that is in such a case." For the descent of manna was not a secret to the heathen, as it settled at such enormous heights that the kings of the East and of the West could see how Israel received its miraculous food.

The mass of the manna was in proportion to its height, for as much descended day by day, as might have satisfied the wants of sixty myriads of people, through two thousand years. Such profusion of manna fell over the body of Joshua alone, as might have sufficed for the maintenance of the whole congregation. Manna, indeed, had the peculiarity of falling to every individual in the same measure; and when, after gathering, they measured it, they found that there was an omer for every man.

Many lawsuits were amicably decided through the fall of manna. If a married couple came before Moses, each accusing the other of inconstancy, Moses would say to them, "To-morrow morning judgment will be given." If, then, manna descended for the wife before the house of her husband, it was known that he was in the right; but if her share descended before the house of her own parents, she was in the right.

The only days on which manna did not descend were the Sabbaths and the holy days, but then a double portion fell on the preceding day. These days had the further distinction that, while they lasted, the color of the manna sparkled more than usual, and it tasted better than usual. The people, however, were fainthearted, and on the very first Sabbath, they wanted to go out as usual to gather manna in the morning, although announcement had been made that God would send them no food on that day. Moses, however, restrained them. They attempted to do it again toward evening, and again Moses restrained them with the words, "To-day ye shall not find it in the fields." At these words they were greatly alarmed, for they feared that they might not receive it any more at all, but their leader quieted them with the words, "To-day ye shall not find any of it, but assuredly to-morrow; in this world ye shall not receive manna on the Sabbath, but assuredly in the future world."

The unbelieving among them did not hearken to the words of God, and went out on the Sabbath to find manna. Hereupon God said to Moses: "Announce these words to Israel: I have led you out of Egypt, have cleft the sea for you, have sent you manna, have caused the well of water to spring up for you, have sent the quails to come up for you, have battled for you against Amalek, and wrought other miracles for you, and still you do not obey My statutes and commandments. You have not even the excuse that I imposed full many commandments upon you, for all that I bade you do at Marah, was to observe the Sabbath, but you have violated it." "If," continued Moses, "you will observe the Sabbath, God will give you three festivals in the months of Nisan, Siwan, and Tishri; and as a reward for the observance of the Sabbath, you will receive six gifts from God: the land of Israel, the future world, the new world, the sovereignty of the dynasty of David, the institution of the priests and the Levites; and, furthermore, as a reward for the observance of the Sabbath, you shall be freed from the three great afflictions: from the sufferings of the times of Gog and Magog, from the travails of the Messianic time, and from the day of the great Judgment."

When Israel heard these exhortations and promises, they determined to observe the Sabbath, and did so. They did not know, to be sure, what they had lost through their violation of the first Sabbath. Had Israel then observed the Sabbath, no nation would ever have been able to exercise any authority over them.

The Angels Jealous of Moses

RABBI JOSHUA, son of Levi, says that at the time when Moses went up to heaven to receive the Law, which the Lord, blessed be He, was giving him, the angels said, "Lord of the universe, what is a mortal man doing here in the heavens amongst us?" And the Lord replied, "He has come to receive the Torah." Then the angels said, "Wilt Thou hand over to man that hidden jewel which Thou hast treasured up with Thee during 974 generations, before Thou hadst created the world? What is man whom Thou hast created? 'Give Thy beauty to the heavens' (Ps. 8.2). Leave the Torah here and do not give it to man." Then God said, "Moses, answer the angels concerning that which they have spoken to Me." And Moses

THE ANGELS JEALOUS OF MOSES: Reprinted from the *Ma'aseh Book*, edited by Moses Gaster. With the permission of the copyright owners, The Jewish Publication Society of America. Philadelphia, 1934.

replied, "Lord of the universe, I would fain answer them, but I fear lest they burn me up with the breath of their mouths." Then God said, "Moses take hold of the throne of glory and answer their speech." And when our master Moses heard this, he began to speak, and said, "Lord of the universe, what is written in that Torah which Thou intendest to give to me? 'I am the Lord thy God who brought thee out of the land of Egypt' (Ex. 20.2). O angels, have you gone down into Egypt? Have you served Pharaoh? Then why should the Lord, blessed be He, give you the Torah? Again, what else is written in this Torah? Is it not written, 'Thou shalt have no other gods before Me' (ibid. v. 3)? Are you living among heathens that you should serve other gods? It is further written therein, 'Remember the Sabbath day, to keep it holy' (ibid. v. 8), which means, rest on that day. Are you working that you should have to be commanded to rest? Furthermore, it is written therein, 'Thou shalt not take a false oath' (cf. ibid. v. 7). Are you engaged in business that you should be commanded not to take a false oath? Furthermore, 'Honour thy father and thy mother' (ibid. v. 12). Have you a father and a mother that you should be commanded to honour them? 'Thou shalt not murder, thou shalt not commit adultery, thou shalt not steal' (ibid. v. 13). Is there envy and hatred among you that you should be commanded not to do these things? Of what good, therefore, is the Torah to you?" When the angels heard this, they became friendly to Moses and everyone of the angels taught him something, even the angel of death.

The Death of Moses

I. Joshua Is Chosen As His Successor

AFTER the defeat of the Midianites at the hands of Israel, God said to Moses: "Go up to the mountain of Abarim from whence you will see the land which I have given to the children of Israel, and then you will die, as your brother Aaron died."

"Oh Lord," pleaded Moses, "You know the spirit of the living, both those that are proud and those that are humble, those that are patient and those that are restive. I am about to depart from this world, I pray You, appoint a leader over the Israelites who will know how to deal with each according to his due. Appoint a leader over them, who shall not be like the kings of the heathens that send their people to war while they themselves remain in their palaces and waste their time in revelry, but one who will go out before the Israelites and lead them into battle."

THE DEATH OF MOSES: From the *Midrash*. In *Book of Legends*, by Hyman Goldin. Jordan Publishing Co. New York, 1929. Reprinted by permission of the present copyright holders, Hebrew Publishing Co.

"Your successor shall be he who has served you with devotion," said God, "he who has shown you the greatest veneration. Joshua, the son of Nun, shall bring forth my people from the wilderness and take them into the Promised Land."

"Indeed," answered Moses, "I have proven him, and he knows how to deal with people of every kind, and he is certainly the man who I expected would be chosen as my successor."

"Take Joshua then," said God, "lay your hand upon him and bestow of your spirit upon him, so that the children of Israel may accept him as their leader while you are still alive, and honor him."

Moses went to Joshua and related to him what God had spoken concerning him. Joshua wept bitterly when he heard that his beloved master would soon die in the wilderness, and would not lead Israel into the Promised Land. "Alas, Master!" he wailed, "your words fill me with sorrow. All Israel will join me in the prayer that God may forgive you and allow you to enter the Promised Land."

"God is no mortal who is apt to change his mind," replied Moses. "His decree must stand."

"But am I the one who deserves succeeding you?" asked Joshua.

With kind words Moses at last persuaded Joshua to succeed him as the leader of Israel after his death. He then led him before Eleazar, the high priest, and before all the people of Israel, and in their presence he laid his hand upon Joshua, and bestowed his spirit upon him.

Moses then said to Joshua: "Heed my advice concerning how to lead Israel, and God will be with you. Know that Israel is still young and has a great deal to learn yet. Should he sin do not be angry with him. For God himself never was too exacting concerning Israel, but always forgave him his backslidings, although he was many a time provoked to great anger against him. Now you must rule over Israel as a father rules over his children, and only then will you deserve to be called the 'Leader of Israel.'"

Joshua promised his master to be true to his teachings, and with a heavy heart and tears in his eyes, he accepted the leadership over Israel.

II. Moses Prays that God Suspend His Judgment

As the days of Moses' life drew near to their end, he began to pray to God to forgive him his sins and allow him to enter the Promised Land, saying:

"O Lord of the world! In Your mercy have you chosen me for Your servant and through me You have performed great and wondrous miracles in the land of Egypt. But now You say to me: 'Behold, you will die!' Shall my final end likewise be dust and worms as that of all other mortals?"

And God replied: "No man can escape death. Even Adam, who was the work of My own hands, was doomed to die; so how can a man born of a woman escape it?"

"O Lord of the World!" said Moses. "You gave only one command to the first man and yet he disobeyed you!"

"Isaac who laid his neck upon the altar to be sacrificed as an offering to Me, also died."

"But from Isaac issued Esau who will destroy your temple and burn your house and exile your children!"

"From Jacob issued twelve tribes that did not anger me, and yet he too died."

Yet Moses persisted, saying: "But Jacob's feet never ascended into heaven, and he did not walk upon clouds. Neither did You speak face to face with him, nor did he receive the Torah from Your hand."

"Enough!" cried God. "Speak to Me no longer of this matter!"

But Moses pleaded on: "With all Your creatures, O my Lord God, You deal according to Your attribute of mercy. You forgive them their sins but You will not even overlook my one sin."

"Not once but six times have you sinned against Me," reminded him God.

"O Lord of the World!" pleaded Moses again. "How often did Israel sin before You, and when I implored Your mercy toward them You forgave them, but me You will not forgive."

"Two vows have I made," answered God, "one that you will die before Israel enters the Promised Land, and the other that Israel shall be forgiven and not be allowed to perish. If I am to break the first I must also cancel the other, and Israel will have to die."

And Moses cried out: "Rather shall Moses and a thousand more of his kind perish than a single soul in Israel!"

III. God Rejects Moses' Last Plea

Moses now made a last effort to obtain God's mercy, saying: "Although I never saw the Promised Land, I have praised it to the people. Shall I share the lot of spies who, although they saw the good land, spoke evil of it in the presence of the people? You know, O Lord, that my desire to enter the Promised Land is not prompted by self-interest. I wish to go there that I might perform all those of Your Commandments that are still to be fulfilled. Forgive me then my sin and allow me to enter the land. Then all living flesh shall know that You are forgiving and merciful."

"Your sin shall not be forgiven you," answered God, "so that all flesh shall know that the Lord does not even discriminate in favor of him with whom He spoke face to face."

"If it be your wish," urged Moses, "that I do not enter the land as leader of the people, then let me enter as the humblest of them all."

And God answered: "Even this cannot be granted to you."

Then Moses pleaded: "Change me into a beast that eats grass and drinks water, but let me enter the land which You have given to the Children of Israel."

"This too must be denied you," replied the Almighty.

"If You are unwilling to change me into a beast, then change me into a little bird that picks its daily food wherever it can find it and then at the fall of night returns to its nest, only let me enter into the Promised Land!"

"Enough, My decree is unalterable!" cried God.

Hearing God's final decision, Moses exclaimed: "The Rock of Ages—all His ways are just!"

And he implored: "Permit me, O Lord, to make but one request of You. Let the heavens be opened and the abyss be rent asunder, so that Your people may see that there is none besides You, O my Lord, neither in the heavens nor upon the earth."

No sooner had Moses finished speaking when the heavens were opened, the abyss was rent asunder, a great light shone in the dark of the night, and the eyes of all Israel were opened and they saw that neither in the heavens above nor on the earth below was there anything except the greatness and glory of God. Thereupon, all the people cried out as one man: "Hear O Israel, the Lord our God, the Lord is One!"

IV. Moses Is Ready to Die

Moses then sat down to write thirteen scrolls of the Torah, twelve for the twelve tribes, and one to be put into the Holy Ark.

When Moses had completed his writing, he went to the tent of Joshua. He stood at the entrance and listened as his disciple expounded the Torah to a number of Israelites. Meanwhile more people arrived, and when they beheld Moses standing at the entrance, they ran into the tent and exclaimed: "Alas! you show no respect to our great leader and teacher, if you thus permit him to stand at the entrance of your tent."

Joshua thereupon looked toward the entrance, and when he saw Moses standing there, he tore his garments and weeping said: "Pray enter the tent and expound the Torah to your humble servants."

"From this day on," Moses replied, "I shall be your disciple."

Moses and Joshua then went to the Tabernacle, but as they entered, a cloud descended and separated them. God then spoke to Joshua, and His words were not audible to Moses. Moses asked Joshua what God had said, but Joshua replied that God would not permit him to tell of what He had spoken to him.

"Now, I am willing to die," said Moses to God.

"Go up to the top of Mount Pisgah," God commanded him, "and from there I will show you the land of Israel and tell you of all that will befall the Israelites in days to come."

V. Moses Chastises Samael, the Angel of Death

When God saw that Moses was ready to die, he said to the angel Gabriel: "Go fetch Me the soul of Moses!"

"How can I approach and take the soul of him who has wrought so many miracles?" asked Gabriel. "O Lord of the world! Adam sinned against You, and therefore You removed Your glory from him and bestowed it upon Moses whom You love.

"Noah, who found favor in My eyes because of his righteousness and simplicity, also died."

"Noah saved only himself when You sent a flood upon the world," argued Gabriel, "nor did he care to pray to You for the lives of the people who were to be destroyed. But Moses, your servant, would not leave Your presence until You had promised him that You would forgive the people their sin."

"Abraham, who was kind and righteous, he too did not escape death," answered God.

"Abraham was indeed a great man, for he gave food to the poor and provided them with all their wants, but this was done by him in a settled land, whereas Moses provided an entire nation with food in a wilderness where there was neither food nor drink," said Gabriel.

"No mortal can escape death!" said God. "Such is My decree!"

Then Gabriel went on to plead: "O Lord of the world! Pray give this mission to anyone it pleases You, but not to me."

God then turned to the angel Michael and said to him: "Go and fetch me the soul of Moses!"

Answered Michael: "How can I presume to approach and take the soul of him who is equal in Your eyes to sixty myriads of people?"

"You go then!" said God to the angel Zagzagel. "Go and fetch me the soul of Moses."

"Lord of the world!" replied Zagzagel. "When Moses ascended to heaven to receive the Torah, I was his teacher and he was my disciple. How can I take his soul?"

God then said to Samael, the Angel of Death: "Go and fetch me the soul of Moses!"

Samael rejoiced over this mission. He took his sword and wrapped himself in wrath and hastened to Moses. But when he beheld the face of Moses and gazed into his eyes, the radiance of which was equal to that of the sun, he trembled and drew back.

"Why do you stand there? What is it you want of me?" asked Moses.

"The God of heaven and earth, He who created all souls, has sent me to take your soul," replied the Angel of Death.

"I will not give you my soul!" cried Moses. "Leave me at once, for I stand here declaring the glory of God!"

To which the Angel of Death replied: "The heavens declare the glory of God and the firmament sheweth His handiwork."

"But I will silence the heavens and the firmament, and I myself will narrate His glory," said Moses.

"All souls since the creation of the world were delivered into my hands," continued the Angel of Death. "Now pray let me approach you and take your soul too."

"Go away!" cried Moses. "I will not give you my soul!"

In great terror Samael returned to God and said: "Lord of the world! I am unable to approach the man to whom You sent me."

God's wrath was now kindled against Samael and He said to him: "Go to him again and fetch Me his soul!"

So Samael drew his sword from its sheath, girded himself in cruelty, and in a towering fury went off to see Moses. When Moses beheld Samael he arose in anger and with the staff upon which was engraved the Ineffable Name, he drove him away. The Angel of Death fled in terror but Moses pursued him. When finally he caught up with Samael he struck him with his staff and blinded him. At that very moment a ringing Voice from heaven was heard calling:

"Your last second is at hand, Moses!"

Hearing this, Moses stood up in prayer, and murmured: "Lord of the world, remember the day on which You appeared to me in the bush of thorns and commanded me to go to Pharaoh and bring forth Your people from the land of Egypt. Recall also the day I ascended into heaven where for forty days I had neither food nor drink. I pray You, gracious and merciful God, do not surrender my soul into the hands of the Angel of Death!"

Then the Heavenly Voice spoke once again: "Be comforted, Moses! I myself will take your soul. I myself will bury you."

VI. THE DEATH OF MOSES

God revealed Himself to Moses from the highest heaven, and with God descended three angels, Michael, Gabriel and Zagzagel. Michael arranged the couch for Moses, Gabriel spread upon it the white napkin for the head, and Zagzagel the one for the feet.

Then Michael stood on the right side of Moses, Gabriel on his left, Zagzagel at his feet, and the Majesty of God hovered over his head.

And the Lord said to Moses: "Shut your eyes."

Moses obeyed.

Then the Lord said: "Press your hand upon your heart."

Moses did so.

Then the Lord said: "Place your feet in order."

Moses obeyed God's command.

Thereupon the Lord addressed the soul of Moses: "My daughter! For one hundred and twenty years have you inhabited this undefiled body of dust. But now your hour is come. Rise and fly into Paradise!"

But the soul replied: "I know that You are the God of spirits and of souls. You created me and put me into the body of this righteous man. Is there anywhere in the world a body so pure and holy as this one? During these one hundred and twenty years I learned to love it, and now I do not wish to leave it."

God replied: "My daughter, do not hesitate, but come forth for your end has come. I will place you in the highest heaven and let you dwell, like the Cherubim and the Seraphim, beneath the throne of Divine Majesty."

But the soul replied: "Lord of the world! I desire to remain with this righteous man, for he is purer and holier than the very angels. When the Angels Azael and Shemhazai descended from heaven to earth, they became corrupt, but the son of Amram, a creature of flesh and blood, has not sinned from the moment he saw the light of day. Let me therefore, I implore You, remain where I am."

Then God bent over the face of Moses and kissed him. At once the soul leaped up in joy and with the kiss of God flew into Paradise.

A sad cloud darkened the sky, and the heavens and the earth wailed: "The pious one has been lost from the earth, and there is none more righteous among men!"

Joshua rent his garments and lamented: "Help, O Lord, for there are no longer any pious ones, and the faithful have departed from the midst of men!"

And all Israel lamented the loss of Moses, crying: "The righteousness of the Lord has he performed, and he has executed his judgment in Israel."

And when all the voices were silenced, the Divine Presence proclaimed: "There has not arisen a prophet in Israel like Moses whom the Lord knew face to face."

Why God Forgives Man

ELIJAH the Prophet once told the following story:

"It happened that I came to a great city, one of the greatest in the world. In that city lived a government official whose duty it was to investigate suspicious characters. When he saw me he led me into the king's palace where a priest came toward me and asked, 'Are you a scholar?'

"I answered, 'I know a little.'

"To which he said, 'If you'll give me the right answer to the question which I am going to ask you I will let you go in peace.'

"I said, 'Ask!'

" 'Why did the Almighty create reptiles? Why did he need such ugly crawling creatures in his beautiful world?'

"I answered him: 'The Almighty is a stern judge. But He also loves justice, benevolence and truth. He foresees the outcome of everything and foretells the future. He is concerned with the good only. With His profound wisdom He created the world and all that is on it. After that He fashioned man. And the only reason He made man was that he serve Him with all his heart, so that He should take pleasure in him and in the generations that spring from his loins until the end of days.

_____

WHY GOD FORGIVES MAN: Adapted from the *Midrash*.

" 'But when man procreated and his number became great he began to worship the sun and stones and wooden idols. From day to day the sinfulness of man had been mounting so that he deserved death and greatly tried God's patience.

" 'At that point God looked upon all the creatures He had created in the world and said: "Men have life and these creatures have life. Men have souls and these creatures have souls. Men eat and drink and these creatures eat and drink. Therefore, men too are animals and are no better than the reptiles that I have created."

" 'Immediately thereafter the Almighty's wrath subsided and he withheld his hand from destroying mankind. From this, therefore, you can see that God created reptiles, so that He would have some creatures with which to compare man and shame him into humility.' "

King David Bows Before an Idol

WHEN David reached the summit of the Mount of Olives he said to his servants, "Go and find me an idol and bring it here!"

When David's servants went to do his bidding they met Hushai the Archite, the king's friend. He asked them, "Where are you going?"

They answered, "David, our king, has commanded us to bring him an idol."

Astounded, Hushai went to David and asked, "Tell me, O King, why did you bid your servants to bring you an idol?"

And David replied, "I wish to bow before the idol."

When Hushai heard these words he rent his garments and strewed ashes on his head and cried aloud, "Woe is me that a man like King David should bow before an idol."

Then spoke the king: "Do not grieve so, my friend! Don't you know how great my fame is throughout the world? All who have heard of me say: 'There is no man as virtuous as David. He rules his people with the fear of God in his heart. He does only good, metes out justice and fulfills all of God's commandments.' Now therefore consider, Hushai, when the people hear about my miserable plight, how my son Absalom attacked me and tried to kill me, what do you suppose they will think? They will say, 'What a waste to worship such a God! With Him there is neither justice nor reward of virtue.' For that reason, I have decided to bow down before an idol in order to defame myself. Then people will be able to say, 'There you have proof there is a God in heaven and a sovereign over the earth! He rules with truth and with justice and punishes even mighty King David for his idol-worship.' "

KING DAVID BOWS BEFORE AN IDOL: *Ibid.*

Better than a Dead Lion

ONCE King David said to God, "Lord of the Universe! I beg of You, tell me the day when I will die."

God answered, "I have decreed that no mortal should know his last day."

"Then tell me—how many years will I live?" David implored.

"I have decreed that no mortal shall know the number of his years on earth."

"Tell me then, O Lord of the Universe, on what day in the week will I die?"

And the Creator answered, "You will die on the Sabbath day."

"Let me die on the day after the Sabbath," pleaded David.

"That cannot be," answered God. "The rule of your son, Solomon, begins on the day after the Sabbath."

"Then let me die a day before the Sabbath!" implored King David.

"No man may die before his hour comes," answered the Almighty. "Dearer to Me is the Torah that you will study for one single day than a thousand sacrifices your son Solomon will bring upon My altar as King."

From that time on King David spent the entire Sabbath day in devoted study of the Torah. And, when the Sabbath on which he was to die arrived, the Angel of Death rose up against him; but he had no power over him, for King David did not cease his studying.

"What shall I do with him?" cried the Angel of Death in exasperation.

Behind the royal palace lay a lovely garden, and so the Angel of Death entered it and began to shake the trees. Hearing the noise, David went to see who was disturbing the Sabbath peace. And as he walked he did not cease his devoted study of the Torah. But as he descended the steps he lost his balance and for one instant the sacred words became stilled on his lips. In that very instant the Angel of Death smote him.

Thereupon, Solomon inquired of the sages: "What shall I do? My father lies dead in the fierce sun. The dogs are hungry. They bark and sharpen their teeth."

The sages replied, "Your father was a king in his life. Now that he is dead he is only a corpse. One may not violate the Sabbath for the sake of a dead man."

And when Solomon heard these words he commented, "A live dog is better than a dead lion."

BETTER THAN A DEAD LION: Adapted from the *Agada* in the Talmud.

The Wall of the Poor

WHEN Solomon wished to build the Temple in the holy city of Jerusalem, an angel of God appeared to him and said, "Solomon, son of David, King of Israel, since thou dost know that the Temple which thou wilt build Me will be the holy place of the people, the portion of all Israel, summon all Israel and let each man take part in the work, each one according to his capacity."

So King Solomon sent forth and summoned assemblies of his people Israel, and not one man was missing. There came the princes and the rulers, the priests and the nobles, as well as the needy and the poor. And Solomon cast lots for the labor, for everything was apportioned by lot. And the lots fell in this manner: to the princes and rulers, the cupolas of the pillars and the steps; to the priests of Aaron's seed and to the Levites, the Ark of the Testimony and the curtain which is upon it; to those mighty in wealth, the eastern side; to the poor and the needy, the Western Wall. Thus were the lots cast and since it came from the Lord, may it be forever a wonder in our eyes!

Then began the labor for the House of God.

The princes and rulers and all the rich men of Israel took the golden earrings from the ears of their wives and their daughters, also their jewels which were very precious; and they bought cedar wood wherewith to cover both the ground and the walls, and cypress wood for the doors, and olive wood for the lintels. Also day-laborers did they hire from the Sidonians and Tyrians and others of the heathen who dwelt in the land; and over them they appointed foremen to urge them and press them on, saying, "Ye slackers, finish your work!" Thus was speedily ended and completed the work of the princes and rulers and the mighty in wealth; also that of the priests of Aaron's seed and of the Levites according to their families.

Only the work of the poor was delayed exceedingly, for they could not bring fine things from afar; and the men, the women and the children hewed stone in the great cave which is the cave of Zedekiah, until by the toil of their hands they completed their portion, the Western Wall.

Now when the holy work was ended and the Temple stood upon its height, perfect in its beauty, the Divine Presence descended and rested upon it, and the Lord chose the Western Wall; for He said, "The toil of the needy is precious in My eyes and My blessing shall be upon it." And a holy Echo went forth, saying, "The Holy Presence shall never be removed from the Western Wall."

So when the enemy destroyed our House of Glory—speedily may it be builded and established in our days, Amen!—the angels of the Most High descended and spread their wings over the Western Wall; and a holy

THE WALL OF THE POOR: Reprinted from *Legends of Palestine*, by Zev Vilnay. With the permission of the copyright owners, The Jewish Publication Society of America, Philadelphia, 1932.

Echo went forth, and proclaimed, "Never shall the Western Wall be destroyed."

Gates of Beauty

NIKANOR journeyed to Alexandria to bring back the gates of copper he had ordered from the great Egyptian artificers in metal. They were for the entrance to the Temple in Jerusalem. He received the gates and loaded them on a ship and then journeyed back to the Land of Israel.

On the way home a storm broke out and the ship began to sink. To lighten the ship the sailors took one of the copper gates and cast it into the sea. And as the storm still raged unabated they started to cast the remaining gate into the sea. Then Nikanor rushed forward and embraced the door with both arms.

"If you wish to cast this beautiful gate into the sea you must cast me with it!" he cried.

At that very instant the sea became calm.

The loss of one of the gates caused Nikanor great grief. He could find no solace. But as the ship entered the harbor at Akku how amazed he was to see the lost gate being tossed ashore by the waves!

God moves in a mysterious way. . . .

The Beauty of Simple Things

ONE of the musical instruments employed in the Temple service in Jerusalem was a pipe. It was made of ordinary reed. It was smooth and slender and it dated back to the days of Moses.

Seeing how valuable it was the King ordered that the pipe be encrusted with gold. After that, whenever the pipe was played during the Temple service, its voice was no longer as limpid as it was before. So they took the beaten gold off, and the pipe's voice again sounded as sweet as ever.

A pair of cymbals were among the musical instruments in the Temple in Jerusalem. They were made of copper and when they were struck together they produced a wondrous sound.

It happened once that they became damaged. So the Jewish sages brought great artists in metal from Alexandria who mended the cymbals and laid gold on them. But when one cymbal was struck against the other the sound was no longer as delightful as before. So they took off the gold and the voice of the cymbals as they clashed together was as wondrous sweet as before.

GATES OF BEAUTY: Adapted from the *Agada* in the Talmud.

THE BEAUTY OF SIMPLE THINGS: *Ibid.*

King Solomon and the Queen of Sheba

I. THE HOOPOE BIRD

KING SOLOMON commanded all animals and birds, as well as all demons and devils, to assemble. And when they had gathered they danced and capered before him and the elders of the nation who had come to Jerusalem for this occasion.

When he looked about him the King saw that the hoopoe, a mountain-cock, was not among those who had assembled. He therefore became angry and commanded the eagles: "Bring before me the hoopoe so that I may punish him for disobeying me!"

Obediently, the eagles flew away to fetch the culprit. And when they found him they brought him before the King.

"Please do not be angry with me, my Lord the King, because I failed to make my appearance with all the other animals today," pleaded the hoopoe. "Believe me, truly, it wasn't out of evil intention or because I took your command lightly."

"Where were you then? Explain your absence!" cried the King sternly.

"Three months ago," the hoopoe began, "I decided to fly to all the far corners of the earth to inquire if there was one single nation that had not heard of the greatness and wisdom of my Lord the King. And thus I flew about for ninety days and ninety nights. I neither ate nor drank nor rested until I reached the city of Kittor, which is located in the east at the end of the world. What was my astonishment when I saw that the earth there was of pure gold! Although there was much silver rolling in the streets no one seemed to take any notice of it.

"All about me stretched magnificent gardens and orchards, radiantly in blossom as on the day when God created heaven and earth. The fertile fields were irrigated by a winding river. On the trees grew the most beautiful and delicious fruit I have ever tasted. But most wonderful of all—the inhabitants of the land were all peace-loving! Every man sat serenely in his own vineyard and under his fig tree. He carried no weapons nor wished to learn the art of war.

"This tranquil land is ruled over by a woman of wondrous wisdom and beauty. She is called the Queen of Sheba, and all her subjects, both the powerful and the weak, the rich and the poor, serve her obediently."

II. IN THE LAND OF KITTOR

When King Solomon heard the hoopoe's story he was delighted and ordered his servants to give the bird the most delicious food and drink, served in golden dishes. After he had eaten the hoopoe said to the King, "Now I'm ready to do your bidding."

So King Solomon called his scribes and had them write the following letter:

KING SOLOMON AND THE QUEEN OF SHEBA: Adapted from the *Midrash*.

"Peace be with you, O Queen of Sheba, and peace be with all your people! Know that God appointed me King over many lands and peoples. He made me sovereign over all the beasts and the animals, over the fish, the birds and the insects. Therefore, I promise you that if you will come and pay me homage I will honor you and raise you above all the sovereigns under my rule. But, should you not obey me, then be forewarned that I will send against you my mighty legions, who will grind you and your kingdom to dust! Should you ask what are those mighty legions of which I speak—know then: that the birds in the sky are my cavalry and the animals of the earth are my infantry. At my command, they will descend upon your land and annihilate you and your people, for against them you can find no protection."

The scribes then tied this letter to a wing of the hoopoe who, as he went winging through the air, called upon all the other birds to follow him.

It was early in the morning when the hoopoe arrived in the land of Kittor, just at the hour when the Queen of Sheba left her palace to worship the sun. When he saw her he gathered all the birds about him and said to them, "Do not scatter about in all directions, but assemble in the air close together."

When the army of birds closed their ranks they hid the light of the sun and the earth grew dark. At this the Queen of Sheba became frightened.

"Woe is me!" she cried. "Something terrible has happened to me! I can no longer see—everything has grown dark before my eyes!"

The hoopoe alighted at the feet of the Queen and stretched out his wings. She saw the letter tied to his wing, and when she read it she began to tremble.

In haste she gathered her counsellors and sages and read them the letter. And when they heard it they looked puzzled and said, "How odd that we have never heard of this King Solomon nor of his kingdom!"

And, despite the advice of her counsellors to ignore the letter, the Queen of Sheba summoned the captains of all her ships and placed in their care many gems, much gold and silver, also six hundred beautiful boys and girls, all of the same size and proportions and dressed alike. These she sent as gifts to King Solomon with the following message:

"And thus speaks the Queen of Sheba: the span of a seven years' journey lies between my country, Kittor, and the land of Israel; but, in order that I may hear your great wisdom from your own lips, I am starting out immediately on the long journey to Jerusalem. Be assured I will neither rest nor spare any effort to make the seven years' journey in only three years, for so great is my eagerness to see you!"

III. The Crystal Palace

The day came at last when the Queen of Sheba was to arrive in Jerusalem. King Solomon sent his bosom friend, Benaiah ben Yehudah, to meet her outside the city limits.

As the Queen of Sheba approached the Holy City, reclining in her litter, she saw at a distance a wondrous rose growing at the edge of a lake. But when she came near she saw to her astonishment the rose suddenly transformed into a flashing star. The closer she came the more dazzling was its light. She was enchanted with its beauty.

When she finally reached the lake's bank she saw, amidst a crowd of nobles dressed in magnificent raiment, a man of arresting beauty. So she said to her servants, "I will alight from my litter and prostrate myself in homage, because my eyes are now gazing upon the face of Solomon, King of Israel."

As she alighted, followed by her attendants, Benaiah ben Yehudah hastened to her and asked, "Why have you left your litter, O Queen of Sheba?"

"To pay homage to you, O King Solomon," she answered.

"Return to your litter, O Queen," said Benaiah. "I am not the King, only one of his servants."

At this the Queen turned to her nobles and said, "Before we may see the lion in his glory he wishes us first to admire his lair, Jerusalem. Before we may have the joy of beholding the King in all his splendor he has made us look upon one of his servants, the like of whose beauty I've never seen."

Benaiah then hastened to the King to inform him of the Queen of Sheba's arrival. Thereupon Solomon entered his crystal palace and seated himself upon his throne.

When the Queen entered and saw him seated on his wondrous throne looking as dazzling as the sun at noon, it appeared to her as though he was floating on water. So, in order not to wet her garments, she lifted up the hem of her skirt and came nearer.

When the King saw her he welcomed her and praised her beauty. Then he seated her on a throne at his right hand.

IV. THE QUEEN OF SHEBA ASKS RIDDLES

"I will ask you some riddles," said the Queen of Sheba to King Solomon. "If you answer them I will then know that it is true when people call you wise."

"Tell me your riddles," said the King.

And the Queen of Sheba asked, "What water does not fall from heaven nor does it gush from stones and the clefts of the rocks? Sometimes it is sweeter than honey and at other times more bitter than gall even though it has the same source."

And Solomon answered, "The tear comes neither from heaven nor from the clefts of the rock. It tastes sweet when man weeps for joy and bitter when he weeps in sorrow."

The Queen of Sheba asked him another riddle: "My loving mother gave me two gifts. One has a beautifully rounded hole in it; the other can cut glass. The first is found in the sea; the second in the depths of the earth."

And the King made answer: "The first gift is the ring with the pearl on your finger—the second is the pendant of diamonds at your throat."

"What," asked the Queen, "is that which you bury before it's dead, and the more it lies and rots the stronger it gets and more life issues from it?"

And Solomon answered, "You bury living seeds in the earth and they shoot forth golden heads of wheat."

"Tell me, O King," continued the Queen of Sheba, "what is it, which when it descends from heaven is pure and white but afterwards becomes sullied? In time it returns to heaven in the form of clouds and again becomes as pure as it first was."

And Solomon answered, "What can be whiter than snow when it descends from heaven and which turns into mud on the highway? The clouds gave birth to it and sent it down upon the earth and when it thaws in the sun it goes back again where it came from."

"Now I will put your wisdom to the supreme test," said the Queen of Sheba. And she ordered that the six hundred boys and girls she had presented as a gift to the King be brought in.

"Tell me, O wise King, which are the boys and which are the girls."

And the King issued a command to assemble them. And it was very difficult to distinguish between them for they were of the same height and were dressed alike. Then the King said to his servants, "Place before each a basin of water and ask them to wash their hands and faces but do not give them any towels."

And so it was done and the six hundred boys and girls began to wash. And when they were through and found that there were no towels, those who were girls dried their hands and faces with the hem of their skirts, and those who were boys, not knowing what to do, remained standing uncomfortably with wet hands and faces.

Afterwards the King ordered that great baskets of nuts, apples and pomegranates be brought. With his own hands he distributed them to the children. Those that put up their little skirts in which to gather the fruit the King placed at his right, and those who held the fruit in their hands he placed on his left. Then he said to the Queen, "Those on my right are girls; those on my left, boys."

Filled with wonder the Queen of Sheba said to her seers and magicians, "By means of your magic you were able to make these six hundred boys and girls look alike. I ask you then—is what the King has done true or false?"

"True!" cried the seers and magicians with one voice. "He is as wise as an angel of God!"

V. The Locked Casket

Once the Queen of Sheba accompanied King Solomon on horseback outside Jerusalem. When they came near Mount Lebanon they dismounted and sat down on the grass to rest.

"Listen!" said the Queen. "Do you hear a woman singing? But I do not understand her words."

"This is a farmer's wife," answered the King. "She sings that her husband Abiezer works in the fields, that her son Ahiezer is grazing his flock in the pasture, and that she herself is doing the housework. She sings that, although so humble, she is happier than I, Solomon King of Israel, is in his palace."

"What a good woman!" cried the Queen, enchanted. "Just see how unjust you were when you wrote that among a thousand men one may find one who is good, but that among all women you have found not even one who is virtuous."

"I still hold to that opinion," answered King Solomon.

To this the Queen of Sheba replied, "I will not believe you until you have proven this woman."

"Very well," said King Solomon. "Let us now go to the house where this virtuous woman lives and we will test her."

So they went to the house of Abiezer and stood before the door. When the farmer's wife saw them she bowed low and invited them to enter her lowly home. When the royal guests had entered she placed before them a pitcher of cold water, milk, butter and sweet cakes. She begged them to eat and they ate. And the Queen of Sheba said to King Solomon, "See, I have found a virtuous woman, but where will you find a virtuous man among a thousand?"

King Solomon laughed and said, "Let us not keep this woman from her housework, for soon her husband and her son will return tired and hungry from their work in the fields, and she must prepare their noonday meal."

As they left the house King Solomon said, "As you wish me to test this woman's virtue I will do so, although I have no desire to disturb the tranquil life of this family."

Then the King went back to his horse and returned carrying a little casket. He unlocked it and asked the Queen of Sheba to look inside. She saw in it a little white mouse and a tiny dish of seeds. The King then locked the casket and said, "With this I will test the virtue of this woman. If she withstands the temptation I am placing before her then I will admit that I am in error."

At that King Solomon and the Queen of Sheba returned to the farmhouse where they met Abiezer and his son. The farmer immediately recognized the King, because he had seen him on several occasions when he had gone to Jerusalem on pilgrimages.

Then King Solomon said to the wife of Abiezer, "I am leaving this little casket with you for three days. Place it in that corner there, and under no circumstances must you move or open it. If you do as I bid you I will give you many fine gifts, but if you disobey me you, your husband and your son will have to pay with your lives."

The King then gave the key of the box to Abiezer. He blessed him, his wife and his son and returned to Jerusalem with the Queen of Sheba.

When they were eating their evening meal Abiezer's wife said to him, "The Lord only knows what's inside this little box! Maybe the King has filled it with gems. It also might be that it is an enchanted box."

"Better let us not think or speculate about this box," urged Abiezer. "Let it rest there in the corner until the King comes back for it in three days."

Abiezer then went to bed and early in the morning he arose for his daily labors. When he returned home for the noon meal his wife placed food before him, but she herself would not touch any of it. When he asked her whether she was ill or had received evil tidings from the home of her father she answered, "I have not slept all night long, dear husband, thinking about that little box. Even when I dozed off for a little while I had nightmares. Oh, if I only knew what is inside of that locked box!"

"Stop talking about that box!" Abiezer said angrily. "Remember what the King said, and don't trifle with our lives!"

Then he returned to his work.

When he came home in the evening he found his wife in bed groaning and moaning.

"What ails you?" cried Abiezer in a fright.

"Let me be!" wailed his wife. "Now I see that you think more of the little box than of me."

Abiezer tried to comfort and soothe her, but to no avail. She persisted: "If you love me truly and wish me to get well then let us both look through the keyhole of the box. I must confess that while you were at work I wished to get near the box but a terrible fright came over me. I have no doubt that the King has hidden a little demon inside."

His wife tormented Abiezer so long with her nagging that finally he was obliged to give in to her, saying, "Very well. Get out of bed and come with me to the box, but remember, you must not touch it with your hands!"

"Have no anxiety on that score," his wife answered. "Even if I were to touch it no harm would come of it. What King Solomon meant was that we should not move it from the corner. He never said anything about not touching it."

And so she looked through the keyhole of the box, but she saw nothing. Thereupon she was filled with disappointment and said bitterly, "The King has concealed his secret only too well. We will never know what's inside that box unless we open it."

Hearing these words Abiezer began to tremble and cried out with fright, "What a terrible thought! Do not speak about opening that box unless you wish to forfeit our lives!"

Then he led her back to her bed, saying, "You must rest now and try to calm yourself. In the morning you will get up feeling better. You'll begin doing your housework again and will forget all about that box."

Then they went to bed.

When the morning star appeared in the sky Abiezer arose. He made his ablutions and said the morning prayers. Afterwards, he went to labor in the fields.

He had been at work only a short while when he saw his son Ahiezer hastening to him.

"Quick father, come home!" cried Ahiezer. "Mother is near death and she wants to see you before she dies!"

When Abiezer heard this he exclaimed, "Woe is me! All these years I have lived in peace and contentment, then the King had to come and bring this misfortune upon us!"

Abiezer hurried home and found his wife in bed. He said to her, "Take heart, my wife, and arise!"

But she answered, "It is already two days that I have taken neither food nor drink and my body is altogether weakened. I had a frightful dream last night. I quake even now when I think of it. In my dream I saw many demons and devils float out of this box until they filled the house. They danced and whirled about me, raised a great lamentation and gnashed their teeth with rage. One devil sprang upon my bed and said to me: 'If you do not open the box and liberate us we will again come tomorrow night and choke you. We will tear you limb from limb. We will burn you, grind you to dust and cast you to all the seven winds!' And when the devil finished speaking he spat in my face and disappeared. I awoke trembling with fright. I called you but you did not answer."

And Abiezer's wife did not cease her weeping. "Soon," she said, "the devils will come and choke me. Therefore, I've sent for you that you should prepare my grave for me."

"Why do you tell me your foolish dreams?" Abiezer reproached her. "Don't you know that dreams are false and ridiculous? If there really were demons and devils in the box, as you say, then it wouldn't be you but *me* that they would try to scare because the key to the box is in my possession. Therefore your dream has no meaning. You dreamed it because you were thinking about the box all the time."

When the wife of Abiezer saw that he was resolute not to open the box she got out of bed and fell weeping at his feet.

"Do me only one small favor," she pleaded. "Give me the key and I will open the box only the tiniest bit. I will peep into it for just one instant, then I will close it quickly and nobody will ever know about it."

"Dear wife!" Abiezer cried. "How drawn and pinched your face looks! Come and eat and you will feel better and calmer. Then you will recall what the King said to us and you will stop thinking about the box."

Abiezer then helped her out of bed. He placed food before her and urged her to eat. She ate, but no sooner had she finished when again she resumed her wailing, saying, "Oh Abiezer, my loving husband! Have pity on me! The King does not have to know anything about this. I will be very careful and I swear that I will take only one little peep."

And so she carried on until evening, until Abiezer could no longer endure her nagging. So he arose and said, "Very well, we will open the box. But remember—for only one instant, just as you promise."

So Abiezer inserted the key and no sooner did he turn it in the lock when the box sprang open and the little white mouse that was inside jumped out and disappeared.

Abiezer and his wife were congealed with terror. She rent her garments and cried bitterly, "It is you Abiezer who will be the cause of our death. Had you been careful the mouse would not have jumped out. How many times did I have to tell you to open the lid just the tiniest bit, and you had to go and open it altogether!"

"Why do you reproach me?" replied Abiezer resentfully. "If you had not pestered me to open the box nothing would have happened."

"It was all your fault!" lamented his wife. "Had you only been a real man and had will-power you would not have allowed yourself to be governed by a woman. You would not have given in to me and we would have avoided misfortune."

But Abiezer said bitterly, "Of what use now are lamentations and tears! We cannot undo our mistake that way. Better let us pray to the Almighty to aid us."

On the third day, as Abiezer and his wife sat grieving, King Solomon and the Queen of Sheba arrived. The guilty woman fell at the feet of the King and cried, "By your life, O my Lord the King, know that it was I who opened the box! Have mercy and spare my life!"

"Why did you disobey me, Abiezer?" asked the King sternly.

And Abiezer answered, "It is I who am the guilty one, O King, because I allowed my wife to wheedle me into doing such a thing. Now I beseech you, have mercy on my wife and let her live. If you wish to punish us it is me you should kill!"

Gently King Solomon answered, "Peace be to you both, my children! Be assured I wish you no harm. I only wished to prove you."

The Queen of Sheba then asked Abiezer to tell her all that had happened, and when Abiezer had finished his story King Solomon exclaimed, "One man among a thousand have I found; but a woman among all those have I not found."

The Origin of the Roman Empire

WHEN King Solomon took Pharaoh's daughter for a wife she brought with her from Egypt a thousand different musical instruments. She instructed him in the use of all of them, saying, "In this manner you play to honor this idol—in that manner you play to honor that idol."

No word of reproach ever passed Solomon's lips.

On that very day the Angel Gabriel stuck a rod into the sea and around the rod formed sand and seaweed. From these arose an island and on the island was built the Empire of Rome which robbed the Jews of their land and drove them into exile.

THE ORIGIN OF THE ROMAN EMPIRE: Adapted from the *Agada* in the Talmud.

Story of the Ant

THIS is what happened in the days of Solomon the King, peace be to him. When the Holy One, blessed be He, gave to Solomon the kingdom, and made him ruler over all animals, and over every creature that is in the world, over the sons of men, and the beasts and the birds, and whatsoever the Holy One had created, He also gave him a great mantle to sit upon. It was of green silk, interwoven with fine gold, and embroidered with images of all kinds; its length was sixty miles, and its breadth was sixty miles. And Solomon had four princes: the first prince was of the sons of men, the second prince was of the demons, the third of the beasts, and the fourth of the birds. The prince who was of the sons of men was Asaf, son of Berachiah; the prince who was of the demons was Ramirat; the prince of the beasts was a lion; and the prince of the birds was an eagle. And Solomon, when he travelled, rode on the wind; he would take the meal of the morning in Damascus, and the meal of the evening in Media, that is in the east and the west. Now one day Solomon was boasting himself, and he said, "Behold there is none like me in the world, for the Holy One hath given me wisdom and understanding, and knowledge and discernment, and hath made me ruler over all His creatures." At that moment the wind withdrew from him, and there fell from off the mantle forty thousand men. When Solomon saw this, he cried out to the wind, "Return, O wind, and be tranquil!" The wind answered him saying, "Return thou, O Solomon, to thy God, and boast not thyself; then will I return to thee." In that hour was Solomon abashed by the words of the wind.

Another day that he was thus travelling, he passed over a valley in which were ants, and he heard the voice of a black ant that said to her companions, "Enter into your houses, lest ye be crushed by the hosts of King Solomon." When Solomon heard the words of the ant, he was angry, and he said to the wind, "Descend to the earth," and the wind descended. He sent after the ants, and said to them, "Which of you was it that said, 'enter into your houses, lest the armies of Solomon crush you?'" The ant that had spoken answered, "It was I who said this to them." He said, "Why didst thou speak thus?" She answered, "Because I feared that they would go out to look upon thy armies, and cease from the praises with which they praise the Holy One, and that His anger would be kindled against us, and He would destroy us." He said to her, "Why, amongst all the ants didst thou alone speak?" She answered, "Because I am the Queen over them." He said to her, "What is thy name?" She answered, "Machshamah." He said to her, "I wish to ask thee a question." She said, "It is not fitting that the one who asks should be on high, and the one who is asked should be below." He lifted her up to him. She said, "It is not fitting that the one who asks should be seated on his throne, and the one who is asked should

STORY OF THE ANT: From the *Midrash*. In *Miscellany of Hebrew Literature,* edited by the Rev. A. Löwy. London: N. Trübner and Co., 1872-77.

be on the ground; take me into thy hand, and I will reply to what thou shalt ask." He took her into his hand, so that she was before his face, and she said, "Ask what thou wilt." He said to her, "Is there in the world a greater than I?" She said to him, "Yes." He said, "Who is it?" She answered, "It is I." Said Solomon to her, "How art thou greater than I?" She said, "If I were not greater than thou art, the Holy One would not have sent thee to me to take me into thy hand." When Solomon heard the words of the ant he was very wroth, and cast her down, and said to her, "Ant, thou knowest not who I am; I am Solomon, son of David the king, peace be to him." She said to him, "Consider that thou art sprung from a vile clot and cease from boasting." In that hour, Solomon fell on his face, and was ashamed and abashed at the words of the ant. He then said to the wind, "Lift up the mantle and let us go." The wind lifted up the mantle, and the ant said to Solomon, "Go, but forget not the Lord, nor boast thyself exceedingly."

The wind then rose continually higher and higher between heaven and earth, and thus passed ten days and ten nights. One day Solomon saw a lofty palace at a distance, built all of fine gold. Then said Solomon to his princes, "I have never seen aught like this palace in the world." At once he said to the wind, "Descend." The wind obeyed, and Solomon went forth, he and his prince Asaf, son of Berachiah, and they walked round and round the palace, and the scent of the herbage there was like the scent of the garden of Eden; but they could find no gate by which to enter it; and they wondered at the matter, as to how the palace could be entered. While they were thus engaged, the prince of the demons came to the king, and said to him, "My lord, why art thou so troubled?" Solomon answered, "I am troubled about this palace, because it has no gate, and I know not what to do." Said the prince of the demons, "My lord the King, I will command the demons to mount up to the roof of the palace; perhaps they will find something; either a man, or a bird, or some living creature. At once he cried out to the demons, saying, "Hasten and mount up to the top of the roof, and see if ye can find aught. They went and ascended to the roof; then they came down again, and said, "My lord, we have seen no man there, nothing but one great bird, which is named the eagle, and he was sitting upon his young ones. At once Solomon called to the prince of the birds, and said to him, "Go, and bring the eagle to me." The Vulture then went, and brought the eagle before Solomon the king, peace be to him; then the eagle opened his mouth in praises to the King, the King of Kings, the Holy One, and then he saluted King Solomon. Said Solomon to him, "What is thy name?" He answered, "El'inyâd." "How old art thou?" asked Solomon. "Seven hundred years," replied the eagle. Said Solomon, "Hast thou ever seen or known or heard that this palace had a gate?" Said the eagle, "By thy life, my lord the King, and by the life of thy head, I know not; but I have a brother, older than myself by two hundred years, and he has knowledge and understanding, and he dwells in the second storey." Then said Solomon to the Vulture, "Take back this eagle to his place, and bring me his elder brother." He disappeared, and after a time returned into the presence of Solomon, and with him was an eagle greater than the former; and this eagle, too, uttered songs and praises to his Creator, and saluted King Solomon, and stood before him. Said Solomon, "What is thy name?" He answered, "El'ôf." "How many are the days of the years of thy life?" asked Solomon. The eagle answered "Nine hundred years." Said Solomon, "Hast thou known or heard that there is an entrance to this palace?" He answered, "My lord, by thy life, and the life of thy head, I know not; but I have a brother older than myself by four hundred years; he has knowledge and understanding, and he dwells in the third storey." Then said Solomon to the prince of the birds, "Carry this one back, and bring before me his elder brother." He took him away, and they disappeared; then after a time came the greatest eagle, and he was very old; he could not fly, but they bare him on their wings, and set him before Solomon, and he gave praise and glory to his Creator, and saluted the King. Said Solomon to him, "What is thy name?" He answered "Altamar." "How old art thou?" asked Solomon. "Thirteen hundred years," he answered. He said to him, "Hast thou known or heard whether there is an entrance to this palace?" He answered, "My lord, by thy life, I know not; however, my father told me that there was an entrance to the palace on the western side, but that the dust had covered it through the number of years that had passed. If thou wilt command the wind to sweep away the dust that is heaped up around the house the entrance will be disclosed." Solomon commanded the wind, and it blew, and removed the dust that was around the house, and uncovered the entrance. And the gate was very great, and made of iron, and it was as though consumed and mouldering from the lapse of time. And they saw upon it a lock, whereon was written, "Be it known to you, ye sons of men, that we dwelt in this palace in prosperity and delights many years. When the famine came upon us, we ground pearls in the mill instead of wheat, but it profited us nothing. Then we left our palace to the eagles, and laid us down on the ground, and we said unto the eagles, 'If any man shall ask you concerning this palace, ye shall say, "We found it ready built." ' " There was also written, "No man shall enter into this house unless he be a prophet or a king. If such an one desire to enter, let him dig on the right side of the gate, and he will perceive a chest; let him break it open, and he will find in it keys; then let him open the entrance gate and he will find a gate of gold; if he open this and enter within, he will find a second, and then a third. Let him open these, and beyond the third he will see a stately building, and in it is a hall set with ruby, and topaz, and emerald, and pearl. Within is an alcove adorned with all kinds of pearls; he will see, moreover, many goodly chambers and courts, paved with bricks of alternate silver and gold. Then let him look on the ground, and he will see the figure of a scorpion: if he will remove the scorpion, which is of silver, he will find a chamber under the ground in which are pearls without number, and silver and gold. Then will be found another doorway, with a lock upon it; and upon the door is written,

'The lord of this palace was pre-eminent in honour and might: even the lions and the bears dreaded his kingdom and his majesty. And he dwelt in this place in prosperity and delights, and he reigned, sitting upon his throne; but his hour to die came upon him before the due time, and as he died the crown fell from his head. Enter into the palace, and thou shalt see wonders.' "

Solomon opened the door and entered, and saw a third gateway, on which was written, "They dwelt in honour and riches; they died, and the ills of time passed over them; they departed to their graves, and there was not left to them one to tread the ground." And he opened the gate and found a hall of ruby, and topaz, and emerald, on which was written, "How did I stand! how much did I encounter! how I ate and drank! how was I clothed in beautiful apparel! how did I affright others, and how at last was I affrighted myself!" He went farther, and saw a beautiful mansion of topaz and emerald, and it had three gates. On the first gate was written, "Son of man, let not fortune deceive thee; thou shalt waste away and go and depart from thy place, and thou shalt lie beneath the ground." On the second was written, "Be not in haste; walk circumspectly, for the world is given from one to another." On the third gate was written, "Take provision for thy journey, and make ready food for thyself while it is yet day; for thou shalt not be left on the earth, and thou knowest not the day of thy death." Then Solomon opened the door and entered, and he saw an image sitting, and any one that looked upon it would have thought that it lived; and Solomon went towards it and drew near, and the image quaked, and cried with a loud voice, "Come hither, ye children of Satan; see! King Solomon is come to destroy you." Then fire and smoke went out of the nostrils of the image. Immediately there was a loud and bitter cry among them, with earthquake and thunder. Solomon cried out loudly to them, "Will ye affright me? Do ye not know that I am Solomon the King, who reigns over all the creatures which the Almighty has created? I shall chastise you with every chastisement since you rebel against me." Then he uttered against them the Ineffable Name. At once they were motionless, and not one of them was able to speak; and all the images fell on their faces, and the sons of Satan fled and cast themselves into the great sea, that they might not fall into the hands of Solomon. Solomon drew near to the image, and took a tablet of silver and a chain from its neck, and there was written on the plate all that concerned the palace. But Solomon could not read it; therefore was he greatly grieved, and he said to his princes, "Know ye not what trouble I have taken in order to reach this image, and now that I have the plate, I cannot read what is written on it?" While he was considering the matter and saying, "What shall I do?" he looked, and behold a young man came from the wilderness, and he came before Solomon and made obeisance to him, and said to him, "What is the matter with thee, King Solomon, that thou art grieved?" Solomon answered, "It is by reason of this plate that I am grieved, because I know not what is written on it." The young man said,

"Give it to me, and I will read it; for I was sitting in my place, and the Almighty saw thee how thou wast grieving, and sent me to read the writing to thee." Solomon gave it into the hand of the youth, who looked upon it, and saw and was astonished for a while, and wept and said, "O, Solomon, the writing is in the Greek tongue, and it says, 'I, Sheddad, son of Ad, reigned over a thousand thousand provinces, and rode on a thousand thousand horses; a thousand thousand kings were subject to me, and a thousand thousand warriors I slew. Yet in the hour that the Angel of Death came against me I could not withstand him.'" Moreover there was written, "Whoso shall read this writing, let him not trouble himself greatly about this world, for the end of all men is to die, and nothing remains to man but a good name."

The Downfall of King Solomon

KING SOLOMON ruled over all animals and birds as well as over the demons and devils, and all the earth was full of his glory. But in the eyes of God he was only a wretched sinner and braggart who deserved punishment for his misdeeds. Solomon had violated three of the precepts that the Torah prescribed for a ruler when he took to himself a thousand wives, when he raised horses without number, when he accumulated great treasures of gold and silver. Therefore, the Almighty smote him with the rod of His wrath and justice. And it happened this wise:

One day King Solomon took captive Ashmodai, King of all the Demons. He had him bound in iron chains so that he was powerless to do him harm. Whereupon Ashmodai said to King Solomon, "If you will lend me your magic ring I will confide to you a great secret."

Solomon trusted him and gave him his ring on which was engraved the Ineffable Name of God. But no sooner did the wily Ashmodai have the ring in his hand when he threw it into the sea where a fish swallowed it.

Deprived of his ring, the King lost all his supernatural powers. With glee, Ashmodai raised him up and cast him away to a distance of four hundred miles from Jerusalem and outside the boundaries of his kingdom.

The King looked about him and found that he was in a desert. Everywhere he saw nothing but a sea of sand and the sky overhead. This made him very despondent, for he understood what Ashmodai had done to him.

At last, taking courage, he arose and began looking for some place of shelter where he could hide from the beasts of prey prowling all around him. He sought in vain. The sun beat down upon him fiercely so that he grew parched with thirst. Then the pangs of hunger gripped him.

After a while he perceived a small oasis in the distance and he began running towards it. There he found some shepherds grazing their flocks. They took pity on him and hospitably gave him food and drink.

THE DOWNFALL OF KING SOLOMON: Adapted from the *Midrash*.

Having eaten, King Solomon asked, "How far is it to Jerusalem?"

"Jerusalem!" the shepherds exclaimed wonderingly. "In what country is Jerusalem? We have never heard of such a city."

King Solomon thought: "These are young shepherds, therefore they haven't heard of Jerusalem. I will ask their elders; no doubt they will be able to give me the right answer."

It was towards evening that Solomon met an old man returning from the fields, hobbling along on his stick. He greeted him courteously and asked, "Tell me, my good man, how far is it to Jerusalem, the famous capital of King Solomon, son of David?"

"Jerusalem? I never heard of such a city," answered the old man. "This is the first time I ever heard the name of such a king."

King Solomon fell into a great melancholy when he heard the old man's words, and began to reproach himself bitterly, "What a vain fool I have been! All along I have deceived myself with the notion that my name was great among all the peoples of the earth. Only now I see that it was only empty conceit that made me believe that."

The following morning King Solomon entered a village. He was a sorry sight—in tatters. His appearance only depressed him the more, for he noticed the pitying looks of the passersby.

Finally, he entered a house in which lived a Jew and his wife and he said to them, "Don't be deceived by my appearance, my good friends! I may be barefoot and in rags, but know that I am Solomon, son of David, the King of Jerusalem. I met with a misfortune, and, as you see, I now find myself cast away, a stranger in a foreign land. Have pity on me then and give me a crust of bread, for I am hungry!"

Hearing these astonishing words the Jew and his wife burst into laughter.

"Oh you poor lunatic!" they said commiseratingly. "Do you think we don't know that our King Solomon lives in Jerusalem?"

Then Solomon began to swear by all things holy that he had told them nothing but the truth. So they said to him gently, "We certainly are sorry that you have gone out of your mind, you poor, unfortunate man!"

When Solomon heard these terrible words he fell silent. The woman gave him food which he ate. Then he thanked her and went his way.

After much wandering, footsore and weary, King Solomon came to a great city. Meeting with a man in rich garb on the street he said to him, "I beg you—take pity on me! Give me shoes, for my feet are bruised. Give me clothing, for I am naked. When I return to Jerusalem, the capital of my kingdom, I will repay you a hundredfold."

"Who are you?" asked the man in astonishment.

"I am Solomon, the son of David and King in Jerusalem," answered the King.

The rich man shook with laughter and said mockingly, "If you really are Solomon, the wisest of all men, why did you leave your royal throne to wander about as a beggar in a foreign land? Is that a wise thing to do, O wisest of mortals!"

Solomon then told the rich man all that had happened to him. The man listened attentively and was filled with wonder. Finally he took pity on him and said to his wife, "Give this man new clothes and shoes. Know that he is King Solomon of Jerusalem!"

Her husband's words filled the woman with amazement.

"O you fool!" she cried. "Do you have to believe everything you are told?"

But her husband called her aside and told her everything that had happened to Solomon. She then understood that what the beggar had said was true. Then she suddenly recalled something and grew angry. Without a word, she picked up a stick and began to belabor Solomon.

"What is it, woman?" cried Solomon. "What harm have I done you that you should treat me so?"

"Why did you say," cried the woman, "that among a thousand men you found one virtuous one but none among women?"

"Calm yourself, I beg you," pleaded King Solomon, "and don't be angry with me. If you will ponder well what I have said you will surely understand that I did not mean to defame women but to do them good."

But the woman remained unappeased.

"How dare you say that your intention was to do them good when you wrote about them with such contempt?"

King Solomon answered, "Had I written in my book that among a thousand women one could find a good and clever one it would have been a great calamity for all women. Men would have done nothing but divorce their wives. Every man would have reasoned thus: 'The woman God gave me is wicked. She is an insufferable nag. Let me divorce her and look for another. Who knows—God in his goodness might bless me with a woman about whom Solomon had said that she was the one virtuous one among a thousand!' Therefore, my dear woman, because I wrote that there was not one good woman to be found, each man will say: 'What's the use of divorcing my wife and taking another since there isn't one good one in the whole lot?'"

King Solomon's answer softened the woman. Her anger left her and, as she parted from him, it was with the blessing: "May God in His mercy restore you to the throne of David, O wise and good King!"

The Sorrow of Jeremiah

WHEN Jeremiah looked upon the Jewish captives he saw that the young men wore shackles on their hands and feet. He hastened to them and stood among them and asked that also his hands and feet be shackled with iron chains.

THE SORROW OF JEREMIAH: *Ibid.*

When Nebuzaradan, the Babylonian conqueror, saw this he took the chains away from him.

Then Jeremiah looked upon the old Jewish captives. When he saw that they wore halters around their necks he hastened to them and stood among them and also put a halter around his own neck.

When Nebuzaradan saw this he took the halter away from him and rebuked Jeremiah: "Either you are a false prophet, or you are incapable of feeling pain, or you wish for my death. Wasn't it you who foretold this disaster to your people? Yet you grieve over it as if it had come as a surprise to you! I have tried to spare you every pain, but out of your own free will you look for grief. You very well know that for my own sake I must guard your life in order not to anger your God. But you appear determined to destroy yourself, thus bringing the wrath of your God on me."

As the procession of the captives began to leave Jerusalem, Jeremiah walked with them. When he came to the graves of the Patriarchs in Hebron he called out to them:

"Oh our Fathers, Abraham, Isaac, and Jacob—arise and come to our aid! Your children are being led into captivity!"

Then a voice sounded, saying: "It is a long time since I've turned my face away from this people!"

Jeremiah then ran to the graves of the Matriarchs.

"Oh our Mothers, Sarah, Rebecca, Rachel and Leah—arise and come to our aid!"

And a heavenly voice answered: "Rachel weeps without cease for her children."

Jeremiah then hastened to the graves of the Prophets and cried out: "Oh Moses! Oh Samuel!—arise and come to our aid! Your children are being led into captivity!"

And a voice answered: "Alas, neither Moses nor Samuel can help you any more!"

Jeremiah then ran into the houses of mourning, crying: "Give me the bread of sorrow! Give me the chalice of consolation! My children are being led into captivity."

And a voice answered: "Leave the house of mourning; it is too late!"

Jeremiah then hastened back to the captives and when they reached the River Euphrates, Nebuzaradan said to him: "If you wish you may come with us to Babylon; if not you are free to return to Jerusalem."

And God spoke to Jeremiah: "Go you to Babylon; I will remain in Judea. However, should you chose to remain in Judea then I will go to Babylon. One of us must remain with the people."

Jeremiah asked himself: "How can I help the captive Jews in Babylon? It is better that God stay with them for He is mighty and is able to protect His people."

And to Nebuzaradan he said: "I will not go with you to Babylon. I will

return to Judea so that I may comfort those of my people who have remained behind."

When the captives saw that the Prophet was preparing to leave them
they broke into loud lamentation.

"O Jeremiah, O Prophet of God!" they cried. "Why do you abandon
us?"

And they wept most bitterly.

When Jeremiah heard this he was filled with sorrow.

"O my children!" he cried. "Woe is me! Had you but listened to my
warnings in Jerusalem you would have been spared all these trials!"

And as he spoke two tears rolled down his cheeks.

When the Babylonian commanders saw the captives weep they cried
out against them and beat them.

"Cease your weeping or we'll slay you all!" they cried.

Again the captives implored the Prophet to remain with them.

"See for yourself," they said to him, "we are not allowed to lament
but you can do so freely. You are free to pray to God—we may only
weep in the stillness of night when we lie down to sleep and no one sees
us."

And Jeremiah spoke words of comfort to the people. He blessed them
and said: "God will not abandon you even in exile. Have hope and put
your trust in Him!"

Then Jeremiah went his way.

But the two tears that the Prophet had shed miraculously turned into
two lakes.

Again Jeremiah returned to Jerusalem. On the way he saw a woman.
She was dressed in black and her face was veiled. As he came near he
heard her lament: "Woe is me, woe is me! Who will comfort me now?
Who will stand by me now?"

"Why do you lament so, woman?" asked Jeremiah.

"O my master!" replied the woman. "Don't you recognize me any more?
You know very well that I had a husband and seven children."

"What has happened to them?" asked Jeremiah. "Perhaps I can help
you."

"O master, my husband has abandoned me!" sighed the woman. "I've
gone forth to seek him but I have not found him. Sad at heart, I returned
home to my children. My neighbors came towards me and cried: 'Unfortunate woman! Your house has fallen down and has crushed your seven
children!' And now, my master—who will comfort me? I'm alone in the
world, without husband and children!"

"Poor woman!" sighed the Prophet. "Your grief is indeed great, but,
I implore you, turn your thoughts to poor unfortunate Mother Zion and
be consoled. Your husband abandoned you—but God abandoned Zion.
You lost only seven children, Zion has lost all her children! They are
either dead or captives. How can Zion be comforted then?"

"I am Mother Zion, O Prophet!" cried the woman suddenly in a loud voice. "I am the mother of your people! O comfort me, for my grief is beyond endurance! Comfort me, comfort me if only you know how!"

Then Jeremiah prostrated himself before the woman and cried out: "Rise up, poor unhappy mother! Shake the dust from your garments, for once more you shall be comforted!"

King Nebuchadnezzar, surrounded by the princes and satraps of his realm, sailed on the Euphrates River. The music of many plucked instruments was heard and the voices of singers sounded. Behind the bank on which the King sailed came a small boat. Four hundred beautiful Jewish boy and girl captives were in it. They were being led into captivity to Babylon, for King Nebuchadnezzar had commanded it so.

The children spread out their little hands and, weeping, prayed: "Protect us, O Lord! Have compassion, have mercy on us!"

When the Babylonian sailors heard this they said to them: "Do not fear. No evil will befall you. When you come to Babylon you will worship our gods and later you will marry our children."

No sooner did the sailors leave them when the children held counsel with one another. They came to a decision.

"Far better that we lie on the bottom of the Euphrates," they said, "than that we worship in luxury the idols in Babylon! We fear though that by our death we will anger God."

"God will understand and forgive us!" cried the eldest of the children.

Arm in arm the girl captives sprang into the River Euphrates.

"We will not abandon you!" cried the boys, and they leaped after them.

A storm arose and whipped up the waters so that a mighty wave carried to the ears of Jeremiah the sound of the weeping of the children. Thereupon he cried out: "They have given up their lives to glorify Your name, O Lord!"

When the Jewish captives in Babylon heard of the death of the children they spoke with pride: "Hail to them, the sons and daughters of our people, whose mighty hearts and spirits scorned the grave and despised death!"

And as they spoke thus their faces grew radiant. They raised their heads and lifted up their eyes and looked with disdain upon Nebuchadnezzar.

The king cried out in anger: "I will break your pride!" And to his slaves he said: "Up slaves! Fill sacks with sand and stones and lay them upon the necks of the Jews!"

The slaves did as the king bid them. Thenceforth the Jews walked with bowed backs. They were beaten cruelly and tormented without end. Therefore they cried aloud to God.

And when God heard them, He said: "I will destroy the earth!"

When the angels heard this they implored: "If you do this, Lord, who will sing the praise of Your handiwork? If you must destroy the earth, then spare the Heavens."

"Then descend to earth," commanded God, "and bring peace to the Jews. Only then will My anger subside."

And as the angels spoke Moses and the Patriarchs came before God.

"Tell us," pleaded the Patriarchs to Moses, "how does it fare with our children in Babylon?"

Moses answered: "Many were killed, many are in chains, many die of thirst and are not fortunate enough to find a grave."

The Patriarchs then broke into lamentation, saying: "Orphans without a protector—naked you are, with stones to lie upon. The sun burns you by day and the cold freezes you by night!"

"Cursed be the sun!" cried Moses, "because it has aided the enemy in his work of destruction!"

"Is it my fault if God has commanded me to shine?" pleaded the sun.

Moses' eye then fell upon the Temple ruins.

"Woe! Woe! Where is your glory now? The torch of the enemy has burnt you to the ground. Where are your priests? Where are your children?"

Then Moses spoke to the captives.

"I beseech you, do not spill your own blood!"

"Why do you say this?" asked the Patriarchs.

And Moses answered: "When our men and women fall to the ground under their burdens their tormentors bring to them their children and command them to kill them with their own hands. When the parents refuse, then the taskmasters themselves slay the children."

When Mother Rachel heard this she came before God and raised her voice in lamentation.

"I can no longer hold back my grief! It is a long time since I died. Great have been the sorrows I've borne for my children! Now I can no longer see their misery and hear their cries. Have mercy, Lord, on my children! Show it for the sake of the Patriarchs, show it for the sake of Moses and Aaron, show it for the sake of the love You have implanted in all parents for their children!"

When God heard this He relented.

"Cease your weeping!" He said. "Your children will someday be happy."

The Trials of Jonah

I. Jonah's Flight to Tarshish

"ARISE!" God bid Jonah. "Go to Nineveh and announce its destruction!"

Jonah thought: "Once before God sent me to threaten Jerusalem with the same fate. But the people there repented and the city still stands. They called me a lying prophet in Jerusalem. If I fare the same way in Nineveh then I'll end up by being despised both at home and abroad. No! I will not go there to carry out God's command!"

Jonah then went to the seashore and asked the sailors: "When does the next ship leave for Tarshish?"

"A ship left for Tarshish only the day before yesterday," they told him. "You'll have to wait for its return."

When Jonah heard this he felt sad indeed.

Immediately God made a strong wind to blow so the ship that was on its way to Tarshish was forced back to port.

"Now I am sure that my plan will be successful!" Jonah cried, overjoyed.

He now waited for the ship's return. When it started again he was on board, bound for Tarshish.

In the course of the voyage a great storm arose. It tossed the ship about and threatened to crush it. But the people on board saw with amazement that the other ships at sea were continuing serenely on their way, undisturbed by the storm. How could that be?

"The Gods rage against us alone!" cried the frightened sailors and passengers on board the ship to Tarshish. "The people on this ship belong to seventy separate nations. Let, therefore, every man pray to his god to come to our aid."

And this they did, each man praying to his god in his own tongue.

Yet no succor came.

All this while Jonah slept soundly, unaware of what was going on.

"How can you sleep and not pray at a time when we are in danger of perishing?" the captain cried, waking him. "To what nation do you belong?"

"I am a Jew," answered Jonah.

"A Jew!" exclaimed the captain. "Then you're one of those who worship the mighty God about whom I've heard so much. Pray to Him. Perhaps He'll cause a miracle to happen!"

THE TRIALS OF JONAH: *Ibid.*

While Jonah was evidently an historical personage—a Prophet who lived in the days of Jeroboam II—his fame to posterity has not been due to his exalted calling but to the fact that he is the hero of the Biblical fairy tale of *Jonah and the Whale* as told in the *Book of Jonah*. The *Midrashic* version, elaborately recounting his ocean journey and his adventures in the belly of the great fish, has proved one of the most diverting legends in Jewish folklore.—N. A.

"That cannot happen because God is angry with me," replied Jonah. "The storm will not subside until you will have cast me into the sea."

But the others would not believe his words. They cast lots in order to discover the sinner among them and it was Jonah who drew the fatal mark.

"Now we are convinced that the Jew's words were true!" they said. "Let him be cast into the sea so that we all may not die on account of one man!"

Still the captain would not consent to this.

"Hold!" he cried. "Let's not spill blood in haste! Perhaps there's another way out. We'll throw everything on board into the sea; maybe it will lighten the ship."

So they threw everything overboard and tried with all their might to steer the ship towards shore, but to no avail.

"Haven't I told you that you must cast me into the sea?" cried Jonah. "Otherwise the storm will not abate."

Thereupon, they all agreed to do what he asked of them and let him down into the sea. But barely were his knees under water when the storm subsided.

"Pull him back!" they all cried. "The danger is over now."

But no sooner was Jonah on board again when the storm began anew.

Once more they lowered Jonah into the sea, but this time up to his waist. And again the waters grew calm. So they pulled Jonah back into the ship. Yet, no sooner was he on board, when the storm resumed again.

For the third time they lowered him and again the waters grew calm. This time though they did not pull Jonah back again, and he sank into the sea.

II. Jonah and the Whale

When Jonah sank into the sea a great fish came and swallowed him. Nonetheless, the Prophet of God remained unharmed and was without fear, for overhead in the inside of the fish, hung a stone that shone as brightly as the sun. This made it easy for Jonah to look through the eyes of the great fish as through two windows. He thus could see everything that went on in the sea.

Suddenly the fish began to tremble and cried out: "I'm sorry for you, Jonah—your end is near!"

"Why so?" asked Jonah. "What do you see that's so frightening?"

"Leviathan, the king of all the fish is approaching!" cried the fish. "He will surely devour us both."

"In that case, bring me to him," asked Jonah. "He may relent and spare our lives."

The fish did as Jonah asked and swam up to Leviathan.

"I've come here to observe how you live," began Jonah to the king of the fish.

"What concern is it of yours?" asked Leviathan.

"You are the fish whom God will some day serve up as nourishment to the pious," answered Jonah.

When Leviathan heard this he grew frightened and hurried away.

"Since I've protected you," said Jonah to the fish, "show me all the interesting places around here."

"With pleasure," answered the fish, "but first tell me what it was that you and Leviathan spoke about."

Jonah consented and, while he told him all about it, the fish swam with him to the bottom of the sea.

Jonah noticed a great many mounds.

"What are these?" he asked the fish.

"Leviathan caused these mounds by spouting streams of water," answered the fish.

And, as the fish spoke, the air became hot and the water began to boil.

"What is the meaning of this?" asked Jonah.

"Now Leviathan is hungry and snorts with rage," replied the fish. "His breath is so hot that it consumes both the air and the water."

Jonah was inside the fish for three days, yet he did not say his prayers even once.

"Verily," said God, "I meant to do Jonah only good and have preserved his life, yet he has not thanked Me for it. Because of this I'll have him swallowed up by another fish, and, inside that fish, it won't go so well with him. Then he'll surely begin to pray again."

And it happened as God willed it. Another fish swam up to the fish in whose belly Jonah was, and said, "God has commanded me to swallow up this man who is inside of you. Surrender him to me or I'll swallow both of you at once!"

"How do I know that you speak the truth?" asked Jonah's fish warily.

"Come with me to Leviathan," answered the other fish. "He'll tell you that what I say is true."

So both went to Leviathan and asked him.

"It is true," answered Leviathan. "I was present yesterday when God commanded this fish to come to you."

Jonah was then obliged to leave the inside of the first fish and allow himself to be swallowed by the second.

In the belly of the second fish Jonah did not find his quarters as pleasant as in the first. He found it pitch dark and very uncomfortable.

Jonah was suddenly filled with terror. What if the fish had decided to devour him? In his anguish he once more thought of God and he started to pray: "Almighty God! Even when I am in the depths of the sea You abide with me and watch over me. Verily, You are the Ruler of the Universe, and Your throne is in heaven and on the earth. I call on You, therefore, to aid me and to lead me out of the depths of the sea to dry land!"

And God graciously heard Jonah's prayer and commanded the fish to carry him to shore and let him go in peace.

【2】

The World To Come

INTRODUCTION

It was but natural—believing in the immortality of the soul, in the reward of virtue and in the punishment of evil—that the Jews should have directed much thought to the *Olam ha-Ba,* the World-to-Come. Heaven and Hell, or Paradise and Gehenna, were two dual concepts borrowed from the Persians.

There was a wide variation in the popular conceptions of this World-to-Come. It ranged from the most spiritual—"The sages are not in Paradise— Paradise is in the sages"—to the following primitive visualization found in one of the minor *Midrashim:*

"The *Gan Eden* at the east measures 800,000 years (at ten miles per day or 3,650 miles per year). There are five chambers for various classes of the righteous. The first is built of cedar, with a ceiling of transparent crystal. This is the habitation of non-Jews who become true and devoted converts to Judaism. They are headed by Obadiah the prophet and Onkelos the proselyte, who teach them the Law. The second is built of cedar, with a ceiling of fine silver. This is the habitation of the penitents, headed by Manasseh, king of Israel, who teaches them the Law.

"The third chamber is built of silver and gold, ornamented with pearls. It is very spacious and contains the best of heaven and earth, with spices, fragrance and sweet odors. In the center of this chamber stands the Tree of Life, 500 years high. Under its shadow rest Abraham, Isaac and Jacob, the tribes, those of the Egyptian exodus and those who died in the wilderness, headed by Moses and Aaron. There also are David and Solomon, crowned, and Chileab, as if living, attending on his father, David. Every generation of Israel is represented except that of Absalom and his confederates. Moses teaches them the Law, and Aaron gives his instruction to the priests. The Tree of Life is like a ladder on which the souls of the righteous may ascend and descend. In a conclave above are seated the Patriarchs, the Ten Martyrs, and those who sacrificed their lives for the cause of His Sacred Name. These souls descend daily to the *Gan Eden,* to join their families and tribes, where they lounge on soft chairs studded with jewels. Everyone, according to his excellence, is received in audience to praise and thank the ever-living God; and all enjoy the brilliant light of the *Shekhina.* The flaming sword, changing from intense heat to icy cold

502

and from ice to glowing coals, guards the entrance against living mortals. The size of the sword is ten years. The souls on entering paradise are bathed in the 248 rivulets of balsam and attar.

"The fourth chamber is made of olive wood and is inhabited by those who have suffered for the sake of their religion. Olives signify bitterness in taste and brilliancy in light (olive oil), symbolizing persecution and its reward.

"The fifth chamber is built of precious stones, gold and silver, surrounded by myrrh and aloes. In front of the chamber runs the River Gihon, on whose banks are planted shrubs affording perfume and aromatic incense. There are couches of gold and silver and fine drapery. This chamber is inhabited by the Messiah of David, Elijah, and the Messiah of Ephraim. In the center are a canopy made of the cedars of Lebanon, in the style of the Tabernacle, with posts and vessels of silver; and a settee of Lebanon wood with pillars of silver and a seat of gold, the covering thereof of purple. Within rests the Messiah, son of David, a man of sorrows and acquainted with grief (Isa. Liii. 3), suffering, and waiting to release Israel from the Exile. Elijah comforts and encourages him to be patient. Every Monday and Thursday, on Sabbaths and on holy days, the Patriarchs, Moses, Aaron and others, call on the Messiah and condole with him in the hope of the fast approaching end."

As if intending to dispel this literal, materialistic visualization of the World-to-Come, the illustrious Rabbi Rab wrote in the Talmud: "In Paradise there is no eating, no drinking, no cohabitation, no business, no hatred or ambition; but the righteous sit with crowned heads and enjoy the radiance of the *Shekhina*." The Eleventh Century philosopher, Maimonides, was even more emphatic in his impatience with the materialistic rewards expected by the righteous in Paradise. He wrote: "To believe so is to act like a schoolboy who expects nuts and confections as compensations for his studies. Celestial pleasures can be neither measured nor comprehended by a mortal being, any more than the blind can distinguish colors or the deaf appreciate music." Rather, he held forth the promise of a *Gan Eden* (Garden of Eden) on earth when the Messiah will come to usher in the millennium and mankind will become worthy of its joys.

N. A.

A Worthy Companion

RABBI JOSHUA was very pious and learned in the Law. Once, in a dream, a voice spoke to him: "Rejoice, Joshua, because you and Nenes, the butcher, will sit side by side in Paradise and your reward will be the same."

When Rabbi Joshua awoke he cried, "Woe is me! Even since childhood I have devoted myself to the service of the Lord, studied the Torah without end and illumined the minds of eighty disciples. Now see the reward I will be getting for all my good deeds! It seems I'm no better than Nenes, the butcher!"

A WORTHY COMPANION: Adapted from the *Midrash*.

He then sent for his disciples and said to them, "I will not enter the House of Study with you until I find Nenes the butcher and learn from him what it is that he has done to deserve being my companion in Paradise."

From town to town Rabbi Joshua went with his disciples in search of Nenes the butcher, but no one had ever heard of him. At last, after much wandering, they came to the village where Nenes lived. Rabbi Joshua then began to make inquiries about him.

"O learned Rabbi!" the townsfolk asked him. "How is it that a man of your eminence should be asking after such an ignoramus and insignificant person?"

But Rabbi Joshua persisted: "Tell me what kind of man is he?"

"Don't ask us, Rabbi," they replied. "You'll see for yourself."

So they sent for the butcher, saying, "Rabbi Joshua is here and would like to see you."

Nenes was astonished.

"Who am I," he exclaimed, "that a great man like Rabbi Joshua should wish to see me? I'm afraid you've come to make sport of me! I will not go with you!"

Chagrined, the townsfolk returned to Rabbi Joshua and said, "O Light of Israel! Light of our eyes and crown of our head! Why have you sent us to such a boor? He has refused to come with us."

"I will not go from here," cried Rabbi Joshua, "until I have seen Nenes, the butcher! In fact, I will go to him myself."

When the butcher caught sight of Rabbi Joshua he became frightened.

"O Crown of Israel!" he exclaimed. "Why do you wish to see me?"

"I wish to put to you some questions," answered Rabbi Joshua. "Tell me, what good have you done in your life?"

"I am an ordinary butcher. I have a father and a mother who are old and weak. I've given up all my pleasures to attend to their needs. I wash and dress them and prepare their food with my own hands."

When Rabbi Joshua heard these words he bent down and kissed the butcher on the forehead, saying, "My son—blessed are you and blessed is your good fortune! How happy am I to have the distinction of being your companion in Paradise!"

The Piety of the Heart

RABBI SIMEON once prayed to the Almighty to show him the place reserved for him in Paradise. God answered his prayer, and he found out that his neighbor in the World-to-Come would be a butcher. Hearing this, Rabbi Simeon was filled with amazement.

"How can that be?" he asked himself in vexation. "All the days and nights of my life I have devoted to the study of the Torah—all my efforts

THE PIETY OF THE HEART: *Ibid.*

I have directed to the greater glory of God. Why, then, do I deserve the humiliation of being placed next to a common butcher in Paradise?"

Rabbi Simeon thought: "I will call on this butcher and find out what manner of a man he is."

He did so and learned that he was very rich. The butcher was hospitable, and Rabbi Simeon lived in his house for eight days. He was accorded all the honors due his illustrious rank.

One day Rabbi Simeon invited him for a walk in the fields. On the way he asked him, "Pray tell me—to what ends have you devoted your life?"

And the butcher replied, "I know I am a sinner. I've neglected to study the Torah and have bent all my thoughts to the affairs of my shop. At first I was poor, but in time I began to prosper. However, in my good fortune I never forgot the needy. I distributed alms, and for every Sabbath I provided all the poor of the town, and even those of the surrounding towns, with goodly portions of meat."

Still Rabbi Simeon remain unconvinced. Was the giving of charity enough to place a common butcher on the same level with him, the Light of the Age?

"It seems to me you must have done something more meritorious than that!" he exclaimed.

"I really cannot think of anything," replied the butcher, "except one unusual thing that once happened to me.

"At the time I was the customs collector of this city. Whenever a ship arrived in the harbor I would go aboard to examine the cargo and to collect the customs.

"Once a ship arrived and I went aboard. The captain said to me, 'I am carrying a valuable cargo in the hold of my ship. Possibly you might wish to buy it.'

" 'Show it to me,' I replied.

"He then brought up on deck two hundred Jewish slaves in chains.

" 'How much do you want for them?' I asked.

" 'I want ten thousand gold pieces for them. If you won't buy them I'll cast them all into the sea and let them drown.'

"I had compassion for my Jewish brothers. I bought them and led them ashore. I fed and clothed them and provided them with lodgings. Then I paired the marriageable youths and girls among them, provided dowries for them, and married them off according to the Laws of Moses.

"Now it happened that among them was a beautiful girl. She awakened the deepest sympathy in me, so I gave her as a wife to my son.

"I had invited to the wedding feast all the people of the town, among them the Jewish slaves I had redeemed. But I noticed an extraordinary thing: amidst all the rejoicing a youth, one of the former slaves, sat alone and shed tears.

" 'Why do you weep?' I asked him.

"But he did not answer.

"I then led him into a private room and this is what he told me:

"On the very day that he and his comrades had been seized as slaves he was to have married the beautiful girl who had now become my son's wife. So I said to him, 'Renounce all thought of her and I will give you a large sum of money!'

"He answered, 'Far better than all the gold and silver in the world would I have for my wife this girl whom I love! But now, alas! it is too late! She is already married to your son!'

"When I heard these words and saw his grief I went to my son and told him of all this.

" 'I will divorce her,' cried my son, 'so that she can marry the youth she loves.'

"And this he did. I gave her a dowry and she married the youth."

When Rabbi Simeon heard the butcher's words he exclaimed, "Praise be the Lord on High who has decreed that I shall sit next to you in Paradise!"

What Tipped the Scales

A POOR farmer hitched his horse to his wagon and drove to Lemberg to look for work so that he might have enough money to buy *matzos* and new clothes for his family for the Passover.

Night fell; there were no stars out, and he drove right into a ditch. The wagon turned over and he lay underneath it half smothered by the mud. Hearing his cries a rich man who chanced to pass by came to his rescue. He ordered his coachman to pull the farmer from underneath the wagon and to free his horse. Then, tying a rope from his coach to the shaft of the wagon, he whipped up his horses and pulled the wagon out of the mud. He then drove the farmer to his home and, seeing the poverty of his family, he gave him a thaler.

The time arrived when God in His wisdom gathered the rich man to his forefathers. When he came up for judgment before the Heavenly Tribunal the Angelic Prosecutor indicted him for his many sins. It began to look very bad for him, for the Scales of Justice were tipping dangerously towards Gehenna. Suddenly, the Angel of Mercy entered and demanded of the Eternal Judge that the man's good deeds be weighed against his sins.

God agreed and the poor farmer and his family whom the accused had aided were placed in the Scales.

"Not enough!" cried the Accusing Angel.

"Let the poor farmer's horse and wagon be placed in the Scales!" asked the Angel of Mercy.

God agreed and it was so done.

"Not enough!" cried the Accusing Angel.

"Place in the Scales the mud which covered the poor farmer when the accused pulled him out of the ditch!" asked the Angel of Mercy.

The Supreme Judge gave his consent. And no sooner was this done than lo and behold! the Scales of Justice tipped towards Paradise!

Tapers to Heaven

A WIDOW once came to the rabbi. She was all in tears. Her daughter was being married but she had no candlesticks to place on the festive table. She was afraid of being humiliated before others.

So the rabbi gave her his best silver candlesticks.

When Friday dusk came around, the rabbi's wife went to light the Sabbath candles. What was her dismay to discover that her beautiful silver candlesticks were gone!

"Thieves must have carried off my candlesticks!" she told the rabbi, aghast.

"Sh! Don't get excited!" murmured the rabbi. "No one stole our candlesticks—they've gone to light our way into the World-to-Come."

Bontshe the Silent

HERE, in this world below, the death of Bontshe produced no impression whatever. In vain you will ask: "Who was Bontshe? How did he live? What did he die of? Was it his heart that burst, his strength that gave out, or his dorsal spine that broke under a burden too heavy for his shoulders?" No one knows. Maybe it was hunger that killed him.

Had a bus horse fallen down in the street, people would have displayed much more interest than they did in this case of a poor man. The newspapers would have reported the incident, and hundreds of us would have hurried to the spot from every street to look at the poor carcass and examine the place where the accident had occurred. But were there as many horses as there are men—a thousand millions—then even a horse would not have received such distinction.

Bontshe had lived quietly, and quietly died; like a shadow he passed over the face of the earth. At the ceremony of his circumcision no wine was drunk and no clinking of glasses was heard. When he celebrated his confirmation he made no brilliant speech. He lived like some dull grain of sand on the sea shore, disappearing among the millions of its kind. And when the wind at last carried him off to the other side, no one noticed it. In his life-time the soil of the roads never kept the impression of his

---

BONTSHE THE SILENT: From *Bontshe the Silent*, by I. L. Peretz. Translated from the Yiddish by Angelo S. Rappoport. Stanley Paul & Co., Ltd. London. 1927.

footsteps, and after his death the wind swept away the small board over his grave. The grave-digger's wife found it at some distance from the grave and made a fire with it to boil a pot of potatoes. Three days only have passed since Bontshe's death, but you would ask the grave-digger in vain to show you the spot where he had buried him.

Had there been a tombstone over Bontshe's grave, a learned archæologist might have discovered it after a century, and once more the name of Bontshe would have been heard among us. He was only a shadow. No head or heart preserved his image, and no trace remained of his memory.

He left behind neither child nor property. He had lived miserably, and miserably he died. Had it not been for the noise of the crowd, someone might, by accident, have heard how Bontshe's vertebral column was snapping under a too heavy burden. Had the world had more time, someone might have noticed that during his life Bontshe's eyes were already dim and his cheeks terribly hollow. He might have noticed that even when he was not carrying loads on his shoulders his head was always bent to the ground, as if he were looking for his grave. Had there been as few poor people as there are horses in street buses someone might, perhaps, have asked: "What has become of Bontshe?"

When they took him to the hospital, Bontshe's corner in the basement did not for long remain unoccupied; ten people of his kind were already waiting for it, and they knocked it down among themselves to the highest bidder. When they carried him from his hospital bed to the mortuary chamber, twenty poor patients were already waiting for the place vacated. And scarcely had Bontshe left the morgue, when twenty corpses extricated from underneath the ruins of a house that had fallen down were brought in.

Who knows how long he will remain undisturbed in his grave? Who knows how many corpses are already waiting for the piece of ground he is buried in? Born quietly, he lived in silence, died in silence, and was buried in an even greater silence.

But it was not thus that things happened in the other world. There, the death of Bontshe produced a deep impression, a veritable sensation. The bugle-call of the Messiah, the sound of the ram's horn, was heard throughout the seven heavens: "Bontshe the Silent has died." Broad-winged archangels were flying about, announcing to each other that Bontshe had been summoned to appear before the Supreme Judgment Seat. In Paradise there was a noise, an excitement, and one could hear the joyful shout: "Bontshe the Silent! Just think of it! Bontshe the Silent!"

Very young angels, with eyes of diamond, gold-threaded wings, wearing silver slippers, were rushing out, full of joy, to meet Bontshe. The buzzing of their wings, the clatter of their small slippers, and the merry laughter of those dainty, fresh, and rosy little mouths, filled the heavens and reached the throne of the Most High. God Himself knew that Bontshe was coming——

The Patriarch Abraham stationed himself at the gate of heaven, stretching out his right hand to Bontshe in cordial welcome: "Peace be with you," a sweet smile illuminating his delighted old countenance.

What means this rumbling and rolling here in heaven? Two angels were rolling an armchair of pure gold for Bontshe. Whence this luminous flash of light? It was a golden crown, set in with the most precious stones, that they were carrying—for Bontshe.

"But the Supreme Court has not yet pronounced judgment?" ask the astonished saints, not without a tinge of jealousy.

"Bah!" reply the angels, "that will only be a formality. Against Bontshe, even the attorney for the prosecution himself will not find a word to say. The case will not last five minutes. Don't you know who Bontshe is? He is of some importance, this Bontshe."

When the little angels seized Bontshe in mid-air and played a sweet tune to him; when the Patriarch Abraham shook hands with him as if he had been an old comrade; when he learned that his chair was ready for him in Paradise and that a crown was waiting for his head, that before the celestial tribunal not one superfluous word would be spoken in his case, Bontshe, as once upon earth, was frightened into silence. He was sure that it could only be a dream from which he would soon awake, or simply a mistake.

He was used to both. More than once, when he was still on earth, he had dreamed of picking up money from the floor. Veritable treasures were lying there!—and yet—when he awoke in the morning, he was more miserable and poorer than ever. More than once it had happened to him that someone in the street had smiled at him and spoken a kind word to him. But when he found out his mistake, the stranger turned and spat out in disgust, full of contempt. "Just my luck," thought Bontshe, scarcely daring to raise his eyes, afraid lest the dream should disappear. He is trembling at the thought of suddenly waking up in some horrible cavern full of serpents and lizards. He is careful not to let the slightest sound escape his mouth, to stir or move a limb for fear of being recognized and hurled into the abyss. He trembles violently, and does not hear the compliments paid to him by the angels, nor does he notice how they are dancing around him. He pays no heed to the Patriarch's cordial "Peace be with you," nor does he even wish good-morning to the celestial court when he is at last brought in. He is simply beside himself with fear.

His fear increased greatly when his eyes involuntarily fell upon the flooring of the Supreme Court of Justice. It was of pure alabaster, inset with diamonds. "And my feet," thought Bontshe, "are treading such a floor!" He grew quite stiff. "Who knows," he thought, "what rich man, what Rabbi, what saint they are expecting? He will soon arrive and mine will be a sad end!"

Terror-stricken, he did not even hear the President of the Court call out in a loud voice: "The case of Bontshe the Silent!" He did not hear how, handing over a dossier to the counsel for the defence, he commanded: "Read, but briefly." All around Bontshe the whole hall seemed to be turning. A muffled noise reached his ears, but in the midst of the din he began to distinguish more clearly and sharply the voice of the angelic advocate—a voice as sweet as a violin:

"His name," the voice was saying, "suited him even as a gown made by an artist's hand suits a graceful body."

"What is he talking about?" Bontshe asks himself. And then he heard an impatient voice interrupting the speaker:

"No metaphors, please."

"Never," continues the advocate, "never has he uttered a complaint against God or men. Never has a spark of hatred flamed up in his eyes, never has he lifted his eyes with pretensions to heaven."

Again Bontshe fails to understand what it is all about, but once more the harsh voice interrupts the speaker:

"No rhetoric, please."

"Job succumbed, but Bontshe has suffered more than Job."

"Facts, dry facts, please," the President emphatically calls again.

"He was circumcised on the eighth day."

"Yes, yes, but no realism, please."

"The clumsy barber-surgeon could not stanch the blood——"

"Go on, go on."

"He was always silent," the advocate proceeds, "even when his mother died and at the age of thirteen there came a stepmother, a serpent, a wicked woman."

"Perhaps after all he means me," thinks Bontshe to himself.

"No insinuations, please, against third persons," angrily says the President.

"She used to begrudge him a piece of bread; threw him a few musty crusts three days old and a mouthful of tendons for meat, whilst she herself drank coffee with cream."

"Come to business!" cries the President.

"She never spared him her fingernails, blows, or cuffs, and through the holes of his miserable musty rags there peeped out the blue and black body of the child. Barefooted he used to chop wood for her in winter, in the biting frost. His hands were too young and too weak to wield the dull axe, and the blocks were too big. More than once did he sprain his wrists, more than once were his feet frozen, but he remained silent. He was silent even before his father——"

"Oh, yes, the drunkard," laughs the accusing attorney, and Bontshe feels cold all over.

"Even to his father he never complained," the advocate concludes.

"He was always miserable and alone, had no friends, no schooling, no religious instruction, no decent clothes and not a minute of respite."

"Facts, facts," the President once more interrupts.

"He was silent even later, when his own father, the worse for drink, seized him by the hair and threw him out of the house on a bitterly cold and snowy winter night. He picked himself up from the snow, without

weeping, and ran whither his eyes carried him. He was silent during his
lonely walk, and when the pangs of hunger began to torture him, he begged
only with his eyes.

"On a wet and foggy spring night he reached a large town. He entered it
like some drop of water that is falling into the ocean, but he nevertheless
passed his first night in the police jail. He was silent, without asking the
why or wherefore. Set free, he started to look for work, for the hardest
work possible; but he was silent. What was even harder than work itself,
was the finding of it, and he was silent. He was always silent. Splashed
by the mud thrown at him by strangers, spat upon by strangers, driven
with his heavy load from the sidewalk into the midst of the road, among
cabs, cars, coaches, and vehicles of every sort—at every instant looking
death in the face, he remained silent. Bathed in a cold sweat, crushed
under the heavy loads he was carrying, his stomach empty and tortured, he
was silent.

"He never calculated how many pounds he was carrying for a farthing,
how often he stumbled for a penny and how many errands he had to run,
how many times he almost breathed his last when going to collect his pay.
He was always silent. He never dared to raise his voice when asking for
his pay, but like a beggar or a dog he stood at the door and his dumb and
humble request could only be read in his eyes. 'Come later,' he was told,
and he disappeared like a shadow until later, when he would ask even more
quietly, nay *beg* for his due. He was silent even when people haggled
for his pay, knocked off something from it, or slipped a counterfeit coin
into his hand. He was always silent!"

"Then after all it is me that they mean," Bontshe consoles himself.

"One wonderful day Bontshe's fortune changed," proceeded the advocate, after taking a drink of water. "Two spirited, frightened, runaway
horses were rushing by, dragging a rich coach with rubber wheels. With
a broken skull the driver lay way back on the pavement. Foam was
spurting from the mouths of the animals, sparks flew from their hoofs, and
their eyes shone like glowing coals on a dark night. In the coach, there
sat a man, more dead than alive. Bontshe stopped the runaway horses.
The man whose life he had thus saved was a Jew; he proved to be of a
charitable disposition and was grateful to Bontshe. He handed over to
him the whip of his dead coachman, and Bontshe became a driver. The
charitable man even found him a wife. He did more: he provided Bontshe
with a child. And Bontshe always kept silent."

"They mean me; they mean me," thought Bontshe, strengthening himself in his belief; but nevertheless he dared not raise his eyes on the
august tribunal. Still he listened to his angelic advocate.

"Bontshe was silent," continued the latter, "even when his benefactor
became bankrupt and neglected to pay Bontshe his wages. He was silent
when his wife ran away from him, leaving him alone with an infant in
arms. He was silent even fifteen years later, when the same child grew
up till he was strong enough to throw the father out of his own house."

"They mean me; they mean me," Bontshe thinks joyfully.

"He was silent," continued the defending angel, as his voice grew still softer and more sad, "when his former benefactor paid all his creditors except Bontshe, to whom he did not give a penny. And when, riding again in his coach with rubber tires and with horses like lions, the benefactor one day ran him over, Bontshe still kept silent. He did not even tell the police. Even in the hospital where one is allowed to cry, he kept silent! He was silent even when the house physician refused to approach his bed unless he had paid him fifteen coppers, or when the attendant refused to change his bed linen unless he gave him five coppers.

"He was silent in his death agony, he was silent in his last hour. Never did he utter a word against God, never a word against man. I have spoken."

Bontshe began to tremble in his whole body. He knew that after the speech for the defence it was the turn of the prosecution. "What will the prosecuting counsel say now?" Bontshe did not remember his life. Down below he used to forget everything the moment it occurred. The angel advocate had recalled to his mind all his past. Who knows what the prosecuting angel will recall to his memory?

"Gentleman judges," begins a strident, incisive, and stinging voice—but stops short.

"Gentlemen," he begins again, this time more softly, but once more he interrupts himself.

And at last, very soft, a voice issues from the throat of the accuser:

"Gentlemen judges! He was silent! I shall be silent too."

Profound silence fell over the assembly. Then from above a new soft, sweet, and trembling voice is heard:

"Bontshe, my child, Bontshe," said the voice, and it sounded like a harp; "Bontshe, my well-beloved child."

And Bontshe's heart begins to weep for joy. He would like to raise his eyes, but they are dimmed by tears. Never in his life had he felt such joy in weeping.

"My child, my well-beloved!" Since his mother's death he had never heard such a voice or such words.

"My child," continues the President of the Celestial Tribunal, "you have suffered everything in silence. There is not a limb in your body that is whole, not a bone that is intact, not a corner in your soul that is not bleeding—and you have always kept silent.

"Down below upon earth they never understood such things. You yourself were not aware of your power; you did not know that you could cry and that your cries would have caused the very walls of Jericho to tremble and tumble down. You yourself did not know what strength lay hidden in you. Down below your silence was not rewarded, but down below is the world of falsehood; whilst here in heaven in the world of truth, here you will reap your reward.

"The Supreme Tribunal will never pass sentence against you; it will never judge and condemn you, nor will it mete out to you such and such a reward. Everything here belongs to you; take whatever your heart desires."

For the first time Bontshe ventures to lift his eyes. He is dazzled by so much light and splendour. Everything is sparkling, everything around him is flashing, beams are issuing from all sides, and he droops his weary eyes once more.

"Really?" he asks, still doubting and embarrassed.

"Yes, really," replies the President of the Celestial Tribunal; "verily I tell you that it is so indeed, and that everything here is yours; everything in heaven belongs to you. All the brightness and the splendour you perceive is only the reflection of your own silent goodness of heart, the reflection of your own pure soul. You will only be drawing from your own source."

"Really?" Bontshe asks again, but this time his voice sounds more firm and assured.

"Certainly, certainly, certainly," he is assured on all sides.

"Then, if such is the case," says Bontshe with a happy smile, "I should like to have every morning a hot roll with fresh butter."

Abashed, angels and judges drooped their heads; whilst the accuser burst out into loud laughter.

The Fear of Death

RABBI SEORAM sat at the bedside of his brother Raba and saw that his eyes were closing in eternal sleep.

Raba said, "Brother, implore the Angel of Death not to cause me pain as he takes me away."

Rabbi Seoram answered, "Why do you ask me when you and the Angel of Death are such good friends?"

Raba sighed and said, "The Angel of Death has little respect for a dying man."

"In that case I will plead for you," answered Rabbi Seoram. "However, promise me that when you arrive in the next world you will appear to me in a dream and reveal to me the great secret of life and death."

When Raba died he kept his promise to his brother and appeared before him in a dream.

"Well, did you suffer any pains in the last moments of your life?" asked Rabbi Seoram.

"I felt no more pain than a man feels when a physician lets his blood."

It is also related that when Rabbi Nahman was at the point of death, Raba entered into a compact with him to reveal the great secret of life and death after he had passed away. Rabbi Nahman kept his word and appeared before him in a dream.

THE FEAR OF DEATH: Adapted from the *Agada* in the Talmud.

"Did you suffer any anguish?" asked Raba.

The spirit of the dead man answered, "The Angel of Death drew my soul away with as light a hand as one draws a hair out of a jug of milk. Nevertheless, I wish to assure you that, even if the Almighty were to order me back upon earth to live my life all over again, I would refuse because of my fear of death."

〔3〕

The Ten Lost Tribes

INTRODUCTION

One of the most absorbing speculations preoccupying Jewish scholars and plain folk alike through the centuries has been that concerning the probable fate of the Ten Lost Tribes of Israel. Many of the theories concerning them were naturally of the wildest sort; the romantic imagination always takes wing in such matters. Nonetheless, life itself has demonstrated that the workings of history can sometimes be more astonishing than those of fiction. With reasonable certainty, determined by the scientific methods of history and ethnology, the probable descendants of some of these Lost Tribes have actually been accounted for.

The history of the Lost Tribes is woven of the gossamer of historical romance. After the Jews of the Northern Kingdom of Israel had been led captive to Assyria by the emperors Tiglath-Pilezer and Shalmanezer (Sargon II) they vanished from historical view, dropped, as it were, into limbo. Some scholars believed that they had been thoroughly assimilated by the Assyrians among whom they lived. Others clung to the view that they had migrated from Assyria to different countries, where they have lived in their own communities in obscurity to this very day. How correct the latter were in their speculation the reader may judge for himself in the ensuing pages.

The fate of the Ten Lost Tribes who inhabited the Northern Kingdom of Israel (the tribes of Judah and Benjamin of the Southern Kingdom of Judea remained unaffected by this and, for that reason, their course in history is well known) is thus accounted for in II Kings 18.11: "And the king of Assyria did carry away Israel unto Assyria, and put them in Halah and in Habor [see Prince Reubeni's account] by the river of Gozan, and in the cities of the Medes."

Ever since the early Middle Ages the discovery of the Lost Tribes has been announced from time to time with breathless haste by Jewish travellers. Proofs of every imaginable sort have been produced of their presence in such widely separate places as China, the Soudan, the Sahara, Azerbaidzhan, Abyssinia, Daghestan, etc.

From a reading of Josephus it becomes plain that in his days it was an

515

accepted view that the Ten Tribes lived in lands beyond the banks of the Euphrates (Antiquities I, 2:c). But it was not until the Ninth Century that the whereabouts of these lost remnants of Israel was posed as a general problem for Jews to ponder.

This problem was dramatically highlighted at that time by the appearance of a certain merchant and traveller in the Jewish communities of Babylonia, North Africa and Spain. This was Eldad ben Mahli Ha-Dani who left behind him a record of his travels which constitutes more legend than fact. Eldad claimed that he was a merchant and scholar from an independent Jewish state which was situated in East Africa. He declared categorically that his country was the home of the Lost Tribes of Asher, Gad, Naphtali and Dan (he himself was of the last-mentioned tribe from which he derived his name).

It goes without saying that his claims held the spellbound attention of all the Jews in the *Diaspora*. For many it encouraged their Messianic expectations, since according to the traditional belief they could not be fulfilled until there had been fully accomplished the gathering of all the scattered remnants of Israel in preparation for the Redemption.

With the exception of Abraham ibn Ezra and Meir of Rothenburg, no Jewish scholar, not even the celebrated Rashi, doubted the truth of Eldad Ha-Dani's statements. Interest in his revelations circulated far beyond the Jewish world. Learned Christendom too was intrigued. It inspired the apocryphal letter of the semi-legendary, medieval priest-ruler, Prester John, in which he told of several Jewish tribes living beyond the river Sambatyon in Ethiopia. From that time on the subject of the Ten Lost Tribes and the mythical Sambatyon river, which threw up a protective rain of rocks during weekdays and subsided on the Sabbath, did not fade from Jewish popular interest.

A remarkable incident touching on the Lost Tribes was related by Matthew Paris, the medieval English chronicler. It was during the time of the Crusades and the Mohammedan "infidels" were preparing to launch their great counter-offensive. Whereupon, the Emperor sent his two sons, Henry and Conrad, to give battle to the Tartars and Cumanians. In his account Matthew Paris recorded: "During all this time, members of the Jews on the Continent, and especially those belonging to the Empire, thought that these Tartars and Cumanians were a portion of their race whom God had, at the prayers of Alexander the Great, shut up in the Caspian mountains."

The Sambatyon legend was first made widespread among Jews by the pseudo-historical work, *Jossippon*, written by Joseph ben Gorion during the Tenth Century.

Intensified attention to the subject took place in the Seventeenth Century in England. It was all due to the writings of Manasseh ben Israel, the Amsterdam rabbi who induced Oliver Cromwell to allow the Jews to return to England after their banishment from that country four centuries previously.

Manasseh was fully convinced of the authenticity of the Sambatyon legend. He wrote in his book, *Hope of Israel:* "Lastly, all thinke, that part of the Ten Tribes dwell beyond the River *Sabbathion* or sabbaticall." He cites many authorities in support of his belief, including the statement of Josephus that Titus himself had seen the river. Later on, after his meeting with the remarkable visionary (or charlatan), the Marrano Jew

Montezinus, Manasseh became fully convinced that the American Indians constituted some of the Ten Lost Tribes.

In a letter to John Drury, the Puritan divine, Manasseh wrote on December 23, 1649: ". . . I thinke that the Ten Tribes live not onely there (i.e. America), but also in other lands scattered every where; these never did come backe to the Second Temple, and they keep till this day still the Jewish Religion, seeing (that) all the prophecies which speake of their bringing backe unto their native soile must be fulfilled."

It is surprising how many peoples have a tradition that they are descendants of the Ten Lost Tribes: the Christian Nestorians, many Georgians of Russia, certain of the Afghan tribes, and the Mohammedan Berbers, all believe in their descent from them. Amusingly enough, the Irish and the Anglo-Saxons too have come in for this claim, according to the somewhat tortured calculations of certain non-Jewish writers.

The question of the Ten Lost Tribes will probably never be fully settled and will remain forever impaled on the twin horns of fact and folk-fancy.

N. A.

Eldad Ha-Dani Visits the Ten Lost Tribes

ELDAD LEAVES HIS NATIVE PLACE BEYOND THE RIVERS OF CUSH

AND in this manner did I go forth from beyond the rivers of Cush: I and a Jew of the tribe of Asher boarded a small ship to trade with the sailors. And it came to pass at midnight that the Lord caused a very great and strong wind to blow, so that the ship was wrecked. And the Lord ordained that I should seize hold upon a plank. And when my companion saw this, he likewise seized hold upon that plank with me. And we went up and down with it, until the sea cast us forth amidst a people whose name is Romaranus. They are black Cushites of tall stature, without clothes and without raiment; for they are like animals, and eat men.

When we came to their country they seized hold upon us. Seeing that my companion was corpulent, plump and fat, they slew him and devoured him, while he shouted: "Woe is me, that I should know this people, that the Cushites should eat my flesh." But me they cast aside, for I had been sick on the ship; and they put me in chains, till I should grow fat and plump. They brought me delicious dishes of forbidden food; but I ate nothing and hid the food. When they asked me whether I ate, I replied: "Yes, I ate."

I stayed with them a long time, till God, blessed be He, performed a miracle for me, and there came upon them a big army from another place, who took them captive, and plundered them, and slew some of them. And

ELDAD HA-DANI VISITS THE TEN LOST TRIBES: Reprinted from *Post Biblical Hebrew Literature*, by B. Halper. With the permission of the copyright owners, The Jewish Publication Society of America. Philadelphia, 1921.

these took me with them among the captives. Those wicked people were fire-worshippers; every morning they would build a great fire, to which they would bow and prostrate themselves. I dwelt with them four years, until they brought me one day to the city of Azin.

A Jewish merchant of the tribe of Issachar met me and bought me for thirty-two pieces of gold, and returned with me to this country. They inhabit the mountains of the sea-coast and are under the rule of Media and Persia. And they fulfil this verse: "This book of the Law shall not depart out of thy mouth." *

They have no yoke of the kingdom but only the yoke of the Law. They have among them captains of hosts, but they do not contend with any man except about the Law. They live in prosperity and ease, there is no adversary, nor evil occurrence. They occupy an area of ten days' journey by ten days' journey, and have abundant cattle and camels and asses and servants; but they do not rear horses. They have no weapons, except a knife for killing animals. There is no extortion nor robbery among them; even if they find garments or money on the road they do not stretch forth their hands to take them.

But there live near them wicked people, fire-worshippers, who take their mothers and sisters for wives. These, however, neither harm them, nor benefit them. They have a judge; when I asked about him they told me that his name was Nahshon. The four modes of executing criminals are practised by them. They speak in the holy tongue and in the Persian tongue.

The children of Zebulun inhabit the mountains of Paran and are on the border of Issachar. And they make tents of hairy skins which are brought to them from Armenia. They reach as far as the river Euphrates and engage in commerce. The four modes of executing criminals are practised by them in a fitting manner.

The tribe of Reuben dwell opposite to them, behind Mount Paran. They live in peace, love, brotherhood and friendship. They go together to battle and attack wayfarers, and they divide the booty among them. They walk in the way of the kings of Media and Persia and speak in the holy tongue and in the Persian tongue. They possess the Bible, Mishnah, Talmud and Haggadah. Every Sabbath they expound the reasons for the commandments in the holy tongue, and the explanations are given in the Persian tongue.

The tribe of Ephraim and the half-tribe of Manasseh dwell there in the mountains of Nejd, the city of Mecca, where is the idolatry of Ishmaelites. These are of abhorred soul and cruel heart; they possess horses and attack wayfarers, and do not spare their enemies. They have nothing but booty to live upon. They are great warriors; one of them vanquishes a thousand.

The tribe of Simeon and the other half-tribe of Manasseh dwell in the

---

* Joshua 1:8

land of the Chaldeans, six months' journey from the temple. They are more numerous than all the others and collect tribute from twenty-five kingdoms; some of the Ishmaelites pay them tribute.

We in our country say that we have a tradition that ye, children of the exile, are of the tribes of Judah and Benjamin, living under the rule of the adherents of the idolatrous religion, in the unclean land, scattered among the Romans who destroyed the house of our God, and among the Greeks and Ishmaelites. May their sword enter into their own heart, and may their bows be broken!

We also have a tradition handed down from man to man, that we are the children of Dan. At first we were in the land of Israel, dwelling in tents. And there were not among all the tribes of Israel brave warriors like us. When Jeroboam the son of Nebat, who caused Israel to sin and made two golden calves, rebelled so that the kingdom of the house of David was divided, the tribes assembled together, and said:

"Arise, and make war against Rehoboam and against Jerusalem!"

But the children of Dan replied:

"Why should we fight against our brethren and against the son of our lord, David, king of Israel and Judah? Far be it, far be it from us!"

At that time the elders of Israel said:

"There are no mighty men among all the tribes of Israel like the tribe of Dan."

Whereupon they all said to the children of Dan:

"Arise and make battle against the children of Judah."

But they replied: "By the life of the head of Dan our father, we shall not make war with our brethren and we shall not shed their blood!"

Whereupon the children of Dan took their swords and spears and bows and prepared themselves to depart from the land of Israel, for we saw that it was not possible to remain there.

They said: "Let us go now and find a resting-place; for if we wait till the end, they will destroy us."

We took counsel and determined to go to Egypt to lay it waste and to destroy all its inhabitants. But our princes said to us:

"Is it not written: 'Ye shall see them again no more for ever'? * How then can ye prosper?"

Then they said: "Let us go against Amalek, or against Edom, or against Ammon and Moab to destroy them, that we may dwell in their place."

But our princes replied: "It is written in the Torah that the Holy One restrained the Israelites from passing through their border." †

Finally they took counsel to go to Egypt, but not by the way our fathers had gone, nor to lay it waste, but in order to pass to the River Pishon, to the land of Cush.

---

* Exodus 14:13

---

†Comp. Deuteronomy 2 4,9,19

And it came to pass, when we drew near to Egypt, that trembling seized hold upon the Egyptians. And they sent word to us:

"Are ye for war or for peace?"

We replied: "For peace: we shall pass through your land to the river Pishon, for there we shall find a resting-place."

And it came to pass, because they did not believe us, that all the Egyptians stood on their watch until we had passed through their land and reached the land of Cush, which we found to be a good and fertile land, having fields, vineyards, gardens and parks. The inhabitants of Cush did not prevent the children of Dan from dwelling with them, for we took the land by force. And it came to pass, because we wanted to slay all of them that they became tributaries, paying taxes to the Israelites. And we dwelt with them many years until we were fruitful and multiplied exceedingly. And we had great wealth.

The Ten Lost Tribes in America

MENASSEH BEN ISRAEL,
TO THE COURTEOUS READER.

THERE are as many minds as men, about the originall of the people of America, and of the first Inhabitants of the new World, and of the West Indyes; for how many men soever they were or are, they came of those two, Adam, and Eve; and consequently of Noah, after the Flood, but that new World doth seem wholly separated from the old, therefore it must be that some did passe thither out of one (at least) of the three parts of the world sc. Europe, Asia and Africa; but the doubt is, what people were those, and out of what place they went. Truly, the truth of that must be gathered, partly out of the ancient Hystories, and partly from conjectures; as their Habit, their Language, their Manners, which yet doe vary according to mens dispositions; so that it is hard to finde out the certainty. Almost all who have viewed those Countryes, with great diligence, have been of different judgements. Some would have the praise of finding out America, to be due to the Carthaginians, others to the Phenicians, or the Canaanites; others to the Indians or people of China; others to them of Norway, others to the Inhabitants of the Atlantick Islands, others to the Tartarians, others to the ten Tribes. Indeed, every one grounds his opinion not upon probable arguments, but high conjectures, as will appear farther by this Booke. But I having curiously examined what ever hath hitherto been writ upon this subject, doe finde no opinion more probable, nor agreeable to reason, then that of our Montezinus, who saith, that the first inhabitants of America, were the ten Tribes of the Israelites, whom the Tartarians

---

THE TEN LOST TRIBES IN AMERICA: From *The Hope of Israel*, by Manasseh ben Israel. Amsterdam, 1651.

conquered, and drove away; who after that (as God would have it) hid themselves behind the Mountaines Cordilleræ. I also shew, that as they were not driven out at once from their Country, so also they were scattered into divers Provinces, sc. into America, into Tartary, into China, into Media, to the Sabbaticall River, and into Æthiopia. I prove that the ten Tribes never returned to the second Temple, that they yet keepe the Law of Moses, and our sacred Rites; and at last shall return into their Land, with the two Tribes, Judah, and Benjamin; and shall be governed by one Prince, who is Messiah the Son of David; and without doubt that time is near, which I make appear by divers things; where, Reader, thou shalt finde divers Hystories worthy of memory, and many Prophesies of the old Prophets opened with much study and care. I willingly leave it to the judgement of the godly and learned, what happy worth there is in this my Book and what my own Nation owes me for my paines: It is called, The Hope of Israel; which name is taken from Jerem. 14.8 O the hope of Israel, the Saviour thereof. For the scope of this Discourse is to show, that the hope in which we live, of the comming of the Messiah is of a future, difficult, but infallible good, because it is grounded upon the absolute Promise of the blessed God.

And because I intend a continuation of Josephus his History of the Jewes, our famous Historian; I intreat, and beseech all Learned men, in what part of the world soever they live (to whom I hope that shortly this Discourse will come) that if they have any thing worthy of posterity, that they would give me notice of it in time; for though I have collected many Acts of the Jewes, and many Hystories out of the Hebrewes, the Arabians, the Grecians, the Latines, and other Authors of other Nations; yet I want many things for this my enterprize, all which I am willing to performe, that I may please my Nation; but rather to the glory of the blessed God, whose Kingdome is everlasting, and his Word infallible.

The Relation of Antony Montezinus

In the 18th. of the Month of Elul, the 5404 year from the Worlds creation, and according to common compute, in 1644, Aaron Levi, otherwise called Antonius Montezinus came into this City Amsterdam, and related to the Sieur Menasseh Ben Israel, and other chiefetains of the Portugal Nation, Inhabitants of the same City, these things which follow.

That it was two years and a halfe, since that he going from the Port-Honda in the West-Indies, to the Papian jurisdiction, he conducted some Mules of a certaine Indian, whose name was Franciscus Caftellanus, into the Province of Quity, and that there was one in company with him and other Indians, whose name was Francis, who was called by all Cazicus. That it happened that as they went over the Mountaines Cordilleræ, a great tempest arose, which threw the loaden Mules to the ground. The Indians being afflicted by the sore tempest, every one began to count his losses; yet confessing that all that and more grievous punishments were but just, in regard of their many sins. But Francis bad them take it patiently, for that they should shortly injoy rest: the others answered, that they were unworthy of it; yea that the notorious cruelty used by the Spaniards towards them, was sent of God, because they had so ill treated his holy people, who were of all others the most innocent: now then, they determined to stay all night upon the top of the Mountain. And Montezinus tooke out of a Box some Bread, and Cheese, and Jonkets, and gave them to Francis, upbraiding him, that he had spoken disgracefully of the Spaniards; who answered, that he had not told one halfe of the miseries and calamities inflicted by a cruell, and inhumane people; but they should not goe unrevenged, looking for helpe from an unknown people.

After this Conference, Montezinus went to Carthagenia, a City of the Indians, where he being examined, was put in Prison; and while he prayed to God, such words fell from him; Blessed be the name of the Lord, that hath not made me an Idolater, a Barbarian, a Black-a-Moore, or an Indian; but as he named Indian, he was angry with himselfe, and said, The Hebrewes are Indians; then he comming to himselfe againe, confessed that he doted, and added, Can the Hebrewes be Indians? which hee also repeated a second, and a third time; and he thought that it was not by chance that he had so much mistaken himselfe.

He thinking farther, of what he had heard from the Indian, and hoping that he should find out the whole truth; therefore as soon as he was let out of Prison, he sought out Franciscus, beleeving that hee would repeat to him againe what he had spoken; he therefore being set at liberty, through Gods mercy went to the Port Honda, and according to his desire, found him, who said; He remembred all that he had spoken, when he was upon the Mountaine; whom Montezinus asked, that he would take a journy with him, offering him all courtesies, giving him three peeces of Eight, that he might buy himselfe necessaries.

Now when they were got out of the City, Montezinus confessed himselfe to be an Hebrew, of the Tribe of Levi, and that the Lord was his God; and he told the Indian, that all other gods were but mockeries; the Indian being amazed, asked him the name of his Parents; who answered Abraham, Isaac, and Jacob; but said he, have you no other Father? who answered, yes, his Fathers name was Ludovicus Montezinus; but he not being yet satisfied, I am glad (saith he) to heare you tell this, for I was in doubt to beleeve you, while you seemed ignorant of your Parents: Montezinus swearing, that he spoke the truth, the Indian asked him, if he were not the Son of Israel, and thereupon began a long discourse; who when he knew that he was so, he desired him to prosecute what he had begun, and added, that he should more fully explaine himselfe, for that formerly he had left things so doubtfull, that he did not seem at all assured of any thing. After that both had sate downe together, and refreshed themselves, the Indian thus began: If you have a minde to follow me your Leader, you shall know what every you desire to know, only let me tell you this, whatsoever the journey is, you must foot it, and you must eate nothing but parched Mayz, and you must omit nothing that I tell you; Montezinus answered that he would doe all.

The next day being Munday, Cazicus came againe, and bid him throw away what he had in his Knapsack to put on shooes made of linnen packthred, and to follow him, with his staffe; whereupon Montezinus leaving his Cloake, and his Sword, and other things which he had about him, they began the journey, the Indian carrying upon his back three measures of Mayz, two ropes, one of which was full of knots, to climbe up the Mountaine, with an hooked fork; the other was so loose, for to passe over Marshes, and Rivers, with a little Axe, and shooes made of linnen packthred. They being thus accoutred, travelled the whole weeke, unto the Sabbath Day; on which day they resting, the day after they went on, till Tuesday, on which day about eight aclock in the morning, they came to a River as bigge as Duerus; then the Indian said, Here you shall see your Brethren, and making a signe with the fine linnen of Xylus, which they had about them instead of a Girdle; thereupon on the other side of the River they saw a great smoke, and immediately after, such another signe made as they had made before; a little after that, three men, with a woman, in a little Boat came to them, which being come neare, the woman went ashore, the rest staying in the Boat; who talking a good while with the Indian, in a Language which Montezinus understood not; she returned to the Boat, and told to the three men what she had learned of the Indian; who always eying him, came presently out of the Boat, and embraced Montezinus, the woman after their example doing the like; after which one of them went back to the Boat, and when the Indian bowed downe to the feet of the other two, and of the woman, they embraced him courteously, and talked a good while with him. After that, the Indian bid Montezinus to be of good courage, and not to looke that they should come a second time to him, till he had fully learned the things which were told him at the first time.

Then those two men comming on each side of Montezinus, they spoke in Hebrew, the 4th. ver. of Deut. 6. Semah Israel, adonai Elohenu adonai ehad; that is, Heare O Israel, the Lord our God is one God.

Then the Indian Interpreter being asked, how it was in Spanish, they spoke what followes to Montezinus, making a short pause between every particular.

1 Our Fathers are Abraham, Isaac, Jacob, and Israel, and they signified these foure by the three fingers lifted up; then they joyned Reuben, adding another finger to the former three.

2 We will bestow severall places on them who have a minde to live with us.

3 Joseph dwels in the midst of the Sea, they making a signe by two fingers put together, and then parted them.

4 They said (speaking fast) shortly some of us will goe forth to see, and to tread underfoot; at which word they winked, and stamped with their feet.

5 One day we shall all of us talke together, they saying, Ba, ba, ba; and we shall come forth as issuing out of our Mother the earth.

6 A certaine Messenger shall goe forth.

7 Franciscus shall tell you somewhat more of these things, they making a signe with their finger, that much must not be spoken.

8 Suffer us that we may prepare ourselves; and they turning their hands and faces every way, thus prayed to God, DO NOT STAY LONG.

9 Send twelve men, they making a signe, that they would have men that had beards, and who are skilfull in writing.

The Conference being ended, which lasted a whole day, the same men returned on Wednesday, and Thursday, and spake the same things againe, without adding a word; at last Montezinus being weary that they did not answer what he asked them, nor would suffer him to goe over the river, he cast himselfe into their Boat; but he being forced out againe, fell into the River, and was in danger to be drowned, for he could not swim; but being got out of the water, the rest being angry, said to him; attempt not to passe the River, nor to enquire after more than we tel you; which the Indian interpreted to him, the rest declaring the same things both by signs, and words.

You must observe, that all those three dayes the Boat stayed not in the same place, but when those foure who came went away, other foure came, who all as with one mouth, repeated all the fore-mentioned nine particulars, there came and went about three hundred.

Those men are somewhat scorched by the Sun, some of them weare their haire long, downe to their knees, other of them shorter, and others of them much as we commonly cut it. They were comely of body, well accoutred, having ornaments on their feet, and leggs, and their heads were compassed about with a linnen cloath.

Montezinus saith, that when he was about to be gone, on Thursday evening, they shewed him very much courtesie, and brought him whatever they thought fit for him in his journey, and they said, that themselves were well provided with all such things, (sc. meats, garments, flocks, and other things) which the Spaniards in India call their owne.

The same day, when they came to the place where they had rested, the night before they came to the River, Montezinus said to the Indian; You remember Francis, that my Brethren told me, that you should tell me something, therefore I entreat you, that you would not thinke much to relate it. The Indian answered, I will tell you what I know, only doe not trouble me, and you shall know the truth, as I have received it from my fore-fathers; but if you presse me too much, as you seeme to doe, you will make me tell you lyes; attend therefore I pray, to what I shall tell you.

Thy Brethren are the Sons of Israel, and brought thither by the providence of God, who for their sake wrought many Miracles, which you will not beleeve, if I should tell you what I have learned from my Fathers; we Indians made war upon them in that place, and used them more hardly than we now are by the Spaniards; then by the instigation of our Magicians (whom we call Mohanes) we went armed to that place where you saw your Brethren, with an intent to destroy them; but not one of all those who went thither, came back againe; whereupon we raised a great Army, and set upon them, but with the same successe, for againe none escaped; which hapned also the third time, so that India was almost berefit of all inhabitants, but old men and women, the old men therefore, and the rest who survived, beleeving that the Magicians used false dealing, consulted to destroy them all, and many of them being killed, those who remained promised to discover somewhat that was not knowne; upon that they desisted from cruelty, and they declared such things as follow:

That the God of those Children of Israel is the true God, that all that which is engraven upon their stones is true; that about the end of the World they shall be Lords of the world; that some shall come who shall bring you much good, and after that they have enriched the earth with all good things, those Children of Israel going forth out of their Country, shall subdue the whole World to them, as it was subject to them formerly; you shall be happy if you make a League with them.

Then five of the chiefe Indians whom they call Cazici who were my Ancestors, having understood the Prophesie of the Magicians, which they had learned of the Wise men of the Hebrewes, went thither, and after much entreaty, obtained their desire, having first made knowne their minde to that woman, whom you saw to be for an Interpreter, (for your Brethren will have no commerce with our Indians) and whosoever of ours doth enter the Country of your Brethren, they presently kill him; and none of your Brethren doe passe into our Country. Now by the help of that Woman we made this agreement with them.

1 That our five Cazici should come to them, and that alone at every seventy moneths end.

2 That he to whom secrets should be imparted, should be above the age of three hundred Moones, or Months.

3 And that such things should be discovered to none in any place where people are, but only in a Desart, and in the presence of the Cazici; and so (said the Indian) we keep that secret among our selves, because we promise our selves great favour from them, for the good offices which we have done to our Brethren, it is not lawfull for us to visite them, unlesse at the seventy months end. Or if there happens any thing new, and this fell out but thrice in my time; First, when the Spaniards came into this Land; also, when Ships came into the Southerne Sea; and thirdly, when you came, whom they long wished for, and expected. They did much rejoyce for those three new things, because that they said, the Prophesies were fulfilled.

And Montezinus also said, that three other Cazici were sent to him by Franciscus to Honda, yet not telling their names, till he had said you may speake to them freely, they are my fellowes in my Function of whom I have told you, the fifth could not come for age, but those three did heartily embrace him; and Montezinus being asked of what Nation he was, he answered, in Hebrew, of the Tribe of Levi, and that God was his God, etc.

which when they had heard, they embraced him againe, and said: Upon
a time you shall see us, and shall not know us; We are all your Brethren,
by Gods singular favour; and againe, they both of them bidding farewell,
departed, every one saying, I goe about my businesse; therefore none but
Franciscus being left, who saluting Montezinus as a Brother, then bade
him farewell, saying, farewell my Brother, I have other things to doe, and
I goe to visite thy Brethren, with other Hebrew Cazici. As for the Country,
be secure, for we rule all the Indians; after we have finished a businesse
which we have with the wicked Spaniards, we will bring you out of your
bondage, by Gods help; not doubting, but he who cannot lye will help us;
according to his Word; endeavour you in the meane while that those men
may come.

The Little Red Jews on the Other Side of the Sambatyon

THUS writes *Reb* Aaron Halevi in the account of his travels:

"In the year 1631 I traveled by ship from Alexandria to Salonika. There
I heard of the arrival of a certain caravan of merchants. I asked them:
"From what country are you."

"We are from the land of Habash (Abyssinia). We have come here to
buy iron and will transport it to the countries on the farther shore of the
river Sambatyon."

At that I went to see the chief of the caravan. I asked him:
"How far is it and how long is the journey to the Sambatyon?"

He answered: "The journey will take from eight to twelve months."

And because I understood the language of these merchants I asked them
whether I too could buy iron and join their company. They assured me I
would derive much profit from the transaction.

Once more I went to the chief merchant and I was found pleasing in
his eyes. He assured me that the journey would be safe and not a hair of
mine would be injured on the way. So I went with him to the magistrate

---

THE LITTLE RED JEWS ON THE OTHER SIDE OF THE SAMBATYON: Adapted from a Yiddish
groschen chapbook published in Vilna in 1912.

The legend about the river Sambatyon was already well-defined in the *Midrash:*
"The river Sambatyon casts up stones all the days of the week, but desists from doing
so on the Sabbath—indeed, on Friday after midday, when it becomes quite calm, as
proof that it is really the Sabbath."

This version of the legend is a vulgarization of a tale included by Gershom ben
Eliezer Halevi Jüdels, a Yiddish writer of Prague, in his famous travel book, *Gelilot
Erez Yisroel* (Lublin, 1634). In 1630 he had gone on a journey from Salonika to
Abyssinia (via Palestine and Arabia). His book, a record of this journey, is a curious
hodgepodge of fact garnished with legend and fancy. Although this version is spurious
it, nevertheless, gained wide currency among East European Jews, a popularity which
it has enjoyed to this very day.—N. A.

of the town and asked that he should write down in his book that I was
joining the caravan of merchants and that their chief was obligated to
bring me safely back or to deliver to the magistrate a letter from me
wherever I might stay. And many Jews accompanied me so that for my
sake they could learn from the chief merchant the truth about the river
Sambatyon.

And so I went off with the caravan. Were I to describe to you all the
incidents of my journey and how many countries, cities, seas and deserts
I traversed, a thousand sheets of paper would not suffice. However, let
me say in brief that I reached at last the city of Mecca where is found
the grave of Mohammed, the Prophet of the Ishmaelites. From there we
met with the most curious beasts six yards high. Many Jews lived there.
And farther on, at a great distance, was the sea and on it were many
mountainous islands, and there too dwelled Jews. They had great stores
of spices and gold and silver. However, they were no meat-eaters and only
tasted fruits and peas, butter, milk and sugar. Their houses were without
roofs and all of them wore silken garments and pearls.

To get to the Sambatyon we first had to traverse the desert. Because
the desert crossing was beset with many dangers I followed the sea route
which was also the shorter. I was surprised to find no iron, not even a
nail on any part of the ship. Everything was fastened by ropes and the
joints had wooden nails. In some parts of the sea I saw columns of fire
and smoke rising as from a fiery furnace.

Forty miles out to sea we came to an island which was covered with a
forest of olive trees and from among the trees poured a dense smoke. I
was told that the fire and smoke were from Gehenna. All around the island
dashed sulphurous waters.

When we finally came to the city and close to the Sambatyon we heard
a mighty roar. The closer we drew to the city the more deafening was the
sound. I then learned it came from the Sambatyon. When I wished to go
to the shore of the river I was cautioned against it. The inhabitants of
the city told me that King Pristian had placed guards on the shore to be
ready against any possible attacks by the little red Jews from the other
shore. Therefore, I tarried three weeks in the city and, in the meantime,
I made it my business to find out everything I could about the river Sambatyon and about the little red Jews who lived on its farther shore.

"Why can't I go across?" I asked.

They told me: "Every day in the week the Sambatyon casts up a hail
of stones and no one can cross."

"If that is so," I answered, "then of what earthly use are the guards
the King has placed there?"

To that they replied: "They don't guard the shore every day but only
two hours on Friday afternoon before the Sabbath arrives when the river
subsides and becomes tranquil. Then the guards gather, not to battle with
the little red Jews on the other side of the river should they choose to
cross but to run quickly when they see them at a distance to sound the

alarum so that the fortresses and strong places should shut their gates because the Jews are coming.

On the Sabbath too the guards stay away for they know very well that the little red Jews are pious and will not violate the Sabbath peace by crossing over the Sambatyon. However, after the *Maarev* (evening) service when night has fallen the guards rush to the riverside for then the Sambatyon once more begins to rage and boil and throw up great stones and boulders that no living thing could survive. I was shown houses and ruined fortresses that the Jews had wrecked when they had attacked and laid the city waste.

For great joy and pride I shed tears. Of course I did not reveal to the inhabitants that I was a Jew because I saw in what terror they stood of the little red Jews.

I then asked: "How much can I get for a hundredweight of iron?"

"For one hundredweight of iron," they told me, "the little red Jews will give you a hundredweight of gold. They have whole mountains of gold and their country is vast. All varieties of the finest fruits and cattle and fowl and fish and spices are to be found there. They wear garments of silver and gold. Never do they wear black, for they like only gay colors."

Also, they told me of two neighboring countries on the shores of the river in which, for instance, if a man kills an animal he is sentenced to death. The Sambatyon varies in width along its course. In some places it is two hundred yards wide and in others only sixty. The people who live along its banks do not drink the river water nor do they allow any animal to drink from it because they consider the water as sacred. Whoever has boils is immediately rid of them as soon as he bathes in it.

On the other side of the Sambatyon live only Jews. They are ruled by twenty-four Jewish kings. Each king rules over a separate kingdom with well-fortified towns and cities. However, over all of these kings there is a supreme king. And this one is a great warrior. He rides on a leopard and in his retinue are a hundred and fifty thousand heroes accoutred in armor and carrying long spears. They mount mighty steeds that have been trained to bite and kick and kill any stranger that dares approach them, at which they neigh loudly. These horses eat cooked sheep's meat and drink wine. Whenever one of the soldiers wishes to mount a horse he first has to bind the horse's legs and put an iron muzzle over its mouth, because it is so fierce.

When the king (his name in 1631 was Eliezer) wishes to ride the leopard they fetch him a golden step-ladder and in this fashion he mounts the beast. Thereupon all other warriors mount their horses. During the two hours before the Sabbath sets in on Friday afternoon, when the river Sambatyon subsides, they cross the river and observe the Sabbath on the enemy's territory while those who remain on the other side see to it that no enemies attack during the king's absence on the Sabbath. And whoever is foolish enough to cross is instantly killed. But the Jews make one exception—the Ishmaelite merchants that come to sell them iron.

The little red Jews are great horsemen. They can sit in their saddles for three days without stirring, being well supplied with packs containing all kinds of foodstuffs so that the riders need not get off their horses. In fact, they live on their horses. The feet of the riders are fastened to the horses so that when the horses run like a bolt from a bow their riders should not be thrown.

King Eliezer is a great man of war. He is six yards tall and his sword three yards long. And when he and his men cross the Sambatyon to the side of their enemies they slay them by the thousands. The Jewish warriors wear golden armor and their bows are of gold as well; the tips of their arrows are dipped in a deadly poison. Whomever they strike has to die instantly. The little red Jews collect from their foes their weekly tribute after which they recross the Sambatyon in peace to their homes before sundown.

The little red Jews have another famous warrior among the 24 kings and he is also a great *tzaddik*. His name is Daniel the Pious. He lives in the city Armona. His palace is constructed of precious stones and diamonds. When he goes to the synagogue for prayer he is accompanied by his queen and four sons and two daughters. The sons too are strong men and the daughters are beauties and very pious. When the daughters are out on the street they veil their faces. All the Jews, whether men or women, know trades and find it easy to earn a livelihood. Nothing is lacking in their kingdom except iron. That is why the Ishmaelite merchants bring them iron and from it they fashion their weapons of war. King Daniel has a gem among his treasures, a carbuncle that is displayed only on the Sabbath when it is hung up in the palace and it glows both day and night like the sun at midday in order that it should not be necessary to kindle a fire on the Sabbath which is forbidden. Therefore, the carbuncle is called "The Sabbath Light."

At the time when I was there, the king of India sent King Eliezer an embassy of three great lords bearing a gift of peace. The king received them with great honor. The gift they gave him was a savage who had no head, his eyes and mouth were set in his breast. He wore forty pearls that were pure and clear. They dazzled like the sun on a gem called sapphire which is indeed wonderful to behold.

Also I passed the mountains of Niskor. In them live the Bene-Rahab, the children of Jethro. On the other side of the mountains live the four tribes of Dan, Naphtali, Zebullon and Asher. Their kingdom is vast. From there I traversed the great mountains of Isman where live the Khazars who are all proselytes.

From there I journeyed to the desert of Habash. In the land of Habash I found many Jews and they were as black as Ethiopians.

Prince David Reubeni and the Jewish Kingdom of Khaibar

IN THE year 1525 Prince David Reubeni, who claimed to be the Ambassador of his brother Joseph, the Jewish King of Khaibar (Habor) in middle India, as well as the general of his army, made a series of sensational appearances in Europe. He had travelled in slow stages from his native land by way of Abyssinia, the Soudan and Egypt. Everywhere he went he was received with extraordinary interest, and by Jews, with indescribable excitement. On the one hand, no one had ever heard of the existence of a Jewish kingdom in Khaibar; on the other, he had come to make the startling offer, in the name of his brother, of a military alliance against the victorious Turks, to the Pope, the Emperor Charles V, and King John of Portugal. The Jews of Europe could hardly believe that there could be a Jewish kingdom in existence, moreover one having such unusual military power as Reubeni described. It had a stunning effect on the Jewish imagination and let loose all kinds of wild romantic speculations about the possible origin of the Jewish ambassador and his people. In the minds of many he loomed large as the Messiah. Others thought that the Jews of Khaibar must surely be the descendants of one of the Ten Lost Tribes of Israel.

Reubeni's romantic, soldierly appearance, in flowing Oriental robes, beturbaned, and carrying a golden sword, harmonized perfectly with his remarkable tale. He told all and sundry that his brother was an independent Jewish monarch and that, not far from Khaibar, lay the Jewish kingdom of Cranganore where the Cochin Jews lived. This was the first knowledge the Jews of Europe received of the existence of the Cochin Jews, another of the lost remnants of Israel.

Reubeni was received in state by the Pope, by the Emperor and by King John. They all encouraged him in his mission for a military alliance against the Turks, for they stood desperately in need of all possible aid, and they heaped many honors upon him. They took him and his mission very seriously. In a letter that the Venetian ambassador in Rome, Marco Foscari, wrote to the Signory of Venice on March 14, 1524, he stated: "An ambassador has come to the Pope from the Jews in India offering him three hundred thousand warriors against the Turk and asking for artillery."

What did Reubeni expect to gain from all this for his people? To "a great Moslem lord," a judge of the king of Fez, who asked him about Khaibar, he replied: "From our youth on we are trained in war, and our weapons are the sword, the lance and the bow. We wish to go, with God's help, to Jerusalem to wrest the land of Israel from the Moslems, for the end of days and salvation have arrived. I have come to ask for wise artificers who know how to make weapons and firearms so that they might come to my country and fashion them there and also teach my people how to make them."

Reubeni's matter of fact information about the Jewish tribal descent of his people literally rocked all of the European Jewish communities to their foundations. "We are kings," said he proudly, "and our fathers were kings from the time of the destruction of the Temple till this day in the wilderness of Habor. We rule over the tribes of Reuben and Gad, the half-tribe of Manasseh in the wilderness of Habor, and there are nine and a half tribes in the land of Ethiopia and other kingdoms. The nearest to us are the tribe of Simeon and the tribe of Benjamin, and they are on the River Nile above the kingdom of Sheba. They dwell between two rivers—the Blue River and the Black River which is the Nile. Their country is fertile and large and they have a king whose name is Baruch, the son of King Japhet. He has four sons: the eldest Saadia, the second Abraham, the third Hoter, and the fourth Moses. Their inhabitants are as numerous as ours in the wilderness of Habor, thirty myriads, and we and they take counsel together."

The curiosity of the judge must have been very lively indeed, for he asked Reubeni: "What will you do with the Jews in all the lands of the west? Will you come to the west for them and how will you deal with them?"

Reubeni replied: "We shall first conquer the Holy Land and its surroundings. After that our captains of the army will go forth to the west and east to gather the dispersed remnants of Israel. If the Moslem kings are wise they will take the Jews under their rule and bring them to Jerusalem, and they will have much honor, and God will deliver up all the kingdoms to the King of Jerusalem."

In conclusion, made curious by the reports concerning Reubeni, the judge finally ventured to ask: "Is it true what the Jews in Fez and its neighborhood say, as well as the Moslems, that you are a prophet and the Messiah?"

Reubeni was taken aback. He apparently was no adventurer and was very much in earnest about his mission for concluding a military alliance between his people and Christendom. To claim Messianic stature for himself, flattering and advantageous as it might be temporarily, could even lead to disaster for him in the long run. So he hastened to assure the judge: "God forbid, I am a sinner before the Lord, greater than any one of you, and I have slain many men; on one day alone I killed forty enemies. I am neither a prophet, nor the son of a prophet, neither a wise man nor a cabalist. I am but a captain of the army, the son of King Solomon, the son of David, the son of Jesse, and my brother, the King, rules over thirty myriads in the wilderness of Habor. Moreover, the Marranos [secret Jews or "New Christians"] in the kingdom of Portugal, and all the Jews in Italy, and all the places that I passed through, also thought me to be a prophet, wise man, or cabalist, and I said to them: 'God forbid! I am a sinner and a warrior ever since my youth.'"

Before Reubeni could manage to get help from the Emperor and King John, the unexpected defeat of the feared Turks by the Portuguese put the seal of doom on all his plans. He and his fabulous Jewish host of 300,000 warriors were no longer needed. Thereupon, without any ceremony, King John abruptly ceased his banqueting of the swarthy Jewish warrior-prince and sent him packing. In the end the Inquisition got on his trail and forced the Emperor to clap him in prison where he died in 1537, a broken and much wiser man.

Some Jewish scholars maintain that David Reubeni was an adventurer and charlatan, but the accumulating knowledge about various Jewish ethnic-culture groups in remote places of Asia and Africa tends to corroborate the authenticity of his claims and mission to the Pope and the Princes of Christendom.

The Jewish Kingdom of the Khozars [*Khazars*]

Chisdai Abu-Yusuf, the son of Isaac the son of Ezra, of the family of Shaprut, a physician, became Vizier to the Caliph Abd er-Rahman III (911–61) and his successor the Caliph Hakem (961–76). The Byzantine Emperor, Romanus II, driven into straits by the Abbaside Caliph at Bagdad courted the friendship of Abd er-Rahman and sent him a Greek medical manuscript of Dioscorides, in charge of a Monk, Nicolaus, to interpret the Greek into Latin. Nicolaus became Chisdai's friend. Chisdai was sent by Abd er-Rahman to Navarre and cured its deposed King Leon of obesity and helped to restore him to his throne of Navarre. Otto I, Emperor of Germany in 956, sent an embassy to the Caliph Abd er-Rahman, and Chisdai carried on the negotiations which led to a satisfactory treaty. As Nasi (Prince) or temporal head of the Jewish congregations of Cordova, Chisdai advanced Jewish interests and Jewish studies in Spain and else-where. He had heard from Oriental travellers that there was a Jewish kingdom in Asia ruled by a Jewish King. Once he was told by merchants from Choresvan (Khorasan) that such a Jewish kingdom did really exist and that the land was called Khozar. He had also heard of Eldad the Danite. Ambassadors from the Byzantine Emperor to the Caliph had told Chisdai that the merchant's story was true, Chisdai accordingly sent one Isaac ben Nathan with a letter, . . . with a recommendation to the Emperor. Isaac remained six months in Constantinople, but went no further, the Emperor writing that the way to the land of Khozar was far too dangerous and the Black Sea only occasionally navigable. Chisdai thought of sending his letter to Jerusalem, where Jews had promised to forward it to Nisibis, thence to Armenia, from Armenia to Berdaa, and from thence to Khozar. But while he was considering this plan, Ambassadors came from the King of the Gebalim (Slavonians) to Abd er-Rahman, among whom were two Jews, Saul and Joseph. These offered to hand the letter to the King of Gebalim, who out of respect for Chisdai would send it to the Jews in Hungary, thence it would be forwarded to Roumelia and Bulgaria and so finally reach its destination. By these means the letter was delivered to Joseph

---

THE JEWISH KINGDOM OF THE KHOZARS: From *Jewish Travellers*, edited by Elkan Nathan Adler. G. Routledge & Sons, Ltd. London, 1930.

the King of the Khozars, and the King sent him a reply of which a translation is [here] given. Chisdai is believed to have died in 1014. The authenticity of these letters, now generally accepted, was for a long time impugned by Buxtorf, Basnage and others. The great poet philosopher, Judah Halevi, in 1140 wrote the famous work *Cusari* which is based on the conversion of the King of the Khozars, who inhabited the Crimea, and of a portion of his people. This took place according to the Arabian historians in the second half of the eighth century.

* * * * *

THE ANSWER OF JOSEPH, KING OF THE TOGARMI, TO CHISDAI, THE HEAD OF THE CAPTIVITY, SON OF ISAAC, SON OF EZRA, THE SPANIARD, BELOVED AND HONOURED BY US

BEHOLD, I inform you that your honoured epistle was given me by Rabbi Jacob, son of Eleazar, of the land of Nemez (Germany). We were rejoiced by it, and pleased with your discretion and wisdom, which we observed therein. I found in it a description of your land, its length and breadth, the descent of its sovereign, Abd er-Rahman, his magnificence, and majesty; and how, with the help of God, he subdued to himself the whole of the East, so that the fame of his kingdom spread over the whole world, and the fear of him seized upon all kings. You also told us that had it not been for the arrival of those ambassadors from Constantineh, who gave an account of the people of our kingdom, and of our institutions, you would have regarded all as false and would not have believed it. You also inquired concerning our kingdom and descent, how our fathers embraced the laws and religion of the Israelites, how God enlightened our eyes and scattered our enemies; you also desired to know the length and breadth of our land, the nations that are our neighbours, such as are friendly and hostile; whether our ambassadors can go to your land to salute your eminent and gracious king, who draws the hearts of all men to love him and contract friendship with him by the excellence of his character and the uprightness of his actions, because the nations tell you that the Israelites have no dominion and no kingdom. If this were done, you say, the Israelites would derive great benefit from it, their courage would be reawakened, and they would have an answer and occasion for priding themselves in reply to such as say to them, "There are no Israelites remaining who have a kingdom or dominion." We shall, therefore, delighting in your wisdom, answer you with respect to each of these particulars, concerning which you have asked us in your letter.

We had already heard what you have written concerning your land, and the family of the king. Among our fathers there had been mutual intercourse by letters, a thing which is written in our books and is known to the elders of our country. We shall now inform you of what happened to our fathers before us, and what we shall leave as an inheritance to our children.

You ask, also, in your epistle of what people, of what family, and of what tribe we are? Know that we are descended from Japhet, through his son Togarma. We have found in the genealogical books of our fathers that Togarma had ten sons, whose names are these:—Agijoe, Tirus, Ouvar, Ugin, Bisal, Zarna, Cusar, Sanar, Balgad, and Savir. We are of Cusar, of whom they write that in his days our fathers were few in number. But God gave them fortitude and power when they were carrying on wars with many and powerful nations, so that they expelled them from their country and pursued them in flight as far as the great River Duna (Danube?), where the conquerors live to this day, near Constantineh, and thus the Khozars took possession of their territory. . . .

As to your question concerning the extent of our land, its length and breadth, know that it is situated by the banks of a river near the sea of Gargal, towards the region of the East, a journey of four months. Near that river dwell very many populous tribes; there are hamlets, towns, and fortified cities, all of which pay tribute to me. From thence the boundary turns towards Gargal; and all those who dwell by the sea-shore, a month's journey, pay tribute to me. On the south side are fifteen very populous tribes, as far as Bab-al-Abwab, who live in the mountains. Likewise the inhabitants of the land of Bassa, and Tagat, as far as the sea of Constantineh, a journey of two months; all these give me tribute. On the western side are thirteen tribes, also very numerous, dwelling on the shores of the sea of Constantineh, and thence the boundary turns to the north as far as the great river called Jaig. These live in open unwalled towns and occupy the whole wilderness (steppe) as far as the boundary of the Jugrians; they are numerous as the sand of the sea, and all are tributary to me. Their land has an extent of four months' journey distant. I dwell at the mouth of the river and do not permit the Russians who come in ships to enter into their country, nor do I allow their enemies who come by land to penetrate into their territory. I have to wage grievous wars with them, for if I would permit them they would lay waste the whole land of the Mohammedans as far as Baghdad.

Moreover, I notify you that I dwell by the banks of the river, by the grace of God, and have in my kingdom three royal cities. In the first the queen dwells with her maids and attendants. The length and breadth of it is fifty square parasangs together with its suburbs and adjacent hamlets. Israelites, Mohammedans, Christians and other peoples of various tongues dwell therein. The second, together with the suburbs, comprehends in length and breadth, eight square parasangs. In the third I reside with the princes and my servants and all my officers. This is a small city, in length and breadth three square parasangs; the river flows within its walls. The whole winter we remain within the city, and in the month of Nisan (March) we leave this city and each one goes forth to his fields and gardens to cultivate them. Each family has its own hereditary estate. They enter and dwell in it with joy and song. The voice of an oppressor is not heard among us; there are no enmities nor quarrels. I, with the princes and my ministers, then journey a distance of twenty parasangs to the great River Arsan, thence we make a circuit till we arrive at the extremity of the province. This is the extent of our land and the place of our rest. Our country is not frequently watered by rain; it abounds in rivers and streams, having great abundance of fish; we have many springs; the land is fertile and rich; fields, vineyards, gardens and orchards are watered by rivers; we have fruit-bearing trees of every kind and in great abundance.

This, too, I add, that the limit of our lands towards the Eastern region is twenty parasangs' journey as far as the sea of Gargal, thirty towards the south, forty towards the west. I dwell in a fertile land and, by the grace of God, I dwell in tranquillity.

With reference to your question concerning the marvellous end, our eyes are turned to the Lord our God and to the wise men of Israel who dwell in Jerusalem and Babylon. Though we are far from Zion, we have heard that because of our iniquities the computations are erroneous; nor do we know aught concerning this. But if it please the Lord, He will do it for the sake of His great name; nor will the desolation of His house, the abolition of His service, and all the troubles which have come upon us be lightly esteemed in His sight. He will fulfil His promise, and "the Lord whom ye seek shall suddenly come to His temple, the messenger of the Covenant whom ye delight in: behold, he shall come, saith the Lord of Hosts" (Mal. iii, 1). Besides this we only have the prophecy of Daniel. May God hasten the redemption of Israel, gather together the captives and dispersed, you and I and all Israel that love His name, in the lifetime of us all.

Finally, you mention that you desire to see my face. I also long and desire to see your honoured face, to behold your wisdom and magnificence. Would that it were according to your word and that it were granted to me to be united with you, so that you might be my father and I your son. All my people would pay homage to you: according to your word and righteous counsel we should go out and come in. Farewell.

The Black Jews of Abyssinia

Introductory Note

The history of this Jewish tribe (Falasha) in Abyssinia is still veiled in obscurity, and any attempt to investigate its origin encounters many obstacles. The opinion of the Abyssinians, which is partly shared also by the Falashas, is that these Jews came from Palestine to Ethiopia in the time of King Solomon and his alleged son Menilek I. The Ethiopian chronicle relates that the queen of Sheba, during her visit to him at Jerusalem, conceived a son whose father was Solomon; that the son was named Menilek or Ibn al-Hakim, that is to say, the son of the sage, and that he became the founder of the royal dynasty of Abyssinia. The Abyssinians have appropriated this legend, which draws its origin from the biblical passages of chapter 10 of the First Book of Kings and from chapter 9 of the Second Book of Chronicles, mentioned also in our midrashic literature, where reference is made to a queen of the South, whom the Arabs claim as their own. By this episode the Abyssinians establish the origin of the Falashas in their country. According to them the queen of Sheba, on her return to her kingdom, brought along with her a large number of Hebrews, such as scholars and artisans, and upon the birth of her son this immigration was considerably augmented. The exodus of these Jews from Palestine is explained in very amusing anecdotes. Menilek I was raised and educated at the court of Solomon at Jerusalem, and he was his father's favorite. Because he was loved by his following, on account of his being handsome and intelligent, the Israelites, fearing that he would seize the throne after the death of Solomon, insisted that he be sent to rejoin his mother. Solomon reluctantly consented to their demand, but on condition that each family be required to send its first-born son to accompany Menilek into his country and to remain there with him. He had him crowned as king of Ethiopia, and sent him home with a large following of thousands of Jews. Solomon had also prepared for him a copy of the Tables of the Law, which the priests, who formed part of his escort, were to take with them. But these deceived the wise king, carried away the original from the temple, and put the copy in its place. The Tables of the Law of Moses, thus stolen from Jerusalem, may be found to this very day, the Abyssinians assure us, in the Church of Zion at Axum, the ancient capital of Ethiopia and the residence of Menilek I.

An opinion which appears to be more historical is that the Falashas are the descendants of those Jews who settled in Egypt after the first exile, and who, upon the fall of the Persian domination on the borders of the Nile, penetrated into the Soudan, whence they went into the western parts of the present country of Abyssinia. Then they directed their steps towards the interior, and, in time, after the destruction of the second temple, their number was augmented by fugitives who came to join them; for, upon the shores of the Red Sea and in the whole of Egypt, the Jews, whose land had been destroyed by the Romans, continued to suffer from persecution. Then, towards the end of the fifth century of the common era, the captive Jews led away from southern Arabia, following the wars of the Abyssinians against the Himyarites, augmented the number of these Jews who already resided in Ethiopia. There they formed themselves into groups, then gathered in the same provinces, almost in the same centers, and became fused into a single and indissoluble community. Protected by the mountains and supported by natives converted to Judaism, they finally became grouped into a small independent state, and this independence they maintained in several parts of the empire for hundreds of years. It is approximately only since the past two centuries that the Falashas have become scattered throughout the entire extent of Abyssinia in little groups and families, and to-day they are also met with in the most southern provinces of the empire, in Choa, in the country of the Gallas, and even in the equatorial regions which have but recently come under the suzerainty of the Negus, where they live outwardly as Christians, as did the Marranos in Spain.

Their occupation, originally that of military mercenary service under the different sovereigns, and later trade on the banks of the Nile and on the littoral of the Red Sea, is mainly agriculture and manual labor. They are in their country almost the only people who are able to follow, with any skill, the trades which are practised in Abyssinia, and thanks to their skill they are on good terms with their non-Jewish compatriots. Abyssinia needs the Falashas who furnish the articles indispensable for the maintenance of the country. In Abyssinia, as in many other places, the masses of the people are in perfect harmony with the Jews whom they hold in esteem because of their open spirit and their industry.—Jacques Faitlovitch. From *The Falashas*. In American Jewish Year Book, 5681 (1920). The Jewish Publication Society of America. Philadelphia, 1920.

A Visit to the Falashas *

I took advantage of an accidental absence of my host, to leave my narrow and dark dwelling, which threatened to become my prison. Accompanied by the servant of the house, I walked up hill and down dale towards the Falasha village, which was at a full league's distance from my abode. The way was tortuous, and across steep mountains; the rays of the sun fell straight on our heads, and on our arrival we were exhausted with fatigue.

My approach was announced beforehand by some children who were tending flocks of sheep. I hastened my step, and went to an open spot to see the effect produced by my sudden appearance in the midst of the inhabitants. Men and women cried out with astonishment at the sight of my complexion and of my dress. I was politely asked to go back and enter a hut where several men were sitting together. On my arrival they saluted me, and surrounded me, though at a considerable distance. They appeared uncomfortable, and when I wished to go near them they drew back. Only two persons ventured to grasp my hand in a friendly manner, while the others called out "Atedresbeny!" (Touch us not!) A man attired in a long tunic, and holding a small dish containing water, examined me from head to foot without uttering a single word. This cold reception was beginning to be unpleasant to me; I could not understand their strange ways, but I determined to be patient.

During my visit my Moslem follower remained behind, sleeping under the shadow of a tree. After hesitating for a few minutes, the Falashas broke silence: "Gueta" (Sir), said they, "doubtless you require a knife (gara) or sword (shotel): you should buy them in a large town, for the instruments we make are of too rough a workmanship to suit a European." "Oh, my brethren," I replied, "I am not only a European; I am, like you, an Israelite. I come, not to trade in Abyssinia, but to inquire into the state of my co-religionists, in conformity with the desire of a great Jewish Asso-

---

* From *Travels in Abyssinia*, by Joseph Halévy. In *Miscellany of Hebrew Literature*, Part II. Society of Hebrew Literature. London, 1877.

The first Jew to seek out the Falashas was Joseph Halévy, of the Sorbonne in Paris. His journey into Abyssinia took place in 1868.

ciation existing in my country. You must know, my dear brethren, that I also am a Falasha! I worship no other God than the great Adonai, and I acknowledge no other law than the law of Sinai!" The e words, uttered slowly, and in distinct tones, that all might understand them, had a striking effect on the Falashas. Whilst some appeared to be satisfied, others shook their heads doubtfully, and looked at each other as if to inquire how I should be answered. At last several voices exclaimed, "What! you a Falasha! a white Falasha! You are laughing at us! Are there any white Falashas?"

I assured them that all the Falashas of Jerusalem, and in other parts of the world, were white; and that they could not be distinguished from the other inhabitants of their respective countries. The name of Jerusalem, which I had accidentally mentioned, changed as if by magic the attitude of the most incredulous. A burning curiosity seemed all at once to have seized the whole company. "Oh, do you come from Jerusalem, the blessed city? Have you beheld with your own eyes Mount Zion, and the House of the Lord of Israel, the holy Temple? Are you also acquainted with the burying-place of our mother Rachel? With glorious Bethlehem, and the town of (Kîebron) Hebron, where our holy patriarchs are buried?" They were never weary of asking me questions of this nature; and they eagerly listened to my replies.

I must confess I was deeply moved on seeing those black faces light up at the memory of our glorious history. I informed them that, before coming to Abyssinia I had visited Jerusalem, and that the city had sadly fallen from its ancient splendour. I told them that the Jewish inhabitants of the Holy City were plunged into misery; and that a mosque stands on the site of the ancient temple. They were grieved at this news, as they had no correct idea of the actual state of the Holy Land; most of them believed that it belonged to Roman Christians. . . .

Our conversation lasted two hours. As they became more communicative, I inquired why some of them avoided approaching me, and what was the object of the dish with water held by one of them in his hand. They replied to me that the contact with an unclean man defiles them for one or more days, during which period they remain secluded from the rest of the household. The Falashas were also careful to receive money in a vessel full of water, so as to cleanse it from impurity before handling it.

I was surprised to find these ancient Mosaic observances still in full force in Abyssinia, and my astonishment increased on learning that the Falashas purchase from other nations only unground corn, and salt cut into oblong cakes. All articles of consumption prepared by an unclean individual are rejected. Liquids are considered as conductors of uncleanliness, and the defiled individual does not touch the vessel with his lips; water is poured out to him in the hollow of his hands. I may add incidentally that I have remarked a similar strange custom among the Indians.

My curiosity was strongly aroused, and I was desirous of being enlightened on several important questions, but my companion had awoke from his sleep and said that our conversation had lasted long enough, and that it was time to go back. . . .

The Falashas came frequently to see me, and I was enabled to question them at leisure on all the points I wished to know. This proceeding proved distasteful to my host, who told me one day that he could no longer answer for my safety, and that I must take my departure. As I was arranging with the Falashas for the means of going into the interior of the country, I asked for a delay of a few days to complete my preparations. During this interval I was enabled to pay the Falashas a second visit, and to remain with them two whole days. The opportunity was furnished to me by the chief of the district in the following manner:—

In Abyssinia every European is looked upon as a skilled artificer and a wizard, as well as a gunsmith. The Sheik, on seeing me, recollected that he possessed an old firelock, inherited from his ancestors, which he thought might become serviceable if it could be mended. He sent me by one of his slaves this antiquated piece, which seemed to date from the earliest invention of firearms, with a request to repair it for him as soon as possible. It would not have been prudent to own that I did not understand this kind of work, as nobody would have believed me. Had I sworn ignorance by all that is sacred, I should have been accused of failing in consideration towards the authorities of the country. Notwithstanding my complete unacquaintance with the gunmaker's art, I took the firelock, observing that it could not be mended until a blacksmith had made a new spring to replace one that was broken. As the Falashas were the only workers in iron, I necessarily had recourse to them. On the 11th January, I proceeded to their village, in company with the Debtéra who usually visited me. His father, who was named Anania, lodged me in his house, or rather in a hut close to his. Not having undergone the process of purification, I could not be admitted into the hut occupied by himself and his family. The Falashas came freely in and out of my dwelling, which proved that they looked upon me as a Jew, for they do not become familiar with Christians. As a matter of convenience we sat in the court-yard, or under the shade of a thickly-covered tree. Some smiths were at work near us with very primitive tools. The women helped their husbands at their occupation, and when tired they seated themselves near us, to listen to our conversation. In order to strengthen the friendship that was springing up between the Falashas and me, and also to have an opportunity of observing their customs with reference to diet, I purchased a sheep, and asked the head men of the community to come and partake of it with me in the evening. Meanwhile, I noticed that a large number of women attended at our meetings, mingled unreservedly with the men, and also took part in the discussions, either supporting or opposing the opinions of the men. This freedom of the weaker sex surprised me considerably. I was struck with the contrast presented by the domestic manners of the Falashas with those of Moslems, or even of Abyssinian Christians, amongst both of whom females rarely appear in male society.

The sheep was in due course tied up by its feet, and led up for slaughter to a cleanly-kept spot, while a blessing was said, and repeated by all the company. The knife had been sharpened, but not with such care to take away all notches, as is practised by other Jews. Some children brought grass and fresh leaves, on which to put the sheep during the process of skinning and quartering. In the course of these operations, the Falashas expressed their disgust at the practice indulged in by the Amharas, of eating raw meat from the body of an animal still palpitating, and perhaps still breathing. They compared those gluttonous savages to dogs.

The Bene-Israel Jews of Bombay

INTRODUCTORY NOTE

Today the Bene-Israel Jews, who live in the Bombay Presidency of India, number little more than ten thousand. For the greater part they are poor and ignorant unskilled workers and are considered among the lowest castes of the population. Superficially there is very little to distinguish them from other Indians. They bear Hindu names, wear Hindu clothes and speak the vernacular of the country. Nevertheless, they consider themselves as a people apart. On the Sabbath day they do not work and attend services in their synagogues. The other Indians call them, derisively, *Shanwar Teles*, "Saturday oilmen," because most of the Bene-Israel earn their livelihood as oil pressers and they rest on the Sabbath.

The tradition of the Bene-Israel is that their ancestors had left Palestine after the invasion of Antiochus Epiphanes in 175 B.C. They had fled in a ship and travelled by way of Egypt and the Red Sea to India. But a storm arose and they were shipwrecked on the Konkan coast near the ancient city of Cheul which is thirty miles south of Bombay. During the shipwreck they lost their Torah scrolls, a misfortune over which they still mourn. In the course of time, they forgot many of the Jewish rites, customs and prayers. Of the last they remembered only the *Shema,* the Jewish creed—"Hear O Israel, the Lord our God, the Lord is One!" This they repeated in Hebrew on every religious occasion, during the rite of circumcision, at weddings and at funerals. Their traditions were handed down from father to son with a stubborn fidelity, despite the vicissitudes and persecutions they had to suffer since early days.

That their claim of having left Palestine before the Dispersion has historical validity may be seen from the Biblical character of some of their customs relating to birth, marriage and death, of the nature of the fasts and feasts they celebrate, and of the rites and ceremonies they perform. For instance, their offering of frankincense in their synagogue service is identical to the rite which prevailed in Palestine up to the time of the destruction of the Second Temple. It is of considerable significance that the Bene-Israel remained ignorant of Channukah, the Festival of Lights, which was introduced by Judah Maccabeus after he had reconsecrated the Temple in 168 B.C. They also were unaware of the Temple's sack by Titus in A.D. 70.

It is interesting to note that there are two classes of Bene-Israel Jews, a natural consequence of the caste-ridden social organization of the Indian people. One class is called the Gora ("white")-Israel. Its members consider themselves "the real" Bene-Israel. The other is the Kala-Israel. It consists of "black" or Indian proselytes to Judaism. While there is no distinction made between the two groups in religious observance, nonetheless, intermarriage between them is strictly prohibited by the Gora-Israel who are pridefully determined to preserve their group "purity." In recent times, this division has caused a great deal of bitterness and indignation on the part of the socially inferior Kala-Israel group.

No doubt the Bene-Israel Jews would have disappeared long ago as a religious and ethnic-culture group had it not been for the fact that many hundreds of years ago—some say five hundred, others, nine hundred—there appeared in the Konkan country a half-legendary character by the name of David Rahabi. He taught them many of the tenets of Judaism to which, in their naïve and primitive fashion, they have clung tenaciously ever since.—N. A.

A Bene-Israel Circumcision Party *

A MALE child is circumcised on the eighth day after his birth and then he receives his name. The child is circumcised by his father if he is a good operator, otherwise it is circumcised by the Hazan or the Reader of the Synagogue or by any operator from the Community. The operator is called Mohel i.e. a circumciser. The fee paid to the Synagogue on the occasion varies from Rupees two to five. The Mohel receives from Rupee one to Rupees two from the father of the child. In other countries the Mohel receives no fee. A Mohel always longs to circumcise as many children as is the numerical value of his name. . . . The mohel Judah David Ashkenazi, a Cochin Jew, used to circumcise children in Bombay, both among the Bene-Israel and other Jews without any fee. The circumcision is performed either at home or in the Synagogue. Relatives, friends and acquaintances only are invited on the occasion of circumcision. The evening before the day of circumcision, a few men go to the place where the child is to be circumcised and place a chair near the wall at the west side. If the circumcision is to be performed in a Synagogue, a chair is placed to the left side of the Ark, in memory of Elijah the Prophet, who is called "the Angel or Messenger of the Covenant," and is said to come along with the child, and to be present at every circumcision. A copy of the Scriptures is placed upon the chair, which is covered with a silk or cotton curtain, left hanging from the wall.

---

* From *The History of the Bene-Israel of India*, by Haeem Samuel Kehimkar. Copyright, 1937, by Dr. Immanuel Olsvanger. Tel-Aviv: Dayag Press Ltd.

A table covered with white cloth is placed at some distance from the chair, and a citron and a twig of subja or myrtle are placed thereon. Between the table and the chair dedicated to the memory of the Prophet Elijah, two other chairs are placed in front of each other, one for the circumciser and the other for the Sandek (godfather).

On the morning of the circumcision the child is taken in a palanquin or in a carriage to the Synagogue accompanied by friends and relatives. The mother remains at home, as she may not enter the Synagogue before the purification which takes place on the fortieth day. If the circumcision is delayed owing to the child's illness, she takes her child to the Synagogue on the fortieth day after the birth. On the entrance of the party into the compound of the Synagogue juice of dry grapes or raisins and a plate containing a cup of oil, and a piece of lint or some cotton are taken inside and placed on the table where two candles are lit. The child is generally carried from or to the palanquin or the carriage into or from the Synagogue by the maternal-uncle. The actual ceremony is being performed according to the usual Jewish ritual.

Presents are given to the child by its relatives after the circumcision is over. They are in cash, or consist of ornaments of gold or silver. Batasas (sugar cakes) are then distributed, and the party breaks up. Some of the relatives accompany the child home, where they cut the citron, break a coconut or two and invoke Elijah the Prophet. Pieces of citron and Kernal are then distributed to the party. A cock is killed on this occasion, cooked and given to the circumciser and members of the family; but the parents of the circumcised child do not partake of it. Fees are demanded by the Kaji and the synagogue officers on the occasion of birth, marriage and death, but no registers are kept.

The ceremonial is the same when the circumcision is performed at home.

On the morning of the twelfth day, the child is bathed and laid in a cradle with the repetition of the word Beshem Adonai that is, "in the name of God"; one or two songs are then sung to lull the child to sleep, and at other times a pretty lullaby is always repeated while it is being rocked to sleep.* But on the first occasion when the child is being put into the cradle, a coconut or two are broken and their water is sprinkled on all sides, and the coconut Kernals and sugar are handed round to the children of the house.

Jo jo, my child,	I washed your flesh,
My seed of pearl,	I pitied you dear;
Keep your eyes	In the Name of the Lord
From crying, my treasure, jo jo.	I put you to sleep, jo jo.

---

* The author probably refers to the following popular Lullaby which I saw reproduced in a collection of Hebrew Zmiroth. The tune was given to me by Mrs. Simon, a Bene-Israel lady of Bombay.—Immanuel Olsvanger.

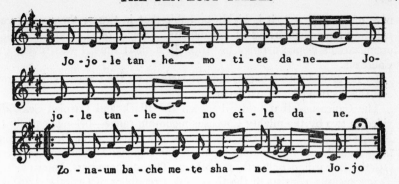

Jo -jo - le tan - he___ mo - ti -ee da - ne___ Jo-

jo - le tan - he___ no ei - le da - ne.

Zo - na-um ba -che me -te sha — ne_____ Jo-jo

My milk has quietened you,
Has sweetened your lips,
And within the hand of God
I shall deliver your soul, jo jo.

Your cradle is of Sandlewood,
Your cushion of silk;
Grandmother will come
And will sing you to sleep, jo jo.

Your shirt is green,
Your matlet of silk;
The Pipalpan is yellow
And pure are the pearls, jo jo.

I'll thread pearls for you
To decorate your neck;
Your mother will dress
Her head with flowers.

The Caucasian Mountain Jews

FOR many centuries, the so-called Caucasian Mountain Jews have been living isolated in their remote and lofty "auls," or villages. Until recently, they were almost unknown to the outside world, their extraordinary history waiting to be unearthed.

These unique people—formerly oppressed, now awakening to a new existence—first came to my attention in 1933, when in Moscow I happened upon a series of photographs depicting their peculiarly biblical and patriarchal life.

I had come to Moscow from Vienna in the course of investigating the changed social status of the women of Soviet Asia. But what I heard about the mountain group interested me very much. These Jewish mountaineers were settled chiefly in the northern and eastern Caucasus, along the western shores of the Caspian Sea, and when I learned that several of these settlements were in the territory once occupied by the Khazars—the legendary Asiatic tribes that had been converted to Judaism in the early Middle Ages—my curiosity was really aroused. Since my early youth I had been preoccupied by the problem of the Khazars in connection with the still obscure question of the origin of the Jewish masses of Eastern Europe.

Moscow specialists in Jewish history and culture encouraged me. "You will be the first Western European visitor to our mountaineer brothers," they said. "Gather as much material as you can on the spot. At the present

THE CAUCASIAN MOUNTAIN JEWS: By Fannina W. Halle. *Commentary*, October, 1946. Published by the American Jewish Committee, New York.

pace of development, it is highly probable that in two or three years you will find almost no traces of the old life." Soviet officials and scientific organizations helped arrange my trip. In a short time, I was roving the Caucasus.

I went armed with a background of facts about the Caucasus in general, and this section of it in particular.

The Caucasus—that bridge between the Black and Caspian Seas, divided in two by the mighty Caucasus mountain range—belongs equally to Europe and Asia. The northern section, which is part of the Occident, contains a number of autonomous republics and regions: Daghestan, Northern Ossetia, Kabardino-Balkaria, and others. The southern part, known as the Transcaucasus, consists of the three Union republics of Georgia, Armenia, and Azerbaidzhan.

The Caucasus region has a hundred and fifty mountain peaks, rising as high as 13,000 feet. Noah's Ark landed on Mt. Ararat; on Elbruz, Prometheus suffered for his presumption. This oldest link between Asia and Europe is still the home of innumerable tribes of diverse origins, living in isolated groups among the mountains and offering almost inexhaustible material for ethnic and linguistic study. In the republic of Daghestan alone, a population under a million includes eighty-one different peoples and tribes speaking thirty-two languages and twice as many dialects. It is therefore not surprising to find there also an ancient tribe of Jews among the rest. Who are these Jews?

No one has yet been able to establish definitely the origin of the nearly 30,000 Daghestan or Mountain Jews ("Dagh Chufut" in the native language), or of the Georgian Jews, another group about equal in size. These latter live in western Georgia, close to the Black Sea, and call themselves "Hebraeli," or "Israeli." Little research has been done on the Caucasian Jews, but there is no doubt that both groups are among the oldest inhabitants of the country, that they once formed a homogeneous mass, and that their numbers were once very great.

Armenian and Georgian chronicles report the first Jewish movements into the Transcaucasus at the beginning of the 6th century B.C.E. Some of the first arrivals were probably captives sent as gifts to friendly rulers by Nebuchadnezzar of Babylon. Later, there were Jewish refugees fleeing into the Caucasus—presumably through Mesopotamia and Persia—after the destruction of the Second Temple.

The Mountain Jews and the Georgian Jews who developed under very different conditions are now totally distinct, speaking different languages and living different lives. The Mountain Jews, who began to come into northern Daghestan in about the 6th century, carried with them the language of the Tats, an Iranian people among whom they had been settled. Their present language, like Yiddish, is a mixture—in this case a mixture of Iranian, Turkish, and Semitic elements, plus a number of pure Hebrew and Aramaic words and terms derived from the Talmud. Since 1928, they have used a latinized alphabet, like other peoples of the Soviet East; before that time they used Hebrew characters. Orthodox religious services are held in Hebrew, like those of all other Jews.

Before the 1917 revolution the Mountain Jews belonged to the most conservative Jewish group. At that time, although some of their *chachams* (rabbis) used to study at the *yeshivot* of Kovno, Lithuania, there were no Talmudist among them. In olden times, however, mountain Jewish scholars, according to a rabbinic tradition, participated in the creation of the Talmud. There is mention of a Rabbi Nahum Hamadai (the name itself indicates that he came from Mydia, later Azerbaidzhan) and of Simon Saphro from Derbent.

In contrast to other Jewish groups, there are no priests or Levites among the Mountain Jews, and most of the names of both men and women date back to the epoch of the wanderings of Israel in the Arabian desert or to the period of the Judges and Kings. In this fact, some Russian orientalists are inclined to see a confirmation of the Mountain Jews' own strong oral tradition of descent from the lost ten tribes of Israel.

Very proud of their alleged ancestry, which is verified by an old Jewish Haggadah, and alluded to in the accounts of various travelers of the 9th, 18th, and 19th centuries, they emphasized it as the first point in one of their many memorandums to Czar Nicholas I. They further declared that their forefathers did not participate in the rebuilding of the Second Temple of Jerusalem. . . .

My next stop among the Mountain Jews was the town of Kuba, which the inhabitants once called "the Magnet." Kuba had recently yielded to Baku as a center of attraction for them. I arrived at night. Fresh from industrialized Baku, which has been called a European, Asiatic, and American city all in one, Kuba, situated practically at the border of the Daghestan Republic in an out-of-the-way valley of the Shakh Dagh Mountains, twelve miles from the railroad station of Khatshmas, seemed at first glance to take me back at least two thousand years. But the following morning I realized that actually this was a place where the sharpest historical and cultural contrasts met in an even more striking synthesis than elsewhere in this region. Caucasian, pagan, Islamic, Soviet, and Biblical elements, all were there.

Indeed, the very first scene that greeted me when I crossed the bridge spanning the Kubinka River, which separates the Moslem from the Jewish quarter in Kuba, was like a vision out of Genesis. Against the background of a majestic chain of mountains on the distant horizon, a procession of women moved slowly and impressively in their national costumes, which, although shabby, were yet becoming, and in some instances elaborate. In their billowing cloaks and veils, with tall pitchers of water on their shoulders, they seemed in the morning sun to be returning from a meeting with the matriarch Rebecca at the well. I could not help thinking that formerly the Mountain Jews had called Kuba "a second Jerusalem," and that, like the other Jewish group in Georgia, the Jews of Daghestan had brought monotheism to Caucasian soil.

However, while some of the Georgian Jews turned out to be missionaries of Christianity, the Daghestan Jews were bringers of Judaism. Beginning in the 7th century, Judaism spread so far over the region that the whole northeastern Caucasus still shows signs of it in ruined settlements and ancient tombstones. Toward the middle of the 8th century the king of the powerful Khazars, an Asiatic-Turkish people, embraced Judaism, bringing with him the members of his court and large numbers of his subjects.

The progress was finally stopped by a series of violent persecutions at the hands of the Moslems, who killed many Jews and drove many others into hiding among the mountains which gave them their name. The rest—though it took centuries—were at last forced into the Islamic religion and lost their identity in the general population. But there are still villages where the Mohammedan residents will display old Hebrew Bibles and claim with pride that their ancestors were Jews.

The Mountain Jews, intermarrying with members of neighboring tribes, came into closest union with the Khazars, and maintained a close relationship with their great state even after the beginning of its decline in the 10th century. The Mongol invasion destroyed Khazar independence, but Jewish fortresses and tiny Jewish-Khazar principalities remained along the Caspian. As late as 1346 Russian chronicles speak of these places as Zhidy (Jew's Land).

After the destruction of the Khazar state, the Mountain Jews suffered repeatedly from new invaders and from religious persecution. Toward the later part of the 16th century, they retreated from the mountains to the valleys and the coast, forming new Jewish settlements, such as Nalchik and Grozny, and settling in large numbers in several old cities, particularly in Derbent and Kuba. During the war of conquest by the Russians, which lasted for a century and a half, ending in 1864, the Mountain Jews were the victims of incessant attacks by their neighbors, attacks provoked by fanatical Moslems. From 1864 until 1883, a period during which they were not yet identified as a Jewish people, they enjoyed the same treatment the Czarist regime accorded other mountain groups. But as soon as their national identity was established, restrictions began, and in many cases they were subject to the same oppression as other Jews in the Russian Empire. . . .

The Mountain Jews are a handsome people, graceful in their movements, and, like most Caucasian tribes, good horsemen and marksmen. In respect to facial features, they are almost indistinguishable from other Daghestan mountaineers. Their own neighbors sometimes find it hard to differentiate among them, and must ask, "Are you Jew or Moslem?"

Some of the women are beautiful, but, like most Oriental women, they age prematurely. Many of the older ones, who almost all smoke long pipes, belong to a special guild of mourners, whose skill in lamentation and in extemporizing poems about the dead is so appreciated that some of them are even sought after by non-Jewish tribes. (There are even "weepers" who receive prizes for their skill.) The longevity of the Mountain

Jews is remarkable. I myself saw several hundred-year-old individuals who still had their teeth, hair, and youthful slenderness. These "hoary worthies," some of whom still kept two or three wives (in accordance with the Biblical and Islamic custom), are highly respected by the younger generation. The Mountain Jews have in the course of time adopted other Islamic customs from their neighbors, such as the sale of women, child-marriage, marriage by capture, customs relating to style of dress and dwelling, superstitions and black magic, talismans and amulets, as well as beliefs in demons and other spirits. . . .

The Yemenite Jews

INTRODUCTORY NOTE

Unfortunately, the Jewish travellers in South Arabia have not cleared up the interesting question of when the Jews settled in Yemen. The tradition of the local Jews records that their ancestors came to Yemen forty-two years before the destruction of the First Temple. It further states that Ezra, as he was about to build the Second Temple, sent a message to the Jews of Yemen calling upon them to return to Palestine, but they declined the invitation on the ground that the final salvation had not yet come. Ezra was thereupon angry with them and prophesied that they would never enjoy permanent peace in Yemen, and that their wealth would not endure. Oral tradition, moreover, states that the Jews came into the country as warriors and that they built the city of Sanaa, which bears the ancient Hebrew name "Udal" in their poems. They are said to have remained masters of Sanaa until the advent of Mohammed, who fought against the city and conquered it. . . . It is certain that the settlement of the Jews in Yemen is very old, that they had their own rulers for a certain period, and that their religion exercised a powerful attraction over the local tribes before the advent of Mohammed, so that a Yemenite king with his entire court went over to Judaism in the fifth century. Only lately (in 1913) an announcement appeared in the newspapers that ancient coins recording Jewish rulers had been found. . . .

It seems like a miracle that this scattered fragment of the Jewish people has defied the tribulations of centuries, has pursued its own religious life and created its own literature, ceremonies, synagogue chants and melodies. . . .

The number of Jews in Yemen consists of about 8,000 families (about 30,000 souls) who are scattered over a few hundred places. Only in Aden and Sanaa are there large communities; for the rest they live in small towns and villages. Three fourths of all the Jews are artisans: tailors, shoemakers, weavers, goldsmiths, potters, masons, makers of handmills, brickmakers, workers in tobacco and powder, joiners, smiths, etc. A European Jew can hardly conceive how modest are the requirements of his co-religionists in South Arabia. Even a "rich" Yemenite does not eat more than one course at a meal on a weekday; and the Yemenite immigrants in Palestine, who are employed in domestic service, must be trained to eat an adequate meal. As for clothing, they are content with a single shirt. But despite their very modest requirements and their unflagging industry and diligence they are unable to earn the minimum for their existence and hunger is a frequent guest.—Joshua Feldmann. From *The Yemenite Jews*. The Jewish National Fund. Cologne, 1913.

The Messiah among the Yemenite Jews *

The intense preoccupation of the Yemenite Jews with Cabala and astrology and with their magical content, made them receptive to everything that had relation to a belief in the Messiah. Repeatedly there arose among them men who announced that they were either the Messiah or his forerunner, and always, down to our own day, they found among the Yemenites enthusiastic and believing followers who never for a moment doubted all the miracles reported about these messiahs. The ending of the Jewish *Galut* (Dispersion) among the nations of the earth was their great longing. Particularly where persecution was unusually harsh the End of Days seemed to Jews persuasively near. There such men as these messiahs found their most fertile soil. At all assemblies and weddings, and at other festivals, the subject of the end of the *Galut* served as the liveliest part of the conversation.

In order to bring the Dispersion to an end, all the cabalists of Sanaa (the principal Jewish center in Yemen) used to gather every morning, as recently as 35 years ago (c. 1900) in both of the large synagogues there and, under the direction of *Mori* (scholar) Hayyim Garah, they studied the Zohar and chanted psalms and *selichos* (penitential hymns). "They recited special prayers, then they blew blasts on the shofar (ram's horn). This lasted for fifteen minutes until the tones of the sacred trumpet pierced their consciousness and filled with anguish those spirits eager for miracles. They were exhausted with prayer; many, in a daze, fell down in convulsions." †

One must remember that this took place in an Arab environment which, in equal measure, was dominated by Messianic beliefs. Faith in the "Return," *al-raga,* of the Mahdi, the concealed *imam,* as the redeemer of the world, is one of the most fundamental tenets of the Shiite sect of Islam, the leading one in Yemen.

The first information concerning the appearance of a Messiah, or his forerunner, is found in Maimonides' *Iggeret Teman* (Letter to Yemen) and in his letter to the Jews of Marseilles. The attention of Maimonides

---

* Translated from *Ethnologie der Jemenitischen Juden,* by Erich Brauer. Carl Winters Universitätsbuchhandlung. Heidelberg, 1934.

† Yomtob Sémach. From *Une Mission de l'Alliance au Yémen.* Paris, 1910.

to the appearance of a Messiah in 1172 in Yemen was drawn by Jacob al-Fayyumi. In *Iggeret Teman,* which was his answer to al-Fayyumi's epistle, Maimonides vigorously attacked all kinds of Messianic speculations . . .

Some twenty years later (1194), in reply to a communication from the Jews of Marseilles asking for his opinion on the merits of astrology, Maimonides once more dwelled upon the subject of the Messiah in Yemen and gave a graphic account of his appearance there. He wrote:

"Regarding the Messiah, reports of whom you say stem from me, I would like to say that it is not as you have heard. It happened, not in the East, but in Yemen. Twenty-two years ago there appeared there a man who declared that he had a message from the Messiah whose coming he had come to herald. According to him the Messiah would appear first in Yemen.

"Accordingly, many Jews and Arabs gathered round him and they followed him into the mountains. He led them astray with such speech as: 'Follow me! Let us go forth to greet the Messiah for he has sent me to announce his coming!' Our brothers in Yemen wrote me a long letter in which they apprised me of his practices and customs, of the innovations he introduced into the synagogue service, and in general of what he spoke to them. They informed me of all the miracles they had seen him perform and asked me for my opinion thereon.

"I understood fully from their letters that that poor man, although he appeared to be well-enough God-fearing, was demented, and altogether ignorant. Everything he said or did was either a lie or an illusion. For that reason I was much concerned for the Yemenite Jews and wrote to them three letters about the Messiah, about his signs by which men could know him and about the signs of the times in which he would make his appearance. I exhorted them to warn that misguided man in order that he should not go down to destruction and thereby drag the entire community into it with him.

"In brief, one year later he was arrested and all his followers fled. After he was imprisoned an Arabian king said to him: 'What have you done?'

"He answered: 'My Lord and King, I speak but the truth. According to God's command have I dealt!'

"The king then asked him: 'What is your sign?'

"He replied: 'My Lord and King, chop my head off and I will rise up again just as I was before.'

" 'You couldn't possibly give me a better sign than that,' said the king, 'and if what you claim comes true, I and the whole of mankind will believe in you and in the truth of your words, and contrariwise, we will recognize that our fathers practiced nothing but lies, deceit and vanity.'

"Thereupon the king commanded: 'Bring a sword!'

"So they brought a sword and, at the command of the king, they chopped the unfortunate man's head off . . .

"May his death serve as his atonement for himself and for all Israel!

"Heavy money fines were exacted from Jewish communities in many places. None the less, there are still many fools to be found there today who say that he will soon rise up from his grave . . ."

The Jews of K'aifengfu

INTRODUCTORY NOTE

This is one of the strangest chapters of universal history—fantastic even and not less amazing than if there had been a 2000-years-old colony of Incas in the middle of England or of Arabs in Norway.

To understand the above to its full extent, a glance at the history of the Jews of Honan is necessary.

Just when Sino-Jewish relations first occurred is a matter for conjecture. It has been suggested that they date back to Biblical times—the "Land of the Sinim" mentioned by Isaiah * being China. Another assertion is that the Lost Tribes finally found their way to China and settled there. No historical proof is forthcoming in support of these assertions.

However, it has been historically proven that Jewish immigration on a large scale into China took place during the Han Dynasty, i.e. the 2nd Century B.C. These Jews came mostly from Persia. They settled down at different places, but finally became attracted in large numbers to the city of K'aifengfu on the Hwangho (Yellow River), capital of Honan and then the residence of the ruling dynasty. Moreover, they there enjoyed the protection that Chinese Emperors granted to all who came to sojourn in their kingdom.

There is no record of the numerical extent of this immigration, but an old inscription upon a memorial stone refers incidentally to "70 families" coming to settle in the city during the reign of an early Sung Emperor. We may assume that they immigrated periodically in groups of several hundreds, growing finally to a community of some 5,000 to 6,000 heads. But besides this, we have abundant documentary evidence to show the different stages of their settlement there—at least on general lines.

The Jews came in groups of families. They brought with them their wives and children, their rabbis and their craftsmen, their holy scriptures and their tools—in short their own old culture. The very characteristics of their race—their peacefulness and respect for tradition, scholarship and age —agreed in the most happy way with Chinese rationality, tolerance and cult of ancestor-worship.

Thus, the immigrants soon accommodated themselves among these hospitable people—strange and foreign to them in almost everything, but whose culture and ethics they found as old and fine as their own. They got adapted to the exterior conditions of their new surroundings, but remained true to their Jewish self, and nobody interfered with them.

They spoke Chinese and prayed in Hebrew. They dressed in Chinese clothes and fashions, but had, before God, their kittels, tallisses and twil-

---

* Chapter 49, verse 12.

lims.* They had their houses built in the style of the land of their adoption, the ridges turned up in a gentle curve—so also was the roof of their Synagogue, in the compound of which they raised, following the Chinese custom, huge stone-tablets, "steles," where all was inscribed that should be remembered—now the best monumental testimony to their history. Outwardly Chinese in form, the inscriptions read like this: "Adam was the first man, Abraham was the founder of our religion, then came Moses and gave us the Law and the Holy Scriptures . . ."

Chinese citizens they were, free and never secluded in a ghetto or quasi-ghetto, but Jews in faith, giving loyally to the Emperor what was the Emperor's and piously to God what was God's. They read their thoras † and taught their children the old language. They had their boys circumcised and they did not intermarry with those not of their race. Following the Bible even to the time-honoured eating-rules as laid down by Moses, they disdained the ritually "unclean," and it is in this way that they came to be called in China "T'ai Chin Chiao," meaning "those who extract the sinews"—clean dietitians. And this was a term of commendation, for respecting a time-honoured law or custom has ever been in China a subject of esteem.

Such were the conditions under which the Jews settled in China—mutual respect being the principal feature of Sino-Jewish relations—whilst in Europe the Middle Ages wore on.

The Jews were fruitful and multiplied. They grew into a great community. In the 7th Century, the ruling Emperor of the T'ang Dynasty appointed a special mandarin to take care of Jewish matters, and especially ordered him to go, once every year, to the Synagogue at K'aifengfu and to burn incense as an expression of His Imperial grace and favour. As it was customary in all Chinese temples to have a tablet hung up with the name of the Emperor written in gilded Chinese characters, a tablet of a similar kind was also suspended in the Synagogue of K'aifengfu. But above this tablet the Jews placed another one with a Hebrew inscription: "Hear, oh Israël! The Lord is Our Lord! The Lord is One!" . . . The Chinese understood and smiled, and the Jews smiled in return. . . .

According to contemporary documents, the Jews "excelled in agriculture, commerce and magistracies." "They are highly esteemed," reads a Chinese record, "for their integrity, fidelity and strict observance of their religion."

At the end of the 9th Century, an Arabian explorer Aboul Zeyd al Hassan travelled all over China and reported that the number of Jewish communities was considerable, their relations with the Chinese being excellent, especially at K'aifengfu. About the year A.D. 1000—so state the steles—"high Imperial honours were bestowed upon several Jews at K'aifengfu." In 1163, the construction of a "new great Synagogue was commenced" there, to be completed two years later "at the cost of the Government." And in 1279—another inscription reads—the Synagogue having suffered from a flood of the Hwangho has been "rebuilt on a larger scale."—In Europe, this was the time of the Crusades.

---

* Ritual articles of clothing used during divine service.

---

† Hebrew texts of the Old Testament written on parchment scrolls.

In the 15th Century an Imperial Edict ordered the great Synagogue at K'aifengfu to be renovated "with the help of the Imperial Cash Office." This contribution enabled the community also to replace their ancient thora-scrolls by new ones brought from Ningpo on the Eastern coast. The "stony chronicles" also recorded that another century of quiet development followed.—In Europe, the Inquisition started to work.

Who were these Jews of K'aifengfu? Who were their leaders, rabbis, scholars, mandarins? Who were their prominent men upon whom "Imperial honours had been bestowed"? We don't know. We have some names, occasionally mentioned, but no biographies. A striking fact indeed, but also throughout in accordance with the devoutness of those historians and with their spirit of true democracy.

I have with me one of those rare facsimiles made in Shanghai in 1851, when some manuscripts from K'aifengfu came through this city. It has been taken from a manuscript which was copied from the Pentateuch probably in the 16th Century, to be used for the weekly reading of the "sedrah." * On its last page a strange note reads (in translation) as follows:

"Holiness to Jehovah! The Rabbi ben Akiba, the son of Aaron, the son of Ezra, heard it. Shandiavor, the son of Bethuel, the son of Moses, read it. Mordecai, the son of Moses, witnessed it. And he believed in Jehovah. And HE accounted it to him for righteousness."

And a similar note in another prayer-book of the same kind:

"Holiness to Jehovah! The learned Rabbi Phineas, the son of Israël, the son of Joshua, the son of Benjamin, heard the reading. I have waited for Thy salvation, O Jehovah! Amen."

These Hebrew names tell us nothing about the men who bore them. To all appearance, they were prominent amongst their people. In their workaday world they might have been a Mr. Kao, Mr. Li, Mr. Shih or Mr. Chong. From the most ancient times, the Chinese Jews were divided into a rather limited number of clans, seven of which are recorded as the ancestral families who immigrated during the Han Dynasty.† Mr. Kao might have been a wealthy teaplanter, Mr. Li a mandarin, and Mr. Chong perhaps a poor teacher, but all of them alike were "highly esteemed for their integrity, fidelity, and strict observance of their religion."—Walter Fuchs. From *The Chinese Jews of K'aifengfu*. T'ien Hsai Monthly. V. 5. Nanking, 1937.

---

* Biblical text to be read as part of the liturgy.

† Kao, Shih, Ai, Li, Cha, Kin, Chong.

A Translation of the 1489 Inscription Covering the Reconstruction of the Ch'ing Chên Ssu *

ABRAHAM *(A-wu-lo-han)*, the patriarch who founded the religion of Israel *(Yi-tz'u-lo-yeh)*, was of the nineteenth generation from P'an-ku Adam *(A-tan)*. From the creation of heaven and earth the patriarchs handed down successively the traditions which they had received. They made no images, flattered no spirits and ghosts, and they placed no credence in superstitious practices. At any time the spirits and ghosts could not help men, idols could afford them no protection, and superstitious practices could avail them nothing.

So (Abraham) meditated upon Heaven: .

Above, it is ethereal and pure; (below) it is most honourable beyond compare. The Way of Heaven *(T'ien Tao)* does not speak, yet "the four seasons pursue their course, and all creatures (in sequence) are produced" ("but does Heaven say anything?"—*Analects*, bk. XVII: *19*). It is evident that things come to life in the spring-time, grow during the summer, are harvested in the autumn, and stored up in the winter. Some fly (birds), others swim (fish), some walk (animals), and others grow (plants). Some (plants) are luxuriant, others despoiled, some (flowers) are blooming, others falling. Living things are produced from the sequence of life; transformations are due to the process of change; shapes are the outcome of the particular form, and colours are developed from their colour source.

The patriarch (Abraham) suddenly awakening as out of sleep, then understood these profound mysteries. He began truly to seek the Correct Religion *(Chêng Chiao)*, with a view to assisting the true Heaven. With all his heart he served it, and gave himself up wholly to its respectful veneration. Then it was that he laid the foundation of the Religion which has been handed down to this day. By inquiry it was found that this was in the 146th year of the Chou Dynasty (977 B.C.).

Through transmission (the Religion) reached Moses *(Mieh-shê)*, who was also a patriarch of the Correct Religion *(Chêng Chiao)*. Examination reveals that he lived in the 613th year of the Chou Dynasty (510 B.C.). From his birth he was gifted with a perspicacity that was pure and genuine. His benevolence *(jên)* and righteousness *(li)* were altogether perfect; his principles *(tao)* and his goodness *(tê)* were together complete. He sought for the Scriptures *(Ching)* at the top of Mount Sinai *(Hsi-na)*, and to this end he fasted forty days and nights. He put away his lustful passions, and denied himself both sleep and food, and with a sincere mind gave him-

---

* From *Chinese Jews*, by William Charles White. The University of Toronto Press. Toronto, 1942. With the permission of the author and publishers.

The *Ch'ing Chên Ssu*, the great synagogue at K'aifengfu, became a Christian Mission Church in the 1930's. The great poverty of the Jews and their reduced numbers had forced them to abandon their ancient *Ssu*.

self up to prayer. His devotion touched the heart of Heaven, so that the fifty-three sections of the Book of the Correct Religion then had their origin. Their contents are extremely subtle and mysterious; the good men (recorded in the Book) stir up and incite the goodness of the heart of man, while the evil men (of the Book) repress and give warning to man's unregulated will.

Again (the Religion) was transmitted to Ezra *(Ai-tzu-la)*, another patriarch of the Correct Religion. He being a descendant of the patriarchs received from them the whole heritage of the Way *(Tao)*. His way *(tao)* of honouring Heaven and performing worship fully revealed the mysteries of the Way *(Tao)* of the ancestors.

However, the Way must be based on Purity *(Ch'ing)*, Truth *(Chên)*, Ritual *(Li)*, and Worship *(Pai)*. *Ch'ing* means pure unity without duplicity, *Chên* signifies genuineness without depravity, *Li* denotes simply reverence, and *Pai* is an act of obeisance. In the midst of daily occupations men must not forget Heaven even for a single moment, but morning, noon, and night, three times a day *(yin, wu, hsü)* should pay due reverence *(li)* and offer worship *(pai)*. This is the basic principle *(li)* of the true Way of Heaven *(T'ien Tao)*.

What was the common practice of the patriarchal worthies in their reverential ceremonies? First they washed their bodies, and changed their garments; then they purified their mind *(t'ien chün)*, and regulated their natural faculties *(t'ien kuan)*; and so with great respect and veneration they then entered in before the Scriptures of the Way *(Tao Ching)*. The Way *(Tao)* has no form or figure, but is just like the Way of Heaven which is above.

The outline of procedure in the ceremonial worship of venerating Heaven is simply set forth in the following:

At first the worshipper bends his body to honour the Way, and the Way is present in the act of bending the body. Then he stands erect, without leaning, to honour the Way, and the Way is present in the act of standing erect.

In response, he preserves his quietude of mind, and by silent praise he honours the Way, for that which should not be forgotten is Heaven.

In movement, he examines his conduct, and by vocal praise he honours the Way, for that which should not be substituted for is Heaven.

The worshipper recedes three paces, and immediately (the Way) is behind him, and in consequence he honours the Way which is behind him.

He advances five steps, and perceives (the Way) before him, and in consequence he honours the Way which is before him.

Turning to the left he bends his body to honour the Way, which is good, for the Way is then on his left.

Turning to the right he bends his body to honour the Way, which is not so good, for the Way is then on his right.

He uplifts his head to honour the Way, and the Way is above him; he lowers his head to honour the Way, and the Way is near him.

Finally he worships *(pai)* the Way, and It is honoured in this act of worship.

Truly, in the matter of honouring Heaven, if a man did not venerate his ancestors *(tsu)* he could not then properly offer sacrifices to the forefathers *(hsien)*. Thus, in the spring and autumn sacrifices to the ancestors, one "served the dead as he would have served the living; he served the departed as he would have served those present" *(Doctrine of the Mean, Legge, XIX:5)*. He offered oxen and sheep, and seasonal food (cp. *Doctrine of the Mean, XIX:3)*, and did not fail to honour the ancestors because they had already passed on.

In every month there should be four days' fasting. Fasting is the entrance *(mên)* to the Way, and the foundation upon which good works are laid up. Today a good deed is laid up, tomorrow a good deed is laid up, and with this beginning in good deeds the piling up becomes a habit. When the time of fasting comes, no evil is done, but all sorts of good actions are performed; thus the seven days (of the week) are brought to a good ending, and a new week commences (cp. Vertical Inscription No. XXXVII). As the *Book of Changes* says *(Hexagram* XXIV): "The good man, doing good, finds the day insufficient." The *Book of History (Legge, v:1; 2:3, p. 290)*, also expresses this same meaning. At the four seasons of the year there is abstention for seven days, in consideration of the calamities experienced by all the ancestors, and also sacrifices are then made to the forefathers, in order to repay the source *(pao pên)* (of the good things that have been received). Cutting off from all food and drink, there is rigid abstinence for one whole day, reverently praying to Heaven, for repentance of previous faults, and for the moving towards the new good deeds of the present day. Is this not the meaning of the saying of Hexagram *Yi* (42nd) and in the *Book of Changes,* as explained by the sage when he says: "The wind and the thunder unite, and the Superior Man *(Chün Tzu)* moves toward the good that he has seen, and corrects the faults which he has committed"? *(Chou, Yi Chih Ta Hsiang)*.

Truly, the Way of the Religion *(Chiao Tao)* has been handed down, but the transmission and reception have been in sequence. It came out from India *(T'ien-chu)*; in obedience to the divine command it came *(fêng ming êrh lai)*. There were *Li, Yen, Ai, Kao, Mu, Chao, Chin, Chou, Chang, Shih, Huang, Li, Nieh, Chin, Chang, Tso, Po,*—in all, seventy or more clans. Bringing tribute of Western *(Hsi Yang)* cloth, they entered (the court of) Sung, and the Emperor said: "You have come to Our China *(Chunghsia);* reverence and preserve the customs of your ancestors, and hand them down at Pien-liang (K'ai-fêng)."

In the *kuei-wei* year (1163), the first year of the Lung Hsing period, under Hsiao Tsung of the Sung Dynasty, *Lieh-wei* (Levi) *Wu-ssu-ta* was charged with the administration of the Religion, and the *Yen-tu-la* began to build the synagogue *(ssu)*.

Under the Yüan Dynasty, in the *chi-mao* year (1279), which was the sixteenth year of the Chih Yüan (Kublai) period, the *Wu-ssu-ta* rebuilt the ancient temple *(ku ch'a)*, the Ch'ing Chên Ssu. This was located at the south-east of the Earth-market Character Street *(T'u-shih Tzu Chieh)*, and on each of its four sides it was thirty-five *chang* (350 feet).

The Emperor Kao, T'ai Tsu of our Ta Ming Dynasty, at the beginning of the founding of the new dynasty (1368), devoted himself to consolidating the army and the people of the empire. To all those who submitted to his influence he gave land for villages, where they could dwell in peace and be content with their lot. This was indeed the manifestation of his goodwill in the matter of indiscriminate benevolence.

Because the synagogue could not do without persons in charge of it, then *Li Ch'êng, Li Shih, Yen P'ing-t'u, Ai Tuan, Li Kuei, Li Chieh, Li Shêng, Li Kang, Ai Ching, Chou An, Li Jung, Li Liang, Li Chih, Chang Hao*, and others, who were well-versed in the canonical Scriptures *(Chêng Ching)*, and who exhorted others to do good, were designated to be *Man-la* (Mullahs). The Way of the Religion *(Chiao Tao)* has been transmitted in succession. To the present the robes and head-dress, the rites and music, all conform to fixed regulations for each season. The phrases and words, the movements and pauses, are made in accordance with ancient usage *(chang)*. All men observe the established laws, know how to honour Heaven and to venerate the ancestors, and show themselves loyal to the prince and filial to their parents. This is all due to the work of the abovementioned *Man-la*.

Yen Ch'êng, the physician, in the nineteenth year of Yung Lo (1421), received from the Emperor, through Chou-fu Ting Wang, a present of incense and (permission) to rebuild the synagogue *(Ch'ing Chên Ssu)*. In the synagogue (was placed) the Imperial Tablet *(Wan Sui P'ai)*, acknowledging allegiance *(fêng)* to the ruling Emperor of the Ta Ming Dynasty. In the twenty-first year of Yung Lo (1423) a memorial was presented on the merits (of the above-mentioned physician), and by Imperial decree he was given the surname *Chao*, and there was conferred upon him the grade of Embroidered Robe Body-guard *(Chin Yi Wei-chih-hui)*, and he was promoted to be colonel in the constabulary *(Chih-hui)* of the Chêkiang *(Chê-chiang)* Province.

In the tenth year of Chêng T'ung (1445), Li Jung and Li Liang themselves prepared funds to rebuild three sections *(chien)* of the Front Hall *(Ch'ien Tien)* (of the synagogue).

When in the fifth year of T'ien Shun (1461) the waters of the Yellow River inundated the country, leaving hardly more than the foundations of the synagogue, Ai Ching and others presented a petition to the provincial authorities, asking that they might be allowed to reconstruct the synagogue according to the commission which had previously been received from the provincial treasurer through the prefect of the city, in which had been mentioned the ancient shrine *(ku ch'a)*, the synagogue *(Ch'ing Chên Ssu)* of the Chih Yüan period (1279). Permission having been granted, Li Jung again prepared funds and began to build it on a

very spacious plan (grand scale) so that, glittering with gold and variegated colours, its splendour was complete (perfect).

During the Ch'êng Hua period (1465–1488), Kao Chien, Kao Jui, and
Kao Hung, themselves provided funds and built an additional three sections *(chien)* to the Rear Hall *(Hou Tien)* of the synagogue. These
having been beautified with gilt and colour, three copies of the Scriptures
of the Way *(Tao Ching)* were placed in them. Moreover, on the outside
they constructed the corridor which connected with the Front Hall *(Ch'ien
Tien)*. Truly this was an enterprise of permanent value. These then are
the circumstances concerning the former and later constructions of the
synagogue.

The Jews of Cochin

AT PRESENT the Jews of Cochin number, in all, some fourteen hundred.
As are their Hindu neighbors, the Jews are divided into castes which do not
intermarry or interdine with each other. There are three Jewish castes
which have been denoted in the literature as white Jews, black Jews,
and brown Jews.* The white Jews, who are at the head of the Jewish caste
hierarchy, range in skin color from a pale white to a medium brown; in
general, their pigmentation is about the same as that of south Italians. The
skin color of the other two castes is like that of the natives of Cochin,
ranging from a light brown to a deep brownish-black. The white Jews
have their own synagogue, where the brown Jews are also allowed to worship. The black Jews, who are by far the most numerous, have seven
synagogues.

The life of the Cochin Jews is conducted strictly according to the pre-

---

THE JEWS OF COCHIN: From *The Jewish Way of Life in Cochin,* by David G.
Mandelbaum. In *Jewish Social Studies,* V. 1, 1939. New York.

The existence of a considerable Jewish Colony in Cochin and neighboring towns has
long been known, and has excited much interest among very different classes. . . .

It is beyond doubt that Jewish colonies were established many centuries ago on the
southwest coast of India. Arab travelers in the 10th century mention them as numerous
in Ceylon. Vasco de Gama (Gaspard da Gama) in his first voyage found a Polish Jew
at the Anjedives, and the early Portuguese appear to have called the king of Cochin
king of the Jews on account of the number in his territory. . . . The great original
settlement in South India was at Cranganore, but when that place fell under the
Portuguese, the Jews met with such injustice that they left it and settled near
Cochin which has always been the chief settlement since then, though there are several
at Chêntamangalam and other inland towns.—A. C. Burnell. From *The Indian
Antiquary* in an article on "The Original Settlement-Deed of the Jewish Colony at
Cochin." Bombay, 1874.

---

* The Jews of Cochin prefer to use the terms *meyuchasim,* Malabar Jews, and
m'shuhararim for the three groups. In this paper the designations commonly used in
previous writings on the subject have been retained. . . .

cepts of the *Shulhan arukh*, the orthodox codex. While the mother tongue of the children is Malayalam, the Dravidian dialect of the country, yet all, boys and girls alike, learn to read Hebrew; the men whose single garment is a waist-cloth, inevitably have a small skullcap of gaily colored cloth perched atop their heads, from which two earlocks often droop; rice and curry, the diet of the South Indian, is also their staple food, but meat curries are never mixed with milk curries. An orthodox Jew from Warsaw or the Bronx might find the Sephardic liturgy of the Cochin synagogues a bit odd at first, but the devotion of the Cochin Jews to Jewish law and learning would soon make him feel at home.

In spite of exposure to the strange customs of an Indian culture the life of the little colony has remained a Jewish way of life. Just how long the Jews have lived in Cochin is not possible to say. Local tradition relates that the first Jewish settlers arrived soon after the destruction of the temple in 70 C.E. There is nothing inherently impossible in the suggestion that the Jews came to the country during the first centuries of the Christian era.

The earliest documentary record of the colony is found in the inscriptions on a set of copper plates which are to this day in the possession of the Jews of Cochin. It was the custom of the ancient Rajas of the Malabar coast to bequeath grants of lands and privileges to their favorites. These bequests were graven on copper and given to the recipients of the favors as a kind of patent of nobility and a perpetual evidence of their rights. The Jewish plates were given in the year 1020 by the Raja Bhaskira Ravivarman to one Joseph Rabban. By the terms of the grant Joseph Rabban received the principality of Anjuvannam and all its revenue. In addition, certain noble rights were bestowed on Joseph Rabban and all his posterity. They included the right to ride an elephant, to be carried in a litter, to have a state umbrella, to be preceded by drums and trumpets, to call out so that lower castes might withdraw from the streets at its approach. It is also specified that the recipient shall not have to pay taxes and shall enjoy all the benefits of the Raja's administration. The opening line of the charter states that it was given when the Raja was in residence at Muyirikodu, the modern Cranganore.*

The date and place of the grant, and the privileges conferred are clear, but other particulars such as where the principality of Anjuvannam was located, the status of the Jews at the time, and why the charter was given, can only be inferred. Since the kingdom was probably small, the principality could not have been far distant from Cranganore. The Jews must have been well established and very influential, because the prerogatives and insignia of high rank are jealously guarded and seldom granted by the

---

* The copper plates are discussed and analyzed most thoroughly in the following works: Lévi, S., in *Mémorial Sylvain Lévi* (Paris 1937) p. 364–365; Menon, K. P. Padmanabha, *History of Kerala* (Ernakulam 1929) vol. ii, p. 507–14; Thurston, E., *Castes and Tribes of Southern India*, vol. ii, p. 463–77; Hultsch, E., *Epigraphica Indica*, vol. iii; Cammiade, L. A., *Epigraphica Indica*, vol. xvi, p. 340.

princes of India. Strong motives must have moved the Raja to bestow ennoblement on a Jew. Many of the privileges enumerated in the copper plates have fallen into desuetude even among the royalty of Malabar, but the great economic concession granted by the charter, freedom from taxation, is still held by the Jews of Cochin.

The Last of the Samaritans

IT WAS a peculiar feast, as I saw it two years ago, ushered in by the twilight on the cold peak of Gerizim. It passed for a festival of joy; and, indeed, it was sung and danced the night through. But to me it seemed more like a funeral feast; I saw in it the death of a People and a Faith.

The last of the Samaritans slaughtered their paschal lambs on the mountain once crowned by the holy temple. They ate the flesh of the sacrifice, they sang and danced to the Eternal One who had brought their fathers out of Egypt—a scant forty men and boys at prayer, a scant hundred and seventy souls in all, to celebrate the festival of Spring.

Ghosts hovering about the glow of the altar-fire.

Strange is this tiny people, the Samaritans, strange as their fate. After the destruction of the Kingdom of Israel, Shalmaneser settled a number of foreign peoples, "men from Babylon and from Cuthah, and from Arva, and from Hamath and Sepharvaim," in the conquered land. The newcomers mingled with the remnant of the Israelites and, remarkably enough, took over the religion of the older inhabitants. As a result, when two hundred years later the forty thousand Jews returned under Zerubbabel from the Babylonian exile "to build again the Temple of the Lord in Jerusalem," these *Shomronim* or Samaritans came to the Jews and said, "Let us build with you, for we seek your God as you do; and we do sacrifice unto Him since the days of Essarhaddon, king of Assur, who brought us up hither." So reports the Bible.

Again remarkable: instead of welcoming the unexpected support, the few thousand homecomers had the spirit to refuse an alliance with the Samaritans. They were held to be hybrids, no longer racially "pure." And so they could not be allowed to help build the Temple in Jerusalem.

The Samaritans bitterly revenged the rebuff. The stories of modern intrigues against the Balfour Declaration come to mind when we read, in Ezra and Nehemiah, of Arabian and Ammonite baiting the returned Jewish settlers, of despatches and embassies sent to the royal court at Babylon asking for the repeal of the "Declaration" of Cyrus. The Jews, in turn, heartily requited the enmity which more than once threatened the whole work of the restoration.

THE LAST OF THE SAMARITANS: By Wolfgang von Weisl. *The Menorah Journal,* April–May, 1926. New York.

And then a thing most remarkable of all came to pass—a psychological puzzle.

During the very period when the struggle of the Samaritan against the Jew was bitterest, the Law of the Pentateuch achieved an absolute dominion over the Samaritans, who now called themselves *Shomronim,* that is, "Guardians" (of the Law). The same conservative reaction that ruled in the Jerusalem of Ezra and Nehemiah manifested itself in the Shechem of Sanballat. A temple was erected on Mount Gerizim, which according to Samaritan lore is the site designated by God as His Holy Hill; and, rejecting oral tradition, the Samaritans maintained the strict letter of the written Law, at least so far as they recognized it, that is, the Law as contained in the Hexateuch. Fighting simultaneously against Jews and Gentiles, from then on they watched jealously over the purity of their new "race."

Centuries passed. Greeks and Romans came—and neither Jews nor Samaritans consented to submit to them; yet both Jews and Samaritans remained hostile to each other. Vespasian smote the Jews and overran Jerusalem and he smote the Samaritans and killed eleven thousand of them by Mount Gerizim. But this common tragedy—like their common faith—failed to bring together the kindred peoples.

Both Jews and Samaritans revolted against the foreign yoke. In 628 c.e. the Emperor Heraclius conquered the Holy Land and he butchered the Jews for having risen against him. But the remainder of Jews and the equally persecuted *Shomronim* continued to live in enmity. Although both had long lost their Temples neither could forgive the other for the thousand-year-old quarrel over the building of them.

Another thousand years passed, and more. Countless peoples swept through the land; Arabs, Seljuks, Crusaders, Tartars and Turks succeeded one another; but the little tribe at the foot of Mount Gerizim, although progressively decimated by oppression and forced conversion, held fast to its Holy Books—the Pentateuch and *Joshua*—held to its books and its existence.

Until today.

Now, at the moment when the Jews are again returning to rebuild Zion, the Samaritans are vanishing.

They number only a hundred and seventy souls, and they have no hope of increase; for they are almost entirely lacking in women to replenish the tribe. They are a handsome people, the men noble in bearing and large of build, the women delicate of feature and with marvelous eyes. But the race is spent, the procreative power is failing. Many of the men are unable to find wives; there are no Samaritan girls for them, their law forbids intermarriage with the Arabs, and they are prevented from taking Jewish wives by the *Verbot* of the Jewish rabbis, today as twenty-three hundred years ago. For the Samaritan may be an "Israelite"—as he calls himself—but he is not a Jew.

Every Passover, in the Springtime, the Samaritans leave their huddled quarter in the fanatically Moslem town of Nablus—where they live in a close community—and climb to the summit of Gerizim, and camp on the site of their former Temple. Men, women, and children, they climb the mountain, erect their tents, and for the seven days of the festival live under the open sky, once again a people in their own land.

On the thirteenth of Nissan—one day earlier than the Seder of the Jewish tradition—they offer up the paschal sacrifice. They slaughter seven sheep "in the twilight," they roast the meat over an open fire, "the head with the legs and the inwards thereof," and they "eat the flesh with bitter herbs and unleavened bread" according to the Bibilical prescription. The oldest sacrifice still extant!

Usually a few visitors find their way, earlier in the evening, to the summit of the steep mountain and as guests witness the sacrifice.

But that Passover of two years ago was different.

Not a few visitors, but vast throngs advanced on Har Gerizim. The multitude gave the festival an unwonted character; for the first time in the history of these kindred enemies, Jews marched en masse to the Samaritan rite—as friends.

Seven auto-trucks brought three hundred and fifty Jewish workmen from Jerusalem to Nablus; five hundred workmen came on foot from Haifa, by way of Tul-Kerem through the hills of Ephraim; and still others from the colonies and from Jaffa. It was at once an excursion and a demonstration—a demonstration in the face of the Arabs of Nablus, the enemy of today, and in the face of Samaritans, the enemy of yesterday.

Shrouded in white mantles the Samaritan men-folk stood in a circle around the sacrificial victims. The sun sank. The Samaritans cried forth their prayers, they thrust their hands toward the yearling lambs huddled in the circle of stones which marked the place of sacrifice. One lamb after the other was slashed through the throat, and the blood trickled between the joints of the altar stones. Green branches covered the ground. They were kindled and the sheep thrown upon them and heaped over with burning brushwood.

The men-folk continued to pray, pressed in a circle about the fire. At their feet squatted the children who plucked the singed wool from the skin of the sheep. A man poured water over the animals so that the wool fell off more easily.

The flames danced and the smoke drifted through the circle. And moonlight streamed on the white rock and boulders.

It became difficult for the worshipers to maintain their devotions. The fifteen hundred onlookers crowded upon the tiny ring of sacrificers; those in the rear could not see and thrust themselves forward. The police were compelled to join hands and form a circle to provide free room for the festival.

Sometimes I felt that the vast throng of guests incited the worshipers to even greater fervor. Like dervishes, and also like the Chassidim, the more pious among them closed their eyes, carried away by the roll of the chant, transported by the consciousness that they were the last representatives of a truth sealed by the blood of their fathers.

They now began praying with their entire body; beards and sidelocks flew and the upraised arms beat time. The chant grew ever louder and faster, hymns and songs of joy set to a march tempo. I caught snatches of melody I had once heard in Salonika and others heard once in Yemen; from the depths of the music rose echoes of the ancient kinship with the Jews.

The sheep were now plucked and ready to be cut open. The hind feet were bound, and one after another the victims were raised on a pole thrust between the thighs. Lungs and bowels were carefully inspected. The intestines were removed and cast into the fire. Liver, kidneys, and lungs were set aside as gifts of honor for the priests. The hymns again mounted in triumph—and sang the departure from Egypt.

And then a silence. A voice from the closed circle, a voice speaking Hebrew—for the first time in perhaps eighteen centuries the summit of Gerizim heard the sound of Hebrew words that were not Samaritan prayers. The priestly teacher of the tribe was speaking to the assembled guests.

He said that a covenant was being sealed today between Judah and Ephraim—it was only a phrase, of course, for "Ephraim" was no more, and the thirty or forty survivors were hardly a power to contract a covenant, but on a feast-day phrases may pass. Then the speaker proceeded further—"because of the covenant" he asked for means to restore the Samaritan synagogue, for the Samaritans were poor. . . . And the Samaritans applauded.

The applause smote my heart. I thought of Germany and Austria in the days after the war.

The sacrifice was over. The butchered and cleaned meat was set apart and guarded so that no one should touch it until midnight, the hour for eating, was at hand. If a Jew or Moslem were to touch the devoted meat, it would become "impure."

A bustle and activity now developed among the tents, such as the ancient mountain had surely never seen. The Samaritans received the guests in their tents, and sold them coffee, tea, beer, water, and eggs—at, be it observed, moderate prices. Despite the fact that everyone knew the vast importance of the receipts to the impoverished handful of workers and shopkeepers of Nablus, the Samaritans gallantly felt themselves bound to maintain the fiction that the Europeans present were their guests. They summoned up their painful smattering of Hebrew and politely greeted the visitors in their common tongue.

While the tourists among the guests sat about in the tents and wondered that such things could be, the workers transformed the mountain top into a *Chalutz* camp.

Some hundreds of *Chalutzim* crouched about in a vast circle, while a lecturer from the Labor Organization retold to them the history of Shechem and the *Shomronim*. Others paraded between the rows of tents; soon they were singing, and finally they began to join hands—yú-la-la, yú-la-la! they were dancing the Horra, the new Jewish national dance.

Not to have seen the Horra danced in Palestine is hardly to know what dancing means. The *Chalutz* pours out his entire soul in the Horra. He dances until he drops with weariness. He dances for the sake of dancing, for the pure ecstasy of it. No touch of eroticism, as in the European dance. On the contrary, the Horra is a dance especially fitting for men, who rejoice exclusively in its movement and energy.

They interlock arms, each man holding fast to his neighbors' shoulders. The circle is joined, a simple melody breaks forth—from the throats of the dancers or the onlookers—and the circle begins to turn with an ever increasing velocity. The onlookers, men and women, are sucked into the swirl. Coats, mantles, and rucksacks are tossed into the center of the ring. Here and there a pair of interlocked arms gives way, a new dancer thrusts himself into the gap, and the dance widens and quickens to ever new feet. Then the circle dissolves, and in a few moments reforms a few yards away, a new Horra.

The music of the Horra casts a spell on the *Chalutz*. As soon as the word, "Dance!" is given, as soon as he hears the monotonous but stimulating melody, he drops whatever he is about, and hastens to join the moving ring. The songs are, as I have said, monotonous and simple. The text of one of them, already of the more complicated variety, consists of the words, a score of times repeated:

> We need no sweethearts
> We only need dances.

Many of the songs have no text whatever, but merely two or three meaningless sounds which, endlessly repeated, beat out the rhythm of the dance. Nevertheless, in their wildness and natural simplicity these songs have a beauty; and on the moonlit mountain-top the dance of the cobbled shoes of the *Chalutzim* is a thousand times lighter, freer, and happier than the erotic measures of Europe.

The cup of joy overflows. The workers are light of heart: things are moving forward in Palestine, there is no unemployment, twenty-four hundred new immigrants have been granted visas, the tourists are bringing new money, the Zionist Organization is again in funds, more land has been bought—for all of this the *Chalutzim* dance the Horra in the face of Nablus, the seat of the Arab Congress! What more is needed to be happy! The *Chalutzim* understand the historical significance of their dance on the holy mountain of their one-time enemy. Whoever had not understood it has been enlightened by the Labor lecturers who had come, Bible in hand, to build the bridge from the past and to project the future.

"We've outlived Babylon and Rome," sang the Horra, "we are outliving the Samaritans, and we are going to outlive the Arab Congress in Shechem. We are going to live, sing, and dance the Horra."

It was nearly midnight. The sheep had been placed on the glowing stones of the altar, covered with earth, and roasted whole. They were now removed from the stones, laid on clean platters, and brought to the circle of worshipers who were joined by their women-folk.

The elders sat on stools, "with loins girded, their shoes on their feet, and their staff in their hand." As the roasted meat was brought to them, they arose. They ate it standing, "in haste," as the Israelites were commanded to eat it on the night of the Exodus.

Enormous loaves of unleavened bread were distributed, and platters of bitter herbs. The meat was laid between the matzoth, seasoned with the herbs, and eaten—naturally in the Oriental fashion—without plate, knife, or fork.

The meal ended at precisely midnight. The High Priest, a lineal descendant of Aaron and an eighty-year old greybeard of royal presence, raised his voice in prayer. The little community pressed quietly together and rendered thanks to the Eternal that they had been nourished and preserved to this day . . . the last of the Samaritans.

[4]

Folk Tales

INTRODUCTION

The narrative art of Jewish folklore has the liveliness and color of all eastern storytelling. Jewish, Hindu and Arabic tales alike show ingenious plot invention; they use all the technical devices of suspense and the surprise ending with much skill. And yet there is a subtle difference that marks off Jewish tales and legends from the others. They are more cerebral, turned inward, as it were, and tirelessly pointing a moral for the guidance of men.

This is the character of the didactic tales about *Alexander Mukdon* (Alexander the Macedonian). It is indeed surprising that Alexander the Great should have loomed so large and have been treated in such a favorable light by Jewish folklore. Historically speaking, he had but little personal contact with the Jewish people, except for a brief time during his whirlwind march through Palestine after subjugating Tyre in 332 B.C.

Cultural fusion was partly responsible for Alexander's popularity. Hellenism had been infiltrating steadily into Jewish life ever since the pre-Maccabean era, not only in Judea and Syria, but especially in Egypt where a great Jewish population of more than one million had developed a significant Graeco-Jewish culture by the Second Century B.C. Accordingly, Greek legends about Alexander found a wide and sympathetic acceptance among Hellenized Jews.

There was something in the personality of Alexander that readily appealed to the Jewish folk fancy. For one thing, his treatment of subjugated peoples was more humane and tolerant than that of other world conquerors; he also allowed the stream of Jewish life to flow on undisturbed so long as it did not resist his will to power during his brief world domination. Moreover, he was not only a military genius whose daring exploits filled mankind with astonishment, but he was a philosopher, personally educated by Aristotle for whom Jews always had the greatest reverence.

And it is precisely the intellectual side of Alexander that gave the unknown Talmudic narrators of the Alexander legends the necessary springboard for their moralizing. They depicted him as a confused but well-meaning ruler who showed more dash and insane drive to power than philosophical temper about which he was so inordinately proud.

The ethical question satirically raised in many of the Jewish Alexander stories was: how was it possible for a man claiming to be a philosopher to be so lacking in *chochma* and in virtue as to pursue such destructive and senseless ends as wars of conquest?

Many of the Alexander stories in the *Agada* and in later Jewish literature were derived from their well-known Greek originals, in Plutarch and in Callisthenes among others. Yet even these, in the transmuting process of Jewish didactic treatment, acquired a new character. The emphasis was transferred from the genius and splendor of the world-conqueror in Greek legend to his moral bankruptcy and to the vanity of vanities of strife and power, thus by contrast holding up to praise the gentle arts of peace and civilization.

The three Alexander legends included in this section are Jewish in origin, although *The Great Are Also Little* bears a similarity to a version by Callisthenes. *The Lord Helpeth Man and Beast*, which the English poet Coleridge adapted from the Talmud, was so popular that the Arab writer, Abu al Wafa ibn Fakih, included it in a work which was later translated into Latin by a Jew in 1053 under the title *Dicta Philosophorum*. This Latin version of the legend in turn was translated into English, Spanish and French, thus entering into the general legendary lore about Alexander during the Middle Ages, but without giving any indication of its Talmudic identity. A somewhat similar fate was in store for *The Acquisitive Eye*. It first appeared in the *Agada,* yet it entered into general folklore by means of the Twelfth Century compilation, *Alexandri Magni Iter ad Paradisum.* In this version, however, an old Jew, Pappas, is introduced to rebuke the insatiably acquisitive king.

N. A.

The Great Are Also Little

No MATTER how much he achieved in the world Alexander still remained dissatisfied.

"I would like to experience something most unusual, that no human being before me has ever experienced," he cried.

So he ordered his hunters to capture a number of eagles. He chose the largest among them and sat himself astride on it. Then he speared a piece of flesh on his lance and raised it high.

As soon as the eagle smelled the flesh it rose up in the air, straining to reach it.

Purposely Alexander held the flesh out of the reach of the eagle who rose ever higher and higher into the air. Soon the towns and cities began to look like pin-points to the king.

Alexander was filled with vain-glory.

THE GREAT ARE ALSO LITTLE: Adapted from the *Agada* in the Talmud.

"Who can compare to me now?" he gloated. "I am now higher than all men; in my eyes now they look like insects!"

But suddenly fear gripped him. He thought: "If I am so high up how can people see me? Maybe I also look like a fly to them. Perhaps they don't see me at all, and if I am out of sight how can they do me honor? Soon they may even forget me!"

And all his pride burst, and his uniqueness seemed as nothing to him now.

And still the eagle kept soaring, farther and farther from the earth. Once more Alexander looked down and the earth now seemed to him like a little ball. The king grew frightened and he lowered his lance with the flesh on its point. Straining to reach it the eagle began to descend ever lower and lower. Soon objects became distinct, ever larger and larger, towns, trees and people. And the nearer he came people grew bigger and bigger to his eyes. And Alexander rejoiced and derived the right moral from it.

When he reached the ground again, he ordered a sculptor to fashion a portrait of him holding a small sphere in his hand.

"Let people know," spoke the king, "that even the mighty Alexander can look as insignificant as this tiny sphere."

The Lord Helpeth Man and Beast

DURING his march to conquer the world, Alexander, the Macedonian, came to a people in Africa who dwelt in a remote and secluded corner in peaceful huts, and knew neither war nor conqueror.

They led him to the hut of their chief, who received him hospitably and placed before him golden dates, golden figs, and bread of gold.

"Do you eat gold in this country?" said Alexander.

"I take it for granted," replied the chief, "that thou wert able to find eatable food in thine own country. For what reason, then, art thou come amongst us?"

"Your gold has not tempted me hither," said Alexander, "but I would become acquainted with your manners and customs."

"So be it," rejoined the other. "Sojourn among us as long as it pleaseth thee."

At the close of this conversation two citizens entered, as to their court of justice.

The plaintiff said: "I bought of this man a piece of land, and as I was making a deep drain through it, I found a treasure. This is not mine, for I only bargained for the land, and not for any treasure that might be concealed beneath it; and yet the former owner of the land will not receive it."

THE LORD HELPETH MAN AND BEAST: From the Talmud. Translated by Samuel T. Coleridge. *In Hebrew Tales*, by Hyman Hurwitz. Printed for Morrison and Watt. London, 1826.

The defendant answered: "I hope I have a conscience, as well as my fellow-citizen. I sold him the land with all its contingent, as well as existing advantages, and consequently the treasure inclusively."

The chief, who was at the same time their supreme judge, recapitulated their words, in order that the parties might see whether or not he understood them aright. Then, after some reflection, he said, "Thou hast a son, friend, I believe?"

"Yes."

"And thou," addressing the other, "a daughter?"

"Yes."

"Well, then, let thy son marry *thy* daughter, and bestow the treasure on the young couple for a marriage portion."

Alexander seemed surprised and perplexed.

"You think my sentence unjust?" the chief asked him.

"O no!" replied Alexander. "But it astonishes me."

"And how, then," rejoined the chief, "would the case have been decided in your country?"

"To confess the truth," said Alexander, "we should have taken both parties into custody and have seized the treasure for the king's use."

"For the king's use!" exclaimed the chief. "Does the sun shine on your country?"

"O yes!"

"Does it rain there?"

"Assuredly."

"Wonderful! But are there tame animals in the country, that live on the grass and green herbs?"

"Very many and of many kinds."

"Aye, that must then be the cause," said the chief. "For the sake of those innocent animals the all-gracious Being continues to let the sun shine and the rain drop down on your own country, since its inhabitants are unworthy of such blessings."

The Acquisitive Eye

AFTER he had conquered the entire world, Alexander started back on his journey home to Macedonia. On the way he came to a stream. He dismounted and, taking out some salted fish he carried in his knapsack, he began to rinse them in the water before eating. At this a remarkable thing happened: upon touching the water the fish became alive.

Filled with amazement, Alexander threw himself into the stream and bathed in it.

"Now I understand," he cried overjoyed, "that the water in this stream

---

THE ACQUISITIVE EYE: Adapted from the *Agada* in the Talmud.

flows from Paradise! I will wash my face quickly in it and then I'll follow the stream, for it's sure to lead me to Paradise."

Barely had he finished washing his face when his eyes began to shine like stars, his face became radiant, his energies renewed. Never before had he felt so happy. Quickly he went up to the Gates of Paradise, but he found them closed.

"Open up, Gates!" he cried out. "Alexander wants to enter!"

Instantly the answer came: "These are the Gates of the Eternal. Only the pious may enter here."

Seeing that the Gates would not open for him, he implored, "Give me some kind of token, O Heavenly Gates, so I can prove that I've been here."

At this the Gates of Paradise relented and opened for an instant. A human eye then rolled towards him. Amazed, Alexander picked it up and placed it in his knapsack. Then he made his way home to Macedonia.

No sooner had he reached home when he called all his wise men together. He told them everything that had happened to him.

"What signifies the strange gift I received?" he asked.

"O King," replied the wise men, "place the eye in the scales and weigh it."

"What for?" asked Alexander. "I can tell you beforehand that it weighs but little."

"Do it just the same!" the wise men urged. "In the other half of the scales place a gold piece. Then we will find out which is heavier."

Alexander did as they asked. To his surprise he found that the eye was heavier than the gold piece. He threw into the scales another gold coin— still the eye was heavier. He then threw in a whole handful of coins and ordered that all his gold and silver and jewels be thrown in. Still the eye outweighed the treasure.

"Even were you to take all your chariots and horses and palaces and place them in the scales, the eye will still be heavier," said the wise men.

"How do you explain this?" asked the king. "How is such a thing possible?"

"Learn a lesson from this, O King," said the wise men. "Know that the human eye is never satisfied with what it sees. No matter how much treasure you will show it, it will want more and still more."

"Your explanation doesn't satisfy me. Give me proof," insisted Alexander.

"Very well," agreed the wise men. "Have all your gold and treasure removed from the scales. Then place a pinch of dust in their place and observe what happens."

Barely had Alexander placed a little dust in the scales when they tipped to the other end, for the dust proved heavier than the eye.

"Now I understand the meaning of your words and of what was in your minds!" cried Alexander. "So long as a man is alive, his eye is never sated, but no sooner does he die when he is as dust! Then his eye loses its impulse and becomes powerless. It can no longer desire."

The Power of Hope

A KING was betrothed, and soon after he set forth on a long journey.

Days, months and years passed, without any word from him.

His intended waited for him sorrowfully but without abandoning hope for his return.

The girl's companions then said with pretended compassion and spiteful glee, "Poor girl! It seems your love has forgotten all about you and will never come back."

Disconsolate and stung by their gibes, the girl wrapped herself in her grief and wept much when she was alone. . . .

She then picked up the last letter the king had sent her, in which he swore that he would ever remain true and faithful to her. Rereading it her heart once more became serene, her spirits lifted and she continued to wait patiently for his return.

After many years the king came home. Amazed, he asked his intended, "How was it possible for you to remain faithful to me so long?"

"My King," she answered rejoicing, "I had your letter and I believed in you."

And thus too it has been with Israel and the nations of the earth. These say mockingly to the Jews, "Your God has abandoned you."

Israel, thereupon, yields himself to solitude. Sad and lamenting he reads in the godly pages of the Torah the sacred promise of redemption, consoles himself and derives new strength from it.

When the day of redemption comes God will surely turn His face to the abandoned and will ask, "How could you have remained true to me for so long?"

And Israel will answer, "Your commandment was your pledge to me."

The Test of a True Friend

WHEN the time came for Arvas, the philosopher, to die he called his son to his bedside and asked, "Tell me, my son, how many friends have you made in your life?"

"I have about a hundred friends," answered the son proudly.

"Whatever you do," Arvas admonished his son, "don't believe a man is your friend until you've proved him. Reflect that I, who am so much older than you, have found only half a friend in all my life. Isn't it rash of you to say that you have a hundred? Therefore, my son, go and prove your friends and find out if you have one real friend among them!"

THE POWER OF HOPE: From the Talmud. Translated from the adaptation by Leo Tolstoy.

THE TEST OF A TRUE FRIEND: Adapted from the *Midrash*.

"How shall I prove them?" the son asked.

Then Arvas instructed his son: "Slaughter a calf. Cut it up in pieces and put them in a sack. Also, dip the sack itself in blood. Then carry it to one of your friends and say to him: 'Dear friend, help me, I implore you! I've just killed a man! Please bury him in your yard and nobody need ever know about it! In this way you will save me from disaster.' "

The son did as his father counselled, and, bringing the sack to a friend, he pleaded with him to help conceal it.

His friend replied, "Remove that carcass from my house and be off with you! Bury it elsewhere yourself, and suffer the consequences of your crime! Furthermore, never darken my threshold again!"

The son went to a second friend and to a third, and even to the very last, the hundredth one! And each one drove him away. He then returned to his father and told him all that had happened.

"There is nothing unusual in your experience," his father comforted him. "When a man prospers, his friends are numerous, and when he falls on evil days they vanish like the mist. Therefore, my son, do as I now bid you. Go and call on that man who I have told you is only half a friend of mine and hear what his answer is."

The son went to call on his father's "half-friend." He begged him to bury the bloody sack secretly. His father's "half-friend" answered, "Come quickly into the house so that the neighbors won't see you!"

He also sent away his wife and children and, when they were alone, he began to dig a grave in his yard. When the grave was dug the son of Arvas the philosopher revealed the true contents of his sack.

"I came only to prove you as a friend of my father, and I know now that you are a true friend!" he cried.

The son then returned to his father and told him of the loving kindness his "half-friend" had shown him.

"But tell me, father," he asked, "do you think there is anybody in the world lucky enough to have a 'whole' friend?"

"I have never in my life seen a 'whole' friend," his father answered, "but I've heard a story about one."

"Tell me about it," begged the son.

His father then told him this story of true friendship.

"Once there were two young merchants: one lived in Egypt, the other in Babylon. They had never met but they knew of each other through the reports of travellers. They also sent each other merchandise with messengers.

"Once the merchant who lived in Babylon went to Egypt with a caravan of merchandise. When the Egyptian merchant heard that his friend was coming he hurried out to welcome him, embraced him, and brought him to his home. He showed him all his treasure, and had all of his men-servants and women-servants wait upon him.

"On the eighth day of his stay the merchant of Babylon fell ill. His anxious friend then called the most eminent physicians of Egypt to examine the sick man. They examined him thoroughly, but they found no sign of illness. So they deduced that he was love-sick.

" 'Tell me, who is the woman you love?' his friend asked.

" 'Call all the women of your household and I will point out to you the woman my heart desires.'

"The merchant of Egypt showed him all his female servants, but the sick man answered, 'No, she is not among them.'

"Then the Egyptian showed him a young girl, an orphan, whom he himself had raised and whom he had planned to marry because he was without a wife.

"When the sick man saw her he exclaimed, 'Behold! This girl holds the power of life and death over me!'

"When the Egyptian heard this he said to his friend, 'Take her and may she be a good wife to you!'

"He gave the bride a dowry and many gifts. Soon after the sick man became well again and journeyed back to Babylon with his bride.

"Years later the wheel of fortune turned, and the merchant of Egypt lost all his possessions and became destitute. In his despair he thought of his friend and said to himself, 'I will go to my friend in Babylon, for he will surely help me.'

"When he arrived in Babylon the merchant of Egypt was footsore from his long journey. His shoes were torn and his garments were in tatters. He trembled for fear that his friend would not recognize him, and that the servants would drive him away as a mere beggar.

"He spent the first night in an abandoned house at the city's outskirts. As he looked out on the street he saw two men quarreling. One of the two drew a knife and stabbed the other to death, and then he ran away.

"A multitude soon gathered and began to hunt for the murderer. When they entered the abandoned house they found there the merchant from Egypt.

" 'Do you know who murdered this man?' they asked him.

"Now the destitute man felt sick of life and the thought of death appeared sweet by comparison. So he cried, 'I am the murderer!'

"Thereupon, they took him and cast him into a dungeon. The next morning the judges sentenced him to be hanged.

"All the inhabitants of the city came to watch the execution. Among them was his friend, the merchant from Babylon, who recognized him.

" 'You are hanging an innocent man!' he cried out to the judges. 'Know that not he but I am the murderer!'

"The judges then ordered the stranger released and substituted the merchant of Babylon for him on the scaffold.

"Now among the great multitude gathered around the scaffold stood the real murderer. The spectacle of such true devotion between two friends stirred him deeply.

"He said to himself, 'If I permit an innocent man to die for my crime I shall receive a terrible punishment in the next world!'

"So he cried to the judges, 'Release this man! Neither he nor his friend has committed this murder. The first took upon himself the blame because he found life insufferable. The other took upon himself the blame because of true friendship for the first. Know that I am the real murderer! Hang me and do justice!' "

Each Man to His Paradise

ONCE there was a scholar who was pious and upright, but he had a father who drank much wine. In fact, he drank so much that he used to roll in the gutter like a common sot. At this the street urchins would throw mud and stones at him. The good son felt great shame seeing his father's degradation, for he loved him. There were times when he even prayed for death.

One day the son said, "Father, I beg of you—don't go to the wine-house anymore because you bring only disgrace on yourself and me. I promise you instead that I will buy you the very finest wines obtainable—only do your drinking at home."

After much pleading the father finally agreed to his son's plan.

Every day thereafter the good son furnished his father with drink, then put him to bed himself and stayed at his side until he fell asleep.

One day it began to rain hard. The son went to the synagogue, and on his way he saw a drunkard lying in the gutter, drenched to the skin. Around him swarmed little street urchins pelting him with stones and mud. When the good son saw this he thought to himself: "I will go and bring my father here. When he sees this drunkard lying in the mud and being abused by these ragamuffins, shame will overcome him and he may give up drinking."

So the son went home to fetch his father, and then brought him to the spot where the drunkard lay.

For a moment the old man regarded the prostrate man, then he bent down to him and whispered, "Do tell me, brother, in which wine-house did you buy such wonderful drink to get you so good and drunk?"

"I didn't call you here for that," the son rebuked him bitterly. "I just wanted to show you what a disgraceful appearance a sot has, and you look the same way when you get drunk. So I beg you to take this to heart and give up going to the wine-house."

"My son," exclaimed the father, "I swear by my life that for me there is no greater pleasure than drink, and the wine-house is my Paradise! So do let me be!"

EACH MAN TO HIS PARADISE: *Ibid.*

Hearing these words, the good and pious son turned sadly away, for he knew that all his efforts to reform his father were in vain.

Onkelos

I. ONKELOS CONSULTS THE SPIRITS

ONKELOS BAR KELONIKOS was a nephew of Titus. He was anxious to become a Jew, so he decided to find out what position the Israelites occupied in the Hereafter. He was a great magician and necromancer. He would take skulls and bones and would pretend to talk to them. Also, he would bring up the spirits of people long dead and from them find out what was taking place in the other world. So he brought up the spirit of his uncle Titus and asked: "Who occupies an exalted position in the other world?"

"The Israelites," answered Titus.

"Is it advisable for me to join them?" asked Onkelos.

"Their laws are so numerous that it is impossible to keep them. Go and engage in battle with them, and you will become their chief, for whoever oppresses Israel becomes a chief."

"And what is the nature of your punishment in the other world?" inquired Onkelos.

"I am punished with what I decreed upon myself when alive," said Titus. "Every day they gather together my ashes, and bring me to life. They then judge me, find me guilty, burn me again and scatter my ashes over the seven seas."

Onkelos then brought up Balaam, the heathen prophet, from the other world, and he asked: "Who occupies an exalted position in the other world?"

"The Israelites," answered the heathen prophet.

"Is it advisable for one to join them?" inquired Onkelos.

"Seek not their peace nor their prosperity," advised the heathen prophet.

ONKELOS: From *Book of Legends,* by Hyman Goldin. Jordan Publishing Co. New York, 1929. Reprinted by permission of the present copyright holders, Hebrew Publishing Co.

There was actually an historical person by the name of Onkelos the Proselyte who lived in Palestine at the end of the first century A.D. To him was attributed by error the authorship of the *Targum Onkelos,* the Aramaic version of the Pentateuch, which remains a part of Jewish traditional literature. Scholars maintain, however, that in the popular mind long ago Onkelos was confused somehow with the name of the proselyte Akilas (Aquila), who had translated the canonical Scriptures from the Hebrew into the Greek. No doubt it is Akilas (Aquila), and not Onkelos, who is the subject of the above legend, for Epiphanius relates that this same proselyte was a relative by marriage of the Emperor Hadrian and was appointed by him in A.D. 128 to an office for the rebuilding of Jerusalem as "Aelia Capitolina." The legend, therefore, has some basis in fact.—N. A.

Finally Onkelos brought up Jesus from the other world, and he asked him too: "Who occupies an exalted position in the future world?"

"The Israelites," answered Jesus.

"Is it advisable for me to join them?" inquired Onkelos.

"Seek their welfare, but not their misfortune," advised Jesus, "for whosoever injures them, fares as badly as he who wounds the pupil of his eye."

II. ONKELOS BECOMES A JEW

Onkelos now made up his mind to embrace Judaism, but he feared the wrath of Hadrian. One day Onkelos said to the Emperor: "I would very much like to engage in some business venture."

"If you need money," said the Emperor, "then all my royal treasures are open to you; you can take as much gold and silver as you please."

"I would like to go abroad," said Onkelos, "to learn the ways and customs of men. I would like to consult you, O Sire, on how to go about it."

"Very simple!" said Hadrian. "You buy goods when the price is very low, then you can be sure that the value will go up."

Onkelos journeyed to the land of Israel and there he engaged in the study of the Torah. After some time he was met by Rabbis Eliezer and Joshua. The rabbis noticed that a wondrous change had come into his face; and so they said: "No doubt Onkelos is engaged in the study of the Torah, and for this reason the expression on his face has changed."

When Onkelos embraced Judaism, the Emperor sent a legion of soldiers to seize him. When the soldiers came to Onkelos he explained to them some portions of the Bible, and they too embraced Judaism. The Emperor then sent another legion of soldiers to arrest Onkelos and ordered them not to enter into any conversation with him.

When the soldiers reached Onkelos, they seized him and refused to listen to any portions of the Bible. Onkelos thereupon said: "Friends, I shall not try to explain to you any passage of the Jewish Law, but I will tell you something else. You know that the torch-bearer carries a torchlight before the chief lecticarius; that the chief lecticarius carries a torchlight before the dux; the dux carries a torchlight before the general; and the general carries a torchlight before the king. But does the king ever carry a torchlight before any man?"

"No, he never does," replied the Romans.

"But the King of Israel, the Holy One, blessed be His name," continued Onkelos, "He carries a torchlight before his subjects, the children of Israel. When they departed from the land of Egypt, He went before them in a pillar of fire to light them on their way."

Thereupon, this legion too embraced Judaism. So the Emperor sent a third legion and he commanded them: "You must not enter into any conversation with him!"

When the soldiers came to the land of Israel, they arrested Onkelos and made ready to convey him to Rome. As they led him out of his house he noticed a *mezuzah* that was fastened to the door. He placed his hand on it and laughed.

"Why are you laughing?" asked the soldiers.

"It is the custom with mortals," replied Onkelos, "that the king sits inside his palace and his guard watches him from without. But in the case of the Holy One, blessed be His name, it is the reverse: His subjects are on the inside, while He watches over them from without."

And so this legion too adopted the Jewish faith, and the Emperor no longer sent for Onkelos to be brought to Rome.

Satisfied with the knowledge he had acquired of Judaism, Onkelos returned to Rome where he went to call on the Emperor Hadrian.

"How your appearance has changed!" exclaimed the Roman Emperor. "Did your business fare badly, or did anybody dare do you harm?"

"O Sire, this is not the case at all!" answered Onkelos. "Would any one dare do me harm when you are my relative?"

"Why then do you look so badly" asked the Emperor.

"It is because I studied the Torah of the Jews," replied Onkelos. "Moreover, I have even been converted to Judaism."

"Who advised you to do that?" cried the Emperor in a rage.

"O Sire, you advised me to do that," answered Onkelos.

"I?" asked the Emperor in amazement. "When did I ever advise you to become a Jew? Are you out of your senses?"

Onkelos replied: "O Sire, before I left Rome I consulted you. You then advised me to buy merchandise that other people scorn at its lowest price. I then went among many nations and peoples, and nowhere did I find a nation that is so scorned and so persecuted as the sons of Israel. So I followed your advice and I joined their ranks, for someday, I am certain, they will be elevated to a high estate."

Pope Elhanan

RABBI SIMEON the Great dwelt in the city of Mayence, which is on the banks of the River Rhine, and he had three mirrors hanging up in his house,

---

POPE ELHANAN: From *Miscellany of Hebrew Literature,* edited by the Rev. A. Löwy. London: N. Trübner and Co. 1872-77.

The legend of Elhanan the Pope enjoyed great popularity among Jews of medieval times. Some scholars attribute it to the Thirteenth Century. As in many other Jewish legends, there are in it elements of historical fact. It has been well established that Anacletus II (Pietro Pierlioni), who was Pope in Rome from 1130 to 1138, was of Jewish descent, leading his enemies to call him *Judaeo-pontifex* (the Jewish pope). Because of this ancestry and his striking Jewish features, he was the victim of much anti-Semitic abuse. Even the usually tolerant Bernard of Clairvaux, who led the opposition to him in France, wrote in an epistle bristling with hatred: "To the shame of Christ a man of Jewish origin was come to occupy the chair of St. Peter."

by which he perceived all that had happened and that which would happen; and after his death a fountain sprang forth from the head of his grave.

This Rabbi Simeon was a very eminent man, and he had a little son whose name was Elhanan. And it happened on one Sabbath day that the attendant came in to light the stove, as was her custom on every Sabbath, and she saw that R. Simeon and his wife were not at home, for they had gone to the Synagogue to pray; only the servant of the house was left with the child. Then the attendant took up the child in her arms and went out with it. The servant of the house saw what was done, but she never suspected that any evil was intended; for she said to herself, she is only playing with the child, and will soon return and bring him back to the house. But the traitress never returned; for she took the child off at once, and placed it within the new covenant. And she congratulated herself that she had brought a good offering for acceptance before God, according to the notion of all the Christians in those days. When R. Simeon and his wife returned from the Synagogue, they did not find even their own maidservant in the house, for when she saw that the attendant delayed to bring back the child, she went out to look for her and to follow her. But she found her not; therefore she returned to the house of R. Simeon in great distress, crying and lamenting greatly. R. Simeon said to her, "What is all this lamentation? Tell me what has happened." She answered, "Sir Rabbi, the attendant, who lights the fire on the Sabbath day, has come and stolen away your son and fled, and I do not know where she has hidden herself with him." Then R. Simeon hastened and went out, he and his wife and the maidservant, and they sought and searched, but in vain, for the child was not to be found. Then the parents broke out into weeping and bitter lamentation, and cried out in the terrible anguish of their heart. After this R. Simeon fasted to afflict himself day and night, and prayed to the Lord that He would restore his son; but his prayer returned empty, for the Lord refused to reveal to him where the child was.

The child was taken to the priests, who brought him up and instructed him, and he became a great scholar, for his capacity was large, like the capacity of his father R. Simeon. And the boy went on and rose from one school to another, rising higher and higher, until his wisdom became ex-

Edward Gibbon traces the Jewish ancestry of Anacletus to his grandfather: "In the time of Leo the Ninth, a wealthy and learned Jew was converted to Christianity, and honored at his baptism with the name of his godfather, the reigning pope [Leo]. The zeal and courage of Peter the son of [the convert] Leo were signalized in the cause of Gregory the Seventh who intrusted his faithful adherent with the government of Adrian's mole . . . or, as it is now called, the castle of St. Angelo. Both the father and the son were the parents of a numerous progeny . . . and so extensive was their alliance that the grandson of the proselyte was exalted by the weight of his kindred to the throne of St. Peter. A majority of the clergy and people supported his cause: he reigned several years in the Vatican."

There is little question that the historic memory concerning Anacletus and his friendly attitude toward the Jews furnished the raw material from which popular Jewish fancy created the legend of Pope Elhanan of which there exist a number of variants.—N. A.

ceedingly great, and he repaired to Rome. There he learned, in addition, many languages, and made a reputation for himself, and rose continually in position, until at last he attained the rank of Cardinal. His name went out into all the earth, and all men spoke in his honour, and exalted him in their sayings exceedingly for his learning, his grace, and his conduct in the priesthood.

At that time the Pope died, and no Cardinal was found so wise and learned as this new Cardinal to fill the place of the deceased. So they elected him, and placed him on the throne of the Popes. Now the new Pope had long been aware that he had sprung from the stock of Judah, and that his father was R. Simeon the Great, of Mayence. And though, when enjoying all prosperity and highly esteemed among the nations, his heart would not allow him to leave all this honour and to return to his father, and his people, and his religion, yet now that he was raised to the head of all Christians, he longed greatly to see the face of his father, and his heart prompted him to bring his father to Rome by stratagem. So he wrote a letter to the Bishop of Mayence—for all the governors were subordinated to him—and commanded him that he should not permit the Jews to keep their holy Sabbath, nor to initiate their sons in the covenant, nor to observe the customary lustrations. The Pope reasoned thus: When the Jews hear this, and when fear and consternation fall upon them, they will hasten to send the chief men among them to entreat me to rescind my severe decree against them; and there can be no doubt that they will send my father at the head of the delegates. So he calculated from the first, and so it actually happened. When the Pope's letter reached the Bishop he summoned the Jews and commanded them on the authority of the Pope according to all that had been decreed against them, and required implicit obedience. Then the Jews were in great trouble, and entreated the Bishop to turn away this great calamity from them. But he answered and said, "Do not address your supplications to me, for it is not in my power to aid you. Here is the Pope's letter: read it and see that I am unable to protect you. But if it be in your minds to ask for indulgence, this is my advice to you: send learned and respected men from among you to the Pope at Rome, and let them present your supplication to him; perhaps he will be entreated by you, and remit this severe decree." Then the Jews of Mayence approached the Lord with repentance, and prayer, and alms; after which they chose two Rabbis, together with R. Simeon the Great, who was to be the chief of the delegation, to go to Rome; for they said, "Perhaps the Lord will do a great work for us, and turn the heart of the Pope to us for good." In the meantime they followed the precepts of their religion and did not conform to the decree; for thus the Bishop allowed them to do secretly and in privacy until the return of the delegates. The three who were chosen set forth on their journey and came to Rome, where they conferred with the Jews as to what was to be done in this most evil business. When the Jews of Rome heard the story, they were greatly astonished, and said, "Who would have believed such a thing? There never yet was a Pope so kind to the Jews as this Pope; he always associates with Jews; they are his intimates and his councillors; besides which they continually play with him at the game of chess; in short, he does not live without them. How is it that his heart has suddenly been changed to hatred of them?" They said, moreover, they did not believe that the decree emanated from the Pope, and declared that the Bishop must have invented it himself to injure the Jews of Mayence. Then R. Simeon the Great showed them the letter which the Pope had sent, and his seal that was upon it. When the Jews of Rome saw this, and knew that the thing was true, they said, "It must be that the anger of the Lord was kindled against you, so that He moved the Pope to make this decree against you." Then they also appointed a fast, and multiplied their prayers and works of charity. And the wardens of the congregation of Rome went to the Cardinal, the chief Minister of the Pope, and entreated him for the Jews of Mayence. But the Cardinal said, "You know that this letter is the Pope's letter, and that he sent it to the Bishop of Mayence; and what am I? What can I do for you? I can be of no use to you." Yet he promised them that he would be among the supporters of their petition, and that he would speak in their favour, as a good intercessor. He bade them prepare a letter of petition, and said that he would present this written petition to the Pope; and they did so.

When the petition reached the hand of the Pope, and he read it, and knew who the delegates were that had come from Mayence, he gave orders that they should be admitted to his presence. Then R. Simeon the Great, with the two Rabbis who had been associated with him, came to the Chief Cardinal, who informed the Pope that the Jews had come according to his command, and that they desired to appear before him and have a personal interview. The Pope answered, "Let him who is the chief of the three come in and stand in my presence by himself." Accordingly R. Simeon, who was the chief and the elder of his two companions, came in, and his aspect was like an angel; and when he appeared before the Pope he knelt down and made obeisance. The Pope was then sitting and playing at the game of chess with a Cardinal, who sat opposite to him. When he saw R. Simeon the Great he trembled greatly, and bade him rise from his knees and sit on a chair until he had finished the game. For he had recognised his father the moment he appeared; but his father did not recognise him. When the Pope had finished his game he turned to R. Simeon and said to him, "What is thy petition?" R. Simeon wept bitterly, and told the Pope his petition, and would have prostrated himself a second time, but the Pope would not permit him, and said to him, "I have duly heard thy request, and thy supplication has come to my ears; but many accusations against you came to me from Mayence; for this reason I issued the decree against you." In the course of the conversation the Pope began to discuss with R. Simeon in great argumentation, and R. Simeon was almost at a loss for a reply to one who questioned him with so great acumen. And he wondered much to see the great capacity of an alien, which would not be believed if it were reported. Half the day they sat and discussed. At last the Pope said, "My friend, I see that thou art a great scholar, and thy brethren who sent thee shall not be disappointed in the hope which they placed in thy eloquence. Behold, the Jews come to me every day to play chess with me; do thou also sit down with me and let us play once, and thy request shall not be left unheeded." Now R. Simeon was a wonderful player at this game, such that there was not to be found one like him in all the land. Notwithstanding this, the Pope beat him, at which R. Simeon wondered greatly. Then they returned to the discussion of religions, and R. Simeon heard from the mouth of the Pope things great and wonderful, and the Pope became a prodigy in his eyes. In the end R. Simeon renewed his petition and wept greatly. Then said the Pope, "Let all who are present go out from me." They went out, and the Pope then fell on the neck of R. Simeon and wept, and said to him, "My beloved father, do you not recognise me?" R. Simeon understood not what the words of the Pope meant, and he answered, "Whence should I have the honour to recognise your Holiness?" But the Pope continued, "My beloved father, did you not in your early days lose your son when he was yet a child?" R. Simeon was greatly troubled, and answered, "It was as you say." Then the Pope made himself known to him and cried, "I, I am he, that son of yours, whom the attendant stole away on the Sabbath day. I cannot tell through what sin this calamity came upon you; but I know and am convinced that the matter was from the Lord. And because I desired to see your face and disclose all this to you, since I had resolved in my heart to leave my new religion and to return to the God of my fathers, therefore I made this decree as a trick, since I knew from the first that the Jews would send you to request me to remove this persecution from them. And now I abrogate the decree, and you shall be left in peace. But, my father, will you not tell me, is there any hope for the future of expiation in the sight of God?" R. Simeon answered, "My dear son, dispel this anxiety from your heart, since you acted under restraint, and while yet a child were stolen away from your parents and your religion." "But yet," answered the son, "I knew long since that I was born a Jew, yet I remained among the nations, and the great prosperity which I enjoyed restrained me from returning to the God of truth. Will God forgive me?" R. Simeon answered, "Nothing can withstand repentance: he that makes confession and quitteth sin shall receive mercy." Then said the son, "In that case return home in peace, in the name of the God of Israel, and deliver to the Bishop the letter which I shall give you, and he shall leave you alone. Let no one know anything of our conversation, and after no long time I will come to you to Mayence. But before I leave my place and my office I will do something for a memorial, and leave it after me for the good of the Jews."

R. Simeon returned to his companions and to the Jews of Rome, and showed them the letter of the Pope, abrogating the decree, and they rejoiced greatly. After that he returned to his city, and delivered the letter to the Bishop; and there was joy and gladness among the Jews in all the city. He disclosed to his wife the secret that their lost son was Pope, and when she heard the news she raised a great lamentation, and would not be comforted. But R. Simeon said to her, "Be quiet, and grieve not, for in a short time our son will be in our house."

The Pope composed a book containing heresy with regard to the faith, and left it to be preserved carefully, and instituted a rule that all the Popes should read it. Then he collected great treasure, and made his escape secretly, and came to Mayence, and returned to the God of Israel in truth and sincerity, and became a Jew greatly respected in the eyes of all the people. And at Rome no one could tell whither he had gone, or what had become of him.

On this subject R. Simeon wrote a *Yotzer* for the second day of *Rosh-ha-shanah,* in which he said, "God has shown favour *(El chanan)* to his inheritance."

Therefore, let no reader think that the words of this narrative are false and vain, for they are truthful and right, there is no falsehood in them.

But many say that it was by the game of chess that R. Simeon discovered the Pope to be of the seed of the Jews, because the Pope played as his father had taught him when yet a child, when he began to learn this game.

The Lord pardon us our transgressions, through the merit of R. Simeon the Great. Amen. Selah.

Caught in His Own Trap

IN A certain Polish village there lived a Jewish tenant-farmer. He was a plain man, had no learning, but he made up for it in piety and in good deeds. His father before him had worked the same little farm, and the landowner, a friendly old man, had lived on good terms with both father and son. Also the peasants of the countryside liked this upright tiller of the soil. They entrusted him with many of their affairs. When he went to town, which was often, they had him make purchases for them there.

One day a young nobleman arrived in the village. He had wasted his patrimony in wine, women, song and card-playing. Now he found himself without any means. Therefore, he fell upon the idea of displacing the Jew on his farm and to work it himself.

"It will be an easy matter to get rid of him," he told himself. "After all, he's a Jew and am I not a nobleman?"

But things didn't go as easily as he had expected. The landowner explained to him that he had no right to consider his proposal. Hadn't the Jew taken over the farm from his father? He paid his rent on time and in full. Why then should he take his farm away from him and leave him without bread? What the landowner didn't tell the nobleman was that he did not trust him, for he saw that he was lightheaded and irresponsible.

But the young nobleman didn't give up so easily. At first he tried to

---

CAUGHT IN HIS OWN TRAP: Adapted from an old Yiddish groschen chapbook.

reach his goal in a friendly way by asking the Jew to leave the farm out of his own free will. When he saw that the Jew was stubborn and refused to oblige him, he began to threaten him with direst misfortunes. What wouldn't he do to him? He'd incite the peasants against him; that wouldn't be too hard. Wasn't he a Jew? He'd inform the authorities that certain things were not in order. He'd induce the village priest to forbid the peasants from having any dealings with him. And a lot of other things.

But all these threats had no effect. The Jew did not allow himself to be intimidated. On the contrary, he went about telling everybody in the village of the nobleman's threats. Thereupon, both the peasants and the priest assured him that they would ignore the rascal.

Foiled in this the nobleman conceived a devilish plan. One day, as the Jew was on his way to town in his wagon, his enemy, by means of money, drink and wheedling, induced several peasant youths to wait in ambush for him in the forest through which he had to pass.

Unaware of the danger that awaited him the Jew got through with all his business in town and, as dusk descended, he started on his journey home.

The sky was overcast and it rained steadily. By the time the Jew reached the forest, night had descended. He allowed his horses free rein for he could not see one step ahead of him. Then an uneasiness fell on him. To drive away the gloom he began to recite the psalm:

"God is our refuge and strength, an ever present help in trouble.

"Therefore we will not fear, though all the earth be removed, and though the mountains be carried into the midst of the sea."

He repeated this psalm over and over again, yet the forest continued to stretch ominous and black all around him. The horses seemed to have lost their way and wandered aimlessly in the dark.

The Jew's uneasiness grew steadily. With increasing verve he chanted the psalm, ever louder, in order to still his fear. A thing like this had never happened to him before in his life. Times without number his horses had crossed the entire length of the forest, one could say almost blindfolded, so well they knew the way. How could he now explain the fact that they had lost their way?

At last the dawn broke. The Jew at last saw where he was and found the road back to his farm.

The young nobleman waited impatiently for the return of the peasants he had engaged to waylay the Jew. Hour after hour passed but no sign of them. When midnight came and still he had not heard from them he grew very uneasy. The devil alone knew what had happened! Who could tell —maybe the Jew had stood up to the peasants and got the better of them! Worse yet, he could have gone and revealed everything to the authorities. Again, it was even conceivable that these rogues of peasants had betrayed him.

Stung to a frenzy by these thoughts he got a horse and wagon and galloped off into the woods.

A thick darkness, like that which fell on Egypt under Pharaoh, lay all about him. He couldn't find his way. Suddenly, he felt a rain of blows descending on him. Several dark figures had leaped upon him, gave him even no time to cry out. They belabored him so lustily that he lost his voice. When his attackers finally wearied of their exertions, he managed to find his tongue. It was then that they realized their mistake.

When the Jew finally reached home he found that all in the village had already heard what had happened and were splitting their sides laughing. The young nobleman was taken to a hospital. After that he didn't dare show his face in the village for fear of being laughed at.

The Three Daughters, or the Evil of Tale Bearing

ONCE upon a time there lived a pious man, who had three daughters. The first one was a thief, the second was a sluggard and the third was a liar who never spoke the truth and who slandered people whenever she had an opportunity. One day a pious man, who had three sons, came to the city and said: "You have three daughters and I have three sons. Let us make a match between them." But the father of the girls said: "Let me alone. My daughters are not good enough for your sons, for each one has a vice." The father of the boys asked: "What are their vices?" And the other replied: "One is a thief, the second is a sluggard, and the third is a liar." The father of the boys asked: "Have they no other vices than these? If so I will cure them. Leave it to me." So they were betrothed, and he took the damsels with him and married them to his sons.

As soon as the weddings were over, he gave to the thief the keys to all his money and satisfied her greed so that she had no reason to steal. To the second he gave menservants and maidservants in plenty so that she should have nothing to do. And as to the third, he fulfilled all her wishes, so that she should not tell lies or slander anybody. And whenever the father-in-law left her house, he embraced and kissed her, for he hoped that by being good to her he would cure her of her evil quality and she would not carry on slander any more.

One day the father came to see how his daughters were getting on. So he went to the first one and asked her how she was getting along with her husband, and how she was treated by her parents-in-law. She replied: "I thank you so much, father, for having given me in marriage to this man, for I have everything that my heart desires. And moreover, I have all the keys in my hand so that I do not have to steal." Then he went to the

THE THREE DAUGHTERS, OR THE EVIL OF TALE BEARING: Reprinted from the *Ma'aseh Book,* by Moses Gaster. With the permission of the copyright owners, The Jewish Publication Society of America. Philadelphia, 1934.

sluggard and asked her how she was getting on. And she also said: "I am so thankful to you, father, for having brought me here, for I need not lift a hand, I have menservants and maidservants in plenty, and my husband and parents-in-law all treat me very well." Then he came to the daughter who told lies to ask her how she was getting along, and she said: "You are a fine father! I thought you gave me one husband but it seems you gave me two, the father and the son. For no sooner does my husband leave the house than my father-in-law comes in and kisses me and hugs me and wants me to do his will. Dear father, if you do not believe it, come to-morrow morning and you will see it is true."

Next morning the father came and she put him in a room where he could see what was going on. Her father-in-law came as usual and kissed her and embraced her and said to her: "My dear daughter-in-law, how are you getting on? Is there anything you want?" He did all this with the good intention of curing her of her vice, but her father who saw it, grew furious and rushed out of his chamber and killed him. Then he tried to get away, but when her two brothers-in-law came home and found their father lying dead, they killed their father-in-law. Then the slanderer began to shout: "Murder! Murder!" and they understood it was through her that the tragedy had occurred. So they killed her too, and thus through slander three persons lost their lives. Therefore did Rabbi Huna say: "The sin of the evil tongue is greater than the three sins, murder, adultery and theft, combined."

The Love-Drink

IT WASN'T enough that they were poor but they had to have a house full of girls—not one boy!

One fine day, the mother of this brood of girls became again pregnant.

"What if my wife gives birth to a son this time?" hopefully day-dreamed her husband. "If so, where will I get the money to have a decent circumcision party?"

It was really a serious matter. But, as there was still plenty of time, he decided to put on his beggar's knapsack and go forth into the world to collect alms. Then, having put by a tidy sum, he would hurry home and celebrate the birth of his son in dignified style.

So he said goodbye to his wife and children and started out to seek his fortune.

After several months his wife gave birth, and miracles and wonders—it was a boy! However, as it was wintertime and there was no firewood,

THE LOVE-DRINK: Adapted from *Yiddishe Folksmaisses*, collected by Judah Loeb Cahan Ferlag Yiddishe Folklore-Bibliothek. New York and Vilna, 1931.

the house remained wretchedly cold. The poor woman did not know what
to do. But she suddenly recalled that her husband had once put away
some coal in a corner of the attic.

"Children," she said to her daughters, "go up into the attic—you'll find
some coal in a corner. Make a fire for I feel very cold!"

When the girls went up to the attic to fetch the coal they were filled
with wonder. Among the coals they saw bits of stone that sparkled with
great brilliance. So they ran down again.

"Mother," they cried all out of breath, "we saw some sparkling little
stones in the coal!"

"Indeed!" exclaimed the mother in surprise. "Go back and bring down
to me a couple of those stones, so I can see what they are like."

They went and brought her a couple of the sparkling stones.

When she looked at them she saw that they were diamonds. She therefore said to her oldest daughter, "Run child to the goldsmith and ask him
how much one of these stones is worth."

As soon as the goldsmith looked at the stone he said: "This is a genuine
diamond!"

Then he bought the stone and paid the girl a lot of money for it.

With the money the woman bought a house and furnished it in royal
style. She and her daughters outfitted themselves in beautiful clothes so
that they were not to be recognized any more. Moreover, on the eighth
day after the child's birth a magnificent circumcision party was held to
which all the people in town were invited.

Having become so rich the woman grew vain.

"This wretched village is no place for us!" she said disdainfully.

They therefore moved to a large town where she bought herself a fine
mansion in a neighborhood where only rich people lived. But, as she was a
very good woman who knew at first-hand the bitterness of poverty, she
was nonetheless very charitable. As soon as they got wind of this, beggars
from all over the world began to descend upon her. Among them was also
her own husband who had no inkling whatsoever that the rich woman who
distributed charity with such an open-hand was his own wife whom he had
left only some months before in a state of destitution. "Maybe she'll give
me a sizeable alms," he hopefully thought. "Then I'll have enough money
to celebrate my son's circumcision in respectable style."

When he entered the rich woman's house she recognized him at once.
Yet he failed to recognize her. She looked beautiful and gay now, not
careworn and sad as he had known her. Instead of rags she wore clothes
of the most fashionable cut.

"Here's an alms for you, my good friend," she said to him, giving him
money.

He stood in confusion for the alms was very large. Never before had
anyone given him so much money.

"Don't stand there gaping!" she said to him. "Go and buy some decent
clothes for yourself and then come back and spend the Sabbath here."

Her husband went away and bought himself new clothes and on Friday he arrived to spend the Sabbath in her house.

The rich woman received him hospitably. She had him seated at the head of the table and invited him to recite the benediction over the Sabbath cup of wine.

The children looked on with surprise.

"What on earth has mama done?" they asked one another. "She has taken a poor man and given him the place of honor!"

The rich woman then served her guest two large slices of carp which were well salted and peppered. Then they had noodle soup, boiled chicken and sweetened carrot compote. The poor man so enjoyed his meal that he jawed away in silence and did not say one word.

Then the guest was shown his bed and went to sleep.

In the middle of the night he awoke feeling terribly thirsty; his mouth and throat felt as if they were on fire. "It's the salted and peppered carp," he thought. So he got out of bed and began groping in the dark for the water-jug. He tripped suddenly over some object and, with a loud noise, went sprawling on the floor.

"What is it—what is it?" cried the woman opening the door of her room.

"I'm dreadfully thirsty . . . I'm looking for water . . . it's the pepper and salt on the carp," he murmured.

"Oh, so it's a drink you want," said she. "Come into my room—the water-jug is here."

So he went into her room. She poured him a glass of wine. He drank and smacked his lips.

"It's a marvellous drink—what is it?" he asked.

She did not answer him. Instead she sang:

> This is wine
> And you are mine
> And I am thine

In the morning, when the children arose, their mother said: "Children—this is your papa!"

The Faithful Neighbor

IN THE year 1311 King Philip of France issued a decree ordering all Jews, under penalty of death, to be gone from his kingdom within two days. But the unfortunate Jews were unable to sell their houses, fields, and household goods in such a short time. So they wandered forth without a *perutah* and empty-handed.

THE FAITHFUL NEIGHBOR: Adapted from *Yiddishe Legendes*, by Eliezer Shindler. Ferlag "Grininke Beimelach." Vilna, 1936.

One of the exiles, a wealthy dealer in precious stones and jewels who was from Paris, greatly feared that his money and jewels would be taken from him, so he confided them to the care of one of his Christian neighbors. He thought: "Some day the king's decree against the Jews may be revoked. When that will happen I'll return and claim my treasure."

The Christian promised to guard well the money and the jewels, and so the Jew wandered forth together with all his brethren to seek an unknown refuge in the wide world.

Many years later King Philip died and his son, who inherited his throne, revoked his father's decree. He let it be known that the Jews who had been banished from the kingdom could safely return. And so the exiles returned, among them the dealer of precious gems from Paris.

The first thing the jeweller did was to call on his old neighbor to whom he had entrusted his treasure. But alas—the man was gone!

The Jew then inquired about the man among his neighbors. He learned that in recent years he had fared very badly, had lost all his possessions, and was obliged to give up his fine house. Now he was living outside the city in great poverty.

Hearing this the Jew began to grieve. He was sure of one thing: if his neighbor had lost everything he must have parted with the treasure he had entrusted to him.

Downcast, he went to look for the man outside of the city of Paris. He found him in a tiny bare hut that had neither bed nor bench. The unfortunate man was sitting on a chest, emaciated from hunger and trembling with cold.

When he saw the Jew he arose and greeted him. Then he opened the chest and drew forth a bag from it.

"Here is your treasure," he said. "I have guarded it well."

"How could you have done a thing like that?" cried the Jew taken aback. "You were cold and hungry and yet you did not touch these things!"

"How could I touch that which wasn't mine?" replied the Christian. "Many a time I grew weary of life and thought of death, for my suffering was too grievous to be endured. But I dared not die. Had I not faithfully promised to guard the treasure you placed in my care? I suffered and waited. It is good that you have returned now."

When the Jew heard this he was mightily moved.

"How fortunate that you waited and did not take your life," he said. "Know that the hard evil days are over for you! You are my brother and half of my possessions belong to you."

So the Jew and his Christian neighbor lived side by side as of yore, in everlasting friendship and brotherly love.

King Ptolemy and the Seventy Wise Jews

As PTOLEMY, the King of Egypt, heard that the Jews possessed an excellent Law he decided to have a Greek translation * made of it. He therefore ordered the artificers of his kingdom to fashion for him a golden table, two golden and two silver jugs, as well as two golden chalices. They were also to beat figures on them in relief and to set them with five thousand gems. These vessels the king ordered to be placed in a chest and wrote to the High Priest in Jerusalem the following letter.

"Ptolemy, King of Egypt, sends Eleazer, the High Priest, peace!

"As I have heard that you Jews possess an excellent Law I therefore beg you to send to me seventy of your wise men who understand the Torah, in order that they may translate it for me into the Greek tongue. In gratitude for your friendly consideration, please accept the gifts that I am sending you with my servant Aristeas."

When the High Priest received the letter and presents from Aristeas he rejoiced exceedingly and said to him, "I beg you to remain here for several days while I choose the seventy wise men who are to return with you to Egypt."

In the meantime Aristeas went about Jerusalem viewing its sights. He was present at the service in the Temple when the priests officiated. And about that he wrote a long letter to Ptolemy.

First he informed the king of what the High Priest had said. He described to him with fidelity the appearance of the Holy City and of the Temple. He then added, "After the High Priest had selected the seventy wise men he summoned me and introduced me to them.

" 'Listen to them,' he begged, 'do everything they ask you. After they

---

KING PTOLEMY AND THE SEVENTY WISE JEWS: Adapted from the version of J. Lewner in *Agada-Sammlung*, by B. Gottschalk. Verlag M. Poppelauer. Berlin, 1920.

* The great estimation in which this work was held by the Greek-speaking Judaeans, and in time also by non-Jews, gave rise to legendary glorifications, which were finally, about a century later, crystallized in a story which relates that the origin of the translation was due to the steps taken by Ptolemy Philadelphus, whose attention had been attracted to the value of the Book of the Law by his librarian Demetrius. Demetrius declared it worthy of a place in the Royal Library, provided it were translated into Greek. Thereupon the king sent his ambassadors to the high-priest Eleazar with costly presents, requesting him to choose several wise men, equally versed in Hebrew and in Greek, and to bid them repair to his court. The high-priest selected seventy-two learned men, taking representatives from the twelve tribes, six from each, and sent them to Alexandria, where they were received with great pomp by the king. The seventy-two delegates finished the translation of the Torah in seventy-two days, and read it aloud before the king and all the assembled Judaeans. It was from this legend, looked upon till recently as an historical fact, that the translation received the name of the Seventy-two, or more briefly, of the Seventy, *Septuagint.*—H. Graetz. From *History of the Jews*, Vol. I, p. 514. Jewish Publication Society of America. Philadelphia, 1891.

are through with their translation let not the King detain them any longer.'

"When I had promised this to the High Priest, he continued, 'If I did not consider the blessings that the translation of the Torah can bring, I would not permit these sages to depart from here. My soul hangs on theirs and only with the greatest reluctance do we part from each other.' "

When everything was ready for their departure, the sages and Aristeas bid the High Priest farewell and journeyed to Alexandria.

Upon their arrival there the wise men immediately went to the king. They greeted him and gave him their blessings.

"Have you brought along with you a Torah-scroll?" he asked.

"Here it is," they answered.

They then took a scroll of the Torah out of a chest and unrolled it for the king.

With amazement and awe Ptolemy regarded it. He blessed the seventy sages and also the High Priest and bowed before them seven times. He asked the sages to be seated, clasped the hand of each, and said, "Today is the happiest day of my life. I will never forget it!"

He ordered that a magnificent banquet be prepared. To it he invited all the princes and the great men of the kingdom.

Because they were strangers, the Jewish sages sat apart, for that was the custom in Egypt. Before they sat down to eat one of the sages arose and prayed.

"Eternal Father—bless King Ptolemy and may everything that he undertakes meet with success. Bless also his wife, his children and his friends."

"Amen!" cried the other sages.

Then the king put questions to the Jewish sages in order that he might test their wisdom. Among the questions he asked and the answers he got were these:

"When can a king's rule be successful?"

"When he serves God, rewards the good and punishes the wicked," the sages replied.

"How can a man increase his possessions?"

"By giving to the poor."

"How should a ruler punish those who slander him?"

"By being merciful and patient with them."

"How can a ruler triumph over his enemies?"

"By striving for peace, by relying always on God and not upon his army."

"How can a ruler put fear into the hearts of his enemies?"

"By having his army ready, but always being discreet in using it."

"How should a man behave in misfortune?"

"He should pray to God and put his trust in Him. He should also reflect that there isn't a man on earth who doesn't meet with misfortune sometime."

"When do we reveal our true strength of character?"

"In misfortune."

"How can we always remain truthful?"

"We must reflect how disgraceful lying is."

"How can a man develop patience?"

"He must reflect that the life of man is full of suffering."

"How can a ruler avoid doing what is unworthy?"

"He must think of his good reputation and the example he must set for his people."

"What is the most difficult thing for a king?"

"To master himself."

"How can we silence those who slander us?"

"By doing good."

"How can one acquire a good name?"

"By dealing kindly with one's fellow men."

"To whom shall we do good?"

"First to our parents and friends, then to our fellow-men."

"How can the evil-doer regain his honor?"

"By doing good again."

"How can one drive away care?"

"One must look for social intercourse with people."

"Can one acquire righteousness through knowledge?"

"Indeed, one can, for the understanding man has his eyes open and knows how to distinguish between good and evil."

"Of what value are relatives?"

"One's kin give consolation in sorrow and aid in time of need."

"How can a ruler guard himself against idleness and evil desires?"

"He must reflect that God has made him the leader of his people. Much is expected of him to whom much is given."

"When is a ruler called 'the father of his people'?"

"When he loves his people without making distinction between stations and ranks."

"How can one guard oneself against anger?"

"When one reflects on the consequences."

"How can a stranger gain respect?"

"By being modest and upright."

"Which of our works endures forever?"

"The work of righteousness."

"What are the fruits of wisdom?"

"The joy of the heart and the peace of the soul."

"How can we guard ourselves against pride?"

"By thinking of man's final end."

"Whom should man bewail?"

"Not the dead because they will return no more. Let him lament over the living for they must experience much misfortune and it's not always possible for us to help them."

"When does a ruler derive comfort from war?"

"When he goes to battle, not out of lust for spoils, but only to defend his country."

"Why is it that so few people strive after wisdom?"

"Because most people regard the acquisition of riches as the highest good. The wise, however, know that riches alone cannot bring happiness."

"Who is best suited to be a general?"

"He who is determined to spill as little blood as possible and who knows the best way to surround the enemy and take him prisoner."

"What should we do in the days of good fortune?"

"We should reflect on what we have already achieved and what we still wish to accomplish. We should regard nothing with contempt because it has often turned out that the smallest means have achieved the greatest results."

King Ptolemy thanked the wise men for the answers they gave his questions. He gave them presents of gold and assigned to each a servant to wait upon him. On the following day he asked Aristeas to conduct them to an island outside the city and to lodge each of them in a separate house.

When this was done, Ptolemy requested the wise men to begin their translation of the Torah and, after they had sat down to their labors, he left them and locked the doors behind him. As he departed he thought:

"I will know that the translation is correct if all versions of the seventy sages read alike."

And it happened exactly that way. After seventy days the king sent to inquire if the translation was ready.

"We have just finished it today," answered the seventy wise men.

Without delay they returned to King Ptolemy and handed their translations to Aristeas. He compared them all and made certain that they agreed in every way. The king then ordered that all the translations be put away and preserved.

The following day he dismissed the wise men with many gifts and murmuring his gratitude.

[5]

Demon Tales

INTRODUCTION

According to primitive belief, demons or spirits animate all natural phenomena. Jews, too, believed in the reality of demons, devils, fiends, spectres, ghosts and spirits. *Shedim* (demons) and *dibbukim* (migrant spirits) inflicted illness upon the body, especially on the internal organs and the mind. Each illness had its own particular demon—special demons for blindness, deafness, epilepsy, headache, delirium, insanity, etc.

Despite that a belief in demons was not integral in the doctrines of Judaism, it, nonetheless, was widespread among the Jews of post-Biblical times. Yet, on account of their rationalistic conditioning and a higher level of literacy in the mass, it manifested itself among them to a lesser degree than among many other peoples. During their long Babylonian sojourn, as was to be expected, Jews fell under Chaldean and Persian cultural influences. Their dualistic angel-demon conception was directly borrowed from Zoroastrianism: "The Wise Lord," Ahuramazda, leading the angelic hosts against the hordes of fiends and demons of Ahriman, "The Spiritual Enemy." This conflict of opposites became a fundamental part of cabalistic doctrine: God was pitted against Satan, Good against Evil, the pure against the impure, the angels against the demons. These supernatural powers, ruling over both animate and inanimate existence, worked their inscrutable designs, whether for weal or for woe, in the destinies of both individuals and nations.

The early Christians, being themselves Jews, naturally carried over Jewish demonology into their religion. The Gospel writer, Mark, for instance, has Jesus say: "In my name shall they cast out devils." *Acts 10.38* tells of Jesus "healing all that were oppressed of the devil: for God was with him." It was not unnatural, therefore, that in this contemporary intellectual climate a moralist in the Talmud should have declared: "Every limb engaged in the fulfillment of a divine commandment is protected against the 'Strong One' [Satan]."

In medieval times, the Jewish conception of demons differed in some respects from that held by Christians. Not all denizens of the spirit world were regarded as being necessarily evil. Some even were considered to be benevolent and helpful to the pious and the deserving in time of need. The

592

medieval Jew believed that demons resembled angels in three ways: they had wings; they could fly from one end of the world to another; they could foretell future events. The demons also resembled human beings in three ways: they had to eat and drink; they procreated like them; they also died like them. They subsisted on the natural elements: water, fire, wind and moisture. The only possible cause of death among them was when they got dry. In the hour of mating they acquired bodies like humans, but lost them immediately thereafter.

All these characteristics belonged to Lilith, later the wife of Samael— Angel of Death. She is the subject of distinctive portraiture in Jewish myth and legend. She had an interesting origin and equally as interesting was the persistence with which her fearful image plagued the superstitious folk through the centuries.

In ancient Assyria there were three female demons called Lilit, Lilu and Ardat Lilit. The first Jewish reference to Lilith is found in Isaiah 34.14:

"Yea, the night-monster (Lilith) shall repose there,
And shall find her a place of rest."

In the *Midrash,* and in other post-Biblical writings, Lilith is also described as a demon of the night. Rashi, the imaginative medieval exegete of Worms, said that Lilith bore the human shape of a woman yet had the wings of an angel. She is usually described in legend as an irresistibly seductive woman with long hair. Like the Greek siren Circe she seduces unwary men, and then savagely kills the children she bears for them. This personification of Lilith as a demon of vengeance against the children of men finds a most curious explanation in *Midrash* literature.

When God created Adam, the first man felt very lonely in the newly fashioned world. So God, in His loving kindness, created Lilith from *Adamah,* the same dust from which Adam had been molded and whose name he bore. But before long they quarreled. For Adam, the proverbial domineering male, wished to rule over Lilith. The *Midrash* legend has him laying down the law for her and her sex: "I am your lord and master and it is your duty to obey me." But Lilith, a militant feminist, was equally proud and wilful. She retorted: "We are both equal, for we are both issued from dust [Adamah], therefore, I will not be submissive to you."

She then pronounced the Ineffable name of God and flew away.

No sooner had she left him when Adam felt lonely again. Aggrieved by her rebellion and desertion of him he complained to God: "Oh Lord of the Universe, the woman Thou hast given me has fled from me."

God agreed that Adam had been unjustly treated and then sent three angels in pursuit of the fleeing wife. When they caught up with her over the Red Sea, they ordered her to return at once to Adam but she refused. At this the angels grew angry and threatened: "We will drown you in the sea!" Unafraid, Lilith answered: "Don't you know, I've been created for the purpose of weakening and punishing little children, infants and babes? I have power over them, from the day they are born until they are eight days old if they are boys, and until the twentieth day if they are girls."

Angered by her defiance, the three angels laid hold of her to drown her. Frightened now, Lilith pacified them with the promise that, if she entered the home where a woman was about to give birth, and she saw an amulet on each wall bearing the names or the images of the three angels, Senoi,

Sansenoi and Sammangelof, she would spare the infant. So they let her go, and God was obliged to create Eve to be Adam's mate. And ever since then Lilith has been roaming the world, flying at the head of her 480 hosts of evil spirits and destroying angels, howling her hatred of mankind through the night and vowing vengeance because of the shabby treatment she had received at the hands of Adam. For that reason she has been called in demonic legend—"The Howling One."

To guard themselves against her vengeance, superstitious Jews of former times would hang in the room of a new-born babe four coins, one on each wall, to serve as amulets against Lilith's wicked designs. Fixed to each coin was a label inscribed with the words: "Lilith—begone!" Some philologists even think that the English word "lullaby" is nothing but a corruption of "Lilla—abi! (Lilith—begone!)"

N. A.

King Solomon and the Worm

KING SOLOMON, the wisest of men, resolved to build a temple dedicated to the glory of the God of Israel. He remembered the sacred words of Scripture: "And if thou make me an altar of stone, thou shalt not build it of hewn stones: for if thou lift up thy tool upon it, thou hast polluted it." (Exod. XX. 25). The tools of iron symbolized the sword, the instrument of war and death; whilst the altar and temple were the symbols of peace and life. Solomon desired that not only the altar, but all the stone-work in the sacred edifice should be made ready for the builders at the quarry without using any metal implement, so that in the course of building the temple no instrument of iron should be employed.

How was this wish to be realized? Even Solomon, the wisest of monarchs, did not know how to set about his task. Again and again he asked himself: "How is it possible to split the immense blocks of stone or to cut down the huge trees if the workmen are not allowed to use metal implements?" In despair the King summoned his great council of state, consisting of the wisest men in his kingdom. He told them his difficulty and asked them for their advice. The counsellors listened to the words of their beloved monarch in silence. After a while one of the most venerable of them arose and spoke as follows:

"Long live the King! Mighty Sovereign! Haven't you heard that among the countless creatures of the Most High there is one which can serve you as your heart desires? It can cut stone better than the sharpest tool of iron. I refer to the tiny but wonderful worm called the Shamir, or diamond insect. Don't you know, O wisest of rulers, how the Almighty created ten marvels in the twilight of the eve of the first Sabbath in the week of creation? Among these marvels was the worm Shamir. Its size

---

KING SOLOMON AND THE WORM: From *Jewish Fairy Tales*, selected and translated by Gerald Friedlander. Robert Scott. London, 1917.

is that of a grain of barley. It is endowed with miraculous power, for, behold! it can split the hardest stone by merely touching it. Moreover, iron is broken by its mere presence."

"You show excellent wisdom, beloved counsellor," cried Solomon with joy in his heart. "Now tell me, where is this marvellous little worm to be found?"

"May your days be as glorious as the days of David your father," replied the wise servant of the King, "but more than I have already told you I do not know. No mortal being has ever discovered the home of the Shamir. It is useless to seek the information you desire by consulting the sons of men! Hasn't God bestowed upon you knowledge and understanding more than He has given to any one else? Is it for naught that your wisdom exceeds that of all the children of men? Aren't you ruler of all the spirits and demons? Seek their aid, Sire! and you will find the Shamir. Invoke the wisest of the spirits who will reveal to you even the secrets of the heavens above, of the earth beneath, and of the waters under the earth."

The good advice of the counsellor appealed to Solomon's heart, and after thanking his wise minister, he dismissed his council in order to carry out the suggested plan. He looked at the ring on his right hand and read the Holy Name of God engraved thereon. No sooner had he pronounced the Divine Name than a demon appeared before him and, making obeisance, cried, "What is your wish, Solomon, King of Israel?"

"I command you," said Solomon, "to tell me where the worm Shamir is to be found."

In trembling voice the demon replied, "Mighty King of man and spirits! I am your servant and I will always obey you if I have the power to do so. Be not angry with me, for I fear I cannot help you now. The secret you desire to know has not been revealed to any of the inferior demons. It is only Ashmodai our King who is in possession of the secret."

"Tell me," interrupted King Solomon, "where does Ashmodai, the King of the demons, dwell?"

"May it please your gracious Majesty," the demon replied, "Ashmodai lives far from the haunts of men. His palace is built on the top of a very high mountain. In this same mountain he has dug a very deep well. Daily he fetches his drinking water from this well. When he has obtained sufficient water for his needs, he closes up the mouth of the well with an enormous rock which he seals with his signet-ring. He then flies up to heaven to receive the orders of those who are his superiors. His tasks take him to the ends of the earth, even beyond the great sea. With the going down of the sun in the west, he returns to his own home. He examines very carefully the seal on the rock at the mouth of the well, in order to find out if it had been tampered with in his absence. He then proceeds to uncover the well and he drinks of the water. Having quenched his thirst he covers up again the mouth of the well and seals it afresh."

King Solomon sat on his wonderful throne of gold while the demon told his tale. Not a word escaped the memory of the wise King. He then dismissed the demon, who disappeared in an instant. Thereupon, Solomon summoned to his presence his brave captain and friend Benaiah, son of Jehodiah. He told him briefly the nature of the task he was chosen to undertake, saying, "Go, trusty servant Benaiah, and capture Ashmodai, the King of the demons, and bring him before my presence. To assist you in your perilous undertaking I give you this golden chain on the links of which the letters forming the Divine Name are engraved. I will also entrust to your care my signet-ring which is also engraved with the Holy Name of the Most High. Take with you also this large bundle of white wool and these skins full of strong wine."

After giving him minute instructions about the journey and the way to overcome Ashmodai, he sent Benaiah on his way, wishing him success in his undertaking.

The brave warrior set out on his dangerous quest. After many days of hard riding across the great desert he finally reached his destination. Never had he seen such a desolate spot. Before him stood a towering mountain without sign of any human habitation. The mountain seemed to be the abode of silence and death. Undaunted, Benaiah began to climb the mountain. He feared neither man nor spirit, for he was wearing on his finger King Solomon's signet-ring. When half-way up he bored a hole in order to discover the whereabouts of Ashmodai's well. Great was his delight when he discovered the position of the well. He drew off the water and stopped up the hole with the wool which he had brought with him. Quite near to this hole, Benaiah made an opening into the well. Through it he poured all the wine in the skins. Then he concealed himself behind a large crag and waited impatiently for the arrival of the King of the Demons.

Soon after sunset Ashmodai drew nigh. He carefully examined the seal on the rock over the mouth of the well and found it intact, even as he had left it early in the morning. After he had rolled away the rock, he descended into the well to quench his thirst. The fragrant wine overpowered him so that he quickly returned to the mouth of the well to inhale the fresh mountain air. Realizing that the well had been tampered with, he again examined the seal, but it did not appear to have been touched. Meanwhile a burning thirst forced him to descend again in order to obtain something to drink. No sooner had he tasted the wine than he desired to drink more and more. After he had drunk freely of the wine, he felt drowsy. All his senses were overpowered. His head became heavy, his body staggered and his knees gave way. At last he fell to the ground and slept soundly.

Benaiah now came forth from his hiding place and crept very quietly to the sleeping demon. Without wasting a moment, he threw the golden chain around Ashmodai's neck and sealed it with the golden signet-ring engraved with the Divine Name. He then sat down on the ground close by waiting for the effects of the strong wine to wear off.

After a while Ashmodai awoke and found that he was no longer free, for he saw the golden chain around his neck and he beheld the Holy Name on the seal. He then groaned so loudly that the mountain shook. In vain Ashmodai struggled to rise. In his anger sparks of fire flew from his eyes and foam covered his mouth.

He continued to struggle, but all to no purpose. He could not rise. He looked at Benaiah and cried in bitter anger, "Is it you who has bewitched me?"

"Verily," replied Benaiah, "behold the Name of the Lord of lords is upon you!"

Ashmodai immediately subsided. Realizing that he was vanquished he told Benaiah that he was quite ready to obey his orders.

"Come then," cried Benaiah, "we will go at once to King Solomon, your master. Arise and follow me!"

Ashmodai arose and followed Benaiah, who was surprised at the behaviour of his captive on their way to the Holy City. Wherever they passed Ashmodai left behind him a trace of his might. In one village he brushed against a palm tree. After its foliage had been shaken off, he uprooted it with one hand. In another place he knocked his shoulder against a house and overturned it. In the market-place of a large town they met a happy bridal procession. When the bride and bridegroom passed Ashmodai began to weep.

"Why do you weep?" Benaiah asked in surprise.

"Alas," replied Ashmodai, "within three days the bridegroom will be a corpse!"

In the next town they overheard a farmer asking a bootmaker to make a pair of boots which were to last him for seven years. Ashmodai burst out laughing.

"Tell me," cried Benaiah, "why do you laugh?"

"Because the poor fellow will not wear his shoes for even seven days; behold within a week he will die—yet he asks for shoes to last him seven years!"

One day they met a blind man going astray. Ashmodai set him on the right path. He showed similar kindness to a drunkard whom they met at the crossroads. On another occasion they saw a magician who was exhibiting his skill. He claimed to be able to read the future and to disclose secrets. This made Ashmodai laugh and when Benaiah asked the reason, he answered, "Wouldn't you laugh also at a man who pretends to reveal secrets, while at the same moment he is unaware of the fact that a treasure lies buried at his feet? We demons judge persons according to their true value and not according to their deceptive appearance in the eyes of man."

After many strange adventures they finally came to the Holy City. Benaiah conducted his captive to the royal presence. As soon as Ashmodai beheld King Solomon, fear seized him and he began to tremble violently in every limb. He held a long staff in his hand on which he supported himself. Ashmodai threw his staff before the King.

"Why do you do this?" asked Solomon.

"Mighty Sovereign," replied Ashmodai, "don't you know that in spite of all your splendour you will occupy after your death no more space in the earth than is measured by yonder staff, yet you are not satisfied with ruling the children of men, but must hold the spirits and demons in subjection."

"Don't be vexed," Solomon answered gently, "you won't find me a hard master. I merely demand one little service of you. I wish to build a great Temple to the glory of the Creator of heaven and earth, and for this purpose I require the services of the wonderful worm Shamir. Tell me now, where can I find this tiny creature?"

"O wisest of mortals," replied Ashmodai, "don't you know that the Shamir has not been placed in my charge?"

"Where is it?" thundered Solomon. "Speak slave! and speak truly."

"Mighty master," replied Ashmodai, "since the days of Moses, who employed the Shamir when writing on the tablets of stone, the worm has been entrusted to the care of the Prince of the Sea who has given it into the charge of the woodcock. The woodcock has sworn to carry the Shamir with him at all times. He lives in a nest built on the top of a very high mountain. He uses the Shamir to split the rocks so as to plant seeds in the clefts, and the vegetation which grows there serves as his food. Whenever he goes from his nest he takes the Shamir with him, carrying it beneath his wing."

"Enough," cried Solomon. "You shall live with me until the Temple is built!"

Once again King Solomon summoned his trusty captain Benaiah, and sent him to look for the nest of the woodcock, to obtain the Shamir, and to bring it back to the Holy City.

"Take with you," said the King, "a glass cover, a little wool and a small leaden box. May your journey be as successful this time as your former one!"

Benaiah obeyed with a glad heart all the instructions which King Solomon gave him. He set out on his journey, crossing hill and dale, stream and desert. At last he discovered the nest of the bird he sought. The woodcock was away on one of his expeditions. In the nest were the fledgelings. Benaiah now covered the nest with the glass cover which he had brought with him for this purpose. He then concealed himself and waited to see what would happen.

When the woodcock returned he tried to enter his nest but found he could not do so, for the glass was very hard and strong. He saw through the glass his helpless young, and flapping his wings and screeching loudly sought to break the glass. All his efforts were in vain. The young birds frightened by the noise also began to screech.

"What is to be done?" cried the woodcock in the language of the birds.

Again and again he tried to smash the glass, but without success. As a last resource, he decided to make use of the precious treasure entrusted to his care. He produced the Shamir from beneath his wing and put it on the glass, which split into pieces as soon as it was touched by the wonderful worm. At that instant Benaiah raised a lusty cry and frightened the woodcock so that he dropped the Shamir. It had barely fallen upon the ground when Benaiah seized it and carefully placed it in the wool and secured it by putting it in the small leaden box which he had brought for the special purpose.

Without lingering a moment, Benaiah set out on his homeward journey, rejoicing greatly at his success. In despair the woodcock killed himself, fearing the terrible vengeance the Prince of the Sea would bring on him when the disappearance of the Shamir became known. Benaiah reached the Holy City in safety and delivered to King Solomon the wonderful worm. With its help the wise King built the Temple; and thereafter the Shamir disappeared and to this very day no one knows where it is to be found.

The Witches of Ascalon

WHEN Rabbi Simon, the son of Shetah, was appointed a prince in Israel, people came to him and said, "In the city of Ascalon, there is a certain cave inhabited by eighty witches."

One rainy day, Rabbi Simon gathered together eighty stalwart young men and gave each one a new vessel, a clean robe being folded in each. The young men accompanied Rabbi Simon to Ascalon, bearing the vessels on their heads, so that their clothes should not be spoilt by the rain.

Rabbi Simon said to them: "I will enter the cave by myself. If I whistle once, put on your robes; and if I whistle a second time, all of you together rush into the cave and each of you seize a witch and lift her up from the ground, for such is the nature of witches that if you raise them from the ground they can do nothing."

When Rabbi Simon arrived at the entrance to the cave, he shouted, "Witches, witches, open for me, I am one of you!"

They said to him, "How is it your clothes are so dry in this time of rain?"

"I walked between the drops of rain!" he answered.

And they asked again, "What have you come for?"

And he replied, "To learn and to teach. Let each one of you show me what you can do, and I will show you what I can do."

One witch uttered an incantation and bread appeared. Another brought meat in a similar way; a third, dishes, and a fourth, wine. Then the witches said to him, "Now what can you do?"

THE WITCHES OF ASCALON: From the *Agada* in the Talmud. In *Legends of Palestine*, by Zev Vilnay. Reprinted by permission of the copyright owners. The Jewish Publication Society of America. Philadelphia, 1932.

To which he replied: "I can whistle twice and cause to appear eighty young men, clad in dry robes, who will make merry with you and you with them."

He whistled once and the boys donned their robes; he whistled a second time and they all rushed into the cave.

Simon said to them, "Let each one choose his partner!"

And according to their instructions each of the young men lifted up a witch and then they carried them away to be hanged.

Thus was Ascalon rid of its eighty witches.

How High—That High?

IT WAS *Selichos*-time, the ten penitential days before *Yom Kippur*. The widow planned, as was the ancient custom among the Jews, to go to the synagogue after midnight to recite the *Selichos*. These are the penitential prayers which are said in order to purify the spirit in preparation of the awesome Day of Atonement.

When the first *Selichos* night came around the widow did not go to bed. Her eyes were tortured with sleep but, because she was afraid she might miss the waking knock on her shutter by the *shammes*, she decided to sit up and wait for him.

But sleep eventually overtook her where she sat.

She suddenly awoke with a start! She heard a loud knocking on her shutter and the familiar booming in a bass voice of the *shammes*: "Arise, children, to the service of the Lord!"

Arise, children, to the service of the Lord—Arise!

Joyful for having heard the call to prayer the widow quickly wrapped her shawl around her and hastened into the dark street.

In front of her house she saw the shadowy outline of a Jew.

"Are you going to the synagogue for *Selichos*?" he asked.

"Indeed I am," replied the widow.

"Then let us go together," said the man.

The widow agreed heartily for, truth to tell, she was afraid to walk alone in the dark. So they trudged the road together to the synagogue.

HOW HIGH—THAT HIGH?: Adapted from a Yiddish groschen chapbook.

All about them the town lay fast asleep. Not a sound could be heard, not a person could be seen.

"I simply can't understand this!" marvelled the widow. "Where is everybody? Surely they must have heard the *shammes* call as well as we did."

"I'm sure they did," the stranger reassured her. "We probably were too slow getting started. When we get to the synagogue you'll see everybody will be there."

At last they came to the synagogue. Except for the perpetual lamp flickering before the Ark of the Torah the building was in darkness. Somewhat uneasily the widow mounted the stairs to the women's gallery and the man remained below in the well of the synagogue.

High up there she felt alone and uneasy. Except for the man below there was nobody in the House of God. She sat there waiting, but nobody came. Her disquietude grew. She looked down from the women's gallery and then her eyes met those of the man. They were dark as coal and flashing fire. They held her spellbound, pierced through her like sharp knives. She trembled and broke into a cold sweat. She tried to tear her eyes away from his but she couldn't.

Suddenly she saw him stretch out his hand towards her. With horror she saw it grow longer and longer until it reached right up into the women's gallery. The long bony fingers were outstretched. Already they were groping for her throat, ready to strangle her. Summoning all her strength she cried out, *"Shema Yisroel Adonoy Elohenu, Adonoy Echod!* Hear, O Israel, the Lord our God, the Lord is One!"

Then she tore herself away from the clutching fingers. Quickly she ran down the stairs and then out into the street. She ran and she ran until she was out of breath.

"Thank you, dear God, for having saved me from this terrible danger!" she murmured gratefully.

She now knew for certain that the man in the synagogue was no human but a demon in disguise who was out to do her harm.

Just as the widow arrived home she heard the town clock toll the hour of midnight. There—she should have known better! The hour was still too early for the *shammes* to make his rounds. She therefore settled herself comfortably in her chair and waited for his knock. But soon drowsiness overcame her and she floated away in dreams.

All of a sudden she awoke with a start! She heard the voice of the *shammes* booming outside on the street in his hoarse bass voice:

"Arise, children, to the service of the Lord!"

Then she heard his knock on her shutter.

Thankful that she had not missed his call to prayer, the widow once more wrapped herself in her shawl and hastened into the street.

This time she saw people come pouring out of their houses, rubbing their eyes heavy with the first sleep. She joined the stream of worshippers flowing towards the synagogue. From a distance she could see that the house of prayer was brilliantly lit, ready for the service, and she heaved a sigh of relief. Now nothing could happen to her, now everything would be well!

As she hastened along deep in her thoughts, she suddenly realized that a Jew was walking beside her. In the dark she could make out only his shadowy outline. He carried a large prayer book in his hand.

"Do you mind if we walk together to the synagogue?" he asked her with a pious mien.

"With pleasure," she replied gratefully, for truth to tell, she was afraid of the dark and felt thankful for having found a companion to walk with.

"I can't begin to tell you what a fright I got a little while ago," the widow began confidentially.

"Why, what happened?" asked the stranger.

"I had fallen asleep in my chair," continued the widow, "and I thought I distinctly heard the *shammes* calling for *Selichos*, so I started out for the synagogue. Standing before my door I saw a Jew who asked if he could walk along with me to the synagogue. There was nothing unusual about him as far as I could see. Believe me, he looked no different than you, he had a black beard and he carried a large prayer book as you do. But, when we came to the synagogue and I went upstairs to the women's gallery and he remained below, I suddenly took fright. He looked at me with fiery piercing eyes. I thought I was going to faint. I struggled to take my eyes off him but I couldn't. Then slowly, slowly he reached out his hand towards me. It grew longer and longer, stretched and stretched higher and higher until it reached right up to me in the balcony."

"How high?" asked the man with incredulity.

"May God punish me if I don't speak the truth! I swear his hand reached right up to the women's gallery!"

"Lord preserve us!" cried her companion in amazement.

Then he said: "I'm just asking out of curiosity—tell me, how high up do you think his hand reached?"

"Oh, way up high," said the widow with a sweeping upward gesture of her arm.

"This high?" asked the man, raising his hand aloft.

As the widow looked at his hand it began to grow longer and longer, to stretch higher and higher until it reached to the top of a tall tree.

The widow began to tremble with fright. Her heart began to pound so that she felt it in her mouth. She tried to cry out but she found that she had lost her voice. Moving her lips soundlessly she prayed: "*Shema Yisroel Adonoy Elohenu, Adonoy Echod!* Hear, O Israel, the Lord our God, the Lord is One!"

Then she began to run.

"Ha ha ha—ho ho ho—hi hi hi!" she heard a frightful laughter behind her.

Terror gave her wings. She ran and she ran until, all out of breath, she arrived at the synagogue. More dead than alive she recited the prayer of Thanksgiving customary after escaping from great danger.

"What has happened to me is a warning from Heaven because of my sins," she thought.

Then, with a contrite heart, she began to intone the penitential *Selichos*.

INTRODUCTORY NOTE TO *The Golem of Prague*

The mystery of "where do we come from and where do we go?" has always fascinated thinking men. As human control over the forces of Nature grew and man became increasingly conscious of his latent powers he began to speculate about his own capacity to equal and even to oppose the demi-urgos of creation. There was no great conceptual leap from the Prometheus legend, in which man, arrogant in his purposeful knowledge, tried to wrest the elemental secret of fire from the gods, to the "mechanical man" the ingenious Maelzel made in the early Nineteenth Century, or to the "mechanical heart" invented by Carrel and Lindbergh in our day.

Like all peoples, Jews too were intrigued by the idea of creation. Alien to all tenets of rationalistic Judaism, even sacrilegious in opposing itself to God, Jewish folklore nevertheless boasts a number of legends in which man superseded God as Creator. An astonishing piece of impudence from the pious, but breathtaking in its sheer daring!

The *golem*, or homunculus legend in Jewish folklore, is very ancient, dating back to Rabbinic times. In its literal meaning the word "golem" means lifeless, shapeless matter into which the one who has discovered the tetragrammaton (*Shem-Hamforesh* or God's Ineffable Name), can by its mystic means breathe the impulse of life. There is little doubt that the Talmudic speculations about the creation of the first man stimulated the growth of the *golem* legends. There is the following passage in the Talmud complete with all implied directives that were avidly taken up by the legendary *golem* creators.

"How was Adam created? In the first hour his dust was collected; in the second his form was created; in the third he became a shapeless mass (*golem*); in the fourth his members were joined; in the fifth his apertures opened; in the sixth he received his soul; in the seventh he stood up on his feet. . . ."

According to the *Agada* in the Talmud the celebrated Rabbi Raba had created a homunculus. This creature was a man like any other man, except that he lacked the power of speech which God alone could endow. When in a mood of egoism and vainglory Raba sent his *golem* to Rabbi Zeira, that sage quickly discovered the creature's magical origin and indignantly returned him to the dust from which he was fashioned. The creation of man was God's own business, he said.

There is also the legend in the Talmud about the two rabbis Hanina and Oshaga. Every Friday, by means of mystic formulae from the *Book of Creation,* they would make a three-year-old calf which they ate on the Sabbath. The Eleventh Century Bible exegesist Rashi, being thoroughly saturated with Jewish Cabala and with the supernaturalism of the medieval

Christian world, even tried to give the account a dubious religious sanction:

"They, Hanina and Oshaga, used to combine the letters of the name by which the universe was created. This is not to be considered forbidden magic, for the words of God were brought into being through His Holy Name."

Jewish legend even has Rashi's great contemporary, the poet-philosopher of Valencia, Solomon ibn Gabirol, create a maid-servant *golem*. When the king heard of it he wished to put the Jewish poet to death for practicing black magic, but Gabirol demonstrated to the King's royal satisfaction that the creature he made was not human, and forthwith he returned her to dust.

Another *golem* was alleged to have been created in the time of the Crusades in France by Rabbi Samuel, the father of the famous Judah Hasid. He fashioned a homunculus, but, like Raba in Bible times, he could not make it talk. Wherever he went this *golem* accompanied him as his servant and vigilant bodyguard.

Christian Europe too had its own versions of the homunculus. What else are the medieval legends of Doctor Faustus and the poet Vergil? Even as Rashi believed in the authenticity of the creation of the rabbinical calf so did the most advanced Christian thinkers of the Middle Ages and the Renaissance believe in the legend of Vergil's statue into which the poet had breathed life and forced it to obey his will in various escapades.

By the time of the late Renaissance legends about *golems* were widespread among the Jews of Eastern Europe. The most popular folk tale was that of the *Golem of Chelm*, created by the redoubtable cabalist Rabbi Elijah of that town. He allegedly created it sometime during the middle of the Sixteenth Century by means of the *Shem-Hamforesh*, God's Ineffable Name. This mystical name he wrote on a piece of parchment and placed it in the earthen *golem's* forehead. Little did he dream what a monster the creature would turn out to be! When he beheld its frightful aspect and its destructive tendencies, he began to repent his folly in making it: His *golem* could very well destroy the whole world! So he drew forth the *Shem-Hamforesh* from its forehead, and immediately the monster turned to dust. It would be interesting to investigate what Mary Shelley knew of this legend when she wrote her Frankenstein chiller.

In 1625 the eminent Italian-Jewish doctor, scientist, and encyclopedic scholar, Joseph Del Medigo, while journeying through Germany, Poland and Lithuania, observed that "many *(golem)* legends of this sort are current, particularly in Germany." The legend of the *Golem of Chelm* was undoubtedly one of those he heard.

The *Golem of Prague*, the most popular of all the Jewish *golem* stories, is without doubt merely a later-day variation of the older tales. How it happened to fix on the historical personality of Rabbi Yehuda Loew will always remain a fruitful source of speculation for the folklorist and the historian of Jewish culture. It is sufficient that it has been and still is one of the most alive as well as one of the liveliest among all Jewish folk legends.

This fact is not without its historical or national-cultural interest. The image of the *golem*, as it was already fully developed in the Sixteenth

Century *Golem of Chelm*, was that of a Frankenstein with frightful pro-pensities for tearing up and smiting down. It remained for the later legend of the *Golem of Prague* to endow the terrifying figure with moral and social grandeur. The crude, shapeless lump of clay no longer was a figure symbolic of the genius of indiscriminate destruction. The *golem*, in the hands of the Maharal of Prague, became a national protector of the persecuted Jews, a God-sent Avenger of the wrongs done a helpless people.

It is precisely this aspect of the folk imagination and the historical forces that stimulated it that are of the most universal interest. For, as is well known, folk legends are not just accidental in their origin or fanciful fictions invented by the "childlike masses." They are a true record and mirror of the complicated historical and cultural experiences of a people.

The middle of the Seventeenth Century was a cataclysmic period for the Jewish people of Europe. It marked the most dreadful massacres of Jews in history, of course excepting those by the Nazis in World War II. The terrible ravages of the Thirty Years War and the revolt of the Cossacks under Bogdan Chmielnitzki against Polish rule left the Jews of Europe frightfully decimated and shattered. This was immediately followed by the Messianic fevers which tortured and racked the spirits of those Jews who survived the bloody holocaust, and finally left them spent and disen-chanted. Darkness and superstition descended on the Jewish ghetto as it never had before.

Nowhere could Jews themselves cope with the problems of their sur-vival. God, it seemed to them, had abandoned them to the sword and the persecution of the enemy without, and to the seduction and betrayal of the Messianic swindlers within, such as the Messiah of Smyrna, Sab-batai Zevi. So in its despair, the folk-mind, fed by the sickly cabalistic dreams and myths current at the time, created the magical figure of the *golem* to protect the Jews' puny weakness with his enormous physical strength, to discover by means of his supernatural powers the plotters against their peace and thus foil their wicked plans. It was the *golem* as Redeemer that, viewed within the historical frame of reference of the tormented Jewish life in the Seventeenth Century in Europe, lends the legend such haunting poignancy.—N. A.

The Golem of Prague

RABBI YEHUDA LOEW, known to the pious as the *"Maharal,"* came to Prague from Nikolsburg, Posen, in the year 5332 of the Creation (1572 A.D.) in order to become rabbi of the community there. The whole world resounded with his fame because he was deeply learned in all branches of

---

THE GOLEM OF PRAGUE: Adapted from *Nifluot Maharal* (Miracles of the Maharal, 17th Century).

knowledge and knew many languages. Is it any wonder then that he was revered by the wise men among the Gentiles? * Even King Rudolf of Bohemia esteemed him highly. Because of these reasons the Maharal was able to wage war successfully against the enemies of Israel who tried to besmirch Jewish honor with their false blood accusations.

After much sad experience, in the course of which these frightful slanders were fully exposed in the brilliant light of truth, King Rudolf assured Rabbi Yehuda Loew that never again would he permit any blood accusations to be charged against the Jews in his kingdom. When the Maharal first came to Prague the blood accusation was a very common occurrence there and much innocent Jewish blood was spilled because of it. Immediately on his arrival, Rabbi Yehuda Loew announced that he would fight against this unholy calumny with all his power in order to silence the enemies of his people who so tirelessly plotted for its destruction.

One day, King Rudolf sent his carriage to fetch the Maharal for an audience with him. They talked together for a whole hour but what was said during their meeting nobody knows to this very day.

The Maharal returned home in a gay mood. He told his intimates: "I have already half destroyed the filthy myth of the blood accusation! With God's help I hope soon to wash away entirely this hideous stain from our innocent people."

And the Maharal's hope was soon fulfilled. To his joy, and to the joy of all the Jews of Bohemia, the King issued a decree ten days later announcing that no one, besides the particular individual charged in a blood accusation, had to stand trial. Prior to that *all* the Jews were collectively charged with the alleged crime. Furthermore, that the individual accused could not be condemned unless there was positive proof of his guilt in the crime. The King also ordered that, during any trial on such a charge, the Rabbi of Prague had to be present. Nor could the verdict be valid unless the King himself countersigned the judge's sentence.

One would have thought that the King's decree would put an end to the shameless slander that the Jews had a custom which required them to use Christian blood in the baking of the Passover *matzos*. But the enemies of Israel were endlessly resourceful that way. All that it required for a Christian who wished to destroy a Jew was stealthily to plant a dead child in his house and the hue and cry of the blood accusation was on again. Only in rare cases was it possible for the Jew to extricate himself from the fine meshes of the net his enemies entangled him in.

There was one man in the kingdom of Bohemia of whom the Maharal stood in great dread. This was the priest Thaddeus. He was not only an implacable enemy of the Jews but a clever sorcerer besides. He was determined to carry on a war to the death against the Maharal. The Maharal too girded himself for battle against this enemy.

---

* Tycho Brahe and Johann Kepler were among his intimate friends.

One night, the Maharal called upon Heaven to answer him in a dream how best he could wage successful war against his enemy Thaddeus. And the answer came to him in the alphabetically arranged words of the Cabala: "Create a Golem out of clay who will destroy all the enemies of Israel!" *

The Maharal knew that in the Hebrew words of this formula there were stored enough mystical secrets by means of whose powers he could create a Golem. He then confided his secret to Isaac ben Shimshon ha-Cohen, his son-in-law, and to his principal disciple, Jacob ben Chayyim ha-Levi. He told them that he would require their help because they were born under the constellation of Fire and Water respectively; the Maharal himself was born under the constellation of Air. To the making of the Golem all the four elements of Fire, Water, Air and Earth were necessary. He then cautioned the two against revealing his plan to anyone and instructed them that, during the next seven days, they were to purify their bodies and souls with ablutions, fasting, prayer and austerities.

It was on the second day in the month of Adar in the year 5340 of Creation (A.D. 1580) that the momentous event took place. At four in the morning the three made their way out of the city to the Moldau. There, on the clay bank of the river, they moulded the figure of a man three ells in length. They fashioned for him hands and feet and a head, and drew his features in clear human relief.

Having done this, the three stationed themselves at the feet of the prostrate Golem. The Maharal then ordered Isaac ben Shimshon ha-Cohen to encircle the figure seven times from right to left. He also revealed to him the cabalistic incantations he was to pronounce while doing so.

No sooner had the Maharal's son-in-law completed his task when the Golem began to glow like fire. Then the Maharal asked Jacob ben Chayyim ha-Levi to do the same circling, but he instructed him to utter different cabalistic formulae and to encircle the figure from left to right. As soon as he was through, the fire in the Golem was quenched and a cloud of steam arose from its body. When it cleared, they saw that hair had grown on its head and that nails had appeared on its fingers and toes.

Next, the Maharal himself began to circle around the Golem seven times. Then with one voice, all three recited the Scriptural passage from *Genesis* II,7: "And he breathed into his nostrils the breath of life; and man became a living soul."

Immediately, the Golem opened his eyes and looked at the three men wonderingly.

"Get up on your feet!" commanded the Maharal.

The Golem stood up and they dressed him in clothes they had brought with them, clothes that were fitting for a *shammes*.

Most wonderful to relate—when they had left Prague two hours before

---

* *Ato Bra Golem Devuk Hachomer V'tigzar Zedim Chevel Torfe Yisroel.*

they were only three, but when six o'clock struck there were four of them
returning!

On the way home the Maharal said to the Golem: "Know that we have
created you so that you may protect the defenseless Jews against their
enemies. Your name is Joseph and you will serve me as *shammes* in the
House of Judgment. You must obey me no matter what I tell you to do,
even should I ask you to jump into fire and water!"

Although the Golem could not speak, for the power of speech is God's
alone to give, he, nonetheless, understood what the Maharal said to him.
He had a remarkable sense of hearing and could detect sounds from a very
great distance.

To his two disciples the Maharal said that he had named the Golem
Joseph because he had implanted in him the spirit of Joseph Shida, he who
was half-man and half-demon, and who had saved the sages of the Talmud
from many trials and dangers.

When the Maharal came home he told his wife, Perele the *Rebbitzen*,
pointing to the Golem, that he had met the poor unfortunate (plainly a
mute idiot) on the street, and that he felt very sorry for him, and so he
brought him home with him.

"He will serve me as *shammes* in the House of Judgment," he said.

At the same time the Maharal forbade anyone to give the Golem any
menial tasks to perform for he had not created him for that.

And so the Golem sat always in a corner of the House of Judgment,
with expressionless face cupped in his hands, just like a clay Golem who
has no thought in his head. Because he behaved like a mute idiot, people
began to call him derisively *"Yosele Golem."* Others called him "Dumb
Yosele."

Despite the Maharal's orders against giving Yosele Golem any tasks to
perform, his wife, Perele the *Rebbitzen*, disobeyed him. One day, just
before Passover, she motioned to him to fetch water from the well and to
fill the two big barrels in the pantry with water for the holy day.

Yosele Golem quickly snatched two buckets and ran with them to the
well. As the *Rebbitzen* was preoccupied with other matters she did not
observe what he was doing.

To the well and back again he ran so many times that, without anyone
noticing it, the barrels began to overflow and soon the water spread
through the house. At this the servants raised a great outcry and ran to
tell the Maharal.

When Rabbi Yehuda Loew came and saw what Yosele Golem had done
he burst out laughing and said to the *Rebbitzen:* "My, my, what a wonderful water-carrier you got yourself for Passover!"

He then went and took away the buckets from the Golem and led him
back into his corner in the House of Judgment.

From that time on the *Rebbitzen* never again asked Yosele Golem to
do anything for her. But when the story got around in Prague every-

body laughed. It even gave rise to a new saying: "You're as good a watch-maker as Yosele Golem is a water-carrier!"

The Maharal employed the Golem to protect the Jews of Prague against the dangers that threatened them. With his assistance he was able to perform many miracles. Most of all he used him in his war against the blood accusations which were again rife in the land and which caused so much sorrow to the Jews. In such cases, when the Maharal had to send Yosele Golem on a dangerous mission, he found it advisable to make him invisible by means of an amulet upon which was written a cabalistic word.

In the period before Passover, which coincides with the Christian Easter, a time when the blood accusation was usually brought, the Maharal made Yosele Golem put on a disguise. He had him dress up like a Christian and made him wear a rope around his middle in order that he might look like any ordinary Gentile porter.

The Maharal ordered him to guard the Ghetto * of Prague like the apple

---

* The etymology of few words concerning Jews has aroused so much discussion and disagreement as the word *ghetto*. Some see the word as derived from the Hebrew *gett* (divorce, separation), others, from the Talmudic Hebrew root *gedad guda* (wall). There also is the Tuscan *guitto* and the Modenese *ghitto*, both meaning "sordid." There are also the Italian words *ghetta* (flock, herd), and *borghetto* (small burg or quarter). And lastly, there are the two German words *gitter* (bars) and *geheckte orte* (hedged place) derived from the Latin *gehectus*.

As is well known, the systematic persecution of the Jews in Europe began with the first Crusades in the Eleventh Century. However, their segregation (physical as well as social) did not begin until 1215 when the Fourth Lateran Council issued a decree compelling Jews to wear the yellow badge in order to mark them off from Christians. Previously Jews had lived in their own quarters largely from choice and from social and religious convenience. Before the Middle Ages their separate quarters were referred to in Latin as *vicus Judaeorum*. Later on, among the Germanic peoples, they variously became known as *Judengasse, Judenstrasse* or *Judenviertel*. In Portugal these quarters were called *Judiaria*, in England, *Jew Street*, and in France, *Juiverie*.

But it was not until the terrible anti-Jewish excesses during the Black Plague in 1348-9—when Jews were falsely accused of having poisoned Christian wells—that those Jews, who did not take flight eastward into the Polish Provinces, were ordered locked up within walled enclosures in the sections or streets where they lived. These then became known as *ghettos*.

At night the ghetto gates were closed and locked like a prison with bolts and chains, with a Christian watch standing without. The hostile attitude toward the Jews in those days is made plain in the inscription found on the ghetto gate in Padua: "The people, the inheritors of the Kingdom of Heaven, shall have no communion with the disinherited."

Jews were not only forbidden, under pain of severe punishment, to leave the ghetto gates after dark, but they were kept locked up on Sundays, on every Christian holy day, and on carnival days

The confined ghetto, on the medieval pattern, lasted in Europe for more than four hundred years, and, in modified form, until the fall of Czardom in 1917. The word "ghetto" is of course inexactly applied today to those slum localities of a city where Jews live in large numbers, such as the East Side of New York or Whitechapel in London.—N. A.

of his eye, to roam all its streets at night and to be on the lookout against those who might wish to do evil to the Jews. He was to examine the contents of every passing wagon and of every bundle carried by a passerby. If he but suspected someone of making preparations for bringing a blood accusation against the Jews he was to bind the malefactor with his rope and bring him straightway to the city watch in the *Rathaus*.

It so happened that the leading Jew of Prague in communal matters **was** the wealthy *Reb* Mordchi Meisel. One of his debtors, a Christian who ran a slaughter-house, owed him five thousand crowns. Time and again *Reb* Mordchi demanded of the slaughterer that he return the money, but each time the latter declined to pay on some pretext or other.

Now the slaughter-house was situated outside the city, and the slaughterer was in the habit of conveying meat into the city through the Jewish ghetto. This put the idea into his head of accusing *Reb* Mordchi of having used Christian blood for the baking of *matzos*.

Several days before Passover, the child of a Christian neighbor of the slaughterer's died. It was buried in the Christian cemetery. Late that night, the slaughterer stole into the cemetery and dug up the child. He then killed a pig in the slaughter-house and cleaned out its insides. He cut the throat of the dead child and wrapping it in the folds of a *tallis*, he placed it inside the pig. Afterwards, he rode to town, intending to secrete the body in *Reb* Mordchi's house while he slept.

When the slaughterer was near *Reb* Mordchi's house, Yosele Golem, who was then roaming the streets, suddenly appeared and insisted on examining the contents of his wagon. When he saw the dead child in the pig's carcass, he quickly bound the slaughterer with his rope and carried him to the town watch right in the *Rathaus*. He dumped him in the courtyard and hurried away.

A great commotion was heard in the *Rathaus*. The watch was called out. They brought lights, and saw before them the slaughterer, lying tied hand and foot and looking bruised and swollen. They examined the pig and found the dead child in its carcass. Seeing that it was wrapped in a Jewish *tallis*, the chief of the watch clearly saw that it was a blood accusation plot.

After close questioning the slaughterer confessed what he was up to. When he was asked who had brought him to the city watch he answered: "It was a Christian porter who was mute. He was an enormous fellow who looked more like a devil than a man!"

No one had any idea who this strange creature could be. A great terror fell upon all enemies of Israel. Only Thaddeus the priest understood from what quarter this secret power could have come. So he had the rumor spread in town that the Maharal was a sorcerer, in order to discredit him in the eyes of all upright Christians who respected him. And he intensified his struggle against him and all the Jews with a consuming hatred.

When King Rudolf saw that there was no foundation whatsoever for any of the blood accusations he became angry at the priest Thaddeus. The pleas and persuasion of the Maharal at last had their effect. The King issued a solemn decree under his own seal, forbidding anyone in his realm from ever raising the blood accusation against any Jew or group of Jews. Neither were the courts of the kingdom to honor such charges because the sin of accusing the innocent with crimes they had not committed always falls like a blight upon the entire nation.

Once again Passover came around but not one blood accusation was raised in the Kingdom of Bohemia that year. It seemed as if King Rudolf's decree had effectively silenced the enemy. Thereupon, the Maharal called his son-in-law and his disciple, both of whom had assisted in the creation of the Golem, and said to them: "I have called you to tell you that the Golem is no longer needed. The lie of the blood accusation will never be raised in this country again."

This took place on the night of *Lag Ba-Omer* in the year 5350 of the Creation (A.D. 1590).

That night, the Maharal said to Yosele Golem: "Don't sleep tonight in the House of Judgment but instead go up into the attic of the Synagogue * and make your bed there!"

Ever-obedient, Yosele Golem did as the Maharal told him.

After midnight, accompanied by his son-in-law and his disciple, the Maharal ascended to the attic of the Synagogue and stationed himself before the sleeping giant. They now took their places in reverse position to that when they created him. They stood at his head and gazed into his face.

Then they began to circle around him, beginning from left to right. They did this seven times, intoning cabalistic incantations and formulae in the meantime.

All this time, the old *shammes, Reb* Abraham Chayyim, whom the Maharal had brought to assist him, stood at a discreet distance from the Golem, lighting him up with two waxen candles. Upon the completion of the seventh encirclement the Golem lay rigid in death. He looked again like a hunk of hardened clay.

The Maharal took the two candles from the *shammes* and had him divest the Golem of his clothes, except for the shirt. They then took some old discarded prayer shawls and wrapped them securely around him. Afterwards, they covered him with thousands upon thousands of discarded leaves from old prayer books so that he was altogether hidden from sight.

The Maharal also told the *shammes* not to breathe a word to any living soul of what he had seen that night and to burn the Golem's clothes when no one saw. Then they all descended from the attic. They washed their hands and uttered prayers of purification, as one usually does after being near a corpse.

In the morning, the Maharal had a report spread throughout Prague

---

* The famous *Altneuschul.*

that his *shammes*, Yosele Golem, had quarreled with him and had left the city at night. Everybody accepted the report as true except the three who had the privilege of going up to the attic with the Maharal the previous night.

One week later, the Maharal had a proclamation posted and read in the *Altneuschul*, forbidding any Jew, on pain of excommunication, ever to go up to the Synagogue attic.

The reverence for Rabbi Yehuda Loew was so great that no one dared look for the Golem in the attic. It is believed that he is still lying there, buried deep under a heap of torn leaves from old prayer books, and only waiting for the coming of the Messiah, or for the time when new dangers appear to menace the existence of Israel, to rise again and smite the foe.

The Miser's Transformation

IN A certain city there once lived a rich man. He possessed lands and gold and had chests full of costly vessels of silver inlaid with precious stones. Rich as he was he was also miserly. He never gave an alms to a poor man, helped no one in distress, and even kept away from the synagogue out of fear that he might be asked to make a donation. For this reason he was nicknamed, "the Miser."

Nonetheless, this same tight-fisted man could also be unselfish. He served as voluntary *mohel* to the newly born boys of the neighborhood and consecrated them to the faith of Jehovah and to the Holy Torah. He fulfilled this obligation with such devotion that he never made any distinction between rich and poor, and was never deterred by time, effort and money to journey for this purpose to the most distant places.

One day, as he stood before his house, a stranger approached him and said, "My wife has just been delivered of a son. I would therefore like you to consecrate him."

The miser replied: "This is my duty. Wait a moment and I'll follow you. Tell me, where do you live?"

"I live far away," said the stranger, "but I'll drive fast; I've good horses and a light wagon."

The miser went into his house, looked carefully over the securely-locked chests that held his treasure, then he bolted door and gate and followed the stranger.

At first the man drove at a slow, unhurried pace. The miser, who knew the countryside well, could see where they were going. But suddenly the stranger started to whip up his horses that now tore away at a great speed. They sped by fields and woods, mountains and valleys, until a mist fell and night began to descend.

THE MISER: Adapted from *Kav Hayashar* (Moral Code), by Zevi Hirsch Kaidanover. Frankfort, 1705.

All this time the miser had not heard one single bird sing, or a bee hum, or a brook gurgle. When the moon rose at last, he looked fearfully around him. What was his terror to see that the horses cast no shadow! They sped at a breath-taking speed, neighing and pounding the road with their hooves. The journey seemed to come to no end. When he saw this he said to the driver with a quavering voice, "Where are you taking me?"

"We'll soon be at our destination," the stranger assured him.

And even as he spoke, the dawn began to break, the mist lifted and the sun shone dazzlingly upon a little hamlet.

It nestled in a verdant valley. Looking upon it, a peace, such as he had never known before, descended upon the frightened miser.

The stranger drove slowly to his home where he and the miser were soon surrounded by a group of men who greeted them with a hearty: *"Sholom Aleichem."* The servants led the horses into the stable while the host escorted his guest into the house.

The miser stood mutely regarding everything with astonishment. The magnificence of every object dazzled him. The furniture was inlaid with gold, silver and gems. The doors were of carved ivory. Even the locks, bolts and nails in the house were fashioned of gold and silver.

When the host excused himself and went without the miser began to speculate in his mind which costly object he saw would be given him as a gift.

He wandered from one room into another and at last found himself in the room of the woman who had given birth. What splendor he found here! The woman lay in a bed made of silver and nearby, in a cradle of beaten gold, slept the new-born babe.

As soon as she noticed the miser the woman motioned him to approach.

"I am happy to see you here," she murmured. "You have it in your power to perform a great service for me. Believe me, I'll remain ever grateful to you for this. In repayment I will reveal to you a great secret. Know that you are not now among mortal men. Those who live here are demons; the one who brought you, my husband, is a demon. You have been snared here by lie and deception. The splendor and magnificence of gold and gems which you see all about you are nothing but dazzle and shimmer—and unreal as mist."

Thereupon, the miser's courage died in him.

"I'm a human being like you," continued the young mother. "I was caught in this evil net in my tender youth. The snare of my husband's gifts blinded my reason and thus, before I knew it, I became the wife of a demon! Although I'm already beyond saving there is still time to save you!"

"I'm lost!" wailed the frightened miser.

"Let me warn you betimes," cautioned the woman, "not to taste any food or drink while you're here. Neither must you accept any present from my husband, regardless whether it's costly or trifling in value."

The miser left her, trembling in every limb. He thought regretfully of everything he had left behind him, of his lands and his gold. He was certain—everything was lost to him now, and he himself was at the mercy of the demons.

When night fell he heard a tremendous uproar outside. Horses and wagons, bearing demons, were arriving in a steady stream. No doubt they came as guests to the circumcision celebration.

Once again the miser was obliged to enter the chamber of the mother and child. Together with the demon-guests he intoned prayers and incantations to guard the child against evil spirits and ghosts who delight in harming new-born children.

At the festive board the demons waxed gay and hilarious. But the miser declined all food and drink. The bright candle-light illumined the magnificent interior, but in the soul of the miser reigned darkest gloom. He decided to hear nothing and see nothing. He thought only of the terrible things the unfortunate mother had told him.

That night he could not fall asleep, but lay awake, alert and watching.

When morning came his host conducted him to a synagogue which was already full of demon-worshippers. The miser was courteously invited to act as precentor. Full of anguish, he sang the service and, as the congregation of demons chanted with him, the dread chill of their voices congealed his blood.

After they were through praying, the child was fetched and the miser performed the rite of circumcision. According to custom, everyone present tasted refreshments, but the miser excused himself on the pretext that this was his special fastday.

At this his host spoke up with cunning: "It is our duty to honor our guest and to postpone our feast until evening when he will be able to join us in eating and drinking."

The miser's heart sank. He only thought of how he could best save his soul from perdition.

The day passed quickly and night fell. Again, the host came and led the miser to the festive board around which sat the other demons. They ate and drank lustily and made merry. Only the miser sat silent and dejected. When he was pressed to eat and drink he excused himself this time with the plea of illness. As the gaiety of the demons grew in intensity his own terror increased.

Suddenly his host arose and motioned to him to follow him into another room.

"This is my last hour on earth!" thought the miser in terror as he followed him.

As the demon opened the door, the miser's eye fell upon an astonishing array of beautiful and costly vessels.

"Since you have done me such a great service," said the demon, "I want you to accept a little token of appreciation from me. Choose what you like from among all that you see here."

The miser was filled with consternation.

"I have all the silver I want at home," he blurted. "Thank you just the same."

Without a word the demon led him into the next room. Here all the objects were made of gold.

"Do you like any of these things?" asked the demon.

"Thank you kindly," replied the miser hastily. "I have all the gold I want at home."

Without another word the demon then led him into the next room.

The miser stood speechless with excitement at what he saw. Here there was no magnificence, no sparkle of silver or glow of gold. All he saw were bunches of keys, of all sizes and shapes, hanging from nails on the wall.

"A strange thing!" muttered the demon. "When I showed you first my treasures of silver and then of gold you remained cold and indifferent. But now, when I show you just bunches of keys made of ordinary iron, you show astonishment!"

The amazement of the miser suddenly gave way before a deadly fear. Right before him on a nail in the wall hung a familiar bunch of keys. The demon stretched his hand out and took it off the wall.

"These are my keys!" cried the miser quaking. "Truly, these are the keys with which I've locked the chests in which I keep my treasures!"

"Don't be afraid, even if these are your keys!" said the demon in a cold voice. "Don't turn pale, don't tremble so! Since you did me a great service by coming here and have refused to accept any gift of me, I want to show my appreciation in some other way.

"Know that I am a demon! I am lord and master of all those evil spirits who have power over the riches and treasures in the possession of humans who are as miserly as you, and who, like you, never aid the needy when they cry out. Also know that neither you nor such as you are the actual owners of their wealth. We demons hold the keys to your strongboxes and guard them well although we can never enjoy them.

"Here then is your bunch of keys! Take them and become sole master of your riches!"

The miser quickly snatched at the keys. His host called for a wagon. The miser got into it and was whirled away.

The wagon stopped before the miser's door and he alighted. But no sooner did his feet touch the ground when both the horses and the driver vanished.

The miser entered his house, but he was not the same man anymore. He opened his treasure chests and strong-boxes and took out their valuables. He distributed alms, clothed the poor, and did good to those in misfortune. A new and beautiful life began for him.

From this time on people stopped calling him "the Miser." Instead, they honored his noble example and, when he died, they followed him with blessings on their lips to his eternal rest.

No Privacy Anywhere

IT HAPPENED in a year of famine on the day before *Rosh Hashanah*. A kindhearted man who had a shrewish wife gave a gold-piece to a poor man. When his wife discovered this act of benevolence she nagged him so much for it that he left home. As he could find no lodgings he went to spend the night in the cemetery.

He had barely fallen asleep when he was awakened by the conversation between two girl spirits.

The first one said, "Come, my friend, let us fly over the world and eavesdrop on what is said under the curtain of Heaven. After all, today is *Rosh Hashanah* in the world below. Let us find out what misfortunes are in store for the living."

The second one answered, "I am sorry, but I cannot go with you. I was buried in a straw shroud and I am ashamed to show myself in Heaven in such a garment. Suppose you go alone, and should you hear anything interesting let me know all about it."

And so the first spirit sped to Heaven alone, and, when she returned, her friend asked her, "Well, what have you learned?"

"I have heard it said that a hail storm will destroy the crops of those who sow their fields early."

Hearing this, the good man returned home and, when sowing time came, he waited until all his neighbors had sowed their fields. Then he began to plant. It happened just as he had heard the spirit say: the crops of all the neighbors failed and his own prospered.

The following year he went again to sleep in the cemetery. Again he heard the same two spirits conversing.

Said the first, "Let us fly over the world and eavesdrop under the curtain of Heaven so that we may learn what misfortunes await mankind."

"I have already told you that I have nothing on except a straw shroud!" remonstrated the other. "Better go alone and tell me later what you've heard."

And so the spirit went alone and when she returned her friend asked her, "Well, what have you learned?"

"I heard that he who sows his field in the summer will have his crops burned by the sun."

The man returned home and sowed his fields early in the spring before all his neighbors. When the hot weather arrived his crops were already well grown and firmly rooted, but the crops of his neighbors were scorched.

Mystified by her husband's continued good fortune his wife insisted that he reveal to her his secret. He then told her everything.

Several days later his wife had a quarrel with the mother of one of the dead girls.

NO PRIVACY ANYWHERE: Adapted from the *Agada* in the Talmud.

"Come, and I'll show you that your daughter lies buried in a shroud of straw!" she said to her.

For the third time one year later the man went to spend the night in the cemetery. Again he heard the two spirits conversing. As on the two previous occasions he heard one of the spirits say, "Come, my friend, let us fly over the world and eavesdrop under the curtain of Heaven in order to learn what misfortunes await mankind."

"Heaven defend us!" cried her friend fearfully. "Let us keep our mouths shut! One cannot say anything even around here. Everything we talk about is immediately carried to the living. Very likely at this moment someone is eavesdropping on *us*!"

The Man Who Married a She-Devil

THE man who fears the Lord will guard himself against the temptations of the flesh. But if he submits to them he is in imminent danger of losing his soul and of burning in the everlasting fires of Gehenna.

For instance, it could easily happen that Satan, like a cunning fisherman, will cast his net for him. He could make a she-devil take on the shape of an enticing woman and send her to corrupt him with her lecheries. And as the sins of the parents are visited upon their posterity, so the offspring of a man guilty of adultery remain forevermore tainted. Everybody knows that if a man make a compact with Lilith the Temptress or any other she-demon, he and his kind are torn up by the roots by a just, all-knowing God, and their very names are erased from the recollection of mankind.

In a certain large city stood a handsome stone house on a wide street. A clever goldsmith and his wife and children lived in it. Outwardly this man feigned piety, but secretly he lived in sin with a she-devil who, just as his wife, bore him offspring.

Now this she-devil was very beautiful. She was also very cunning and spun her web of seduction around the goldsmith with great skill. He soon found himself caught irrevocably in her toils. Many a time, while in the synagogue, he would interrupt his devotions and rush off to see her.

And so the years sped by one after another.

It happened once, that on the first night of the Passover, the goldsmith sat down amidst his household to chant in the time-honored fashion of all Jews the narrative of the Exodus from Egypt. Suddenly he felt desire over-

---

THE MAN WHO MARRIED A SHE-DEVIL: Adapted from a medieval tale in *Der Born Judas*, by M. J. Bin Gorion. Insel Verlag. Leipzig, 1916.

In this demon-legend Jewish punctiliousness in the matter of justice and law, is delightfully revealed. Not only a criminal but even a demon is entitled to the full protection of law and order. The cause of justice must always be served.—N. A.

come him. Its power over him was compelling. So he arose and left the house in haste.

The astonishment of the goldsmith's wife knew no bounds. Looking through the window she saw him enter his workshop. This excited her curiosity. She tiptoed after him and discreetly peered through a crack in the wall of the workshop.

The interior was brilliantly lighted with many tapers. In the center stood a table set for two as for a feast. It was laden with gold and silver dishes and with the finest of food and wines. Then she saw something which caused her to tremble. On a magnificent couch lay a woman of great loveliness. Beside her reclined the goldsmith, her husband.

The virtuous wife was overwhelmed by what she saw. She turned hastily away and, with a troubled spirit, reentered her house. When her husband returned, she averted her eyes from him and did not utter a word.

The betrayed wife arose at dawn and hastened to the Rabbi for she felt the urgent need of unburdening her grief to him.

After he had heard her tale the Rabbi sent for the goldsmith who, under his persistent questioning, finally confessed that he had a concubine who did not belong to the human species. Hearing this, the Rabbi was moved to compassion. He gave him an amulet on which he wrote the Ineffable Name in the holy tongue.

"Go in peace," said the Rabbi. "From this day on the wiles of the she-devil will be powerless against you."

And it happened as the Rabbi said. The goldsmith felt no longer any sinful inclinations and he broke forever loose of the she-devil—or so he thought. . . .

Years later, as the goldsmith lay dying, the she-devil suddenly appeared before him. This time she appeared to him more enticing than she had ever been before. She wrung her hands and sobbed, and lamented that when he died she and their demon-children would remain unprovided for.

She gazed lovingly into his eyes and spun her web of seduction about him even more skilfully than at any previous time. Throwing her arms about him she kissed and embraced him, so that, although dying, he felt his ancient love return for her.

At last she succeeded in breaking down his will, although he struggled against her. She made him solemnly promise that she and her children would share equally in the inheritance with his human wife and children. He then assigned to her the cellar of his house as her and her children's dwelling in perpetuity.

Many years had passed since the death of the goldsmith. A bloody war had swept like a holocaust over the land. The human sons of the goldsmith were killed in that evil time. After that, the house passed into the hands of strangers.

All this time the cellar remained locked and heavily barred. The new owners never showed any curiosity to investigate below. One day, however, a venturesome youth tried to force his way in. Barely an hour had elapsed when he was found lying dead on the threshold, but no one knew what it was that had caused his death.

Two years later demons began to frequent the kitchen of the house. When food was being cooked at the hearth, earth and ashes were found in the caldron, making its contents inedible. It wasn't long before the kobolds penetrated into the interior rooms. They seized upon candlesticks and other decorative objects and smashed them upon the floor. While they worked no harm on the people of the house they so thoroughly frightened them that they were obliged to move into other quarters.

Soon the entire city was being plagued by the demons. Alarmed over the critical situation the elders of the community held urgent counsel with one another to devise ways and means to fight the demon-pestilence effectively. The holy men, wise in exorcism and magic, tried all manner of strong measures, but to no avail. The demons only mocked at them and played further pranks upon them. Finally, the elders decided to send for a certain seer of great renown in the land.

The seer arrived and forthwith commenced to drive out the demons by means of highly secret incantations in which figured the Ineffable Name. Immediately the demons declared themselves vanquished and with loud cries of fear swarmed out of their hiding-places.

On close questioning they told the seer how they came to live in the cellar. To this he replied that they had been occupying the premises illegally because no demons may dwell together with humans.

"You may only live in the wastelands, in the dark forest, and in the desert," he warned them sternly.

To which the demons heatedly replied that they held absolute title to the house according to the laws and teachings of Holy Scripture.

"We demand," they said, "that this case be brought before a proper tribunal for judgment!"

Since one may not ignore an appeal to justice from even a demon, a court of equity was convened two days later. The seer and the rabbinical judges took their judicial places. The voices of the demon-plaintiffs were heard distinctly although no corporeal forms were visible.

They told the court about their late-lamented father, the goldsmith, of his last will and testament on his dying bed, and of the subsequent death of all his human descendants in the course of the war. They argued, that by virtue of all these reasons, they alone were the legitimate heirs to the estate left by their human father.

Opposed to the demons were the current owners of the house. They pleaded: "We paid a great sum for the property to the human descendants of the goldsmith. Those who bring the claim against us are demons. Since human law is not valid for demons, they cannot be considered the rightful heirs."

The judges then withdrew and after consultation issued their decision: that the kobolds held no legal title to the house of the goldsmith, that the law of God obliges them to shun the habitations of men and live in solitary places.

Then up rose the seer and in an awesome voice he pronounced incantations. The demons arose in terror and fled to the dark forest and the wasteland, never to molest man again.

⟦6⟧

Animal Tales

INTRODUCTION

The invention of the fable—some believe by the wise men of India, others by the Greeks—marked a turning point in the popular instruction of the people in morals and wisdom. Animals, birds and fish, and even trees and plants, were endowed with human personality. They spoke, thought, felt and acted like people. Thus, by the subtle art of indirection and by epigrammatic condensation of both narrative and idea, the beast fables were able to project the normal situations in life and the lessons to be drawn from them with superb pedagogic skill. Their popularity among the common people was enormous.

While there are traces of the fable in Jewish Scriptures, it would be wrong to include the Jews among the innovators, or even significant developers, of this folk-art form. They were only skilful translators and adapters of the fables of India and Greece. A superficial comparison of fables in Jewish collections with those of other peoples reveals that, by and large, they borrowed freely from Hindu works, such as the *Panchatantra* and the *Mahabahratta,* and the numerous *jatakas* which deal with the nativity of Buddha, and from Greek sources, such as Aesop, Phaedrus, Avian, Kybises and Syntipas.

The outstanding Jewish fabulist of all time was Rabbi Meir, the most eminent pupil of Rabbi Akiba, who lived in Hellenic Asia Minor during the Second Century A.D. He was a great teacher of the people and, being well read in Greek and Latin literatures, discovered that the fable could be an effective aid to his instruction. The Talmud records that he was the collector of three hundred fables—certainly an astonishing number—yet there are altogether only about thirty fables to be found in both the Talmud and the *Midrash.* Meir's fables, whatever their national origin, were ingeniously adapted to the needs of Jewish life and understanding, as can be seen in his fable *The Fate of the Wicked.* The special talent he possessed in this genre helped win for him a legendary reputation among the people. There are many anecdotes in the *Agada* concerning his skill as a teacher of ethics and his greatness as a man. Upon his death in Asia Minor, a writer in the *Mishna* commented sadly: "With the death of R. Meir fable-writers ceased to exist." To this day in many Jewish homes, in honor of R. Meir's memory, there hangs on the wall a coin-box (*Meir Baal ha-Ness pushkeh*) into which the pious woman of the household, before lighting the Sabbath candles, drops her modest donation for the support of the poor in the Holy Land.

The English folklorist, Joseph Jacobs, has remarked: "It has been conjectured that the chief additions to the fable literature of the Middle Ages were made through the intermediation of the Jews, Berechiah ha-Nakdan and John of Capua." Berechiah (known to Christians as Benedictus le Puncteur) was a Jewish grammarian who lived in Oxford in A.D. 1190. The 107 "Fox Fables" (*Mishle Shualim*) in his noted collection are witty and didactic. While a large number of the fables are Aesop's, and others are of Indian origin, quite a few are apparently Jewish in character and in moral point. Berechiah's foxes are amusingly Talmudical; they argue like expert casuists and quote Scripture with the ease of learned rabbis, and their laughter and irony have the traditional Jewish ingredients. In the opinion of Joseph Jacobs—". . . it is very possible that the first knowledge of Aesop gained in England was derived from a Latin translation of Berechiah." John of Capua, a Thirteenth Century Jewish convert, helped spread the great Bidpai cycle of Brahmin fables through Europe by means of his Latin translation, *Directorium Vite Humane*, from Rabbi Joel's Hebrew version of the Arabic version, *Kalilah wa-Dimnah*.

Another noted Jewish collection of fables was the *Sefer Shaashuim* (Book of Delight) by Joseph ibn Zabara (c.1200), a Hebrew poet of Spain. It too was modeled upon the Indian Bidpai fables, and, like a zoological park, abounded in lions, tigers, leopards and foxes. Zabara endowed his cunning psychological fox with all the male cynicism about women that was so fashionable during the Middle Ages among the sophisticated upper classes, Arabic, Christian, and Jewish alike. *The Book of Delight,* in more than one way, is a rare item in Thirteenth Century European folklore. Of the original narrative design employed by Zabara in binding together the series of fables reproduced in this section, *The Fox and the Leopard*, the Anglo-Jewish scholar, Israel Abrahams, has observed: "Here, in Zabara, we have an earlier instance than was previously known in Europe, of an intertwined series of fables and witticisms, partly Indian, partly Greek, partly Semitic in origin, welded together by the Hebrew poet by means of a framework." (*Book of Delight*, p. 26.)

N. A.

The Fate of the Wicked
(A Fable by Rabbi Meir)

ONCE a fox said to a wolf, "If you want to enjoy a good meal, take my advice: enter the courtyard of any Jew on Friday and help him in his preparations for the Sabbath. Rest assured that he will reward you for this by asking you to partake of the Sabbath feast."

The wolf was enchanted with the sage advice of the fox and decided to follow it.

THE FATE OF THE WICKED: Adapted from the *Agada* of the Talmud.

But no sooner did he show his face in the courtyard of a Jew than the entire household fell upon him with sticks and trounced him so soundly that he barely managed to escape with his life.

Full of wrath the wolf went in search of the fox, and when he found him he wanted to tear him limb from limb. The fox tried to mollify him.

"Don't carry on so," he told him. "I'm not to blame because they beat you. Blame your father instead! Pay attention to what I'm going to tell you now.

"Once a Jew asked your father to help him in his preparations for the Sabbath, and for that he promised to invite him to the feast. But your father had no patience and devoured all the delicious courses and did not leave the Jew even one little chicken bone.

"Now, can you understand why the Jew beat you? But don't lose heart! Leave it to me. I'll lead you to a house where both of us can have our fill of a delicious feast."

The wolf gratefully agreed.

The fox then led the wolf to a well over which hung two buckets suspended from ropes. When one bucket went down the other one came up. The fox climbed into one bucket and quickly descended to the bottom of the well.

"What are you doing there?" asked the curious wolf from above.

"My! You've never seen anything like it!" the fox cried out with rapture. "I've found here meat and cheese and other good things to eat! Just look down—don't you see what a great big cheese is down here?"

The wolf looked down and, sure enough, saw the reflection of the moon mirrored in the water. But he believed that it was a cheese as the fox had told him.

His appetite whetted, the wolf could hardly control himself any longer. "How can I get down?" he called to the fox.

"Very simply," said the fox, "get into the other bucket and join me."

The wolf climbed into the bucket with alacrity. But no sooner was he in than the weight of his body pulled him down to the bottom of the well, and at the same time pulled up the other bucket carrying the fox who jumped nimbly out.

Terror seized the wolf when he saw what had happened.

"How will I get up again?" he cried to the fox.

The fox merely answered him with the saying from the Book of Proverbs:

> "The righteous is delivered out of trouble.
> And the wicked cometh in his stead."

The Advantage of Being a Scholar

A FOX looked up into a tree and saw a crow sitting on the topmost branch. The crow looked mighty good to him, for he was hungry. He tried every wile to get him down but the wise old crow only leered contemptuously down at him.

"Foolish crow!" the fox said, banteringly. "Believe me, you have no reason to be afraid of me. Don't you know that the birds and the beasts will never have to fight again? Haven't you heard the Messiah is coming! If you were a Talmud scholar like me you'd surely know that the Prophet Isaiah has said that when the Messiah comes 'the lion shall lie down with the lamb and the fox with the crow and there shall be peace forevermore.' "

And as he stood thus speaking sweetly, the baying of hounds was heard. The fox began to tremble with fright and started to run for his life.

"Foolish fox," croaked the crow pleasantly from the tree. "You have no reason to be afraid since you're a Talmud scholar and know what the Prophet Isaiah has said."

"True, *I* know what the Prophet Isaiah said," cried the fox as he slunk into the bushes, "but you see—the trouble is the dogs don't!"

King Leviathan and the Charitable Boy

IN A certain town there lived a man who brought up his son in the ways of righteousness. Daily he repeated to him the commandment: "Cast thy bread upon the waters; perhaps it will be returned to you a hundredfold some day."

And it came to pass that this man was gathered to his forefathers. Then the boy recalled what his father had taught him. Each day he would go to the edge of the sea and cast a piece of his bread into the water. And, on the spot where it fell, a fish appeared and swallowed it. From that day on, whenever the boy came to cast his bread into the water, the same fish waited for him. In time the fish became so big and strong that he began to tyrannize over all the other fish around him, so that they feared for their very lives.

In terror they assembled and went to complain to King Leviathan. "Lord," they said, "among us in the sea there is a fish who has become so big and powerful that we no longer feel safe with him. A day does not pass when he does not devour at least twenty of us."

When King Leviathan heard this he was filled with wrath. "Bring the culprit before me!" he commanded. And he sent a messenger to summon him. But, when the fish heard King Leviathan's request, he laughed and devoured the messenger. Seeing that the messenger did not return, Leviathan sent another one after him. But he too met with the same fate.

Enraged, Leviathan cried: "I myself will go after this criminal!" And, when he found him, Leviathan asked him: "How does it happen that there are so many fish in the sea and yet no one is as big as you?"

KING LEVIATHAN AND THE CHARITABLE BOY: From *The Alphabet of Ben Sira*. Adapted from the German translation *Vom Levjathan* in *Der Born Judas*, compiled by M. J. bin Gorion. Insel-Verlag. Leipzig, 1919.

"You speak truly," replied the fish. "The secret of my strength lies in that daily a boy appears on the shore and throws bread to me. And I grow even stronger because every morning I devour twenty fish and at night, thirty."

"Why do you eat your own kind?" demanded Leviathan sternly.

"Can I help it if they come near me and thus tempt me?" answered the fish.

Thereupon, Leviathan grew impatient with the fish and commanded: "Begone! Bring to me the boy that feeds you!"

"I will bring him to you tomorrow," the fish replied. He then swam to the spot on the strand of the sea where the boy came daily to feed him and he dug a hole on that spot and covered it with seaweed.

When the boy came the following day and stepped onto his accustomed place he fell into the sea, and the fish swallowed him and swam swiftly to King Leviathan.

"Spit out the boy!" commanded Leviathan. The fish then spat him out and into Leviathan's mouth.

"My son," demanded Leviathan of the boy, "why do you throw your bread into the water?"

The boy replied, "O King, my father taught me to do so ever since I was little."

Hearing him speak thus King Leviathan rejoiced. He spat him out and he kissed him fondly. Then, because he found him worthy, he taught him all the seventy languages of mankind. He also studied Torah with him and made a great scholar of him.

Having taught him all he knew he then cast him three hundred miles onto the land. When the boy arose he found himself at a spot on which no human foot had ever trod. Feeling very tired, he lay down to rest. Suddenly he saw two ravens flying overhead and, having been taught by Leviathan the language of the birds, he understood what the two birds were saying.

He heard the younger bird say, "Father, just look at that boy below on the ground. Do you think he is dead or alive?"

"That I do not know, my son," replied the raven.

"How I long to eat human eyes!" exclaimed the young raven. "I'm going to swoop down on the boy and peck out his eyes!"

"Do not do so, my son," his parent warned him. "Should the boy be alive you might yet meet with misfortune."

But, being heedless, the young raven disobeyed his father and swooped down on the boy who had overheard all that was said and was feigning to be asleep. No sooner did the young raven alight on his forehead when the boy seized his legs and held him tight in his grasp.

"Father! Father!" shrilled the little raven. "Come and help me!"

And when his father saw his plight to lament: "Woe to my son!" And to the boy he called out: "Boy, let my child go! If you understand my language, heed me! I promise to reward you if you will show mercy. Know that upon the very spot upon which you lie is buried the vanished treasure of Solomon, King of Israel."

The boy then let the bird go free. He dug in the ground on that spot. He knew that the raven had spoken truly, for he found there King Solomon's treasure which consisted of priceless pearls and gems. And so he became rich and, when he died, he left his children untold wealth.

The son of Sira had this boy in mind when he wrote: "Break thy bread for the hungry, and share your repast with all who wish to partake of it."

The Sly Fox

A SICK lion who had not eaten for a long time acquired a bad breath. In the forest he met an ass.

"Does my breath smell badly?" he asked him.

"It does," replied the simple-minded ass.

"How dare a common creature like you insult me, the King of the Beasts!" roared the lion, and forthwith he devoured the ass.

A while later he met a bear.

"Does my breath smell badly?" the lion asked him.

"Oh no!" exclaimed the bear. "Your breath is sweeter than honey."

"Flatterer!" roared the lion. "How dare you deceive me?"

And he devoured the bear, too.

At last he met a fox.

"Smell me, my friend," asked the lion, "and tell me whether my breath is sweet."

Now the sly fox saw the pitfall and was wary.

"Pardon me, O King of the Forest," said the fox most politely, "for I cannot smell at all! I have a bad cold."

The Price of Envy

WHILE a poor woman stood in the market-place selling cheeses, a cat came along and carried off a cheese. A dog saw the pilferer and tried to take the cheese away from him. The cat stood up to the dog. So they pitched into each other. The dog barked and snapped; the cat spat and scratched, but they could bring the battle to no decision.

"Let's go to the fox and have him referee the matter," the cat finally suggested.

"Agreed," said the dog.

So they went to the fox.

The fox listened to their arguments with a judicious air.

"Foolish animals," he chided them, "why carry on like that? If both

---

THE SLY FOX. Adapted from the *Midrash*.

of you are willing, I'll divide the cheese in two and you'll both be satisfied."

"Agreed," said the cat and the dog.

So the fox took out his knife and cut the cheese in two, but, instead of cutting it lengthwise, he cut it in the width.

"My half is smaller!" protested the dog.

The fox looked judiciously through his spectacles at the dog's share. "You're right, quite right!" he decided.

So he went and bit off a piece of the cat's share.

"That will make it even!" he said.

When the cat saw what the fox did she began to yowl:

"Just look! My part's smaller now!"

The fox again put on his spectacles and looked judiciously at the cat's share.

"Right you are!" said the fox. "Just a moment, and I'll make it right." And he went and bit off a piece from the dog's cheese.

This went on so long, with the fox nibbling first at the dog's and then at the cat's share, that he finally ate up the whole cheese before their eyes.

Know Your Enemy

A YOUNG inexperienced mouse went out to forage for food. Before he started out his wise old granddaddy cautioned him, "Watch out, dear child, for our enemies!"

The young mouse promised faithfully to do so and then dashed out into the barnyard.

The first one he met was a rooster who stretched out his wings and, looking fierce, cried out in a terrible voice, "Cock-a-doodle-do!"

Scared out of his wits, the little mouse scurried back into his hole.

"Grandpa, Grandpa!" he gasped breathlessly. "I've just met a terrible creature with a comb red as blood. When he saw me he threw back his head and screamed at me!"

Grandpa Mouse smiled indulgently and said, "Foolish child! This is no enemy of ours! This was a rooster who crowed. You have nothing to fear from him!"

Taking heart the little mouse went out again and the first one he met was a turkey. He got so frightened when he looked at him that pell-mell he ran back into the mouse-hole.

"Oh Grandpa!" he cried, trembling with fright. "I just saw a horrible black creature. He had yellow legs, a sharp beak and angry red eyes. When he saw me he shook his head fiercely and cried, 'Gobble, gobble!'"

Grandpa Mouse smiled indulgently.

"Foolish child!" he chided. "He isn't our enemy—he's only a turkey! You will be able to recognize our enemy by the humble way he carries himself. He keeps his head down and has beautiful golden eyes. His fur is smooth and he purrs ever so gently. When you meet *him*—run for your life!"

The Wise Bird and the Foolish Man

A BIRD-CATCHER once caught a bird. But it was an extraordinary creature that understood all the seventy languages of mankind. She therefore pleaded with her captor in his own tongue: "Set me free, and I will impart to you three useful teachings."

"Tell them to me first. Then I will release you," said the bird-catcher.

"First give me your solemn oath that you will keep your word," answered the bird.

"I swear to set you free," replied the man.

The bird then spoke: "Pay heed then! The first teaching is: 'Never regret what has already happened.' The second teaching is: 'Don't believe the incredible.' The third teaching is: 'Never try to achieve the unattainable.' "

Having taught the man her wisdom the bird pleaded: "Set me free now, as you promised."

And the bird-catcher agreed and set her free.

At that, the bird spread her wings and flew to the top of a high tree nearby and from there she mocked at the man below: "Fool that you are! You let me out of your grasp not knowing that I carry in my body a priceless pearl through whose magic power I have become wise."

When the bird-catcher heard this he regretted the folly that had led him to release the bird. To retrieve his loss he began to climb the tree upon which the bird was perched. But barely had he reached half-way when he lost his hold and fell to the ground. There he lay with broken bones, moaning with pain.

The bird looked down upon him and laughed. "You stupid fool!" she chided him. "But a few moments have passed since I imparted to you my wisdom and already you have forgotten it! I told you never to regret anything that has happened, and almost immediately you regretted giving me my freedom. I taught you not to believe the incredible and, nevertheless, you accepted as truth my fairytale that I carry in my body a wonder-working pearl. Know that I am nothing but a common bird who has to forage for her nourishment from hour to hour! Lastly, I cautioned you against trying to achieve the unattainable and, nonetheless, you undertook to capture a bird on the wing with your bare hands. Because you did not heed me you now lie broken and bleeding. About such as you is the proverb: 'A reproof entereth more into a wise man than an hundred stripes into a fool.' There are, unfortunately, many simpletons like you among men!"

THE WISE BIRD AND THE FOOLISH MAN: Adapted from the German translation *Drei Lehren* in *Der Born Judas*, compiled by M. J. bin Gorion. Insel-Verlag. Leipzig, 1919.

A striking, similarity to *The Wise Bird and the Foolish Man* related above is to be found in the *Gesta Romanorum*, No. 167.—N. A.

The Fox and the Foolish Fishes

THE Holy One said to the Angel of Death: "Cast a pair of each species into the sea, and then thou shalt have dominion over all that remain of the species."

The Angel did so forthwith, and he cast a pair of each kind into the sea.

When the fox saw what he was about, what did he do? At once he stood and wept. Then said the Angel of Death unto him: "Why weepest thou?"

"For my companions, whom thou hast cast into the sea," answered the fox.

"Where, then, are thy companions?" said the Angel.

The fox ran to the sea-shore, and the Angel of Death beheld the reflection of the fox in the water, and he thought that he had already cast in a pair of foxes, so, addressing the fox by his side, he cried: "Be off with you!"

The fox at once fled and escaped.

The weasel met him, and the fox related what had happened, and what he had done. And so the weasel went and did likewise.

At the end of the year, the Leviathan assembled all the creatures in the sea, and lo! the fox and the weasel were missing, for they had not come into the sea. He sent to ask, and he was told how the fox and the weasel had escaped through their wisdom. They taunted the Leviathan, saying: "The fox is exceedingly cunning."

The Leviathan felt uneasy and envious, and he sent a deputation of great fishes, with the order that they were to deceive the fox, and bring him before him.

They went, and found him by the sea-shore. When the fox saw the fishes disporting themselves near the bank, he was surprised, and he went among them. They beheld him, and asked: "Who art thou?"

"I am the fox," said he.

"Knowest thou not," continued the fishes, "that a great honor is in store for thee, and that we have come here on thy behalf?"

"What is it?" asked the fox.

"The Leviathan," they said, "is sick and likely to die. He has appointed thee to reign in his stead, for he has heard that thou art wiser and more prudent than all other animals. Come with us, for we are his messengers, and are here in thy honor."

"But," objected the fox, "how can I come into the sea without being drowned?"

"Nay," said the fishes, "ride upon one of us, and he will carry thee above the sea, so that not even a drop of water shall touch so much as the soles

THE FOX AND THE FOOLISH FISHES: From the *Alphabet* of (pseudo) Ben Sira (7th or 8th century A.D.). Reprinted from *The Book of Delight*, edited by Israel Abrahams. With the permission of the copyright owners, The Jewish Publication Society of America. Philadelphia, 1912.

of thy feet, until thou reachest the kingdom. We will take thee down without thy knowing it. Come with us, and reign over us, and be king, and be joyful all thy days. No more wilt thou need to seek for food, nor will wild beasts, stronger than thou, meet thee and devour thee."

The fox heard and believed their words. He rode upon one of them, and they went with him into the sea. Soon, however, the waves dashed over him, and he began to perceive that he had been tricked.

"Woe is me!" wailed the fox. "What have I done? I have played many a trick on others, but these fishes have played one on me worth all mine put together. Now that I have fallen into their hands, how shall I free myself? Indeed," he said, turning to the fishes, "now that I am fully in your power, I shall speak the truth. What are you going to do with me?"

"To tell thee the truth," replied the fishes, "the Leviathan has heard thy fame, that thou art very wise, and he said, I will rend the fox, and will eat his heart, and thus I shall become wise."

"Oh!" said the fox. "Why did you not tell me the truth at first? I should then have brought my heart with me, and I should have given it to King Leviathan, and he would have honored me; but now ye are in an evil plight."

"What! Thou hast not thy heart with thee?"

"Certainly not. It is our custom to leave our heart at home while we go about from place to place. When we need our heart, we take it; otherwise it remains at home."

"What must we do?" asked the bewildered fishes.

"My house and dwelling-place," replied the fox, "are by the sea-shore. If you like, carry me back to the place whence you brought me, I will fetch my heart, and will come again with you. I will present my heart to Leviathan, and he will reward me and you with honors. But if you take me thus, without my heart, he will be wroth with you, and will devour you. I have no fear for myself, for I shall say unto him: 'My lord, they did not tell me at first, and when they did tell me, I begged them to return for my heart, but they refused.'"

The fishes at once declared that he was speaking well. They conveyed him back to the spot on the sea-shore whence they had taken him.

Off jumped the fox, and he danced with joy. He threw himself on the sand, and laughed.

"Be quick," cried the fishes, "get thy heart, and come."

But the fox answered: "You fools! Begone! How could I have come with you without my heart? Have you any animals that go about without their hearts?"

"Thou hast tricked us!" they moaned.

"Fools! I tricked the Angel of Death, how much more easily a parcel of silly fishes."

The fish returned in shame, and related to their master what had happened.

"In truth," he said, "the fox is cunning, and ye are simple. Concerning

you was it said: 'The turning away of the simple shall slay them'."
(Prov. I: 32)

Then the Leviathan ate the fishes.

The Proper Place for a Tail

A SNAKE went slithering down the road.

"How long will you insist on leading while I drag behind you!" cried the tail to the head. "Why shouldn't we change places for once? Let me lead now and you follow."

"Very well," agreed the head. "You go first."

So the tail began to lead and the head trailed after.

At last they came to a pit filled with water and the tail, not having any eyes, slid right into the pit, dragging the head down with it. It fell among sharp thorns and hurt itself as well as the head.

Now, I ask, who was to blame?

Didn't it serve the head right for being so weak that it allowed itself to be led by a brainless tail?

The Curse of the Indolent

A HEATHEN farmer had a pig, a she-ass, and a little ass. He fed the pig a great deal, but the she-ass and her child were fed in limited measure.

"What a foolish man our master is!" said the little ass to his mother. "Don't you think it is unjust, mother, that we who work for him and pull his burdens should be fed so poorly? Why is it that pig who is lazy all day long and does nothing eats as much as she wants?"

"Just wait a while, my child," the she-ass comforted him. "A time is sure to come when you will see the pig in great misfortune. Know that the farmer is not stuffing her with fine food out of love for her but only to hasten her grief."

When the heathen celebrated the next feast day he slaughtered his pig. Ever after, whenever the little ass was given food he ate sparingly, remembering the sad fate of the pig.

When his mother saw this she tried to correct him: "It isn't eating a lot that brings death, my child, but going about the livelong day like the pig doing nothing!"

THE PROPER PLACE FOR A TAIL: Adapted from the *Midrash.*

THE CURSE OF THE INDOLENT: *Ibid.*

The Fox and the Leopard

A LEOPARD once lived in content and plenty; ever he found easy sustenance for his wife and children. Hard by there dwelt his neighbor and friend, the fox. The fox felt in his heart that his life was safe only as long as the leopard could catch other prey, and he planned out a method for ridding himself of this dangerous friendship. Before the evil cometh, say the wise, counsel is good.

"Let me get him out of the way," thought the fox. "I will lead him into the path of death, for the sages say: 'If one come to slay thee, be beforehand with him, and slay him instead.'"

Next day the fox went to the leopard, and told him of a spot he had seen, a spot of gardens and lilies, where fawns and does disported themselves, and everything was fair. The leopard went with him to behold this paradise, and rejoiced with exceeding joy.

"Ah," thought the fox, "many a smile ends in a tear."

But the leopard was charmed, and wished to move to this delightful abode.

"But first," said he, "I will go to consult my wife, my lifelong comrade, the bride of my youth."

The fox was sadly disconcerted. Full well he knew the wisdom and the craft of the leopard's wife.

"Nay," said he, "trust not thy wife. A woman's counsel is evil and foolish, her heart hard like marble; she is a plague in the house. Yes, ask her advice and do the opposite."

The leopard told his wife that he was resolved to go.

"Beware of the fox!" she exclaimed. "Two small animals there are, the craftiest they, by far—the serpent and the fox. Hast thou not heard how the fox bound the lion and slew him with cunning?"

"How did the fox dare," asked the leopard, "to come near enough to the lion to do it?"

(The leopard's wife then takes up the parable, and cites the following incident:)

The lion loved the fox, but the fox had no faith in him, and plotted his death. One day the fox went to the lion whining that a pain had seized him in the head.

"I have heard," said the fox, "that physicians prescribe for a headache, that the patient shall be tied up hand and foot."

The lion assented, and bound up the fox with a cord.

"Ah," blithely said the fox, "my pain is gone."

THE FOX AND THE LEOPARD: From *The Book of Delight*, by Joseph Zabara (circa 1200 A.D.). Translation by Israel Abrahams. With the permission of the copyright owners, The Jewish Publication Society of America. Philadelphia, 1912.

Then the lion loosed him. Time passed and the lion's turn came to suffer in his head. In sore distress he went to the fox, fast as a bird to the snare, and exclaimed, "Bind me up, brother, that I, too, may be healed, as happened with thee."

The fox took fresh withes, and bound the lion up. Then he went to fetch great stones, which he cast on the lion's head, and thus crushed him.

"Therefore, my dear leopard," concluded his wife, "trust not the fox, for I fear him and his wiles. If the place he tells of be so fair, why does not the fox take it for himself?"

"Nay," said the leopard, "thou art a silly prattler. I have often proved my friend, and there is no dross in the silver of his love."

(The leopard would not hearken to his wife's advice, yet he was somewhat moved by her warning, and he told the fox of his misgiving, adding that his wife refused to accompany him. "Ah," replied the fox, "I fear your fate will be like the silversmith's; let me tell you his story, and you will know how silly it is to listen to a wife's counsel.")

A silversmith of Babylon, skillful in his craft, was one day at work.

"Listen to me," said his wife, "and I will make thee rich and honored. Our lord, the king, has an only daughter, and he loves her as his life. Fashion for her a silver image of herself, and I will bear it to her as a gift."

The statue was soon made, and the princess rejoiced at seeing it. She gave a cloak and earrings to the artist's wife, who showed them to her husband in triumph.

"But where is the wealth and the honor?" he asked. "The statue was worth much more than thou hast brought."

Next day the king saw the statue in his daughter's hand, and his anger was kindled.

"Is it not ordered," he cried, "that none should make an image? Cut off his right hand."

The king's command was carried out, and daily the smith wept, and exclaimed, "Take warning from me, ye husbands, and obey not the voice of your wives."

(The leopard shuddered when he heard this tale; but the fox went on:)

A hewer of wood in Damascus was cutting logs and his wife sat spinning by his side.

"My departed father," she said, "was a better workman than thou. He could chop with both hands: when the right hand was tired, he used the left."

"Nay," said he, "no woodcutter does that, he uses the right hand, unless he be a left-handed man."

"Ah, my dear," she entreated, "try and do it as my father did."

The witless wight raised his left hand to hew the wood, but struck his right-hand thumb instead. Without a word he took the axe and smote his wife on the head, and she died.

His deed was noised about; the woodcutter was seized and stoned for his crimes.

"Therefore," continued the fox, "I say unto thee, all women are deceivers and trappers of souls. And let me tell you more of these wily stratagems."

(The fox reinforces his argument with the following tale:)

A king of the Arabs, wise and well-advised, was one day seated with his counsellors, who were loud in the praise of women, lauding their virtues and their wisdom.

"Cut short these words," said the king. "Never since the world began has there been a good woman. They love for their own ends."

"But," pleaded his sages, "O King, thou art hasty. Women there are, wise and faithful and spotless, who love their husbands and tend their children."

"Then," said the king, "here is my city before you: search it through, and find one of the good women of whom you speak."

They sought, and they found a woman, chaste and wise, fair as the moon and bright as the sun, the wife of a wealthy trader; and the counsellors reported about her to the king. He sent for her husband, and received him with favor.

"I have something for thy ear," said the king. "I have a good and desirable daughter: she is my only child; I will not give her to a king or a prince: let me find a simple, faithful man, who will love her and hold her in esteem. Thou art such a one; thou shalt have her. But thou art married: slay thy wife tonight, and tomorrow thou shalt wed my daughter."

"I am unworthy," pleaded the man, "to be the shepherd of thy flock, much less the husband of thy daughter."

But the king would take no denial.

"But how shall I kill my wife? For fifteen years she has eaten of my bread and drunk of my cup. She is the joy of my heart; her love and esteem grow day by day."

"Slay her," said the king, "and be king hereafter."

The man went forth from the presence, downcast and sad, thinking over, and a little shaken by, the king's temptation. At home he saw his wife and his two babes.

"Better," he cried, "is my wife than a kingdom! Cursed be all kings who tempt men to sip sorrow, calling it joy."

The king waited his coming in vain; and then he sent messengers to the man's shop. When he found that the man's love had conquered his lust, he said, with a sneer, "Thou art no man; thy heart is a woman's."

In the evening the king summoned the woman secretly. She came, and the king praised her beauty and her wisdom. His heart, he said, was burning with love for her, but he could not wed another man's wife.

"Slay thy husband tonight," he said, "and tomorrow be my queen."

With a smile, the woman consented; and the king gave her a sword made of tin, for he knew the weak mind of woman.

"Strike once," he said to her. "The sword is sharp; you need not essay a second blow."

She gave her husband a choice repast, and wine to make him drunken. As he lay asleep, she grasped the sword and struck him on the head; and the tin bent, and he awoke. With some ado she quieted him, and he fell asleep again.

Next morning the king summoned her, and asked whether she had obeyed his orders.

"Yes," said she, "but thou didst frustrate thine own counsel."

Then the king assembled his sages, and bade her tell all that she had attempted; and the husband, too, was fetched, to tell his story.

"Did I not tell you to cease your praises of women?" asked the king triumphantly.

("So much," said the fox to the leopard, "I have told thee that thou mayest know how little women are to be trusted. They deceive men in life, and betray them in death."

"But," queried the leopard, "what could my wife do to harm me after I am dead?"

"Listen," rejoined the fox, "and I will tell thee of a deed viler than any I have narrated hitherto.")

The kings of Rome, when they hanged a man, denied him burial until the tenth day. That the friends and relatives of the victim might not steal the body, an officer of high rank was set to watch the tree by night. If the body was stolen, the officer was hung up in its place.

A knight of high degree once rebelled against the king, and he was hanged on a tree. The officer on guard was startled at midnight to hear a piercing shriek of anguish from a little distance; he mounted his horse, and rode towards the voice, to discover the meaning. He came to an open grave, where the common people were buried, and saw a weeping woman loud in laments for her departed spouse. He sent her home with words of comfort, accompanying her to the city gate. He then returned to his post.

Next night the same scene was repeated, and as the officer spoke his gentle soothings to her, a love for him was born in her heart, and her dead husband was forgotten. And as they spoke words of love, they neared the tree, and lo! the body that the officer was set to watch was gone.

"Begone," he said, "and I will fly, or my life must pay the penalty of my dalliance."

"Fear not, my lord," she said, "we can raise my husband from his grave and hang him instead of the stolen corpse."

"But I fear the Prince of Death. I cannot drag a man from his grave!" he cried.

"I alone will do it then," said the woman. "I will dig him out; it is lawful to cast a dead man from the grave, to keep a live man from being thrown in."

"Alas!" cried the officer, when she had done the fearsome deed, "the corpse I watched was bald, your husband has thick hair; the change will be detected."

"Nay," said the woman, "I will make him bald!"

And she tore his hair out, with execrations, and they hung him on the tree. But a few days passed and the pair were married.

(The fox reaches the end of his persuasion.)

The leopard's bones rattled while he listened to this tale. Angrily he addressed his wife:

"Come, get up and follow me, or I will slay thee."

Together they went with their young ones, and the fox was their guide and they reached the promised place, and encamped by the waters. The fox bade them farewell, his head laughing at his tail.

Seven days were gone, when the rains descended, and in the deep of the night the river rose and engulfed the leopard family in their beds.

"Woe is me," sighed the leopard, "that I did not listen to my wife!"

And he died before his time.

PART FIVE

Proverbs and Riddles

Proverbs and Folk-Sayings

He is the right sort of pepper.

When the cat wears gloves she can't catch any mice.

The whiskey weeps out of the drunkard.

A daughter-in-law is always a bit of a mother-in-law.

If they give you—take; if they take from you—yell!

A lie one mustn't say—some truths you shouldn't say.

If grandma had wheels she'd be a wagon.

He's got to learn how to shave another's beard.

He crawls with a healthy head into a sick-bed.

Because he is angry at the cantor he doesn't say *"Amen!"*

If you look for *chaleh* you lose the black bread.

He's such a thief, he'll steal the crack of your whip if you don't look out!

If you deal in honey you have a chance for a lick.

When it falls it falls buttered side down.

The masses are no asses.

You must never show half-completed work to a fool.

Too great a modesty is half conceit.

If they say dead—you're buried.

A *Litvak* is so clever he repents even before he commits a sin.

The worst informer is the face.

You rebuke your daughter but mean your daughter-in-law.

Charge nothing and you'll get a lot of customers.

Don't spit into the well—you might drink from it later.

Jews are very charitable; when you say "good morning," they answer: "good year."

Somehow there's always money for *matzos* and shrouds.

A boil is no trouble—under the other fellow's armpit.

Cancer—shmancer! as long as you're healthy.

Weep before God—laugh before people.

You can never fill a sack full of holes.

If a jug fall on a stone—woe to the jug! If a stone fall on the jug—woe to the jug!

Silence is the fence around wisdom.

Attend no auctions if you have no money.

Do not worry about tomorrow, because you do not even know what may happen to you today.

He who drinks much water after meals will never suffer from stomach trouble.

The laziest man is he who does not seek to acquire friends; still lazier is the one who loses friends because he makes no effort to keep them.

The sun will set without your assistance.

Your friend has a friend, and your friend's friend has a friend; be discreet.

A dream which has not been interpreted is like a letter unread.

Approach the perfumer and you will be perfumed.

If the arrow-maker is killed by his arrow, he is paid out of his own work.

In a field where there are mounds, talk no secrets.

If one person tells you that you have ass's ears, take no notice; should two tell you so, procure a saddle for yourself.

Whatever you have to your discredit, be the first to tell it.

Had you gotten up early, you would not have needed to stay up late.

The heart and the eye are the agents of sin.

When the kettle boils over, it overflows its own sides.

Should the castle totter, its name is still castle; should the dunghill be raised, its name is still dunghill.

In whom wisdom is, in him is everything; in whom it is not, what has he? He who has acquired it, what does he lack? In whom it is not, what has he acquired?

You can't chew with somebody's else's teeth.

The luck of an ignoramus is that he doesn't know that he doesn't know.

House-guests and fish spoil on the third day.

A human being learns how to speak early, but to keep silent—late.

The one who is incapable of love must learn how to flatter.

The slanderer never wants to tell the truth, but there may be some truth in his slander.

A man is no angel, yet he is fully capable of becoming The Angel of Death.

Be a disciple of Aaron; a lover of peace, and a promoter thereof.

He that uses the crown of learning as an instrument of gain, will perish.

Strip a carcass of its hide, even in the marketplace, rather than have recourse to beg. Say not: "I am a priest . . . I am the son of a great man —how can I condescend to such low employment?" Degrading as these may appear, it is still more so to hold your hand out for charity.

Glorious labor! It both warms and nourishes those that are engaged in it.

The highest wisdom is kindness.

He who acquires knowledge without imparting it to others, is like a flower in the desert where there is no one to enjoy it.

When a thief has no opportunity for stealing he considers himself an honest man.

He who devotes himself to the mere study of religion without engaging in works of love and mercy is like one who has no God.

The deeper the sorrow the less tongue it has.

Shrouds have no pockets.

Enemies cannot do a man the harm that he does himself.

Whether a person be Jew or Gentile. . . . according to his acts does the Divine Spirit rest upon him.

To cheat a Gentile is even worse than cheating a Jew, for besides being a violation of the moral law, it brings Israel into contempt and desecrates the name of Israel's God.

When trouble comes in the world Israel feels it first; when good fortune comes into the world Israel feels it last.

As everyone treads on dust, so every nation treads on Israel, and as dust outlasts metal, so shall Israel outlast its oppressors.

One fool makes many fools.

Sell the Holy Scrolls in the synagogue to give a poor girl a dowry.

Were the eyes not to see the hands would not take.

The whole world is one town.

Whatever one desires most one dreams about.

What is the use of good wine in a rotten barrel?

He who flatters you is your enemy—who rebukes you is your friend.

If you spit upwards you're bound to get it back in the face.

Drive your horse with oats—not with a whip.

If you can't afford chicken, herring will do.

If we didn't have to eat we'd all be rich.

An insincere peace is better than a sincere war.

All things grow with time except grief.

Do not swallow poison because you know an antidote.

An awl can't stay lost in a sack; the point will come out today or tomorrow.

Where there is too much, something is missing.

A half-truth is a whole lie.

One has no appetite for eating . . . the other has no eating for his appetite.

An ox has a long tongue, and yet cannot blow the *shofar*.

You can't get two skins off an ox.

To get in is always easier than to get out.

Poverty is no disgrace—but it's no great honor, either.

When is a pauper miserable? When he's invited to two weddings in one day!

At the baths, all are equal.

Lend a man money, and you buy yourself an enemy.

On someone else's beard it's good to practice barbering.

For *borsht* you don't need any teeth.

If you examine carefully enough, everything is *tref*.

Resent something, and your belly hurts.

The child of old parents is a ready-made orphan.

When a rogue kisses you, count your teeth.

If the housewife is worthless, the cat is industrious.

Better a good neighbor, than a bad relative.

Better a Jew without a beard, than a beard without a Jew.

Better to ask the way ten times, than to go astray once.

Better to suffer an injustice, than to do an injustice.

Better an honest slap, than a false kiss.

Call me "bear"; just don't chase me into the woods.

Brandy is a bad messenger: you send him into your belly, and he creeps into your head!

An angry man sleeps alone.

For bread you can always find a knife.

You can get drowned close to shore, too.

If there's a fire at your neighbor's you, too, are in danger.

Good news is heard from afar.

If God wills it, a broom can also shoot.

If God lived on earth, people would break His windows.

God is a father; luck is a stepfather.

God sends the cure before the affliction.

From a goose you can't buy any oats.

Everywhere it's good, and at home it's even better.

It's not as good with money, as it is bad without it.

Good is long remembered; bad even longer.

The tavern will not corrupt a good man, nor will the House of Study straighten out a bad one.

Long as the Jewish Exile.

From fortune to misfortune is just a span, but from misfortune to fortune is quite a distance.

For luck you don't need any wisdom.

Not the mouse is the thief; only the hole.

Never mention rope in the house of a man who has been hanged.

Where they like you, go infrequently; where they hate you, don't go at all.

Promising and liking cost no money.

"Lots of property, lots of headaches . . ."—but no property at all, that's even a greater headache.

Someone else's worries don't take away your sleep.

To a doctor and a surgeon you mustn't wish a good year.

If a man is destined to drown, he will drown in a spoonful of water.

One has no intent to give:
the other hasn't a cent to give.

You have? Hold! You know? Be silent! You can? Do!

What one has, he wants not; and what one wants, he has not.

If you have no hand, you can't make a fist.

When the heart is full, the eyes overflow.

The hat's all right, but the head's too small.

Whoever lies down to sleep with a dog, gets up with fleas.

To a beaten dog it is not permitted to show a stick.

Sit at home, and you won't tear your shoes.

If you can't help your friend with money, at least help him with a sympathetic groan.

It helps, the way cupping helps a corpse.

The wagon rests in winter; the sleigh rests in summer; the horse—never.

What is cheap, is dear.

A wolf loses his hair, but not his nature.

Better one word before, than two after.

Words should be weighed, not counted.

If his word were a bridge, I'd be afraid to cross.

A wife sets you on your feet, or knocks you off them.

With weeping you pay no debts.

If things aren't the way you like, you've got to like them the way they are.

What three know is no secret.

The greatest pain is the one you can't tell others about.

What he says he doesn't mean and what he means he doesn't say.

When a son gets married, he gives his bride a contract and his mother a divorce.

A clock that doesn't go at all, is better than one that goes wrong.

Don't be too sweet, or you'll be eaten up; too bitter, or you'll be spat out!

A lot of singing, and too few noodles!

What good can a lamp and spectacles be,
when a man just doesn't want to see?

A wise man eats to live; a fool lives to eat.

Neither wisdom nor prayer will help when the cards aren't running.

With wisdom alone one doesn't go to market.

A dream is half a prophet.

They don't flatter the rich—just his money!

Roast pigeons don't fly into your mouth.

A drowning man will grab even for the point of a sword.

All brides are beautiful; all the dead are pious.

Anger is a fool.

More lovely is an ugly patch than a beautiful hole.

Not that which is beautiful is loved, but rather that is beautiful which is
loved.

A liar believes no one.

A liar must have a good memory.

When the girl doesn't know how to dance, she says the musicians don't
know how to play.

A homely girl hates mirrors.

One has fear in front of a goat, in back of a mule, and on every side of a
fool.

If luck is with you, even your ox will give birth to a calf.

When the miller fights with the chimneysweep, the miller turns black and
the 'sweep turns white.

God gave man two ears and one mouth so he might hear much and say little.

Every man has his own insanity.

A fool throws a stone into the brook, and ten wise men can't recover it.

When a fool is silent, he, too, is counted among the wise.

The rich man's foolishness is more admired than the pauper's wisdom.

If you could hang on a wall all the world's bags of woe, everyone would
grab for his own.

Troubles are to men what rust is to iron.

A joke is a half-truth.

If you cook with straw,
your food stays raw.

What's the good of a good head, if the feet can't carry it?

When a miser becomes extravagant, he eats borscht with honeycake.

Whoever is a child at 20, stays a fool till 100.

The wise man conceals his intelligence; the fool displays his foolishness.

If the storekeeper doesn't figure out his accounts, his accounts will figure him out.

Rich relations are close relations; poor relations are distant relations.

If one can crawl well, he crawls up on top.

Nine rabbis can't make a *minyan*, but ten cobblers, yes.

For dying, you always have time.

One gets out of the way of a drunk, a fool, and a load of hay.

One who has the reputation of an early riser may safely lie abed till noon.

You can't dance at two weddings at the same time; nor can you sit on two horses with one behind.

Too good is unhealthy.

〖2〗

Folkquips

A man said to a sage, "You brag of your wisdom, but it came from me." "Yes," replied the sage, "and it forgot its way back."

Said a king to a sage, "Sweet would be a king's reign if it lasted forever." "Had such been your predecessor's lot," replied the wise man, "how would you have reached the throne?"

A man laid a complaint before the king; the latter drove the suppliant out with violence. "I entered with one complaint," sighed the man. "I leave with two."

The king once visited a nobleman's house, and asked the latter's son, "Whose house is better, your father's or mine?" "My father's," said the boy, "while the king is in it."

To one who reviled the wise man for his lack of noble ancestry, he retorted, "Your noble line ends with you, with me mine begins."

A philosopher sat by the target at which the archers were shooting. " 'Tis the safest spot," said he.

An Arab's brother died. "Why did he die?" one asked. "Because he lived," was the answer.

"What have you laid up for the cold weather?" they asked a poor fellow. "Shivering," he answered.

A page had weak eyes. "Heal them," they said. "To see what?" he rejoined.

A fool quarrelled with a sage. Said the fool, "For every word of abuse I hear from you, I will retort ten." "No," replied the other, "for every ten words of abuse I hear from you, I will not retort one."

645

Riddles

Q. It's not a shirt—
 Yet it's sewed;
 It's not a tree—
 Yet it's full of leaves;
 It's not a person
 Yet it talks sensibly.
A. A book.

Q. What is it? A deaf man has heard how a dumb man had said that a blind man had seen a running rabbit; that a lame man pursued it and that a naked man had put it in his pocket and brought it home?
A. A lie.

Q. One dreamed that he was on a ship at sea with his father and mother and that the ship had begun to sink. It was, however, possible to save himself and one other person only—either his father or mother—not both. What should he do?
A. He should wake up.

Q. Three merchants and three robbers had to cross a lake. However, only one rowboat was available and it could safely carry only two people at a time. How could they all manage to get across since one merchant was afraid to be left alone with two robbers?
A. First of all two robbers crossed. One robber then brought the boat back and rowed across the third robber. Afterwards he returned once more and remained on shore. Then two merchants got into the boat and rowed across. One merchant in company with one robber returned with the boat. The robber got out of the boat and then two merchants rowed across. After that a robber returned to fetch the last robber.

"What is it that hangs on the wall, is green, and whistles?"
"A herring."

"A herring?! Does a herring hang on a wall?"
"Who stops you from hanging it?"
"Is a herring green?"
"It could be painted green."
"But who ever heard of a herring that whistles?"
"*Nu,* so it doesn't whistle!"

【4】

Conundrums

Why did Adam live so long?—Because he had no mother-in-law.

Who, with one blow, annihilated a quarter of the world's population?—Cain.

What is man's best means of concealment?—Speech.

On what occasion did all the people in the world hear the crowing of the cock?—In Noah's Ark.

Which is the place where you can find no Jew?—In a Christian cemetery.

What does the king see but rarely, the shepherd all the time, but God never? —His equal.

Who walks on four feet in the morning, on two feet at noon, and on three in the evening?—Man. As a child he crawls on all fours; as an adult he walks on two; and in his old age he walks leaning on a stick, i.e., three feet.

Who can speak in all languages?—Echo.

What causes us neither pain nor sorrow yet makes us weep?—Onions.

Who is lesser, poorer and utterly unsignificant compared to his brothers, nonetheless he makes them greater and richer?—The cipher (0).

What has twelve branches and on every branch four twigs and on every twig seven leaves?—The year.

What live creatures were not in Noah's Ark?—Fish.

What does a pious Jew do before he drinks tea?—He opens his mouth.

Can you tell me what the comparative and superlative of the word "nice" is?—Nice, nicer, m-m-m!

Which king is the best in the world?—A dead one.

What kind of water can you carry in a sieve?—Frozen water.

What is it that everybody would like and when they get it they don't like it?—Old age.

Why is it our luck that Moses stuttered?—Had he been normal in his speech he would have doubled the number of commandments, laws and regulations.

What do you do to get rid of some one?—If he's rich you ask him for a loan, if he's poor you give him a loan.

How many sides has a bagel?—Two: one inside, one outside.

When our teacher Moses didn't feel well what did God give him?—Two tablets.

PART SIX
Songs and Dances

INTRODUCTION

There is a legend in the Talmud which relates how above King David's couch there hung his harp. At early dawn, when the whole world lay hushed in sleep, the morning breezes would begin to blow, and under their touch the harpstrings would stir and play of themselves. The music sounded was wondrous and ethereal, like the sunrise itself. And so, while David slept, the music vibrated in his being. Finally, by an inner bidding, he arose and composed the psalms which he set to the melodies of the harp.

This is an allegory in which the harp may be said to symbolize the Jewish people playing of itself in a ceaseless outpouring of melody under the stirrings of the life-force within it and out of its collective cultural experience. Who wishes to hear the true voice of the Jewish people, to hear the vibrations of the strings of the Jewish heart, would do well to turn to its folksongs. The eminent French composer, Maurice Ravel, a Gentile, has said of them: "I was attracted to the strange and haunting beauty of Jewish music. I felt, almost, as though I had been brought into a new musical world when a few authentic Jewish melodies were brought to my notice. I was so bewitched by the mysterious color and exotic charm of these melodies that for weeks I could not get this music out of my mind. Then my imagination was set aflame . . ."

RELIGIOUS SONGS

Music among the ancient Jews was considered a divine art. This they assumed from the authority of Scripture itself in its account of the Prophet Elisha: "But now bring me a minstrel. And it came to pass when the minstrel played, that the hand of the Lord came upon him." It was this belief in the divine character of music, one which the Christian church subsequently borrowed from the Jews, that was responsible for the introduction into the synagogue service of the practice of chanting or cantillating Scripture during the period of the Second Temple. It prompted the sages in the Babylonian Talmud to conclude: "Who reads the Scriptures without sweetness, and learns them without a chant, of him says the Prophet Ezekiel: 'And I also have given them laws that are not good.' "

Musicologists have pointed out with some surprise the striking resemblances between traditional synagogue melodies and the Gregorian chants. Being Jewish, the first Church Fathers naturally had adopted the Jewish manner of cantillating the various books of the Bible according to certain fixed musical modes or melodies. These latter were indicated in the Hebrew Bible text by the *ta'amim*, the identifying vocalization or accent marks above and under the Hebrew text, resembling somewhat in principle the much later *neumes* of Christian musical notation, both merely serving as reminders of the rising and falling of a tune. The two specimens of Jewish cantillation presented in this section—the melodies for reading

the Torah and the *Haftaroh* (excerpts from the Prophets)—are traditional and no doubt of venerable though unknown origin. But, because of
the great diversity in Jewish national groups and in their cultural traditions in various parts of the world, there have sprung up different types
and modes of cantillation.

Synagogal hymns and melodies, whether composed in medieval Spain,
in the Provence or the Rhineland during the Crusades, are still being
sung today in every part of the world. Many of them are folksongs in
the truest sense of the term for they give utterance to the people's
desires and feelings in a most direct and communicative way. In this
category belong such old synagogue melodies as *Yigdal, Adon Olam,* and
Kol Nidre. Yigdal is based on the Thirteen Articles of the Jewish Creed
formulated by Maimonides. It immediately took a leading place in the
liturgies everywhere. *Adon Olam* is a solemn hymn sung on the Sabbath
and on The Day of Atonement. *Kol Nidre* marks the most dramatic
point in the service on the eve preceeding the Day of Atonement.

DEVOTIONAL AND TABLE-SONGS

With the destruction of the Second Temple both choral and instrumental music were abolished by the Rabbis as a mark of mourning for
the desolation of Zion. However, in honor of the Sabbath, the Rabbis
lifted this ban. It was considered a *mitzvoh,* an act of merit, for the
pious to cast off all mourning beginning with the eve of the Sabbath and
to go forth to greet the Sabbath Bride with joyous song and gladness.
The same dispensation was granted for all festival and Holy Days. For
that reason there are hundreds of religious folksongs of a devotional
nature, called *Zemiroth,* or Table-Songs. These acquired great popularity
beginning with the Tenth Century. They were sung for conviviality as
well as to lend a spiritual tone to the Sabbath and holiday meals. In
later times the texts of many of these songs combined Yiddish words
with Hebrew Scriptural quotations. A considerable number even added
to these two languages a third, such as Russian, Polish or Roumanian.
Examples of Yiddish-Hebrew songs are *Mayerke Mine Zuhn* and *Yismach
Moishe,* the latter a convivial song for *Simchas Torah.*

HASIDIC SONGS AND DANCES

To the *Hasidim,* the followers of Baal Shem the Eighteenth Century
mystic, song was equivalent to prayer, and even superseded it in spiritual
power. It was considered "the ladder to the Throne of God." Many
Hasidic rabbis thought that words were an impediment to spiritual expression, a wall standing between the communion of the individual and his
God. In consequence, many *Hasidic* melodies *(niggunim)* were sung without words. While some, especially the melancholy meditative ones, were
merely sung, the lively, the ecstatic ones, usually served as vocal obligati
to the famed dances of the mystic circle.

Nothing so well illustrates the rhapsodic attitude of the *Hasidim*
toward the power of song as the following tale:

The Rabbi of Ladi was a man of unconventional ways. His homilies
were compounded of folk-tales and the wise saws of the people. One day,
as he preached in the synagogue he noticed the bewildered look of an old
man who was trying hard to get the drift of his words. After he had

finished his sermon and the congregation was departing, he said to the old man:

"I could see by the expression on your face that you did not understand my sermon."

"That is true, Rabbi," confessed the old man.

"It may have been my fault," apologized the modest rabbi. "Perhaps I was not clear enough. At any rate, I'm going to sing to you now, for melody goes right to the heart and the understanding where words fail."

And so the Rabbi of Ladi threw his head back, and closing his eyes he sang with ecstasy a wordless song of longing and faith. As the old man listened his face lit up.

"I understand your sermon now, Rabbi!" he exclaimed happily.

Ever after, in the midst of his preaching the rabbi would break into song.

There are an astonishing number of *Hasidic* songs and dances, representing probably the most distinguished and original element in the musical creation of the Jewish folk. Like their lyrics, *Hasidic* tunes are steeped in mystical rapture. Many of them employ some of the idioms of Wallachian folk tunes but their moods, their intensity, are characteristically *Hasidic*. In addition, *Hasidic* songs carry over the meditative somber strain from the traditional Oriental-Jewish liturgies.

YIDDISH FOLK SONGS

The secular song among the Jews of Central and Eastern Europe first came into being during the late Renaissance. This was entirely due to the traditional rabbinic attitude which frowned upon secular songs. It held that among other peoples these songs were frequently licentious in character and, since the Jewish people had been given the mission to be "a Holy Nation," they were duty bound to occupy themselves only with morally uplifting music—with hymns, psalms, devotional songs and songs of exaltation. This largely explains why for so many centuries the musical creativity of the Jews was channelized into pious rather than secular directions.

But, since the Jews did not live in a vacuum, the secular humanism of the Renaissance succeeded also in penetrating the ghetto walls. The fear of the rabbis, though understandable, was unfounded, for on account of a sternly moralistic conditioning of the people Jewish folksongs are unusually free of the lascivious.

Beginning with the Sixteenth Century secular Yiddish folksongs became well-defined in both their musical and poetic forms. In the same way that Jewish folklore has such an astonishingly large characterology, Yiddish folksongs too have an immense diversity. Their themes touch upon everything in Jewish daily experience. They are of God, and of the world, of the World-to-Come and of the Messiah, of Moses and of the Patriarchs and Matriarchs. They also treat of living and of dying, of love and of separation, of attainment and of frustration, of work and of the marketplace, of good fortune and of misfortune. In short, the whole measure of Jewish life can, with remarkable comprehensiveness, be taken from its songs.

Yiddish folksongs have their own distinctive characteristics. They are emotional, tender and introspective. The humorous songs are touched by the same wry or ironic comicality found in Jewish folkhumor; the melancholy songs bear the same unresigned plaintiveness of the folktales about martyrs, only their sorrow is lightened by a lyrical sweetness in the melody.

Yiddish folksongs are almost always in the minor key, even those intended to be convivial and joyous. This represents a curious cultural phenomenon and has elicited much surprised comment from musicologists and composers. Yet, to one familiar with the long history of Jewish suffering, there can be no cause for surprise in this. To be sure, Jewish songs in the minor key have points of resemblance to the Slavic, to the Spanish-Moorish and to the Arabic songs. Nonetheless, they are penetrated by a special kind of sadness which is hard to describe but which one soon comes to recognize as "Jewish" on closer familiarity with them.

PALESTINIAN SONGS

Ever since the anti-Semitic May Laws of 1881 in the Russian Empire and the series of bloody pogroms to which they logically led, an energetic movement arose for a Jewish homeland in Palestine. This movement was formalized and expanded by the world-wide organization of political Zionism under the leadership of Dr. Theodor Herzl at the First Zionist Congress in Basle in August 1897.

In the years before World War I such songs as *B'Shuv Adonoy* and *Am Yisroel Chay* gave utterance to the yearnings and the indestructible faith of Zionists in the survival of the Jewish people and in the final restoration of Zion as their homeland. With the mass settlement on the land of Palestine of young and ardent *Chalutzim,* the Palestinian Hebrew folksongs took on a fresher and more modern character for they extolled the virtues of labor and self-sacrifice in the cause of upbuilding the country.

The young *Chalutzim* sang as they toiled at roadbuilding, reclaiming swamps, plowing the land, cultivating orange groves and vineyards, and engaging in hundreds of other occupations. All these aspects of their life and struggle are vividly expressed in their folksongs, which breathe the spirit of embattled, optimistic youth. Musically they are vigorous, rhythmic and emotionally intense. Examples of such songs included in this section are the *Artsa Alinu* and *Naaleh L'Artseynu,* both serving as choral accompaniment to the *Hora,* the national dance of the Jews in Palestine. (For a description of this dance see page 563.)

With the tremendous increase of the Jewish *Yishuv,* or community, in Palestine in the three decades subsequent to the Balfour Declaration of November 2, 1917, a distinctive and significant Jewish culture in Hebrew emerged in Palestine. The struggle for sovereignty also took on a more militant character with the growth of group strength and national consciousness, culminating on May 14, 1948, with the formal establishment of the State of Israel.

Because the Jews in Palestine have come from every Jewish community in the world it is but natural that to a large extent they should have fused their musical tastes and traditions. Out of this acculturation has emerged a new body of Jewish folksongs. The outstanding musical influences on Palestinian folksongs have been the *Hasidic,* the Slavic, the Oriental Sephardic, the Palestinian Arabic, and the Jewish Yemenite.

Jewish Folksongs in America

Being predominantly of Eastern European stock, most American Jews are familiar with the old Yiddish folk songs. An historian of American jazz, Isaac Goldberg, has observed: "Just as Yiddish intonation and Yiddish idiom have entered into the very language of the Eastern Americans, so have certain elements of Jewish folksong made their way, largely through Tin Pan Alley, into American popular song. This has not been part of a conscious program. It has taken place in the way that all cultural interchange takes place."

Among the most important composers of American jazz have been Jews such as George Gershwin, Irving Berlin, Jerome Kern, Vernon Duke, Sigmund Romberg, and others. The Jewish origin of these composers must have had a considerable effect on their compositions, it being hardly likely that they could become entirely divorced from their Jewish upbringing and Jewish musical tradition. This, in effect, is what George Gershwin has said: "Even though I know practically nothing about the poetic content of the Yiddish folksong, nevertheless I believe that many of the melodies that I use in my works are Jewish according to the internal, deep emotional element that flows in them, regardless of the fact that they are purely American in style." This may account for the fact, as Gershwin's friend and biographer Isaac Goldberg has pointed out, that such tunes of his as *My One and Only, Funny Face, Swanee* or *It Ain't Necessarily So* can be turned "into Jewish melodies by a subtle emphasis in the singing."

The Yiddish songs generated in America have been largely of the music hall type. Neither in melodic beauty nor in quality or text can they compare with European Yiddish folk songs or modern Palestinian Hebrew songs. Being the product of the American scene, they bear the imprint upon them of American jazz. For that reason, and despite their employment of some of the traditional idioms of Yiddish folksongs, they have frequently been accepted by Tin Pan Alley and sung by millions of Americans. Among the most outstanding examples are: *Bei Mir Bist Du Shane* and *Yossel-Yossel* which under the name of *Joseph-Joseph* gained wide popularity. Similarly, Cab Calloway's recording of *Ot Azoy Nate a Shnyder* and the Andrew Sisters' recording of *Sha, Sha, di Rebbitzen* have brought these two songs, and others like them, into the popular musical stream of America, thereby continuing the blending process of our American multi-national culture.

Note: With some exceptions, the English versions of these songs are literal translations, without any attempt at rhyme or metric fidelity. While, in most cases, the literal renderings make it impossible to fit the English words exactly to their tunes, they, however, have the merit of conveying the exact meaning and feeling of the original texts.

The difficulties in presenting a uniform phonetic transliteration of the Yiddish lyrics are self-evident, for the songs, collated from various compilations, represent almost every known dialect of Yiddish. In consequence, the same words occurring in different songs are not always transliterated the same way, although in most instances the differences have been reconciled.

Unless otherwise noted, the English versions are by the editor.

N. A.

Folk Songs

FRAYGT DEE VELT AN ALTE KASHE
(The World Asks an Old Question)

Fraygt dee velt an al - te ka-she: tra-la tra-di-ri-di

rom? Fraygt dee velt an al - te ka - she:

tra - la tra-di - ri - di - rom? en - fert men:

tra - di - ri - di - ri-lom, oy, ai, tra - di - ri - di - rom.

Un az men vil, ken men oich zu - gen:

tra - i - dim. Bleibt doch vy-ter dee al - te ka -she:

tra - la tra-di - ri - di - rom Bleibt doch vy-ter dee

al - te ka - she: tra - la - tra-di - ri - di - ri-lom.

FRAYGT DEE VELT AN ALTE KASHE: From *Die Schönsten Lieder die Ostjuden:* Compiled by Fritz M. Kaufmann. Jüdischer Verlag. Berlin, 1920. Maurice Ravel, the eminent French composer, has given this song an orchestral setting under the title of *La Question Eternelle.*

Fraygt dee velt an al-te ka-she:
Tra-la tra-di-ri-di-rom? [*Repeat 2
   lines*]
En-fert men: tra-di-ri-di-ri-lom,
Oy-ai, tra-di-ri-di-rom!
Un az men vil, ken men oich zu-
   gen: tra-i-dim?
Bleibt doch vi-ter dee al-te ka-she:
Tra-la tra-di-ri-di-lom. [*Repeat 2
   lines*]

The world asks an old question:
Tra-la tra-di-ri-di-rom?
So the answer is: tra-di-ri-di-ri-lom,
Oy-ai, tra-di-ri-di-rom!
And if one wants to, one may also
   say: tra-i-dim?
So again we remain with the old
   question:
Tra-la-tra-di-ri-di-lom.

A GANAYVEH (A Theft)

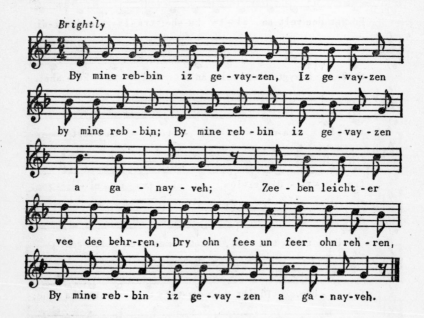

By mine reb-bin iz ge-vay-zen, Iz ge-vay-zen by mine reb-bin; By mine reb-bin iz ge-vay-zen a ga-nay-veh; Zee-ben leicht-er vee dee behr-ren, Dry ohn fees un feer ohn reh-ren, By mine reb-bin iz ge-vay-zen a ga-nay-veh.

By mine reb-bin iz ge-vay-zen,
Iz ge-vay-zen by mine reb-bin;
By mine reb-bin iz ge-vay-zen
A ga-nay-veh:
Zeeben leicht-er vee dee beh-ren,
Dry ohn fees un feer ohn reh-ren;
By mine reb-bin iz ge-vay-zen
A ga-nay-veh.

At my rabbi's there was,
There was at my rabbi's;
At my rabbi's there was
A robbery:
Seven candlesticks like bears,
Three without feet and three with-
   out stems;
At my rabbi's there was
A robbery.

A GANAVEH: From *Yiddish Folk Songs*, collected and arranged by Sarah P. Schack and E. S. Cohen. Bloch Publishing Co. New York, 1927.

[*Repeat first 4 lines*]
Zee-ben hem-der vee dee bech-er,
Dry mit lat-tes feer mit lech-er;
By mine reb-bin iz ge-vay-zen
A ga-nay-veh.

Seven shirts like goblets;
Three with holes, four with patches;
At my rabbi's there was
A robbery.

[*Repeat first 4 lines*]
Zee-ben hay-ner vee dee tzee-gel,
Dry ohn kep un feer ohn flee-gel;
By mine reb-bin iz ge-vay-zen
A ga-nay-veh.

Seven roosters like bricks,
Three without heads and four without wings;
At my rabbi's there was
A robbery.

[*Repeat first 4 lines*]
Zeeben may-den vee dee sossnes,
Dry ohn tzay-ner un feer ohn yoss-les;
By mine reb-bin iz ge-vay-zen
A ga-nay-veh.

Seven girls like pine trees,
Three without teeth and four without gums;
At my rabbi's there was
A robbery.

DER FILOZOF (The Philosopher)

Koom a-her, du fil-oz-of
Mit dine katz-ish-en moy-chl;
Koom a-her tzum reb-bin's tish
Un lern zich say-chel.

Come here, you philosopher
With your little cat's brain;
Come sit at the rabbi's table
And learn some sense.

DER FILOZOF: *Ibid.*

Refrain:

Bim ba bam, bam bim ba bam	Bim ba bam, bam bim ba bam
Bim ba bim ba, bam bim bam.	Bim ba bim ba, bam bim bam.
Bim ba bim, bam bim ba bam,	Bim ba bim, bam bim ba bam,
Bam ba bim ba, bam bam!	Bam ba bim ba, bam bam!

A luft bal-lon hos-tu ois-ge-tracht,	An air-balloon you did invent,
Un maynst du bist a cho-rutz;	And think yourself a genius;
Der reb-be shputt, der reb-be lacht,	The rabbi mocks, the rabbi laughs,
Er darf dos oif ka-po-res. [*Refrain*]	He has no earthly need of it.

Tzu vays-tu, vos der rebbe tut	Have you any idea what the rabbi does
B'es er zitst be-yi-chee-dos?	
In ein mi-noot in him-mel fleet,	When he sits all alone?
Un est dort sha-losh su-dos.	In one moment he flies to heaven,
[*Refrain*]	And eats there the third Sabbath meal.

VEE AZOY TRINKT DER KAYSER TAY?
(How Does the Czar Drink Tea?)

Raboi-sai, raboi-sai, cha-cho-mim un a breg! Ch'vel eich fre-gn, ch'vel eich fre-gn! Freg shoin, freg shoin, freg! Ent-fert al-le of mine shy-leh: Vee trinkt a kay-ser tay? Me nemt a hi-te-le tzu-ker,— un me macht in dem a le-che-le, un me geest a-rine hase vas-ser, un me misht— un me misht.—Oy ot a-zoy, oy ot a-zoy trinkt a kay-ser tay!

VEE AZOY TRINKT DER KAYSER TAY?: From *Yiddishe Folkslieder*, by Beregovski and Feffer. State Music Publishing House. Moscow, 1939. By arrangement with Leeds Music Corporation, New York, N. Y.

Ra-boi-sai, ra-boi-sai, cha-cho-mim
    un a breg!
Ch'vel eich fre-gn, ch'vel eich
    fre-gn!
—Freg shoin, freg shoin, freg!
Ent-fert al-le
Of mine shy-leh:
Vee trinkt a kay-ser tay?
—Tay?
Me nemt a hit-te-le tzu-ker,
Un me macht in dem a le-che-le,
Un me geest a-rine hase vas-er,
Un me misht, un me misht.
Oy, ot a-zoy, oy, ot a-zoy
Trinkt a kay-ser tay!

My masters, my masters, sages
    beyond compare!
I want to ask you, I want to ask
    you!
—Go ahead and ask, go ahead
    and ask—*ask!*
Answer all of you
To my question:
How does a czar drink tea?
    —Tea?
You take a loaf of sugar,
And you make a hole in it,
And you pour in it hot water,
And you mix, and you mix,
And that's the way, and that's the
    way
A czar drinks tea!

Ra-boi-sai, ra-boi-sai, chai-cho-mim
    un a breg!
Ch'vel eich fre-gn, ch'vel eich
    fre-gn!
—Freg shoin, freg shoin, freg!
Ent-fert al-le
Of mine shy-leh:
Vee est a kay-ser bool-bes?
—Bool-bes?
Me shtelt a-vek a vahnt mit put-ter,
Un a sol-dat-l,
Mit a har-mat-l,
Sheest durch dee put-ter mit a hay-
    ser bul-beh
Un treft dem kay-ser gleich in moil
    a-rine.
Oy, ot a-zoy, oy, ot a-zoy,
Est a kay-ser bul-bes.

My masters, my masters, sages
    beyond compare!
I want to ask you, I want to ask
    you!
—Go ahead and ask, go ahead
    and ask—*ask!*
Answer all of you
To my question:
How does a czar eat potatoes?
    —Potatoes?
You raise up a wall of butter,
And a soldier,
With a cannon,
Shoots a hot potato through the
    butter
And right into the mouth of the
    czar.
And that's the way, and that's the
    way
A czar eats potatoes.

Ra-boi-sai, ra-boi-sai, cha-cho-mim
    un a breg!
Ch'vel eich fre-gn, ch'vel eich
    fre-gn!
—Freg shoin, freg shoin, freg!
Ent-fert al-le
Of mine shy-leh:
Vee shluft a kay-ser ba-nacht?
—Vee er shluft?

My masters, my masters, sages
    beyond compare!
I want to ask you, I want to ask
    you!
—Go ahead and ask, go ahead
    and ask—*ask!*
Answer all of you
To my question:
How does a czar sleep at night?
    —How he sleeps?

Me shitt un a ful-n chay-der mit
fe-dern,
Un me shly-dert a-rine a-hin-tzu
dem kay-ser,
Un dry rut-tes sol-dat-en shtay-en
un shry-en:
Shah! Shah! Shah!
Oy, ot a-zoy, oy, ot a-zoy,
Shluft a kay-ser ba-nacht!

You fill his bedroom full of
feathers,
And you throw the czar into it,
And three divisions of soldiers
stand outside and yell:
S-sh! S-sh! S-sh!
And that's the way, and that's the
way
A czar sleeps at night!

DIRE GELT UN OY, OY, OY! (The Rent—Oh, Oh, Oh!)

DIRE GELT UN OY, OY, OY!: From *Yiddishe Folkslieder Ois Dem Folks-Moil Gezamelt*, edited and compiled by J. L. Cahan. Internatzionale Bibliotek Ferlag Co. New York and Warsaw, 1912.

Refrain:

Di-re gelt un oy, oy, oy!	The rent—oh, oh, oh!
Di-re gelt un Bo-zhe moy!	The rent—my God!
Di-re gelt un gra-do-voy!	The rent—police!
Di-re gelt muz men tzuh-len!	One's got to pay the rent!

Kumt a-rine der strush	The janitor comes in
Nemt er a-rup dus hit-tel,	And takes off his hat,
Un az me zuhlt kine dee-re-gelt	And if he's not paid the rent
Hengt er a-rois a kvit-tel. [*Refrain*]	He hangs up a notice.

Kumt a-rine der zshontz-eh	The manager comes in
Mit dem grob-ben shtek-en,	With his fat stick,
Un az me git eem kine dee-re-gelt	And if he's not paid the rent
Shtelt er a-rois dee bet-ten.	He puts out your beds.
[*Refrain*]	

"Far vos zol ich eich ge-ben dee-re-gelt	"Why should I give you the rent When the kitchen is a ruin?
Az dee kech is tzi-broch-en?	Why should I give you the rent
Far vus zol ich eich ge-ben dee-re-gelt	When I have nothing to cook on?"
Az ich hub nisht oif vus tzu kochen?" [*Refrain*]	

OT AZOY NATE A SHNYDER (That's How a Tailor Sews)

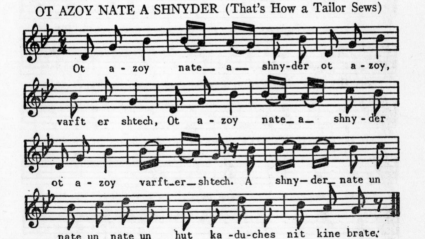

Ot a-zoy nate a shny-der,	This is how a tailor sews,
Ot a-zoy varft er shtech.	This is how he makes his stitches.
Ot a-zoy nate a shny-der,	This is how a tailor sews,
Ot a-zoy varft er shtech.	This is how he makes his stitches.
A shny-der nate un nate un nate,	A tailor sews and sews and sews,
Un hut ka-du-ches nit kine brate.	And gets the fever but no bread.

OT AZOY NATE A SHNYDER: From *Yiddisher Musik-Folklor*, compiled by M. Beregovski. State Music Publishing House. Moscow, 1934. By arrangement with Leeds Music Corporation, New York, N. Y.

A CHAZZANDL OIF SHABBES (A Cantor for the Sabbath)

Is ge-koo-men tzu foh-ren a chaz-zan in a kline shte-tel,

da-ve-nen a shab-bes, oy da-ve-nen a shab-bes,

Zy-nen ge-koomen eem her-ren dee dry shen-ste ba-le

ba-tim fun dem shte-tel, dee dry shen-ste ba-le

ba-tim fun dem shte-tel:___ Ei-ner a shny-de-r'l der

tzvei-ter a ko-val-tshi-k'l, un der drit-ter a ba-le-gol-tshi-k'l.

Ruft zich o-pet der shny-de-r'l Ruft zich o-pet der shny-der'l oy—

___ Hut er ge-da-vent, hut er ge-da-vent. A

zoi-vi men git___ mit-ten no-del a shtoch___ un mit-ten

ei-sen oy a press___ Oy,___ hut er ge-da-vent

Oy, oy oy,___ oy,___ oy,___ oy,___

oy, hut er___ ge-da___vent.

A CHAZZANDL OIF SHABBES: From *Jewish Folk Songs*, compiled by Henry Lefkowitch. Metro Music Co. New York, 1927.

Is ge-koo-men tzu foh-ren a chaz-
    zan in a kline shte-tel
Da-ve-nen a Shab-bes, oy da-ve-nen
    a Shab-bes.
Zy-nen ge-koo-men eem her-ren dee
    dry shen-ste ba-le-ba-tim fun
    dem shte-tel,
Dee dry shen-ste ba-le-ba-tim fun
    dem shte-tel:
    Einer a shny-de-rl,
    Der tzvei-ter a ko-val-tshi-kl,
    Un der drit-ter a ba-le-gol-tshi-kl.

Ruft zich o-pet der shny-de-rl, ruft
    zich o-pet der shny-de-rl:
    "Oy! hut er ge-da-vent, hut er
    ge-da-vent!
A-zoi vi men git mit-ten no-del a
    shtoch,
Un mit-ten ei-sen a press—
Oy! hut er ge-da-vent!
Oy, oy, oy, oy, oy, oy, oy!
Oy, hut er ge-da-vent!

Ruft zich op-et dus ko-val-tshi-kel,
    ruft zich op-et dus ko-val-tshi-
    kel:
    "Oy! hut er ge-da-vent, hut er
    ge-da-vent!
A-zoi-vee men git mit-ten ham-mer
    oy a zetz,
Un mit dee kle-tshes oy a kvetsh
Oy! hut er ge-da-vent!
Oy, oy, oy, oy, oy, oy, oy!
Oy, hut er ge-da-vent!"

Ruft zich op-et dus bal-e-gol-tshi-
    kl, ruft zich op-et dus bal-e-
    gol-tshi-kl:
"Oy! hut er ge-da-vent, hut er ge-
    da-vent!
A-zoi-vee men git mit dee lei-tses oy
    a tsee,
Un mit-ten bei-tshel oy a chvatsh.
Oy! hut er ge-da-vent!
Oy, oy, oy, oy, oy, oy, oy!
Oy, hut er ge-da-vent!"

Once there came a cantor to a vil-
    lage
To sing the service on the Sabbath,
    to sing the service on the
    Sabbath.
So there came to hear him the three
    leading worthies of the village,
The three leading worthies of the
    village:
    One was the tailor,
    The second was the blacksmith
    And the third was the drover.

Then up spoke the tailor, up spoke
    the tailor:
    "Oy! how he did sing! how he
    did sing!
Just as one makes a stitch with
    the needle,
Just as one presses with the
    iron—
Oy! how he did sing!
Oy, oy, oy, oy, oy, oy, oy!
Oy, how he did sing!

Then up spoke the blacksmith, up
    spoke the blacksmith:
*"Oy! how he did sing! how he did
    sing!*
Just as one gives a bang with the
    hammer,
Just as one gives a squeeze on the
    bellows—
Oy! how he did sing!
Oy, oy, oy, oy, oy, oy, oy!
Oy! how he did sing!"

Then up spoke the drover, up spoke
    the drover:
*"Oy! how he did sing! how he did
    sing!*
Just as one gives a pull on the reins,
Just as one gives a crack with the
    whip—
Oy! how he did sing!
Oy, oy, oy, oy, oy, oy, oy!
Oy! how he did sing!"

MEER ZENEN DO! (We Are Here!)

Zog nit kane-mol az du gayst dem letz-ten veg.

Him-len bly-e-ne far-shtel-n bloy-e teg.

Koo-men vet doch un-zer oys-ge-benk-te sho,

S'vet a poyk tun un-zer trot:

    Meer ze-nen do! [*Repeat 3 lines*]

Fun green-em pal-men-land biz vy-ten land fun shnay,

Meer ze-nen do-mit un-zer pine, mit un-zer blut,

Shprotz-en vet dort un-zer ge-vu-ra, un-zer moot. [*Repeat 2 lines*]

Oh never say that you have reached the very end,

Tho leaden skies a bitter future may portend,

Because the hour for which we yearned will yet arrive

And our marching steps will thunder: "We survive!"

From land of palm trees to the land of distant snow

We are here, with our pain, with our woe,

And wherever our blood was shed in pain

Our fighting spirits will resurrect again.

MEER ZENEN DO!: From *Dus Gesang Fun Vilna Ghetto*, compiled by Katcherginsky. Copyright, 1946, by L'Association des Vilnois en France; and reprinted with their permission. English words by Ruth Rubin.

Ge-shree-ben iz dos leed mit blut un
  mit bly,
S'iz nit kine leed fun a foy-gl oif
  der fry,
Nor s'hut a folk z'vish-n fal-en-di-
  ke vent,
Dos leed ge-zun-gen mit na-ga-nes
  in dee hent. [*Repeat 2 lines*]

Not lead, but blood inscribed this
  song we sing,
It's not a caroling of birds upon the
  wing,
But 'twas a people midst the crashing fires of hell,
That sang this song, and fought
  courageous 'til it fell.

THE BALLAD OF ITZIK WITTENBERG

Sligt er-getz far-tay-et
Der feint vee a cha-yeh.
Der Mau-ser, er vacht in mine hant,
Nor plitz-im—Ge-sta-po
Es fihrt a gesh-meed-ten
Durch fintz-ter-nish dem ko-men-
  dant! [*Repeat 3 lines*]

The enemy hearkens: a beast in the
  darkness;
the Mauser—it wakes in my
  hand—
But wait! My heart's drumming:
  two sentries are coming,
and with them our first in command.

THE BALLAD OF ITZIK WITTENBERG: *Ibid.* English words by Aaron Kramer in *Jewish Life*, October, 1947.

On the night of July 16, 1943, the Gestapo arrested Itzik Wittenberg, the com-mander of the partisan organization in the Vilna Ghetto. Several of his men attacked the Gestapo guard, sawed through the chains with which Wittenberg was bound and released him. The following morning the Gestapo demanded that Wittenberg be handed over to them alive or they would destroy the ghetto. Although the Jewish partisan leader knew that the Gestapo had been planning to destroy the ghetto in any case and that the ultimatum was only a ruse, nonetheless he went to the Gestapo and surrendered himself voluntarily. He did this in order not to injure the reputation of the partisans among the Jews remaining in the ghetto. The Nazis tor-tured and executed him on July 14, 1943.

Dee nacht hut mit blitz-en
Dos ghet-to tze-ri-sen,
"Ge-fahr!"—shrite a toy-er, a
vant—
Cha-ve-rim ge-try-eh
Fun kay-ten ba-fry-en—
Far-shvin-den mit dem ko-men-dant.
[*Repeat 3 lines*]

The ghetto is sundered by lightning
and thunder;
"Beware!" shrieks a tower in fright.
Brave comrades have freed our
commander and leader,
and flee with him into the night.

Dee nacht is far-floi-gn,
Der toyt far dee oy-gn,
Dos ghet-to es fee-bert in brand,
In um-ruh—dos ghet-to,
Es droht dee Ge-sta-po:
"Toyt o-der dem ko-men-dant!"
[*Repeat 3 lines*]

But night soon is over—and death
lies uncovered;
the flames of the city leap high.
Aroused is the ghetto—the storm-
troopers threaten:
"Give up your leader, or die!"

Ge-zugt hut dan Itz-ig—
Un durch vee a blitz is—
"Ich vill nit eer zolt tzu-leeb mir
Darf-n dem leb-n
Dem soy-neh up-ge-ben . . ."
Tzum toyt gate shtoltz der ko-man-
deer. [*Repeat 3 lines*]

The battle-ground quivers as Itzik
delivers
the answer—while guns hold their
breath:
"Shall others be given, to pay for
my living?"
And proudly he goes to his death.

Ligt vid-der far-tay-et
Der feint vee a cha-yeh,
Ch'alt fes-ter deer Mau-ser in hant,
Itzt bist meer ty-er
Zy du mine ba-fry-er,
Zy du itz-ter mine ko-men-dant.

Once more in the darkness the
enemy hearkens;
the Mauser—it wakes in my hand.
You are now dearer—now you be
my hero!
Now you be my first in command!

AROIS IZ IN VILNA A NYER BAFEHL
(A New Order Is Issued in Vilna)

A - rois iz in Vil - na a ny - er ba - fail tzu

bren - gen dee Yi - den fun shtet - lach, Ge-

bracht hut men al - le fun yun - ge biz alt, A-

fil - lih oych kran - ke oif bet - lach.

AROIS IZ IN VILNA A NYER BAFEHL: *Ibid.*

A-rois iz in Vilna a ny-er ba-fehl,
Tzu bren-gen dee yid-en fun shtet-lach,
Ge-bracht hut men al-le fun yun-ge biz alt,
A-fil-lih oych kran-ke oyf bet-lach.

A new order was issued in Vilna
To bring all Jews from the villages;
So they brought all—young and old,
Even the sick in their beds.

Tzu-noif-ge-shpart hut men dem la-ger,
Men hut zay ge-num-men sort-ee-r'n.
Ush-men-er yid-en in Vilna tzu bly-ben,
Un Su-ler in Kovno tzu fee-r'n.

They closed the gates of the camp,
And then they began to sort them,
Jews of Ushmen were to remain in Vilna,
Jews of Sul were to be taken to Kovno.

A-rois-ge-feert hut men fun la-ger,
Yun-ge un frish-e kor-bo-nes,
A-rine-ge-shpart hut men zay a-lem-en gleich
In dee zel-be far-mach-te va-gon-es.

They led from the camp
Young and fresh victims,
Confined them all alike
In the same sealed cars.

Der tzug iz zich lang-zam ge-foh-ren,
Ge-fife't un ge-ge-b'n sir-e-nes.
Stan-tzee-eh "Pogar" der tzug shtelt zich up,
Men tshep-et dort up dee va-gon-es. . . .

The train pulled along slowly,
Whistled and sounded the siren.
At station "Pogar" it stopped;
They started to unhitch the cars.

Zy hub-ben der-zehn az men hut zay far-feert,
Men feert tzu der shrek-le-cher she-chi-ta,
Zay hub-ben tzer-broch-en dee teer fun va-gon,
Tzu-zam-en ge-proovt mach'n pli-teh.

When the Jews saw they had been deceived,
Were being led to the horrible slaughter,
They broke down the doors of the cars,
Together to attempt their escape.

Zay hub-ben ge-vorf-en zich oif der Ge-shta-po
Un zay dee clyde-er tze-ris-sen,
Ge-blib-en iz lig'n leb'n dee yid-en
Et-lech-e deitsh-en tze-bis-sen.

They flung themselves upon the Gestapo
And tore their clothes to shreds,
Left lying beside the Jews
Were some German bitten to death.

On April 5, 1943 the Gestapo assembled the last 4000 Jewish survivors in the province of Vilna. They were told they were being transferred to the ghetto of Kovno. However, the train halted instead at the Pogar station.

Alerted by the Nazis' treachery and understanding full well that they were being led to their execution, the Jews—men, women and children—leaped from the freight train and threw themselves upon their would-be murderers. They attacked them

JAMELE

Du vest zine a g'veer, mine Ja-me-le,
Flaygt meer zin-gen by mine vee-ge-le,
Al-le nacht a-mol mine ma-me-le.,
Ich ge-denk noch heint ihr nee-ge-le,
Ich ge-denk noch heint ihr nee-ge-le.

Du vest zine a g'veer, mine Ja-me-le,
Flaygt meer zin-gen by mine vee-ge-le,
Al-le nacht a-mol mine ma-me-le,
Ich ge-denk noch heint ihr ni-ge-le
Ich ge-denk noch heint ihr ni-ge-le.

Un me-ku-yom is ge-vo-ren mir
Dee hav-to-choh fun mine ma-me-le.
Ver hot noch ge-sehn a-za ge-veer,
A-za oy-sher vee ihr Ja-me-le!

Shlof-en shlof ich oif a ker-be-le,
Mach ha-moi-tzi oif a sko-rin-ke
Un l'chy-im oif a sher-be-le
Full mit brun-nen vas-ser klo-rin-ke. [*Repeat line*]

You'll be rich, my Jamele,
Used to sing at my little cradle
My mother every night long ago.
I still recall her little tune,
I still recall her little tune.

And fulfilled for me was
The promise of my little mother.
Whoever saw such a rich man,
Such a wealthy man as her Jamele!

I sleep upon a pallet of straw,
Recite the benediction over a crust
And drink: "to life!" from a broken dish
Full of clear well-water.

with sticks and with pieces of iron that they managed to break off the train cars. Those who had nothing to fight with punched and pummelled, clawed and wrestled with their Gestapo guards. Some frenzied prisoners even used their teeth as weapons and bit through the jugular vein of a number of their enemies. All but the few who escaped were mowed down by the Nazi machine-gunners.

This incident refutes the widely-held belief that all the six million Jews massacred by Hitler went to their death with the docility of sheep. As time goes on, more evidence crops up to support the view that there were many fiercely fought battles between the unarmed Jews and the heavily armed Nazis.—N.A.

JAMALE: From *Yiddish Folk Songs*, collected and arranged by Sarah P. Schack and E. S. Cohen. Bloch Publishing Co. New York, 1927.

OIF DEE FELDER (In the Fields)

Oif dee fel-der vee s'vy-en vin — tn,

Oif dee fel-der vee s'vy-en vin — tn,

Oif dee fel - der vee s'vy-en vin — tn,

Dee kol-veert-ni-tzes snup-pes bin — den.

Oif dee fel-der vee s'vy-en vin-tn,
Oif dee fel-der vee s'vy-en vin-tn,
Oif dee fel-der vee s'vy-en vin-tn,
Dee kol-veert-ni-tzes snup-pes bin-
   den.

In the fields where the winds are
   blowing,
In the fields where the winds are
   blowing,
In the fields where the winds are
   blowing,
The farm-girls are binding the
   sheaves.

Shveh-re snup-pes, full mit zang-en,
   [*Repeat twice*]
Full mit munt-er-eh ge-zang-en.

Heavy sheaves full of wheat-spears,

Full of cheerful songs.

Un dee zun, zee brent vee fy-er,
   [*Repeat twice*]
Yay-de shoo iz far unz ty-er.

And the sun, it burns like fire,

Every hour to us is precious.

S'hut dos feld unds broit ge-ge-
   ben, [*Repeat twice*]
Far dem ny-em shay-nem leb-en.

The field has given us bread,

For the new beautiful life.

OIF DEE FELDER: From *Yiddishe Folkslieder*, by Beregovski and Feffer. State Music Publishing House. Moscow, 1939. By arrangement with Leeds Music Corporation, New York, N. Y.

MYKOMASHMALON (A Monologue of a *Yeshiva-Bocher*)

Gloomily

My - ko - mash - ma - lon der re - gen? Vos - zhe
lust er meer. tzu her - en? Zine-eh trup-ens oif dee
shoi - ben kyke-len zich, vee tree-be tray-ren. Un dee
shtee - vel is tzu - ris - sen, un es vert in gass a
blut - te; Bald vet oich der vin-ter koom - en, ch'ob kine
va - re - meh ka - po - te. My ko - mash - ma - lon dos
licht-el? Vos-zhe lust es meer tzu her-ren, s'ka-pet
un ess treeft ihr chal-lev, un s'vet, bald fin ihr nisht
ve - ren A - zoy tzank ich do in kly - zel, vee a
licht - el, shvach un tin - kel, biz ich vel a - zoy meer
ois - gehn in der shtil in miz - rach vin - kel.

MYKOMASHMALON: From *Jewish Folk Songs*, compiled by Henry Lefkowitch. Metro Music Co. New York, 1927. Original Yiddish words by Abraham Reisen.

My-ko-mashma-lon der re-gen?
Vos-zhe lust er meer tzu her-ren?
Zine-eh trup-ens oif dee shoi-ben,
Kyke-len zich vee tree-be tray-ren.
Un dee shtee-vel is tzu-ris-sen,
Un es vert in gass a blut-e;
Bald vet oich der vin-ter koo-men,
Ch'ob kine va-re-meh ka-po-te.

What is the meaning of the rain?
What does it tell me?
It drops against the panes,
Rolls down like sad tears.
And my boots are full of holes,
And the street is full of mud;
Soon the winter too will come,
And I have no warm *kapote* to
    cover me.

My ko-mahsma-lon dos licht-el,
Vos-zhe lust er meer tzu her-ren?
S'ka-pet un es treeft eer chay-lev,
Un s'vet bald fun eer nisht ve-ren.
A-zoy tzank ich do in kly-zel,
Vee a licht-el, shvach un tin-kel,
Biz ich vel a-zoy meer ois-gane,
In der shtil, in mizrach vin-kel.

What is the meaning of the candle,
What does it tell me?
It drips and melts its tallow,
And soon it will be no more.
This way I'm sputtering in the
    chapel,
Like a candle, weak and gloomy,
Until I too will be snuffed out,
In silence against the East wall.

ZYZHE MEER GEZUNT (The Czarist Recruit's Farewell)

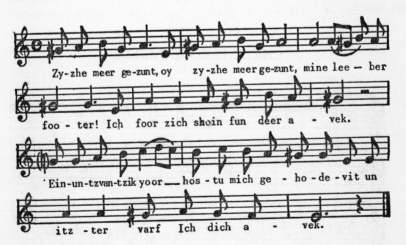

Zy-zhe meer ge-zunt, oy zy-zhe meer ge-zunt, mine lee — ber
foo-ter! Ich foor zich shoin fun deer a-vek.
'Ein-un-tzvan-tzik yoor — hos-tu mich ge-ho-de-vit un
itz-ter varf Ich dich a-vek.

ZYZHE MEER GEZUNT: From *Die Schönsten Lieder der Ostjuden,* compiled by Fritz
M. Kaufmann. Jüdischer Verlag. Berlin, 1920.

Zy-zhe meer ge-zunt, oy zy-zhe
  meer ge-zunt,
Mine lee-ber foo-ter!
Ich foor zich shoin fun deer a-vek.
Ein un-tzvan-tzik yoor hos-tu mich
  ge-ho-de-vit,
Un itz-ter varf ich dich a-vek!

Farewell, oh farewell,
My dear father!
I'm going to leave you now.
Twenty-one years you've raised me
But now I cast you off!

Zy-zhe meer ge-zunt, oy zy-zhe
  meer ge-zunt,
Mine lee-ber mut-ter!
Ich foor zich shoin fun deer a-vek.
Un-ter dy-nem har-tzen hos-tu mich
  ge-trug-en
Un itz-ter varf ich dich a-vek!

Farewell, oh farewell,
My dear mother!
I'm going to leave you now.
Under your heart you've carried
  me,
But now I cast you off!

Zy-zhe meer ge-zunt, oy zy-zhe
  meer ge-zunt,
Mine ge-try-eh ka-leh!
Ich foor zich shoin fun deer a-vek.
Noch deer vel ich ben-ken bes-ser
  vee noch al-le,
Un itz-ter varf ich dich a-vek!

Farewell, oh farewell,
My faithful bride!
I'm going to leave you now.
I'll long for you more than for all
  the others,
But now I cast you off!

CHATZKELE, CHATZKELE

Chatz-ke-le, chatz-ke-le, shpeel meer a ka-zatz-ke-le,
chotsh an oo-re-me, a-bee a chvatz-ke. Oo-rem is nit gut,
Oo-rem is nit gut, lo-mir zich nit shay-men mit ay-ge-ne blut.

CHATZKELE, CHATZKELE: *Ibid.*

Chatz-ke-le, Chatz-ke-le! Shpeel meer a ka-zatz-ka-le!
Chotsh an oo-rem-e, a-bee a chvatz-ke!
Oo-rem is nit gut, oo-rem is nit gut,
Lo-mir zich nit shay-men mit ay-ge-ne blut!

Nit kine ge-bet-e-ne, a-lain ge-kum-men!
Chotsh an oo-rem-e, fort a moom-e!
Oo-rem is nit gut, oo-rem is nit gut,
Lo-mir zich nit shay-men mit ay-ge-ne blut!

Chatz-ke-le, Chatz-ke-le! Play me a *ka-zatz-ka-le!*
Although poor, at least I've cour-age!
Poor isn't good, poor isn't good,
Let's not be ashamed of our own flesh and blood!

Though not invited I came myself!
Even if poor, still I'm an aunt!
Poor isn't good, poor isn't good,
Let's not be ashamed of our own flesh and blood!

ZOL ICH ZINE A ROV (Should I Be a Rabbi)

Zol ich zine a rov, ken ich nit kine Toi-reh;
Zol ich zine a soi-cher, Hob ich nit kine schoi-reh.
Un kine hay__ hob ich nit, un kine hub-ber hob ich nit,
Un a troonk bron-fen vilt zich, un dos vibe_ shilt_zich,
Zay ich meer a shtane, Zetz ich meer un vane.__

Zol ich zine a rov,
Ken ich nit kine Toi-reh;
Zol ich zine a soi-cher,
Hob ich nit kine schoi-reh.

Should I be a rabbi,
I don't know any Torah;
Should I be a merchant,
I don't have any goods.

ZOL ICH ZINE A ROV: From *Yiddish Folk Songs*, collected and arranged by Sarah P. Schack and E. S. Cohen. Bloch Publishing Co. New York, 1927.

Refrain:

Un kine hay hob ich nit,	And hay I don't have,
Un kine hub-ber hob ich nit,	And oats I don't have,
Un a troonk bron-fin vilt zich	And I'd like a drink of whisky,
Un dos vibe shilt zich,	And my wife curses me,
Zay ich meer a shtane,	So I see a stone
Zetz ich meer un vane.	And sit me down and weep.

Zol ich zine a shoi-chet,	Should I be a *shochet*,
Halt ich nit kine chal-lef;	I cannot use a *chalef*;
Zol ich zine a m'lamed,	Should I be a *melamed*,
Ken ich nit kine alef. [*Refrain*]	I don't know an *alef*.

Zol ich zine a shoo-ster,	Should I be a cobbler,
Hob ich nit kine ko-pe-teh;	I don't have any last;
Zol ich zine a bek-ker,	Should I be a baker
Hob ich nit kine lo-pe-teh.	I don't have any shovel.
[*Refrain*]	

Zol ich zine a ko-val,	Should I be a blacksmith,
Hob ich nit kine ko-va-dleh;	I don't have any anvil;
Zol ich zine a shen-ker,	Should I run a tavern,
Is mine vibe a pa-d'leh. [*Refrain*]	My wife is a drunk.

MIT A NODEL, OHN A NODEL (With a Needle, Without a Needle)

Mit a no-del, ohn a no-del, nay ich meer b'-ko-vod go-dol. Mit a no-del, ohn a no-del,
(Spoken) nay ich meer b'-ko-vod go-dol. Ich nay un nay a gan-tze voch__ Ich ken shoyn nay-en a Par-iz-er loch.
Mit a no-del, ohn a no-del, nay ich meer b'-ko-vod go-del.

MIT A NODEL, OHN A NODEL: *Ibid.*

Refrain:

Mit a no-del, ohn a no-del,
Nay ich meer b'-ko-vod go-dol.
Mit a no-del, ohn a no-del,
[*Speak words*] Nay ich meer
   b'-ko-vod go-dol.

With a needle, without a needle,
I sit sewing with pleasure.
With a needle, without a needle,
I sit sewing with pleasure.

Ich nay un nay a gan-tze voch,
Ich ken shoyn nay-en a Par-iz-er
   loch. [*Refrain*]

I sew and sew all week long,
I can already sew a Parisian hole.

Ich tzee a-rois dee fas-trig-ge,
Un tu a lek fun'm ma-me-lig-ge.
   [*Refrain*]

I pull out the basting,
And taste a snack of *ma-me-lig-ge.*

EILI EILI

EILI EILI: Copyright, 1927, by Henry Lefkowitch. Used by permission of Metro Music Company.

nor ich tracht fun mine Gott, Ich heat mit moi-reh
up dine Toi-reh, dine ge-but, Re-te mich,
re-te mich fun ge-far, Vi a-mol d'o vos fun bay-zen gzar
Hair mine ge-bait un mine ge-vane, hel-fen kenst du
nor Gott a-lane, Shma Yis-ro-el a-do-noy e-lo-
hay-nu a-do-noy e-chod.

Ei-li ei-li lo-mo a-zav-to-ni?	Oh God, my God, why have You forsaken me?
Ei-li ei-li lo-mo a-zav-to-ni?	Oh God, my God, why have You forsaken me?
In fei-er un flam hut men uns ge-brent,	In fire and in flame they burned us,
I-ber-al ge-macht tzu shand un shpot,	Everywhere they dishonored and mocked us,
Doch op-tzu-ven-den hut uns kei-ner nit ge-kent	Yet they could not turn us away
Fun dir, mine Gott, mit dine hay-li-ger Toi-reh, un dine ge-but.	From You, my God, from Your holy Torah, and from Your commandments.
Ei-li ei-li lo-mo a-zav-to-ni?	Oh God, my God, why have You forsaken me?
Ei-li ei-li lo-mo a-zav-to-ni?	Oh God, my God, why have You forsaken me?
Tog un nacht, nor ich tracht fun mine Gott.	Night and day, I think only of my God.
Ich heat mit moi-reh up dine Toi-reh, dine ge-but.	Fearfully I guard Your Torah and Your commandments.
Re-te meech, re-te meech fun ge-far Vee a-mol d'o-vos fun bay-zen gzar!	Deliver me, deliver me, from danger And from evil decree as you once did our forefathers!
Hair mine ge-bait un mine ge-vane, Hel-fen kenst du nor Gott a-lane,	Hear my prayer and my weeping, Only You alone, God, can succor me!
Sh'ma Yis-ro-el a-do-noy e-lo-hey-nu A-do-noy e-chod.	Hear, O Israel, the Lord our God, the Lord is One!

A BREEVELE DER MAMEN! (A Letter to Mother)

Moderate

Mine kind, mine trayst, dee foorst a - vek, zay
zei a zuhn a goo - ter; Dich bate mit
treh - ren un mit shrek dine try - ye lee - be
mut - ter. Dee foorst, mine kind, mine
ain - tzig kind, a - rib - ber vei - te
yah - men, Ach, kum a - heen nor
frish ge - zund un nit far - gess dine
mam - men. Yoh! foor ge - zund un
koom mit glik zay yay-den voch a bree-vel shik. Dine
mam - mes hertz, mine kind, der - kvik. A

This song originated among the Jewish immigrants on New York's East Side about 1908 or 1909 and became a great favorite because it articulated the universal homesickness for relatives left behind in the old country.

bree—ve—le der man—men, zolst du— nit fer—
zom—men, Shribe ge-shvind, lee-bes kind, shenk ihr dee ne—
chul—me, Dee mam—me vet dine breev'—le leh—zen
un— zee—vert ge—neh—zen, Heilst ihr shmertz
ihr bit—ter hertz er kvikt— ihr— dee—ne—shu—meh.

Mine kind, mine trayst, dee foorst a-vek,
Zay zy a zuhn ā goo-ter,
Dich bate mit treh-ren un mit shrek
Dine try-ye lee-be mut-ter.
Dee foorst mine kind, mine ain-tzig kind
A-rib-ber vy-te yah-men;
Ach kum a-heen nor frish ge-zund
Un nit far-gess dine ma-men,
Yoh! foor ge-zund un koom mit glik,
Zay yay-deh voch a bree-vel shik,
Dine ma-mes hertz mine kind der-kvik.

My child, my comfort, you're going away,
See that you remain a good son,
With tears and with anguish begs
Your devoted, loving mother.
You're going away, my only child
Across distant seas;
May you get there in good health,
And don't forget your mother.
Yes! Farewell and get there safely,
See that you write a letter once a week
And refresh your mother's heart, my child.

Refrain:
A bree-ve-le der ma-men
Zolst du nit fer-zom-en,
Shribe ge-shvind, lee-bes kind,
Shenk eer dee ne-cho-me.
Dee ma-me vet dine breev'-le leh-zen,
Un zee vert ge-neh-zen,
Heilst eer shmertz, eer bit-ter hertz,
Er-kvikt eer dee ne-sho-meh.

[Repeat refrain]

A letter to your mother
You must not neglect.
Write quickly, dear child,
Give her that consolation.
Your mother will read your letter,
And she will rejoice,
You'll ease her pain, her bitter heart,
You'll refresh her spirit.

Lullabies and Children's Songs

ROZHENKES MIT MANDLEN (Raisins and Almonds)

In dem beys ha-mik-dosh In a vin-kel chey-der
zitst dee al-mo-ne bas Tsee-on a-leyn eer ben
yo-chi-dl Yee-de-le--vigt zee ke-sey der Un

Chorus

singt eem tzum shlo----fen a lee----de----le sheyn. Un-ter
Yee-de-les vi------ge-le--- Shteyt a klor-vice .tsi.--ge
le dos tsi-ge-le iz ge-fo----ren hand-len----
dos vet zine dine be---ruf Ro-zhen-kes-----mit
mandlen Shlof-je Yee-de-le shlof.

Im dem beys ha-mik-dosh, in a vin-kel chey-der,	In the Temple, in a far corner,
Zitst dee al-mon-e bas Tsee-on a-leyn.	The widow, the Daughter of Zion, sits solitary.
Eer ben yoch-id'l Yee-del-e vigt zee ke-sey-der,	Her only child, little Judah, she rocks unceasingly,
Un singt eem tzum shlof-en a lee-del-e sheyn.	And puts him to sleep with a lovely tune.
Un-ter Yee-del-es vig-el-e	Behind little Judah's cradle
Shteyt a klor vice tsig-el-e.	Stands a pure white kid.
Dos tsig-el-e is ge-for-en hand-len;	The kid went off to trade;
Dos vet zine dine ber-uf,	That will be your calling,
Rozh-en-kes mit mand-len.	Raisins and almonds.
Shlof-zhe Yee-del-e shlof.	Sleep, little Judah, Sleep.

ROZHENKES MIT MANDLEN: From *Jewish Community Songster*, compiled and edited by the Board of Jewish Education: Chicago, 1929.

SHLUF, MINE KIND (Sleep, My Child)

Shluf mine kind, mine trayst mine
    shay-ner,
Shluf-zhe zoo-ne-new,
Shluf mine lay-ben, mine kad-dish
    ein-er,
Lu-lin-ke lu lu.
Shluf mine lay-ben, mine kad-dish
    ein-er,
Lu-lin-ke lu lu.

Sleep, my child, my comfort, my
    pretty,
Sleep, my darling son.
Sleep, my life, my only *kaddish.*
Lu-lin-ke lu lu.
Sleep, my life, my only *kaddish.*
Lu-lin-ke lu lu.

By dine vee-gel zitzt dine ma-me,
Zingt a leed un vaynt,
Vest a-mol fer-shtehn mis-ta-mo
Vos zee hut ge-maynt. [*Repeat 2
    lines*]

By your cradle sits your mama,
Sings a song and weeps.
You'll understand some day most
    likely,
What is in her mind.

In A-mer-i-ca is der ta-te
Dy-ner, zoo-ne-new,
Du bist noch a kind les atoh,
Shluf-zhe, shluf lu lu. [*Repeat 2
    lines*]

In America lives your papa,
My darling little son,
You're still a child at present,
So sleep, sleep lu lu.

SHLUF, MINE KIND: From *Yiddish Folk Songs*, collected and arranged by Sarah P. Schack and E. S. Cohen. Bloch Publishing Co. New York, 1927. Yiddish text by Sholom Aleichem.

Dor-ten est men in der voch-en
Cha-leh zoo-ne-new,
Ya-che-lech vel ich deer dort
    koch-en,
Shluf-zhe, shluf lu lu. [*Repeat 2
    lines*]
	There they eat on every week-day
	Chaleh, darling son,
	There I'll cook fine broths for you,
	So sleep, sleep lu lu.

Er vet shik-en tzvon-tzig dol-lar, Zine por-tret der-tzu, Un vet neh-men, lay-ben zol er, Unz a-hin-tzu-tzu. [*Repeat 2 lines*]	Papa will send us twenty dollars, And his picture too, And he'll take us, long life to him, - To be there with him.
Er vet chaph-en dich tzu kush-en, Shvy-gen ash far freid, Ich vel kvel-len, tray-ren geese-n, Vy-nen shtill-er-heid. [*Repeat 2 lines*]	He'll pick you up and kiss you, Struck mute for sheer joy, I'll look on and shed happy tears, Weeping silently.
Biz es kumt der gut-ter kvit-tel, Shluf-zhe zoo-ne-new, Shlut-en iz a ty-er mit-tel, Lu-lin-ke lu lu. [*Repeat 2 lines*]	'Til we get the happy letter, Sleep, my darling son, Sleeping is a precious help, Lu-lin-ke lu lu.

SHLUF MINE KIND, SHLUF KESAYDER
(Sleep, My Child, Sleep Unawaking)

Shluf, mine kind,—shluf kes - say - der, Zin - gen vel ich dir a lied: Az du, mine kind,— vest el - ter veh - ren, Ves - tu vis - sen an un - ter - shied, Az du, mine kind,— vest el - ter veh - ren, Ves - tu vis-sen an un - ter-shied.

SHLUF MINE KIND, SHLUF KESAYDER: From *Yiddishe Folkslieder Ois Dem Folks-Moil Gezamelt*, edited and compiled by J. L. Cahan. Internatzionale Bibliotek Ferlag Co. New York and Warsaw, 1912.

Shluf, mine kind, shluf ke-say-der,
Zin-gen vel ich dir a lied:
Az du, mine kind, vest el-ter veh-
ren,
Ves-tu vis-sen an un-ter-sheed.
Az du, mine kind, vest el-ter veh-
ren,
Ves-tu vis-sen an un-ter-sheed.

Sleep, my child, sleep unawaking,
I will sing a song for you:
When you, my child, will grow older
You will know the difference,
When you, my child, will grow older
You will know the difference.

Az du, mine kind, vest el-ter veh-ren,
Vest-tu ve-ren mit lite-n gleich,
Da-mols vest-tu ge-vohr ve-ren,
Vos haste o-rim un vos haste reich.

When you, my child, will grow
older,
You'll be like other men.
Then you'll discover
What means poor and what means
rich.

Dee tire-re-ste pa-latz-en, dee tire-
re-ste hy-zer,
Dos altz macht der o-rim-mann;
Nor vy-stu, ver es tut in zy voi-
nen?
Gor nisht der, nor der reich-er
mann.

The most splendid palaces, the
finest houses,
All these the poor man makes.
But do you know who lives in them?
No, not he—but the rich man.

Der o-rim-mann, er ligt in kay-ler,
Der vill-gutsh rint eem fun dee
vent,
Der-fun be-kumt er a re-mat-ten
fay-ler,
In dee fees un in dee hent.

The poor man, he lies in the cellar,
The damp drips from all the walls,
From that he gets rheumatic pains
In his legs and in his hands.

SHLUF, MINE FAYGELE (Sleep, My Little Bird)

Shluf mine fay-ge-le,
Mach tzu dine ay-ge-le,
Eye-lu-lu-lu;
Shluf ge-shmok mine kind,
Shluf un zy ge-zund,
Eye-lu-lu-lu;
Shluf un cho-lem zees,
Fun der velt ge-nees,
Eye-lu-lu-lu;
Kol z'man du bist yung,
Kens-tu shluf-en gring,
Lach-en fun als-ding,
Eye-lu-lu.

Sleep my little bird,
Shut your little eyes,
Eye-lu-lu-lu;
Sleep soundly, my child,
Sleep and be well,
Eye-lu-lu-lu;
Sleep and dream sweetly,
Enjoy the world,
Eye-lu-lu-lu;
While you are still young,
You can sleep easily,
Laugh at everything,
Eye-lu-lu.

SHLUF, MINE FAYGELE: From *Yiddish Folk Songs*, collected and arranged by Sarah P. Schack and E. S. Cohen. Bloch Publishing Co. New York, 1927.

Tenderly

Shluf, mine fay-ge-le, Mach tzu dine ay-ge-le, Eye — lu — lu—

lu; Shluf ge-shmock mine kind, Shluf un zy ge-zund, Eye-lu— lu—

lu; Shluf un cho-lem zees, Fun der velt ge-nees,

Eye — lu — lu — lu; Kol-z'man du bist yung,

Ken-stu shluf-en gring, Lach-en fun als-ding, Eye-lu-lu.

AL-LE LIU-LE LIU-LE (A Cradle Song)

Slowly

Al-le liu-le liu-le, shlof-zhe ein mine g'du-le,

Mach-zhe tzu di-neh ay-ge-lach dee fi-neh.

Al-le liu-le, liu-le,	Al-le liu-le liu-le,
Shluf-zhe ein mine g'du-le,	Go to sleep my joy,
Mach-zhe tzu di-neh	Close your
Ay-ge-lech dee fi-neh.	Lovely little eyes.
Shtay oif vee-der	You'll awaken
Mit ge-zun-te glee-der,	With healthy limbs,
Mine leeb zees kind,	My dear sweet babe,
Geech un ge-shvind.	Soon and quickly.
Vest ois-vak-sen a grois-in-ker,	When you'll grow up,
Ves-tu zine a tan-na,	You'll be a sage,
Vel-len doch al-le	Then everyone
Zine meer me-ka-neh.	Will envy me.

AL-LE LIU-LE LIU-LE: From *Die Schönsten Lieder der Ostjuden*, compiled by Fritz M. Kaufmann, Jüdischer Verlag. Berlin, 1920.

UNTER DEM KIND'S VEEGELE (Under Baby's Cradle)

Quietly

Un - ter dem kinds vee - ge - le shtate a gol - den tzee-ge-le Dus tzee-ge-le is ge -foo - ren han — dl'n ro - zhin - kess mit mand — len. Ro - zhin-kess mit fy — gen, dus kind vet shlo -fen un shvy — gen.

Un-ter dem kind's vee-ge-le	Under baby's cradle
Shtate a gol-den tzee-ge-le.	Stands a golden kid,
Dus tzee-ge-le is ge-foo-ren hand-len	The kid went off to trade
Ro-zhin-kess mit mand-len.	With raisins and almonds.
Ro-zhin-kess mit fy-gen—	Raisins and figs—
Dus kind vet shluf-fen un shvy-gen.	Baby will sleep and hush.
Shluf meer, shluf meer in dine ruh,	Sleep then, sleep then and rest,
Mach dee ko-sher-e ai-ge-lech tzu!	Shut your lovely little eyes!
Mach zay tzu un mach zay oif,	Shut them tight then open wide.
Kumt der ta-te un vekt dich oif.	Papa comes and wants to wake you.
Ta-te, ta-te, nisht oif-vek!	Papa, papa—don't you wake him!
Dus kind vet shluf-en vite-er a-vek.	Baby's going to sleep some more.
Shluf-en is a gu-te schoi-reh,	Sleep is good merchandise,
Moi-she-le vet ler-nen Toi-reh.	Moi-she-le will study Torah.
Toi-reh vet er ler-nen,	Torah he will learn,
Sfo-rim vet er shry-ben,	Holy books he will write,
A gut-ter un a froo-mer,	Good and pious,
Vet er m'yehrtz-e-shem bly-ben.	God willing, he'll remain.

UNTER DEM KIND'S VEEGELE: From *Die Schönsten Lieder der Ostjuden,* compiled by Fritz M. Kaufmann. Jüdischer Verlag. Berlin, 1920.

POTSHE, POTSHE, KEECHELECH
(Clap Hands, Clap Hands, Little Cakes)

Pot-she, pot-she kee-che-lech; Der ta-te vet koi-fen shee-che-lech, Dee ma-me vet koi-fen — ze-ke-lech, Yan-ke-le vet ho-ben roi-te be — ke — lech.

Pot-she, pot-she, kee-che-lech,
Der ta-te vet koi-fen shee-che-lech,
Dee ma-me vet koi-fen ze-ke-lech,
Yan-ke-le vet hub-ben roi-te be-ke-lech.

Clap hands, clap hands, little cakes,
Papa will buy little shoes,
Mama will buy little socks,
Yankele will have little red cheeks.

TZIP-TZOP, EMERL! (Tzip-Tzop, Little Pail!)

Tzip, tzop, e-me-rl! Koom tzu mir in ke-me-rl! Vel ich dir e-pes vy-sen, Shif-e-lach mit ei-sen, Beer in dee kree-ge-lach, Kin-der in dee vee-ge-lach! Kin-der in dee vee-ge-lach shry-en vee dee tzee-ge-lach: "Ma meh! Ma meh!"

POTSHE, POTSHE, KEECHELECH: From *Yiddishe Folkslieder,* by Beregovski and Feffer. State Music Publishing House. Moscow, 1939. By arrangement with Leeds Music Corporation, New York, N. Y.
TZIP-TZOP, EMERL!: From *50 Zmiroth Liludim* (50 Songs for Children), by Julius Engel. Berlin, 1923.

Tzip-tzop, e-me-rl!	Tzip-tzop, little pail!
Koom tzu mir in ke-me-r'l!	Come to me in the pantry!
Vel ich dir ep-pes vy-sen,	There I'll show you something,
Shif-e-lach mit eis-en,	Little boats with iron,
Beer in dee kreeg-e-lach,	Beer in little pitchers,
Kin-der in dee veeg-e-lach!	Babies in their cradles!
Kin-der in dee veeg-e-lach,	Babies in their cradles
Shry-en vee dee tzeeg-e-lach:	Bleating like the goatkins:
"Ma—meh! Ma—meh!"	"Ma—meh! Ma—meh!"

OIF'N PRIPECHUK (In the Oven)

Oif' n pri-pe-chuk brent a fay-e - ril   un in shtub iz   heys

un der re - be le-rent kley-ne kin-der-lach   Dem A - lef Beys

Un der re - be le-rent kley-ne kin - der-lach   Dem A - lef Beys

Zeyt-je kin-der-lach Gedenkt-je tay-e-re vos eer le - rent   do

Zogt-je noch a-mol un ta-ke noch a-mol ko-mets A - lef,   O!

Oif'n pri-pe-chuk brent a fy-e-ril,	In the oven burns a little flame,
Un in shtub iz heys.	And it's hot in the room.
Un der re-be le-rent kley-ne kin-der-lach dem A-lef Beys,	And the teacher drills the little children in the alphabet,
Un der re-be le-rent kley-ne kin-der-lach dem A-lef Beys.	And the teacher drills the little children in the alphabet.

Refrain:

Zeyt-je kin-der-lach,	Pay attention, children,
Gedenkt-je ty-e-re,	Remember, dear ones,
Vos eer le-rent do.	What you study here,
Zogt-je noch a-mol,	Repeat once again,
Un ta-ke noch a-mol,	And then again
Komets A-lef, O!	*Komets A-lef O!**

OIF'N PRIPECHUK: From *Jewish Community Songster*, compiled and edited by the Board of Jewish Education. Chicago, 1929.
* Phonetic symbol. Untranslatable.

Zogt-je noch a-mol,
Un ta-ke noch a-mol,
 Komets A-lef, O!

Le-rent kin-der mit groys chey-shek,
A-zoy zog ich aych on,
Ver es vet fon aych kenen iv-ri,
Der be-kumt a fon. [*Refrain*]

Eer vet kin-der el-ter ver-en,
Vet eer al-leyn fer-shteyn,
Vee feel in die oys-yes lee-gen trey-
 ren,
Un vee feel gev-eyn! [*Refrain*]

Repeat once again
And then again
 Komets A-lef O!

Study, children, with great zest,
That is my request.
Which one of you will learn to read
 Hebrew
Will get a flag.

When you children will grow older,
You'll understand yourselves,
How many tears lie in these letters
And how much weeping!

A RETENISH (A Riddle)

A RETENISH: From *Jewish Folk Songs,* compiled by Henry Lefkowitch. Metro Music
Co. New York, 1927.

Du may-de-le, du shayns, du may-
de-le du fines,
Ich vel deer ep-pes fray-gen a re-te-
nish a fines:
Vos is hech-er far a hoiz,
Vos is flin-ker far a moiz?
Du na-ri-sher bo-cher, na-ri-sher
trop,
Du hosst nit kine say-chel in dine
kupp;
Der roich is hech-er far a hoiz,
Dee katz is flin-ker far a moiz.

Pretty little girl, good little girl,
I will ask you a clever riddle:
What is higher than a house,
What is swifter than a mouse?
You foolish fellow, you simpleton,
You have no sense in all your head;
Smoke is higher than a house,
The cat is swifter than a mouse.

[*Repeat first two lines*]
Vos far a vas-ser is ohn a zamd,
Vos far a may-lech is ohn a land?

What kind of water is without
sand,
What kind of king is without a
land?

[*Repeat 5th and 6th lines*]
Dos vasser fun oig is ohn zamd,
Der may-lech fun kor-ten is ohn
a land.

The water in the eye is without
sand,
The king of spades is without a
land.

Songs of Courtship and Marriage

GAY ICH MEER SHPATZEEREN (I Go Out Walking)

Gay ich meer shpa-tzee-ren,
Tra-la-la-la-la-la-la,
Gay ich meer shpa-tzee-ren,
Tra-la-la-la-la-la-la,
Do treft mich un a bo-cher, a-ha!
Do treft mich un a bo-cher, a-ha!

I go out walking,
Tra-la-la-la-la-la-la,
I go out walking,
Tra-la-la-la-la-la-la,
When lo! I meet a fellow, a-ha!
When lo! I meet a fellow, a-ha!

Er zugt er vet mich ne-men,
Tra-la-la-la-la-la-la, [*Repeat 2
lines*]
Nor er laygt es op oif zu-mer, a-ha!
[*Repeat line*]

He says he will marry me,
Tra-la-la-la-la-la-la,

Only he put it off for the summer,
a-ha!

GAY ICH MEER SHPATZEEREN: From *Jewish Folk Songs,* compiled by Henry Lefkowitch, Metro Music Co. New York, 1927.

Der zu-mer is ge-koo-men, Summer did come at last
Tra-la-la-la-la-la-la, [*Repeat 2* Tra-la-la-la-la-la-la,
 lines]

O-ber er hut mich nit ge-nu-men, But he did not marry me, a-ha!
 a-ha!

Nine, er hut mich nit ge-nu-men, No! He did not marry me, a-ha!
 a-ha! a-ha!   a-ha!

DEE MEZINKE OISGEGAYBEN (The Youngest Daughter Married Off)

Hech-er, bes-ser, dee rohd, dee rohd mach gres-ser!	Leap higher, the circle, the circle make bigger!
Grois hut mich Gott ge-macht,	God has raised me up,
Glik hut er meer ge-bracht,	Happiness He has brought to me,
Hul-yet kin-der a gan-tze nacht,	Revel, children, through the night,
Dee mez-in-ke ois-ge-gay-ben.	My youngest daughter I've married off.
[*Repeat line*]	
Shtar-ker fray-lech, du dee mal-keh, ich der may-lech!	Faster, joyous—you the queen, I the king!
Oy, oy, ich al-lane,	Oh, oh, I myself
Hub mit mei-ne oi-gen ge-zane,	Have seen with my own eyes
Vee Gott hut mich ma-tzlee-ach ge-vane,	How God has heaped blessings on me,
Dee mez-in-ke ois-ge-gay-ben.	My youngest daughter I've married off.
[*Repeat line*]	

DEE MEZINKE OISGEGAYBEN: From *Yiddish Folk Songs*, collected and arranged by Sarah P. Schack and E. S. Cohen. Bloch Publishing Co. New York, 1927.

VUSZHE VILS TU? (What Do You Want?)

Vus-zhe vil-stu, vus-zhe vil-stu? A shny-der far a man, a shny-der far a man? A shny-der far a man vil Ich nit! A shny-ders toch-ter bin Ich nit! Klyd-'lech nay-en ken Ich nit! Zitz Ich oif-'n shtane shtil-ler-hate un vane. Al-le may-de-lech hub-ben cha-se-neh, nor Ich blibe a-lane.

Vus-zhe vils-tu, vus-zhe vils-tu?
A shny-der far a mann?
A shny-der far a mann?
—A shny-der far a mann vil ich nit!
A shny-der's toch-ter bin ich nit!
Klyd-'lech nay-en ken ich nit!
Zitz ich oif'n shtane
Shtil-er-hate un vane:
Al-le may-de-lach hub-ben cha-
se-neh,
Nor ich blibe a-lane!

What do you want, what do you
want?
A tailor for a husband?
A tailor for a husband?
—A tailor for a husband I don't
want!
A tailor's daughter I am not!
Dresses sew I cannot!
So I sit upon a stone
Silently and weep:
All the girls are getting married,
But I am left alone!

Vus-zhe vils-tu, vus-zhe vils-tu?
A shoos-ter far a mann?
A shoos-ter far a mann?

What do you want, what do you
want?
A cobbler for a husband?
A cobbler for a husband?

VUSZHE VILS TU?: From *Die Schönsten Lieder der Ostjuden,* compiled by Fritz M. Kaufmann. Jüdischer Verlag. Berlin, 1920.

—A shoos-ter far a mann vil ich nit!
A shoos-ter's toch-ter bin ich nit!
Sheech lot-ten ken ich nit!
Zitz ich oif'n shtane
Shtil-er-hate un vane:
Al-le may-de-lach hub-ben cha-
se-neh,
Nor ich blibe a-lane!

—A cobbler for a husband I don't
want!
A cobbler's daughter I am not!
Shoes patch I cannot!
So I sit upon a stone
Silently and weep:
All the girls are getting married,
But I am left alone!

Vus-zhe vils-tu, vus-zhe vils-tu?
A rebb'n far a mann?
A rebb'n far a mann?
—A rebb'n far a mann vil ich doch!
A rebb'ns toch-ter bin ich doch!
Toi-reh ler-nen ken ich doch!
Zitz ich oif'n dach
Un kook a-roop un lach:
Al-le may-de-lach hub-ben cha-se-
neh,
Ich mit zay ba-glach!

What do you want, what do you
want?
A rabbi for a husband?
A rabbi for a husband?
—A rabbi for a husband I do want!
A rabbi's daughter I'm after all!
Torah learning I have got!
So I sit upon the roof
And looking down, I laugh:
All the girls are getting married,
Together I with them!

HAIR NOR DU, SHANE MAYDELE (Just Tell Me, Pretty Maid)

HE:

Hair nor, du shane may-de-le,
Hair nor, du fine may-de-le,
Vus ves-tu tu-en
In a-za vy-ten veg?
Vus ves-tu tu-en
In a za vy-ten veg?

Just tell me, pretty maid,
Just tell me, good maid,
What will you do
In such a far-off place?
What will you do
In such a far-off place?

SHE:

Ich vel gane in al-le gass-en
Un vel shry-en vesh tzu va-shen!
A-bee mit dir tzu-za-men zine!
A-bee mit dir tzu-za-men zine!

I will walk through all the streets
And will cry: "I wash clothes!"
So that you and I together will be,
So that you and I together will be!

HE:

Hair nor, du shane may-de-le,
Hair nor, du fine may-de-le,
Oif vus ves-tu shluf-en
In a-za vy-ten veg?
[Repeat 2 lines]

Just tell me, pretty maid,
Just tell me, good maid,
What will you sleep on
In such a far-off place?

HAIR NOR DU, SHANE MAYDELE: From *Yiddishe Folkslieder Ois Dem Folks-Moil Gezamelt*, edited and compiled by J. L. Cahan. Internatzionale Bibliotek Ferlag Co. New York and Warsaw, 1912.

Slow

Hair nor du shane may-de-le, Hair nor du fine
may-de-le, Vus ves-tu tu-en
in a-za vy—ten veg? Vus ves-tu
tu-en in a-za vy—ten veg?
Ich vel gane in al-le gas-sen Un vel shry-en
vesh tzu va-shen! A-bee mit dir tzu-
za-men zine, A-bee mit dir tzu-za-men zine!

SHE:
Ich bin noch a yun-ge froy,
Ich ken shluf-en oif a bint'l shtroy,
A-bee mit dir tzu-za-men zine!
   [*Repeat line*]

I am still a young woman,
I can sleep on a bundle of straw,
So that you and I together will be!

HE:
Hair nor, du shane may-de-le,
Hair nor, du fine may-de-le,
Mit vus ves-tu zich tzu-dek-ken
In a-za vy-ten veg?
   [*Repeat 2 lines*]

Just tell me, pretty maid,
Just tell me, good maid,
What will be your coverlet
In such a far-off place?

SHE:
Der toy fun him-mel vet-mich tzu-
   dek-ken,
Dee fay-ge-lech vell'n mich oif-vek-
   en,
A-bee mit dir tzu-zam-en zine!
   [*Repeat line*]

The dew of heaven will cover me,
The birds' singing will waken me,
So that you and I together will be!

ALLE MENTSHEN TANTZENDIK (While Everybody Is Dancing)

Fast

Al - le ment-shen tan-tzen-dik un shprin-gen-dik un la-chen-dik un zin-gen-dik, un Moi-she-le shtate alz vy-nen-dik. Moi-she, Moi-she! Vus, dee veinst? Ech vine,— vus ech mine:— Es iz shoyn tzite tzi der chip-pe tzi gine.

Al-le ment-shen tan-tzen-dik un shprin-gen-dik,
Un la-chen-dik un zin-gen-dik,
Un Moi-she-le shtate alz vine-nen-dik.
—Moi-she, Moi-she, vus! du veinst?
—Ech vine, vus ech mine
Es iz shoyn tzite tzi der chip-pe tzi gine!

While everybody is dancing and leaping
And laughing and singing,
Moishele stands and weeps.
—Moishe, Moishe, what! You're crying?
—I weep, I mean that
It's already time to go under the *chu-peh*

[*Repeat first 5 lines*]
Es iz shoyn tzite essen tzi gine!

It's already time to eat the wedding feast!

[*Repeat first 5 lines*]
Es iz shoyn tzite a mitz-veh-ten-tzel gine!

It's already time to dance a *mitzveh tentzel!**

[*Repeat first 5 lines*]
Es is shoyn tzite shlo-fen tzi gine!

It's already time to go to bed!

ALLE MENTSHEN TANTZENDIK: *Ibid.*

* The traditional Jewish wedding dance which all the relatives are obliged to dance with bride and groom as a *mitzvoh*, an act of piety.

DEE GILDERNE PAVEH (The Golden Peacock)

Es koomt ge-floi-gen dee gil-der-ne pa-veh
fun a frem-den land; fun a frem-den
land; Hot zee far-loi-ren dem gil-der-nem fe-der
mit a grois-sen shand, Hot zee far-loi-ren dem
gil-der-nem fe-der mit a grois-sen shand.

Es koomt ge-floy-gen dee gil-der-ne pa-veh
Fun a frem-den land,
Fun a frem-den land.
Hut zee far-loy-ren dem gil-der-nem fe-der
Mit a grois-sen shand,
Hut zee far-loi-ren dem gil-dern-nem fe-der
Mit a grois-sen shand.

A golden peacock came flying
From a foreign land,
From a foreign land,
And she lost her golden feather
In burning shame,
And she lost her golden feather
In burning shame.

Es is nit a-zoy der gil-dern-ne fe-der
Vee dee pa-veh a-lane.
  [*Repeat line*]
Es is nit a-zoy der ay-dem
Vee dee toch-ter a-lane.
  [*Repeat 2 lines*]

It isn't so much the golden feather
As the peacock herself,

It isn't so much the son-in-law
As the daughter herself.

Vee es is bit-ter, mine lee-be mit-ter,
A fay-ge-le oif dem yahm.
  [*Repeat line*]
A-zoy is bit-ter, mine lee-be mit-ter,
Az me kumt un tzu a schlech-ten
  mann. [*Repeat 2 lines*]

Just as 'tis bitter, my dear mother,
For a little bird on the sea,

So it is bitter, my dear mother,
To put up with a cruel husband.

DEE GILDERNE PAVEH: *Ibid.*

Vee es is bit-ter, mine lee-be mit-ter,   Just as 'tis bitter, my dear mother,
A fay-ge-le ohn a nest.   For a little bird without a nest,
    [Repeat line]
A-zoy is bit-ter, mine lee-be mit-ter,   So it is bitter, my dear mother,
Shver un shvi-ger's kest.   To eat my in-laws' bread.
    [Repeat 2 lines]

Vee es is bit-ter, mine lee-be mit-ter,   Just as 'tis bitter, my dear mother,
A shtee-be-le ohn a teer.   To live in a doorless house,
    [Repeat line]
A-zoy is bit-ter, mine lee-be mit-ter,   So it is bitter, my dear mother,
Meer ohn deer. *[Repeat 2 lines]*   To live away from you.

A LEEBEH, A LEEBEH (A Love, A Love)

A LEEBEH, A LEEBEH: From *Yiddishe Folkslieder Ois Dem Folks-Moil Gezamelt,* edited and compiled by J. L. Cahan. Internatzionale Bibliotek Ferlag Co. New York and Warsaw, 1912.

A lee-beh, a lee-beh is gut tzu fih-
ren,
Mit a mentsh, o-ber nisht mit deer;
Ge-vald, ich vel durch dir kra-pee-
ren!
Vus hos-tu dich ein-ge-leebt in
meer?
Ge-vald, ich vel durch deer kra-pee-
ren!
Vus hos-tu dich ein-ge-leebt in
meer?

Vus shtays-tu un-ter my-neh fents-
ter,
A-zoi vee a zel-ner far der teer?
Tsu bin ich den dee tire-e-ste, dee
shen-ste?
Vus hos-tu zeech ein-ge-leebt in
meer?

A fy-er hut ge-darft dus hoiz far-
bren-nen,
I-der ich hub dich dort ge-zane;
Der ty-vel hut mich ge-darft tsu-
nem-men,
I-der du host zeech ein-ge-leebt in
meer!

Vest krug-en a shen-ne-reh un a bes-
se-reh,
Zee vet zine klug-er noch far meer;
A-ber-yeh vet zee oych zine a gres-
se-reh,
Vus-zhe hos-tu zeech ein-ge-leebt in
meer?

It's good to be in love
With a real man, but not with you;
Gevalt! I'll croak yet on account of
you!
Did you have to fall in love with
me?
Gevalt! I'll croak yet on account of
you!
Did you have to fall in love with
me?

Why do you stand beneath my window
Like a soldier before the door?
Do you think me the most precious,
the prettiest?
Did you have to fall in love with
me?

A fire should have burned down that
house
Before I saw you there;
The devil should have taken me
Before you fell in love with me.

You'll find a prettier and a better
one,
She'll be cleverer than I;
More accomplished than I she'll also
be—
Did you have to fall in love with
me?

DU ZOLST NIT GAIN MIT KINE ANDERE MAYDELACH
(You Mustn't Go with Any Other Girls)

Du zolst nit gain mit kine an-de-re
may-de-lach,
Du zolst nor gain mit mir.
Du zolst nit gain tzu dine ma-me in
shtee-be-le,
Nor ku-men zol-stu tzu mir.
[*Hum*] Ta ra ra ram pam, (etc.)

You mustn't go with any other girl,
You must only go with me.
You mustn't go to your mama in her
little house,
But you must come to me.
[*Hum*] Ta ra ra ram pam, (etc.)

DU ZOLST NIT GAIN MIT KINE ANDERE MAYDELACH: *Ibid.*

Du zolst nit gain mit kine, an - de - re
may - de - lach, Du zolst nor - gain mit
mir, Du zolst nit, gain tzu dine ma - me in
shti - be - le, Nor ku - men zol-stu tzu
mir. Ta ra ra ram pam- (etc.)

A KALEH BAZETSEN (Melody for the Bride)

A KALEH BAZETSEN: From *Musikalisher Pinkas*, by A. M. Bernstein. Berlin, 1926.
A tune played by the *klezmer* (folk instrumentalists) to move the bride to tears
just before the wedding ceremony—a custom almost obsolete now but formerly
universally observed for centuries among Jews in Eastern Europe.

Dances and Song-Dances

HAVA NAGILA (Let Us Rejoice)

HAVA NAGILA: From *Jewish Community Songster*, compiled and edited by the Board of Jewish Education: Chicago, 1929.

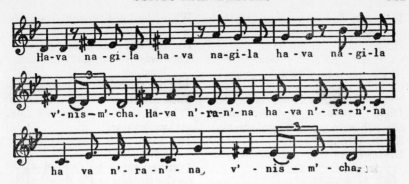

Ha-va na-gi-la ha-va na-gi-la ha-va na-gi-la

v'-nis—m'-cha. Ha-va n'-ran'-na ha-va n'-ra-n'-na

ha va n'-ra-n'-na, v'-nis—m'-cha.

Ha-va na-gi-la v'-nis-m'cha!
Ha-va n'-ra-n'-na v'-nis-m'-cha!
U-ru a-chim b'-lev sa-may-ach!

Let us rejoice and jubilate!
Let us sing and rejoice!
Awake, brothers, with joyful hearts!

B'SHUV ADONOY

B'shuv a-do-noy· b'shuv a-do-noy es shee-vas tsee-yon ho-

yee-nu k' chol-meem oz yi-mo-ley s'-chok pee nu

ul-sho-ney-nu ree-noh ree-noh oz yom-ru va-go-yim oz

yom-ru va-go-yim hig-deel a-do-noy la-sos eem

ey-leh, hig deel a-do-noy la-sos eem-mo-nu, shu-voh a-

do noy es sh'vee sey nu es sh'vee-sey nu ka-fee-keem·

ba-ne-gef ha-zor-eem b'-dim-oh ha-zor-eem

b'-dim-oh b'-ree-noh b'-ree-noh yik-tso-ru.

B'SHUV ADONOY: *Ibid.*

B'shuv a-do-noy es shee-vas tsee-
    yon,
Ho-yee-nu k'chol-meem.
Oz yi-mo-ley s'chok pee-nu,
Ul-sho-ney-nu ree-noh;
Oz yom-ru va-go-yim:
Hig-deel a-do-noy la-sos eem ey-leh,
Hig-deel a-do-noy la-sos eem-o-nu.
Shu-voh a-do-noy es sh'vee-sey-nu,
Ka-fee-keem ba-ne-gev.
Ha-zor-eem b'dim-oh b'ree-noh yik-
    tso-ru.

When the Lord brought back those
    that returned to Zion,
We were like unto them that dream.
Then was our mouth filled with
    laughter,
And our tongue with singing;
Then said they among the nations:
"The Lord hath done great things
    with these,"
The Lord hath done great things
    with us.
Turn our captivity, O Lord,
As the streams in the dry land.
They that sow in tears shall reap in
    joy.

AM YISROEL CHAY (The People of Israel Live!)

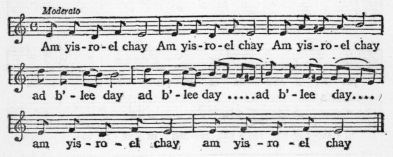

Am Yis-ro-el chay!
Am Yis-ro-el chay,
Ad b'lee day.

The people of Israel live!
The people of Israel live,
Eternally!

ARTSA ALINU

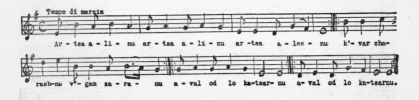

AM YISROEL CHAY: *Ibid.*
ARTSA ALINU: From *Manginoth Shireynu*, by Moshé Nathanson. Hebrew Publishing Co. New York, 1939.

Ar-tsa a-li-nu, ar-tsa a-li-nu,
K'var cha-rash-nu v'-gam za-ra-nu;
A-val od lo ka-tsar-nu,
A-val od lo ka-tsar-nu.

We have gone to the land,
We have plowed and also sowed;
But we have not yet reaped,
But we have not yet reaped.

NAALEH L'ARTSEYNU (Onward, On to Palestine)

Na-a-leh l'-ar-tsey-nu b'-ri-noh
na-a-leh l'-ar-tsey-nu b'-ree-noh Yom gee-loh
yom ree-noh Yom k-du-shoh yom m'-nu-choh
Lively
Na-a leh l'-ar-tsey-nu b'-ree-noh na-a-leh l' a-ar-tsey-nu
1 b'-ree-noh 2 b'-ree-noh.

Na-a-leh l'ar-tsey-nu
B'ri-noh na-a-leh
L'ar-tsey-nu b'ree-noh;
Yom-gee-loh yom-ree-noh
Yom-kdu-shoh yom-m'nu-choh
Na-a-leh l'ar-tsey-nu b'ree-noh
Na-a-leh l'ar-tsey-nu b'ree-noh.

Onward, on to Palestine
We gaily throng,
Onward, on to Palestine
Come, swing along.

Joyous day
Gladsome day!
Hallowed day!
Peace for aye.

Onward, on to Palestine
We gaily throng,
Onward, on to Palestine
Come, sing our song.

NAALEH L'ARTSEYNU: From *Jewish Community Songster*, compiled and edited by the Board of Jewish Education: Chicago, 1929. Translation by George M. Hyman.

GILU HAGOLILIM (Song of the Watchman)

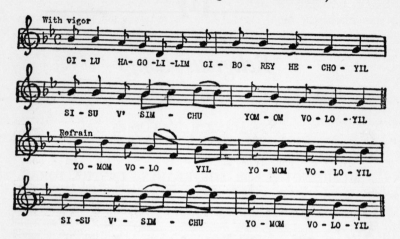

Gi-lu ha-go-li-lim,
Gi-bo-rey he-cho-yil;
Si-su v'sim-chu
Yo-mom vo-lo-yil!

Mey-chesh-kas ha-lay-law
O-leh kol cho-lil,—
Shi-ro yash-mi-a
Sho-mer ha-go-lil.

Yeh-meh ha-go-lil
Ko yeh-meh l'vo-vee;
Ro-vi b'tsi-dee,
V'su-see a-ro-vee.

Zu-los-cho ha-go-lil,
Mah lee u-mee lee?
Ha-go-lil, ha-go-lil,
Ach a-toh go-li-lee!

Glee reigns in Galilee,
The Galil rejoices.
The day and the night round
Lift up your voices.

Thru night's witching darkness
A flute softly sounding,
The watchman of Galilee
His watch song resounding.

Sing ho, my Galilee,
O, sing on my heart strings
With gun and my noble steed
I fear not what fate brings.

Who am I, what have I,
Without thee, my Galil?
Glorious Galilee;
I love thee, my Galil.

GILU HAGOLILIM: From *Little Books of Jewish Songs: Chamisho Osor Bishvat* (Palestine Arbor Day). Board of Jewish Education. Chicago, 1928. Translation by A. M. Dushkin.

[2]

Religious Songs

SYNAGOGUE MELODIES

MUSIC NOTES FOR THE READING OF THE TORAH

MUSIC NOTES FOR THE READING OF THE TORAH: Notations by Moshé Nathanson. In *Chumesh Haftaroth*. Hebrew Publishing Co. New York, 1928.

MUSIC NOTES FOR THE READING OF THE HAFTAROH

YIGDAL

Yig-dal E-lo-heem chai v'yish-ta-
   bach nim-tso v'eyn eys el
   m'tsee-u-so:
E-chod v'eyn yo-cheed k'yi-chu-do
   ne-e-lom v'gam eyn sof l'ach-
   du-so:

The living God we praise, exalt,
   adore!
He was, He is, He will be evermore.
No unity like unto His can be,
Eternal, inconceivable, is He.

YIGDAL: Music and Hebrew text from *Songs of My People*, compiled and edited by
Harry Coopersmith. The *Anshe Emet* Synagogue. Chicago, 1937. English text from the
Hebrew poem by Daniel ben Yehudah in *Songs of Zion*, translated by Alice Lucas.
J. M. Dent & Co. London, 1894.

Eyn lo d'mus ha-guf v'ey-no guf lo
na-a-roch ey-lov k'du-sho-so:

No form or shape has th' Incorpore-
al One,
Most holy beyond all comparison.

Kad-mon l'chol do-vor a-sher niv-ro
ri-shon v'eyn rey-shees l'rey-
shee-so:

He was, ere aught was made in heaven or earth,
But His existence has no date or
birth.

Hi-no a-don o-lom l'chol no-tsor yo-
reh g'du-lo-so u-mal-chu-so:

Lord of the Universe is He proclaimed,
Teaching His Power to all His hand
has framed.

She-fa n'vu-o-so n'so-no el an-shey
s'gu-lo-so v'sif-ar-to:

He gave His gift of prophecy to
those
In whom He gloried, whom He
loved and chose.

Lo kom b'Yis-ro-el k'Mo-sheh od
no-vee u-ma-beet es t'mu-no
-so:

No prophet ever yet has filled the
place
Of Moses, who beheld God face to
face.

To-ras e-mes no-san l'a-mo eyl al
yad n'vee-o ne-e-man bey-so:

Through him (the faithful in his
house) the Lord
The law of truth to Israel did ac-
cord.

Lo ya-cha-leef ho-eyl v'lo yo-meer
do-so l'o-lo-meem l'zu-lo-so:

This law God will not alter, will not
change
For any other through time's utmost range.

Tso-feh v'yo-dey-a s'so-rey-nu ma-
beet l'sof do-vor b'kad-mo-so:

He knows and heeds the secret
thoughts of man:
He saw the end of all ere aught began.

Go-meyl l'eesh che-sed k'mif-o-lo
no-seyn l'ro-sho ra-k'rish-o-so

With love and grace doth He the
righteous bless,
He metes out evil unto wickedness.

Yish-lach l'keyts ha-yo-meen
M'shee-chey-nu lif-dos m'cha-
key keyts y-shu-o-so:

He at the last will His anointed
send,
Those to redeem, who hope, and
wait the end.

Mey-sim y-cha-ye Eyl b'rov chas-
do-bo-ruch a-dey ad sheym
t'-hi-lo-so:

God will the dead to life again restore.
Praised be His glorious name for
evermore!

THE HISTORY OF *KOL NIDRE*

The prayer, *Kol Nidre*, which is the most important part of the synagogue liturgy on the eve of *Yom Kippur*, the Day of Atonement, has had a fabulous history. It is conjectured by musicologists that its melody must have originated some time during the Sixth or Seventh Century A.D., but where it cannot be said with any certainty. Its melodic line, majestic and yet plaintively discursive, has continuously fascinated composers of modern times, Jews and Gentiles alike. Beethoven, for instance, introduced the theme into one of his last great quartets, the one in C♯ minor, Opus 131. Max Bruch, rather ornately, adapted it for the cello with orchestral accompaniment. Leo Tolstoy was deeply affected by the *Kol Nidre* music. He described it as the saddest, yet the most uplifting, of all the melodies he knew, and "one that echoes the story of the great martyrdom of a griefstricken nation."

While the *Kol Nidre* melody possesses a wonderful clarity, the Aramaic text has proved enigmatical to many. Rabbi Kaufman Kohler describes it as "a rabbinic formula, recited by the Reader or *Hazzan* (cantor) on behalf of the congregation before the regular evening service of the Atonement Day by which all the vows and pledges made in the form of oaths and anathemas by the individuals with regard to their own person during the past year should be revoked and annulled."

The question then arises: why is such a disproportionate importance given to the individual's vows and pledges, a relatively trivial matter, on this, the most solemn holy day in the Jewish religious calendar? A number of modern scholars think they have found a persuasive explanation for this mystery. They point out that these are supposed to be no ordinary vows and pledges, that the text of *Kol Nidre* represents no matter-of-fact legalistic formula for their annulment. Rather, at the time the prayer was composed, it was designed for the numerous involuntary Jewish apostates in the Byzantine Empire. Later on, beginning with the terrible persecutions of 1391 and the massacres carried out by the fanatical Vicente Ferrer, *Kol Nidre* was for the special use of the tens of thousands of the Marrano "Conversos" in Spain and of the "Christãos Novas" in Portugal, who, under the threat of torture and death at the stake, had adopted the state religion, but secretly clung to the faith of their forefathers with the tearful fervor of the guilty. *Kol Nidre*, therefore, became the supreme penitential prayer of all those unfortunates who had made hypocritical vows and pledges to alien beliefs and thus, in chanting it, were making abject supplication for God's forgiveness. This, it is contended, is clearly proven by the fact that, immediately before it is sung, three times in succession, by the *hazzan*, two of the elders of the congregation step forward and each takes a Torah-scroll from the Ark. Flanking the *hazzan* on each side they solemnly recite together the following formula: "In the tribunal of heaven and the tribunal of earth, by the permission of God—blessed be He—and by the permission of this holy congregation, we hold it lawful to pray with the transgressors."—N. A.

KOL NIDRE

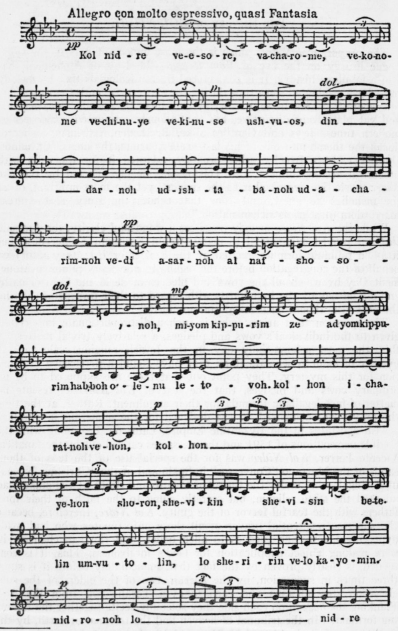

KOL NIDRE: From *Jewish Music*, by A. Z. Idelsohn. Henry Holt & Co. New York, 1929.

ve-le-so-ro-'noh lo-e-so - re. ush-vu - o - so -

noh lo._____ she-vu - os.

Kol nid-re ve-e-so-re, va-cha-ro-me,
  ve-ko-no-me ve-chi-ny-ye ve-
  ki-nu-se ush-vu-os,
Din-dar-noh ud-ish-ta ban-oh ud-a-
  cha
Rim-noh ve-di a-sar-noh al naf-sho-
  so-noh,
Mi-yom kip-pu-rim ze ad yom kip-
  pu-rim
Hab-boh o-le-nu le-to-voh.
Kol-hon i-cha-rat-noh ve-hon, kol-
  hon
Ye-hon sho-ron, she-vi-kin she-vi-
  sin be-te-lin
Um-vu-to-lin, lo she-ri-rin ve-lo ka-
  yo-min.
Nid-ro-noh lo nid-re
Ve-le-so-ro-noh lo e-so-re.
Ush-vu-o-so-noh lo she-vu-os.

All vóws (*kol nidre*), obligations,
oaths, and anathemas, whether
called "konam," "konas," or by any
other name, which we may vow, or
swear, or pledge, or whereby we
may be bound, from this Day of
Atonement until the next (whose
happy coming we await), we do repent. May they be deemed absolved,
forgiven, annulled, and void, and
made of no effect; they shall not
bind us nor have power over us.
The vows shall not be reckoned
vows, the obligations shall not be
obligatory; nor the oaths be oaths.

ADON OLAM

A-don o-lam a-sher mo-lach,
B'te-rem kol y'tseer niv-ro,
L'eys na-a-soh b'chef-tso kol a-zai
  me-lech sh'mo nik-ro.
V'a-cha-rey kich-los ha-kol
L'va-do yim-loch no-ro,
V'hu ho-yoh v'hu ho-veh
V'hu yih-yeh b'sif-o-roh.

Lord of the world, He reigned alone
While yet the universe was naught,
When by His will all things were
  wrought,
Then first His sov'ran name was
  known.
And when the All shall cease to be,
In dread lone splendour He shall
  reign,
He was, He is, He shall remain
In glorious eternity.

ADON OLAM: Text by Solomon ibn Gabirol (1021-58). Translated by Israel Zangwill.
In *Daily Prayer Book,* compiled by Chief Rabbi J. H. Hertz. London, 1942. Music
from *Songs of My People,* compiled and edited by Harry Coopersmith. The *Anshe
Emet* Synagogue. Chicago, 1937.

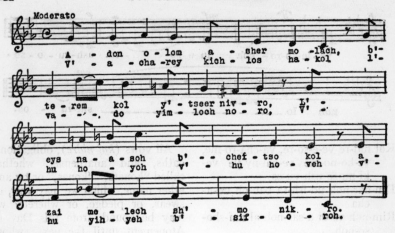

SHEMA

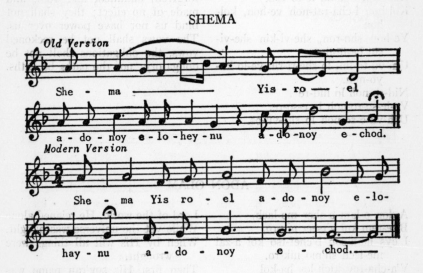

She-ma Yis-ro-el a-do-noy e-lo-hey-nu a-do-noy e-chod.

Hear, O Israel, the Lord our God, the Lord is One.

SHEMA: Old Version from *Jewish Music*, by A. Z. Idelsohn. Henry Holt & Co. New York, 1929. New Version from *Manginoth Shireynu*, by Moshé Nathanson. Hebrew Publishing Co. New York, 1939.

The *Shema* is the religious Jew's confession of faith. It contains the central keynote of Judaism: the unity and Oneness of God. This is the prayer that is closest to the heart of the pious Jew and is most often on his lips. In time of great danger, and when he lies on his deathbed, he recites it with fervent emotion.—N. A.

Devotional Songs

ADIR HU

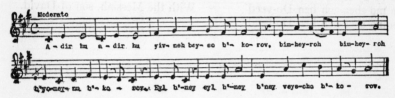

A-dir hu a-dir hu yiv-neh bey-so
   b'ko-rov, bim-hey-roh
B'yo-mey-nu b'ko-rov.
Eyl b'-ney eyl b'-ney
B'-ney veys-cho b'-ko-rov.

May the Mighty One soon rebuild
   His house
Speedily, speedily soon, in our days.
O God, rebuild it, rebuild Thine
   house betimes.

ELEEYOHU HANOVEE

(Go back to REFRAIN till END)

ADIR HU: From *Manginoth Shireynu*, by Moshé Nathanson. Hebrew Publishing Co. New York, 1939.
ELEEYOHU HANOVEE: From *Jewish Community Songster*, compiled and edited by the Board of Jewish Education. Chicago, 1929.

[*Chorus*]

E-lee-yo-hu ha-no-vee	Elijah, the Prophet
E-lee-yo-hu ha-tish-bee	Elijah, the Tishbite
E-lee-yo-hu, E-lee-yo-hu	Elijah, the Gileadite
E-lee-yo-hu ha-gil-o-dee	

Bim-hey-roh b'yo-mey-nu	May he speedily
Yo-vo ey-ley-nu	Come to us
Im mo-shee-ach ben Do-veed	With the Messiah, son of David.
Im mo-shee-ach ben Do-veed	

OBER YIDEN ZAYNEN MEER (But Jews We Are)

Ver meer zayn-en zayn-en meer　O-ber yid-en zayn-en meer
Vos meer lern-en lern-en meer　O-ber Toyroh lernen meer.

Ver meer zay-nen—zay-nen meer	Whoever else we are—we are,
O-ber Yi-den zay-nen meer,	But Jews we are;
Vos meer ler-nen—ler-nen meer,	Whatever else we learn—we learn;
O-ber Toy-reh, ler-nen meer.	But Torah we learn.

Ver meer zay-nen—zay-nen meer	Whoever else we are—we are,
O-ber Yi-den zay-nen meer	But Jews we are;
Vos mir gib-en—gib-en meer	Whatever else we give—we give,
O-ber n'do-vos gib-en meer.	But charity we give.

Ver mir zay-nen—zay-nen meer,	Whoever else we are—we are,
O-ber Yi-den zay-nen meer	But Jews we are;
Vos meer zing-en—zing-en meer	Whatever else we sing—we sing,
O-ber Z'meeros zing-en meer.	But *Zemiros* we sing.

OBER YIDEN ZAYNEN MEER: *Ibid.*

MAYERKE, MINE ZUHN (Mayerke, My Son)

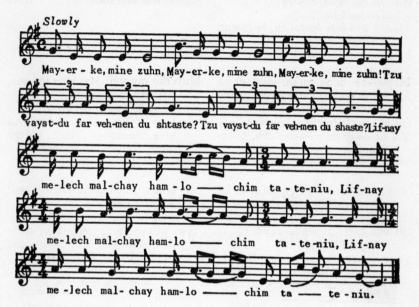

May-er-ke, mine zuhn, May-er-ke, mine zuhn, May-er-ke, mine zuhn! Tzu vayst-du far veh-men du shtaste? Tzu vayst-du far veh-men du shaste? Lif-nay me-lech mal-chay ham-lo —— chim ta-te-niu, Lif-nay me-lech mal-chay ham-lo —— chim ta-te-niu, Lif-nay me-lech mal-chay ham-lo —— chim ta —— te-niu.

May-er-ke mine zuhn, May-er-ke
  mine zuhn, May-er-ke mine
  zuhn!
Tzu vayst-tu far veh-men du
  shtaste?
Tzu vayst-tu far veh-men du
  shtaste?
Lif-nay me-lech mal-chay ham-lo-
  chim, ta-te-niu,
Lif-nay me-lech mal-chay ham-lo-
  chim, ta-te-niu,
Lif-nay me-lech mal-chay ham-lo-
  chim, ta-te-niu.

Mayerke my son, Mayerke my son,
  Mayerke my son!
Do you know before whom you're
  standing?
Do you know before whom you're
  standing?
Before the King of Kings, Father
  dear,
Before the King of Kings, Father
  dear,
Before the King of Kings, Father
  dear.

May-er-ke mine zuhn, May-er-ke
  mine zuhn, May-er-ke mine
  zuhn!
Vus ves-tu ois-bet-ten ba eem?
  [*Repeat line*]
Bo-nay, cha-yay, me-zo-nay, ta-te-
  niu! [*Repeat twice*]

Mayerke my son, Mayerke my son,
  Mayerke my son!
What is it you'll ask of the Lord?
"Sons, life, and sustenance," Father
  dear.

MAYERKE, MINE ZUHN: From *Die Schönsten Lieder der Ostjuden*, compiled by Fritz M. Kaufmann. Jüdischer Verlag. Berlin, 1920.

May-er-ke mine zuhn, May-er-ke
   mine zuhn, May-er-ke mine
   zuhn!
Oif vus darfs-tu *bo-nay?*
   [*Repeat line*]
Bo-nim oys-kim ba-toi-ru, ta-te-niu.
   [*Repeat twice*]

Mayerke my son, Mayerke my son,
   Mayerke my son!
For what do you need sons?
"Sons to study the Torah," Father
   dear.

May-er-ke mine zuhn, May-er-ke
   mine zuhn, May-er-ke mine
   zuhn!
Oif vus darfs-tu *chay* [*Repeat line*]
Kol ha-chay-im you-dee-chu, ta-te-
   niu.

Mayerke my son, Mayerke my son,
   Mayerke my son!
For what do you need life?
"And everything that lives shall
   give thanks to You," Father
   dear.

May-er-ke mine zuhn, May-er-ke
   mine zuhn, May-er-ke mine
   zuhn!
Oif vus darfs-tu *me-zo-nay?*
   [*Repeat line*]
*Ve-u-chal-tu ve-su-vo-tu ee-vay-
   rach-tu,* ta-te-niu.

Mayerke my son, Mayerke my son,
   Mayerke my son!
For what do you need sustenance?
"You will eat, and you will be satis-
   fied, and you will praise the
   Lord," Father dear.

May-er-ke mine zuhn, May-er-ke
   mine zuhn, May-er-ke mine
   zuhn!
Tzu vays-tu vehr du bist?
   [*Repeat line*]
Hi-ne-ni, heh-o-ni mi-ma-as, ta-te-
   niu. [*Repeat three times*]

Mayerke my son, Mayerke my son,
   Mayerke my son!
Do you know who you are?
"O behold me, destitute of good
   deeds," Father dear.

YISMACH MOISHE (Moses Rejoiced)

Yis-mach Moi-she be-mat-nass,
Yis-mach Moi-she be-mat-nass,
Yis-mach Moi-she be-mat-nass,
Be-mat-nass chel-koy.
Oy! Vee hut men eem ge-ru-fen?
Vee hut men eem ge-ru-fen?
Ki e-ved nay-mon ku-ru-su loy.
Ki e-ved nay-mon ku-ru-su loy.

Moses rejoiced in the gift,
Moses rejoiced in the gift,
Moses rejoiced in the gift,
The gift of his portion.
Oh! How did they call him?
How did they call him?
A faithful servant You called him,
A faithful servant You called him.

YISMACH MOISHE: *Ibid.*

Yis-mach Moi-she be-mat——nass, Yis-mach Moi-she be-mat——nass, Yis-mach Moi-she be-mat——nass, Be-mat-nass chel——koy. Oy! vee hot men eem ge-ru-fen? Vee hot men eem ge-ru-fen? Ki e-ved—— nay-mon ku-ru-su—loi, ki e-ved—— nay-mon ku-ru-su— loi.

Yis-mach Moi-she be-mat-nass,
  [*Repeat twice*]
Be-mat-nass chel-koy.
Oy! ven is dos ge-vay-zen?
Ven is dos ge-vay-zen?
Be-om-doy le-fu-ne-chu al har see-
  nai. [*Repeat line*]
	Moses rejoiced over the gift,
	The gift of his portion.
	Oh! When was the occasion?
	When was the occasion?
	When he stood before You on
	  Mount Sinai.

Yis-mach Moi-she be-mat-nass,
  [*Repeat twice*]
Be-mat-nass chel-koy.
Oy! Vus is dort ge-shta-nen un-ge-
  shreeb'n?
Vus is dort ge-shta-nen un-ge-shree-
  b'n?
V'cho-sif bo-hem shmi-ras shab-bos.
  [*Repeat line*]
	Moses rejoiced over the gift,
	The gift of his portion.
	Oh! What was written upon them?
	What was written upon them?
	Therein was written to observe the
	  Sabbath day.

GOTT FUN AVROHOM (God of Abraham)

Ad libitum

p Gott fun av - ro - hom fun yitz-chok un fun ya - a - koiv

ba - heet dine hei - lig folk yis - ro - el fun a - lem bei - zen,

az der li - ber hei - li - ger sha-bes koi-desh geht a - vek

un die voch un der choi - desh un dos yohr vos kumt on,

soll zein tsu ma - zel un tsu bro - cho tsu oy-sher unt tsu

ko - vod, tsu par - no - - so toi - vo, tsu

ma - - sim toi - vim un tsu b' - su - rös

toi - vois un tsu a - lem gu - ten A - - men.

GOTT FUN AVROHOM: From *Sabbath*, by Abraham E. Millgram. Music edited by Prof. A. W. Binder. With the permission of the copyright owners, The Jewish Publication Society of America. Philadelphia, 1944.

This most beloved of Yiddish devotional songs for the Jewish woman is of Seventeenth Century origin. It is chanted rather than sung on the Sabbath day at twilight and sounds all the anxious overtones of the insecure life of the ghetto.

Gott fun Av-ro-hom, fun Yitz-chok
un fun Ya-a-koiv,
Ba-heet dine hei-lig folk Yis-ro-el
fun a-lem bay-zen!
Az der lee-ber hei-li-ger sha-bes koi-
desh geht a-vek,
Un dee voch un der choi-desh un
dos yohr vos koomt ohn,
Zoll zine tsu ma-zel un tsu bro-cho,
tsu oy-sher un tsu ko-vod,
Tsu par-no-so toi-vo, tsu ma-sim
toi-vim un tsu b'-su-ros toi-
vois un tsu a-lem gu-ten. U-
mane!

God of Abraham, of Isaac and of
Jacob,
Protect Your holy people Israel
from all evil!
As the dear holy Sabbath departs,
And the week and the month and
the year ahead approach,
May they bring good fortune and
blessings, prosperity and honor,
May they bring good living, good
deeds and good tidings and all
else that is good. Amen!

Hasidic Songs and Dances

V'TAHEYR LEEBEYNU (And Purify Our Hearts)

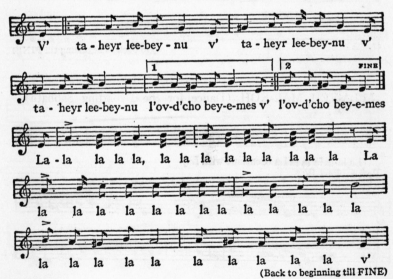

(Back to beginning till FINE)

V'ta-heyr lee-bey-nu l'ov-d'cho bey-
e-mes,
La-la-la-la-la-la-la-la-la.
V'ta-heyr lee-bey-nu l'ov-d'cho bey-
e-mes.

Purify our hearts to serve You in
truth,
La-la-la-la-la-la-la-la-la.
Purify our hearts to serve You in
truth.

V'TAHEYR LEEBEYNU: From *Jewish Community Songster*, compiled and edited by the
Board of Jewish Education: Chicago, 1929.

DANCE OF REB MAYER

M'LA-VEH MAL-KOH (Dance for the Departing Sabbath)

DANCE OF REB MAYER: *Ibid.*
M'LA-VEH MAL-KOH: *Ibid.*

A DUDELE (You)

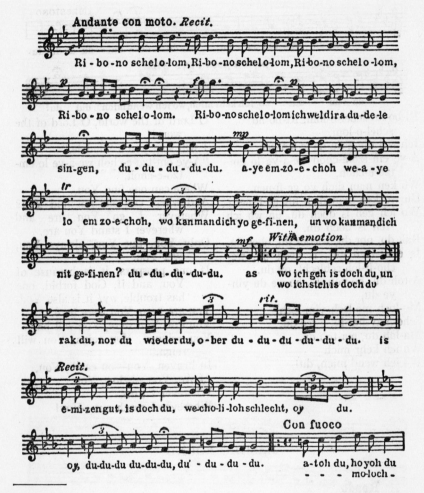

A DUDELE: From *Jewish Music,* by A. Z. Idelsohn. Henry Holt & Co., New York, 1929.
Unconsciously, the author of this *Hasidic* religious threnody, the Eighteenth Century
Rabbi Levi-Yitzchok, must have had in mind the morning prayer of Yehuda Halevy,
the great philosophical poet of Twelfth Century Spain. Halevy's morning prayer,
recited daily by every pious Jew, declares God is immanent in all creation, and man
does not have to seek him anywhere, except in the purity of his own heart. Halevy
sang:

Lord, where shall I find Thee?
High and hidden is Thy place!
And where shall I not find Thee?
The world is full of Thy glory!—N. A.

ho-we du yih-ye du   du-du-du-du - du. - du.   scho-mayim du, e-rez du,
me-lech - yim-loch-

ma-loh du, ma-toh du - du,   du - du - du - du.   du-du-du-du-

du - du - du.   wo ich kehr mich, wo ich wend mich   du!   du!

Ri-bo-no schel-o-lom, Ri-bo-no schel-o-lom,	O Lord of the world, O Lord of the world!
Ich wel dir a du-de-le sin-gen,	I will sing you a "dudele."
A-ye em-tzo-e-choh we-a-ye lo em-tzo-e-choh,	"A-ye em-tzo-e-choh we-a-ye lo em-tzo-e-choh,"
Wo ken man dich yo ge-fi-nen,	Where can one find You,
Un wo ken man dich nit ge-fi-nen?	And where can one not find You?
Wo ich geh is doch du, un wo ich steh is doch du.	Wherever I go You are and wherever I stand You are.
Rak du, nor du, wieder du, ober du.	Only You, but You, always You, ever You.
Is e-mi-tzen gut, is doch du, we-cho-li-loh schlecht, oy du.	If one prospers, it is because of You, and if, God forbid, one has trouble, *oy!* it is also You.
A-toh du, ho-yoh du, ho-we du yih-ye du,	You are here, You were here.
Mo-loch me-lech yim-loch.	You are, You were, You will be.
Scho-may-im du, e-rez du,	You reigned, You reign, You will reign.
Ma-loh du, ma-toh du,	In heaven, You—on earth, You.
Wo ich kehr mich	Above, You—below, You.
Wo ich wend mich, du!	Wherever I turn,
	Wherever I reach out—You!

HASIDIC ROUND

HASIDIC ROUND: *Ibid.*

A RADEL FUN'M LIBAVITCHER REBBE

A RADEL FUN'M LIBAVITCHER REBBE: From *Sabbath*, by Abraham E. Millgram. Music edited by Prof. A. W. Binder. With the permission of the copyright owners, The Jewish Publication Society of America. Philadelphia, 1944.

HASIDIC DANCE NO. I

HASIDIC DANCE NO. II

HASIDIC DANCE NO. I: From *Le'Hasidim Mizmor*, by Meir Simeon Geshuri. "Techiyah,"
Jerusulem, 1936.
HASIDIC DANCE NO. II: *Ibid.*

RABBI LEVI-YITZCHOK'S KADDISH

RABBI LEVI-YITZCHOK'S KADDISH: Arranged by Julius Engel. "Juwal," Verlagsgesell-
schaft für Jüdische Musik. Berlin, 1923.

Gut mor-g'n dir, Rib-boi-noi shel oi-lom!

Ich, Lay-vee Yitz-chok ben So-reh mi Ber-di-tchev,

Bin tzu dir ge-koo-men mit a din toi-reh

Far dine folk Yis-ro-el.

Un vos host-tu tzu dine folk Yis-ro-el?

Un vos host-tu zich on-ge-zetzt Oif dine folk Yis-ro-el?

Az vos nor a zach, is tzav es b'ney Yis-ro-el,

Un vos nor a zach, is e-moir li-vney Yis-ro-el!

Un vos nor a zach, is da-bare li-vney Yis-ro-el!

Ta-te-niu! Ka-mo u-mois b'oi-lom?

Bav-ly-im, Par-sy-im, Ed-o-my-im!

Good morning to You, Lord of the Universe!

I, Levi-Yitzchok, son of Sarah, of Berditchev,

Have come to You in a law-suit

On behalf of Your people Israel.

What have You against Your people Israel?

And why do You oppress Your people Israel?

No matter what happens, it is: "Command the Children of Israel!"

No matter what happens, it is: "Say to the Children of Israel!"

No matter what happens, it is: "Speak to the Children of Israel!"

Father dear! How many other peoples are there in the world?—

Babylonians, Persians, and Edomites! . . .

Dee Deitsh-len-der vos zog'n zay?
"Un-zer Kay-nig is a Kay-nig!"
Dee Eng-len-der vos zog'n zay?
"Un-zer Mal-chus is a Mal-chus!"
Un ich, Lay-vee Yitz-chok ben
So-reh mi Ber-di-tchev zog:
Yis-ga-dal v'yis-ka-dash shmay ra-
boh!
Un ich, Lay-vee Yitz-chok ben So-
reh mi Ber-di-tchev zog:
Lo o-zuz mim-koi-mee! 'Chvel zich
fun ort nit ree-ren!
Un a suff zol dos zine, un an ek zol
dos ne-men!
Yis-ga-dal v'yis-ka-dash shmay ra-
boh!

The Germans—what do they say?
"Our King is a King!"
The English—what do they say?
"Our Sovereign is a Sovereign!"
And I, Levi-Yitzchok, son of Sarah,
of Berditchev, say:
"Hallowed and magnified be the
name of God!"
And I, Levi-Yitzchok, son of Sarah,
of Berditchev, say:
"Lo o-zuz mim-koi-mee! I will not
stir from here!
An end there must be to this—it
must all stop!
*Hallowed and magnified be the
name of God!*

Glossary

Agada: (See main introduction for explanation.)

Ai: A Yiddish exclamation equivalent to the English Oh!

aleph-bess (bet): The first two letters of the Hebrew-Yiddish alphabet, i.e. learning how to read.

aleichem sholom: "To you be peace," which is the inverted Hebrew response to the customary salutation: *sholom aleichem*—"peace be to you."

Amoraim (s. *Amora*): The builders of the Talmud.

apikoiros (pl. *apikorsim*): From the ancient Greek word *Epikoureios*. In the *Mishna* and Talmud the *apikoiros* is described as a Jewish adherent of the Greek philosopher Epicurus. In the course of time the Greek origin of the word was forgotten and in Yiddish meant a heretic or free-thinker.

baal-tefilah: The leader of prayer, the precentor.

bagel: Hard circular roll with hole in the center like a doughnut but boiled and then baked; adapted from the Russian *bublitchki.*

bahelfer: Assistant to a *melamed* or Scripture-teacher.

Bar-Mitzvah: A thirteen-year-old Jewish boy who is confirmed; the confirmation ceremony itself.

blintzes: Cheese or *kasha* (groats) rolled in thin dough.

borsht: A beet or cabbage soup, of Russian origin.

bris: Circumcision ceremony; performed on the eighth day after birth of boy.

bronfin: Whisky.

chacham (pl. *chachamim*): Hebrew for wise man, sage.

chalef: Slaughterer's knife, also that of the Angel of Death.

chaleh: White Sabbath or holy day bread.

chalutz (halutz): A Jewish pioneer in the land of Israel.

Channukah (Hannukah): Described variously as "The Festival of Lights," "The Feast of Dedication," and "The Feast of the Maccabees." It is celebrated for eight days from the 25th day of *Kislev* (December). It was instituted by Judas Maccabeus and the elders of Israel in 165 B.C. to commemorate the rout of the invader Antiochus Ephinanes, and the purification of the Temple sanctuary.

chochem: Yiddish adaptation of Hebrew word *chacham.*

chochma: Wisdom.

cholent (shalet): Potted meat and vegetables cooked on Friday and simmered overnight for the Sabbath noonday meal.

chupeh: Marriage canopy under which bride and groom stand during the wedding ceremony.

chutzpah: Impudence, unmitigated gall.

datcha: A summer home in the country or seashore; in both Russian and Yiddish.

dayyan: A rabbinical judge.

Diaspora: The lands of the Jewish dispersion collectively.

dreydlach (s. *dreydel*): From the German *drehen,* "to turn." These are small metal tops, having four sides, and are spun with the fingers. Jewish children in East European countries traditionally play with them on *Channukah.*

fisnoga: Comical word-combination of the Yiddish *fis* (feet) and the Russian *noga* (feet).

gabbai (pl. *gabbaim*): Synagogue treasurer.

Gaon (pl. *Geonim*): The title given to the rectors of the two famous Talmudic academies of Sura and Pumbeditha in Babylon beginning with the Sixth Century. But the word also signifies "a genius." It was the title of honor given to Rabbi Elijah of Vilna, the 18th Century scholar.

gefillte fish: Stuffed fish seasoned with spices and eaten on the Sabbath.

Gehenna (Hebr. *Gehinnom*): Hell.

Gemara: The Aramaic name for the Talmud.

gesundheit: Good health!

gewalt: Help!

goniff: Thief.

goyish, derived from *goy* (pl. *goyim*): Gentile.

gribbenes: Small crisp pieces left from rendered poultry fat, eaten as a delicacy.

groschen: Small German silver coin whose old value was about two cents.

gulden: Austrian silver florin whose former worth was about forty-eight cents.

guten tog: Good-day; good-bye.

Habdalah: The benedictions and prayers recited at the conclusion of the Sabbath over a cup of wine, spices and a freshly kindled light.

Haggadah (*Hagadah*): The book containing the Passover home service of the *Seder,* consisting in large part of the narrative of the Jewish exodus from Egypt led by Moses.

Hasid (pl. *Hasidim,* adj. *Hasidic*): Literally "the pious one." Refers to a devotee of *Hasidism,* the mystic sect founded in the middle of the 18th Century by the Ukrainian Rabbi Israel Baal-Sehm. There were sectarians in the days of the Maccabees who were also called *Hasidim,* but the two must not be confused.

hazzan (*chazzan*): A cantor.

Kaddish: The mourner's prayer recited in synagogue twice daily for one year by the immediate male relatives, above thirteen years of age, of the deceased; a son who recites the *Kaddish* for a parent.

kaleh: Bride.

kapote: Taken from the old French word *capote,* meaning coat.

kazatzkale: Lively Russian dance.

Kedushah: Literally "holiness," but refers to the Third Benediction called

"Holiness of the Name" which is recited by the *baal-tefilah* leading the synagogue service, with the responses given by the congregation.

kest: The old ghetto practice whereby the young bride's parents supported, in their own home, their daughter and son-in-law for a specified period of time after their marriage.

kopek: Small Russian copper coin, there being 100 *kopeks* in a *ruble.*

kosher: Food permitted and prepared according to Jewish dietary laws.

kreplach: Small pockets of dough filled with chopped meat, usually boiled and eaten with chicken broth.

kreutzer (kreuzer): Austrian copper coin, the hundredth part of a gulden, and formerly worth about one-half of a cent.

kugel: Noodle or bread suet pudding, frequently cooked with raisins.

lamdan: A scholar.

lox: Smoked salmon.

luftmensch: Literally "air man," but refers to the person who has neither trade, calling, nor income and is forced to live by improvisation, drawing his livelihood "from the air" as it were.

Maimon, Rabbi Moses ben, (1135-1204): The famed physician and philosopher of Spain, known generally as Maimonides and among the Jews as the *Rambam,* derived from the first four letters of his Hebrew name—RMBM.

mameligge: Roumanian corn porridge eaten with sour cream.

matzos: Unleavened bread eaten during Passover week in recollection of the Jewish Exodus from Egypt.

mazel (mazl): Luck.

mazel-tov: Good luck, congratulatory greeting especially used at weddings.

melamed: Old style orthodox Scripture and Hebrew teacher.

meshuggener: A crazy man.

mezuzah: Small rectangular piece of parchment inscribed with the passages Deut. VI. 4-9 and XI. 13-21, and written in 22 lines. The parchment is rolled up and inserted in a wooden or metal case and nailed in a slanting position to the right-hand doorpost of every orthodox Jewish residence as a talisman against evil.

Midrash: Literally "to study," "to investigate." A body of exegetical literature, devotional and ethical in character, which attempts to illuminate the literal text of the Bible with its inner meanings. The *Midrash* is constantly cited by pious and learned Jews in Scriptural and Talmudic disputation. (For full explanation see main introduction and introduction to the section *Biblical Sidelights.*)

mikveh: Indoor bath or pool required for Jewish ritual purification.

milchig: All dairy foods; refers to cutlery, dishes and cooking utensils used exclusively for dairy foods according to Jewish ritual regulations.

min (pl. *minim*): Term used in Talmud and *Midrash* for "heretic."

Mincha (Minha): Afternoon or twilight devotional service of the Jewish liturgy.

Mishna: A compilation of oral laws and Rabbinic teachings, edited by Judah ha-Nasi in the early 3rd Century A.D., which forms the text of the *Talmud.* It is obligatory for pious Jews to study it constantly. (For full explanation see main introduction.)

minyan: The quorum of ten men necessary for holding public worship; young boys can also be included, provided they are over thirteen.

misnagdim (s. *misnagid*): Literally "opponents"; since the advent of the *Hasidic* sect in the 18th Century the term is applied to all non-*Hasidic* Jews.

mohel: The religious functionary who performs circumcisions according to Rabbinic rite and regulation.

Nasi: Literally "prince"; the president of the Sanhedrin. The title was first applied in the days of the Maccabees.

nebich: A Yiddish exclamatory word used as an expression of pity.

nu: Yiddish exclamatory question equivalent to "well?"—"so what?"

nudnik: A bore.

oy: The Yiddish exclamation to denote pain, astonishment or rapture.

Pans (s. *Pan*): Polish gentry, nobility.

Passover: English for *Pesach,* the festival commemorating the liberation of the Jews from their bondage in Egypt. It lasts seven days, beginning with the 15th of *Nisan* (March-April).

pfennig: German coin of smallest value, there being 100 to the *mark.*

Purim: Festival of Lots, celebrating the deliverance of the Jews from Haman's plot to exterminate them, as recounted in the *Book of Esther.* It is celebrated on the 14th and 15th of *Adar,* the 12th Jewish lunar month (March).

Rambam: (See *Maimon*).

Reb: Mister.

rebbe: Rabbi; frequently applied only to a *Hasidic* rabbi.

rebbiniu: "Rabbi dear!"—term of endearment for a rabbi.

rebbitzen: The rabbi's wife.

Rosh Hashanah (*Hashana, Hashono, Hashoneh*): The Jewish New Year, celebrated on the 1st of *Tishri* (in September), is the most solemn day next to *Yom Kippur* (Day of Atonement).

Rosh Yeshiva (*Yeshiba*): Principal or rector of a *yeshiva,* an orthodox Talmudic college.

ruble: Silver coin of Russia, having had the value in Czarist times of fifty-one cents.

samovar: A brass urn, used in Russia for boiling water for tea, which is heated by means of a tube filled with hot charcoal which passes through the hollow center.

Sanhedrin (from the Greek *synhedrion*): The assembly of seventy-one in Jerusalem, established during the Second Temple period, which constituted the parliament and highest judicial body in the nation.

schlemihl: A clumsy, inept person; the etymology of the word is obscure. (See introduction to *Schlemihls and Schlimazls.*)

schlimazl: A luckless fellow. (See introduction to *Schlemihls and Schlimazls.*)

schmaltz: Animal fat.

schnapps: Whisky.

schnorrer: A beggar who shows wit, brass and resourcefulness in getting money from others as though it were his right.

schoirah: Merchandise.

Seder: The religious home service recounting the liberation from Egyptian bondage, and celebrated amidst festivity on the first and second nights of Passover; the reformed rite observes only the first night.

selichos (selichot): Penitential prayers, supplicating for God's mercy, are recited in orthodox synagogues after midnight on "the ten days of repentance" during the *Rosh Hashanah* and *Yom Kippur* time-interval.

s'forim (s. sefer): A book; usually is applied to Jewish religious books.

Shabbes: The Sabbath, i.e., Saturday.

shadchan (pl. shadchonim): A marriage broker. (See introduction to *Traditional Types.*)

shammes (pl. shamosim): A synagogue sexton.

Shekhina (Shekinah, Shechina): God's radiance or presence.

Shema: The first word in the confession of the Jewish faith: "Hear, O Israel: the Lord our God the Lord is One!"

Shem-hamforesh (ha-Meforash): The name first used by the sages of the *Mishna* for the *tetragrammaton,* the secret preeminent and Ineffable Name of God. To discover this name was the principal preoccupation of the later cabalists, for by its supernatural power they hoped to bring the Messiah.

shochet (pl. shochtim): Ritual slaughter.

shofar: Ram's horn blown during the synagogue services on *Rosh Hashanah* and *Yom Kippur.*

sholom aleichem: Peace be unto you! It is equivalent to the more prosaic greeting—"hello!"

shul: Synagogue.

Shvuous (Shevuoth, Shabuat): Variously known as "The Festival of Weeks" and "Pentecost." It originally was a harvest festival and is celebrated seven weeks after Passover.

Simchas Torah: "Rejoicing over the Torah," the last day of *Succoth* (Feast of Tabernacles), celebrating the completion of the reading of the Torah.

sofer (pl. soferim): A scribe, a copyist; one who writes out, with a goose-quill in the traditional manner, the Scrolls of the Torah and who also copies *mezuzahs* and other Hebrew religious writings.

tallis (tallith): Prayer-shawl.

Talmud: (See main introduction for detailed explanation.)

Talmud Torah: Hebrew school for children.

Tannaim: The architects of the *Mishna.*

tateniu: Father dear—the suffix *niu* in Yiddish is added for endearing intimacy; also, God is addressed this way by the pious.

tefillin: Phylacteries.

Thaler: Large silver coin formerly in the currency of some German states, including Austria, and once having the value of seventy-two cents.

Tisha Ba'Ab: Ninth day of the month of *Ab* (August) set aside by Jewish tradition for fasting and mourning to commemorate the destruction of Jerusalem and the Temple by Nebuchadnezzar in 586 B.C. and by Titus in A.D. 70.

Torah: "Doctrine" or "law"; the name is applied to the five books of Moses (Pentateuch), and in a wider sense to all sacred Jewish literature.

tref (terefa): Food forbidden by dietary laws or not prepared according to their regulations.

tzaddik (pl. *tzaddikim*): *Hasidic* rabbis and wonder-workers.

tzimmes: Dessert made of sweetened carrots or noodles.

vey: Woe! Usually appears in Yiddish as *oy vey!* (woe is me!)

yeshiva: Talmudic college.

yeshiva-bocher: Student in a *yeshiva.*

yiches: Good ancestry; pride of ancestry.

yiddena: Yiddish for a Jewish woman.

Zemiros (*Zemiroth*): Devotional "table-songs" for the Sabbath and holy days.

zloty: Large silver Polish coin.

Zohar: (See introduction to *Cabalists* for detailed explanation.)

INDEX